1954

Pepper Pace

Editor
FirstEditing

©**Pepper Pace Publications**

ISBN: 9798836268336

Praise for 1954!

"This is Genius!!"
Reviewed in the United States on July 14, 2021

This is genius. Bailey is so right. 1954 reminds me of The Truman Show. I knew that Pepper Pace would rock the hell out of this story. I love the characters and the bond that is forming. They are acting but they are feeling each other as well!! I'm so ready for more..."

"Another great story from the mind of Pepper Pace!"
Reviewed in the United States on November 1, 2021

This is such a good story. I was hooked from the first page. I feel like I'm transported in time to the 50's...

"Wonderful Story!"
"Reviewed in the United States on September 27, 2021

I love this story! It really draws the reader into the emotions of the characters. And it has everything I love about a book- it's creative, intriguing, it keeps me entertained, and it addresses important issues. Please read this series- you'll be so glad you did!"

Sign-up to the Pepper Pace Newsletter!
http://eepurl.com/bGV4tb

A note from the author

Thank you for joining me on this journey. 1954 feels like a wonderful odyssey! It was previously published as an episodic series. It worked perfectly for that platform, but I knew that it was always meant to be a book.

I sent it to the editors and thought that I might condense it. But this tale didn't need to fit into the tidy little format that most books fall into. The storyline needed no adjustments.

That is why the story that you are getting is the equivalent of three books in one!

No worries because there really isn't a dull moment in the lives of these folks. Enjoy!

-Pepper Pace,
June 2022

Contents

1954 Pepper Pace

ACT I

1954 Pepper Pace

Chapter One

Bailey opened the email and reread the short message for the third time.

Miss Westbrook, you have been selected to move to the next phase of audition. Please dress in the appropriate manner based on your character outline. Authenticity is a key to moving onto phase three of this project.

The email then provided the time and location for the audition. However, there was no script for her to rehearse.

She navigated to the Facebook group called Rising Stars! It gave encouragement to up-and-coming actors and actresses, and sometimes even provided leads to auditions, mostly for commercials and local plays. But sometimes there was a heads-up for a part as an extra on a performance set to play at the Aronoff Theater. As a twenty-two-year-old would-be actress that had never been involved in any acting gig beyond her high school productions, Bailey needed as many tips and as much free guidance as she could get.

After locating the Facebook post that was entitled simply 1954, she reread it, confirming that it was still just as mysterious and vague as it had been when she first saw it.

Hi guys and gals. If you are an up-and-coming actor/actress located in the Greater Cincinnati area and able to devote one year to a fully immersive project, then you may be what we are looking for! You must be willing to relocate (location to be announced and all fees and travel expenses are fully covered).

This is an interactive play that will require improvisation skills and the ability to stay in character at all times. Phase one of the audition will require each applicant to provide an outline of their character in a 1954 Midwestern setting. Authenticity is the key, so remember that there are no cell phones in 1954. Use of era verbiage and slang is a plus.

Other than an email address to submit the character outline, there was nothing else listed.

Bailey had allowed her mind to roam with the idea of living in 1954. Of course, as a Black woman in the '50s, she would most likely have been relegated to a job as some white family's maid. Her commute to work would have required her to sit at the back of a bus. If she had to do the shopping, she would have been required to wait until after all the white customers had been served first. She would not have been able to make eye contact with any white person that she crossed paths with, and if she passed a white person while walking down the street—even a white child—she would have been required to step off the sidewalk and into the grass, dirt, or road to give them the right of way.

The '50s, for some, might have been a golden age in American history—but for others, it would have been a nightmare.

Bailey had toyed with the idea of writing an outline of a young woman with that history—but there was another side to the idea of that era in time, and that included the pinup girls, the '50s housewife, the wholesome '50s family unit, and even the not-so-wholesome bad boys that wore leather jackets, highwater pants, and carried switchblades.

So, she had spent the weekend writing a fantasy tale about a day in the life of a young wife in 1954. She had forgotten all about it until today, when she'd gotten the email about moving onto phase two. It had instructed her to appear for an audition next Saturday.

She was intrigued, despite her confusion. But if she only had until Saturday, she needed to get on the ball and find herself an outfit.

Bailey fired up her laptop to research online stores that specialized in '50s-era attire. There were several cute options, but none could deliver a dress in less than seven days. Would thrift stores have '50s-style dresses? She thought it was doubtful, so instead, she decided to look up theatrical costume shops and found one in downtown Cincinnati that said they had what she was looking for. She was at the store within an hour.

They had two options that she could make work with a few alterations, which they said could be done in twenty-four hours. While the red suit with the matching waist-length jacket and pencil skirt initially caught her eyes, the plaid dress with the billowy skirt best represented her role as a simple housewife.

The store owner reminded her that if she was going for authenticity, not only would she need the dress but also a hat, gloves, and a handbag that matched her shoes.

And that is how a dress that would have cost her forty bucks ended up costing her nearly three times that.

She wasn't sure why she had splurged. She wasn't rolling in dough. But when she saw everything laid out together, she knew that wearing those items would not just allow her to act, but to become the part.

While the shop worked on the alterations, Bailey assessed her natural hair. No way was she going to take down her braids, not even for a role. If people understood the pain and time it took to get micro-braids, it would be self-explanatory. Instead, she went out searching the wig stores until she found a perfect Betty Boop style wig.

She cringed when she took stock of the money she'd spent today. Why couldn't this have been a simple, scripted rehearsal? More importantly, why was she so excited about playing the role of a 1950s housewife? It sounded like some renaissance festival shit, but she was still intrigued.

When she got the dress back after alterations, Bailey was anxious to put it on. She had gone out to the Wal-Mart and purchased a pair of thigh-high nylons. She'd hit a thrift store and found some costume jewelry, including a jewel-encrusted hair barrette that looked like it would have been worn as some woman's crown and glory; perhaps a humble housewife that didn't have much money to splurge but wore her grandmother's jewelry with pride.

She put on the dress and all the props, and once the wig was in place, her breath caught in her throat. She stared at herself in the floor-length mirror that was hooked to her bathroom door.

She barely recognized herself. She did a slow spin. From the simple heels to the hat that she'd pinned carefully on her head, Bailey looked like pictures she'd seen of Black women in the '50s, crowding into old-fashioned passenger cars so they wouldn't have to break the bus boycotts. She looked like the beautiful aunties and grandmothers that dressed in their Sunday best.

She smiled proudly at herself.

On Saturday she drove to the audition, praying that it was aboveboard—even if it did turn out to be some experimental theater thing.

She pulled up to a Chinese restaurant, double-checked the address, and then with a shrug, she went inside. There were several other people sitting in the restaurant's waiting area and each turned to look at her as soon as she entered.

She was relieved when she saw that they were all dressed in '50s attire.

The host, an older Asian man, greeted her.

"Please have a seat. Auditions have begun," he said while gesturing to the benches that lined the wall.

"Thank you," she said politely, and took a seat next to a man dressed in a business suit and hat. He looked nervous but authentic. He even smoked a cigarette. She didn't really want to be inhaling his cigarette smoke but took the seat anyway because he looked like the safest option.

Also present was a woman that looked to be in her thirties. She was wearing a '50s-style bathing suit with *pinup girl* written all over her. Despite being under-dressed, she looked comfortable in the attire. There were two other men, one dressed like a mechanic. He even wore grease-stained coveralls with the name **Bobby** stitched onto his breast pocket. His blond hair was heavily oiled and flopped in his eyes as he waited. He reminded her of an actor named James Dean. He was talking to the other man who wore an old suit that looked too big with dusty, old shoes. The second man didn't look like he was from the '50s, he just looked a little bit like a bum.

She was the only Black person present.

The man sitting next to her gave her a quick look.

"I hope this gig is on the up-and-up," he said. "I've been out of work for a few weeks now." He offered his hand. "I'm Marty."

She accepted his hand. "Hello. I'm Bailey." She looked around curiously. "What a strange place to hold an audition..." She could see that there were people eating in the restaurant. Strangely, they were all dressed in '50s attire as well.

"I'm not here for an audition," Marty said while squashing out his cigarette in a nearby ashtray. Wait...restaurants outlawed smoking in restaurants ages ago...

"I'm hoping to get a sales position at the new Chevy dealership. I used to be a sales manager at Luke's GM." He spoke in a suddenly mocking tone. "We had a snazzy jingle. Lucky Luke's..." Marty sighed. "Wasn't so lucky for me. I got canned because everybody wants a Chevy these days."

Bailey glanced at the ashtray and then out to the diners in the restaurant, and then she recalled what the host had said; "Auditions have begun."

She eyed the man named Marty and then smiled. "We can't afford a car right now. My husband just got back from Korea. But maybe soon."

"Well, I'd like to shake your husband's hand. Say, if I get this job at the dealership, you have your husband come down. I'll set him up with a good deal."

"Thank you. I'll be sure to let him know." Bailey's heart was beating a mile a minute. Fully immersive was what this play was described as.

"I hear it's sometimes hard for the boys coming home. How's your husband holding up?" Marty asked.

She gave him a troubled smile and a slight shrug. "Things have been slow. Joe and I got married right before he was shipped over. His mother's been kind enough to allow us to live in one of the apartments she owns. She's giving us a break on the rent...but she lives in the unit next door. And...well, you can imagine that it's not always good to live so close to your mother-in-law." Marty chuckled. She noticed that some of the others waiting were watching them.

Bailey continued, warming up to the role-play. "I know Joe wants me to stay home and take care of the house, but I'm hoping I can bring in a little money to help out." Bailey rolled her eyes. "His mother hates that I want to work outside of the house. But she's so old-fashioned. Since the war, women *have* to get jobs. Look at her. After Joe's dad passed away, she had to rent out the other half of the house just to make ends meet."

"We all have to pull our weight," Marty agreed.

"Don't fret yourself." The woman in the bathing suit pulled out a cigarette. The mechanic with the nametag that read **Bobby** leaned over with a flip-top lighter and lit her skinnier than normal cigarette.

"Times are changing," she continued after a quick thank you to the mechanic. "I'm here to audition for a modeling gig in a new gentlemen's magazine and I don't care who knows it." The woman opened the small cigarette case and withdrew a vintage compact. She quickly powdered her nose and then replaced it. She looked around the room with a haughty expression. "People say that I have the curves of Marilyn Monroe."

"Va-va-va-voom..." the bad boy mechanic said. He let out a low wolf whistle. "I can attest to that."

The woman batted her eyes at him. "How would you know? Unless you're Mr. DiMaggio."

"DiMaggio is a scrub. I hear they're splitsville, anyway," Bobby said while eyeing the woman. "Besides, your gams are much better than *Mrs.* DiMaggio's."

Bailey looked from one to the other, wondering if they knew each other. Were they in on this? Or were they just improvising the way she was?

"Well if you like my gams, just wait until you take a gander of me in a bunny costume."

"A bunny costume?" Bobby asked incredulously. "What kind of sham magazine would put a dame in a bunny getup?"

"You'll just have to pick one up, mister. It's called *Playboy Magazine*, and all the models wear heels, bathing suits, and bunny ears. Oh, and cute, fluffy bunny tails."

The guy wearing the second-rate thrift store costume looked at the flirtation going on between the man sitting next to him and the woman across from them. He sighed.

"Anybody know when this thing is supposed to get started?" He pulled out his cell phone and checked the time. "I've been here for nearly half an hour." He looked at her. "What time did they tell you auditions were happening?"

She glanced at the others. They all seemed to be waiting—as if they were some weird characters from a *Twilight Zone* episode.

"Uh...I was told to be here at two o'clock," she replied politely.

He frowned. "I was told to be here at one forty-five. What about you guys? You three were here when I got here."

Marty shrugged. "Yeah. I need to get going myself. I'll just have to reschedule." He stood and put on a coat and then he tipped his hat in her direction and in the direction of the pinup model.

"Good luck to you," he said before leaving. He opened the door and a young man wearing a vintage army uniform came in. Everyone looked at him. The host greeted him and told him to have a seat and that auditions had begun.

The man took the recently vacated seat beside her while the bum scowled.

"Why is this man saying the auditions have begun but they're not calling anyone back?" He sighed in annoyance and then jumped up and went to the host. "Excuse me, how much longer will it be?"

The host opened a reservation book. "Your name please?"

"George McHenry."

"Please follow me, Mr. McHenry." The man looked pleased as he straightened his lapel and was guided out of sight.

She saw Bobby and the pinup girl smirk briefly before Bobby eyed the G.I.

"Hey, pal. How long have you been home?"

The young actor frowned in confusion. "What?"

"Did your noggin get scrambled over in Korea? How long have you been Stateside?"

He did the same thing she had. He took in the cigarette being smoked by Miss Pinup, the way Bobby was speaking to him as if he was actually in 1954, and he quickly acclimated.

"Oh, sorry. I've been home about a week now." He looked at Bailey curiously. "I...uh...thought I'd have a job waiting for me. But they couldn't hold it. So, I'm hoping to get anything."

"Poor guy," Miss Pinup said. "I think it's lousy how you boys are treated when you get home. Mrs. Bailey over there said her husband just got shipped home and she has to go out and find work."

He nodded at the pinup girl. "Thank you, ma'am, but I didn't sign up expecting a handout. I'm willing to work for my keep."

The host was suddenly in front of Bailey. "If you will follow me?"

She gave him a surprised look but got up and quickly nodded at the others in the room.

"Pleasure to make your acquaintance," she said, chastising herself for suddenly switching to a southern accent. This was the Midwest, not the south, for God's sake!

Her stomach grumbled as she was guided past people that were eating Chinese food—lo mein, General Tso chicken, yummy egg rolls—all kinds of food that had never been eaten in China. And everyone present was dressed like they had been transported from the dinner scene of *A Christmas Story*.

"You have been selected for the next phase of audition," the man said after leading her to an office. "Someone will be with you shortly. Please stay in character at *all times*."

Once the door was closed and she was alone, Bailey blinked. What kind of craziness was this?

Chapter Two

Five minutes later, a man entered the room. He too was dressed in vintage '50s clothing, although he looked like a studio head or a businessman in a nice suit with hair that was kept in place by some type of slicking gel.

She stood and he offered his hand. "Bailey Westbrook?"

"Yes."

After they shook, he gestured to the door that she'd just entered. "I'm Bruce Adams. Come with me, please." She followed him out the door, happy she was wearing a pair of sensible heels.

"You've made it to the final phase of auditions. If you're successful, you will be offered a position in 1954." Mr. Adams talked fast and walked faster. He paused abruptly to consult a notebook and she nearly stumbled into him.

"There has been a slight script change. Your husband, Joe, has been renamed. You are now Mrs. Bobby Banks. Your husband was never in Korea and has been working the last two years as a typesetter at the *Gazette* — which is the only newspaper in town."

Mr. Adams closed the notebook with a snap while Bailey tried to absorb the information. They were poised near the restrooms, preparing to enter the dining area. She could clearly see the front door where another person had arrived to replace the pinup girl.

"Bobby has brought you here to celebrate his good news. Are you ready?"

"I-I'm ready."

He gently clapped her shoulder. "You did great at your audition. Just continue improvising and you will be fine." She was encouraged by his words and followed him back into the restaurant again. This time, she was led to a table where a man was waiting. He smiled when he saw her and stood to pull out her chair.

He wasn't bad-looking, reminding her of a younger and slightly better-looking version of Leonardo DiCaprio.

"Hi, honey. I already ordered for us," he said.

Bailey placed her bag on the table and unpinned the hat from her head as she tried to think of an engaging response. "I'm so sorry I'm late. I've been on pins and needles since you told me that you had good news."

"Give me a moment to order us a drink. We're celebrating, after all." He raised his hand and a waiter appeared. "Waiter, give me your best bottle of champagne. My wife and I are celebrating good news."

"Champagne?" she said in surprise. After the waiter disappeared, she leaned in and whispered. "Bobby, can we afford champagne?"

He took her hand. "Honey, that's what we're celebrating. I got a raise!"

She smiled in excitement. "A raise? Bobby, that's wonderful news!"

"Now you won't have to get a part-time job. You're looking at the newest editor at the *Gazette*."

"An editor? Bobby, I can barely believe it!" she said with the perfect inflection of excitement.

"And best of all is that I can write bylines now; my name in print. Can you imagine that, Bailey?" he asked in what seemed like genuine excitement. His blue eyes even sparkled. Damn, he was one good actor.

"Like a real reporter?" she asked in awe, edging her improvisational skills up a notch.

"Yes. If I create my own stories, I get a byline."

"Honey, that is wonderful news. You've worked so hard for this."

The waiter appeared with the champagne and she dutifully covered her mouth as she giggled in anticipation as the cork was popped. The waiter filled two champagne glasses with the bubbly liquid and Bobby lifted his glass and stared into her eyes.

"I want to toast to the most beautiful wife that any man could dream of having. You've been supportive and patient, and now it's time to start fulfilling your dreams."

"You already have, Bobby," she said sincerely. "From the first second that you walked past me, stopped and pretended to drop something so you could retrace your steps just to get a second look at me, I knew you were someone special."

He gave her a gentle smile, his light eyes holding her with love and warmth that nearly shook her with its sincerity.

"I love you, Bailey," he whispered. "Here's to us." They clinked glasses and she sipped her wine. It was surprisingly good. Dinner was served a few moments later while the two of them made plans to move out of his mother's apartment and get a brand-new house of their own. He speculated about a new car but she laughed and said that a used car was better than no car at all and they might not want to get in over their heads. He kissed her hand and said that she was both smart and beautiful.

He "taught" her how to use chopsticks while she oohed and aahed at all the strange flavors.

"Bobby, you should write an article about how good the food is here."

"Well, I was hoping to write stories about things that are more important, like Brown versus Board of Education. I know how important that ruling was for you. You had a good education, but not all Negroes do."

Bailey gave him a surprised look. He was acknowledging her race. So he wasn't treating her like an amalgamation of the '50s housewife. He was giving her the ability to incorporate the story of her people into this world.

"That's what I love about you, Bobby Banks. You see what others choose to close their eyes to."

His eyes seemed to flinch, but then he smiled. She hoped that she hadn't gotten too sappy.

"Shall we call it a night, Mrs. Banks?" he said smoothly.

"Let's. I need to start ordering catalogues to decorate our new home."

Mr. Adams suddenly appeared. "Very good job, Miss Westbrook. Please follow me so we can discuss the terms."

"I got the job?" she asked in excitement.

Mr. Adams's eyes suddenly darted to Bobby. Bobby's smile had disappeared and Mr. Adams seemed to blanch. "Sorry, Bobby," he said quickly.

Bobby's eyes looked far away. He didn't respond. Mr. Adams gestured to Bailey. "Please follow me." And then he quickly hurried her out of the area. Although the man did everything quickly, she understood that he was rushing them out of Bobby's presence.

Once they were back in the office, he sighed. "Miss Westbrook, you must never break character. Ever."

"Ever?" she asked incredulously.

Mr. Adams shook his head. "You'll understand once you read the contract." He picked up a folder and dug through it for papers, which he handed to her. "You've been offered a position in 1954. If you accept, you will be paid for one year of your time. You will be required to relocate and, with the exception of twenty-four hours a week, you will be required to stay in character."

"Wait...*what?*" They expected her to work straight through, morning, noon, and night?

Mr. Adams just held up a hand, requesting she let him finish. "For your time, you will be compensated one hundred twenty thousand dollars—"

"Shut the front door!" she gasped.

He continued as if she hadn't interrupted. "— which will be broken into twelve equal payments. If you willingly leave the production prior to the twelve months, you will be required to repay twenty-five percent of what you were paid. Or you will be sued to the highest extent of the law." He paused to look at her. Bailey nodded in understanding.

Got it.

"Should you be fired from the show, you will be required to repay fifty percent of what you were paid.

"In addition to the compensation, you will receive a weekly stipend based on the wages of your individual character." Bailey frowned.

She didn't work a job...her character was married. Hold up! Was she supposed to be married to some strange guy for the next year?!

"Excuse me, Mr. Adams. Sorry, I'm breaking character—"

"You can break character in this room and a few other designated areas."

"Are you saying that my character will be married? Can I rewrite my script?"

"No. Rewrites are done by the board. Your placement in 1954 is contingent upon you playing the role as written. If you accept the terms, then your new script—with the revisions that we discussed—will be emailed to you by close of business Monday. Now, Miss Westbrook, I know you have a lot of questions, but many of them can be answered by reading this handbook."

Mr. Adams opened a metal file cabinet and withdrew a pamphlet with 1954 written in bold, black letters on the cover. A drawing of a '50s-era family could be seen picnicking in the park on its glossy background.

"After you read this, you can email me your questions. My email address is in the back of the pamphlet. And, Miss Westbrook—"

"Can you just call me Bailey?" she asked while leafing through the pamphlet.

"Bailey," he continued. "You did very well. We made rewrites before your final audition, and that rarely happens."

"Mr. Adams—"

"Bruce. Call me Bruce."

"Bruce. Is this on the up-and-up?"

"It is."

"Because it's a lot of money," she continued.

"We ask for a lot, and we expect our money's worth."

"One hundred twenty thousand dollars is a lot for a twenty-two-year-old that's living in a studio apartment."

Bruce smiled and led her out the door. "Bailey, read the pamphlet. You'll understand things a lot better, and you'll understand why we don't put too many details in our open call." He opened the back door to the restaurant and ushered her out. "I hope you sign the contract. Bobby really liked you."

"Bobby? How do you know that? You barely talked to him."

"The monitor. Eyes in the sky watches everything…well, not the bathrooms, of course. We're not that kind of production."

Bailey tried not to cringe. Well, that's not creepy. Not one bit.

She finally turned to go and when she turned back to wave goodbye, the door was already closed.

Chapter Three

The moment Bailey got home, she slipped out of her heels — she'd already removed the wig and hat while in the car — and she draped her coat over the living room chair.

She was already reading the pamphlet entitled 1954 as she dropped into an armchair.

If you received this publication, then you have been offered a role in our project, 1954. As such, you have been given a unique opportunity, because 1954 is not a play or a movie: it is a way of life.

Bailey blinked in confusion. *What is this insanity?* She continued reading.

Developed by a modern-day visionary, 1954 took three years of hard work to bring to life a fully functioning town. We currently have seventy-two cast members in the fictional location of Wingate, Ohio. It began with its exciting inauguration in 1953 and we believe that 1954 will be even more successful.

Yes, you are correct that this way of life is going into its second year of production. We do refer to it as a production because in exchange for your annual salary, you will be assigned a character outline and you will be recorded for broadcast.

If you agree to our terms, you will be included in our growing cast and while there may be challenges, you will find that 1954 can be satisfying in its simplicity.

Here are the terms that you must agree upon. Once you have signed your contract our production

manager, Bruce Adams, will provide you with character outlines and a set map.

1. We (The '50s Experience LLC) will pay you twelve equal payments of $_____ over the course of twelve months of employment. Payment will be automatically deposited into your account of choice.

The money line was left blank, but she would assure that it was properly filled in if she took this weird-ass gig.

2. You will receive a weekly stipend that is equal to the position you hold in the town. This is considered your living expenses and it will be more than adequate to live comfortably in 1954—however, it is up to you to maintain your obligations and to pay your bills timely. Failure to do so will have the same result as it would in real life (referred to henceforth as irl).

3. You will be assigned a job/career. Our workday is limited to five hours unless you choose to work overtime (if available). Payday is every Friday.

4. You will remain in character at all times during production and will only be allowed to break character during allotted script changes, meetings, and while taking leave.

5. You agree to be filmed at all times while in active production with the following exceptions: no after-hour bedroom scenes, no restroom scenes, no sex scenes, and there will be no filming whenever the pause filming light has been engaged. The pause filming light will cause a member of production to

interview you and may be viewed and treated as an infraction.

Bailey wiped her brow. What the — ? Infractions? This was starting to sound like some weird cult. What was the end game? They were being recorded, but this wasn't supposed to be a play or a movie. Wait...was it like that movie *The Truman Show*? It was about some guy that had been filmed secretly all his life for the entertainment of the rest of the world. He lived in a fictional world with actors for friends and family.

Would there be some strange child hidden away that they had to play to? She continued reading, very anxious about the reason for all of this.

6. **Failure to comply with your agreement will result in monetary infractions that will be deducted from your next monthly pay. These infractions are at the discretion of the production crew and begin in $100 increments. Should you leave the production, you will forfeit any <u>remaining</u> monthly deposits and will be subject to a mandatory 25% repayment of any amounts <u>previously</u> paid. In the event that you are asked to leave the show, you will be charged a mandatory 50% repayment fee, including the loss of <u>future</u> deposits. Failure to return all required payments will result in legal charges.**

7. **Once weekly there will be a team script reading in which script changes may be requested. You may attend this meeting while out of character. This time is also to be**

used to conduct research for the era and your character. You may also make and receive phone calls after the meeting has adjourned.

8. You will be provided 24 hours of personal time to do as you please. Personal time allows you to break out of character, leave set, research and enjoy family time irl. For obvious reasons, you will not be allowed on set while on personal time. However, if you would like to shorten your leave, it can be banked for use at a later time. Please read more about clock-time and time reporting in the *Welcome Aboard* handbook.

9. You may only leave set during your personal leave. As this is a closed set, you will not be able to make or receive communications until your allotted personal leave, however, as previously stated, personal communications will be allowed after the weekly script meeting has adjourned.

10. This set is closed. This means that no visitors are allowed. Should there be an emergency that requires your immediate attention the production manager, Bruce Adams, will be your point of contact. Please see Bruce Adams with any personal needs that may require you to leave set. Please be reminded that an unscheduled leave will impact your employment with this production.

Now you may have asked yourself how this is possible. 1954 and its predecessor, 1953, is broadcast to members of an exclusive online subscription service. Members pay upwards of $5000 dollars a month to watch the interactions of our little town.

We are most popular in Japan, Iceland, Denmark, Sweden, and Korea, with subscriptions growing in Canada and South Africa. 1954 will begin providing translations in several languages beginning with our new season.

Some subscribers have favorite characters, as well as not-so favorite characters. This keeps the dynamic interesting. Do not be concerned with the mundane quality of life in 1954. That is the appeal. Our subscribers watch in order to live vicariously during an era that has been seen as a golden age in Americana.

If you have any questions, please contact Bruce Adams at his email address: BruceAdams@The50sExperiencecom.

Bailey leaned back, not realizing that she had been tensely reading the entire publication. Five hundred dollars a month subscription? Who in the hell could afford that? Well, obviously enough people to allow them to pay over seventy people a hundred and twenty grand a year.

Where do I sign?

She immediately sent Bruce an email stating that she was accepting the job and he sent her a return email within the hour with a simple contract. She was to sign it and mail it back by the end of the week. Things moved quickly after that. Bailey was emailed her *Welcome Aboard* handbook. It included a map of the town and a list of reoccurring characters.

There was a mayor named Stewart George and his wife, Lucy. The sheriff was Abe (no last name given), the doctor was Fred Geyer, and his head nurse was Adelaide (also no last name given). There was a milkman named Curtis, a butcher shop, barber shop, boardinghouse, beauty shop, two grocery stores, two restaurants, and the town newspaper—which she already knew was called the *Gazette*. There was a packaging factory simply referred to as "the factory," and several small and large farms.

The handbook explained that Wingate was almost completely self-supporting, yet certain things could only be accomplished behind the scenes. Some examples were waste management, water and energy control, and supply of authentic retro products whenever possible. The factory would repurpose the packaging of modern-day products for use in town by making them appear vintage.

It was all very interesting. Despite her many trepidations about the unknown, Bailey found herself becoming excited about being involved in this production.

She sent Bruce an email with a list of question, mostly about the script, and Bruce replied that they had hired a number of new cast members and that scripts were being finalized.

He suggested that she start the process of moving, as shooting would begin October 1, but she was expected on set the day before for orientation. That gave her a little over a month to either store her belongings or find them new homes.

Luckily for her, the efficiency that she rented had come furnished, and all she needed to do was to pack up her clothes. Upon her arrival at Wingate, Bailey would be supplied with a complete wardrobe.

Bailey considered her hair. She'd been natural since the age of sixteen and she loved it. But it was not reasonable to think that she would wear a wig day in and day out for the next year. Now that she understood people across the world would be looking at her, she felt anxious about putting out the right vibe.

She knew if she didn't take care of this in real time, there was no telling how a white 1950s beauty salon would tackle her 4c hair.

She visited an urban hairdresser for a relaxer, but refused to allow the stylist to cut it into one of the up-to-date dos. Instead, she asked the woman to summon the ancestors of her granny and aunties to make her look like she was on her way to a Wednesday church service.

The results were on point. It reminded her of how Aunt Mae looked back when she was a kid after her visit to the hair salon.

Yeah, it was old-fashioned, and that made it perfect.

With a sigh, she figured it was time to tackle her family. The only people she had to consider were her Aunt Mae and Uncle Dewbug. They'd raised her after her mother died because granny was too old, plus her aunt and uncle had never been blessed with their own children. Aunt Mae was actually granny's younger sister, and both she and her husband were getting up in years.

Bailey's sister, Adrienne, was married and lived in North Dakota with her husband and kids, and her younger brother, Cedric, was a Marine stationed in Hawaii. That left the care of her aunt and uncle squarely on her shoulders. There wasn't much that needed to be done for them, it was *she* that really needed *them*.

Bailey spent every holiday and each of her birthdays with them. She loved spending hours on the phone chitchatting about silly, unimportant things with her aunt—but things that entertained them both.

Bailey had learned the hard way that when there wasn't much family left, you valued every moment you had with those that were special to you.

"I don't understand this at all," Aunt Mae said as they sat at the older woman's kitchen table drinking sweet tea and eating ginger snap cookies. They were stale—just the way Aunt Mae (and her dentures) preferred them, and the way Bailey had gotten used to.

"What do you mean?" Bailey asked. She'd already explained it *three* times. What was there not to get? Well…she supposed there was a lot not to get, but she was too close to the situation. No…she had too much *hope* invested in this.

1954 would be the answer to her dreams. At the end of this project, she would have a hundred and twenty grand to live on while she found the roles she could only dream about. She could afford to travel, maybe even move to LA or New York.

No. She couldn't live that far away from her aunt and uncle. But she would at least be able to fly out for auditions.

"This all sounds too good to be true," Aunt Mae replied while wrinkling her nose as if she smelled something foul. "They goin' to pay you all that money but you ain't never heard about this so-called movie? Have you even tried to look it up on the Internet?"

Bailey nodded. "Yes, I have, and I found it. The thing is, because it's a subscription service, I couldn't see more than just a trailer describing something that sounded like show *Big Brother*. Do you remember? It was a big deal, but when you watched it, it was actually pretty boring."

"And this won't be boring? You just walking around pretending you live in 1954? You mark my words, they're going to have you on set acting un-Godly, sleeping around and fighting with each other like all those housewife shows they got on cable TV."

Bailey shook her head. "Maybe, but there won't be any sex or nudity. And I get the feeling 1954 is supposed to be wholesome. You see, they market it as a return to the golden age of America."

Aunt Mae rolled her eyes. "That weren't no golden age. I worked in two houses as a maid back in 1954. In one of them, I had to watch two little girls while their parents sat reading the newspaper or fancy magazines.

"I was the one that bathed them, fed them, and put them to bed each night. *And* they had designated times when they could 'bother' their mama and daddy.

"Chile, the '50s for Black people was terrible! If whites struggled, then you can imagine what the Blacks did. We ate cornpone and dandelion greens when there wasn't any meat. When we had meat, Daddy got the main piece, Mama the next, and we kids had to split the bones between us! And you best believe we sucked whatever meat there was off that bone!

"Whites used to help themselves to our crops and there wasn't a damn thing you could do about it. Do you know how far I had to travel just to get a decent job that gave me a few dollars a week? Then half of that went to my mama and daddy."

Bailey absorbed everything she said with an intense expression.

"I read about how Blacks were treated back then. But the Internet doesn't go into all the details you just did. You were my age in the '50s," she suddenly realized.

Aunt Mae nodded. "I could tell you some stories—"

"Yes, but not only about the bad things. There has to be stories about good things."

Her aunt sighed. "Yeah. We lived in a community where everyone was poor. So, we found ways to have fun. We partied, drank, listened to music, and when there was extra money, we bought records. Dancing became the only thing you could do for fun.

"We'd go to house parties for a penny to enter and we ate barbecued ribs, collard greens, chess pie, and drank homemade hooch. We would have the best time—until the older boys got to fighting and it got shut down.

"Truth be told, we lived in our own world. Whites didn't come around us, and we only went around them when we had to."

Aunt Mae continued talking about her life as a young woman in the '50s while Bailey listened as if she was a child sitting on Uncle Dewbug's lap.

When Bailey went home that night, Aunt Mae was no closer to understanding why she would choose to do something like this—but Bailey was even more inspired to find a place for herself in this production.

Chapter Four

A month later, when Bailey first set eyes on Wingate, she finally understood that this was no prank. 1954 was no minor production someone had created on a whim.

This was the real deal.

It began when she drove through the gated entrance and a uniformed guard checked her name off his clipboard. It didn't look like a uniform from the '50s but then again, how would she know? She was told to drive her car to a nearby one-story building where she could then park in its garage.

While she did not see a town, she did see several people rushing to and fro, driving skids, pushing carts, and wheeling equipment.

It certainly looked like the set of a big production.

After being instructed by a busy receptionist to wait for Mr. Adams in the waiting area, Bailey's fear began to build. That was until she saw a man introduce himself as Drew Davies. He was the young soldier she had talked to at the audition. He seemed equally relieved to see her.

Included in their small group of newcomers was a middle-aged woman named Nadine. She explained she was a stand-up comic needing inspiration and Quinton, a man in his thirties, who had been in several small movies and just needed one big break.

As Bruce gave them a tour of the building, Drew confessed he thought she was one of the actors in on the audition.

"I tried to give you a hint the audition had already begun," she whispered, "but speaking to a lone Black person in a room full of white people isn't really true to actual 1954."

Drew's laughter burst out and she found herself already liking him.

"Well, Bruce told me there is no racism in Wingate."

She gave him a surprised look. "He did?" she whispered. Bruce was still leading them to the meeting rooms and wasn't talking about anything, so they were able to continue whispering to each other as they trailed along after him.

"Yep," Drew nodded. "But that also means there won't be any sit-ins, no boycotts—which actually didn't really start catching on until 1955." He pointed to his temple. "I've done my research."

She smiled, but it worried her that 1954 might get whitewashed.

They finally got on a bus that would take them to Wingate—a retro Greyhound. Bailey was also worried about leaving her personal care products behind. But Bruce explained that under no circumstances would modern items be allowed on set. Even their cell phones would be confiscated and held in lockers at the production office.

Well, they would just have to work something out because she could *not* rely on just any 1950s shade of makeup. She was too brown for that!

When they finally stopped at the curb in what appeared to be the middle of a bustling town, each of the newly hired cast members sat in stunned silence.

Wingate was a real town. People walked down the streets briskly, carrying packages, briefcases, and in one instance, a lady was even pushing a pram with an actual kid in it.

"What the...?" Quinton said in awe.

Bruce was standing at the front of the bus with a bemused smile. "Welcome to Wingate. Shall we begin our tour?" They stepped off the bus and looked around as if they were tourists.

"Under normal circumstances, you wouldn't be allowed on set wearing modern clothes, but our last stop will be to wardrobe.

"First stop is the grocery store." He gestured to a quaint storefront and they entered.

There were actually people there already shopping. The customers tipped their hats or nodded, "How d'do," before continuing their shopping. They seemed to be picking up everything from food to shoe polish. One lady even had a Tiffany-style lamp to purchase.

These folks had been here a while and knew what they would need to make it work.

Bruce seemed to read their minds when he explained that everyone in town had been included in the cast of the previous production, 1953.

Now these were the people she would really need to speak to in order to get a feel for life on the set. Bruce began pointing out the location of the hidden cameras.

"You are never to look directly into the camera, but you must play to them as much as possible. The production team does amazing work in splicing the footage, but it helps if you are aware."

Bailey saw that the cameras looked like small bulbs, much like the ones that went into appliances. She could also tell they were easy to conceal.

"This is one of the switches to indicate you want to cut filming." Bruce headed for the entrance where there was a normal-looking, push-button light switch on the wall by the door. Instead of a plain cover, it was surrounded by a colored motif that actually fit in with the whole retro décor.

"I can't imagine any reason you would want to cut filming for the entire store." He gave them a serious look. "And should that ever happen, I'm sure it would result in a severe infraction."

They all looked at each other, fully understanding the stakes.

Bruce smiled again. "There shouldn't be any worries with mistaking the cut filming switch with a light switch. The lights are all controlled by the up-and-down flip switches."

Next, Bruce showed them the butcher shop and Quinton asked if they butchered the meat on site. The butcher explained the meat and lots of other things were shipped in already prepared.

Nadine walked around marveling at items she admitted she hadn't seen since being a kid. She suddenly looked excited.

"I must admit, I'm impressed. This is perfect. Absolutely perfect," she said.

When Bruce led them out of the shop, she called over her shoulder that she would be back for the pork chops.

Bruce nodded his approval. "Now that's the kind of enthusiasm we're looking for. Well done, Nadine."

When they returned to the bus, they had seen all of the shops and salons, including the police station, and knew the location of all the cameras inside and outside. They'd spoken to a few people that gave them enthusiastic greetings and words of encouragement.

"Did all the previous cast return for 1954?" Drew asked.

Bruce shook his head. "Not everyone. Some were not invited back and others weren't cut out for a year-long production. But lucky for us, our casting call netted four new stars with their very own story lines. Now let's get you to wardrobe and I'll show you your new homes for the next three hundred sixty-five days."

Wardrobe was the best part of the day. They were led to huge rooms and then allowed to "shop" for their clothing. Tailors and seamstresses were available to help and when Bailey tried on an outfit that didn't quite fit, a seamstress would appear who immediately fixed it, right there on the spot.

They were given strict limits though. Bailey's character was only allowed two pieces of jewelry, and only in the mid-range price line. She selected a pair of pearl and a pair of diamond-ish earrings. She was given a wedding band that made her feel weird and caused her to start worrying about her husband, Bobby. Or maybe the man that looked so much like Leonardo DiCaprio had been recast. There was so much she still didn't understand, and so much to learn.

"What about my makeup? I use Fenty and Black Opal." Bailey's meaning was to impress upon the fact that those brands didn't exist in the '50s, and they were for use by Black people.

The seamstress smiled. "You get to shop for that too, and believe me when I say we have shades from pale to ebony and brands from Natasha Denona and Fenty to Kat Von D. But if you don't find your preferred brand or color, just leave the information with me and I'll make sure we order it, send it to the factory for re-packaging, and you'll have it in a few days."

Bailey gave the woman a skeptical look but when she was led to the makeup section, she discovered that not only did they have the shades that complemented her complexion, but they had brands (discovered on the bottom of the packaging) she could not have ever afforded to buy herself.

At this point, she couldn't even manufacture anything to complain about.

When her wardrobe was selected—which included several pairs of shoes but only one pair of heels, some panties, two petticoats, pointy brassieres, a scratchy wool coat, several pretty hats, a nice, big apron, a shit-ton of nylons (no socks), a pretty pair of slippers, two modest nightgowns and a robe, three everyday dresses, one Sunday dress, a formal gown, some blouses, some skirts, one pair of slimming pants, and finally, several sweaters—she was told her items would be shipped over to the house.

Poor Quinton didn't fare very well in the wardrobe department. He got three pairs of pants that looked exactly alike, three white shirts, undies that looked scratchy, socks, a pair of used shoes, one suit jacket, a wool winter coat, and one hat. No wedding ring—lucky him.

Nadine got a *box* of vintage jewelry. It seemed her character was a bit more well-off than Bailey's, because she also got more shoes and party dresses.

"I'll show you where you live. The fellas first, since you both live in town," Bruce announced.

They took Quinton to the boardinghouse, and his room was simple and unimpressive. When he sat on the bed it squeaked and his expression went blank to hide his disappointment. In addition to a bed there was a desk, which held an old suitcase, a wooden chair, and a bookshelf containing a clock and a small radio.

Bruce gave him a half smile. "No worries, Quinton. You will sell enough of those encyclopedias to move your way right out of the boardinghouse and into your own place. You'll see. We scripted it that way.

"The other fellas will show you the ropes. And as a plus, Miss Grady, the owner, sure can cook. But just a heads-up, you'd better be prompt for your meals because if you miss one, you're out of luck. And do *not* offer to help with dishes. That's her job. Remember, your place is to go out on the porch after dinner and enjoy a cigarette with the fellas."

"I don't smoke," Quinton said.

Bruce nodded. "Duly noted." But he offered no other guidance.

After leaving Quinton, they boarded the bus to take Drew to his residence. The young man leaned in and whispered to her and Nadine.

"Quinton sure got screwed."

"Royally," Nadine replied. "But it's his own fault for writing himself as a door-to-door salesman...unless he intends to screw all the housewives in town."

"I don't think this is that kind of story," Drew said.

The bus came to a stop in front of a house. It was small and pretty, with flowers planted in the front yard surrounding the wide front stairs that led to a large porch. A lone metal chair with a handmade cushion was situated by the door, and to Bailey, it looked as if a woman had sat in this very spot for years shelling peas or talking to her next-door neighbors.

"This is where you grew up and where you've come to get back on your feet after being shipped home from Korea," Bruce said to Drew. They entered the house after a quick knock.

"Bruce here. I brought Drew."

A woman came from the kitchen, wearing an apron and drying her hands on a dish towel. A man came from one of the back rooms.

"Drew, this is your mother and father." An older woman appeared at the top of the stairs. "And that's your grandmother."

"Oh, God," the older lady said. "You and I are going to have to switch rooms, sonny. I can't make it up these stairs for the next year. This is some bullshit."

Bailey gave her a surprised look and tried not to laugh.

"Now, Midge. You shouldn't cuss, even when the cameras aren't rolling. You might accidentally let something slip."

Midge came down the stairs slowly with a scowl. "I ain't a damn fool, Bruce. I know how to act professional when I need to."

Drew greeted each member of his new family. "Sure, Granny. We can switch rooms. I got no problems with that."

"I already like you, kid," Granny said.

"Well, I got to finish up these two meat loaves," Drew's new mom said. She looked at Bailey and Nadine. "We eat this stuff about three days a week. I toss it in the freezer and save time so I don't have to cook during my prime time."

Bruce told Drew his things would arrive soon and the rest of his family would get him trained on what to do when the cameras began to roll.

Nadine, Bruce, and Bailey boarded the bus and the butterflies were really flapping around in Bailey's stomach.

Was it just her, or was Bruce intentionally vague about what they needed to do? She couldn't ask Nadine with Bruce so close, so she just tried not to focus on how hungry she was. Breakfast had just been orange juice and an egg and cheese McMuffin at the butt-crack of dawn.

Nadine's house was the next stop and as they drove, Bailey asked about her story line.

"Well, I wrote it as the mysterious woman that's come back to town since being a teen. It turns out much like real life; I got knocked up; but unlike real life, my character puts her kid up for adoption.

"The script got rewritten." She squinted at Bruce, who was listening intently. "I'm not sure if I'm allowed to tell the twist."

"You can tell. There's no secrets between the cast members," he replied.

"Well, it turns out I used to date Mayor George back when we were teens. He's the secret father of my child. But he doesn't know it. I've come back to town to enlist his help in finding our love child."

"Oh," Bailey said. "You actually have some intrigue going on. I'm just a simple housewife. Well, the script was rewritten; I'm a newlywed. We were living with my husband's mother for the first few months and we just bought a new house. It's kind of boring compared to your story line."

"Mundane is what the people like," Bruce said. "You're attractive, your husband is attractive, and you're interracial. The people are curious about how you live."

"We're interracial!" Bailey said excitedly. "So, we will talk about race?"

Bruce chuckled. "We have some great scripts coming up about it. Just because there isn't racism in Wingate doesn't mean we won't delve into racial issues."

That was good to know. She wasn't sure why she had been so worried about the racial issue—maybe because she sensed there weren't going to be many Blacks in Wingate. She didn't want them to rewrite her out of the show if she made waves of the racial variety.

They drove out of the main area of town to a nearby suburb. These were real houses, most with vintage cars parked in the driveway. People bustled about, moving things in, gardeners cutting the grass wearing old-fashioned uniforms and using old-fashioned push lawnmowers.

And that's when Bailey finally saw the Black people. They were the gardeners.

She and Nadine exchanged quick looks. She'd noticed it too. They got out of the bus in front of a large house.

"I live here?" Nadine asked in surprise.

Bruce grinned. "Yes, ma'am. You did well once leaving Wingate and you've come home to roost."

They went inside and saw a nicely decorated house that was richly furnished. Boxes were against the walls that still needed to be unpacked. But it didn't take away from the expansive foyer, which contained a gigantic chandelier.

"I didn't know I was rich!" Nadine said while looking around.

"You're not," Bruce replied. "At least not as rich as you're trying to appear. You're living well above your means."

Nadine made a face. "Well, okay. Just like reality..." Bailey tried not to laugh. Nadine was a hoot. She hoped her story line would be successful.

"No worries, Nadine. Your house staff will fill you in on the script changes. Good luck."

Nadine gave them a wary look as they retreated, and Bailey knew exactly how she felt. There was no script like something you could rehearse to. There was only a vague outline of where their story line was going. They would either sink or swim.

The bus driver finally headed to the place she would call home for the next year.

Now that she had Bruce all to herself, she decided to pick the man's brain.

"How many Blacks are in Wingate, Bruce?"

He looked up into the air as if taking a mental count. "Well, there's you, Curtis the milkman, Pastor Jimenez — although he does double duty as a Hispanic cast member. There are the cooks at Miss Maple's Restaurant...I'd say, including the housekeeping and gardening staff, we have twenty or twenty-five Black characters."

"They seem to mostly be servants of some type," she said.

"Well, it is 1954. And *you're* not in the service industry." Oh, lucky me. And just in case he wasn't aware, there were Black professors, Black doctors, Black business owners in the real 1950s. But she wisely didn't say what she was thinking.

"How does playing a Black woman work in 1954 among the white suburbanites?"

"It won't be discussed beyond the neighbors commenting on it. You and Bobby have an amazing story line. You just wait and see."

Again with the vagueness. But she was not trying to rock the boat.

Chapter Five

The bus pulled to the curb of a ranch-style house. If she had read an advertisement for ranch-style houses, this would have been the picture gracing the ad.

It was a brick house with an attached garage, an expansive yard (probably with some Black gardener to keep it manicured). Neat boxwood shrubs flanked an old-fashioned, windowed front door. There was a huge front bay window Bailey could imagine filled with decorative pots of plants.

This was her house! she thought happily. Well, hers and her unknown husband's.

She saw some of her neighbors bustling about. These would be the people that would either welcome her or gossip about her...or she guessed both could be possible.

She waved to a man dragging a box of supplies into the house. He gave her a friendly wave in return. Well, this wasn't the real 1950s, that was for sure.

Bruce opened the door. "Bobby? We're here."

Bailey was surprised to see that the living room was practically barren. There wasn't even a rug, just some wall sconces. Was this going to be furnished by tomorrow?

Bobby came hurrying into the room. His hair wasn't perfectly coiffed the way it had been when she'd seen him during auditions. Blond bangs flopped into his eyes. He wore slim-fitting khaki-colored pants and his casual bowling shirt was untucked and slightly rumpled. He was wiping his hands on a rag that he tucked into a back pocket.

His blue eyes moved to Bailey first before acknowledging Bruce. He shook the man's hand.

"Hey, Bruce." His attention moved back to Bailey and he shook her hand with a gentle grip. "Hi, Bailey. Nice to see you again."

"Hi, Bobby. Is that your real name?"

He nodded. "We try to use everyone's real first names just to prevent mistakes." He turned his attention back to Bruce. "I can take it from here, Bruce. I'm sure you have lots to do."

Bruce gave him a relieved look. "There's plenty to do," Bruce agreed. "Good luck, Bailey. You're in fine hands," he added when she gave him a wary look.

"Your things arrived. They're in the bedroom," Bobby said. "But I can show you around first, if you want."

"Sure."

"What do you think so far?" Bobby asked as soon as Bruce was gone.

She looked around. "Well, it's emptier than I thought—"

"I mean, about Wingate? We just bought this house, so we're going to open our scene with it mostly empty. But what do you think about the world we created?" He looked excited, which caused him to look like a kid instead of a man she guessed was in his early thirties.

"Wingate is magnificent, especially in the details. That's not even factoring in that everything is real; real houses, real stores, real cement streets."

"Everything is in the details. Let me show you the kitchen. A lot of the shots take place in the kitchen." She followed him into the next room, where she saw the retro appliances people in modern days spent loads of money for.

Bobby took pride in turning on burners to the gas stove, showing her how to operate the oven and finally, how to work the percolator.

"Not many houses have these," he said. "But since we're a young couple that is moving up financially, we're going to have some of the bells and whistles. The attached garage has a washer and dryer. No dishwasher though. They had them in 1954, but they cost an arm and a leg up until about the '70s."

"I never use the dishwasher anyway," she said. "And I have no complaints about anything after seeing how Quinton, one of the new cast members, is living," she joked.

"Quinton," he said, and squinted. "The salesman. He starts out humble, but I wrote him to move up pretty fast. He'll appreciate where he goes if we all see how he started."

Bailey gave Bobby a surprised look. Did he just say *he* had written Quinton's script?

"You write scripts?" she asked.

"Yeah. I'm the producer," he replied.

Her eyes widened. "You're the producer? Of this entire production?"

He shrugged and looked a little embarrassed, but for some reason, she didn't think his reaction was fake. "I'm the producer and creator of 1954. I'm Robert Chesterfield Jr. You may have heard of me." The last was not a question. Of course she had heard of him—well, maybe not him specifically, but the Senior was well known. Who in the *world* hadn't heard of him?

Robert Chesterfield Sr. had nearly won the Republican nomination for president of the United States. The only reason Donald J. Trump had gotten the nomination instead was because of the scandal Chesterfield was embroiled in.

At the height of the #MeToo movement, Chesterfield had been accused of several instances of sexual misconduct with women, men, and underaged girls.

Not only did he lose the presidential bid, he lost his congressional seat—and his marriage. After several years, Chesterfield was still in jeopardy of serving prison time.

Bobby was watching her closely for her reaction, so Bailey didn't show how deeply shocked she was. She had been one of the people that had shared memes about the candidate and posted negative social media comments, raging against the entitlement that had allowed him to get away with sexual assault for so many years.

There was nothing she could say that could possibly glaze over the seriousness of this man's father's supposed crimes.

"The scandal left our family in shambles." Bobby sighed. "And for the record, none of my siblings have anything to do with our father. Even before he became a congressman, he wasn't really there for anyone but himself." Bobby shrugged. "But I'm not him. I would never do the things he's been accused of. So, if you have any questions about it, I guess we should get it out of the way now, so we can leave it behind us."

Bailey stared at him.

I'm going to be playing opposite this man whose father was accused of rape. A man that certainly lived a life of excess and entitlement, and who may have been touched by an environment that celebrated rape culture. And I will be in close quarters with him for the next year...

Her expression became closed. "I'm not going to lie. I'm...surprised. But I won't pass judgement on you, and I don't have any interest in your private life. I just want to excel in this role."

He nodded and gave her a sad smile. Perhaps it was the response he needed, but not the one he wanted.

Bobby continued showing her around the house, suggesting what items they would need to discuss filling the house with so they would be prepared during filming.

"Should we rehearse?" she asked when he mentioned his character would probably like to fill the office with books and a secondhand desk.

"Rehearsing can sometimes detract from the story. In 1953, when the cast tried writing out their dialogue, they started sounding like kids in a sixth-grade play.

"The script is just a guide. For instance" — he hurried to a box in the living room and retrieved a huge book — "we need to decorate this house. The script says you use the Sears and Roebuck catalogue to do that." He passed it to her. "How you do it, what you pick, is not scripted."

Bailey's brow rose. "Do you mean I get to choose how this place is furnished?"

"No," he replied. "We have a design team for that. In fact, you can expect a furniture delivery tomorrow afternoon. But you will get to choose how it's decorated."

"But what about you? Don't you want a say in the decor? You'll be living here too."

"It's not my place," he said. "We try very hard to adhere to the norms both in script as well as out of it. It just...helps to prevent mistakes."

She was busy leafing through the catalogue and didn't pay attention to his quiet contemplation of her.

"My auntie used to have a Sears and Roebuck catalogue sitting on the bathroom floor," she chuckled. "I guess Uncle Dewbug needed something to do while he was handling his business."

Bobby cocked his head at her and blinked. "Yes, Bailey! That's the type of thing I want you to do when the camera's running. I can't script that."

She was surprised by his reaction to her simple statement. But she nodded. "I understand. You want everything to sound natural."

He nodded. "Yes. As if we know everything about each other."

"Okay." She wanted to joke about being an actor but something about him made her think he wouldn't like that.

"Here's our bedroom," he said, and gestured into one of the rooms.

Ours? They had to share a room?

The cluttered bedroom had boxes presumably filled with her new wardrobe, bed railings that were being put together, mattresses and a box spring propped against the wall, a dresser, and a vintage, floor-length mirror that still had Bubble Wrap securing it.

It was such a mess—but there was also a white vanity with a white satin chair. It had gold inlays, and the legs were thin but curved so it gave a rounded appearance. It was absolutely beautiful, and it was hers—where she would sit each day and apply her makeup and do her hair.

"I was putting our beds together," he said, and she turned her attention back to him before she could gush about how beautiful everything was.

"It's a trundle bed, but no one should be able to tell once it's put away. You'll get the main bed and at night I'll sleep in the pull-out trundle. Sorry we can't have our own bedrooms, but our house isn't big enough." He was talking fast and looked worried about her reaction, so she made sure not to reflect one.

"I understand. Thanks for making a trundle bed."

He nodded in relief. "All the couples have them except people that are in real relationships with each other."

"There are people really in relationships?" she asked.

"Oh yes. There is a couple that got married last year in front of the cameras. We've also had a breakup or two, but they were just minor story lines. A few people have kids. Obviously, we can't have school-aged children on set, but it works for now."

"Do you see this going on year after year?"

He smiled. "Of course."

She looked around without asking him why 1954. All that mattered is she was guaranteed a nice payday. "We have a lot to do. We'd better get started," she said.

He seemed to appreciate the help, but she wondered why he didn't just hire a crew to do this. For instance, when they'd dropped Drew off at his "parents'" house, his mother had been cooking dinner. If the butcher had his meat delivered, why couldn't they have the meals done the same way? Just pop it in the oven and pretend they'd prepared it?

Thinking of food was making her hungry. It was late in the day, and she had missed lunch and it was now approaching dinnertime.

"What do we do for food between filming?"

They'd just gotten the bed put together and he was gathering up all the wrapping paper to take out for trash pickup. He explained that the garbage truck would run every few hours to make sure the garbage pails only contained "normal" garbage when filming started.

She thought that was a crazy thing to worry about, but didn't say anything.

"I'm sorry, are you getting hungry? The catering truck is also running today. But it's just soup and sandwiches."

"That sounds great to me." She helped gather the trash, which they stuffed into garbage bags and carried to the kitchen.

She followed him into the kitchen, where he pulled out a worn menu looked like it belonged to a restaurant.

"They had delivery in 1954?" she asked in surprise.

"No, I don't think so. It's just that everything has to look like a prop. Authenticity."

"Authenticity," she agreed.

Chapter Six

Bobby and Bailey sat at the kitchen table eating remarkably delicious double-decker sandwiches and cups of broccoli cheddar soup. There was cold Coca-Cola in old-fashioned glass bottles—and for some reason, it tasted even better than what was sold in the plastic containers. Maybe it was old enough to contain trace amounts of cocaine.

Bobby appeared more at ease as they talked about all that would happen tomorrow.

"You and I won't start filming until nine a.m." He stood and hurried out of the room. When he returned, he carried with him a leather binder—because of course, authenticity wouldn't allow him to carry a cheap cardboard one. He passed her a few sheets of paper.

"This is your weekly outline. It goes in your notebook, which is in the kitchen drawer by the stove. Your notebook looks like a ledger for doing the budget. So if you need to refer to your script, you can...but try not to do it often during the shoot."

She quickly scanned her outline as he spoke. The first few paragraphs detailed her backstory. Bailey was a graduate of Wilberforce University. It was a primarily Black college. So far, so good.

An only child whose parents lived out of state, Bailey's character had been forced to drop out of college due to lack of money. But instead of returning to Tennessee, where her prospects were slim, she got a job as a bank teller in Wingate.

One day while she was waiting to catch the bus to go home, Bobby Banks walked past a lady so pretty he had to retrace his steps pretending he had dropped something, just so he could take a second look.

Bailey liked that the story line she had developed in the audition was now part of the permanent script. She continued reading.

After a whirlwind marriage, the newlyweds moved into a duplex owned by Bobby's mother, and after Bobby's raise at the *Gazette*, the two had just received the keys to their new home.

She turned the page. At the top was listed the date for the current week, and then in bold letters it described each day.

Day 1: Bailey's excitement at having a new house and new car is contagious. It becomes obvious she's not used to such nice things as she expresses her joy to her husband at every new object.

Bailey discreetly rolled her eyes as she continued to read.

Bailey's inexperience with running her own household will provide humor as well as ingratiate her to the audience. It is a learning experience for both her and the viewers.

She is left in charge of furnishing the house and goes through the Sears and Roebuck catalogue wistfully, knowing they are not yet able to afford all of the finery she may want.

Day 2: Bailey must navigate the new town and goes grocery shopping. She may not know how to cook well, but Bobby would never tell her so.

On and on it went, with meeting new neighbors and finding ways to occupy herself while she waited each evening for Bobby to return home.

When she finished reading the "script," Bailey sighed and looked at Bobby in disappointment. She had been hoping for more substance—something meatier than this. But it was as if they were writing this for a child, or maybe a Black Lucile Ball.

Bobby looked down at the rejected script and surprised her with a smile. "Before you say anything, I intentionally left a lot open-ended so you can fill it in. What you do all day when I'm at work is something I won't know. But what I do know is you have to be *cute*—not cute in looks, but *fun*. You don't have to be the comic relief, Bailey. But you have to fulfill our viewers' desire to see exactly what a '50s housewife is.

"The character outline you wrote talks about your excitement at going grocery shopping without your mother-in-law so you could prepare your first meal for your husband by yourself. I want that in the story line!

"When I first read your script, what stood out is how fulfilled you were, not just by serving your spouse, but for your own accomplishments—like how you made pie that had too much sugar, but your husband just put less sugar in his coffee and then had two slices.

"It was perfect!" Bobby exclaimed. "When I finally met you, you gave me the same idealistic feeling I'd gotten from your outline. It was fresh. *You're* fresh."

She smiled in appreciation; his enthusiasm once again fired her up. But then he dashed it with his next statement.

"Uhm"—he averted his eyes—"I think you should probably look at your notebook."

"My notebook? Okay..." She got up and opened the drawer next to the stove, where she saw a binder that did resemble a ledger.

She brought it back to the table and opened it. He gave her a sheepish look. "You have to follow the cleaning schedule. All the housewives do. But," he added quickly, "feel free to adjust it to whatever order you want."

After flipping to the first page, she found a page that was completely filled with tasks.

"I'm sorry," he said quickly. "We don't make enough money to get a maid."

Bailey chuckled. "Well, there's a lot here. But I come from an old-fashioned family and we know how to clean. I can have this done in a couple of days—"

"Well...you're supposed to do this every day."

"Every day!" Her eyes practically bugged from her head. "Well, this has like twenty things to do. It says here I have to dust, vacuum, mop. And I need to clean the bathroom every single day?"

"And prepare meals, do the grocery shopping— but you only have to wash the windows once a week."

She gave him an incredulous look. "But if I do all this, how will I have time for anything else?" She pointed at the list. "It says here I have to exercise every morning. And why do I only eat toast and coffee for lunch?"

"Because you won't have time for anything else. You also get to go to the beauty salon once a week. And there's money enough to get your nails done—"

She almost sputtered, but he continued.

"Bailey, this is what people are paying hundreds of dollars a day to see. This is the kind of thing a 1950s housewife did. Why do you think it's so special? People in real life wouldn't do this. But in 1954, women were judged on how well they maintained their households—while wearing a full face of makeup *and* heels."

"This sounds like...a fetish series."

He shrugged and gave her a rueful smile.

"You're right. Of course, that's all this is. It's geared for those that want to peer into an age when people lived their lives this way."

She got a sudden understanding. "There are no shortcuts because this isn't just about the output. This is about really being in 1954."

He just smiled.

"How many scriptwriters are there?" she asked.

"Everyone gets input on their script, but I get the final say. We'll have a weekly team meeting where we go over the script for that week. While I'm 'supposedly' at work at the *Gazette*"—he made air quotes—"I'm actually doing a lot of the production and writing. My story line is relatively small because of that. I want you to look at me as if I'm *your* prop. I'm a supporting character to you."

She was surprised but pleased at his words. "Ok...I feel like I have a starring role."

"You do," he said. "You and the other four new hires. You're real actors. The rest of us just have a passion for this project."

Bailey frowned in confusion. "Are you saying the folks from 1953 aren't actors?"

"Nope. Not a one. But I didn't want them to act. I just wanted them to live." He wasn't looking at her now. It seemed as if he was in deep thought about something that took away his focus.

He finally looked at her again. "Anyway, 1954 now has structure, so it's totally different than 1953. We broke the cast into teams, and each team has a weekly meeting. We pay well to make sure everyone stays in character, and subscription to the project has exceeded our highest expectations."

She liked what he had to say. "When do we get to see ourselves?" She couldn't imagine how she'd look in a 1954 setting. Also, she wanted her aunt and uncle to see her and understand this was a legitimate acting job.

He stood and began gathering their empty food wrappers. "You can watch Sunday after our team's meeting. Have you decided what day you want to take for your weekly leave?"

She stood and helped him clean up. "Not yet. Maybe Sunday after the meeting." He just nodded. "When do you take off?"

"I don't. I guess I'll take a few hours here and there. But I'll let you know when that happens." He leaned against the counter with the half-empty bag of trash in one hand and appraised her.

"What do you think about all this?"

"I think it's exciting, and very smart," she replied.

"What about living with a stranger for a year?" He was watching her closely.

She thought about her honest feelings before answering. "Well, performers stay in close quarters all the time. If I were a musician, I might be spending most of my time on a tour bus with ten other people." She smiled, realizing she didn't really have an issue with spending time in Bobby's company. If what he said was true, then he would be out working most of the time. And although sharing a bedroom with a guy would be an adjustment, she was open-minded and forward thinking. It wasn't like she would be walking around in the nude or anything, and she assumed the same was true for him.

Besides, he wasn't hard on the eyes. Bobby wasn't too tall, or too short. He wasn't too thin, he wasn't too buffed—he was just…perfect, actually.

She could see his arms were well-muscled, as were his thighs, and he had a cute butt that filled out his pants.

He smiled easily, and although his attention seemed to drift, she attributed it to having a creative mind.

She noted he looked relieved at her response and it made her wonder if he'd done this before; lived in a house with a cast member, so she asked him.

"Not really. But I'll be spending so much of my time at the 'office'"—again, he made air quotes—"that I won't be in your space very much. But we do share a bedroom and the bathroom, and of course, we will be playing a married couple. While there is some affection expected between us, I don't want you to think I'll behave inappropriately. There will never be any kissing beyond a peck on the cheek in greeting and hand-holding in public. I'll always respect your privacy."

She nodded. "We'll be fine." She gave him an encouraging smile. "If something happens that makes me uncomfortable, we'll discuss it during the team meeting."

He sighed in relief. "Okay. I'll take out this garbage."

He left through the kitchen door and Bailey smiled. She liked Bobby, and once they began filming, the butterflies that were flapping around in her tummy would finally quiet down.

Chapter Seven

Bobby had to leave her for a few hours to make sure everything was prepared for shooting, but he promised he wouldn't be too long. He offered her a copy of the master script to look over. It contained the story lines for everyone in town.

Instead of scanning it in his absence, she began reading it word for word and by the time he had returned at close to midnight, she had a great deal to talk about.

If he had written this, then the man was a genius. Bruce had stated they shouldn't worry about their lives being mundane. And now she understood, because the day-to-day activities of the people in town were far from boring. It was the small things that made 1954 exciting. She found herself turning each page wanting to know more, to see more about the lives of her neighbors and the other townspeople.

She understood why Robert Chesterfield Jr. had placed so much of his time and energy into recreating 1954. It was because even just reading about the people created a nostalgia and longing for something she'd never experienced. And if just merely reading about it caused that to happen, then she could only imagine what happened when people actually watched it — watched *them*.

Later that night, they lay in their respective beds talking and enthusing about the characters and script. Their conversation didn't feel strained or uncomfortable; in fact it was like the first night of sleepaway camp — only a co-op camp.

Bobby sat propped up with his pillows under one arm, dressed in matching pajama top and bottoms, while she lay on her side facing him, dressed in a linen nightgown that was so modest, it hid more of her body parts than the outfit she'd worn earlier in the day.

His trundle bed sat only a foot from the ground, so he had to prop himself up on his elbow just to get a glimpse of her.

When he finally yawned, while still enthusing about some point in the script, Bailey had to force herself to allow the poor man to get some shut-eye.

"This is like the night before Christmas," she said, not tired even though it was after 1:00 a.m. "I'm anxious for the big day tomorrow, but I can't sleep."

"I know," he said, his eyes bright, which caused him to look like a kid on Christmas Eve. "This is when all of our planning is going to finally be put to the test. 1954 is going to be so much bigger than 1953."

"It's an amazing script. And most everyone has done this before. Get some sleep and try not to worry," she said.

He lay down after fluffing his pillow. "You already sound like my wife."

She reached over and turned off the lamp on her bedside table.

"That's good," she replied. What was a wife but your friend? And she could be that easily.

The next day, she awoke to the sound of water running in the bathtub. She checked the clock on the bedside table and saw that it was just after 5:00 a.m.

He was up already? She jumped up and grabbed her robe and then dashed to the kitchen to brew coffee in the percolator. She got two coffee cups from the cabinet; there was already sugar on the table and a small container of cream in the fridge.

"Bailey?" she heard Bobby call.

She quickly wiped her eyes and patted the handkerchief that kept her hair wrapped in place.

"I'm making coffee!"

He appeared in the kitchen wearing a look of surprise. "I didn't expect you to get up this early—but that coffee is a welcome sight. Thanks."

When he headed for the stove, she stopped him. "No, sit down. I'll get it. I know we're not filming but...we should probably get in the habit, you know...like we're really married."

He nodded. "Right." He took a seat and she poured him coffee.

"Little cups," she commented. "Compared to what we use nowadays." She was thinking of the big mug she had packed away in a box and stored at her aunt and uncle's house with her other belongings.

She fried bacon and scrambled some eggs while he made notes in his ledger.

She proudly placed the meal in front of him. "Sorry there's no grits."

He closed his ledger and smiled at the offering before his brow quirked upward. "What are grits?"

"You've never had grits? It's something that fills your belly the way these bacon and eggs alone won't. So, Mister Banks, it looks like I will be making you grits, if I can find some in town."

He gave her a slow smile at the use of the words *Mister Banks*. "I'll pick some up on the way home from the office." He paused and his smile drooped. "Is it okay if we cue that scene for filming? It's earlier than nine but—"

Bailey looked around. "The cameras are already filming?"

"They started at six a.m. and they will go nonstop for the next year, but you're not cued until nine a.m., so if you still want a little more time—"

"No." The butterflies made a reappearance in her belly. She had just been trying to be cute by calling him Mister Banks, but now it was happening. It was really happening!

She sat down and began to eat, trying to think of something 1950-ish to say. Oh God...her brain was stumped. She sat quietly eating her eggs and bacon while she mentally froze up.

"Thanks for getting up so early to make me breakfast," Bobby said while chowing down on his meal. "I want to get a jump-start on the day before the big boss gets in."

She looked up at him, resisting the urge to pat her head wrap. She wasn't wearing makeup! Egads, why had she agreed to this?!

"That's a good idea," she muttered. Oh God, I'm failing at this!

Should she tell him not to work too hard? No, she should give him some encouraging words.

"What are your plans for the day?" he asked. And then he waited patiently while her face drew a blank. "I suppose you'll be pretty busy getting this mess in order..." he supplied.

Suddenly, she remembered the ledger with her daily outline.

"I need to get this house in order," she muttered, and then cleared her throat. "I need to find the Sears and Roebuck catalog. And you, sir, have quite a lot of books that need to be unpacked." Her brain and tongue finally kick-started.

Bobby gave her a relaxed smile. "Don't worry about the books or my office, honey. I'll tackle that over the weekend."

"Well, there's plenty of unpacking to do." She freshened his coffee and then bent down and kissed his forehead. "Don't work too hard today. I'm going to need you to come home and get some things put together, like connecting the washing machine and putting the light bulbs in the ceiling, and hauling out the empty boxes."

Bobby laughed and then gave her a swift side hug. "Hey, now. You'll work me harder than they do at the paper!"

She gave him an encouraging smile. "You'll be fine. They chose you for this promotion for a reason."

"I hope so, Bae." He shortened her name, and she did not anticipate having that particular nickname. At least it wasn't kitten, or something equally as cringy. "I've worked so hard to become an actual editor," he continued. "But more importantly, you won't have to work. I want to give you the best of the best."

She looked around at the kitchen but then her eyes settled on his. "I already have the best of the best."

He reached out and she gave him her hand. Their fingers intertwined on the tabletop and then he quickly untwined them and jumped to his feet. "I better get going if I want to make sure everyone gets their morning paper."

Bobby came around and kissed her cheek. "Bye. Have a good day, Mrs. Banks."

"You too, Mr. Banks."

He left, and she wanted to check her breath. She hadn't brushed her teeth this morning. But she knew the camera hadn't stopped filming just because he had left.

The hell with this! I'm going back to bed, she thought. She had a few more hours before she was scheduled to be filmed and she was exhausted. Bailey yawned, snatched the last slice of bacon, and munched on it while she put the dirty dishes in the sink to wash later. Yep, that would give them something worthy of filming.

She went back upstairs. Now that she'd done her first "shoot," she wasn't quite as freaked out. In fact, because she couldn't see any cameras or lights, and there was no person calling action, Bailey didn't truly feel as if she had been acting.

Just be natural, she reminded herself as she slipped tiredly between the covers.

Bobby had already made up his trundle bed and had pushed it back into its hidden position. Without him there, her body fell into a natural sleep. *I will set the alarm for 8:30*, she thought as her eyes closed. *Oh, wait...no cell phone.* She glanced tiredly at a brass alarm clock on the nightstand. *How would I even set that thing?* She was too tired to even contemplate it. *Oh, never mind. I'll just close my eyes for a few minutes...*

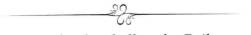

The ringing of a doorbell woke Bailey and she sat up with a jolt and looked over at the silent clock on the nightstand. Oh, Lord! It was 9:05! She had overslept!

She jumped out of bed and threw on her robe, forgoing her slippers. Oh no, this was her first day and she was about to be fired!

She dashed down the stairs, checking that her head wrap was still in place. Bailey rubbed any residual sleep from her eyes and then opened the front door expecting to see Bruce Adams, or some other member of the production team—maybe even 1950s police to escort her off the set.

Instead, she saw a woman holding a covered dish. Both women looked at each other in surprise.

The other woman recovered first. "Hi. Welcome Wagon," she said while slipping on a radiant smile. And yet wasn't there a slight smirk in her smile? Had she intentionally come early in order to catch Bailey at her worst?

Bailey hid her embarrassment and then made sure her robe was tied. "Oh. How kind. It's been a hectic few days," she explained.

"I'm sure," the woman said while giving her a once-over. Again, Bailey got the impression that the woman was being a bit snide. "I'm Helen. Helen Swanson. I live across the street," she said while offering her hand.

She was a bit older, maybe in her mid-thirties. Her short, brunette hair was perfectly coiffed. She wore a plaid dress with a swing skirt that seemed to have petticoats beneath. Petticoats at 9:00 a.m.? Her makeup was on point, making her appear every bit the 1950s housewife.

Bailey shook her hand. "Bailey Banks. My husband, Bobby, is at work."

"Hank is too. He's on the road a lot; trucker." Helen and Hank, Bobby and Bailey...Bailey was feeling a theme here.

"Uh...would you like to come in?" Bailey offered when it appeared Helen wasn't leaving.

"Well, just for a cup of coffee," she said while moving past Bailey into the house. Bailey couldn't hide her displeasure as she shut the door behind her. Who came visiting unannounced at 9:00 a.m. wearing a face full of makeup? Someone that wanted to show you up, that's who.

"Please pardon our..." Bailey couldn't find the words to describe the condition of the living room. It was a mess. There were unpacked boxes, pieces of furniture shoved into corners, and stacks of books that needed to be put away—once there was a bookshelf to do so.

Helen moved right through the room and straight into the kitchen, which was also a total mess, but mostly because Bailey had left the morning dishes unwashed. Most of the boxes had been unpacked, but items still needed to be organized so there were Tupperware dishes stacked on the counter and flour and sugar that needed to be added to the decorative flour and sugar tins.

She remembered Bobby explaining that the housewives of this era prided themselves on how well they managed their home. And now her neighbor would probably go off gossiping that the "Negro woman" kept a dirty house.

"I brought a coffee cake," Helen announced while placing it on the table.

"I'll brew coffee," Bailey said. "Please excuse our mess." She gave Helen a pointed look. "If I had known I'd have a visitor, I would have prepared."

Helen's smile faltered. "No explanations needed, dear. Is there anything I can do to help?"

God no, Bailey thought. So you can run around telling everyone you helped me clean my dirty house?

"No, sit down, Helen, and tell me about yourself. Any children?"

Bailey quickly started the coffee brewing and then found the dishes and utensils for the cake.

Helen certainly was a talker. But she didn't ask Bailey one thing about herself—such as what had brought her to town, how she had met her husband, whether she worked outside of the house. Bailey soon realized Helen was using up her prime time with her own story line. It only made sense that she would, since Bailey did have a starring role. But she didn't like the conniving way Helen was doing it.

"So, you made this coffee cake yourself?" Bailey interrupted. Because it was dry as hell. Helen had been going on and on about the other neighbors. Yep, she was the neighborhood gossip.

"I certainly did. It's my mother's recipe. I'll share it with you," she said proudly.

"Thank you. Bobby and I have only been married a few months. We were living in the apartment owned by his mother and, well…she cooked dinner for us every night." Bailey nibbled a small piece of the dry cake as she spoke. "I want to learn how to cook and do all the things a wife is supposed to do for her husband. But Mother Banks does everything so much better."

"Ain't that the way of the world," Helen said. "It's good you got your husband away from that situation. Is he a mama's boy?"

"Bobby? Oh no. Not at all. But after his father died, he took on a lot of responsibilities—as a good son should. But she doesn't need to take care of him anymore. That's my job."

"Good luck with that. Hank and I moved far away from my mother-in-law so beyond the biannual visit, I don't have to deal with her."

"Well, Mother Banks and I get along well." Bailey stood and gathered their dishes and placed them in the sink. She swept the uneaten portion of her coffee cake into the trash bin while Helen looked on in surprise.

"Well...I should probably get going," the woman said. Bailey smiled politely and waited for her to do so.

Helen stood. "I'll come back later for the dish—"

"No, don't trouble yourself. I'll bring it back. Just show me where you live." And on that note, she escorted Helen to the front door, where the other woman pointed out a pea-green house across the street. Helen opened her mouth to speak—perhaps to begin another long story about herself—but Bailey smoothly interrupted. *I am an actress,* she thought. *And today, I will act as if I have a backbone*—because in reality, she probably would have let this woman talk her to death!

"It was so nice of you to stop by, Helen. Thank you for the coffee cake. And please don't forget, I want that recipe."

Helen plastered on a smile. "Certainly. It was so nice to meet you, Bailey. Say, maybe you and your husband would like to come by and meet some of the other neighbors? We play bridge Saturdays. We can have a welcome-to-the-neighborhood barbecue. How does that sound?"

"Oh..." It actually sounded nice. "I'd like that. Thank you, Helen. I look forward to it. And thanks again for the coffee cake."

Helen finally left, and Bailey went to the kitchen and scraped the remainder of the coffee cake into the trash.

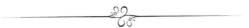

The very next thing she did was get herself cleaned up, being quick about it in case someone else decided to just drop in. Besides, there was supposed to be a furniture delivery later and she was looking forward to seeing what type of furniture she'd be living with for the next year. Also, it was nearly ten, and she hadn't started any of her scripted itinerary — namely, daily chores.

Bailey dressed in the only pair of slacks she owned, along with her tennis shoes and a simple shirt. She tied a decorative scarf neatly around her head to hold her pressed hair in place, hoping she would not sweat through her curls, since she had no curling iron to fix them if that happened.

She knew she was probably expected to put on a full face of makeup, but that seemed ridiculous knowing she was going to be cleaning and unpacking all day long.

So she would at least look presentable for the camera, Bailey defined her eyebrows, applied eyeliner, and added moisturizer to her lips. And that was that. Bailey had a naturally good and youthful complexion without a need for makeup.

She was neither light-skinned nor dark-skinned. She was brown like the shell of a pecan. Her fuller figure was more on the athletic side, and even though her hips swelled and her butt was nicely rounded, her belly was mostly flat—despite her love of carbs and sweets.

Bailey thought she was pretty enough. Although she had no boyfriend, she knew she drew the attention of the opposite sex. But dating had taken a back seat to attending curtain calls instead of hitting a club for some random relationship.

First things first were the bathrooms. If this was going to be her home for the next year, then the place was going to get a good, down-home cleaning! The one off the bedroom had the bathtub, which she scrubbed with Ajax. Using a scrub brush, Bailey cleaned the floor—getting rid of the previous occupant's germs. She made sure to scrub behind the toilet as well because she had learned from an old boyfriend it was possible for a man to pee behind the toilet.

Once both bathrooms sparkled, she tackled the kitchen; sanitizing the cabinets, drawers, and all of the surfaces. Helen might think she didn't know how to keep a clean house, but the viewers would know. Her house was about to be the cleanest in Wingate!

While the kitchen floor dried from another hands-and-knees scrubbing, she decided she needed to get cracking on the living room.

She dragged boxes filled with Lord knew what into the spare bedroom, the one designated to be Bobby's office. She just needed a clean slate for the furniture delivery and then she'd go through the boxes later; maybe that could be a project for her and Bobby. She certainly hoped he didn't expect her to do all the unpacking by herself.

The hardwood floors were scuffed and dull, and badly needed mopping and waxing. She remembered this chore from living with her aunt and uncle that had done things the old-fashioned way. She took out the floor polisher and floor wax and got going. It was tedious but rewarding when an hour later, all of the floors gleamed.

By now her back ached and her shoulders screamed as if she'd just hit the gym without warming up.

I am not *doing this every day.*

But she stood proudly with hands on hips, looking at her handiwork. There was still lots to be done—she'd just hidden most of it in Bobby's office.

It was now after one, and she realized she had skipped lunch. But she wanted to work on the bedroom so the deliveryman could set up the much-needed furniture, and then she could finally unpack her personal belongings. In the meantime, she stacked her and Bobby's boxes in the spare bedroom—which was beginning to look like a hoarder's paradise, and then went to work mopping, waxing, cleaning windows, and scrubbing baseboards.

At close to three, her stomach began to growl at its neglect.

I need food and a nap. She was literally whupped. She remembered she was technically at work. *You get no nap!* Right, because although she doubted anyone would be truly watching her doing nothing more than cleaning for hours on end, she had to assume some weirdo probably found it entertaining.

She rubbed her sore shoulders, wondering if there was Motrin or Ibuprofen packed away in one of the boxes. Before she could go to the kitchen to reheat the coffee and figure out what to eat, the deliverymen arrived and her energy perked right back up.

She forgot about her fatigue as she let them in and was pleasantly greeted with a surprise on her doorstep. There was a glass container of milk, a smaller container of orange juice, a carton of eggs, butter, and a block of cheese. She picked up the items, desperately happy to have more provisions to put in her nearly empty refrigerator.

She then instructed the deliverymen on where to put the furniture, warning them not to scuff her floor. She was simply too tired to care if that made her sound like a bitch—but there was just too much hard work that had gone into making them shine.

Once everything was in and they were gone, Bailey looked at the house that would be her home.

She had to admit, she didn't hate it the way she had expected. Thankfully, nothing was floral. But she had a purple couch.

That was definitely not expected. It was vintage but strangely, also chic and cool. They were playing the role of a young, cool, forward-thinking couple. This is how they would decorate.

The purple sofa was joined by two salmon-colored chairs, an oval cocktail table, and two side tables where two slender lamps sat. There was an area rug that hid much of her gleaming floors, but again, she didn't hate it. Despite the muted purple color, it fit.

They now had a floor-model television. She was tempted to turn it on but was afraid it might just be a prop, even though it had the obligatory rabbit ear antennae.

She ran her hands over the velvety upholstery and then found a rag to polish away any fingerprints from the wooden surfaces. Yeah, she was falling in love with this room. With a few personal touches, it could be dynamic. Her old place certainly wasn't this chic.

In the bedroom, they had delivered a dresser and mirror, and then a desk, chair, and bookshelf had gone into Bobby's office. They had politely refrained from mentioning the crowded condition as they placed the furnishings however it would fit.

She wanted to unpack her clothes and personal items but there was no time. It was getting late, and she had no idea what she was supposed to make for dinner. Besides, she was a hot mess, and she did not want her fake husband to come home and see her looking like this. He might want to fire her and hire someone cuter!

Bailey quickly ran a hot bath, wishing she could linger. What time was he supposed to get home? Maybe he'd work late, she hoped. Because a true 1950s housewife would be dressed to the nines with dinner waiting and a cocktail in hand for him as he walked through the door—and frankly, that decidedly was *not* going to happen today.

If they had liquor, it was packed away in a box. And the only thing in the pantry was a box of Kraft dinner and a bag of potatoes, but at least she would look presentable.

Bailey dug through her unpacked boxes for one of her dresses—a cute, beige dress with no pattern. She slipped on a pair of nylons, kitten heels, and then she applied her makeup. She styled her hair, pleased to see that the kerchief she'd worn on her head all morning had done its job in keeping her curls in reasonable order.

There you go, viewers. I can clean up nicely.

Her legs were sore from bending and hauling boxes all morning, so she had to work hard not to limp. That would not be cute. She hurried to the kitchen to boil the water for the mac-n-cheese and before she could grab a pot, she heard Bobby's car pull into the driveway.

Bailey's tummy flipped in anxiety as she gnawed on her lip and looked at the clock. It was 5:19 and she had no dinner to present to her husband. She hadn't tackled even a quarter of the chores she was scheduled to do; she hadn't even looked at the Sears and Roebuck catalogue or eaten even one bonbon. She was failing as a 1950s housewife.

Chapter Eight

Bailey went outside to meet Bobby. She plastered on a happy smile but was actually worried. Had he seen all the ways she had messed up today?

She had already sensed he was a perfectionist. Living with the big boss was not going to be an easy task for someone who was on the more easygoing, chill side.

He was already heading up the walkway carrying a briefcase in one hand and a small sack in the other. But when he saw her, he stopped and beamed.

"What a sight for sore eyes," he said.

She clasped her hands in front of her shyly. She had never been great with compliments — but this was only acting.

He kissed her cheek and gave her a brief hug.

"Sorry I'm a little late. But I found grits." He handed her the sack and she looked inside.

"You remembered!" She had barely remembered.

"How was your day?" he asked as they headed into the house.

"Uh, busy. I didn't — "

"Bailey!" His mouth fell open and he placed his briefcase on the floor right inside the door. He looked around the newly furnished living room with an expression of awe on his face. He turned to her quickly. "You did all of this? By yourself?"

She gave him a half-smile and shrugged. "Yes…" Was she not supposed to do it? The script hadn't really addressed it.

"Honey, I was not expecting you to tackle all of this alone!" But he wore a pleased smile on his face as he walked around the room, admiring the furnishings. "You were right about this sofa. It is rad." He looked at her. "I need to trust your decisions more."

Oh, so she was to get the blame for the tripped-out color scheme.

She smirked. "Don't worry, honey. I left plenty for you to do." She took him straight to his office. When he opened the door, he laughed so hard she began to laugh too. He closed the door without taking one step into the room.

"I'm sorry," she said, her worried expression returning. "I didn't get a chance to make dinner—"

He faced her and placed his hands on her hips. "Don't be silly, Bae. You've worked harder than me today."

She felt a quick zing at his semi-intimate touch. It wasn't even truly intimate, but it was familiar—and not quite uncomfortable.

"Oh! I didn't even ask you about your day," she said.

He took her hand and led her to the front door. "How about we go out and grab a bite to eat and I'll tell you all about it?"

Thank you, Jesus! She was so hungry. "Are you sure? Because there's a box of macaroni and cheese calling your name in pantry," she joked.

"I feel the need to celebrate," he said. "New home, new furniture, new job—"

"And no mother-in-law," she said.

"We can invite her," he replied with a winning smile. Wow, he was so easy to improv with!

"Uh, no," she said with a shake of her head.

Bobby smirked and then headed for the stairs. "Let me get changed. I'll be right back."

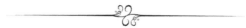

Bailey did not realize there would be a camera in the car, but there must have been because Bobby stayed in character and told her about his hectic day instead of waiting to arrive at the restaurant, where she would have thought he would have saved it for the viewers.

"Where are we going?" she asked when her tummy growled.

"Maybelle's. I think we both could use some good, Southern home cooking," he replied.

Maybelle's…was that the Black-owned restaurant? "I love Maybelle's."

"I'm just happy you introduced me to it," Bobby replied. "Miss Maybelle always made me feel welcome, even though it's a Negro restaurant."

Yep, she had guessed right. God, please have some fried chicken…

"You've never been nervous being around Negroes," she replied. And then before he could establish her story line, she continued. "Just like I had to be comfortable with whites, whites are going to need to be comfortable with Negroes. That's just the simple future."

They got to the restaurant in no time, leaving Bailey to wonder how Maybelle was going to prepare for them on such short notice. There were only a handful of Blacks in Westbrook. They'd have to basically get the majority of them to the restaurant in order for there to be any patrons.

But once they entered the restaurant, Bailey was pleasantly surprised. It sounded like a BB King tune was playing on the jukebox. Two couples were sitting at tables eating while an older guy was at the bar having coffee and smoking a cigarette. Indeed, everyone was Black.

An older woman poked her head from the kitchen and then plastered on a big smile.

"Bailey! You back from your honeymoon, chile?"

Bailey plastered on a smile. This must be Miss Maybelle...but she wasn't going to take any chances.

"Yes, ma'am. Bobby and I got back a few weeks ago."

"Hi, Miss Maybelle," Bobby said politely.

"Hi, baby. Y'all sit anywhere you want. You want your regular?" Maybelle asked.

"You know it," Bailey replied.

"I'll have the same," Bobby said, and then helped Bailey off with her coat. He hung them up and a woman went to the jukebox and slipped in a coin. Bailey didn't know the musical group but she was sure they were very hip for the times.

A lady hurried in through the door tying on an apron. She nearly tripped over her feet when she saw Bobby and then, blanching, she continued through to the kitchen.

"Sorry I'm late, Miss Maybelle," she called. "That bus..."

Bailey didn't hear much else.

"I was telling you about Roger. They're sending him to Dayton to cover the air show," Bobby said. He had been talking about that in the car. "The paper pays for everything, including the hotel."

"The *Gazette* sounds like a big-town newspaper," Bailey said.

The waitress rushed to their table. "What will you have to drink?" She placed down their silverware and napkins

Bailey wanted to say water; she didn't want another Coca-Cola. She'd cut back on soft drinks years ago. But did people order water in restaurants in the fifties? "Iced tea," she said.

"I'll have the same," Bobby said.

Bobby and Bailey continued to talk and joke—sharing that same comfortable rapport they'd had back at the house. And then Bailey's stomach began to growl as she finally began to smell good home cooking. A half an hour before, the restaurant just smelled a little stale, but now it smelled like a real restaurant.

Their food came out and Bailey wanted to drool. There *was* fried chicken! There were also mashed potatoes and gravy, and green beans. A plate of biscuits was placed on the table.

"Thank you," Bailey remembered to say before picking up a chicken thigh and chomping into it.

Ah. This tasted just like KFC.

There wasn't anything wrong with that. Bailey looked at Bobby, who was also enthusiastically enjoying his meal.

"How's everything?" Miss Maybelle came out to their table.

"You make the best fried chicken in town," Bobby complimented.

"Oh, now that recipe got handed down three generations before it got to me."

Slaves must have been cooking it, then, Bailey thought.

"Are you getting back on schedule for your weekly hair appointment, Bailey?" Maybelle asked with a smile. "You know Juanita books up fast. I'll be there tomorrow morning, so I can remind her that you want to keep your Saturday appointment."

Weekly?! There was no way she was going to sit in the hairdressers every damn week for two and three hours—if not more. The hairdressers were the main reasons she'd gone with a natural hairstyle.

"I—" she hesitated.

"Honey, there's money to splurge on the hairdresser," Bobby said. She nodded and smiled at Maybelle.

"Will you tell Juanita I'll be there Saturday?"

"Yep. Now are you two ready for dessert?" Maybelle asked.

Bailey could have stood for something sweet, but Maybelle had just low-key pissed her off.

She was beginning to see how people did things. They manipulated themselves or others into the script when they didn't have much of a role. Was there even a Black hairdresser in Wingate, or had Miss Maybelle just created one?

"Maybe next time," Bailey replied. "I'm pretty beat this evening."

"We both are," Bobby replied.

"I'll have Pearl bring out the check. You two take care, and don't be strangers!"

Once they left the restaurant, Bailey realized she truly was bushed—so much so that she forgot not to limp. Even the muscles in her shins ached.

"Honey, do you know if we have any aspirin back at the house?" Bailey stretched her back slightly. "I might have overdone it today."

Bobby gave her a look of concern. "I don't know, but we'll stop at the pharmacy. I'll get some Epsom salts too."

"Oh," she sighed happily. "That would be nice."

"Bae, don't work so hard. It'll all get done," he said while giving her a sincere look.

They drove to the pharmacy and Bobby had her stay in the car while he picked up the painkillers.

When he returned, Bailey was sound asleep. Bobby quietly drove home and then pulled into the driveway, allowing the car to idle. He didn't move to get out and just gazed at the quaint little house.

Bobby shifted his gaze to the woman slumbering next to him. Soft snores could be heard issuing from her nose and he smiled softly before finally turning off the car.

Chapter Nine

"Bailey. We're home," Bobby said, causing her to jump to attention. Her eyes opened wide with confusion before the memory of the last twenty-four hours washed over her.

"Oh, honey!" she exclaimed. "I'm so sorry I fell asleep!"

She was in a car in front of a quaint little ranch house—but in actuality, she was on a set shooting a reality series.

Bobby's brow dipped. "It's okay. Take off your shoes. It'll be all right." Bobby got out of the car and she saw him hurry to her side. He opened the door for her, because of course, it was the 1950s and men were nice like that.

She chuckled. "I'd better not step on a rock," she said while carefully stepping onto the driveway.

Suddenly, Bobby picked her up and she clutched him in utter surprise. She had not expected to be cradled in his arms. He quickly whisked her to the front door before placing her gently on her feet.

He opened the front door for her, bowing slightly with a pleased grin, gesturing for her to enter.

Bailey was at a loss for words, but the grin on her lips was genuine. Never had a man ever lifted her. It was archaic, but also sweet. It was definitely very '50s.

"Why don't you go up and run yourself a hot bath while I make you a drink."

Bobby moved to the bar and then scratched his head. Bailey smiled to herself. There was no liquor at the bar, but she was interested to see how he would play that off.

He smiled at her and grinned. "Okay...orange juice on the rocks?"

Bailey laughed and sauntered up the stairs still holding her shoes in her hand. If she was the director, she would have said, "...And CUT!"

The next morning, Bailey felt much better. The night before, she had popped two aspirin and soaked in the bathtub with the Epsom salts. She had been in bed by eight o'clock.

When she woke up, she simply lay there for a few minutes thinking about her first day of filming. She decided that all in all, it had been successful.

Bailey listened to Bobby's soft snores from his position on his trundle bed and her mind ventured back to when he had effortlessly lifted her in his arms. She remembered the feel of tight muscles beneath his shirt.

Hmmm. Did he work out?

Bailey shook away the thought, returning to yesterday's shoot. She wondered how she looked on film. She could barely wait until this weekend when she would be able to finally see herself. Well, she intended to be better prepared today. She'd definitely make the best of her day and not spend it all on cleaning—regardless of what her script deemed.

Bailey quietly climbed out of her bed so as to not wake up Bobby. It was still a little weird having a guy sleeping in her bedroom—but she had to remember that besides sleeping and changing clothes, he would rarely need to enter the bedroom. This room was her domain. Basically, every room in this house besides the office was hers!

She was definitely going to visit the Sears and Roebuck catalog today.

After visiting the bathroom to freshen up, Bailey went downstairs and put on the coffee, set butter and cream on the table, and then started the water boiling for the grits.

She had put on a cute, billowy robe that matched her cute, billowy gown. It was a bit itchy, but she certainly looked the part. From her research on YouTube, the '50s housewife did not get fully dressed until after breakfast.

Bailey heard Bobby come down the stairs half an hour later, just as the scrambled eggs went onto plates. She had already decided she was not going to get into the habit of frying bacon every morning. Not only was it unhealthy, it was a hassle, and she was the one that would have to clean up bacon grease.

He came up to her while straightening his tie and placed a chaste kiss on her cheek.

"Morning. Feeling any better?" he asked.

"Much better. The Epsom salts did the job—and the OJ on the rocks didn't hurt."

He poured himself coffee while she grabbed bowls and spooned hot grits into them.

Bobby leaned over and sniffed the piping-hot food.

"They don't smell like anything," he commented.

"Put some butter on them. I already added salt. My auntie told me that if you don't start with salted water, you'll never get grits properly seasoned."

Bobby watched as she added butter and then pepper to her own bowl of grits and he did the same. She blew on the piping-hot spoonful and when she saw him scoop up some, she advised him to be careful.

"Hot grits can be used as a weapon."

He raised a brow and then took a bite. Bobby chewed while in deep thought.

"It doesn't have much of a taste…"

"Some people put sugar in them, but I don't do that. Butter, salt, and pepper is all I need."

She picked up a slice of toast and quickly spread jelly on it. "Here. Jelly toast makes it taste even better."

As she watched him, Bailey saw the moment when he truly began to appreciate the Southern breakfast.

"Good, right?" she asked.

"I like it." He finished his eggs, another slice of toast, and even went back for a second bowl of grits.

"Let's have this tomorrow," he said.

"When I was a kid, we had grits almost every day."

"Oh, by the way." He gave her a curious look. "Why was there an entire coffee cake in the trash?"

Bailey palmed her face. "I met one of our neighbors; Helen. Such a pleasant woman, and kind enough to show up at nearly the crack of dawn," she said in a voice dripping with sarcasm. She got up and began putting away the breakfast items.

"Besides, I think she bought that cake from the day-old bread bin at the grocery store. Dry as a drought."

Bobby chuckled. "How dry was it?" he prompted.

She came behind his chair and kissed his cheek for no other reason than she liked seeing him amused.

"Dry as a wheat biscuit."

"She made a good impression, I see," he replied while trying to hold back his laughter.

"Well, to be fair, I overslept a little and when she rang the bell it rattled me. Oh! And we've been invited to a welcome-to-the-neighborhood barbecue this weekend."

"That sounds nice. We definitely have to go." Bobby looked at his watch. "I better get going," he said while standing. He quickly grabbed her hand and pulled her close. "Promise me you won't overdo it again today. Okay?"

"I promise," she said. His eyes stared into hers and lingered.

Bailey blinked. It almost...well that was crazy. But it did feel as if they weren't acting.

As soon as Bobby left, Bailey quickly washed the morning dishes and then grabbed the Sears and Roebuck catalogue. She perched herself at the kitchen table with pen and paper she had found in Bobby's office.

The catalogue was in pristine condition but appeared, in every way, to be authentic. Instead of heading straight to the home goods, Bailey couldn't help checking out every page of the vintage catalog. It was fascinating, and she was soon lost in everything from the styles of clothing to the low prices of the era.

Before she knew it, Bailey realized the morning was getting away from her. She put everything away and then dashed up the stairs.

Her first real day as a '50s housewife was about to begin and she was strangely excited.

Chapter Ten

Bailey quickly dressed in shorts and a sleeveless blouse. It wasn't exactly workout clothing but it would have to do. Actually, she was kind of cute in them. Normally, she would have dressed in sweats and an old T-shirt.

She remembered her list of chores—it would probably be seared into her brain for life. First on the list was to open curtains and windows—weather permitting--and let the sunshine in. Starting in the bedroom she did just that, and lingered there a moment looking out at the rising sun. She lived in a nice neighborhood where the cookie-cutter homes actually gave a pleasant vibe. Yards were decorated to reflect the individual tastes of each homeowner.

More than one house had plastic pink flamingoes, but she also saw a few plastic ducks, and even one large crystal ball. It wasn't as tacky as she might have imagined. It just somehow fit.

She wondered what they would put in their yard to reflect their personality. She grinned to herself when she remembered the Black Lives Matter sign her aunt and uncle had.

She moved to the bed and stripped down the sheets to air them out. She'd never done that before, but it was apparently a thing in the '50s. She then went from room to room throwing open all the curtains and windows.

She returned to the living room and checked the starburst clock that hung on the wall. It was almost eight. Great. Time to exercise. She had spotted a set of exercise records when unpacking and put one on the record player.

She was still a bit sore, but all in the pursuit of authenticity. Fortunately, the record was only fifteen minutes long and only gave her stretching exercises to do — or what they called limbering up movements.

If she had done this yesterday, she wouldn't be in pain today. Hmmm, maybe they did know what they were talking about.

After her workout, Bailey cleaned the kitchen, even setting the table for dinner.

Dinner, ugh. She still needed to go grocery shopping.

But first things first. She dusted the furniture again, ran the vacuum cleaner again, cleaned the bathroom again, and then realized she could be doing all of this while listening to the radio.

She turned on the radio and was pleased when she recognized the song that played. She didn't know the title or the artist, but she remembered some of the lyrics and hummed along to the beat as she resumed her chores.

After the bed was made, Bailey looked around in pride. It was quarter to ten, which meant there was no time to relax.

She retrieved a cookbook from the kitchen shelf and plopped down at the kitchen table to plan out her weekly meal. The music was interrupted by a fast-talking announcer reading several ads; one for Lucky Strikes cigarettes, the other for dish washing liquid, and then he returned to playing upbeat music. Bailey tapped her feet to the beat, actually feeling very domestic.

"What shall we have for dinner tonight?" she asked aloud but to herself...or at least, that's what the audience should think.

For a few moments, she had actually forgotten about the audience. Maybe because none of this actually felt real yet. After she looked at herself on film it might be easier to stay in character.

"Meat loaf," she said as she came to the first dinner. "Nope." She predicted there might be plenty of meat loaf in their future and she wouldn't start out with it.

"Spaghetti and meat sauce!" she read in excitement. She could make one mean spaghetti dish — and then her shoulders sank. But she made it with jarred tomato sauce. This recipe needed too many ingredients to do it from scratch. Next.

"Chicken and dumplings." She scanned the recipe. "Oh my God..." she muttered. "I don't know how to make biscuits. How do they make them so fluffy?" She stared at the photograph with its fluffy peaks. It did look good, and wouldn't require her to buy too much.

Bailey chewed her lip a bit and then began to copy down the ingredients she'd need from the store. "I guess we'll try it. What's next?"

The next page had a recipe for skirt steak. She'd never had it. It didn't look too difficult, though. She wrote down the ingredients for that.

Next was chicken pot pie. "But I need to make dough..." she spoke aloud. She'd never made dough all on her own. She'd never made much of anything, as she rarely cooked for herself. Aunt Mae always cooked extra and she had a Panera right next to her apartment. *Aunt Mae! I need your pie crust recipe so bad.*

She sighed. If she followed this recipe exactly, maybe she could do it. She wrote down the ingredients.

Okay, that was enough for now. There would probably be plenty of leftovers, and it would tide her over until this weekend when she could call her aunt.

She missed her aunt and uncle so much. There was so much to tell them; about the furniture, and Bobby. And all the cleaning.

Bailey returned the cookbook to the shelf and remembered something. She didn't have a car. She'd have to do all this by bus. She scratched her head, and then had an idea.

She hurried to the window and looked out across the street. A smile spread across her face. Helen, her gossipy neighbor, had a car!

Bailey hurried upstairs to quickly freshen up. She began applying makeup, deciding she didn't want to be too extravagant so early in the morning. But then she saw the iconic red 1950s lipstick.

She opened the cap and stared at it. It was matte, and beautiful. If this was good enough for Dorothy Dandridge in the movie *Carmen Jones*, then it was good enough for her.

After her makeup was in place, she unwrapped her hair. Ugh, the curls were nearly gone. Time to pin it up. She twisted her hair into a twirl that ended at the top of her head, then allowed her bangs to drape to the side.

Wow, she was cuter than she expected. She added eyeliner, despite thinking she didn't need to go all-out.

She changed out of her shorts and top and as an afterthought, quickly folded them and put them away, although in a prior life she would have just left them on the chair or bed.

She selected a brown-and-beige shirtdress with a matching belt—mostly because it didn't need a petticoat. It was cute, though. She primped in front of the mirror before remembering she had to get going if she wanted to be back in time to have dinner ready by five.

She put on her hat, pulled on dainty little gloves, and then slipped on a sweater. With low, black heels, Bailey felt like a completely different person.

She took a deep breath and then remembered Helen's dish. Hurrying to the kitchen, she grabbed the dish and tucked her grocery list into her pocketbook.

She liked how she felt as her heels click-clacked across the floor and out the door.

Bailey quickly rapped on Helen's door and then plastered on a smile. In the '50s you didn't call first, you just showed up at people's doors.

The door opened and Helen gave her a bright smile.

"Well, hello there, neighbor," she said.

"Hello. I hope I'm not intruding, but I wanted to return your dish and thank you again for the cake."

"No intrusion at all. Come on in — or were you on your way off somewhere?" Helen asked while scanning the way Bailey was dressed.

"Oh." Bailey's cheeks felt warm. Was she overdressed? She noted Helen didn't wear a petticoat today but a simple skirt and blouse, and yet her makeup was once again on point. Both of them looked as if they should have been starring in an episode of *Mad Men*.

"I need to go grocery shopping," Bailey continued. "And I wondered if you had any shopping to do, if you might want to join me."

"I always have shopping to do!" Helen exclaimed. "Come inside and I'll get my things."

Bailey handed her the dish and followed her into the house while Helen yammered about a sale she'd seen in the newspaper on oranges and grapefruit.

"I heard about a diet where all you need to do is eat grapefruit for breakfast. Can you imagine losing weight just because you added half a grapefruit to your breakfast?"

Bailey raised her brow. "And coffee, of course."

"Oh, I couldn't get through the day without coffee. I think I might give it a go. Hank likes his women more like Doris Day and less like Marilyn Monroe." Helen turned and looked down at her butt while batting her eyes at Bailey. Her form-fitting skirt showed she had indeed been blessed with nice assets.

Bailey chuckled, although she would never believe a man at any period of time wouldn't prefer his woman with a little meat on the bones.

Once inside, Bailey looked around at the neat living room while Helen grabbed her pocketbook and put on a sweater and scarf. The room was furnished in the classic mid-century modern style. She had looked it up on the Internet after learning she'd gotten the part on the show. The style had been their concept of futuristic living. The room had two matching pea-green leather chairs and a large but dainty orange couch. Matching side tables flanked it, reminding Bailey of walking statues with spindly legs. The room was nicely decorated, although she liked her house much better.

Helen grabbed her keys. "Shall we go?"

"Let's." Bailey was happy she wouldn't need to figure out the bus route. She decided she could probably get whatever help she needed as long as she was willing to share some of her screen time.

Bailey slipped into the car, admiring the bench seats. She'd forgotten there used to be such a thing.

"You'd better put on your seat belt," Helen said. "Automatic steering is so underrated!" She put the car in reverse and pulled out of the driveway. "Don't worry. I haven't wrecked yet—but if we do, that metal dashboard is going to fuck us up!" Bailey gave her a quick look, her mouth hanging open. "I can't believe people used to let their kids sit in the front seat without seat belts," Helen continued as she drove.

Not only had Helen said *fuck* and gone out of character, but she didn't even have the same voice. It dawned on her Helen had been using the transatlantic accent the 1930s actors used in movies and radio. How had she not caught on to that? Even the speed at which she spoke was different now, more relaxed and less frantic.

Bailey's eyes were like saucers as she looked around frantically for the camera.

Helen looked at her curiously. "What's wrong? You know they don't film in the cars, right? They still don't like us to go out of character, but who can stand it all day and all night?"

Bailey frowned. "There aren't any cameras in the cars?"

"Nope, and none in the bathroom—and none in the bedroom after lights-out."

Bailey scratched her head. Then why had Bobby been playing for the camera last night when they'd gone to Maybelle's?

Chapter Eleven

"So, how terrible is it living with Bob?" Helen asked while glancing at her as she drove.

"What do you mean?" Bailey asked. There wasn't anything terrible about him. He had been nothing but a gentleman, despite his father's reputation.

"Well, he is the boss," Helen added.

Oh. Well, she had no intentions of gossiping about the big boss. She knew who buttered her bread. "He's cool, and really nice. How was he last year?"

"He didn't do much acting until the end," Helen said. "And then we all believe he only gave himself enough onscreen time to help some of the actors' story lines. But he's a natural."

Bailey nodded in agreement. "He is." It was like he wasn't acting at all.

"What do you think of this gig?" she asked.

"I love it," Helen said. "I get to live rent-free for a year, and the money isn't too bad."

"Don't you think it's weird living with a stranger though?"

"Hank? Nah. He's in production, so I only interact with him on the weekends. Why? Is it weird for you?"

Bailey shook her head—not that she would ever tell Helen if it was. "I don't see Bobby, uh, Bob, much. But he's been very helpful."

"Well, if you ever get bored, come by and see me. I can really use the screen time. You know, the townies only get paid an additional salary based on screen time."

"No. I didn't know that. So, you guys just get paid what someone in your job position in 1954 would get paid?"

"Yep, including a cost-of-living increase. Don't get me wrong, it's still decent money—but nothing like you actors get paid. The real benefit are the fans. Oh my God, they send you gifts! One fan sends me a grand a month! They're all rich, you know."

"What? Are you serious? They send you money?"

"I'm serious. I just have to do something on screen for him. We have a little signal—wait." Helen gave her a quick look. "You won't tell Bob about the signal, will you? He's a real stickler."

"No, of course not." She was still surprised to learn about fans sending them money. "How many fans do you think you have?"

"Last year I ended the year with twenty or thirty. I'd love to double that this year."

"I'll help where I can, Helen."

"I appreciate it. And if you need to talk off camera, then we'll have a secret signal—just say something like, you need to go for a drive."

Bailey smiled at her in surprise at the offer. "You are awesome." She felt bad for thinking so badly of her. "And I'll help you out with your screen time."

"Thanks, Bailey. It will help."

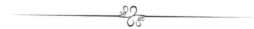

The moment the car pulled up to the curb to park, Helen went right back into character. She touched up her lipstick and then plastered on a broad smile.

Bailey tried not to grimace. Maybe they wanted the townies to be excessively upbeat. Far be it from her to criticize anyone's acting, but she would love to give her a few pointers. It might even help her with gaining new fans. She'd hold off until she knew her better.

They went to the butcher shop and then the grocery store. Bailey ended up adding two grapefruit to her shopping list along with some apples she wanted to try to bake for dessert. Even with two bags of groceries, she'd only spent $12!

She had a household budget of $20 a week, but when a loaf of bread only cost 14 cents, she could afford a little extra. She should probably buy some type of liquor. Wasn't she supposed to meet her husband at the door with a drink? No, that was too much. Orange juice would be their going joke until she had an opportunity to ask what liquor he liked, and then he could make his own drink.

When they were back in the car on the way home, Bailey apologized she couldn't linger to chitchat. But she needed to figure out how to cook one of the recipes.

"You don't know how to make pot pie, do you?" Bailey asked.

"Uh...I don't cook very well. You wouldn't want to ask me. This weekend when we have the barbecue, I would not eat too much of the potato salad. I'm horrible at it," Helen joked.

Bailey smiled. "My aunt won't let me bring food to the church picnic. I'm only allowed to bring ice."

They left the car laughing as if they were new best friends.

When she got to her house, it was half past one.

"Oh no...I'm running late."

She put away the groceries and then pulled out the cookbook. She decided to do the chicken and dumplings, since she would just basically have to throw everything into a pot.

Half the chicken went into the freezer for another day. The chicken stew portion of the recipe didn't bother her; she didn't even need to follow the recipe for it—anybody could make chicken soup! But she nervously studied the recipe for the dumplings. She knew it was basically biscuit dough, but baking had never been her strong point.

When she was twelve, she had tried making biscuits for the first time. They were burnt hockey pucks despite the fact she thought she'd followed the recipe exactly. Then Aunt Mae had tried to teach her, but they never tasted good.

Maybe chicken and dumplings had not been the best first choice...

She got everything prepared and was proud she didn't cut herself when dicing the carrots—although her eyes watered when she cut the onions, and she worried she might ruin her makeup.

After cooking for a while, she tasted the stew. It seemed a bit bland, so Bailey added more salt and pepper. How did Aunt Mae make her broth taste so good? She put something spicy in it but they didn't have hot sauce on set, so Bailey added even more black pepper.

She eyed the pot of bubbling liquid critically. Aunt Mae's had never been this soupy, so she added a few more tablespoons of flour to thicken it up.

While that continued to stew, she prepared two apples for baking. This should be easy. All she needed to do was get them cored and then top them with brown sugar and butter. Easy. She'd slip them in the oven when they started eating.

Dumpling time. She followed the recipe exactly for the soft biscuit dough. She wouldn't add more flour, even though everything in her told her they wouldn't rise.

Just follow the recipe, Bailey.

She took the lid off the pot of stew and saw it didn't look like soup or stew anymore because it had thickened up too much.

"Oh no..." It looked like bad mashed potatoes!

She added water, but it ended up looking like paste. Worse were the huge lumps—lumps that were so bad, she probably didn't need to add the biscuit dough on top.

Bailey fished out as many of the lumps as she could, wishing she could throw the entire batch out and start the whole recipe over. But there was no time to start all over. It was already just after four o'clock and Bobby would be home by five. She dropped the biscuit dough over the top of what remained of the stew and placed the lid on top, praying for the best.

When Bailey heard the car pull up in the driveway, she hung up her apron and then quickly opened the door to greet him.

He gave her a big smile when he saw her, his eyes scanning her hair and makeup. She'd touched it up and dabbed perfume behind her ears.

"Hi, honey," she greeted.

"You look great," he said while pulling her close to kiss her cheek. Butterflies began to flutter in her belly. "Are you feeling any better? You didn't work too hard, did you?" he asked.

"I feel tons better. And I promise I didn't work too hard."

They went inside and he placed his briefcase at the door and took off his hat. He looked at her in surprise. "What smells so good?"

"Chicken and dumplings. I hope you're hungry."

"Starving. Let me get changed and I'll be right down."

"Okay."

She took his jacket and hung it up while he hurried up the stairs. She grinned happily and then went to the kitchen to plate the meal.

She took the lid off the chicken and dumplings and her smile dropped.

The dumplings were like giant pillows! She'd made them too big!

"Okay, okay, okay," she said to herself. He didn't have to see this mess. She grabbed two plates and cut through the dumplings. Half the pot was just dumplings!

She kept digging until she came up with the stew. It was so thick. It was like the biscuits had absorbed all the liquid she'd added. Oh, why had she added more flour?!

She scooped the stew onto the plates, needing to scrape it from the bottom of the pot just to get enough. It was a little stuck, but she didn't scrape up any burnt pieces.

She hid the lumpy stew with spoonfuls of giant dumplings.

Bobby took his seat at the table.

"It smells great in here, Bae."

"Thank you." She placed his plate before him and then spied the apples that needed to be placed in the oven.

She hurried to the stove. "Baked apples for dessert!" she called. Thinking they might not be ready in time, she turned the heat up a little and placed the apples into the oven.

When she turned back around, she saw Bobby staring at his plate of food critically.

She took her seat across from him and he gave her a quick smile. "I hope you like it," she said.

"Of course I will." He picked up his fork and scooped a big piece of dumpling into his mouth.

She waited, without trying to look as if she was.

He chewed for a while and then nodded his head. "This is good."

Bailey didn't know she was holding her breath until her shoulders relaxed. She dug in and the giant, biscuit dumpling wasn't half bad.

"It's a bit mushy in the middle," she noted when she chewed on a bit that wasn't quite cooked completely.

"It's perfectly cooked on top," he commented. "Good job, honey." He dug into the stew and hesitated.

"Is that chicken?" he asked slowly.

She peered closely at what was speared on his fork. "I'm not sure," she said. "There were a few lumps..."

He popped it into his mouth and chewed.

"Lump or chicken?" she asked.

"Lump."

"Oh..."

After Bobby swallowed, he licked his lips rapidly and then drank half of his glass of iced tea. He gave her a nod and a smile.

Bailey ate a small bite of the stew. "It's a little salty," she admitted. It was a LOT salty. That added salt and pepper had been a little too much once the stew had reduced to a paste.

"I like...the pepper in it," he said hoarsely.

"Not too much?" she asked.

He tried to suppress a cough and reached again for the iced tea. "Maybe a little," he finally added. He bravely took another spoonful and nodded enthusiastically.

She couldn't help the smile that spread across her face. He was so nice to pretend he liked it. The food was horrendous.

"How was work?" she asked, giving him an opportunity to stop eating if he wanted. But he continued eating while they talked until he'd cleaned his plate.

Bobby cocked his head. "Is something burning?"

"Oh no!" She leaped up and hurried to the stove. Her apples! She placed the hot dish on the stovetop.

The apples were blackened.

Bobby was suddenly there. He poked at one of the apples with a fork.

"We can take off this crust. I think the sugar is what's burnt." Bailey just sighed in disappointment. "See," he continued. "The apple part is fine."

He took a bite and grimaced when he seared his lip on hot sugar. His eyes watered a little but he managed a smile.

"It's good. Is there cinnamon in it?"

"No." She shook her head. "I think that's just burnt sugar you taste."

"Okay. Let's serve it up," he encouraged.

She gave him an amazed look. This glutton for punishment had to be the bravest, sweetest man ever.

Chapter Twelve

After dinner, Bobby asked if she wanted to watch television.

She did. She had been excited about the television set, but nervous about turning it on and there being nothing but a blank, black screen.

"I need to watch the national news first," he said, giving her an apologetic look. "It's part of my job. But after, we can watch *Kukla, Fran and Ollie* if you want." He turned on the television and then grabbed a notebook and steno pad from his briefcase.

She sat on the couch and sighed in pleasure. She was more tired than she thought. "What do you need the pad of paper for?" she asked.

"I have to search for leads. We get some fed to us, but we're also responsible for finding our own."

She stood, fighting to make it look effortless. "While you do, I'm going to finish up in the kitchen." She left the room, longing to leave the dishes for the morning.

There wouldn't be any leftovers. She swept everything into the garbage. And after the dishes were washed, dried, and put away, she returned to the living room and got comfortable on the sofa.

Bobby glanced at her and then closed his steno pad. He leaned back and placed an arm around her.

"What did you do today?" he asked.

She told him about going to the grocery store with Helen.

"I should have thought to leave you the car —"

"No. I don't mind taking the bus. But we had a lot to get stocked up on. Besides, Helen and I had a nice visit."

Kukla, Fran and Ollie almost put Bailey to sleep. It was in black-and-white; also, the picture was very fuzzy. Technology had surely come a long way. But although boring, it was nice to see a window into another world. She guessed that's how the viewers of 1954 felt.

When she felt herself getting too comfortable and fighting back a yawn, Bailey got up and went to the kitchen to brew tea. She brought a tray containing two cups of tea, a sugar bowl, and wafer cookies. She watched carefully when Bobby added only half a teaspoon of sugar to his tea but he dipped his wafer cookies into it, which made her smile. In some ways, he was like a big kid.

"What do you want to watch next; *Dinah Shore* or *Cavalcade of America*?" he asked after *Kukla, Fran and Ollie* ended.

"*Dinah Shore* this time. *Cavalcade* next time." He got up to change channels and after he sat down, he once again pulled her close as if it was natural for them to cuddle on the couch. She snuggled against him, deciding she would stay awake for a while instead of rushing off to bed.

Bailey woke up when she heard Bobby tiptoe into the bedroom. She looked over at the clock. It was close to midnight. She'd left him hours ago to come upstairs for a bath and to finally go to bed. She'd been sound asleep by ten.

"Hey," she greeted with a yawn.

"I'm sorry. I didn't mean to wake you." He sat in the chair and took off his shoes.

"I just wanted to apologize for dinner." She sat up and turned on the bedside light. She could see he had relaxed his body into the chair and had an amused look on his face.

"No need to ever apologize for the meal you serve me, especially when you put your heart into it."

"I just don't want to make you sick or anything! I don't know how to cook—and that's not faking for the camera."

His brow gathered momentarily. "We shouldn't be talking about this until the weekend." He stood. "I'm going to take a bath and then hit the hay." His voice had gone suddenly lifeless.

"Oh. Okay. I'm sorry. I didn't mean to..." She was unsure how to finish.

He paused with his back to her. "I won't charge an infraction this time, but please don't go out of character again."

She watched in disbelief as he continued to the bathroom, where the door was closed firmly behind him.

Bailey quickly turned off the light and sank beneath her covers. Did he literally just chastise her for apologizing to him? What was so bad about talking after lights-out when the camera wasn't even rolling?

Bailey fumed for a while until she heard the bathroom door open. She quickly closed her eyes and pretended to be sleeping.

Bobby pulled out the trundle bed and settled down. A few minutes later she heard his low, even breathing.

"Bailey?" he said quietly.

She thought about ignoring him. "Yes," she finally replied.

"I'm sorry. I didn't mean to be so sharp." She didn't respond. "You don't have to ever worry about your cooking. I'll eat whatever you set before me because that's my job."

Bailey frowned. "What do you mean, *your job*?"

"I mean, as your husband. Your job is to take care of the household, and my job is to take care of you."

She mulled that over for a while. Her only job, as she saw it, was to get through this year and to be successful enough to finance more acting work. "Okay," she finally replied, because it seemed as if he was waiting.

"And as far as faking for the camera, I can tell you tried hard on that meal. When you put the extra flour into the soup, I thought it was a good idea too, but the ladies in the production office screamed no!" He snorted in amusement.

Oh my God! He had watched her cook through the camera?? Obviously, he saw her on film, but when she thought about it, it made her cringe. It was like being spied on.

"I know you tried hard on dinner. On a personal level, I appreciate it—but on a professional level, your mistakes made for one helluva great show. You are a natural on camera." He sighed. "Don't be sorry for anything you do on camera, okay? As long as you continue to be natural, and you stay in character, then it will be all right."

As long as she stayed in character...

Chapter Thirteen

The next morning, Bailey got up early to begin her daily routine. She was still uneasy after last night's conversation with Bobby, but she was an actress, and she didn't have to show how weird it had made things. Besides, she wouldn't have to be with him for long. She just had to get through breakfast and she'd have the day to herself.

Bailey got the coffee brewing and put four eggs on to boil. He wanted grits again, so she'd make grits again.

She might not be a great cook, but she knew how to make grits and how to boil eggs. If anyone wanted to laugh at her cooking skills, they would need to wait for dinner.

When she heard Bobby come into the room, she lowered the toast into the toaster.

"Good morning, dear," she said with what she hoped was a natural smile. She'd never felt less like smiling in her life.

"Morning." He kissed her cheek, poured himself coffee, and then took his seat at the table. "Did you sleep well?" he asked while watching her.

She placed the toast on the table and took her seat, not meeting his direct stare.

"It might take a while to get used to the new bed and the new house. Thankfully, I'm tired every night, so that helps."

"I told you I'd help this weekend—"

"I know," she interrupted. "I just don't want to spend the day all by myself in a dirty house." She stamped down her annoyance that he seemed critical of how much effort she'd put into making the house presentable. Every day he felt the need to remind her not to work too hard, even though he'd seen the freaking list of chores he expected her to do each day!

She realized she had tensed up and she took a nibble of her toast.

His sky-blue eyes continued to watch her, and it was proving to be too much. There was something about the way he looked at her that gave her a glimpse inside of him. Right now, she glimpsed he sensed her annoyance with him.

"We didn't get married for you to work harder as my wife than you did at the bank—"

"What am I supposed to do when the neighbors drop by and think I don't know how to take care of my own house? Your mother is going to come by, and I know she's going to think I can't take care of things the way she did." There. If an on-air disagreement is what he wanted, then he was going to get it.

"You mean take care of me?" he asked softly.

She looked at him, realizing he was feeding her a new story line—something meatier than just cooking and cleaning.

"Bae." He took her hand. "I know my mother hasn't always been the most supportive. But she knows we are a package deal. If she can't accept you, then she won't have me. And that's all there is to it."

She sighed. "Thanks for saying it, but I already know that. I knew when we said our vows it was going to be me and you against the world." He smiled and kissed the back of her fingers and her tension finally eased. "And thank you for eating dinner yesterday, even though it was terrible."

"It wasn't terrible."

"I told you before we got married I'm not a good cook; plus, your mother never let me into her kitchen so I didn't learn how to make your favorite dishes. When my Aunt Mae raised me, she always said there was only room for one woman in the kitchen."

Bailey smiled as she thought about her aunt because it was something she truly did say. Of course, she had meant there was only room enough for one woman of the house.

This time when Bobby looked at her, his eyes seemed to twinkle. "Now you have your own kitchen, and I am a patient man. If you cook it, then I'm going to love it, because you took the time to do it for us. Okay?"

She nodded and he stood and pulled her gently into an embrace. "I look forward to dinner tonight," he said. "Okay?"

"Okay," she said.

He pulled back and looked into her eyes. "I chose you. Just like you chose me. We will be a success story."

She nodded, reading between the lines. Yes, she would make sure 1954 would be a damn good year.

After Bobby left, Bailey got down to business. Open the windows, air out the sheets, ten minutes of morning stretches, and then get ready for the day.

After that was handled, Bailey looked in the closet for something to wear. She literally could cheat. She could slip on sneakers and then change into heels once Bobby got home. Nice, flat sneakers would be heaven.

But being a 1950s housewife wasn't about taking the easy way out. It was about being extraordinary. She had not known just how hard this was going to be. She was getting paid to do this, but people actually did this kind of thing for free.

She selected a tan skirt and a sleeveless blouse with yellow flowers. She hadn't curled her hair the night before so wearing it down was not a possibility. She pulled it back into a ponytail while swooping her bangs to the side and holding it in place with bobby pins.

Thankfully, she had a hair appointment Saturday. Miss Maybelle had been a godsend for suggesting it—although she had to admit to herself she had not thought so at the time.

It was only Wednesday. She was going to have to figure something out or it was going to get real when she broke out in an Afro.

Next, she sat at her vanity and did her makeup, getting used to the idea of getting dolled up at the crack of dawn. Once again, she reached for the bright-red lipstick. The makeup made such a huge difference. It transformed her from child-like to sophisticated, despite the ponytail and swooped-over bangs. She primped for a moment before remembering she wasn't truly alone.

Finally, she slipped on her kitten heels, checked herself in the full-length mirror, and then quickly made the bed.

Next, Bailey went to the kitchen and did the morning dishes. Was it possible to already be tired?

She needed to check the ledger-slash-notebook. She didn't remember what weekly task she was supposed to take care of today but she hoped it wasn't window washing.

It was window washing.

Bailey tried to hide her annoyance, not wanting to manifest negativity to her viewers. She'd already started the day on a bad note. She thought about Bobby and how pissed off she'd been. But down deep, she sensed that last night, she had disappointed him.

She wasn't sure which bothered her more.

With a resolute sigh, Bailey turned on the radio and found a bucket, which she filled with hot, soapy water and then grabbed a rag.

She was going to do this the old-fashioned way.

Two hours later, Bailey kicked off her shoes, threw her apron on the floor, and then plopped down on the couch. Her eyes drooped in exhaustion. She didn't know what time it was. She didn't care. She was going to take a nap. Period.

Drew, Nadine, or Quinton, one of you is going to have to take over. I'm throwing in the towel for a few hours.

As she drifted off to sleep, Bailey wondered if the other stars were having as much difficulty as she was. She hoped she would have an opportunity —

She fell asleep before she could finish the thought.

Bailey's eyes popped open and she instinctively knew she'd had a nice, revitalizing, *long* nap. She had slept during her prime time—and guess what? She didn't care. She was young, she was a newlywed, and there was no way she was going to get it perfect.

Bailey sat up and stretched, and then instantly regretted it.

"Ow!" Her shoulders and arms were sore and tight from washing every last window in the house. She stood slowly on tender legs, glancing at the clock.

It was just after noon, and she was starving. What she wouldn't do for sushi and a big ramen bowl from The Sushi Palace. Instead, she had a big bowl of Cheerios.

The milkman! She forgot to fill out the order form and to leave him money. Bailey slapped her forehead and found the order form and invoice in the drawer.

First things first; she needed to pee and take a painkiller.

She took care of her business and then assessed the damage to her makeup in the bathroom mirror. She decided then and there she needed to take advantage of the privacy aspect of the bathroom and utilize it more. Needed to fix her panty line? Go to the bathroom. Needed to have a minor breakdown? Go to the bathroom. When you found drool lines on your cheek because you had an impromptu nap at the beginning of shooting your spot as star of a reality show? Go to the bathroom.

Bailey fixed her face, happy at least the eyeliner and lipstick had stayed in place. She went back downstairs in her stocking feet—yeah, she was cheating a little but...but...she wasn't ready to put on the heels!

Since she had to order from the milkman, Bailey decided it was time to work on the budget. She grabbed her pocketbook for the receipts from yesterday's grocery shopping, walking right past the bucket of dirty water and the apron lying on the floor because she was no longer in clean mode. She was in budget mode.

After putting everything into the ledger, Bailey grimaced at how fast twenty dollars was dwindling. She needed to make sure she had enough money left for her hair appointment and a tip.

In her real life, she managed her money on the fly—meaning she was aware of what bills needed to be paid and when. For the first three or four months of her adult life she had tried to keep her checkbook balanced but gave it up after it became too tedious.

After that was done, she grabbed the milk crate, slipped the receipt inside, and left it on the front porch. She looked up and down the street for a neighbor to wave at, but no one was out and about.

Bailey returned to the house and finally looked at the bucket of dirty water. She tied on her apron, slipped on her heels, and then got rid of the bucket. With a sigh, she knew it was time to tackle the thing she most dreaded. Dinner.

Skirt steak.

"Okay." She nodded her head as she went over the recipe. "I can do this." She took the meat out of the refrigerator and examined how skinny it was. The recipe claimed it would cook in as little as fifteen minutes, maybe even less. It said to also allow it to rest for another fifteen minutes after. Theoretically, she could hold off on cooking it until about four thirty.

Perfect. She'd start with roasting the potatoes and making the salad. She smiled to herself. *You got this!*

When that was completed, Bailey knew she should work on the rest of her chores but her body was whupped. Being a 1950s housewife was a better workout than going to Planet Fitness!

She considered leaving it for tomorrow, but honestly, the bathroom should get done. After all, she did share it with another person. She always cleaned the tub before and after using it, so all she needed to do was wipe down the vanity with sanitizer, clean the toilet, and spray down the mirror with the contents of a retro bottle of Windex. Finally, she quickly mopped the floor and was finished in less than fifteen minutes.

Afterwards, Bailey was happy she'd done it. She went downstairs and thought about how quickly dust collected on the pretty wood furniture — all in just one day, which was a little gross. Screw it! She got the duster and quickly went over all the surfaces while thinking about the knickknacks at Aunt Mae's house and how much she'd hated having to keep them shining.

She had always promised herself she'd never fill her house with such atrocities. But the half-empty hutch needed something nice, a vase maybe. She wondered if Bobby could manufacture some wedding pictures. That would be so cute! In the meantime, she might accidentally break some of the delicate-looking cherubs...

After scattering invisible dust all over the place, Bailey got out the bulky Hoover and quickly vacuumed the living room. Nope. Not going to vacuum the bedroom or mop the kitchen floor. Besides, it was getting late.

At a quarter past four, she took stock of her house and felt proud of all she'd accomplished. How quickly she had begun to think of this as *her* house.

Now go and make skirt steak, girl. You got this!

She got the iron skillet and cranked up the heat until it was screaming hot. She quickly placed the seasoned meat on it. Smoke immediately began to rise but she turned on the exhaust fan, since there was no overhead vent.

It began to make a horrendous sound like a jet plane was taking off. She had to open the back door because she didn't think it was getting rid of any of the smoke—in fact, was the vent smoking?! She quickly turned it off.

Grilling inside the house—perhaps not the best idea in the world.

Bobby came home just as she pulled the beautifully roasted potatoes from the oven. Bailey quickly removed her apron and hung it up, then met him at the door.

"Hi, honey," she said while placing her hand on his shoulders and leaning forward for a kiss on the cheek.

One hand was behind his back, but the other slipped around her waist to pull her close in order to deliver that kiss. She really liked this routine. One day, she'd insist her boyfriend do this every time he walked into the house.

"Hello, beautiful." His eyes lingered on her face and she was happy she'd taken the extra steps to add the bright-red lipstick and winged eyeliner. "Dinner smells delicious."

"Why don't you get changed while I finish setting the table—"

His hidden hand came from behind him to reveal a vase of flowers.

Bailey blinked in surprise. She'd never gotten flowers before. Wait—she wasn't getting them now, her character was. But still, her heartbeat quickened in excitement.

"Thank you! These are so beautiful." It was a summer bouquet filled with daisies, pink roses, and baby's breath.

"Not nearly as beautiful as the recipient."

"Wow, I was just thinking…" The hutch needed a vase of flowers…had she said it out loud and he'd heard it through the camera? She had gotten into the habit of talking out loud over the last few days, but she really didn't think she had.

Nevertheless, he would have been watching her clean and could easily see with his own two eyes the house was sadly lacking in the décor area.

She felt a little disappointed, which she knew was unreasonable. This was not her husband. They played characters in order to entertain viewers. Period.

Bobby left the room to get changed and Bailey placed the vase of flowers on the hutch. It really looked good there. She went to the kitchen to cut the steak.

When Bobby returned, he froze in the doorway of the kitchen.

"Uhm…Bae?"

"Yes, honey?" she asked without looking up. She knew what he was going to say, so there was no reason to look up.

"What's that black stuff on the wall?"

She gestured to the exhaust fan where black smoke had come billowing from it soon after she cut it off.

"You mean that black stain?"

He came close to inspect it."

"Yes, that."

"I think there might have been a fire in the exhaust fan."

"Okay…" he said after a moment, as if he hadn't been watching the filming of the entire fiasco. He gave her a quick smile and glanced at the delicious platter of meat.

"Oh my God, that looks amazing."

She grinned and carried it to the table. "Hmph, you sound surprised."

"Not at all!"

"Grab the potatoes—and don't forget to use a mitt! It's still hot."

She got the salad and ranch dressing from the refrigerator and then poured them milk, because she needed to use it up, as she had ordered more for tomorrow.

Bobby's eyes were big when he sat down. She passed him a plate of salad, proud today's meal was a success.

Bobby ate every scrap of food on his plate and even went back for seconds. Poor thing was probably as starved as she was. She had to admit, everything tasted good, even though the center slices of meat were a bit on the bloody side.

Bobby leaned back in his chair and patted his belly. "That was fantastic!"

"Well, there's no dessert—" she began.

"There's no room for dessert," he replied while rubbing his belly. It was actually pooched out. She almost laughed. He had changed into khaki-colored slacks and a light-blue, short-sleeved shirt, which was a bit more formal than the average guy dressed in order to unwind, but it still gave him a relaxed air.

"Well, I'm going to check the vent."

"You are?" she asked as she got up to put away the leftovers. "Maybe we should call an electrician."

"No way. It's probably just a bird's nest."

"Eww, that's gross."

He went out to the garage, laughing.

Why was he so stinking cute? she wondered absently as she rinsed out the empty milk bottle to put on the porch.

Chapter Fourteen

Bailey decided to go through the Sears catalogue while Bobby banged away in the kitchen making a racket.

What did a rich son of a politician know about fixing a vent? He was probably going to get electrocuted.

She folded the edge of pages that interested her as she relaxed on the couch with her feet folded beneath her.

When Bobby hadn't returned to the living room after forty-five minutes, she closed the catalogue and went into the kitchen.

"Wha-a-a?" Her mouth practically flapped open. Her beautiful, neat kitchen was in shambles!

Bobby looked up from a mess of leaves and debris that was strewn across her counter.

"Sweetheart, you might not want to come in here right now—"

"Oh...no..." she said while walking up to stand next to him. Her eyes tried to take in everything at once. Black soot was in her white, porcelain sink. He wore work gloves but had managed to get soot on his face, clothes, and arms.

"I'm going to clean this all up," he said quickly.

"What's that!" She pointed to several big clumps of gray, fluffy stuff.

"I think it's a family of squirrels that got trapped—"

Bailey screeched and ran out of the room.

He followed her as far as the kitchen door. "Bae, I think I fixed it! They were just clogging up the vent from—"

"Oh my God...get rid of those dead bodies!"

Bobby snickered. "Dead bodies? Honey, they're just little squirrels—"

"I'm not going into that kitchen ever again!" She cringed, meaning it with every ounce of her being.

"Okay, okay. I'm going to clean it all up."

After he had gone back into the kitchen, Bailey shuddered and rubbed her elbows.

"Why'd you have to put them on the counter?!" she called, thoroughly grossed out.

He returned to the doorway holding a plastic bag, an amused look still on his face. "I promise, I didn't know that was going to come out of the vent. I just thought it was going to be a bird's nest, or maybe a dead bird."

"Ugh," she groaned.

"I can't believe you're really scared of a few squirrel carcasses. Didn't you go down South in the summers when you were a kid? I know you saw the heads cut off chickens on your aunt's farm—"

"I never had to cut the head off a live chicken!"

"Well, you're lucky. When we went south in the summers, I had to watch my uncle stomp on rats in the barn, and I helped pluck feathers from chickens that were still practically pecking."

"Well, I'm a city girl. So, get rid of that, please."

He chuckled, but did as he was told.

She waited half an hour before looking in the kitchen again. It was no longer in shambles, although there were smudges of soot stains on the counter and sink. The wall behind the stove had been swabbed clean and the vent was back in place as if it hadn't just been a gravesite for a family of rodents.

He was about to vacuum the floor when he saw her. "Almost done."

"Where are those squirrels?" she asked. He gestured with his head to the trash can and she opened her mouth to go off when he laughed.

"No. I took them out to the trash bin and disposed of them properly." He flipped the switch to turn on the vent and it hummed quietly. "All fixed."

Bailey sighed in relief. "Good job. You go take a bath and I'll finish cleaning up."

"Are you sure?" he asked while eyeing the dirty footprints on the linoleum floor.

"Yeah." She gave him a half smile. "There's only room for one person in my kitchen."

"But I'm not a woman—"

"Translation," she interrupted. "I don't trust you to clean it as good as I will."

He nodded. "Ah. True. Okay…well, sorry about the mess." He gave her a boyish grin before leaving the room.

She eyed the mess with hooded eyes.

This is what I get for not mopping the kitchen floor…

It took Bailey forty-five minutes to get the kitchen cleaned and sanitized. By that time, it was close to nine o'clock—her unofficial bedtime. No tea and wafers while they chatted about the events of the day. No after-dinner television, and no snuggle time on the couch.

She had worn slippers while working because she honestly couldn't stand the pain of putting on her heels. This was most definitely slapstick comedy for the audience. But it was taking its toll on her.

While Bobby watched the local news on television, jotting down notes on his pad of paper, she came up from behind him and tiredly wrapped her arms around his shoulders. He turned to kiss her cheek just as she turned to kiss his. Each missed their target and they ended up kissing on the lips.

From there, everything seemed to move in slow motion. Bailey was so close she saw the pupils in Bobby's eyes dilate until there was nothing but a ring of blue coloring deep, dark orbs.

She didn't know if the same thing happened to her eyes, but her heartbeat spiked, slamming with alarm against her rib cage.

Bobby broke the kiss, pulling back quickly while his cheeks grew flushed.

"What was that for?" he asked, his voice slightly stuttering while he tried for a smile.

"That was for being Mr. Handyman in a pinch," she said off the top of her head. Did it make sense? She didn't know. She just wanted to go to the bathroom and hide. Did he think she did that on purpose? Oh no... He had to know it was just an accident.

"I'm going to turn in a bit early." She feigned a yawn.

"No television tonight?" His eyes were still dilated, ringed in blue, and although his cheeks were spotted red, his voice had once again become steady.

"Not tonight."

"Sorry about the mess—"

"Hey, Mr. Handyman-in-a-pinch, you already got the reward. Can't take it back now." Oh, Lord, how was she being so smooth? Her heart was drumming like crazy!

His eyes dropped to her lips and lingered. "Good night, Bae."

"Night, honey." She straightened and left the room as casually as she could.

The moment she was locked in the bathroom, Bailey sat on the closed lid of the toilet and hid her face in her hands. She silently screamed.

I kissed Bobby, or he kissed me, but we kissed...and...I think I liked it!

She was frozen in position, hands covering her face when there was a knock on the bathroom door.

Oh my God! Was Bobby standing outside the bathroom door?

"Bailey?" he asked tentatively. "Uh...I'm sorry. Really, I am! I didn't—"

She opened the bathroom door. "*I'm* sorry. I think I was the one to accidentally...kiss you."

Bobby looked embarrassed as he quickly shook his head. "No, I think I did."

She then shook her head. "We both did, but it was an accident."

"Right," he agreed. "Um...so, I'm really sorry." He turned to go, and the relief she felt erupted into soft laughter. She covered her mouth in embarrassment.

Bobby paused to look at her over his shoulder. "What?"

127

"I'm sorry, it's just the scene with the squirrels was so funny."

After a moment he moved to the door but instead of leaving, he hit the stop filming button with the palm of his hand.

Uh-oh, she'd done it again! She'd gone out of character twice in two days. Bailey cursed under her breath. How did anyone earn an infraction after only three days on the set?!

But when Bobby turned, he had a broad grin across his face.

"Oh my God, that was so hilarious! When you saw those squirrels, you nearly lost it! I have no idea how I didn't fall on the floor laughing."

The tension fell off as she gave in to laughter. "That was so gross! Where did you all find those dead squirrels?"

"That's the beauty of it," he laughed. "They really were stuck in the vent. I had to bring them in from outside, though, and I didn't want to touch them either. I just hoped you wouldn't catch me doing it. Perfect timing on your part!"

"You would actually do anything for the shot," she said in amusement.

He shrugged, still smiling. "Just about." Bobby sat in the chair and began to undo his shoelaces.

"Isn't it kind of early for you to turn in?"

He glanced up and his cheeks were once again spotted with red. "Uhm...I kinda have to turn in now."

"Why?"

"Well, I made it seem as if the reason I turned in early is so..."

Bailey frowned and shrugged, indicating she didn't understand.

"I made the audience believe we were going to finish what we began…" Her expression cleared. Oh! "And I don't want to go back down early because I don't want anyone questioning my stamina."

He was beet red now. Bailey just covered her mouth and laughed until her eyes began to water. "I understand completely. And on that note, I'm going to slather my face with cold cream and take a hot bath."

She retreated to the bathroom and snickered to herself during her entire bath.

When Bailey got out of the bath, the bedroom was dark and quiet. She wasn't sure if that meant that Bobby was sleeping. She climbed into bed, planning to rehash the entire day when Bobby spoke.

"We can't do this again."

She turned to face his trundle bed. What was he talking about? She certainly had no plans to kiss him again.

"Do what?"

"Stop recording. I mean, you didn't do it, I did, and it's something I've never done before. We can't make it a habit."

She mulled over his words. "I don't understand why we can't talk in the bedroom when the lights are out."

"We can talk," he replied. "But only in character."

"But if no one is filming —"

"Because I'll know," he said adamantly. "I'll know."

What she was hearing is that 1954 wasn't for the audience, but for him. That was so odd, to create this entire production just for him.

"Okay, Bobby," she said. "No more out-of-character discussions while on set."

She heard him sigh. "Thank you, Bailey." He sounded relieved.

Chapter Fifteen

Breakfast the next morning was boiled eggs, buttered toast, coffee, and half a grapefruit.

"I think I have a lead on a story for my own byline," Bobby said while putting jam on his slice of toast.

"Oh really?" Bailey asked.

"Yeah. I want to do a story on this new vaccine that's being developed for polio."

"A vaccine against polio? That would be amazing. I know a girl that has to stay in an iron lung. No one knows if she's going to have to live like that for the rest of her life."

"Polio is horrible. I think everyone knows at least someone that has been affected by it."

"That's the perfect story," Bailey said.

Bobby stood and straightened his tie and then came over and gave her a kiss on the cheek. Bailey made sure to keep her head unturned.

"Well, hopefully, it will be in the evening paper," he replied. "I'll see you later, Bae."

"Bye, Bobby."

Bailey was distracted as she went about her morning routine. There was absolutely no good reason for Bobby not to allow them to speak out of character in the bedroom at night when there was no one to see it. And there was no reason he continued to stay in character while in the car the night they'd had dinner at Maybelle's.

Except he'd already told her why it had to happen. It needed to happen for *him*.

She thought back to the day of her interval with Bobby role-playing as her husband for the first time. Bruce Adams had interrupted to announce she'd gotten the job and Bobby had gotten weird. Bruce had to apologize to him for interrupting the role-play.

Was it possible Robert Chesterfield Jr. was... insane?

Bailey had an idea. She hadn't spoken to Helen in a bit and she needed to pick her brain. Helen had been in the 1953 production. She should know if there was something *off* about Bobby. Maybe they could walk instead of doing her morning stretch.

Bailey happily changed into a pair of slacks and a simple sweater. It felt good to wear pants. It felt even better when she put on sneakers.

She sat at her vanity and applied her makeup and then unwrapped the scarf from her head. Things were terrible in the hair department.

There were no curls. She wasn't wrapping her hair in the right way. What did she know about relaxed hair? She'd been natural all her adult life.

There was hair gel, and she knew how to work with that. After parting her hair to the side, she slapped a good amount onto the front of her hair and brushed it to the side. She pulled the rest into a bun at the back of her head, not worrying that it was too severe. It was cute.

Was it appropriate to wear jewelry during a morning walk? Yes. It was appropriate in the 1950s. She put small, white studs into her ears and then a cat broach.

She went out the front door and remembered the morning delivery from the milkman when she saw the metal crate containing two glass milk containers, a pound of butter, and a container of orange juice.

It was nice—like receiving an Amazon delivery package. Why did people stop with the milkman service? She liked the personal touches. She brought it inside, noting it was still cold. She'd have to remember to check for her deliveries after Bobby left for work.

Bobby…yeah. It was as if he thought he really was in 1954. She felt a little sorry for him. He had a predator for a father and despite growing up rich, who knew what his life was really like?

Bailey left the house without her purse or keys. People didn't lock their doors in Wingate, although that went against everything she was comfortable with. She could only afford a small apartment in real life, and it was in the urban area of her city.

Helen answered the door with a broad smile. She would have to get her phone number so they wouldn't have to keep dropping in on each other.

"Hi, Bailey. Come on in," Helen greeted.

"Thanks. Sorry to drop by, but we never exchanged telephone numbers."

Helen led them to the kitchen. "I'll write it down, but feel free to come by whenever you like. With Hank out on the road most days, I get pretty bored." Helen quickly jotted something on a piece of paper. Beneath her phone number was written, "Did you want to go for a drive?"

"I'll write mine down for you."

Bailey grabbed the pad Helen had used but didn't know her phone number. So, she just wrote; "No. Want to walk?"

She passed the note to Helen, who gave it a quick scan before folding it and placing it on her neat counter.

"I'm supposed to be doing my morning exercises but I'd like to take a walk around the neighborhood and get familiar with it. I thought Bobby and I would do that together, but it's been a busy week.

"Anyway, you mentioned wanting to transform your Marilyn Monroe to Doris Day, so I thought you might like to join me."

"Well, not in these heels. Let me change. Have some coffee and I'll be down in less than two shakes. Help yourself!" she called as she hurried out of the room.

Bailey admired Helen's neat, yellow kitchen with its sunflower motif. She had sunflower curtains with matching towels, a sunflower cannister set, and a sunflower cookie jar. It looked straight from the Fingerhut catalogue.

She didn't bother with the coffee, and instead went into the living room to admire her décor. She had little, white porcelain figurines of cats; a cat chasing a butterfly, a cat snoozing, a cat licking its fur.

Would she be forced to have these in her house?

Helen came into the room dressed in form-fitting slacks and a sleeveless blouse. Instead of sneakers, she wore loafers.

"I am so sorry, Bailey! I should have offered to show you around the neighborhood before this." She slipped on a jacket and tied a scarf around her head and neck and then grabbed her sunglasses. "After all, there are people in this neighborhood you will want to avoid. Some are terrible gossips. And some of the men..." — Helen shook her head, speaking a mile a minute — "once they see how pretty you are and realize your husband works during the day, they are going to be all kinds of helpful...if you know what I mean."

"Uh...? Helpful?" Bailey asked.

Helen looked around as if someone was spying on them — which technically was true.

"Did you ever read *Lady Chatterley's Lover*?" she all but whispered, if her loud voice allowed herself to do such a thing.

Bailey had never heard of the book, but with the word *lover* in its title, it had to be scandalous. She shook her head adamantly.

"Let's just say in this neighborhood, there are no shortages of men looking to...help out a lonely housewife."

"I-I'm not lonely," Bailey said quickly.

Helen chuckled. "Let's take that walk."

Bailey's mouth parted and one brow rose. "Helen...are you *lonely?*"

"Hank might be out on the road most of the time, but he makes sure I'm far from lonely when he is home," Helen replied with a wink.

"Oh," Bailey said sheepishly, obviously getting the double meaning.

Helen continued talking as she opened her front door. "Have you met Curtis yet?"

"Curtis? No, I don't think I have."

"He's the milkman. I think you, in particular, will find him interesting. Most women do. I have to admit, he's killer diller."

Bailey barely heard because standing on Helen's doorstep was a cameraman and a soundman holding a boom mic on a length of pole.

Bailey jumped and nearly screeched in surprise but Helen smoothly walked outside, still chattering away.

"You'll meet many of the neighbors at Saturday's picnic. But luckily for you, one of them will not be Mr. Edelman. He is the neighborhood crank."

Bailey tried to ignore the camera. She and Helen walked down to the sidewalk, with the small filming crew trying to anticipate their direction while staying several steps ahead of them.

"Now your neighbors on the right are the Clines. Don't worry, I won't bore you with a lot of names. But they're two true pennies. Has Geneva come by yet?"

"No," Bailey replied with a shake of her head. She focused on Helen, wondering if this walk was a huge mistake. One thing was certain, she wouldn't be able to ask questions about Bobby.

"Well, she and Jeff will be at the barbecue. She said she saw your furniture being delivered and thought it was wild. But I told her it would probably look perfectly fine."

Wait, what? Neighbors she hadn't even met were already gossiping about her?

"Bobby and I think it's very rad," Bailey said indignantly.

"Geneva is old enough to be your mother. She's sensible, even if she comes off as a bit of a know-it-all. Now Haley Brinkman, on the other hand, is wild. She's divorced." Helen whispered the last. She gestured to the house on the other side of Baileys'. "You better keep an eye on Bobby around that one. She has a swimming pool, and has been known to catch a tan with her straps untied. Now I've never witnessed this, but if you happen to catch Bobby peeking through the fence one day..."

Oh boy...

As they rounded the corner, Bailey saw a woman working in her front-yard garden.

"Hello, Camille," Helen waved.

Camille gave Helen a wave and then stood and approached them. She removed her gardening gloves and pushed back her wide-brimmed hat.

"Hi there, Helen. Who do you have here? Did you hire a new girl?"

The smile Bailey had prepared slipped from her mouth. New *girl*?

"As if Hank would spring for a maid. No, this is our new neighbor, Bailey Banks."

"Oh, of course! I'm so embarrassed. I thought you were...well..." She gave Helen a quick look.

"The help," Bailey finished for her in a crisp voice.

"Well, we've never had a Negro in the neighborhood besides Curtis and the garbagemen—"

"But we are progressive here in Westbrook," Helen interrupted.

"Of course we are, dear," Camille added with a big smile. "Bradley and I completely supported

Brown versus Board of Education last year. We believe Negroes won't be able to assimilate—I mean...get along in our society unless they are given similar opportunities."

Bailey stiffened. "I'm a college graduate; therefore, I know the importance of Negroes getting the *same* opportunities as whites."

"Of course," Camille agreed. "In time, of course."

"Will you and Bradley be at Saturday's barbecue?" Helen interrupted.

"We wouldn't miss it for the world! I'd better get back to my gardening. I like to take care of these things before the sun gets too bright. I don't want to turn...uh..." She looked at Bailey in embarrassment.

Okay, what the hell was this? Bailey thought.

"Bye now. We haven't even made our way completely around the neighborhood."

"Oh my. Well, you should probably walk quickly past Mr. Edelman's house," Camille said while turning to head back to her gardening.

"Don't worry. We're not going to walk in that direction."

As they continued down the street, Helen gave Bailey an apologetic look. "I am so sorry. I did not expect Camille to behave like that."

Bailey was now even more anxious than before, and low-key pissed off. But this wasn't 2022, where she would cuss out Camille and put her in her place. In 1955, Blacks were conditioned to tread carefully.

This is how it actually would have been for her if she truly lived in this era—or even worse.

"Let's take our walk past Mr. Edelman's house," Bailey said suddenly.

"Oh…that's not a good idea. He might be outside. And he's not a pleasant person."

Bailey crossed her arms in front of her. "Best to see him so I know who to watch out for."

"I suppose so," Helen said with a sigh.

They walked, with Helen finding several things to comment about if she wasn't directly giving a commentary on a neighbor. She knew whose car was new, and probably what everyone ate for breakfast!

By the time they got to the house with the confederate flag flying on the front porch and the black-faced, red-lipped lawn jockey, Bailey was certain they had come upon Edelman's house.

It was neat—pristine, actually—with red and white flowers adorning the walkway and a perfectly manicured lawn.

"He lives there," Helen whispered. And this time, her whisper was an actual whisper.

Bailey felt a chill run up her spine. The production was really playing this out good because she actually felt nervous being this close to the man that owned the house.

Edelman wasn't outside, but she had a feeling that The '50s Experience LLC would make it a point to put them together in some way.

Chapter Sixteen

They didn't stay out walking much longer, and Helen asked if she needed to go to the grocery store for anything as they stopped in front of her house.

Oh, there was a lot she wanted to talk to Helen about off-camera. A lot. But she was already unsure if she'd have enough money for her hair appointment, and didn't want to go all the way to the grocery store for just one or two items.

She thanked Helen for spending the morning with her and then went inside.

She rolled her eyes, sighed, and then got herself a Coca-Cola and drank it while she finished up her daily chores.

When Bobby got home that evening, there was beef and noodles already on the table for their dinner. It was easy. She had just used the last of yesterday's steak and a package of egg noodles drenched in a can of cream of mushroom soup. She wasn't about to tackle making biscuits, so there was white bread with butter and frozen mixed vegetables she had doctored up with butter, salt, and pepper.

"Hi, Bobby," she said when she greeted him at the door.

He kissed her cheek and then placed his briefcase on the floor at the door — his new norm.

"Hi, Bae. Dinner smells great." He shrugged out of his jacket and took off his hat.

Bailey took them from him and hung them up in the closet — her new norm.

"Get cleaned up. Dinner's already on the table."

She was pouring two frosty glasses of whole — not 2%--milk.

"Guess what?" he said while taking his seat.

"Did you get your byline?" Bailey asked excitedly.

"I did!"

"Oh my gosh! Where's the paper?"

"Patience, honey. Dr. Salk is sending me back his response to some interview questions. We plan to run the story tomorrow — better because Friday is a big news day for the paper!"

"I'm so excited!" Bailey clapped her hands. "Don't we have a bottle of wine somewhere?"

Bobby picked up his glass of milk. "It doesn't matter. We can toast with this."

They clinked glasses while his eyes sparkled happily. She marveled at how he could actually look so excited — as if this was all real.

"If you would have seen George's face when Mr. Adams said I was getting the lead in the news section. George McGee is so used to seeing his name on the headlines, I think he actually went to Mr. Adams and asked for the story."

"Oh, that's low."

"I know, right? Mr. Adams could have given it to him, with me being new."

"Even though it was your idea?"

"Absolutely. It's a very important story." Bobby smirked as he forked food into his mouth. "A little birdy whispered in my ear Mr. Adams told old George McGee he wouldn't have hired me if he didn't think I was capable."

Bailey silently wondered if the little "birdy" that had whispered in Bobby's ear was a hidden camera.

"Your first week on the job and you're getting a byline."

His grin was so broad Bailey couldn't help but take his hand—she was unsure if it was in encouragement or sympathy.

"Helen and I took a walk around the neighborhood," Bailey began.

"Oh?" Bobby replied while chewing a mouthful of noodles and beef. He seemed to really enjoy the meal. "Did you meet any neighbors?"

"I did," she replied with a humorless grin. "Camille Bradley will be at Saturday's barbecue, so you too will get the honor of meeting her."

Bobby paused in his eating. "I see it went well, then."

"Well, besides her thinking I was Helen's maid, or she felt the need to mention I'm the first Negro to live in the neighborhood. Oh! And let's not forget she needed to inform me how she and her husband fully supported Brown versus Board of Education—then yes. I think it went well."

Bobby gave her a wide stare. "Gee, Bae. I'm sorry you had to experience something like that so close to home. We don't have to go to the barbecue—"

"Of course we do," she interrupted. "I can't have her thinking Negroes like me don't know how to *assimilate* to white culture."

He blew out a long breath. "She sounds like an ass."

Bailey laughed in surprise. "Bobby!" He grinned along with her. "But yes, I agree with you."

He sipped his milk and listened with interest to her describe her morning ordeal. "We're going to have to educate our neighbors. I don't think people mean to be ignorant. They were just never exposed to anything different."

"You're not ignorant. And you were exposed to the same things they were."

He nodded. "You're right. My father…" Bobby hesitated. "My father was the kindest man I knew. But he wouldn't give the time of day to a Jewish man, and looked down his nose at the Irish."

"What did he think of Negroes?"

Bobby shook his head. "He had no problems with Negroes—as long as they stayed in their place."

"Meaning, out of their son's bed."

Bobby reached for her hand and caressed it. "He might not have had a problem with that. But certainly, he would not have condoned marriage between our races—or between any different races."

"Thank goodness you didn't turn out like your daddy."

The wide meaning of those words hit Bailey too late. Shit. She should not have said that.

"I'd like to think if my dad had lived long enough, he would have learned from me, and not the other way around." He stood. "Now I must leave you, dear wife. I have a lot of writing to do, so I won't be able to watch *You Bet Your Life*."

"Okay. Are you going back to the *Gazette*?"

"No. I'm going to try to tackle writing in my office."

"Oh...Are you sure about? It's really packed in there."

"I'm just going to have to unload some things onto the floor." He bent down and kissed her temple. "Dinner was great, Bae. Maybe some milk and cookies later?"

"Of course." He left for his office, and Bailey wondered what she was supposed to do for the rest of the evening by herself.

She checked her chores list. Tomorrow was laundry day. No way was she going to start laundry tonight. It would have to be hung out to dry; plus, she didn't know how to use the old-fashioned washing machine.

She suddenly frowned, wondering what was wrong with her.

She had tons of free time, which meant she could do anything she wanted!

She cleaned up the dinner dishes and then decided to chill in the backyard with the newspaper.

Her husband worked for the newspaper, and she had yet to read one.

Husband. That put a smile on her face.

She remembered Bobby putting a portable radio out in the garage when he had been moving boxes and she ran out and got it. It sounded like crap, but it didn't really matter. Just relaxing on the vintage chaise, reading her newspaper and smelling the fresh air, was worth every second of her wasted prime time.

When Bailey stretched in bed the next morning, she felt rested and relaxed for the first time the entire week.

She was getting the hang of this 1950s thing. She went to the bathroom and freshened up, threw on her much-too-frilly robe that was very mismatched to her humble slippers and then headed for the kitchen to start breakfast.

When Bobby entered the room, she had just placed two bowls of Wheaties on the table for them to cover with milk. The coffee was already brewed and in cups waiting on the table. She could only hope he took his cereal naked because they had no fruit, besides the box of raisins that had already been in the pantry when they moved in.

Some might not consider it much, but it was better than the alternative; Bailey's pasty oatmeal.

"Good morning, Bae." He kissed her cheek and took his seat.

"'Morning. How did it go with your article? Sorry I didn't stay up, but I feel like a little old lady these days."

"The prettiest little old lady I've ever met." He winked at her. "Once I get Dr. Salk's interview questions back today, I'm pretty much finished and you can read my article in this evening's paper."

"I'm so proud of you!"

"Thanks!" He beamed. He put cream in his coffee but not sugar, and she discreetly watched to see if he would put any sugar on his Wheaties. If he didn't, then he was a monster. Period.

He sprinkled a teaspoon of sugar over his Wheaties and she cheered internally.

"Do you think we should bring anything to tomorrow's barbecue?" she asked as they ate.

"I don't know," he replied slowly. "I could pick up a few six-packs of beer."

Bailey made a face. "I don't know. I don't want our neighbors thinking we don't have any couth. I could make a gelatin mold."

He gave her a doubtful look. "That sounds kind of hard..."

"It's just Jell-O and a can of fruit cocktail. It should be easy, and everyone likes Jell-O. Besides, we already have the ingredients in the pantry."

"Then I think we have a plan." Bobby stood, straightened his tie, and then leaned over to kiss her cheek. "I'm going to get going. See you this evening."

"Bye, honey."

After he left, Bailey went to the pantry and found the box of Jell-O to check the recipe on the back.

She frowned. "Sweetened condensed milk? Whoever heard of sweetened condensed milk in a Jell-O mold? Cranberry juice...Aunt Mae never put this stuff in her Jell-O." She would just do it the way Aunt Mae did it.

She put the ingredients back on the shelf and then went upstairs to change.

She would have to skip stretching today because she just didn't have time to keep changing clothes. She needed to get dressed for the day in order to tackle the laundry, because the washing machine was in the garage. There was no way she would allow any of her neighbors to catch a glimpse of her looking anything short of perfect—especially that nosey one that had criticized their furniture.

Bailey untied her scarf and then nearly tied it back on. She grabbed the hair gel and plastered her bangs into place and then gave the rest of her hair a French twist, praying it would stay in place with enough bobby pins.

She selected a blue skirt that reminded her of the old-fashioned Catholic school uniforms kids used to wear. She paired it with a sky-blue blouse that didn't look either too fancy or too dowdy.

With makeup in place, Bailey looked at her selection of shoes. No person in their right mind would hang laundry in the backyard wearing heels. She happily slipped on white ankle socks and penny loafers. There was even a bright, shiny penny in each shoe slot.

She stripped the bed linen from her bed before remembering there was no way she could reveal the secret trundle bed beneath hers in order to wash Bobby's sheets.

That she even worried about the condition of Bobby's bedsheets gave her pause.

He'd figure it out.

She carried the hamper downstairs and collected the dish towels and then headed outside for the garage.

When she looked at the washing machine with its wringer attachment and hoses, Bailey was reminded of the story Aunt Mae told of a little girl that had gotten her fingers mangled in the wringer.

But she was an adult, and she knew not to get her fingers too close — at least she hoped not to. That would just be a little too much to give the viewing audience.

147

Thankfully, an old Maytag instruction manual was sitting on top and she read it thoroughly.

Okay, easy enough. She filled the basin with water from the nearby hose, poured in washing powder, and then plugged it in. The basin wasn't very big, so she decided to begin with Bobby's shirts and her blouses and workout clothes.

She pulled the lever to begin the agitator and felt pride when her clothes began to wash.

Bailey went back inside, humming "Rock Around the Clock," since it had played no less than a million times yesterday.

She went around the house opening the curtains and the windows, but then paused and looked at the vehicle that was parked across the street.

Wait. Was that an ambulance?

Was someone hurt? Oh no. She hoped it wasn't Helen.

Her phone rang. It made her jump because this was the first time she'd heard the old-fashioned trill of her phone.

She hurried to answer it, her heart in her throat.

"Hello?"

"Say, 'Oh hi, Bobby'," came a male's voice.

"Oh hi, Bobby," Bailey mimicked without missing a beat. What in the hell was going on? Did something happen to Bobby?

"Ignore the ambulance outside. It's just a precautionary measure." Bailey recognized the voice. It was Bruce Adams, set director and production manager.

"Bobby is calling to tell you he needs to make a stop at the grocery store on his way home and wants to know if you need him to pick up anything. Do you need anything from the grocery store?"

"No. I don't think I need anything from the grocery store—wait, can you pick up a can of sweetened condensed milk and cranberry juice?"

"Now tell him thank you honey and hang up. And don't look at the ambulance."

"Thanks, honey. See you tonight." Bailey smiled to herself and hung up the phone, but she was confused. The cameras were at this very moment focused on her in order to know she'd stared at...

Was that ambulance for *her*?

Was the production company fearful she was going to get her fingers mangled in the washing machine?

Bailey ran to the bathroom and slammed the door shut. She covered her mouth and muffled her laughter. She laughed for nearly five minutes. Every time she thought about opening the door, she would get hit with another fit of laughter.

Oh, my goodness, this crew was so sweet!

She finally got it together and had to hurry back to the garage to stop the agitator before it shredded their clothes.

She filled the basin that sat behind the washing machine with water and then nervously turned on the wringer.

She thought about the ambulance ready to whisk her and her detached fingers to the hospital. This actually was nowhere near funny...

Bailey swallowed and then reached into the cold, soapy water and withdrew a shirt. She placed the shirt against the lower roller and pushed, making sure her fingers were not close. The shirt caught and went through the wringer — without her fingers.

Bailey completed the laundry with no incident and when she returned to the living room to dust, she saw that the ambulance was gone.

Remarkably, there was time for lunch. Between washing and hanging clothes out on the line to dry, Bailey had grilled cheese on fried toast.

She hadn't had buttery fried toast since she was a kid. It was so good, she was tempted to make two. But she had to iron Bobby's shirts.

It was another thing she hadn't done since being a kid.

She brought the laundry to the living room and then turned on the television and watched two soap operas as she ironed.

It wasn't as painfully boring as she remembered, and when she saw the neat stack of folded clothes, Bailey was filled with a sense of accomplishment.

She put away the laundry, made up her bed with the freshly laundered sheets, and then quickly cleaned the bathroom. No vacuuming today, because that was just not going to happen.

She'd thought about dinner all morning, and knew it would need to be something quick and effortless.

Campbell's tomato soup and more grilled cheese sandwiches on fried toast.

But neither Bailey nor Bobby cared about dinner.

Bobby came into the house beaming, carrying a small paper bag in one hand and the evening newspaper tucked beneath his arm.

"Did you...?" she asked the moment he stepped through the door.

He handed her the newspaper, already folded back to his article. She sat on the couch and began reading it aloud. He sat beside her with his arms comfortably around her shoulders.

This was a good day. She wished...

Well, she wished her real life could be as good as this.

Chapter Seventeen

Saturday was finally here. When Bobby came down for breakfast, he was dressed in pajamas and a robe. Bailey raised her brow in satisfaction because she'd been filmed in her nightie for days, and it was nice to be on even ground.

"How did you sleep?" she asked as he took his seat and reached for the cream for his coffee.

He grinned. "I slept like a baby." He scanned the table full of food. "What is this huge spread?"

She placed a bowl of grits beside the scrambled eggs, bacon, and pancakes.

"You have a busy day ahead of you, Bobby. You have some boxes to unpack, your office to clean, and I think you mentioned putting order to the garage."

He nodded good-naturedly. "Yes. Yes, you're right. I did say I was going to take care of all that this weekend."

She took her seat and relented some. "You don't have to do it all in one weekend."

"No," he said while piling his plate with food. "I'm going to take care of it now because next weekend, I want to spend the weekend relaxing with my wife. Maybe we can even catch a movie."

"I'd love that." She checked the clock. "Ugh...this is going to be a busy day. I have a hair appointment this morning, but I need to make the gelatin mold first so I know it will be set in time for the barbecue."

"Or I can pick up beer," he said.

"We're not bringing beer. Do you just not like Jell-O mold?"

"I'm not particularly fond of it."

"What red-blooded American man doesn't like Jell-O?" she mocked.

Bobby quickly raised his hand. "I'll just stick with the burgers and dogs."

"Fine. Oh, by the way, be sure to eat extra potato salad. Helen said she was bringing it and it's a prize-winning recipe." Bailey practically had to bite the inside of her cheeks to stop from grinning.

"I like potato salad."

After breakfast, she let Bobby get changed first while she cleaned up the morning dishes and began the gelatin mold. One can of fruit cocktail didn't seem enough, but she was going to make it work.

Bobby came down dressed in khaki-colored pants, a white T-shirt, and sneakers.

Hubba hubba!

Ooop! She was even thinking in 1950s terms. She mentally amended the thought.

Nice booty!

"Do you need me to drive you to your hair appointment or are you taking the car?"

She wanted to take the car, but didn't know how to get to Juanita's—or whatever the name of her shop was. And since she was a regular, this was something she should definitely know.

"You can drive me. I don't want to keep the car while I'm just sitting, getting my hair done. I'm going to get dressed."

She hurried out of the room and then sat at her vanity to apply her makeup. She spent extra time on it, since she had places to go today. She then slowly unwrapped the scarf from her hair.

It was so tangled, she was embarrassed. She brushed out the old clumps of gel, wishing she could hide and do this in the bathroom, but her hair journey had never been concealed from the cameras and she didn't want to start doing it now.

She brushed it back into a bun and decided she would definitely wear a hat.

Next, she put on a pretty, swing-out dress and slipped on her kitten heels. After checking her appearance, Bailey decided she looked more than acceptable. She'd probably change into something more relaxed for the barbecue.

Bobby was in his office unpacking books. She poked her head in through the door. "I'm ready."

When they got to the car, Bailey turned on the radio to avoid the awkward silence. Now that she knew the car didn't have a camera, she wasn't sure what they should talk about. She definitely had no intentions of going out of character, and she didn't want to waste her witty banter when there was no audience to appreciate it.

"I get paid today," he said after humming a few bars of the Elvis Presley tune that was playing. "I'll run over and pick up my paycheck while I'm in town. The bank opens at eight, so if you want to get your nails done, we have some extra money."

She looked at her nails. She'd never been one to care about manicures, although she did get a pedicure once every summer. But she had to admit, her nails were a hot-ass mess.

"Yes. I think I need that—and to invest in some dish-washing gloves." She'd washed dishes more times this week than she'd probably done in a month back home.

"They're under the sink," he replied.

"Oh." He would know. He probably staged the house before she arrived.

Bailey looked out the window and enjoyed the scenery. This wasn't just a set. People drove and walked dogs. Some were out mowing their lawns with those motorless rotary clippers so they wouldn't disturb their neighbors that wanted to sleep in. People these days should be so courteous.

"Here we are," Bobby said while pulling up to the curb. They were just down the street from the butcher's shop. There was a little storefront with the words JUANITA'S printed in big, white letters on the picture window.

That had not been there earlier in the week. The production did things on the fly; like showing up during her and Helen's walk, or having an ambulance ready and waiting in case she hurt herself. She needed a hairdresser that handled Black hair care, and now there was Juanita's.

Bobby got out of the car and hurried over to open the car door for her. "Call me when you're done." He then reached into his wallet and pulled out two single dollar bills. "That should take care of your hair and your nails."

"Thank you, honey." But how was she going to call when she didn't even know their phone number?

Oh well. It would work its way out.

When Bailey walked into Juanita's hair salon, she was met by the sounds of Charlie Parker's saxophone playing from a portable radio, as well as the eyes of six Black women.

"Hey, Bailey, girl!" a woman she'd never met a day in her life called out to her. She was pretty, with a Dorothy Dandridge vibe. She wore a red dress with a slit on the side, shiny, black heels that put Bailey's kitten heels to shame, and bright-red lipstick that made her look like a movie star.

Was that Juanita? Bailey hoped so, because with that gorgeous hairstyle, she would certainly be in good hands.

An older lady sitting in a salon chair gave the greeter a disapproving look.

"Juanita! Do you have to be so loud? It's too early. I haven't even had my coffee." She lifted her vintage copy of *Jet* magazine and flipped to the next page.

Several people began to snicker, and Juanita pouted her lips at the older woman.

"Somebody pour Miss Baker a cup of coffee," Juanita said with a grin and an eye roll.

"Hi, Juanita," Bailey grinned. "Hi, everyone." She now had two people's names. Only four more to go.

"How's married life treating you, Bailey?" The woman who asked the question had just moved to the coffee pot and was presumably pouring coffee for Miss Baker.

"Bobby is great," Bailey said as she shrugged out of her jacket and hung it up. "I'm just so happy we can start the process of getting on with the rest of our lives."

"Pour me a cup too, Pat," Juanita said.

Three names down; Juanita, Miss Baker, and Pat. These women were good at this.

Pat was petite, and seemed about five or so years older than Bailey. Her hair was also perfectly coiffed.

This had already proven to be a good idea.

Juanita quickly walked to Bailey. "Okay, girl. Let's see what you're hiding under that hat."

Bailey gave Juanita a sheepish grin and it wasn't completely fake.

"My time away from you has taken its toll, Juanita…" she explained before slipping off her hat.

No one said anything for a few beats.

Juanita finally took her arm. "I'm going to take you into the back room and you and me are going to deal with this. Okay?"

"You let that white man see you like that?" Miss Baker asked in awe.

Everyone looked at Miss Baker in shocked surprise.

"Well…" Bailey stammered, and patted her hair. "We're married, and we shouldn't hide anything from each other—" A woman laughed and then quickly covered her mouth. Someone else snorted and then pretended to cough.

"Bobby didn't see my hair like this. I wore a scarf all morning and then put on this hat. Y'all, I need help!"

Everyone burst out laughing, including Bailey. She put the hat back on but Juanita took it off and hung it up. And in moment, she felt completely at ease with these women.

She allowed Juanita to take her to a back room where a curtain was pulled closed after them.

Bailey quickly looked around, noting this room was in shambles. Boxes were stacked haphazardly all around. There was a ladder leaned against the wall and several cans of paint, while drop cloths were balled in the corner.

There was also a professional hair-washing station that looked absolutely modern.

Bailey gave Juanita a wide-eyed look.

"Have a seat. There are no cameras or mics back here."

Bailey sat in the salon chair while Juanita draped a cape around her shoulders along with a towel to keep water from dripping down her neck.

"First of all, I am a certified beautician. I was literally hired just two days ago."

"Really?"

"Yes. These people don't play around. They offered me a regular role making more money than I was making before." She leaned Bailey's chair back and turned on the faucet. "This is some crazy stuff. But we're all here to help you."

Bailey felt the warm water hit her head along with Juanita's soothing touch on her scalp.

"Thank you," Bailey sighed while closing her eyes. "I need all the help I can get."

"Y'all can come in now!" Juanita called.

Bailey was surprised when all the women from the salon crowded into the back room.

"Don't worry," Miss Baker said. "They ain't going to do no filming without you out there."

Bailey wanted to sit up but Juanita began to shampoo her. She did manage to look at the group of women curiously. They introduced themselves. In addition to the other women was Betty, Jackie, and Tracy, who ranged in ages from mid-thirties to possibly fifty.

They all had one thing in common: they all looked ready to walk out of *Jet* magazine.

"We're here to make sure you look good for the camera for all those people out there watching you," Juanita said.

Bailey smiled. "I appreciate that."

"Don't get us wrong," Pat added. "You look good, and you're already the most popular story line in the entire production. That's why they're giving you way more airtime than they're giving anyone else."

Bailey blinked. How did they know all this?

"When we say we want you to look good," Miss Baker added, "we're not just talking about your hair. Girl, you know you're representing Black women for the first time, and Blacks have *never* been given any type of airtime on this show."

"Girl, they will give crusty old granny airtime before they let us do more than be the help."

"Hush," Tracy said to Pat. "You know they're still listening—"

"There aren't any mics back here," Pat said while waving dismissively.

"That was good how you handled that neighbor of yours that made that snippy comment about Blacks in the neighborhood."

"Wait, you guys are watching?" Bailey asked.

"Yes, we are."

"That's the only perk we get," Miss Baker said with an eye roll. "If we don't get no airtime, then we don't get no extra money."

Helen had told her the same thing. "How do you get airtime?" Bailey asked.

"We don't," Pat replied with a hard look. "How do you not have Black people in 1954—one year before the Civil Rights movement begins?"

"If this is truly representative of that era, then we all should be represented," Juanita added.

Bailey listened. She remembered thinking the '50s was one hell of an era to be immersed in for a Black woman. It was one of the other stars, Drew, that had told her there was no racism in Wingate.

Weird he'd been told that but she hadn't—and if it was true, then why was she really here? She wasn't just melting into the background. Bobby spoke openly about their interracial marriage.

"I think 1954 is about to make a turn," she said slowly.

"What do you mean?" Miss Baker, the evident spokesperson, asked.

"I think they're planning for a racism story arc," Bailey said in dawning realization.

"Wouldn't they tell you?" Juanita paused while scrubbing her soapy scalp.

Bailey's lip went up into a mirthless smile. "No. Robert Chesterfield believes the more you know, the less authentic it will be."

"He's not completely wrong," Jackie replied.

"Maybe. But I suspect my neighbor Helen knows a whole lot more than she's letting on—and I feel like it's about to come to a head at the barbecue today."

Helen had asked if she wanted to go to the grocery store but she'd begged off. Maybe she would have told her more if given the chance.

"I wish there was a magic button I could press to say I need help," Bailey said as Juanita dried her hair. "But sometimes, it feels like they're setting me up to fail."

"What do you mean?" Miss Baker asked with a frown.

Bailey didn't completely trust they weren't being listened to so she needed to be careful here.

"I have these notes in my kitchen drawer. And I read them thoroughly before filming ever began. But I don't know my telephone number. I feel as if there's a lot I don't know, and I'd love to signal someone I need help, but I can't."

"Not even Bobby?" Jackie asked.

"Especially not Bobby," she replied. "He's the producer. He's the one who put the rules in place."

"Do you think he wants to see you mess up for the ratings?" Tracy asked. Before Bailey could reply he wouldn't, Miss Baker spoke.

"No." Miss Baker had a severe frown. "He's not going to sabotage his own production. He's too serious for that. Plus, I hear 1954 is set to make twice as much as 1953."

"Besides," Pat gave Bailey a sly look, "The chemistry between you two is off the charts."

Some of the ladies began to chuckle, and Bailey felt her cheeks warm.

"He's just good at role-playing."

"Maybe." Juanita applied leave-in conditioner to Bailey's wet hair. She was grinning widely. "But, girl, just wait until you watch the playbacks. It's like you two aren't even acting. When is your day off?"

"Tomorrow."

"Tomorrow is team meeting," Jackie said. "Tracy and I were invited to yours, since we might be semi-regulars at the hair salon with you, but we'll typically be in Nadine's meeting." Bailey realized she recognized Jackie and Tracy. They had been the maids at Nadine's house. But she still didn't quite follow what they meant about the teams. Did the stars of the show have their own separate meetings?

"This will be the first team meeting I've ever been invited to since joining this show," Pat said bitterly.

"Everyone is going to stop filming at once to go to a meeting?" Bailey asked in confusion.

"No. The meetings are staggered in teams. You got a team, and so do the other stars," Miss Baker replied, confirming her thoughts. "What do you think Bobby's doing all day at the *Gazette*?"

"Holding meetings?"

"And doing script changes," Jackie added.

Bailey wasn't sure why she was surprised by this. Bobby did say he would put script changes into her notebook. Thus far, he hadn't added anything new. She would know, because she had just checked it.

"One more thing before we head back out there," Miss Baker said. "We don't need *them* to tell our story. *We* need to be the ones to tell it."

"Amen," Jackie replied.

Chapter Eighteen

Bailey agreed with the ladies, but was concerned they might be getting the wrong impression about Bobby. She just didn't feel as if he wouldn't be open to new ideas—even if they changed the dynamic of what 1954 was supposed to be about.

"Even before I started filming, I always felt like there should be a true narrative of racial issues. But I don't think Bobby intends to tell a whitewashed story. He's the one that initiates every discussion about race. I think he wants to open the—"

"And we just want to have input on that discussion," Pat interrupted. "You have a lot of influence on him, Bailey. He listens to you."

"Okay," she conceded, still a bit uneasy this might turn into a *them* against *us*.

"You know," Betty grinned at her. "You had me rolling on the floor when Bobby dug that squirrel family out of the vent."

Everyone in the room hollered in laughter and just like that, the mood changed. They spent the next few minutes laughing and mimicking Bailey's facial expressions.

When they all got up to finally leave the room, Jackie stopped and turned. "Oh yeah. You don't need to listen to only white music. You're young. A Black girl your age should be listening to bebop, like Dizzy Gillespie, Charlie Parker, Mary Lou Williams, and Miles Davis. We made a list for you."

"Thank you so much. I still need my phone number so I can call Bobby to pick me up."

"Don't worry," Pat replied. "I'll drop you off on my way home."

Bailey smiled. "Then we should obviously be friends. We're about the same age."

"That would make sense," Pat replied with an appreciative smile.

"Look." Bailey stopped them before Miss Baker opened the curtain. "Will you do me a favor and promise to tell me if I ever look ridiculous?"

Everyone rushed to assure her that her acting was on point.

"You look the way I felt when I was a newlywed," Tracy laughed. "Kinda nervous, a little unsure, but ultra-flirty. Do you notice the way your *husband's* cheeks brighten whenever you flirt with him?"

"Oh, I've seen it!" Pat clapped. "It's so cute. You guys are super adorable. You gotta do more flirting, though! Everyone waits for Bobby to get home to see it."

Bailey was surprised by that revelation.

"Girl, that kiss..." Pat put her hand on her chest and pretended to swoon. "Everybody's talking about that kiss. It's about damn time."

Bailey covered her face in embarrassment. "That was a mistake! I swear it. I thought Bobby was going to give me an infraction."

"What?!" Miss Baker said. "Girl, you two better get with the program! Y'all playing a married couple and y'all still ain't kissing."

Bailey blinked and her brow shot up. "People kiss on the show?"

Tracy rolled her eyes. "All the time. Nadine is making plans to get busy with the mayor and when that happens, it's going to get hot in here!"

"But it's not just about you two together," Pat interrupted. "You alone bring a natural element that was missing from last year's production. All of the new actors do. Girl, to be honest, I stopped watching last year after the first few weeks. But I truly like the new stories. Nadine's story line about having a baby by the mayor when she was a teen is blowing my mind!"

"Oh, that is good," Jackie agreed. "I'm hooked on that."

"I like Drew," Juanita confessed. "He's definitely eye candy."

"Yeah, he is fine," Miss Baker agreed.

Everyone side-eyed the elderly lady. "What? I ain't too old to appreciate a handsome man."

"Look, if you want to make it to that barbecue on time, then I need to get you in hair curlers and under that hair dryer," Juanita said. "And I need to teach you how to pin your curls and wrap your hair at night instead of just slapping on a scarf!"

Everyone hurried out of the room to get into position.

Bailey felt as if her brain was on fire with all the information she'd been given. There was a lot to process. But what stood out most was that the ladies had watched her performance and had enjoyed it. In the end, all the confusion and second-guessing herself seemed worth it.

Bailey was at the hairdressers for about three hours—twice as long as she'd want to spend there on her Saturday mornings. But it was necessary, and well worth her time; plus, she got her nails done, and in total it had only cost her one dollar and fifty cents! Of course, she tipped Juanita, giving her the full two dollars. Visiting the hair salon would be a worthy Saturday routine.

They might not have been starring actresses, but the women in the salon knew how to orchestrate a real beauty salon experience. Random people dropped in to actually get their hair done. The new arrivals sat in the waiting area listening to the bebop music. A man even came by selling donuts, and everyone bought warm pastries from him.

They all chatted and gossiped while eating fresh donuts and drinking coffee. She was so comfortable, she almost didn't want to leave. But at the end of her session, she had a head full of perfectly silken curls, a pocketbook full of duck clips to keep her curls pinned in place, and a list of information that would make her job as Bailey Banks even more successful.

"So, what do you do?" Bailey asked Pat as they drove home in her convertible.

"I work at the factory. It's how I heard about them filming a streaming '50s reality show. They needed people to work in front of and behind the cameras." She rolled her eyes and pressed the cigarette lighter. "Turns out, in pursuit of being authentic, the job positions were based on racial stereotypes, and no one ever tried to find story lines for the maid or the custodian or factory worker or any other person but the whites in town. We got Hispanic people, an Asian couple—I mean, it takes a lot of people to make Wingate run."

She retrieved a cigarette from a pack on her dashboard and lit up.

"You want one?" she asked Bailey, who shook her head.

"And you all live on set?" Bailey asked, still very curious about how it worked behind the scenes.

"Yeah. That side is pretty sweet. You work five days on set and get two days off. I can leave the set or stay. I just can't have any visitors.

"In exchange we get paid a real salary, and it's more than decent. Best is that we live rent-free for a year—with an option to return for future seasons. Girl, my bank account is looking better than it's ever been. Plus, we get to watch the show for free, and we don't have any cameras in our homes. I don't think I could live like. Non-cast members only have to stay in character if we go into town—or when interacting with the cast. But there are still a lot of rules."

"It sounds like you like it, though. Right?"

"For the most part. I just get pissed off when I see the damned butcher getting screen time with a camera following him around on his deliveries when Curtis doesn't get that, and these white women are always wagging their tongues about him."

"Oh…"

Pat grinned. "I'm not an angry Black woman. This is just old; watching history rehash itself over and over."

Bailey nodded, understanding exactly where she was coming from. "Think about your backstory, Pat. Write it down and bring it to tomorrow's team meeting. If you and I are friends, then we're going to need a story line."

Pat nodded enthusiastically. "I can do that. But we probably shouldn't be best friends or anything—at least not yet," Pat said slowly while in deep thought. "Otherwise, you would have been on the phone talking to me this entire week. But we should know each other outside of the hair salon."

"Maybe we used to work together at the bank?"

Pat's brow quirked up. "A teller? I like the idea of being a bank teller. It would explain why I drive a nice convertible while Quinton is driving around in a Studebaker selling those encyclopedias!"

"And I used to confide in you about me and Bobby's interest in each other. And you always supported it, even when other people didn't think it would last."

"Maybe it's not that others didn't think it would last, maybe they just worried Bobby would use you for sex and then drop you."

"That's good!" Bailey agreed. "Work on that in your back story. We'll get it to Bobby to approve."

"Thanks, Bailey." Pat gave her a sincere look of appreciation. "You didn't have to do any of this—"

"Yeah, I do, because I want 1954 to be a success. This will hopefully jump-start my career as an actor— but I also want it to be as real as possible."

"Damn straight."

They pulled up into Bailey's driveway.

"Good luck at the barbecue," Pat whispered.

"Thanks." Bailey got out of the car. "See you later!"

She walked up to the house and opened her front door, worrying if she was going to catch Bobby out of character. Actually, if the cameras were constantly filming her the way the others had suggested, then the production team had called ahead to inform him she was on her way home.

"Bobby, I'm home!" she called while she hung up her coat and hat. She fluffed her hair and saw Bobby coming in from the kitchen.

"Bae, how did you get home?"

His hair was mussed and his clothes were dirty. Okay, so he had been doing something domestic.

"Pat, my friend from the bank, had her appointment at the same time. She drove me home." Bailey frowned at Bobby. "Did you crawl under the house?"

He looked at himself. "No. I mowed the lawn and then went to Mom's house to mow hers. She had a list of chores for me to do, so..." He gave her an appreciative look. "But you look great!" He moved forward to either kiss or hug her, but Bailey held up her hand to keep him at bay.

She had an idea and she wanted to test it. But it scared her down to her bones. She had never been one to make the first moves, but right now she wasn't Bailey Westbrook, but Bailey Banks—newlywed.

She placed a cryptic look on her face. "Oh no you don't. How far did you get with the chores here at home?"

He slouched in feigned disappointment. "Not very far. But I'm going to put a dent in it."

She walked to Bobby and put her hands on his cheeks. She then stared into his eyes. "I'm happy you look out for your mom. Here's some incentive to finish up."

She leaned forward and placed a soft kiss on his lips.

When she leaned back, she saw his blue eyes had rapidly darkened until only thin, blue rings were visible past dark pupils.

Neither spoke for what seemed like a long time before Bobby seemed to remember the ball was in his court.

"That's not going to make me finish. That's only going to cause something else to get started..." he said in a gruff voice.

She released his face and laughed, but at the same time, her heart was racing in her chest. She could not believe her bold action. But it was ridiculous they were kissing cheeks like two people that had been married for a decade. Even Ricky Riccardo kissed Lucy!

"No time for that, dear, I have to call Helen to find out when we should get to the barbecue. And you have a lot of work to finish if we're going to have date night next weekend."

Bobby saluted her as if she was a drill sergeant but dutifully left the room.

Bailey was on autopilot, fighting to act natural. If she stopped to think, she was going to stumble and end up falling flat on her face.

She picked up her pocketbook. Helen's number was still in it and she quickly grabbed the scrap of paper and dialed the number.

"Helen," she said when her neighbor answered. "This is Bailey."

"Oh hi, dear. I hope you're ready for the neighborhood welcome wagon."

"That's the reason I'm calling. What time should we come?"

"Hank's going to fire up the grill at about three, and I told everyone to arrive about four."

"Okay. I'm bringing a gelatin mold."

"Oh, you didn't have to do that, Bailey. We'll have enough food for an annual church picnic! But no one can turn down Jell-O."

"That's what I say," Bailey nodded. "We'll see you at about four."

"See you then, and you'll get to meet Hank. You'll love him. He's sweet."

"Okay. See you then."

Chapter Nineteen

Bailey wasn't exactly sure what one wore to a barbecue in 1954. She had some simple dresses she could pair with flats. It was the end of summer, so shorts wouldn't be out of the question. She didn't want to get too fancy, but she also wanted to look good.

She decided on a pair of denim jeans, which she neatly rolled up to just below her knees. She put on a sleeveless blouse that had a slightly cropped waist that wouldn't show her belly unless she raised her arms. She'd wear a sweater she could take off if she got too warm. She almost put on sneakers before deciding on a pair of beige flats.

After touching up her makeup, she stood in front of the full-length mirror and looked at herself from all angles.

Bobby walked into the room. The door was open, so it was her signal it was okay.

"You look gorgeous," he said while running a hand through his hair and picking at his dirty shirt.

"Thanks, honey. I hope you're going to get cleaned up soon."

"Yep. What time are we going?" he asked while heading for the closet, presumably to search for something to wear.

"In about an hour."

"Oh, there's plenty of time. Check out the office. I put everything away. And I left a pile of stuff we can throw out in the garage. Once I break down the boxes, it's all finished."

"I'm impressed. You finished everything *and* mowed the lawn."

"Two lawns," he reminded her while tossing some clothes onto the bed.

"I have to see this with my own eyes."

"Go ahead. I'm going to take a long, hot bath, and possibly take some aspirin."

"Poor baby."

"I'm fine." He went to the bathroom and shut the door and she headed to his office to check it out.

Everything she hadn't known what to do with had been tossed into the room. It had been so cluttered and piled haphazardly with boxes, it might have even been considered a danger zone.

But now it was in perfect order. The desk was once more visible. A typewriter with a tray of paper sat on its surface. There was also a small globe, a dog-eared dictionary, a mug containing several pens and pencils, and finally, a photo of her and Bobby.

Obviously, it had been photoshopped but it gave her a jolt. It was a wedding photo.

She walked over to the bookshelf, noting it had been polished even though the books were in haphazard piles. There was another photograph, this one of a man and woman; his mother and father?

There was a file cabinet in the corner of the room and next to that, an old leather office chair on wheels.

A corkboard was on the wall with colorful pushpins all ready to hold important facts in place.

She left the room and headed out the back door, slightly ashamed there were unwashed dishes in the sink. She went to the garage and found it was a huge improvement over the way it had looked when she'd done laundry.

She wouldn't call it exactly neat; tools were all over the tool bench and boxes were stacked haphazardly on two steel shelves. Unused furniture was piled in back along with paint cans and empty buckets, gardening tools and the lawn mower. But he had straightened up her laundry area, even placing a rubber mat down so she wouldn't slip on the wet floor.

She nodded in approval and went to the kitchen, where she quickly washed the dishes. And this time she located the rubber gloves under the sink and pulled them on.

Bailey was just about to transfer the gelatin mold to a pretty platter and worrying about whether it was going to come out in one, clean piece or end up as a bunch of slop when Bobby walked into the kitchen.

He wore brown Bermuda shorts that just reached his knees and a brightly colored, short-sleeved Madras shirt was tucked into the shorts. Long, argyle socks encased thick, muscular calves with a pair of moccasins on his feet. A straw porkpie hat sat atop his head.

How was it possible he did not look absolutely ridiculous? This look worked on Bobby Bailey. Maybe not on Hank, or Quinton, or Drew, but it *hella* worked on Bobby.

"Bobby Banks, you are certainly the ginchiest man in all of Wingate!"

He raised his hands in a model pose and did a slow spin.

Oh my God...was that a back belt? Was it possible he could actually bring a resurgence of this style? Yes. Yes, it was absolutely possible.

"We're certainly going to be the hippest cats at the barbecue," he grinned.

"That's for certain. Help me unmold this. I'm scared that if I do it by myself, it's going to end up all over the counter."

He hurried over to help her and the mold came out perfectly.

"That actually looks good," he commented. "I've never seen it with white stuff on the bottom."

"Yeah. That's new for me too. Aunt Mae just had fruit cocktail in hers."

"I'll have a piece," he said while giving it a dubious look.

"Gee thanks, dear. You and I might be the only people who'll eat it."

"Well, we should get going. It's nearly four."

Bailey inhaled nervously. *Here we go.* Whatever was in store for her, she was ready. What did they say about knowledge being power? They hadn't given her a script about what was about to happen, but she knew it was coming...

Chapter Twenty

The barbecue was obvious to Bailey the moment she stepped out of her house. The aroma of grilling meat filled the neighborhood, along with the tunes of some rockabilly singer she didn't know.

By the time they reached Helen's house, a man at the back gate was waving them over.

"Hello, neighbor! You must be Bobby and Bailey. Come on in!"

The man was dressed in colorful matching Bermuda shirt and shorts with black socks that reached his calves. Tan sandals completed the ensemble. He brought visions of Fred Flintstone to mind, or maybe John Goodman from the sitcom *Roseanne*.

Bobby offered his hand. "I'm Bobby and this is my wife, Bailey."

"I'm Hank." His smile was now directed to Bailey. "My wife, Helen, has done nothing but sing your wife's praises—"

"Bailey!" Helen soon joined her husband. "Let me take that from you, dear. We have all the vittles on the table over here. Come on in, you two."

Helen commandeered the gelatin mode and led them to the shindig.

It felt authentically like any backyard barbecue she'd ever attended—except for the two cameramen situated behind the fence. It was going to be tricky to remember not to stand where one of them would end up in her shot.

She gazed at the seven other people present. Each wore broad, welcoming smiles as they watched her and Bobby. The men were gathered by the grill drinking beers and the women were on the other side of the yard sitting in lawn chairs and smoking cigarettes or sipping cocktails.

"Let me get you two drinks," Hank said. "We have soft drinks, beer, wine—"

"I'll have a beer," Bobby replied.

"Same for me," Bailey added.

"Come on." Helen gestured to her. "I'll introduce you to the girls."

Bailey glanced at Bobby, who winked at her as they parted ways. Helen leaned in to whisper to her once they were near the table with the food—and a cameraman.

"Your husband is the cat's meow!"

Bailey grinned. "Yours isn't so bad either."

Helen smiled. "He's no Cary Grant, but he is my big, old teddy bear."

After placing the gelatin mode on the table next to a 7-layer salad, potato salad, and several other side dishes, Helen turned to the women seated in lawn chairs. "Ladies, this is Bailey. Bailey, these are the ladies."

A pretty woman about fifteen years Bailey's senior leaned forward in her bright-yellow lawn chair. Her slender legs were crossed, showcasing brightly painted toenails in strapless heels. She removed a cigarette from between her lips and deftly tapped loose invisible ash.

"Hello. I'm Haley. I live in the house behind you." It was no surprise her voice was as sultry as her looks.

"Nice to meet you," Bailey replied. Haley wore yellow shorts that were much shorter than Bailey's, flaring out like a mini skirt. Although not so short they would raise eyebrows in modern times, they probably did in this era. She also wore a colorful halter with a high collar. The halter showed enough of her cleavage that it certainly would have caught any man's eye in any time period.

She had a '50s bombshell look with bleached-blond hair and heavy make-up that brought images of Marilyn Monroe to mind.

If she remembered correctly, this was the divorcee that was prone to sunbathing in her backyard with the straps of her bikini undone...

Next to Haley sat another woman that was dressed in a simple, plaid dress and brown loafers. With short brown hair and cat glasses, she looked like the town librarian.

"Hi, Bailey. I'm Geneva. My husband, Jeff, is over there talking with your husband. We live next door to you." Geneva rubbed her hands together as she spoke. "Please forgive me for not coming by, but once Helen told us all about the welcome-to-the-neighborhood barbecue, I decided this was the best way to introduce myself."

"Hi, Geneva." She wondered if this was the woman that had criticized the color of their couch. "It's been hectic, but I'm so happy for such a nice welcome. I think this is much better than a quick hello." Geneva looked relieved.

Two other women, Marina and Shirley, also greeted her, each eyeing her curiously. Neither was the woman who had mistaken her for the help. That was a relief.

Hank showed up with her beer and Bailey glanced over his shoulder and saw Bobby talking to several men. He looked at ease—but of course, he would, since he had hired them all.

Haley sat in a fold-out chair next to Helen, who received an affectionate shoulder squeeze from her hubby. "Sorry, we're a little behind on the dogs and burgers."

"I told you we were out of charcoal..." Helen said in a singsong voice.

"Yes. Yes. I should listen," Hank replied contritely.

"We're fine. You go entertain the fellas." Helen shooed him away.

"Bailey, I hear you're a newlywed," Marina said. She held a tall glass of something brown and on the rocks. She had a slight New York accent, and seemed as if she could be Hispanic or Italian. Her black hair was puffed into a regal bouffant. She wore a casual, pastel-pink dress with bright-white gumball-like earrings and matching necklace.

Bailey nodded, trying not to feel as if she was being interviewed. It was not always easy for her in social situations but this was acting, so it should be different. It had to be different because she too had a plan for the evening.

"We've only been married a few weeks," Bailey replied.

"Well, you two are certainly movers and shakers," Haley said while leaning toward her with a raised brow and a broad smile. "My first husband

and I could never afford a house at your age. Not that I'm much older than you are."

Mariana snickered.

"I was a baby when I got married," Haley insisted.

They watched her as if she was expected to explain how they could afford a house.

"I'm sure having a mortgage is going to take some sacrifices."

"Well, this is a very nice neighborhood," Marina said while looking into the air.

Helen nodded. "And I'm sure it will stay a nice neighborhood." She gave Marina a pointed look. Marina suddenly smiled.

"Well, the people that lived there before you were very progressive," Geneva said. "They had friends of all types. You never knew who you might see coming and going." She forced a nervous chuckle. "I saw a man once visit them that had one of those long Jewish beards, and he even wore one of those little hats." Geneva looked around at the other ladies as if for confirmation.

Marina agreed. "Midge never had a problem being around those men Lyle had come to the house. Beatniks were always over there." She nodded at them gravely. "I worried back then about the safety of the neighborhood..."

Bailey just sipped her beer and minded her business.

"They were friendly," Helen said. "They never met a stranger."

"That's a dangerous mentality in this day and age," Geneva said. "Jeffrey and I decided to get a security system."

"No. Really?" Haley asked. "This neighborhood is safe. There's never been issues, not even with Curtis."

Curtis, the Black milkman all the single women supposedly admired. There goes admiring him.

"Curtis is perfectly safe." Haley spoke matter-of-factly.

"You would know." Shirley spoke for the first time.

Haley spun to look at her. "What do you mean by that?"

Shirley smiled. "Just that you are friends with Curtis. You talk to him all the time. So do I. He's a nice one."

Bailey forced herself to sit quietly when all she wanted was to get up and walk away. But out of a sense of curiosity, she did want to see how far this was going to go.

Haley glared at Shirley but didn't say anything else. Bailey sensed there was not much love between them. It was weird because they were very much alike. Like Haley, Shirley also had dyed-blonde hair and heavy makeup, only she fell far short of Marilyn Monroe and was giving off vibes of trying too hard.

Shirley was clearly in her forties, if not older, yet she wore an outfit of a skimpy cropped halter and tight shorts that was far from sexy, as it simply showcased her cellulite and wrinkled, freckled cleavage.

In addition, instead of coiffed blonde locks, Shirley's hair was over-processed and fried, while her makeup was just bad. There was too much rouge, and her lipstick was more orange than red. This was clearly a woman that wished to look a way she could not pull off — at least not in the way Haley did.

"Bailey," Helen said while turning to her. "Was that your husband that wrote the article in the *Gazette* about polio?"

"What?" Marina gasped.

"Yes." Bailey twiddled with her bottle of beer. She hadn't even had more than one sip. "That was Bobby's first byline."

"Well, no wonder he can afford that house!" Marina exclaimed, as if she had solved a puzzle.

"I did have a hand in it," Bailey said mildly. "I worked as a bank teller after graduating college." How many of you rednecks did? she wondered peevishly.

"Oh! You are a credit," Marina said. She looked at Bailey as if she'd grown horns.

"That means you're smart." Helen patted her hand.

Bailey turned and looked over her shoulder at Bobby. "I think I'll see what the hubby's up to. Pardon me," Bailey said politely while standing and hurrying away.

Bobby was talking enthusiastically about football. He put his arm around her shoulder. "Hi, honey." She leaned against him.

"How are you doing on beer? Still babying it?" Hank laughed. "Hope you're enjoying yourself, Bailey."

Bailey took a sip of her beer. "I am. Thanks, Hank."

A leaned forward to shake her hand. His eyes twinkled. He wore a hat low on his head, a bowling shirt and tan slacks. He was tall with a tanned complexion. "Nice to meet you. I'm Alfonso—Al to my friends. Marina is my wife."

"Oh." She gave him a wry smile. "Your wife is a hoot."

Al held onto her hand a bit too long as his eyes quickly scanned her body. Bailey had to slip her hand from his.

The others introduced themselves and she was happy none of them offered to shake her hand.

The conversation fell into a decided lull once she showed up, but she was not interested in returning to the "ladies" as she was expected to do.

The radio announcer enthusiastically announced the new hit song by Etta James.

Hank flipped a burger with a long spatula and began tapping his feet. "I love this music," he announced.

"Ugh. It's filthy," Jeffrey said distastefully while looking away from them. "They shouldn't be playing this music on our channels."

"It's fun," Hank shrugged. "And the kids like it."

Jeff gave him a pointed look. "You know what it's about."

Bailey listened to the lyrics. She'd never heard this particular song before. The singer, Etta James, was telling a guy named Henry to roll with her. Oh...

Al began to clap his hands as he turned his attention to her—actually, his attention had never quite left her. "Bailey," he leered. "What's that dance you young ones do?"

Bailey was appalled. Did this freak actually think she was about to dance for their entertainment?

Bobby tightened his grip on her. "I think I'll introduce myself to the others," he said while leading Bailey to where the women were sitting.

"Aww!" Al called. "Come on, you two. You're the youngest ones here. You gotta keep the party going!"

"Al," Hank warned.

Al looked at him with a broad smile. "I'm just being funny."

Bobby ignored them and took a seat next to Helen. Bailey sat on the opposite side of him, wondering how Bobby planned to handle these racist women.

Chapter Twenty-One

"Hello, ladies. I'm Bobby," he introduced himself politely.

Each woman perked up—specifically, Haley. She uncrossed her legs and then recrossed them in the other direction, making sure attention would go to her perfect legs.

"Hello, neighbor. I saw you mowing your lawn today," she smiled.

"I hope I didn't bother you. I started pretty early."

"Not at all. Watching others do manual labor is my only form of exercise." She laughed with a throwback of her head, even though Bailey didn't think she was all that funny.

"Bailey told us you work at the *Gazette*," Helen said. "I read the article you wrote on the Salk vaccine."

Conversation turned to the horrors of polio; a much more innocent conversation than they'd had with her.

Bailey's attention turned to a man that had come over to the food table. Bailey noted he hadn't said anything other than to introduce himself as Carl, Shirley's husband.

He had taken a slice of her gelatin mold. Bailey held her breath, ignoring everyone else.

He ate a big bite, chewed, and then took an even bigger one.

She got up and walked to the food table.

"How's the gelatin? Any good?"

He gave her a surprised look and seemed to blush at being caught stuffing his mouth. He swallowed quickly.

"I love Jell-O. It's really good. I've never had it with this cream on it before."

"Me either. But I made it, and I was hoping someone would give it a thumbs up."

"Thumbs up," he said politely while giving her the hand sign.

She liked him, and felt a bit sorry he had been matched so inappropriately with a woman like Shirley. He looked normal, and not like he should be married to a wanna-be blonde bombshell. He was dressed in khaki-colored slacks, a polo shirt with a ginormous collar, and scuffed loafers. He was definitely younger than Shirley, with a pleasant face on a tall, thick body.

Hank finally came over with a platter of hot dogs and hamburgers, followed by the other men.

"Come and get it!" Hank called.

"Oh. I've been waiting for this!" Carl's eyes locked onto the food. She thought it was funny. He looked as if he truly hadn't had a good meal in ages. It made her wonder if Shirley was a worse cook than even she was.

Everyone got up to pile their plate with food. She got a burger and bypassed all the things she normally liked on it like onions, tomato, lettuce, mayo, ketchup, and mustard. She stuck with just ketchup, fearful her breath would stink or she'd spill goop on her clothes. She was clumsy at heart, and had never had a burger she didn't end up carrying a portion of on her clothes. This was not the day to be clumsy. She had an important scene she'd have to play and she didn't want a distracting food stain to spoil it.

Bobby came over to stand next to her. "This is nice," he said as he placed two scoops of potato salad on his plate next to a hamburger and hot dog. She almost felt bad about telling him to eat extra potato salad after Helen warned her to stay far away from it. The problem was, Helen had told her while they were OOC — out of character — so no one was in on the joke but her.

She turned away when he took a big bite of the potato salad and only turned back in time to see his shocked expression. Bailey suppressed a grin. He deserved every bit of that for setting her up like this. They were obviously *in on it* — he could have let her in on it too. She quickly returned to her chair without agreeing this was "nice."

Shirley gazed over at her husband, who stood at the table eating without paying her the least bit of attention.

What would it be like if she didn't like the man she had to pretend to be married to for the next year? It was just the first week of filming, and there was always the possibility it could happen…

"How ever did you make such a good catch?" Haley asked while lighting her third cigarette.

Bailey shrugged. "He was the one who did all the catching. I did all the running."

"*You* ran from *him*?" Shirley asked.

Helen gave her a quick look and Shirley looked embarrassed. "I just mean he's quite the catch."

Bailey ignored the jibe and looked at Carl again. While everyone stood at the food table chitchatting,

Shirley's husband didn't say a word to anyone. He just ate. He was like the party crasher that only showed up for the food and booze.

"Your husband seems nice," she commented, turning in time to see a shadow cross Shirley's face. She quickly plastered on a smile. "He is dreamy. He looks just like Tab Hunter. Don't you think?"

Haley rolled her eyes behind Shirley's back.

"I think you're right," Bailey agreed, even though she didn't know who Tab Hunter was.

She caught Al leering at her from his position outside of Bobby's line of vision. When he was caught staring, he winked and slowly licked his lips.

Bailey wanted to hurl. She could not have manufactured the shudders that ran over her body.

Al looked to be in his mid-forties or fifties. It was hard to tell, as he had stark-black hair that had to have been dyed. He was dressed in slacks and a Bermuda shirt. Thankfully he had bypassed the matching shorts.

When she glanced back at him, she saw he was ogling her legs. She decided that was all the attention she would give him. Sexual harassment was not going to play out today — or hopefully, ever. Fighting off a frisky neighbor was not a story line she was interested in playing.

"What do you do now that you're married?" Shirley asked. Bailey gave her a confused look. "You said you used to work at the bank."

Bailey offered a wry grin. "I am doing the hardest job I've ever done in my life. I'm working as a housewife."

Shirley and Haley looked at her as if not understanding the joke before Helen laughed. "I'd like to tell you it gets easier." Helen winked at her. "It doesn't"

Bailey inhaled deeply. "So, what do you ladies do for a living?"

Haley paused in lighting her cigarette. "I collect alimony."

Now the others decided to laugh.

"Hey, it's not easy being a professional woman of leisure," she continued. "There's shopping, and beauty salons, not to mention maintaining my beautiful glow."

Geneva returned to the conversation with her husband, Jeff, now in tow. Both carried a fresh drink and a plate of food.

"Well, if you're not careful, you're going to get wrinkles sitting out in the sun," Geneva said critically.

"Sunscreen, dear. And I slather it on."

Jeff openly ogled Haley's legs. Bailey didn't think Geneva noticed, although she bet the cameraman had.

Carl had gotten another piece of Jell-O and then looked over at Bailey and raised his fork as if to toast. Bailey grinned and raised her half-eaten burger in return.

Shirley looked from one to the other in shock.

"Carl and I were high school sweethearts," she said quickly.

High school sweethearts! She was ten years older — and that was being generous.

"Let me get you all something to drink." Helen stood as if she wanted nothing to do with that story line.

"Just a soft drink for me!" Bailey called.

"Oh, come on. It's a party — *your* party. Live it up! I made margueritas with strawberries! Can you imagine? You can take strawberry concentrate and make all kinds of drinks out of it."

"I'm game." Geneva spoke in a sultry voice while tapping the ash from her cigarette.

"Sure. I'll try anything once!" Shirley said too loudly. Helen hurried to the kitchen for the cocktails, calling for her husband to give her a hand.

Bobby returned to his seat and Geneva wasted no time turning her attention on him.

"So, Bailey tells us you did all the pursuing in your relationship."

Bobby grinned while gazing at his wife. "I saw her first, and did everything in my power to get her to take notice of me."

"Really?" Marina replied in disbelief.

"Really," Bobby confirmed.

Marina gave him a perplexed look.

"I noticed him. I just wasn't sure about his motives," Bailey explained, keeping in mind her and Pat's new story line.

"*His* motives?" Shirley asked in shock. She coughed and looked embarrassed. "I just mean…isn't it illegal for a Negro and a white man to marry?" She whispered the last.

By that time, Marina and Al had returned to the conversation with plates of food.

"It *is* illegal." Marina looked pointedly at Bobby and Bailey.

"Who cares?" Al laughed. "I don't have a problem, as long as it's the way their doing it; a white man and a Colored girl."

Bobby visibly stiffened, but Bailey refused to look at him. She just kept her mouth shut, nearly biting her cheeks to stop herself from speaking.

"Those laws are unconstitutional and have been repealed in Ohio." He reached for her hand and squeezed it gently and she finally gave him a calm look. But if he thought this was going to be *her* show, he was wrong. He'd have to deal with this.

"We are legally married." He continued. "And happily so."

"Well." Marina continued. "I completely understand Bailey running. None of this could be easy on your families."

Bailey finally spoke. "It hasn't been." She cleared her throat nervously. "My aunt and uncle worried I'd have a hard go in life, being with someone who is not like me. And in many ways, they were right. I could have chosen to live in an all-Negro area of town and worked as a maid—because here in Wingate, there is no shortage of Negro servants needed. I could have married a Negro man that would have cut your lawn every week and delivered your packages and picked up your garbage and never been a threat to any whites because we would have never interacted. That's the way it has been for many years in the Negro communities."

Bailey squeezed Bobby's hand and looked at him.

"I could have been content in that world. But fear of leaving that path isn't what caused me to run from Bobby." Bailey looked at the other guests, who watched quietly while the backdrop of an Elvis song played over the radio.

"I ran from Bobby because of the hatred and mistrust. The beatings, the whippings, the burnings, the raping, and the laws that whites put on Negroes to keep us in our place. And because I didn't know what was truly in Bobby's heart when he wanted to spend time with me; if he wanted to leave me with a blond-haired, blue-eyed baby while he ended up with someone he could present to a neighborhood like this."

"You make it sound like it's just us." Geneva spoke in a quivering voice. "Those laws are there to protect you too."

"We just don't want any trouble in our neighborhood," Jeff said flatly, his expression cold and angry.

"If you stay in your place—" Miranda began.

Bobby stood, still holding Bailey's hand. "I think we should take our leave now."

Almost as if on cue, Helen and Hank came out the back door carrying marguerita glasses along with a pitcher of the beverage.

"Sorry it took forever!" Helen exclaimed. "The blender went haywire!"

"There's a mess to clean up in there," Hank chuckled while gesturing to his shirt. "This shirt just got a little bit more colorful."

"Thank you for your hospitality, Helen. Hank." Bobby headed for the gate with Bailey in tow.

"What—?" Helen began

But they were gone in a flash. Even the cameramen had to hurry into position to catch their departure.

When they got into their house, Bobby slammed the door. He opened his mouth but Bailey just ran to him and buried her face against his chest.

She broke down and sobbed. She had never cried so hard in her life.

Every ounce of frustration, trepidation, anger, and outrage burst from her.

Bobby's arms went quickly around her. "Bailey!" he said in alarm. Her sobs continued as he tried to soothe her. He kissed the top of her head and rubbed the back of her neck and spoke apologies.

"Don't cry, Bailey. Please don't cry. I'm so sorry, honey. Shhh. It's okay. It's going to be all right. I promise." He repeated these words over and over until Bailey finally quieted.

After a moment he tried to look into her eyes, but she buried her face in her hands in shame.

He kissed her forehead and stroked what he could touch of her face.

"I'm so sorry. I really am."

"I...need to go to the restroom." She hurried out of the room. When she reached the bedroom, she nearly tripped on the chair, since she had her face almost completely covered. She darted to the bathroom and shut the door, leaning her back against it.

Bailey smiled. Her face was completely free of tears.

And the Grammy for best actress in a reality show goes to Bailey Westbrook...

ACT II

Chapter Twenty-Two

Bailey decided to remove her eye makeup so her eyes would look more lifeless. She had to produce some tears. Bobby was experienced enough to know she had been faking that last scene if there was no evidence on her face.

It wasn't too difficult to pull some terrible memories from her past. Being orphaned at the age of seven channeled enough emotional turmoil to fuel a lifetime of therapy.

She blew her nose, dabbed her wet eyes, and then left the bathroom to join Bobby and his cameras.

He was in the kitchen, where he was busily pouring hot water into cups. He paused and quickly set the pot on the table.

"Hey...I thought you might want some tea."

"Tea would be nice," she replied while taking her seat. She inhaled, turning on her actress persona. "I'm sorry I broke down like—"

"Oh my God, no. Don't apologize." He put down the package of Lipton tea bags and rushed over to her, kneeling at her side. "I'm sorry you had to go through with that! I'm so sorry, Bailey. I'm really sorry."

His blue eyes were filled with shame. As they should be, for not giving her the same opportunity to professionally develop her parts in a scene that was so pivotal to her story line. He was a jerk!

She placed her hand over his. "Honey, you are the remedy, not the sickness. This is not your fault. I know I have to be stronger and smarter." More tears welled in her eyes as she manifested thoughts of her childhood dog having to be put down due to old age.

Bobby gnawed his lower lip and placed gentle hands on her cheeks. "Don't cry. I—we...do you want to move? We don't have to stay in this neighborhood."

She wanted to smile but resisted. Move? Only the most privileged people in society would think that was an answer; to just pick up and move away from their problems. He truly was a Chesterfield—one of the wealthiest families in the United States. In 1954, Blacks did not have that luxury—not many did, whether Black or not.

She placed her hands over his. "We're not going to run from them. We're not going to hide from them. I'm going to make sure I stay in their faces!" She said the last fiercely.

He stared at her, his eyes locking onto hers as if he was trying to see within her soul—or perhaps he did. "I don't want anything to hurt you, Bailey," he whispered.

Speak louder, she thought. The cameras and microphones won't be able to pick up what you're saying.

For a split second, Bailey thought she might lean forward and kiss him. If this really was 1954, and they had just gone through that traumatic experience as a true interracial couple, then she would have. She would have kissed him with unbound passion. And they would have made love—maybe even right here on the kitchen floor. A youthful defiance of the laws of a society that feared two young people that had dared to purchase a home in the middle of a segregated white suburbia.

Bailey exhaled the breath she hadn't even realized she was holding. She released her touch on the back of his hands and turned to reach for her teacup.

His hands slipped from her face.

Bailey and Bobby didn't talk about it anymore. They took their cups of tea to the living room and watched television. She snuggled against him as his arms went around her shoulders, his thumb periodically grazing her arm. And they spent the remainder of the evening in comfortable silence.

When Bailey woke up the next morning, she prepared to get up following a routine that had become familiar; go to the bathroom, wash her face and brush her teeth, swish some mouthwash into her mouth to make sure she didn't have morning breath, make sure her hair scarf was on straight, and then put on her robe and go downstairs to start breakfast.

But before she even moved to get out of bed, she heard Bobby's voice from his position below her on his trundle bed.

"You don't have to get up so early."

"You're awake?"

"I'm always awake before you," he said in amusement. "You snore."

"No..." she said while sitting up quickly.

"It's not loud and I'm used to it now. I probably wouldn't be able to sleep without it."

"Oh my God..."

Bobby chuckled. "Today is your day off. The cameras won't come on at all in the house so if you want to sleep in, you can. But I have to go in. I still have lots to do, so if you want a ride back to the lot, I can drive you. Or the bus will take you there. There's a buzzer you can hit and it will know to come. It goes all over Wingate. It's really one of my better ideas."

Bailey was surprised Robert Chesterfield didn't sound exactly like Bobby Banks. Of course, the voice was the same, but his manner was different. Out of character, Robert seemed more self-assured.

She decided it was hard to be completely at ease when acting opposite someone who you still hadn't learned. Right now, he was just her employer and not her role-play husband.

She reached over and turned on the light and Bobby—Robert—sat up. "I'll ride in with you," she said. "What time is the team meeting?"

"Eight. I try to schedule them as early as possible and get it over with." He stood and stretched, and then began making his bed. "They don't usually last more than an hour. I've been toying with the idea of Zoom meetings, but I wouldn't trust some with keeping an iPad out of sight."

"I'm going to the bathroom," she said while getting out of her bed. She bathed each night so she knew she could be ready to go pretty quickly. And then she'd make up her bed while he took his turn in the bathroom.

"I can make us breakfast," he called. She looked back at him, not expecting to ever hear those words from his mouth.

"Oh?"

199

"I can cook, you know. Bobby might not have ever cooked a day in his life, but I know my way around a stove."

She had been fantasizing about an Egg McMuffin and hash browns for days, but she was willing to make the sacrifice out of sheer curiosity.

"What are you going to cook?"

He paused while plumping his pillow. "That might be a challenge. The lady of the house hasn't filled the pantry yet. I'll surprise you."

"Okay," she said. While turning to the bathroom, her brow raised mischievously. "Maybe if the man of the house gives her more than twenty bucks for the budget, you might see some steaks in the freezer."

"Noted," he replied.

She suppressed her chuckles as she took care of her business. Robert Chesterfield Jr. was probably still a jerk—but maybe not as bad as she had thought.

Once she was finished, she didn't see Robert but heard him moving around in the kitchen. She pulled on the clothes she'd worn the day before and quickly combed her newly curled hair. She'd taken the time to pin them the way Juanita had shown her so they were neat and fresh.

She put on a little makeup, nearly reaching for the bright-red lipstick before remembering Bailey Banks had the day off.

She entered the kitchen and was met with the aroma of bacon. Her belly growled. She hadn't really had much to eat the day before. He was already dressed in slacks and a casual shirt that for once wasn't tucked neatly into his pants.

"Breakfast is almost ready," he said while placing a plate of toast on the table.

Two plates were already made up with two sunny-side up eggs and two bowls of grits.

"You made grits?" she asked in awe. It had taken her years to perfect grits.

"Yep." He moved to take a tray of perfectly prepared bacon from the oven.

Okay…he cooked the bacon in the oven so there was no greasy splattering all over the stove. Really good idea.

"Grab the orange juice from the fridge, please." She did, and he placed three slices of bacon directly onto their plates.

"Coffee?" he asked.

She made to get up. "Yeah. I'll get it."

"No. Sit," he said. "You do all the running around this kitchen every day. Go ahead and eat. I hope you like sunny-side up eggs. The eggs here in Wingate come fresh off a local farm and they are fantastic."

She settled down in pleasure that for once, she was being served. "I don't think I've ever had them quite like this." She admired the eggs. The golden-yellow yokes were still round and unbroken while the whites were perfectly formed with the slightest brown edge surrounding them. They were the prettiest eggs she'd ever seen.

He poured her coffee and then filled his cup before sitting down to eat. She had always been slightly repulsed by raw egg yolk, but when she sliced into the yolk, it stayed mostly in place without running all over her plate. She saw him dunk his bacon into his yolk like it was a spoon and then plop half of it into his mouth. She mimicked him and found she didn't hate it.

"Uh, so how are you finding the job so far?" He gave her a look that wasn't as confident as he'd previously been.

She supposed it was a good question, when one of your actresses broke down in hysterical tears. But she didn't want to talk about yesterday with him.

"It's good," she said simply.

"What?" he asked while holding half a slice of bacon in one hand and his fork in the other. "The food or the job?"

Bailey chuckled. "Both."

He seemed relieved, and grabbed the sugar and sprinkled some onto his grits. Bailey eyed him suspiciously. "Was that really your first time eating grits?"

"No." His brow quirked up. "I was born in Texas, raised in Georgia, so I grew up eating grits."

She was beginning to feel confused at what she knew about the real Bobby and what she was learning about the man playing his character. "If you know about grits, why didn't you put sugar on them when I made them for you?"

"Because Bobby wouldn't know anything about putting sugar on his grits unless you tell him. I like them both ways, so it doesn't matter to me."

"Okay, let's just settle something. Can you please help me figure out what to feed you?"

He covered his mouth and laughed. "No!" he replied adamantly. "That's the fun part!"

"But you don't think I should know? Your mom evidently cooked for you while we lived with her after we got married. I would have seen. It's not cheating."

He settled down but still smiled. "Fine. I'll give you a few of my likes. I like chili, bean soup, sunny-side up eggs, oatmeal, chicken of all kinds, medium to medium rare beef, noodles. Uh…" he thought. "Ham, pork chops, tuna casserole…"

"That's a lot," she sighed when he paused to think.

"Yeah," he agreed.

"How about what you don't like?"

He grimaced. "That wouldn't be so good for the show. Let's say you made my most hated dish. I'd still choke it down without even telling you I hated it. It's just something Bobby would do."

"Okay," she conceded. "Give me something you definitely don't want to see on the menu."

He sighed. "I definitely don't want to see chipped beef or creamed vegetables, like cream of spinach." He shuddered while his lip curled in distaste. "And unless they're minced pretty well, I can live without mushrooms. I can pretty much tolerate anything else. Does that help?"

"Yes. You don't know how much."

Once breakfast was over, Bobby did the dishes while she went upstairs to make the bed. They were done in a flash, and on their way to the lot just as the sun came up.

"There are no cameras in the car?" she asked while watching him closely.

"Nope," he replied while pulling out of the driveway. "There are none in any of the bathrooms, and the ones in the bedroom turn off at lights-out or nine p.m.—whichever comes first." He glanced at her. "Bailey," he said abruptly. "I just wanted to tell you that you are doing an amazing job. You've far exceeded any of our expectations—all of you actors have! But...especially you. I was actually inspired to add new actors to help support the story line."

"Thank you," she smiled.

"This first week of the show was rated higher than any week we ever had for 1953."

Bailey didn't mention she'd already been tipped off as to how popular her role had become. She didn't trust his reaction to knowing she'd gone out of character at some point before the weekend.

"I know...there have been some challenges..." He was suddenly hesitant. When she looked at him, she saw his cheeks were growing red. He met her eyes. "As the guy playing Bobby Banks, I don't always know the appropriate way to handle things. I'm not the actor. You are. So...while I know what Bobby would do, I'm not always sure what *I* should do."

Bailey wasn't sure how to respond because she wasn't sure exactly what he was talking about. Possibly noting the confusion on her face, he rushed on, the words tumbling from his mouth.

"What I'm saying is, I'm happy you took the initiative to kiss me—uh, Bobby."

Her expression cleared and she looked forward out the window in embarrassment.

"Oh, well...it seemed right at the time. But I'm happy you didn't mind me doing."

"I didn't!" he said quickly. "I didn't," he said slower.

"Well...if Bobby feels like it's right...then it's okay for you to kiss me."

He nodded, and then focused on the road.

They arrived at the lot nearly an hour early for the team meeting, so Bobby offered to show her where the meeting would take place.

"So, I'm able to watch the show?"

"Yes. You just log in and you can watch what we're currently live filming—or you can switch to other channels to follow one of the popular characters. You can even go back and view prior episodes."

"Wow, that's amazing."

"Gamers have been doing it for years. We just took what's already out there and piecemealed it for our own purposes. You also get access for your immediate family or...spouse."

"Yeah, but I'm not married."

"A boyfriend, then." He glanced at the floor before meeting her eyes again.

"I don't have one of those either. But I do have an aunt and uncle I'd love to share it with. They don't really understand what this is all about."

"Oh, definitely!" he said happily. "We'll get them their own access code."

"Okay."

"I'm sure they'll be impressed when they see how well you're doing. I'll get it all set up for you and show you how it works."

There were others busily milling around. They greeted Bobby and surprised her when they all greeted her by name—people she knew she'd never been introduced to.

"They all watch you on the show, Bailey," he said, noting her confusion.

"Everyone here watches the show?"

"Everyone here watches *you*, on the show."

She gave him a surprised look. She thought of the conversation she'd had with the ladies at the beauty salon. They talked about her character as if she was in a soap opera—which in a sense, she was.

"They watch us," she said.

He smiled in embarrassment. "Yes, you are right. But they're only watching me because of you." He looked suddenly sheepish as he continued to lead her through the lot.

She was very intrigued at how she looked from behind the camera.

Chapter Twenty-Three

Robert could have had anyone get her account set up, but he handled it himself. When it was completed, he looked at the clock hung on the wall.

"You're all set. We'd better get to the meeting. We're already late."

She was anxious to check out the show but he was right, the meeting should have started five minutes ago. They hurried to the room and when they opened the door, she saw there was a heated discussion going on.

Everyone quieted as soon as the door opened. Bailey recognized almost everyone present. There were the ladies from the hair salon, as well as her neighbors that had been at the party.

"What's going on?" Robert asked as he slowly entered the room.

"What's going on?" the guy that played her next-door neighbor that was married to Geneva said in excitement. "You should know, Robert! You saw the way Bailey cried last night." He suddenly turned to her, his palms up. "Bailey, I'm so sorry! Please understand it...it was just acting."

Bailey's mouth parted in surprise.

"I don't want to be in front of the camera," someone else said. She turned her attention to Carl. He had played the role of the silent, friendly man that paid more attention to the food than to anything else. "I didn't sign up for this—"

Robert ran his hands through his hair. "Carl, you can't seriously want to leave the show."

"Not the show, just being in front of the camera. I'm no fucking actor, Rob!"

"You didn't do any of your lines in the first place," Marina, the Italian lady, commented with an eye roll. "You were supposed to help cause an inciting incident, but all you did was eat."

Carl flashed her an angry look. "Because I'm not going to racially harass someone! I'm a fucking cameraman—not a...racist asshole!" He looked away. "I'm sorry for my language. But I'm done with acting!"

Marina threw her hands up in exasperation. "I'm not ashamed about yesterday! We're paid to be whatever the script tells us to be—including assholes. We're paid to convince our viewers we don't want our *lily-white* neighborhoods sullied by the Negroes!" Geneva gasped, and Marina swung around to look at her. "Oh, chill. I'm an actress. I was hired to play a role. And I'm also biracial. Yes, folks, I'm not Italian, I'm half Black!"

Geneva shook her head and came forward looking as if she was ready to cry. "Bailey, I just want you to know I'm sorry for everything I said yesterday. I'm not a real actress. I just wanted a chance to be on the show. I don't have a racist bone in my body!" She looked from Marina to Bailey as if trying to convince them. "I have Black grandkids!"

Bailey was nodding as nearly everyone rushed forward to apologize for what had happened the night before.

The ladies from the beauty shop just looked angry, complaining in low voices between themselves. Her new best friend, Pat, was the only one loudly voicing her displeasure as she exclaimed this was all bullshit and unnecessary cruelty.

Robert stood there completely quiet, his face pale. He wouldn't meet Bailey's eyes. He wouldn't look at anyone.

Shirley rubbed Bailey's arm, looking totally different without the overdone makeup and inappropriate clothes of a wannabe Marilyn Monroe. This morning she wore short-cropped pants and a plain shirt. Her platinum hair was pulled back into a ponytail. In this moment, Bailey thought with a fresh face clean of makeup, Shirley looked like any housewife she might pass at the grocery store.

And poor Al, Marina's husband who had done all the lascivious flirting, seemed so ashamed he wouldn't even look in her direction.

Helen wrung her hands. "Bailey, I wanted to tell you what was going to happen. I tried to get you to go for a drive so I could warn you. I'm so sorry. I've been so sick about this all week long."

"Guys," Bailey said, still shocked. "Listen to me. You don't need to apologize. In truth, what we all need to do is up our game."

Everyone's attention was now completely on her.

"Yesterday was a good start," she continued. "But it is nothing like what Blacks had to face in the real 1954. It's leading up to the Civil Rights movement for a reason."

Robert turned to look at her, his brow gathered in dawning understanding.

She sighed. "You didn't make me cry. I was just acting."

It was so quiet she could actually hear people breathing.

"Everybody hates us..." Haley finally said while giving her an incredulous look. "You should see the emails and comments..."

Pat just started laughing. "That's a good thing! It means people get it!"

Carl rubbed both hands through his hair in relief. "Are you kidding me?" He whooped loudly, sending a titter of relieved laughter throughout the room. "My mom called me early this morning chewing my ass for not standing up for you! Oh my God, I'm so happy!"

"You're one hell of an actress is all I can say," Al grinned, sounding suddenly at ease. They were actually good actors because right now, Al looked as far from an old pervert as one could get.

This time, the ladies from the beauty shop crowded around her too, congratulating her on a job well done and exclaiming how good her acting was.

"Okay!" Robert yelled. "If we have all of that settled, is it okay if we get back to work?"

The relieved laughter slowed as everyone took their seats around a large conference table. Bailey found a seat and gave her attention to the boss, who suddenly sounded more impatient than she'd ever heard him.

He waited for everyone to come to complete silence before he began.

"For all of the newly hired, welcome to the show. After the meeting, I'll print out your weekly itinerary with all the changes we'll discuss today. Just remember it's just a guide, so own your role. You make your character, not me or the other writers."

He frowned as he scanned his notes. "Even though we want you to feel free to improvise, please don't change your bios. So far, only one person has done that." Robert walked over to Bailey's chair.

"You're supposed to be raised by your mother and father but you changed that by stating you were raised by your aunt and uncle. You mentioned Aunt Mae several times, so we've had to update your biography."

"Oh. I'm sorry about that," she said.

"It didn't cause any conflicts. But you have to be more careful, Bailey."

She gave him a surprised look. "Okay." What the hell? He'd been singing her praises a short time ago and had never mentioned any issues — which he could have done within all the time they were alone with each other. Was he pissed she hadn't actually been distraught over what had happened the night before?

He turned and addressed the others. "The feedback from yesterday's show was phenomenal. You should all be proud of yourselves. You pulled off something that was clearly difficult.

"This story arc is new, but it's important. I think by discussing the racial issues of the '50s, we're placing a mirror to today's issues."

Everyone nodded in agreement at that statement.

"But can you tell the story fully?" Pat asked.

"What do you mean?" Robert asked.

"Can a white man tell the story of the Black struggle?"

"Right," Miss Betty said. "You know the stories. You can feel the emotion and outrage. But until Bailey showed you, did you ever truly feel her frustrated tears, her fear, and her complete demoralization?"

Robert considered her words. "Look, I'm never going to understand what it means to be Black in a society where people still have to be reminded that Black lives matter. But it's not impossible for me to empathize. You saw how the others felt about last night." He gestured to those were at the barbecue.

"We just want to be included in the dialogue and not just the after-affect," Tracy stated. "Don't just show us being mistreated. Show us dealing with it. Show us not dealing with it—"

"Show Curtis when he goes home after being objectified all day by the white women in Wingate," Pat said with an eye roll.

Haley opened and then snapped her mouth closed.

"Everyone is fighting for a place in front of the cameras," Helen said. "Black and white."

"But some of us are fighting more than others," Pat snapped.

"Okay. Okay." Robert raised his hands to quiet the room. "How about you bring me your story lines and I'll take a look at your ideas. If I like them, I'll incorporate them into the story."

Pat exchanged looks with Bailey, who smiled at her in encouragement. Pat came to her feet and sauntered to Robert holding a sheet of paper. She handed it to him and he accepted it in confusion.

"What is this?"

"My story line. I want to be included in the telling of *our* story." And that's when all of the other Black women came to their feet and marched to Robert holding their own sheets of paper.

Bailey suppressed a smile.

Chapter Twenty-Four

Robert placed every biography into a folder without comment and then sat behind his computer.

"Last night's episode was *amazing*." Pat spoke to Bailey in a low voice. "I changed my bio because of it. I feel like if *they* have the right to be passive-aggressive, then there should also be passive-aggressive Blacks."

Bailey raised an interested brow but she had a strong feeling Pat wouldn't have to reach far for aggression.

"I doubt if they'll let *you* play the militant Black, but that's who *I* want to be," she continued.

"I like idea," Bailey said honestly. Someone would have to be fed up enough to be part of the sit-ins and boycotts that would sweep the South.

"Everyone did an amazing job," Robert was saying. He hit a remote control and a projector screen rolled down behind him.

Bailey saw the home screen for 1954, which she'd seen earlier when Robert had showed her how to use the program. It didn't look much different than pulling up a streaming video service on her laptop— only her face appeared in some of the stills on the introductory screen.

Bailey couldn't stop the grin of pride spread across her face. Everything about today was so surreal.

"There were several outstanding scenes that received some of the top reviews of the week." Robert moved to a clip of Bailey making chicken and dumplings. She leaned forward, seeing herself for the first time in action.

The cinematography completely blew her mind. She thought it would look like the show *Big Brother* where certain scenes looked as if they were being filmed from a bubble, plus it was always blurred. But 1954 was nothing like that. It was like watching a movie. They even managed to zoom in for close-ups without a cameraman present.

The only thing that could use improvement was the sound quality. She talked to herself a lot, and it wasn't always easy to hear. But beyond that, she looked authentically distressed at the way her meal was turning out.

While Bailey critiqued herself, she noted everyone in the room chuckled and applauded at the activity onscreen.

"Great job, Bailey," Robert said. "Team Bailey has the top positive comments of all teams. Keep in mind, team; you keep Bailey looking good, and vice versa. Here is the most popular clip of the week for 1954."

Everyone was in good cheer at the news and waited attentively for the next clip. It surprised Bailey, who had expected the squirrel in the vent scene—her personal favorite.

What she saw was the accidental kiss on the lips; their first kiss.

Everyone in the room began to ooh and ahh, and Bailey's eyes flitted to Robert. He had turned red, despite still wearing a smile.

"Okay..." He seemed embarrassed. "That was the most popular clip of the week—followed by the second kiss—no, no. I'm not going to play it." He turned even more red when everyone hazed him about it. People were also clapping her back like children in gym class, and she wondered if someone would start singing Bailey and Bobby sitting in a tree, k-i-s-s-i-n-g. She only hoped she wasn't blushing as hard as he was.

"The third most popular clip is from Nadine confronting Mayor George and finally revealing her mysterious reason for coming back to town." He played the clip, and Bailey could feel the buildup of anticipation in herself even though he'd only played three minutes. It was really good.

The fifth and final clip was of Drew having a PTSD episode in the middle of downtown Wingate.

She was incredibly impressed with both stars.

"How is Quinton doing?" she asked.

"Quinton is doing very well and has a solid following. His comedic timing is spot-on. In fact" — Robert began to rifle through his notes — "You can expect to meet him when his route sends him to your — our — neighborhood in a few weeks."

"Great," Helen said. "I like Quinton's scenes."

"Hoping to add some side-loving?" Hank asked good-naturedly.

Helen swatted his hand. "Maybe — unless you get a truck route closer to home."

Hank chuckled. "That's not likely. I have too much to do with post-production."

"That reminds me," Robert said. "I hope we don't need a course on how to respond to personal comments. You know while tracking, them we've gotten feedback on inappropriate responses..."

Several people looked down — including Helen.

"I won't go into detail, but remember that your comments do reflect on 1954 and everyone who is working hard to make this show realistic. If you get negative feedback, ignore it. We're also in the process of preparing scripts everyone can use for this purpose."

"Trolls don't tend to troll unless they know they're irritating you," Carl added.

"Right. So, our scripts will say something like, 'Thank you for your comments and I will take your ideas into consideration...'"

"Yeah," Al laughed. "Well how good is that going to work when they call you a sex offender that needs to be put in jail?"

Carl clapped his shoulder, and Bailey even looked at him in sympathy. One day she was repulsed by him and the next, she wanted to hug him.

Robert nodded. "Look, guys, we're already getting comments condemning the neighbors for how they treated Bailey, but also...we've gotten the other type." Robert glanced at Bailey, clearly uncomfortable. "The type that praise the neighbors for their treatment of Bailey and supporting that type of behavior."

The sounds of disgust were quick, but Robert raised a hand. "It hasn't been many. And no one can make anonymous comments because we have information on each subscriber. But," he sighed. "I agree, it's distressing. Just be forewarned, and don't engage people in political talks."

"That's easy for you to say," Jeff scowled. "You're playing the role of the good guy."

Robert paused a moment before responding. "I've gotten comments every single day about...personal matters. For many people, specifically those in the United States, I'm far from a good guy. Anyway. I'm printing your weekly schedules and we'll send out revisions as necessary." He turned to the women from the beauty salon who were all sitting together.

"And for anyone who has given me a bio, I will go over them today and get back with you tomorrow. If approved, you'll get a script this week and will be visited by Bruce Adams, who will go over your contract. If your bio is not approved...then we will tell you truthfully if it's your bio or your role-playing abilities.

"Not everyone is suited for role-play. People who think they are doing perfectly well see themselves from behind the camera and realize they're stiff and robotic, or they look into the camera or they're unable to create a sense of realism. So, no doesn't mean no forever. It means no for now." The ladies nodded in agreement, but Bailey had seen each of them acting in the beauty salon and it was as if they hadn't been acting at all. She had a feeling everyone who was sitting in this room had already been approved by Robert Chesterfield Jr.

The meeting adjourned after slightly more than an hour. She left the conference room while reading her weekly script. She headed for the locker room where her modern-day possessions were being held. The others from her team told her goodbye and congratulated her, which made her feel great. Most of them were already on their cell phones as they hurried to the lounge to get caught up with friends.

She continued scanning her script. It was even more scaled back than last week's.

Monday: After Bailey completes her daily chores, she goes grocery shopping. Bailey and Helen will have a discussion about the neighbors. Bailey may not like what she hears but chooses not to rock the boat. Bailey's evening and nighttime routine.

Tuesday: Bailey's daily routine. Learns mother-in-law will come to dinner Saturday. Works on Saturday menu.

Wednesday: Bailey goes back to the grocery store for Saturday dinner menu...

Bailey sighed. Nope. This script was not cutting it. Robert had once said the script was just a suggestion, but these suggestions made her life seem so boring. Besides having her mother-in-law visit, nothing about the upcoming week excited her.

Did Quinton feel that way when he walked around selling encyclopedias? She truly hoped he added to his own story because they surely couldn't depend on the producers to do it.

Once in the lockers, the first thing she did was check her messages. Aunt Mae had called three times! She quickly sat on a bench and listened to the messages, her chest pounding a mile a minute. Didn't she give them Bruce's number to contact her if there was an emergency? She was sure she had.

The first message was just asking if she'd gotten moved in okay. Aunt Mae had ended with, "Call me when you can."

The second message was two days later. "You sure this is on the up-and-up? You ain't been trafficked, have you? Okay, call me when you can."

And then finally the third message was left yesterday. "Well, you said you'd call me Sunday, on your day off, so if I don't hear from you, I'm calling the police! Love you. Call me."

Bailey shook her head in relief now that her heart wasn't in her throat. She called her aunt, who picked up the phone on the first ring.

"Bailey? You all right?"

"Yes, Aunt Mae. I'm fine. How are you?"

Her aunt blew out a long, relieved breath. "Chile, we've been worried sick!" Bailey could hear her uncle Dewbug yelling from the background he wasn't worried and to leave girl alone!

Bailey suppressed a chuckle. "Aunt Mae, I'm about to get changed and then I'm heading out to the house. I'll be there in less than two hours, okay?"

"Okay…well, I guess I'll find out how it went when you get here."

"Yes, ma'am. See you soon."

"Bye, baby."

When they hung up, Bailey sat on the bench for a while just smiling.

When she got to her aunt and uncle's small brick house, it felt like coming home after a long battle — and they greeted her exactly in that way, despite not living with them since being a teen.

But in truth, her apartment never felt as much like home as this house had and because she had given up the apartment, this would be home for one day each week for the next year.

"Ooo!" Aunt Mae said after hugging Bailey. "Did you lose some weight?"

Bailey's brow shot up. "I wouldn't be surprised. The 1950s cleaning routine is definitely no joke."

"Well, I'm about to fatten you up. Come on inside. I made a ham and some green beans and potato salad. I even got that sweet cornbread you like."

Bailey's stomach instantly began to growl. In her opinion, there was no better food than home cooking. "I definitely built up an appetite! And after lunch, I'm going to show you how to watch the show."

"Let's eat fast," Uncle Dewbug said after he'd given her a long hug. Bailey didn't think her uncle was half as interested in the show as he was in getting to the food.

Aunt Mae tugged at one of her curls. "I do like your hair like that."

Bailey patted her curls. "I'll be going to a hair salon once a week to keep it up."

"Then you're one of them rich 1950s housewives. I remember trying to come up with a dollar to get my hair done was hard, if not impossible. And you best not even go if you didn't have no tip money. The next time you showed up, you might get your ear burned with the hot comb!" Aunt Mae chuckled. Bailey stored that information away.

At lunch, she tried to explain the mechanics of how the show worked but they just listened with glazed eyes and she knew they weren't exactly understanding, so she just got caught up with the gossip and other current events.

It was two hours after she arrived that she finally got the show loaded onto their smart television. Her aunt and uncle might be old-fashioned, but they liked their Netflix.

"I'm not going to remember all this," Aunt Mae said with a scowl

"It's easy. It's just like Netflix. Once you sign in, it stays open. And then you skip to who you want to watch."

"Well, that part will be easy," Uncle Dewbug said from where he sat in his recliner. "We only want to watch you!"

"Okay, so this is my channel."

"That's you! That's our Bailey!" Aunt Mae exclaimed as if she just now realized what Bailey had been doing for the last week.

"Yep," Bailey replied proudly. "I'll take you to the beginning, but you can skip around or you can go to the channels for the other main characters. You can watch clips or the entire day of filming. And if you want, you can even write me a review."

"Well play something!" Aunt Mae shooed at her impatiently.

Bailey moved to her first shot where she and Bobby were in the kitchen having breakfast.

"Did you cook food?" Aunt Mae was frowning at the screen.

"Yes, ma'am."

"That's all you cooked that man? Where's the grits or potatoes?"

"We didn't have any. We're playing newlyweds, and we just moved in the day before. But we did get grits later."

Her aunt nodded in approval.

The three of them watched with eyes glued to the screen, although Bailey found herself cringing at every misstep she made. Uncle Dewbug kept asking how much everything cost, and Aunt Mae made several suggestions on how to position the furniture—but thankfully, no one but her thought she seemed stiff or uncomfortable.

Because they were watching her channel, the scene frequently cut until she suggested they watch the edited version, which showed all the main players.

Aunt Mae initially said she didn't care about "them other folks," but quickly got into Nadine's story line.

They watched the show for hours, her aunt and uncle cheering whenever the shot cut back to her.

Right before eight, she told them it was time for her to leave.

"What?" Uncle Dewbug frowned. "I thought you were staying here for the night?"

"I was planning to, but I only get twenty-four hours leave, and since I scheduled my day off on Sundays, part of that time is taken up with our team meeting. I may change my day, but I'll let you know." Bailey had already changed into comfortable jeans and a sweater, more casual than the clothing she had worn on her first day at work.

"Now if you need to contact me, just call Bruce Adams," she reminded. "I left his phone number on the counter. And remember, I won't have access to my phone until Sunday, so don't call my cell phone. And only call Bruce if there's an emergency."

"Okay," Aunt Mae said. "You did good on that show."

Bailey paused. "Really? You liked it?"

"I did. It's like when I used to watch my stories."

Bailey remembered her aunt trying to keep up with various soap operas. It made her feel good she'd compare the two.

"Did you like it, Uncle Dewbug?"

He pinched her cheek. "I loved it, little girl. You are a fine actress."

That made all the sore muscles, confusion, and embarrassment worthwhile.

Bailey got back to the production lot at 10:00 p.m. and decided to relax in the lounge where she could continue watching the show.

The lounge was nice, and there was no one around but her. They had various docking stations, and she selected one that had a lounge chair and laptop.

After getting comfortable, Bailey logged into her account. She'd spent hours watching the show, but her aunt and uncle had gone in order, and she wanted to jump around and look at some things in private, including her personal comments. She was anxious to see what others thought who weren't directly invested in the show, or in her.

First things first, she wanted to see a clip of her kissing Bobby. It wasn't that she had forgotten even the smallest bit of that moment—she just wanted to see if she looked totally stupid doing it.

After locating the correct clip, Bailey looked around to make sure no one was watching before she pressed play.

She felt a surprising zap of electrical current course through her body that quickened her heartbeat when she saw herself kissing Bobby. It wasn't stupid at all. Bobby looked at her as if there was nothing else in the world to look at. The camera had zoomed in enough to see his eyes locked onto her. But the camera had also caught her breathless stare.

In that moment, neither appeared to be acting.

She replayed it once again and then forced herself to stop. Bailey had to admit there was undeniable chemistry between them. She'd seen it early on in watching the playbacks and so had Aunt Mae, who had commented they looked at each other like real newlyweds.

But in all honesty, she'd felt the chemistry long before they'd ever kissed.

She blew out a stressed breath wondering what Bobby—Robert—thought. He had to have seen it, since he put together the scenes.

She navigated to her comments, but soon kissing Bobby was the last thing on her mind.

"What the—??" She had over twelve hundred comments!

She quickly began reading them, but even as she read, more were popping up. Most of the comments had to do with her treatment at the hands of her bigoted neighbors.

"Bailey, my heart goes out to you. Those people are nothing but Godless animals..."

"You are by far the best person on the show. You make me laugh, but yesterday I cried right along with you..."

"I had no idea people could be so cruel..."

"...I hope those people get what's coming to them..."

On and on the comments went. She really needed to respond and let them know they were just acting.

She rubbed her tired eyes. Maybe Robert could help with this. He was probably getting the same messages. She signed off the laptop and headed for the dressing room to change into Bailey Banks's clothes. She was tired, and tomorrow was Monday; the beginning of a new week.

Chapter Twenty-Five

Bailey changed into her 1954 attire and then instead of riding the bus home, she was driven back to her house in an old-timey Ford station wagon. Her driver was a fan, and talked to her nonstop about the show. She was exhausted, but if not for his interest in her part in the show, she would have probably fallen asleep.

"Bye, ma'am," he said after dropping her off in her driveway. "Can't wait to see what you have in store for us next week."

Me either. She waved goodbye and hurried to the house, praying the door would be unlocked. It was.

She slipped out of her shoes and hung up her sweater, being extra quiet so as not to wake up Bobby. She huffed in amusement. He was Bobby when they were on set, and Robert at the production lot. She had to stop thinking in those terms or things would get out of hand pretty quick.

Robert Chesterfield was just one person, a man playing a role, and it didn't matter if she called him Robert or Bobby. They were just actors and she had better remember that.

Besides, the last thing a guy like Robert Chesterfield Jr. would ever be interested in was a no-name actress from Cincinnati, Ohio. And the last thing she should be interested in was a rich politician's son who had never had to struggle for money or equality.

She went into the kitchen for water but ended up drinking a frothy glass of ice-cold milk instead. Then she grabbed her shoes and tiptoed to her bedroom so she didn't wake Bobby.

But she was the one surprised when she saw him in his office, busily scribbling on a pad of paper. He wore earbuds connected to a cell phone, and she eyed them suspiciously.

"So, the rule for no technology on set doesn't apply to the boss?" she asked.

Bobby yelled, jumped half out of his seat and looked ready to throw something at her.

"Oh my God! You scared me!"

Bailey covered her mouth, trying to stop from laughing "I'm sorry! I didn't mean to scare you. I thought you were sleeping."

He took out his earbuds and turned off whatever had been playing through them.

"I didn't expect you back until the morning."

"I didn't want to risk getting caught in traffic or something," she said.

"I was going over some of the bios I got from today's team meeting. They are fantastic! I'm getting so many ideas," he said in excitement.

"Oh? So, are you going to accept them all?"

"Of course—with a few minor adjustments. Pat's ideas are especially intriguing." His expression grew thoughtful. "We might even need to hire more people..."

"What about giving Curtis a speaking role?"

He met her eyes. "We did, a year ago. Curtis said he doesn't want an acting role."

"Really?" she asked slowly.

"Not everyone has the acting bug. He's definitely photogenic, but..." Bobby shrugged.

She thought back to Pat's innuendo that he had ignored people like Curtis. She wondered why Bobby hadn't corrected her assumption.

"I'll let you get back to work. I'm going to turn in."

"Did you get a chance to watch any of the show?" he asked quickly while watching her closely.

"I did. It was strange seeing myself on television. I thought it might be a few years before I saw that," she smiled.

"You're good."

"You are too! You really seem at ease as Bobby."

He smiled and shrugged. "I guess because it doesn't feel like acting. I don't have to read a script or follow some director. I just fall into the role."

"Since you saw all of your shots, in hindsight, is there anything you'd change?" she asked.

"Nothing. Everything enhances the story," he replied, still watching her closely. "What about you? Is there anything you'd change?"

Bailey shrugged. "Nothing. Everything turned out good." There were times in the beginning when she hadn't felt completely confident, but once she forgot the cameras, she easily slipped into her role.

Actually, there was something, and she felt she needed to mention it or it would eat at her.

"There is one thing…"

He cocked his head. "What?"

"You said you don't like to give too much guidance. You don't like the story too scripted. You don't want to reveal too much because you want authenticity."

He nodded.

"But I believe I missed an opportunity to develop my role because you didn't tell me you intended to have me confront racist neighbors."

Bobby nodded and then looked down at his desk with chagrin before meeting her eyes again.

"Yes...that. I'm sorry about that. And of course, you're absolutely right. I should not have sprung that on you for shock value. It didn't give you credit as an actress. But your reaction was completely real; the shock, the hurt, the speechlessness. There were times when I was editing that I didn't know if you'd jump to your feet and curse them all out! I was looking for that type of spontaneity you can't get from sitting in a boardroom and dissecting a script."

She shook her head in disappointment. "But I'd already figured out something like that would happen at the barbecue."

Bobby's brow drew together. "You did?"

"I did. Because that's how I would have written it. I would have even suggested it. That's how I knew I would take all of that abuse, swallow it back, and then go home and break down. I made a plan." Bobby continued to stare at her. "You hired me to act," she tried again. "But then you hindered that."

Bobby inhaled deeply. "I'm sorry, Bailey. You're right. I didn't look at it from that perspective. I think I sometimes forget I'm not the only one that's invested in the show. I'm not saying others don't want it to be successful. But I've had friends convinced that this should be turned into a movie. They totally miss that this isn't meant to be a movie where you sit for ninety minutes and then afterwards talk about how mysterious, adventurous, or romantic it was. It's intended to be a voyeuristic view into the life of the people of Wingate. A flashback to a time that can never return.

"I know I get too close to it. Some might even describe me as a dictator. But this show is my baby. I've dreamed about this for most of my life. When I was a kid...well, let's just say when I got old enough, all I wanted was to bring Wingate to life."

"Did you...create a world you could live in?" she asked softly.

"No. Actually, I didn't even want to be in the story. But I saw a need and I filled it—always on a small scale. Most didn't even realize I was in the show—I kept it low-key.

"No. Wingate is not my playland, but I do find it difficult to look at Bobby as a role because I just do...what feels natural. I don't even like reading my personal comments because it takes me out of the role.

"Anyway. I guess what I'm saying is I like to be deeply immersed in my role, but that doesn't mean it's the only way. I suppose that's what I need to realize."

Bailey stood there for a few moments. That had been a lot. Did it mean he wouldn't hide things from her again?

"It's close to midnight, so I'd better get some sleep or I'll end up taking a nap during my prime time."

He nodded. "Good night, Bailey."

"Good night."

She mulled over their conversation as she sat at her vanity and pinned her hair.

Was it weird that she felt a connection to Bobby but...there was nothing towards Robert?

She slathered Ponds on her face. There was a reason so many actresses fell in love with their leading men.

Oh my God! Did she say fall in love??

Bailey shook her head and used tissues to wipe off her makeup.

"No. Absolutely not," she said aloud.

"What?" Bobby asked from the doorway.

He jump-scared her because she literally had not seen him there. He chuckled and sat in the chair to take off his shoes.

"Gotcha. Turnabout's fair play."

"I got you first," she reminded him.

His brow quirked upward. "Yes. Yes, you did," he muttered.

She gave him a quick look. What did he mean by that?

"I'm going to take a bath," she said while heading for the bathroom. "Can we invest in a shower?"

"Don't you enjoy taking a bath more?"

"I haven't had time to enjoy it. I'm always too tired."

"Well, when you go to the grocery store, be sure to pick up bath beads."

"I'll put that on the list. Anything else?" she asked playfully.

"Can you add that steak you mentioned earlier?"

"Can you give me more budget money?"

"No. We're struggling." He leaned back in his chair.

She crossed her arms. "You need to pack a lunch instead of eating out every day."

She had no idea why she said that. She had no idea what he ate when he wasn't in the house, and it wasn't any of her business.

"I can come home for lunch."

"Do you want to do that?"

"Not all the time...but I could pack a lunch; sandwiches, leftovers, things like that."

"That seems realistic."

"Okay. It's done," he said.

"It's done."

The lights were out when she returned to the bedroom, dressed in one of her new gowns.

Bobby had pulled out his trundle bed and was already under his covers.

Yawning, she climbed into her bed, relishing the cool, clean sheets and plump pillows. She loved this bed, and especially loved that she kept it made up.

"Are you asleep yet?" Robert asked.

"I just got into bed," she replied. "But I will be in a second." She yawned, too tired to even cover her mouth. "What's up?"

"I'm really sorry I didn't tell you about the plan with the neighbors. I truly wasn't trying to make you feel bad. I just didn't think things through. But I promise it won't happen again."

"Thank you. I just don't want to worry about something sneaking up on me when I least expect it." She yawned again.

"Cross my heart."

"Okay," she muttered, half asleep.

"Night, Bae."

Night, Bobby. She wasn't sure if she said the last because she was soon asleep.

Chapter Twenty-Six

The alarm went off all too soon. Bailey rubbed her eyes with a yawn. She was excited to start her week despite being tired. This wasn't just about how well she could cook and clean. She needed to embody the dream because for Bailey Banks, she had attained something many couldn't, regardless of race.

She had married a man that was willing and able to allow her to stay home while he went out to support them both. And in exchange, she had agreed to create a home they both could be proud of.

It was just that simple.

This will be easier. I know what to do and what to expect.

Bailey climbed out of bed determined that she would not allow her list of chores to beat her. She paused, remembering something. Bailey turned in the dark and looked over at where Bobby was lying on his trundle bed.

"Good morning."

"'Morning," he replied.

She smirked and headed for the bathroom. *Snore...I don't think so. The alarm woke you up.*

"Script changes coming later!" he called out to her.

She stopped, surprised he had actually gone out of character all on his own. "Oh?"

"About what we talked about yesterday." She heard him turn in bed and yawn.

She went into the bathroom when he didn't add anything more and got herself ready for the cameras. They had talked about a lot yesterday. But she appreciated him moving out of his comfort zone to even speak out of character. She would just have to keep her eye on her script.

She hurried to the kitchen and put on several eggs to boil and then got the coffee started. By the time Bobby came into the room straightening his tie and looking every bit as if he too was ready to conquer the week, there was cereal and milk on the table along with toast and coffee waiting for him.

"Good morning, honey." She paused where she was spreading egg salad onto bread. "Sorry for the quick breakfast, but I thought we'd save a bit of money if I make your lunch."

He came over to where she was standing and spun her around by the waist. She gave him a surprised look before he lifted her chin and placed his lips on hers.

The electrical current that swooped through Bailey was instantaneous.

"Good morning," he said a moment later once their lips had parted. It had only been a split-second peck, but it had nearly turned her knees into Jell-O.

That's because I wasn't expecting it...

He looked over at the sandwiches. "Egg salad. That sounds good."

Bailey had to force herself to smile. This isn't our third kiss. We've kissed a thousand times. We're married. Kissing Bobby is normal...

But then, she stopped. No. It wasn't normal because Bobby was probably Bailey's first love. He *is* her first love. Kissing him would still be magical. Kissing him would send butterflies through her body—maybe it will still be like that when they are old and sitting in rockers together.

Bailey Banks wouldn't go through any of this, take a chance on marrying him, risk the law and the disapproval of society, along with all the other shit she would have to face unless kissing Bobby would send shock waves through her body.

Bailey touched her chest because her heart was racing.

"Are you all right?" he asked.

"Yep. Eat while I pack your lunch."

"Okay. Okay," he chuckled, and took his seat at the table.

"I'm going grocery shopping today, so I'm sorry you only have carrot sticks with your sandwiches."

"I don't mind carrot sticks, especially if we have some ranch dressing to go along with it."

"We do." She went to the refrigerator for the dressing while he poured milk onto his cereal. "Do you want me to pick up anything while I'm there?"

"Maybe some more fruit," he replied while munching on his Wheaties. "And lunch meat, if you're going to be packing my lunch. I think it's a good idea, by the way. The food truck gets a little pricey."

"Food truck? That food can't be nearly as good as home cooking." She wrapped his sandwiches in wax paper. "At least meals from home will be healthier."

Bobby paused. "Yeah..."

She looked over her shoulder at him. "I'll have you know, Bobby Banks, that while I may not know how to cook yet, I do have cookbooks at my disposal, and if I need to, I can call my aunt for help with recipes."

He plastered on a quick smile. "I have no complaints, Bae. Do you want to keep the car?"

"Well...I was thinking about calling Helen." She sat at the table with a cup of coffee, adding her cream and sugar to it. Bobby stopped eating to look at her. "I didn't like the way we left things after the barbecue," she continued.

"Hmmm. Do you trust her?"

"I think so. She's always been friendly to me. And I truly don't think she expected...what happened to happen."

He sighed and reached over to place a hand over hers. Bailey raised her fingers and their fingers intertwined.

"I love you." He raised her hand to his lips and kissed her fingers. "Very much."

"I love you too." She reached out and cupped his face. "We will be okay."

"It's going to take mighty steps to make a change, Bae. And I know it's hard. But we have to show those people by example. We're no different than them, and they'll see us and know it."

She gave him a grim smile. "I don't want to be like them. I want *them* to be like us. Maybe we don't like everything we see, or agree with every thought every person has. But the difference is, I won't hate someone because of it."

He smiled and kissed her hand again. "You're right. The truth is, having differences isn't the bad part. How we handle those differences is what sets us apart." He looked at his watch. "I've got to get going if I don't want to be late."

She jumped up and handed him his lunch bag. "I need to dig up your lunch box. I think it's in the garage or something…" Translation: we need to get you a retro lunch box.

"This is good for now." He gave her another peck on the lips, paused, and then kissed her again, this time allowing it to linger.

Bailey closed her eyes and returned the kiss.

This time she didn't stop the butterflies from carrying her away.

After Bobby left for the day, Bailey took out her cleaning schedule and spread it out on the kitchen table. She went straight to the living room and turned on the radio. She was going to need music to keep her blood thumping.

A rock and roll tune was playing and she stooped and turned the dial in search for a jazz or blues channel. She stopped at a bebop tune.

Satisfied, she went to the bedroom and changed into her makeshift workout clothing, shorts and a simple blouse, and then she pulled back the sheets to air them. Afterwards, she went around the house opening the curtains and windows, working to the backdrop of the pioneers of soul and R & B music.

She turned off the radio briefly in order to put on her workout record. After her ten-minute workout, Bailey returned to Ella and Miles and a host of others as she went back to the bedroom to get ready for the day.

Today's attire was a baby-blue swing-out skirt (no petticoats, thank you very much) and a flowered blouse. She took down her pin curls and combed them until she found a style she liked.

Next came the makeup. Knowing she'd be heading to the grocery store, Bailey paid particular attention to it, being sure not to go too dramatic on the eyeliner.

Finally, it was time for the lipstick. She applied it with pride, knowing it was the cake topper.

She got up and got her shoes. She'd embrace this role, but that didn't mean she had to embrace these heels.

After slipping them on, she checked herself in the full-length mirror, primped for a while, and then nodded in approval.

Okay. Time to tackle the chores. Let's see how many we can get done.

With each task completed, she mentally checked it from her list:

Wash the breakfast dishes. *Done.*

Mop the kitchen floor. *Done.*

Clean living room; including dusting and fluffing pillows. *Done.*

Vacuum. *Done.*

Make beds and tidy bedroom. *Done.*

Clean bathroom: Scrub chrome fixtures. Mop floor. Disinfect toilet. *Done.*

Review the dinner menu, prepare grocery list...

Bailey flopped down at the kitchen table and focused on what needed to go into her pantry. This should have gone at the top of the list. She was really too tired to even think straight, and nap time was not on the to-do list.

She checked the time. It was after ten. If she was going grocery shopping, she needed to take care of that now — which meant she needed to call Helen and deal with that fiasco.

She looked at the list of items that had been left undone.

Wipe down the refrigerator, inside and out. *Nope.*

Begin dinner prep if necessary. *Not sure what's for dinner yet.*

Dispose of garbage. *Nope, that's Bobby's job.*

Take care of errands, which might take you out of the house. *In the process.*

Have a quick lunch. *Are they serious?? Who has time to eat!*

Set the table for dinner. *Later.*

Prepare the living room for Mister's evening enjoyment. *Hell no.*

Prepare delicious dinner. *I will do my best...*

There was more, but she put the list away. It was depressing.

Bailey grabbed her sweater, hat, and pocketbook, and then headed out the door. Once outside, she noted that the flag was raised on the mailbox.

They had mail! Now that was exciting. She hurried to get whatever the mailman had left.

It was a letter addressed to her and it had Aunt Mae's name on it!

Her heart began to pound. Oh my God, did something happen to her aunt or uncle?

She tore open the letter and saw that it had REVISED SCRIPT written across the top.

Relief ran through her. She quickly folded the letter and stuffed it into her pocketbook. She'd read it while in Helen's car.

So that's how they got the revised scripts out to everyone in an age when there was no Internet.

Bailey hurried across the street, mentally preparing herself for whatever drama awaited.

She rang Helen's doorbell. When the door opened, she saw that her neighbor wore a surprised expression.

"Bailey…"

"Hi, Helen." Oh…maybe she wasn't welcome here anymore. Now that would be a huge script change.

"I was going to come by…Come in!" Helen opened the door and Bailey stepped inside. "Bailey, I'm so sorry about the barbecue. If I'd known—"

"Helen, I don't blame you for that."

"But I put together a welcome party for you and your husband and I made sure to only invite people who were…nice. And I never expected—I'm just so ashamed."

Bailey was relieved Helen wasn't trying to dump her. She rather liked her. But was that normal for this period of time? What should she even say? On one hand, modern-day Bailey wanted to tell her those idiots could go to hell for all she cared.

Wait. 1950s Bailey could say the same—maybe not in those words, but…

"Helen, I've run into people like that all my life, and I'm sure it won't end anytime soon." She reached out and touched Helen's hand.

Helen quickly covered it with her own. "I'm sorry this is the world we live in."

"Me too."

Helen's friendly smile suddenly returned. "So, would you like coffee? There's still plenty of dessert left over from the barbecue."

"I'm going to pass on the dessert. I came by to see if you might want to go to the grocery store. My pantry is almost completely empty."

"That's going to take you weeks to fill."

"I know. And about as much money as our house payment."

Helen laughed. "Let me get my sweater."

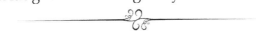

Once in the car, Helen blew out a long breath. "Did you read the script changes?"

Bailey dug into her pocketbook, nearly forgetting about the letter from Aunt Mae. "They scared me to death when I got the letter with my aunt's name on it. I thought something might have happened."

"Oh gosh no. They would call you for something like that. Just prepare yourself for what you're going to read in the new script and what you're going to see in town."

Bailey shot Helen a quick look and then quickly read the updates to her script.

Monday: After Bailey completes her daily chores, she goes grocery shopping with Helen. Bailey and Helen will have a discussion about the neighbors. ~~Bailey may not like what she hears but chooses not to rock the boat.~~

During the shopping, Bailey will be served after all the whites have been served. Bailey will have to step off the sidewalk if walking past a White person. Bailey will pass the COLORED ONLY water fountains without acknowledging them.

Once at home, Bailey will complete her evening routine.

Bailey looked at Helen with her mouth wide open. "Are you shitting me?"

"If what you read is Wingate is now segregated, then I shit you not."

Chapter Twenty-Seven

"I am just happy Robert didn't keep this from you. I was never onboard with that," Helen added.

"Well, I have a feeling if I hadn't chosen to have a conversation with a certain somebody about it, then I still might not be in the know."

"Hank said there's a casting call this week and we're getting new actors; mostly people of color. Real actors."

Bailey nodded as she recalled something her aunt had said. In a segregated world, there wasn't just a White America, there was also a Black one; entire communities made up of Blacks that included Black homeowners, Black businesses, and a Black support system.

Helen parked. They were in town. She gave Bailey a brief smile.

"Are you ready?"

"I am."

"I just want to say," Helen said quickly, "that I hate this. I hate that I never understood until right now—until being a part of this show—what it was really like for Blacks. But I like that I'm part of a production that won't hide it. Because this is pissing people off. Some are learning about it for the first time, some don't want to know. But one thing for certain is Robert's got courage. And he's not going to let them pretend it didn't exist."

Bailey nodded thoughtfully. "Let's get out there."

Helen got out of the car talking a mile a minute about Hank's adventures on the road. Did she prepare these long-winded stories ahead of time?

Bailey chuckled in all the right places as she headed to the grocery store, trying not to see the new water fountain with the large WHITES ONLY sign posted on it.

Luckily, there were no white people walking on the sidewalk in their direction, so she didn't have to step off into the grass.

They walked into the grocery store and Bailey saw a white man glare at her and Helen as if they shouldn't be laughing together.

A week ago, that man would have said good morning to her and probably even tipped his hat.

"I was thinking about what you might need for your pantry," Helen said as they pushed their carts side by side. "Since you can't get everything at once, you should start with the basics. Spices and seasonings. You need your salt, pepper, sugar, and flour. But don't forget your yeast, baking soda, and baking powder."

Bailey grimaced at the thought of baking supplies. She did not want to do much baking, and as long as a loaf of bread only cost 14 cents, she didn't see herself engaging in that activity. But Helen's suggestions did help, so she got everything on her shopping list and Helen's suggested essentials, and then they headed for the checkout counter.

Helen's hands began to tremble despite her happy chatter the closer they got to the checkout.

Helen got in line first, and the cashier rang up her few items. Bailey was behind her and she placed her items on the counter. After Helen was finished, the cashier greeted her politely and rang up her order.

There was absolutely no incident.

Both women were so surprised they didn't say much as they loaded the groceries into the trunk of Helen's car.

"We should go to the butcher's. There's a sale on chuck roast," Helen said hesitantly.

"Bobby sure likes beef," Bailey said. "I think I could make beef and potatoes seven days a week and he'd be perfectly fine."

They headed down the street and once in the butcher shop, she bought a roast.

Again, there was absolutely no incident as they both checked out.

The butcher was polite, and no one treated her as if she was enemy number one.

She and Helen returned to the car, relieved.

Once at home, Bailey decided what she'd make for dinner. Pot roast. It was probably a bit extravagant for a Monday, but Bobby's mother would be coming for dinner Saturday—although Bailey didn't know this yet. And she would need a reason to go back to the grocery store tomorrow after doing all this shopping today.

So, utilizing her critical thinking skills, the pot roast had to be out of the equation for Saturday's meal. *See what happens when one shares information with their coworkers?* she thought to herself. *We make informed decisions.*

Okay. So how do you make pot roast? Yes, she knew there was carrots, potatoes, and gravy along with a side of green beans and buttered rolls. But how did you take this raw slab of meat and turn it into dinner?

Bailey wistfully thought of her aunt's succulent pot roast, and how she'd give up a month's salary if she could just pick up the phone and call her right now.

She sighed. Well, no use wasting time. All she had was Betty Crocker, whose cookbook was her newest literary excursion.

Bailey sat at the table with the cookbook and saw there were three types of roast beef recipes. One would take four full hours to cook, the other three and a half hours, and the final one—Homestyle Roast Beef—only took 2 hours.

Homestyle Roast Beef it was. She read through the ingredients and closed her eyes. It called for parsnips. What even *is* a parsnip? And cornstarch...who buys cornstarch? Oh gosh, she didn't have beef broth! Ugh, she wanted to thunk her head on the table.

The hell with it! In the end, beef broth was just water with salt in it. She'd just have to make do...and this is why the chore list said to prepare a menu...

Bailey put on her apron as if she was a soldier putting on their gear to prepare for battle.

She preheated the oven while she gathered the ingredients they had. Her aunt used Worcestershire sauce, even though the recipe didn't call for it. She'd use it anyway.

She rinsed the meat. It wasn't a rump like Miss Crocker had described. It was a lot flatter; therefore, it would cook faster, she theorized. She seasoned it, added only the onions and garlic and then doused it with beef broth (salted water), covered it, and placed it in the oven.

Wow. That's it? That was simple.

The other vegetables were prepped; the green beans would be easy—just open a can and reheat with some bacon fat she'd saved from breakfast last week. And finally, the dinner rolls just needed a quick reheating.

She was starving. It was after one, and she'd only had a few bites at breakfast. She made herself a sandwich with the last of the egg salad and had a huge glass of ice water.

It was so good. She literally rolled her eyes because it was so nice to sit and relax, even for just a few minutes. She even grabbed the Sears and Roebuck catalogue so she could order baubles and knickknacks for the house.

After an hour she checked the pot roast, envisioning Aunt Mae's thick, rich gravy and juicy roast beef—but saw a slab of grey meat in bubbling water.

Oh...that's why they said broth, because broth is brown. Sheesh.

She took the watery concoction from the oven and stared at it. Is the meat going to turn brown at some point? She added the vegetables dubiously and returned it to the oven for the last forty-five minutes of cooking.

At least the house smelled good. Bailey did a final walk-through of her neat home, checking steps off her mental checklist.

She looked at the neatly dusted living room and thought about leaving the newspaper on the cocktail table for *Mister's evening enjoyment.* No! I'm not going that far with this. But then she grabbed the newspaper and checked to see if Bobby had a byline. None. She placed it on the cocktail table for his evening enjoyment.

By then, the vegetables were sufficiently cooked in the watery broth that looked nothing like gravy. She removed the meat to a platter. It fell apart, but that didn't bother her. It just meant it was not going to be dry. The color was still not pleasing but when she took a taste, it wasn't bad.

Now she had to place the Dutch oven on the burner and turn the water into gravy. With no cornstarch, she would have to add flour. She stopped short of adding it directly into the simmering pot. She'd made that mistake before with the chicken and dumplings and had ended up with lumpy clumps.

Miss Crocker said to put the flour in a small bowl with water and then add that to the liquid. She followed the steps and watched as it slowly began to thicken. She'd made gravy! Real gravy! It was white instead of brown and it tasted a bit bland — maybe even a bit pasty — but she would not over-correct it by adding salt. That was the kiss of death!

When Bobby got home, she smoothed her dress and greeted him at the door. Her heart was racing. He'd kissed her last, now it was her turn to kiss him.

Don't make it awkward. Don't make it awkward...

Before he even had his hat off, Bailey put her arms around him and kissed him.

Bobby dropped his briefcase at his feet and put his hands around her waist. He made a soft humming sound against her lips. And when the kiss ended their faces stayed close, cheeks touching.

"Am I ever going to get tired of that?" he whispered.

"I hope not," she whispered in return.

Oh. My. God.

Why did he kiss better than any man she'd ever known? Why was her heart going crazy right now?

She smiled and took the hat off his head and turned to place it in the closet.

When she turned back, he was smiling too. His hands went back around her waist but he didn't pull her in for a kiss. "You look extra gorgeous today. Dinner smells great. Did you have a good day?"

"The best." She kissed his cheek and reached down to carry his briefcase to the living room, where he no doubt would work on something or other while they watched television later.

"Helen and I had a long conversation and she's not like the others. I like her."

"Good. Maybe we can have them over for dinner soon. I like Hank. He seems like good people." Bobby said the last over his shoulder as he left to get changed.

A short time later, he sat at the table. "Dinner smells really good." He peered at the platter of meat and potatoes. The gravy was next to it in a pretty gravy boat she'd found. "What is it?" he asked.

"Pot roast." It was the ugliest pot roast she'd ever seen in her life.

Bobby blinked. "Okay." He smiled and dug in.

He ate two plates of the meal—although he did cover it in hot sauce she had luckily added to the grocery list. But he ate every bite.

She had to admit that while it wasn't pretty to look at, it did at least taste good.

"That was delicious." He wiped his lips with his napkin.

"It was supposed to be brown," she replied.

"Hey. We're not roast beef racists in this house."

Bailey laughed. "You're right. This is a no judgement zone."

"I need to finish up a few things in my office. Want to meet at the sofa in about half an hour?"

"You have a date." Bailey quickly cleaned the kitchen and put the small amount of roast beef into the refrigerator, not sure who would bother to eat it—certainly not her.

She brought two glasses of iced tea and met Bobby at the sofa. They watched the evening news and then George Burns and Gracie Allen.

...do not be concerned with the mundane quality of life in 1954. That is the appeal...

But Bailey's evening felt anything but mundane, snuggled in Bobby's arms, kissing during each commercial—of which there were many.

The audience should enjoy this. Maybe the production company would splice together all their evening kissing scenes and air them between dramatic shots of the other stars.

Well, the audience wouldn't enjoy the scenes as much as she surely was. She lay her head against Bobby's shoulder, snuggling close. He gave her shoulders a gentle squeeze and kissed her forehead. Damn, could this be any more perfect?

I have fallen in love with Bobby Bailey…

Chapter Twenty-Eight

Bailey slept well. For the first time in a while, she didn't want to get out of bed. She'd had a dream she wanted to recapture, trying to hang onto the lingering memory of how it made her feel.

In the dream she was married, and it wasn't a reach that her husband was Bobby. They lived in a house that was a hybrid of her apartment back home and the house she was in now. They lived in this modern era, but he acted like a 1950s husband, including the way he dressed. She kept showing him modern things, teaching him how to use a cell phone and her laptop.

It was only natural she'd dream about him. They'd spent most of the evening kissing. She couldn't stop the smile that spread across her face.

Yesterday had been far from acting. He should feel like a stranger to her, but it wasn't like that. She felt as comfortable with him as if that dream was real and he truly was her husband.

Was it possible to fall in love with a character from a show?

Of course, she knew she was only talking about characters in a streaming video production. She didn't feel anything for Robert Chesterfield. But if the viewers could be swept away by them as actors, then why couldn't she?

Bobby Bailey isn't real...so having a crush on him was no different than crushing on Michael B. Jordan when she watched *Black Panther*.

Bailey climbed out of bed when it was evident the beautiful dream was on its way to becoming a distant memory. She covered her mouth as she yawned, since she knew Bobby was more than likely already awake and listening for her to get up and start her day.

Thinking about him in the room put a smile on her face. It should have been creepy, but it gave her a special feeling. It was like discovering a new love, or the first day at your dream job.

She was beginning to see things in a better perspective. Even this world had developed a strange appeal. She looked forward to facing the day and her list of chores. She knew soon she would conquer that list just like she was conquering this role.

Bailey headed for the bathroom, stopped and looked over her shoulder.

"Good morning."

"'Morning," Bobby replied.

She smiled and then went into the bathroom.

Breakfast was oatmeal and she'd purchased fruit, which she left on the table. Frosty glasses of milk sat by each bowl along with warm, buttered toast. She poured coffee into their cups and then was giving everything a once-over when Bobby came into the kitchen.

Okay, she thought nervously, anticipating their morning kiss.

Bobby straightened his tie as he walked into the kitchen looking calm, cool, and collected. He then locked eyes with her and she could see a sudden onset case of nerves as he swept his fingers through his neatly combed hair, instantly messing up the work he'd obviously just spent time perfecting.

"Good morning, Bae." Bobby cleared his throat and then walked to her.

"Good morning, dear." She wiped her hands on the dish towel she was holding and stepped forward to meet him.

It felt like they moved in slow motion as Bobby placed his hands on her waist and gently pulled her forward.

She was beginning to realize it was something he always did, as if he would never chase the kiss but would own it completely.

Once their bodies were pressed against each other, his lips followed, pressing against hers. It was just a peck but he lingered long enough to stare into her eyes before they finally separated.

"What's for breakfast?"

Bailey was so lost in those blue eyes it took a moment for her to understand the question.

He gave her a quirky half smile and in that instant, her anxiety melted away.

"Fruit!"

"Fruit?" His brow went up in amusement.

"And oatmeal."

He moved to take his seat.

"You know, the house is really coming along. I think we should have Mother come for dinner and give her a tour."

She grabbed a piece of toast and nodded. "I guess we should. I'll have to figure something to make for dinner. When should we do it?"

"How about Saturday?"

She made a face. "I thought that was going to be date night."

"Oh, right. We can move date night to Sunday. Is that okay?"

"Yes. That's fine. But I don't know what I'll cook for dinner. We already had the roast beef…"

"Maybe something simple," he suggested after spooning oatmeal into his mouth. "She doesn't like anything spicy or extravagant."

"Hmmm. How about ham?"

"Mom likes ham."

"I'll need to go to the grocery store again."

"If you want to drive me to work I can leave the car with you."

She thought about getting dressed and looking presentable so early in the morning. She did not want to do that.

"I'll just take the bus."

"Are you sure?"

"Yes. It's fine."

"I've been thinking about a new story idea."

"Oh great. What is it?"

"Well, you know how they don't allow us to cover big news stories since they get their national news feeds from New York?"

She nodded, although she didn't know.

"Since the tide has changed on McCarthy and anticommunism, I'd like to get opinions on how people now feel about the subject. When my dad was alive, he followed everything McCarthy said and was sure the government was on the verge of being infiltrated.

"But now that everyone knows McCarthy's just a crackpot, I'm curious how people actually feel."

"Your dad sure had a set of ideas," Bailey said.

Bobby reached out and took her hand. "He did, but luckily, I have my own mind and didn't let his ideas influence me."

"And what about your mother?"

He blew out a breath. "It's hard to tell with her. I don't know if she just went along with Dad to pacify him or if she truly believed the way he did."

Well, Saturday should prove to be interesting.

Bobby talked about his idea a while longer before he drained the last of his coffee and stood.

"I'd better get going." He bent to kiss her. "Love you."

Her heart gave a hard thump. "I love you too. Have a good day."

"You too." He left.

Bailey had done her morning exercises and cleaned the kitchen before she remembered to go outside to retrieve her milk delivery. Sure enough, two half gallon jugs of milk, a jug of orange juice, and a package of butter were waiting on her stoop. Bailey looked up and down the street but didn't see Curtis or his milk truck.

She shrugged and brought her items into the house. One day, she'd catch sight of the elusive Curtis the milkman.

She got dressed and decided to wear the brown plaid shirtdress she'd worn the week before. It looked good with her complexion and was very fifties.

She spent some extra time on her makeup, not just because she needed to go into town to pick up the ingredients for Saturday's dinner, but because she liked the way Bobby's eyes roved her face when she made the extra effort.

Bailey smiled to herself as she thought about Bobby at work watching her now through the cameras. It made her a little more self-conscious, so she had to put it out of her mind and focus.

She went into the kitchen and pulled out the trusty Betty Crocker Cookbook and searched for the ingredients to make ham. She knew she'd need a can of pineapple rings and some cloves, but she was sure she would need something elusive she could never imagine.

"What?" she laughed. "Cornstarch again!" Either Betty Crocker had stock in cornstarch or it was as popular as salt and pepper.

When she finished looking over the recipe, she saw neither pineapple nor cloves. There was another ham recipe and although it called for cloves—the ground variety—it also had mustard and honey, but no pineapples.

Was aunt Mae just creating these recipes off the top of her head?

She jotted pineapple rings and toothpicks onto her list. She quickly scribbled down maraschino cherries.

When she had her list complete, Bailey got her sweater, hat, gloves, and pocketbook and then headed out the door.

She didn't even flinch when she saw the lone cameraman standing by her mailbox waiting for her.

Bailey walked down the street. She had passed the bus stop several times when riding with Helen, Pat, as well as Bobby, and she was happy it was just around the corner from the house, especially since she was wearing heels.

Bailey had no idea what the bus fare might be, but made sure she had several coins in her wallet.

The bus stop was empty — except for her and the cameraman. There was a covered bench and she took a seat, remembering what Bobby had said about a hidden button that would call for it.

She spotted a metal button on the pole near her seat and she pressed it, hoping it wasn't a hidden camera. It wasn't, because the bus rounded the corner about two minutes later.

When she stepped inside, Bailey noticed two things; the fare was only a nickel and secondly, she recognized the bus driver. It was the nice man that had given her a ride from the production lot to the house. He had gone on and on about how much he admired her and the show. She half expected his animated smile but he was expressionless — which, since they had technically never met, his demeanor was normal.

The door closed, leaving the cameraman still standing on the sidewalk. That meant there most likely would be cameras and microphones on the bus.

There were only about five or six people on the bus. She sat down and thought about the first time she'd ridden the bus into Wingate. She had been so impressed with how realistic everything looked; the town, the houses —

"Girlie." Bailey looked up, realizing the bus hadn't taken off and there was no one else getting off or on. The bus driver had turned in his seat and was looking at her.

She gave him a questioning look.

"Back of the bus," he snapped.

She looked at him in confusion. Back of the bus? What? She noticed everyone was staring at her. One man who had been reading his newspaper closed it and glared at her.

"Get your ass to the back of the bus," he spat, his face turning red in anger.

It finally sank in. She had taken a seat in the front. Bailey quickly came to her feet, not sure if she wanted to just get off the bus or if she should comply and move to the back.

There were no Blacks present—only white faces looking at her as if she was a criminal.

Bailey moved to the back of the bus and took a seat. The bus finally took off and she looked out the window for a minute, digesting what had just happened.

She finally peeked up at the front of the bus and at the bus driver. She could see his face reflected in the rearview mirror and she waited to see if he'd meet her eyes and give her a wink letting her know they were in this together and this was a shit story line.

But he didn't.

Chapter Twenty-Nine

When Bailey got off the bus, she contemplated calling someone to pick her up; preferably Pat. She needed a Black friend right now, but she wasn't sure about Pat's new story line. Even though she was sure Robert had approved it, most people were working during this hour.

As a Black 1950s housewife, Bailey would definitely be considered a rarity.

In the end, she had no choice but to pull up her big girl panties, since a cameraman was waiting for her at the stop. She swallowed down her emotions and headed for the butcher shop.

It was a quiet day in Wingate. There were a few women around, but they seemed to be moving busily. She saw a few in the salon, another leaving the post office and another entering the grocery store. By the time she reached the butcher's shop, Bailey's heartbeat had calmed.

She went up the canned goods aisle hoping to see canned pineapple so she wouldn't have to pay a visit to the grocery store and could get home as quickly as possible.

She was in luck, and saw just what she was looking for. She checked the wrapper and saw a recipe for the exact ham recipe her aunt made!

In the same aisle they had whole cloves and maraschino cherries. She needed to diversify her cookbooks. Did the Sears and Roebuck catalogue have soul food cookbooks?

Bailey placed a carton of cornstarch and two cans of broth into her basket. Any more than this and she wouldn't be able to carry her groceries home on the bus.

She had to suppress a groan thinking about the bus ride and that man that had cursed at her.

Shaking the thought out of her head, she went to the meat counter and searched for the smallest ham she could find.

"Excuse me," she said to the two busy butchers. "Do you have any ham smaller—"

"You're going to have to wait," one of the men said while glancing at her from where he was trimming a piece of beef.

Her brow went up because there wasn't anyone at the counter. So, what was she waiting for? She almost asked, but thought better of it.

Bailey waited while the two butchers ignored her. She didn't recognize these men. She'd always been helped by the same butcher, a pleasant, older man that always smiled and greeted her kindly.

A full minute later, the man that had told her to wait turned to her.

"What can I get you?"

"I need a small ham. Smaller than the ones you have displayed."

The man sighed tiredly. "These are the smallest bone-in hams we have. Do you want me to cut one in half?"

"Yes, please." He nodded and got one of the larger hams. After placing it on the cutter, he gestured with his butcher's knife where she wanted it sliced. Once she had the size she wanted, he cut it and carried it to the counter.

He stopped and looked at someone behind her. A broad smile suddenly appeared on his face.

"Yes, ma'am. How can I help you?"

A woman walked from behind Bailey and stood next to her, her finger resting on her lip as she considered the meat on display.

"How fresh is that ground beef?" she asked.

"Freshly ground this morning, ma'am."

Bailey glanced at the other butcher. He wasn't helping anyone, just slicing meat. He could have helped this woman...but regardless, she knew in 1954 she had to wait for the white people to be served—although it was stupid to stop right in the middle of helping her to help someone else.

Bailey adjusted her hold on her basket. It was beginning to get heavy. Plus, her feet were growing sore after standing in one spot.

She quietly looked at the other meat on display, waiting for this asshole butcher to give her the ham.

She exhaled. She shouldn't be mad. This wasn't real. This was acting.

After a full five minutes, the woman had selected her meat and left. The butcher moved back to the counter, where he finished wrapping her ham, weighed it, and slapped a sticker on it. It literally took thirty seconds.

"Thank you," she said, forcing a pleasant comment.

"Yep." He returned to his duties without sparing her a look.

Asshole.

Bailey moved to the counter to pay for her food. There were only two other people in the store, so hopefully this would go quickly and without another incident.

She didn't bother to speak to the cashier. The woman was older, and had the look of someone would turn her nose up at a Colored person.

"Have a good day," the cashier said as Bailey gathered her two bags.

Bailey paused and glanced at her. "You too." And then she quickly left.

You can't judge a book by its cover, she thought as she headed out the door.

The cameraman was waiting for her outside the door. That made her suspicious. What was he trying to capture? No one had ever followed her down the street in Wingate before.

She hefted her bags and headed for the bus stop. One bag had just the ham, and although it was relatively small, it was still unruly to handle. Her other purchases were in another bag and her pocketbook dangled from her wrist.

As soon as she got to the bus stop, she'd have to put down her packages in order to fish out the nickel from her wallet. Bailey was so distracted, she barely saw the man that was hurrying up the sidewalk in her direction.

He bumped into her and one of her bags dropped. She heard the faint sound of splintering glass.

The man paused long enough to glance at her from over his shoulder. "Watch where you're going!"

Bailey's mouth opened and she almost called him an asshole. Almost. Instead, she crouched down at her torn bag and checked for the damage. The maraschino cherries were no more.

She'd have to pack everything into one bag. Why did she wear heels today? Her feet were screaming.

"Are you all right?" A man crouched beside her and he scared her so badly she nearly fell on her butt. An added surprise was seeing a Black man.

"Oh!"

He smiled. "Sorry if I scared you."

He was good-looking—movie star good-looking!

He had the type of brown skin that reminded her of polished dark wood. His short hair was shaved on the sides with military precision. He had gorgeous, dark eyes that seemed concerned despite his gentle smile.

She definitely had never seen him before.

Bailey looked at the mess on the ground. Maraschino cherry juice was already spreading across the sidewalk and the paper bag had developed a hole in its bottom.

"I think I made a mess." She began to unpack her items into the other bag.

The man picked up the ruined paper bag containing the broken shards of glass and cherries. He carefully carried it to a nearby garbage can. Bailey stood, hoping her heavy package wouldn't tear.

"Thank you," she said.

He nodded good-naturedly, but then glanced past her in the direction of the man that had knocked into her. A shadow crossed his face.

"No problem." He met her eyes again and smiled. "I'm Curtis. Curtis Jackson."

Curtis! As in Curtis the milkman.

"You're the milkman!"

"I am."

"I'm Bailey Banks...you delivered milk to me today."

"What street?" He cocked his head curiously.

Bailey gave the street and he nodded. "Yes, that's today's route. Who do you work for?"

"Oh. I'm a housewife," she replied.

"On Stewart Street?" His brow dipped in surprise. "Mrs. Banks..." And then his expression cleared. "Oh." His smile slipped away.

The change in Curtis was instantaneous. He virtually shut down. Even his deep, dark eyes went cold. He looked past her.

"I better go," he said stiffly. "Have a good day." And then he walked right past her.

Bailey's mouth fell open, but she didn't turn to look after him. She didn't even try to mask her shock. Her stomach felt as if it had dropped to her knees.

She quickly moved to the bus stop, past the new sign at the water fountain that said WHITES ONLY, and past the woman that walked toward her, being sure to step off into the grass so they wouldn't touch.

Again, there was no one at the bus stop. The cameraman was standing at a distance, and she was so happy he wasn't doing a closeup because no amount of acting could help her hide the hurt that filled her. She even forgot to press the button for the bus but it didn't matter, because it showed up within moments of her arrival.

Bailey boarded and slipped her nickel into the slot. Again, she entered the bus alone, the door feeling like a cell door as it shut behind her. This time, she didn't look at the bus driver and just moved to take a seat at the back of the bus.

The moment she sat down Bailey turned to the window, not caring whether or not the bus cameras could see her. Tears slipped from her eyes but she was too embarrassed to wipe them away.

Bailey had pulled herself together by the time the bus let her off around the corner from her house. It was a good thing, since another cameraman was at the stop to greet her.

She was thinking about how much she literally resented them when she stopped in her tracks.

Oh my God...

Camille, the woman that had thought she was Helen's maid, was in her garden pulling non-existent weeds.

Bailey looked around as if there was another way for her to get to her house—and there was, if she wanted to walk all the way around the block.

She just couldn't do that—not now, when she was dog-tired and emotionally whipped.

Today had been a lot.

Bailey hurried down the street and when she was in front of Camille, the older woman looked up and pushed back her hat. Bailey tried to pretend she didn't see her.

"Hello." Camille got up and walked to her.

Bailey stopped walking and closed her eyes briefly.

Enough is enough, Robert Chesterfield! Enough is enough...I get it. I'm your scapegoat to show the world just how racist 1954 was for Blacks.

But she was twenty-three years old and had never had to deal with anything like this. There was no script, nothing to memorize or to guide her. She just had to base her actions on her limited knowledge of Jim Crow segregation and her own feelings.

And right now, all she felt was the need to lash out, and burying those feelings, even for the show, was soul-crushing.

"Bailey, wasn't it?"

"Yes. Hello."

"I'm sorry I didn't make it to the welcoming party. Uh, my husband was feeling a bit under the weather."

"It's perfectly fine."

"Say"—she rubbed her chin—"I'm looking for some help around the house; just a few hours a week and nothing heavy. You don't happen to know anyone who might be interested, do you?"

Bailey pretended to think about it. "Maybe Helen. She talked about being bored during the day."

Camille's eyes went wide. "Helen? Well, I couldn't have a wh—a, uh, neighbor working for me."

"I'm sure I don't know anyone," Bailey said while walking away. "I have to get home...I couldn't find the Negro restroom in town. Goodbye!"

Camille stood on the sidewalk with a shocked expression as she watched Bailey hurry away.

269

The first thing Bailey did when she stepped into the house was kick off her shoes and leave them in the middle of the floor. She went into the kitchen and set the groceries on the counter along with her pocketbook and then returned to the living room, where she slumped back into the armchair, still wearing her sweater and hat.

Bailey closed her eyes and sat that way for a full five minutes before she pulled herself out of the chair.

She had put everything into perspective. *This is your job. Nothing more, nothing less.*

She hung up her sweater and put away her hat and then slipped on her heels.

Bailey turned on the radio, where a female crooner sang a soulful song about her no-good man. She went into the kitchen and unpacked her groceries. She had to wipe off the broth and carton of cornstarch because it looked like someone had tried to murder them. She put them in their places in the pantry.

Bailey pulled the ground beef from the refrigerator and fried it with diced onions and peppers, and then added a jar of marinara sauce. She put on a pot of water to boil for the spaghetti and pulled together a quick iceberg lettuce salad.

By the time Miles Davis began blowing his trumpet, the garlic bread was coming out of the oven. Bailey checked the time and saw it was just after four o'clock.

She went to the bathroom and then touched up her makeup, removing the trail of tears that had dried on her cheeks. She fluffed her hair and then did a quick walk-through of the house. She put the newspaper on the cocktail table in the living room just when she heard Bobby's car pull up.

She met him at the door, noting his broad smile. Bailey studied his eyes, trying to determine if that smile reached them. She wasn't sure, but he did seem happy to see her.

"Hi, honey," she said. She put her arms around him and kissed him. When she pulled back, their eyes locked. Both wore smiles, but they both looked a little tired and a little beat up. Bailey figured he hadn't had a good day either. But she bet hers had been worse.

She didn't know about him, but she had felt nothing with that kiss.

Chapter Thirty

"How did your idea go over with your boss?" Bailey asked as she placed spaghetti noodles onto Bobby's plate.

He stared at the food in pleasure. "It went good, but let's talk about this spread. Dinner looks amazing, Bae."

She smiled. "It's the least I can do for my hubby." Bailey took her seat and placed her napkin under her chin; otherwise, she was sure to stain the dress. "So, what did he say?" she asked, being very attentive.

"Mr. Adams thought the idea was a swell one...but it would take some added legwork we don't really have. We're going to have to rely on volunteer labor. I thought maybe we could get some of the spouses and kids to go door-to-door." He smiled at her as he chewed his spaghetti and sauce. "How about it, honey? Want to go door-to-door for the cause?"

Bailey stared at him. In that instant, she wanted to throw her plate of spaghetti at him, right square in the face like one of the clowns got pied at the fair.

"How soon did you want to do it?" she asked slowly.

"The sooner the better. Maybe you could lead it — but don't try to take on everything yourself. Get some team leaders — maybe Helen might want to help."

"I'd love to help, Bobby. I'll talk to her about it this evening. I'm sure she'll want to be included." Bailey sighed, deciding it was time for her to write her own script. After all, Robert had added a doozy of a story line, and it was time to manifest racial equality in Wingate.

She pushed the food around on her plate listlessly, even though she was starving since she had skipped lunch—again.

He looked up at her with his cheeks pooched out with food. He really was enjoying the meal—it was one of the more decent ones she had prepared, and he certainly intended to get his fill.

"You okay, honey? You look a little tired. You haven't been working yourself too hard, have you?"

Damn, this man was a good actor. He didn't look at all as if he hadn't just orchestrated the most hellish day on Earth for her.

"I'm fine. It's just…"

"What?" He put down his fork, a look of confusion and worry growing on his face.

Yeah, Robert Chesterfield. You didn't write this scene in your little script, did you? But you can thank yourself because you're the one who just gave me the idea…

"They got a new butcher today. The nice old man I used to see wasn't there."

"Hmmm, maybe he retired."

"I guess. But one of the new fellows wasn't nearly as nice."

Bobby's frown deepened. "What do you mean?"

"He made me wait until after he finished working on whatever he was doing, and then right in the middle of my order he began helping another lady—a *white* lady."

Bobby's jaw clenched. "I can go down and have a talk with this fella—"

"Well, and a man cursed at me on the bus—"

"What?!" Bobby jumped to his feet. "What man? What did he say?!"

Bailey stood and placed a calming hand on his arm. He sure did look authentically mad. His face had gone red and a pulse was beating in his forehead. How do actors make pulses beat in their forehead?

"Honey, you can't do anything about man—"

"Well, I don't want you riding the bus again!" he yelled.

"Or shopping at the butcher shop? Or walking down the street? Or trying to find the Black Only water fountain and toilet?"

His chest was rising rapidly up and down. "I'm going to have a talk with that butcher—"

"For doing his job? Sit down, baby. Calm down, okay?" Bobby reluctantly took his seat.

"What did the man on the bus say to you?" he asked, his words slow.

"He told me to get my ass to the back of the bus."

Bobby's eyes locked onto her so hard she saw them move from one of her eyes to the other.

"I didn't—I accidentally sat near the front. I just wasn't thinking—"

He grabbed her hand and squeezed it gently. "There shouldn't be any laws saying you have to sit in the back! It's stupid as hell. They take your money the same as they take everyone else's!"

She closed her eyes and shook her head. "I know the rules, okay? They're not going to magically change just because I married you."

"I know—"

"A man bumped into me today because I didn't step off the sidewalk fast enough—"

"Oh my God, honey, are you okay?" He made to stand up again but she pulled him back down to his chair.

"Yeah, he knocked the bag with the maraschino cherries out of my hands and it broke all over the place. But that's not even the important part."

Bobby just sighed in frustration and ran the hand that wasn't holding hers through his hair.

"What do you mean that's not the important part? My wife has been accosted and mistreated!"

She squeezed his hand and shook it slightly until he looked at her again.

"The important part is, you are not married to a white woman."

He cocked his head in confusion. "I don't understand...of course I know you're a Negro—"

"Right. You accept me completely—but those people out there don't." She gestured to the door. "You ask me to go door-to-door just days after my neighbors told me, in not so many words, they don't want me around—"

"But—"

"And I agreed to do it, because I *can*. But not in the white neighborhoods. I will gladly go door-to-door to poll my Black neighbors. I'll go to the Black businesses and speak to the Black leaders." Her brow drew together. "And while there isn't a Black bus service I can take, I'll be going to the Colored butcher shop from now on."

Bobby's stared at her. He'd gone speechless.

Bailey didn't crack a smile although part of her really wanted to.

Touché, Mr. Chesterfield. You better build that all-Black community sooner rather than later.

"I wanted to make you a part of all facets of my life so badly, I didn't stop to realize what I was asking you to do. I'm sorry, Bailey. I'm so sorry. What else am I not seeing? I want to know."

That one surprised her. If only she really could tell him how she felt about him right now...

"Bailey? Is there something else?" He stood and pulled her gently from her chair and put his arms around her. "What is it?" His expression was a mixture of confusion and wariness. "Did something else happen?"

Bailey lightly bit her lip and then she slowly nodded. "When...those things happened to me today, I realized that when my friends and family warned me about marrying outside of my race..."

He frowned and pulled her closer. "Yeah?"

"I didn't realize how some days—a day like today—I might not want to see a white person's face."

His surprise at her words went beyond acting. Bobby froze and after a few heartbeats, he exhaled slowly. His hands slowly fell from her.

"I'm..." he said softly while studying the floor.

"I'm sorry," she said softly. "Because I know what I just said to you is all kinds of horrible. You've never hurt me—or anyone else that I'm aware of. And while I have no regrets in marrying you, living with you, making a home with you—I can't always look at you and not see the people that hurt me."

Bobby met her eyes again. "I think I understand. As long as you don't want to end this—"

"No! No, I don't want us to end! When I look at you, most days, I don't even see color. I just see the man I want to spend the rest of my days with." She took his hands in hers. "But when I get hit with this white hatred day after day after day…" Bailey chewed her lip and looked away. "I just want to lick my wounds."

"I won't lie and say what you just said doesn't hurt." They locked eyes again. "But mostly because I can only imagine the frustration of being treated like you have been. I want to hurt something! I want to hurt somebody!" He swallowed. "I guess all I can do in the end is be your rock. If you need me to hold you up, I'm going to always do that."

He closed his eyes and leaned towards her until their foreheads touched. She was so thankful he understood that right now was not the time to kiss — and she had no idea when that time would return.

They finished dinner quietly, with very little small talk. Afterwards, Bobby apologized and said he needed to work on his story idea in his office, but offered to meet her for their normal date in front of the television set.

She told him maybe tomorrow would be better and he gave her a crooked smile and gently squeezed her arm before closing himself in his office.

Yep. That man certainly had a lot of things he was going to need to take care of.

When he was out of the room she went to the telephone and called Pat, who answered immediately.

"Hello?"

"Hi, Pat. This is Bailey..."

"Hey, girl. Are you okay? You don't sound so good."

"I'm...not really."

"Did something happen?"

"Yes. I was in town today and...so much happened, and I need someone to talk to."

"Okay," Pat responded quickly. "You're not hurt, are you?"

"No." Bailey suddenly wondered if they were capturing Pat's end of the conversation since she was now a regular. This actually sounded like a real conversation. "I hate bothering you—"

"You are not bothering me, Bailey. We are friends."

"Do you think we can meet and talk? I tried to wait until after I thought you were off work—"

"Hmphf. Don't worry about work. I got canned the other day."

"What? But why? You're one of the best tellers at the bank."

"Yeah, but Mandy Sue started training there last week and all of a sudden, they don't think they need a Black teller for the Black customers...so Mandy has my job."

"Oh, Pat, that's lousy." Bailey was certain both sides of this conversation were being filmed or Pat would not have revealed that juicy bit of information over the phone. That story line was just too good not to get on film. "I can come pick you up and we can go someplace to talk. I think we both need an ear."

Bailey looked back towards Bobby's office. "Yeah, we can. I'll let Bobby know I'll be out for a while."

"Okay, I should be there in about fifteen minutes."

"Thanks, Pat. You don't know how much I need this."

"See you soon, sis."

After hanging up with Pat, Bailey went to the kitchen and poured a glass of milk and then put several cookies on a plate.

She carried them to Bobby's office and managed to knock on the door without spilling anything.

"Come in."

Bobby gave her a surprised look and then saw the cookies and milk. He smiled in appreciation. Paper was strewn all over his desk. Wow, he really was working.

"Sorry to disturb you, honey. I thought you might like a little snack for later. I called my friend Pat. We used to work at the bank together."

"Okay," he nodded.

"She and I are going out for a bit."

"Sure, Bae." He looked at the mess of papers and notes on his desk. He had probably stashed his tablet in his drawer when she knocked. "It looks like I'm going to be busy for a while and there are things I could use at the office, so I might just go over there for a few hours."

"That's fine, honey." She inhaled and placed her hand on his shoulder. "I'm sorry about today—"

"I hate what happened to you today," he interrupted while covering her hand with his. "But I hate for you to apologize to me too. Because you are the last person in this situation that should be apologizing to anyone. I just want you to go out with your friend and have fun, Bae. Have fun." He kissed her hand and she nodded and left the room.

Chapter Thirty-One

Pat arrived with a short toot of her car horn.

"Pat's here!" she called.

"Bye, hon. Have fun!" she heard Bobby return. Bailey went outside. There was no cameraman waiting for her outside…because there was one in the back seat of Pat's car.

Oh my God! The show truly didn't want to miss any of this!

She got into the car, ignoring the man with his huge camera and microphone.

"Hi, girl!" Pat said happily.

"Hi. Thanks for picking me up." She put on her seat belt.

"I think you needed someone to talk to just about as much as I did. We can go to Maybelle's. I just had dinner, but I wouldn't mind some peach cobbler. Or if you prefer, we can have a drink and listen to some bebop. A guy I know opened a juke joint in the back of his grandma's house." Pat chuckled. "It's kind of loud and crowded, so I don't know how much talking we'll accomplish, but I guarantee we'll feel better after a few bottles of beer."

Bailey was curious about the juke joint. It reminded her what Aunt Mae had said about paying a penny to go to a house party.

But talking was the purpose, not dancing and partying.

"Let's go to Maybelle's."

"Maybelle's it is."

"I can't believe the bank let you go."

"Let me *go*? That's what they do to white people. They fired me. And for some girl that hasn't had a job since she graduated from high school. Although they tell me she did take an accounting class." Pat rolled her eyes and grabbed a cigarette. "You're lucky you got out of there when you did."

"Yeah," she replied quietly, because it hadn't been luck. She'd married a man that allowed her to leave all of that behind. That was a lot to digest—and she would, but not here in the car with a camera pointed at her. "What are you going to do for a job?"

"The bank gave me severance pay. That will hold me over until I get on at the factory. I put in my application yesterday. Hopefully, I'll hear something back this week."

"That's good. I'm happy you have something lined up."

"Yeah, but...it's the factory. I didn't see myself working there."

"Well, maybe it's just for now. You're smart, Pat. I know you'll find something else."

"Thanks, Bailey," she smiled. "So, what's going on with you?"

"I had one of those days. But actually, it began with a backyard barbecue my new neighbor threw to welcome me and Bobby to the neighborhood."

"Ow." Pat made a face. "And you were the only Negro?"

"How did you guess?"

"Sounds like fun."

"Not *everyone* hated me. But it was bad—and it happened in front of Bobby—I think that's the worst."

"Holy hell. What happened?"

Bailey recounted the highlights of Saturday's barbecue, including her breakdown once they got home.

Pat parked in front of Maybelle's restaurant. It was good, since Bailey's anxiety had spiked once they drove into town. She definitely did not want to have to step off the sidewalk again today.

This is just a role. How in the hell is it making her feel like she's really being mistreated? Isn't this what she wanted? She didn't want a whitewashed 1950s story line, but...

They went inside the restaurant. A Little Richard song was playing on the jukebox and Bailey was pleasantly surprised to see there was a nice amount of people present. There were probably fifteen or twenty people eating! Also, the smell of cooking food was present. Maybelle's had become a real working restaurant.

Bailey recognized the waitress from her last visit, but couldn't remember her name for the life of her. She was happy she wore a name tag on her blouse. Pearl.

Pearl greeted them. "Have a seat wherever you want. I'll be right with you." The poor girl looked busy for real.

They found a seat and removed their hats. Pat was dressed in a slimming skirt, heels, and a turtleneck sweater. Pat looked way cooler than her. Even her short hair with the tapered neck seemed trendy.

"So, what happened today, sis?" Pat asked while pulling out another cigarette.

"The same thing that always happens, a man told me to get my ass to the back of the bus." Pat's brow rose.

"Yeah, I know. I should have been on the back of the bus."

"I didn't say anything…"

Pearl came by. "You ladies ready to order?"

"I'll just have the peach cobbler and a cup of coffee," Pat said.

That sounded good. "I'll have the same."

"Do you want ice cream?"

Hell yeah! "Only if the cobbler's warm."

Pearl smiled. "That's the only way to have it. I'll bring it right out."

Pat tapped the ash of her cigarette into the ashtray. "One day, when I was about fifteen, I got on the bus and there weren't any seats in back. There were a few empty ones in front—a couple of them weren't even next to a white person. So, I sat in one of those seats.

"The bus driver told me to stand up. I had to stand up on a bus that had empty seats until an old Black man got up and let me have his. This poor guy kept stumbling, so I got up and told him he could have his seat back. But he wouldn't take it.

"You know, I saw a few whites looking over at us as if they were ashamed, but they didn't say one thing. They never spoke up." Pat squished out her cigarette. "I have absolutely nothing to say about you sitting in the front of the bus, sis."

Bailey stared at the other woman. "There are millions of stories like ours, aren't there?"

"And worse."

"Pat, when I got home…I really laid into Bobby."

Pat straightened. "What?"

"I feel so bad about it. But in that moment, I was so mad! I was mad at the butcher that made me wait, and the man that knocked into me because I didn't step off the sidewalk. And Bobby asked me if I wanted to go door-to-door for something he's doing at work.

"I just…I'm trying to avoid as many whites as I can and he asks me to go door-to-door, as if he has no idea what's going on out there in Wingate, in the world!"

"Sis…" Pat said sympathetically. Pearl came out then with their orders. After she left, Pat leaned forward.

"Jeez, Bailey. You've only been married a few weeks. Are you having second thoughts about marrying—"

"God, no. I'm in love with Bobby. But when those things happen to me, I just can't stand to be around him. It's so terrible, and…I told him."

"Oh my God. Bailey!" Pat said with shock.

"I know…I feel so bad."

"What did he do?"

"He said he understood and he went to his office to do some work. I think he just wanted to give me some space because of what I said. But I feel so bad—"

"Look. I'm going to be honest with you. When you first said you were seeing a white man, I thought you were crazy. I didn't know how you could ever trust him. But Bobby never tried to keep his relationship with you a secret.

"I don't think he sees color. And I know that's a messed-up thing to say because a person like me is proud to be Black. I'm proud of my culture, and I don't want someone who can't see it."

Bailey sat back in her seat and sighed.

"But hear me out," she continued quickly. "Bobby might not see color because in his eyes, you two are the same. Being a Colored girl is just a part of who you are. But it's not all you are, Bailey. You're a wife, a niece, a friend, and your own individual."

Bailey digested Pat's words. "I should apologize to him—"

"Don't be so quick to feel bad about what you said. Was it true?"

Bailey nodded. "In that moment, it was true."

"And now?"

"I said it in anger...but it was true."

"You gotta speak your truth, Bailey." Pat pulled her cobbler to her and sliced into it with her fork. She took a bite and her eyes rolled up. "Oh, man, the best cobbler in Ohio. You better eat it before I steal it."

Bailey smiled and took a bite. The ice cream had begun to melt, which only turned it into a silky sauce because the cobbler was still warm. Somebody's grandma had to have baked this. It was delicious!

"I feel better now that I talked to you," Bailey said honestly.

"We gotta be tough; and you more than most—considering your choice in hubbies." Both ladies smiled. "When I told you about those people on the bus that day, and how they saw what was wrong about what was happening, but they chose not to stand up and say anything, Bobby isn't like that.

"Bobby took you as his wife in front of God and all the world. And he sounds like he will shield you from anybody that tries to hurt you, just like you said he did at the party."

Bailey blinked at Pat.

"I can only imagine the mess Bobby has to deal with being married to you. There's probably a lot of stuff he won't ever tell you. His mama isn't jumping up and down, I bet?"

"No. But she wasn't as bad as the people at the picnic. In other words, she doesn't particularly care for me, but I don't think it's because she hates Negroes. I think she doesn't think any woman is good enough for her son."

"Right. And does he hang out with his friends anymore?"

"Well...no."

"I think you're the prize, Bailey," Pat said while scooping up the last of her cobbler and ice cream.

"The prize?"

"The one that makes it all worth it. The question is, is he your prize?"

Bailey chewed her lip. "I think I should go home...after I pick up an extra slice of cobbler for my sweetie."

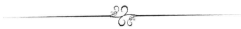

Bailey felt much better. The story line was solid, and going in the direction she wanted it to go. Taking things personal was probably not completely abnormal, considering the story's content and the climate in the United States. But she was acting like a kid that was role-playing on the Internet with a bunch of strangers and then forgetting none of it was real.

She wasn't being professional at all. But Bailey intended to do things better. No more crushing on her boss's character. It was crazy, and it was affecting her acting. He wasn't real. Bobby Bailey is not a real person.

"You gotta come to the juke joint with me sometime," Pat said as they drove back to the house.

"How would that look? A married woman hanging out at a juke joint?" Bailey chuckled.

"Bring your husband."

"The white man?"

"The white man's married to a Negro." Pat laughed next.

"Hmmm. I'll think about it. But definitely, we need to get together more often."

"I agree, sis. How about Saturday, after our hair appointment?"

Bailey made a face. "I didn't tell you, but I'm making dinner for Mother Banks for the first time."

"Oh. Sounds like fun."

"Yeah. She's not terrible, but I'm certainly not her favorite person."

"You'll win her over. There is just something about you that's so likeable."

Bailey chuckled. "I wish you would have told that to the folks at Saturday's picnic." She turned suddenly to look at Pat. "Bobby wants me to go door-to-door to take a poll on McCarthy and communism. I told him I'd go to every Negro house in Wingate—but I could really use some help. How about it?"

"Girl, why would Negroes be concerned about communism when we can barely walk down the street in peace? But I guess I can. I'm not currently working. Besides, if we don't give our opinions, then we don't count."

"Thanks, Pat. You're a doll!"

They pulled into Bailey's driveway. Bobby's car wasn't present and the sun had just begun to set. He was still out. He was going to be tired. She felt bad about pushing the story line and forcing him to create the Black community so fast. She had faith he would carry it out.

Bailey said goodbye to her friend and then went inside her house. She kicked off her shoes and then jotted a quick note for Bobby, which she left on the table.

Hi, honey. I had a much-needed talk with Pat and she helped me to put things into perspective. I just want you to know I am devoted to making this work. I love you. Check in the fridge. I got a delicious surprise for you.

~Bae

Bailey took a long, hot bath and pinned her curls while marveling at the fact that she had not known about this miraculous thing about pinning her curls a week ago.

She got ready for bed and by the time she climbed between the sheets, Bobby still hadn't come home. She fell asleep, tired but ready to turn a new leaf.

Bailey was sound asleep when the lights turned on.

She blinked and looked up. Bobby was standing inside the doorway, looking at her.

"W-what?"

"We need to have a talk. Now," Bobby said coldly.

Chapter Thirty-Two

Bailey sat up in bed and looked at the clock. 2:12…a.m.?

"What?" she asked, trying to pull herself out of her sleep haze.

"You might want to get up. Grab a robe and meet me in the living room. The cameras won't be running." He turned and left, but she noticed his brow was gathered and he seemed far from happy.

What the – ?

It took her a moment to clear her head, and then like a splash of water, she recalled the events of the previous day.

Bailey jumped out of bed and grabbed her robe. She rubbed her eyes and slipped her feet into her house shoes and then she was out of the bedroom and heading to the living room, suddenly fully awake.

Bobby had turned on the living room lamp but otherwise, the house was dark. He stood in the middle of the room watching her. When she entered the room, he sighed and crossed his arms and the expression he wore caused Bailey to wonder if she was out of a job.

"Bailey," he said with barely controlled annoyance. "Your actions today jeopardized the production." Her mouth fell open, but he continued. "As a trained actress, I would think you would know in any improv, unless you are *trying* to sabotage the show, you wouldn't rewrite an entire production!"

"I'm not trying to sabotage the show! I want the show to be the best it can be—"

He shook his head and gave her an incredulous look. "Are you trying to tell me that you didn't see an issue with rewriting my script—"

"What script?" she interrupted. "Because my script is really limited, Bobby. You, yourself, said I'm in charge of my character's actions—"

"*Your* character's actions, not the actions of the entire production!" He placed a hand on his forehead and turned to pace before speaking again. This time, his voice was low and controlled. "Just in case you don't understand, we hired the women you acted with at the beauty shop and were in the process of hiring eighteen other people—mostly people of color; African American, Hispanic, and Asian.

"We began the all-Black community of Garden Hills right outside of Wingate. The cost for that is out of this world! My production team is screaming at me, as are our funders. But I know it's necessary, and hey, since we added you, our streaming subscription has more than quadrupled!"

Bailey listened quietly, not used to seeing Robert Chesterfield with his boss's hat on. She didn't dare speak, even though she wanted to point out this was something he was already planning to do…

"But the script was for you to go door-to-door and run into Mr. Edelman—your cranky, racist neighbor. And Mr. Edelman has his script all ready to go. But because of what you did, he won't be able to do any of what we planned."

Bailey's heart began to pound in her chest as she realized just how much her actions had affected others.

"I'm sorry. I didn't know," she whispered.

Robert stopped pacing and rubbed his eyes tiredly. "I had to scrap all of the scripts for the people that were supposed to be interviewed by you. Those people have already been living here and are already established, and all we would have needed to do is give them a little coaching." He stared at her again. "But we can't use *any* of that now. That was hours of my work just wasted."

Bailey bit her lip and then sat down slowly. "I didn't realize. I'm really sorry."

He sat down across from her, looking more tired than angry. "Look, I understand why you did what you did — or at least I think I understand. But you can't do things like that anymore. It also happened when you and Pat established her story line before it was ever approved. I let it slide because it gave me some new ideas."

She could barely look at him as he stared at her with intensity, explaining something so elementary to her.

"The nature of this show is that you act, but within your confines — and just like with any improvisation, you never direct what another actor is required to do."

She nodded, feeling foolish because this was absolutely something she already knew.

"I know it's been a real sticking point with you about not having direction in your script. I thought by allowing you to do what would come natural for a young, African-American newlywed, you'd bring more to your story line than I could ever write. But maybe I should be giving you a real script that you have to follow exactly — "

She quickly shook her head. "No, don't do that. It's not the lack of direction in my script." She tried to meet his eyes, but was incredibly embarrassed at having to be talked to like this. "I just don't always know what to expect. I didn't expect to see the Whites Only sign—"

"I made sure it was part of your script changes—"

"You did," she said quickly. "And I appreciate it. But I didn't know Bailey was going to face so much racism. Helen tipped me off to that. Why is it she knows before I know?"

He looked confused. "Because that's a part of *her* script. Do you want to see everyone's script?" He was back to being annoyed. "Because I can give you a copy of what everyone is expected to accomplish in a week—or better yet, I can give you access to my master copy..."

Bailey sighed in frustration. "I don't need all of that. But you can't tell me you couldn't tip me off that some guy was going to force me off the sidewalk, or the butcher was going to make me stand there for five minutes while he chatted it up with another customer!"

"But that's what I'm saying." His hands went up in exasperation. "Those are real actors, so I didn't tell them how to do what I wanted to have accomplished. In Wingate, there will be some racists. Some are completely open-minded, while there are others that are split in the middle.

"I don't tell them ahead of time what to do. I trust that they are going to do what their prepared bio tells them they should do."

Good Lord. Bailey stared at Robert in awe. He wasn't telling *anyone* what to say. It wasn't just her. No one on this entire show had lines they had to read…

He leaned forward and propped his elbows on his knees, locking his hands in front of him. He stared at her, his blue eyes intensely locking onto her brown ones.

"Here's the thing. And I want you to think about this very hard. Do you want to continue working on this show?"

The blood felt as if it was draining from Bailey's face.

"I do—"

"Okay." He continued without allowing her to say more. "Now that I've added this element to 1954, I don't intend to put an end to it, whether you're married to Bobby or not. Bobby and Bailey can break up if you don't feel as if you can continue working intimately with me—"

"No, I can!" she said adamantly.

"Good, because I'm trying not to make things difficult between us. I know how hard it can be playing opposite your boss, and I appreciate that you've done it with ease. They believe you. The world believes *us*. But if at any point you don't believe you can continue, let me know, and while I want to see Bobby in an interracial relationship—I think it's important to see him in one—I can have someone else become his love interest. Pat maybe."

"Pat…"

What in the hell was he saying? Did he want to replace her with Pat?

"Pat's character is being developed for a starring role. She is getting incredible feedback from the viewers, and we'd like to see Pat develop into the woman that will head the boycotts and sit-ins when they eventually come to Wingate.

"That's why I feel as if we really need to showcase as much of the truth about racism as I can, in order for the civil rights movement to give a good payout."

Everything he was saying was really good, but Bailey couldn't get past two things; Pat replacing her as Bobby's love interest, and Pat ushering in the civil rights movement...

Wasn't she the one that was being affected by racism almost on a daily basis? It just seemed that it would be her character that would want to fight for equality in her community.

"I kind of thought Bailey would be the one to help with equal rights. She's dealing with it every day—"

"But Bailey is more the comic relief. Think in terms of Lucille Ball. She's great, and everyone loves her in that capacity. Which is not to say Bailey won't have some tough decisions. We are using her as a catalyst for what's to happen with Pat's story line."

The comic relief? But that's exactly what she didn't want! But then again, isn't that how she'd played it? But every human was multi-dimensional, she wanted to yell at him. That didn't mean being fun or funny, or sweet and kind, meant she couldn't be that bitch if she needed to be!

Too bad she'd only been that bitch behind the scenes...

He stood. "Let me show you something." He sounded excited, almost like he had when they'd first met the evening before shooting began.

She followed him into his office where he had files and folders laid out cluttering his desk. He went to his briefcase and removed a long, rolled sheet of paper.

He pinned it to the corkboard on the wall and then gazed at it proudly. It was a map.

She looked at it, closely.

"This is Wingate." His hand swept a broad section of the large map, but then moved upward. "And this is Garden Hill. We'll have restaurants, a theater, even a lounge." His fingers scanned another area. "Pat has a house here. She'll be moving into one her bio says was passed down from her parents. She'll be one of the few single Black homeowners in the entire show.

"There's going to be rowhouses here and farmland here." He looked at her again. "It takes time, but I'm pushing for it to be completed by mid-fall. We have people working around the clock and the show can't afford that. I'll be pulling from my own pockets to fund this, but it will be worth it in the long run because Wingate will be real."

He had a dreamy look in his eyes, but then he looked at her again. "That's why it was so devastating when you said you'd go door-to-door to the Negroes in the community, because we don't really have that—yet."

She shook her head, feeling terrible, but unsure how many ways she could apologize for what she'd done.

"Maybe we can just write that all out by having Bailey suck it up and face her neighbors the way you originally —"

He just smirked. "Well, it sounds like you'd rather be a writer for the show than an actor. As much as I don't mind an actor's input, I hope in the future you will leave the writing and development to the production team. Do you see any flaws in my ideas?"

"No." She shook her head and it was the truth. Now might not be the right time to suggest she have a bigger role in the upcoming civil rights movement. It sounded like she had to watch her back so she continued with a job.

"Trust in the process, Bailey." He looked at his wristwatch. "It's getting late and I need some shut-eye. Script changes are in your folder in the kitchen drawer. You can look them over tomorrow when you're doing your daily chores.

"Also, another change is, I'll be in your bed in the morning."

What?

He shook his head, apparently noting the surprised look on her face.

"I don't mean we'll be sleeping together. Bobby is going to oversleep in the morning...because honestly, I could use the extra hour of sleep. After you get up to make breakfast, I'll tuck in the trundle bed and get in your bed so you can do a scene waking him up in the morning."

"Okay." She nodded, being agreeable to about anything he had to say.

He headed for the bedroom. "I'm going to take a quick bath, and you should get some sleep. Six a.m. is going to get here pretty fast."

"True." She followed him into the bedroom but was preoccupied with the script changes he'd mentioned. While Bobby gathered his pajamas and underwear to take into the bathroom with him, she climbed back into bed.

"Good night," he said while giving her a grim look. "And I'm sorry if that conversation got heated."

"If it got heated, it's because I needed it," she said truthfully. "See you in the morning."

He cut off the light and then went into the bathroom.

Bailey lay in the dark, mulling over everything Robert had said. She thought about the Reddit post; Am I the Asshole? where people described scenarios in which they wanted an opinion on who was right and who was wrong.

I think on this one, Bailey Westbrook, you are the asshole.

Chapter Thirty-Three

Despite being troubled by her conversation with Robert, Bailey had fallen asleep before he climbed into his trundle bed. She didn't wake up until the shrill of the alarm sent her hand slapping at the device.

For once, she heard the signs of Bobby's sleep as his loud snores were briefly interrupted by a short snort. She heard him toss and snuggle against his pillow and then the snoring resumed.

She lay in bed rehashing her conversation with him, waves of embarrassment hitting her until she felt she would turn into a nervous wreck if she didn't stop replaying his words.

She had to work in front of cameras that captured her every expression, her every thought, and she had to be authentic while it happened. She simply could not do that unless she put everything about yesterday out of her mind. She would have to pretend everything was all right. It was a good thing she was an actress. Pretending is what she did.

She listened for a few more moments at the male snores that filled the room. Why had she not ever noticed that before? Probably because she was too busy snoring herself. After a long yawn, Bailey threw off her blankets and tiptoed to the bathroom.

She splashed her face, brushed her teeth, gargled, and then straightened her head scarf, making sure her hair pins peeked through just perfectly.

She studied herself in the mirror. Ugh, her eyes were puffy. She'd just have to put on a little eye makeup. After that was complete, she grabbed her robe—wishing for the hundredth time it wasn't so frilly—and then headed to the kitchen.

She saw her note to Bobby still on the kitchen table and then went to the refrigerator to see if the cobbler was gone. It was still there.

Hmph. He could have it for lunch, then. She tossed the note into the trash and then got out the items she wanted for breakfast. Today was a good day for Wheaties and sliced bananas. She was really too tired for anything else.

As the coffee brewed, she retrieved her organizer from the kitchen drawer and scanned her script changes while pretending she was just consulting her list of chores.

Wednesday: Bailey will complete ALL of her chores in preparation for mother-in-law's visit (since Bailey changed script by going grocery shopping yesterday instead of today!). Today is window cleaning day.

Wait. What? She checked yesterday's script and saw she *was* supposed to have spent time working on Saturday's menu.

She closed her eyes at what had been written. Someone had been in a pissy mood when they'd written that!

Woosah…

She closed the book and returned it to its proper place, promising herself she'd do better about keeping track of things.

She prepared Bobby's lunch and decided in addition to the peach cobbler, she would use the last of the roast beef (since he had apparently liked it so much), and she made him a sandwich with mustard and mayonnaise.

Once it was packed, she checked the clock and pretended to listen for Bobby to enter the room.

She poured herself a cup of coffee and added her cream and sugar, and when he still hadn't entered the room, she frowned and went into the bedroom as he had instructed her to do.

Uh-oh. She hoped he hadn't really overslept and had woken up long enough to move from the trundle bed to the big bed. She should have woken him up!

But when she entered the bedroom, she saw him in her bed and the trundle bed was securely in its place underneath.

What to do, what to do? Should she A: Throw cold water into his face to wake him up. Or B: Slather him with morning kisses?

She went with B, but was really feeling A.

She hurried to the bed and sat down on its edge. She leaned over and placed a gentle kiss on his cheek. He didn't move, but his snores stopped. He looked so different with his hair tussled and 5 o'clock shadow covering his rugged jaw.

She leaned forward again and kissed his jaw and then his chin and finally his lips.

His hands came up and wrapped around her waist, pulling her closer while also surprising her. Her hands moved up his chest to rest on his shoulders and she couldn't stop from thinking his muscles there were really hard.

She felt his lips part and the next thing she knew, he had captured her bottom lip between his.

Electricity rocketed through Bailey as the gentle, sweet kiss was instantly transformed.

Bobby's hand suddenly cupped her cheek. He held her there as the kiss deepened, his lips moving from one to the other.

And then he suddenly sat up. He actually shot up in bed, eyes wide.

Oh shit...had he been dreaming? Oh my God, he had been sleep-making out with her!

He looked at her, stunned, and then quickly covered his crotch with his hands!

Oh my God, he had morning wood!

They sat like for a few seconds before she realized getting them out of this mess was going to be on her shoulders because he was still trying to pull himself out of a sleep haze—and possibly the prelude to a wet dream.

"Honey," she chuckled. "You overslept. What time did you get in last night? I didn't even hear you come to bed."

She waited for him to say his part, to say anything. *Come on, Bobby, wake the hell up...*

"Jeezel Petes! What time is it?" He finally got it together.

"Quarter to seven—"

"I'm going to be late for work!" He made to throw back the sheets and jump out of bed, but then he probably remembered his morning wood and hesitated.

Uh...well, the cameras would most likely follow her, so she jumped up and waved her hands. "Babe, you better hurry." And with that, she dashed out of the room and went back to the kitchen.

Oh God…she wasn't sure what to do. She'd made out with Bobby…

She went to the table and poured milk into his bowl of cereal and then quickly sprinkled sugar over it. She then sat down to eat her own cereal, although food was the last thing on her mind. It was just the only thing she could do to keep things moving.

Had the cameras picked up on his erection even though she hadn't? And as a matter of curiosity, how big had that erection been?

Bailey! Stop tingling. This is not appropriate!

But it felt as if they had just been interrupted during foreplay. Lord have mercy! Maybe she needed to get laid. She hadn't had sex in over a year, and most times, was too preoccupied with memories of bad relationships to think much about the lack of it.

But she was obviously in need if she couldn't stop lusting after her boss!

She wasn't lusting! Not exactly…

But Lordy, the tingles weren't stopping.

Bobby finally rushed into the room, pulling on his jacket, his hat already on his head and briefcase in hand. He looked at her, but then his eyes swiftly shifted, not meeting hers.

"I'm sorry, honey! I'm late. No time for breakfast!"

She stood and grabbed his cup of coffee. "Not even time for coffee?"

He accepted it and took a drink. "Thanks, Bae. But I gotta go. Mr. Adams wants to talk to me about my ideas, and I need to have everything organized for the meeting."

He thrust the cup back to her after drinking half of the hot liquid and then turned to leave.

"Don't forget your lunch!" she called, and then grabbed it to give to him.

He gave her a crooked smile and accepted the lunch. "I'm sorry, Bae. Thank you." He stopped to give her a peck on the lips, but actually hesitated before doing it.

When their lips touched — even though it was just for a moment — Bailey felt as if her heart had jumped from her chest and was now in her throat.

When Bobby slowly pulled back, his blue eyes locked with hers and she visibly saw his dark pupils dilate. His lips parted and he swallowed.

"Have a good day," she said.

He blinked, and the spell came to an end. "You too!" He hurried out of the room.

Bailey had never wanted to press stop on the cameras as badly as she did in moment. But she knew how to remedy that. She went to the bathroom and shut the door, where she stayed hidden for a full fifteen minutes.

When Bailey left the bathroom, she had sufficiently pulled herself together and was dressed in her shorts and a blouse. Luckily, she had tossed them in the bathroom hamper, although they weren't the least dirty. How could they get dirty after ten minutes of stretching?

She stripped the covers down on the bed and opened the shades — it was a bit too chilly this morning to open the windows. She kept her mind blank as she went about her morning tasks.

She did her morning stretches while mentally saying, Don't think about Bobby. Don't think about Bobby.

As she dressed and unpinned her hair, she had to remind herself that just last night he had yelled at her. But even when she applied her makeup, she did it wondering if he liked the way she looked.

She put on a wrap dress, nothing fancy, since it was going to be a day of cleaning. She wore the heels for those that were surely subscribed to the stream just for the purpose of watching her clean while wearing heels and a full face of makeup.

But she was in no way fetish-shaming. To each his own.

Bailey made up the bed, resisting the urge to smell the pillows Bobby had used. She liked the way he smelled, even though they used the same soap. It smelled different on him, though.

After the bed was made she turned on the radio, tackled the kitchen, and left the half of chicken from the week before in the sink to thaw.

Today was window day, but she would be damned if she was going to wash all the windows in the house once a week. Maybe once a year.

But she would wash all of the windowsills. She imagined her mother-in-law roaming through the house with a white glove searching for dirt.

She grabbed a bucket of hot, soapy water, put on her gloves and then cleaned every sill in the house. There were twelve. And it took a long time.

When was done, she decided to give the furniture a waxing instead of just hitting it with the duster. This was something she actually enjoyed. The mid-century furniture was so pretty — and expensive.

The flowers from last week were half dead so she threw them out and put away the vase. Before her mother-in-law's visit, maybe she'd go out and buy more.

Bailey pulled out the vacuum cleaner next. But as she was going over the floors, she noticed the baseboards were in dire need of cleaning.

Out came another bucket of hot, soapy water, and Bailey cleaned the baseboards in the kitchen and living room. That hadn't been on any to-do list so once it was accomplished, she felt good.

With the house smelling of lemons and pinecones, Bailey consulted the Betty Crocker Cookbook for recipe ideas for the chicken.

She could make fried chicken, but didn't want the house smelling like grease after all the work she had put in.

Chicken and rice casserole! Nice. She'd eaten that as a kid and always liked it; plus, she had all the ingredients. She went to the pantry to grab them when the telephone rang.

Surprised, she grabbed the kitchen phone.

"Hello?"

"Hi, Bae." It was Bobby.

"Hi, Bobby. Is everything okay?"

"Yep, I just wanted to tell you I won't be home for dinner. We're going to be working late tonight. I'm so sorry."

She made a face. "It's fine, honey. Do you want me to bring you dinner? I can have Helen or Pat drive me —"

"No. Don't worry about that. I'll grab a burger. But I don't want you to wait up for me. I might be late."

"I understand, but I don't want you to work too hard..."

"I know. But it can't be avoided. You should take it easy today. Maybe you can call Helen or your friend Pat and go out."

"I don't know..." she said reluctantly. "I spent a lot of money this week already —"

"Don't worry, there's money in the bureau. I have to go, honey, we're in the middle of a huddle. Oh! Thanks for the sandwich and cobbler — everything was amazing." She smiled. "Love you, gotta run!"

"Bye, honey." She sighed and hung up the phone. She put the chicken in a dish and placed it in the refrigerator.

Well, that was one task off her list. She stretched and felt her back crack.

Bailey kicked off her shoes, and removed her apron and hung it on its hook in the pantry. She tried not to limp to the couch where she sank down into it with a sigh.

You might want me to go out to further Pat's story line, or use Helen as a catalyst to torture me racially — but I am going to take a long nap and figure out the rest later.

It didn't take much for her to get comfortable, and within moments, Bailey was sound asleep.

Chapter Thirty-Four

Bailey jerked and her eyes opened. She remembered the cameras and quickly wiped the corner of her mouth, just in case she had drooled.

It was just after four. She sat up and hurried to the bathroom and saw she only needed to do a little touch-up on her makeup.

Now ready to face the cameras, Bailey slipped on her heels and touched her growling belly. She couldn't think about eating right now when she had to figure out what was going to come next for her.

Should she allow herself to be racially profiled in front of Helen, or should she further the story line of her possible replacement?

With a sigh, she picked up the telephone and dialed.

"Hello?"

"Hey, Pat. Are you busy?"

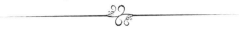

"I can't believe you don't know Billy. He's everybody's friend."

"Well, I was raised in Dayton, so unless I saw him at the bank, I wouldn't know him."

Pat took a draw from her cigarette and nodded. "I keep forgetting you weren't raised here in Wingate." The three of them were in Pat's car; her, Pat, and of course, the back seat cameraman.

"He's a hoot, and the juke joint he's running ain't half bad. He's got all the latest music, beer and liquor, plus his granny cooks all the food."

"That sounds good, because I am starving."

"I'm just happy you're stepping out and letting your hair down, sis. I know you think married women aren't supposed to do that. But when a married woman's husband tells her to go out and have fun, then you can't blame nobody but him!"

Bailey grinned. "I guess you're right."

Pat hummed to the tune playing on the radio and after a few moments, the cameraman lowered the camera. Bailey looked over her shoulder at him quizzically.

He answered before she asked. "There's no filming out here until Garden Hills is finished. We'll pick up again once we get to the juke joint."

"Girl, they are working day and night trying to get everything done. I can barely get any sleep with all the heavy equipment and banging." Pat was smiling broadly despite the complaint. She put out her cigarette and rolled down the window. "You should see the house they're building for me! I love it. They actually shipped in an old farmhouse. Can you believe?"

"They shipped in your house?" Bailey asked in surprise.

"Yep. You're not going to believe this, but they're giving me a starring role!"

"I heard," she grinned. "Congratulations."

"They want everything in the house authentic, since I'll have scenes filmed there. You should see the old, retro-style refrigerator and stove. They actually scare the living daylights out of me!" she laughed. "I can't believe all the things that's happening to me. Robert said he wanted a vibrant young Black woman to usher in the upcoming civil rights movement. I just can't believe it all!"

Bailey couldn't believe it either. Robert had actually shared his vision with her? Because he sure wasn't all interested in "sharing" with her.

"I am so excited for you, Pat. What about the other ladies from the beauty shop?"

"They all got hired as regulars!"

"And you're the only one that got a starring role?"

"So far. But they're still hiring."

"Well, I'm happy for you."

"This is good for all of us! I love the direction Robert's taking this show."

Bailey smiled and nodded.

When they reached Billy's house, Bailey saw several cars parked up and down the street. They weren't the only ones arriving, either. The camera began filming again and the two friends hurried up the walk where a man wearing a bowling shirt and fedora hat was greeting his guests. She saw the man accepting a dollar from the new arrivals.

Pat turned to her. "I forgot to tell you, it costs a dollar to enter, but it's on me. I'm just so happy you came out."

"Are you sure?"

"Yeah, you can get us beers once we're inside."

"Pattycakes!" The host called when he saw them. He and Pat hugged.

"Billy, this is my friend Bailey."

Billy gave her a long, up-and-down look. "Bailey. I see. Nice to meet you." He took her hand and then gallantly kissed her knuckles.

Pat laughed. "Maybe I should have introduced her as *MRS.* Bailey Banks."

Billy immediately released her hand. "Oh. That will be two dollars, please."

Pat slapped two dollar bills into his hand and then pushed her way past him and into the house.

"Nice to meet you," Bailey called while hurrying after Pat. The house was a nice two stories. The furniture had been pushed against the walls to give space as several couples danced in a rapid style in the center of the room. Foldout chairs—the kind found at church potluck dinners—had been situated around, but most people were dancing or standing around.

The music was loud, but nice. Several people saw Pat and greeted her, but Pat didn't spend much time talking to others and took her hand and led her to a table where an older woman had a cooler filled with drinks.

"Let's get some beers," Pat said while shaking her hips to the music.

"Maybe we should eat something first," Bailey suggested.

"Y'all want some food?" the older lady asked. Presumably, she was Billy's grandma. "That'll be five cents a plate."

"Yes, ma'am." Bailey dug into her pocketbook for the coins and passed them to the woman, who dropped them into a change-holder she retrieved from her brassier. After she put it back into place, she got up and shuffled over to a buffet table where she began uncovering various trays of food.

She piled each plate with a healthy helping of collard greens, two pieces of spareribs, potato salad, and cornbread while Bailey looked on in amazement.

Her belly groaned in hunger as she accepted her plate.

"Y'all want a beer or pop?" the old lady asked.

They got a drink too? Hell yeah! She got a Coke while Pat got a beer, then they took seats off to the side of the dancing bodies.

The food was finger-licking good and no sooner did they finish eating than Pat pulled her up and onto the floor to dance.

"Come on! Let's cut a rug, Bailey!"

Bailey quickly wiped her hands on her napkin while being dragged along by Pat. She couldn't help but laugh as the two danced together. She knew nothing about the dance steps of this era, and some of these people looked like they were straight from the Cotton Club in Harlem. But in the end, the music was lively, the crowd was enthusiastic, and her feet began to move while her hips went into a shimmy.

Bailey had to admit, she needed this. Everything about 1954 had been work, and when not work, it had been about pretending not to want to drop down into a sleep coma. She had enjoyed making out with Bobby, but this was the first time she'd actually had fun.

Billy's juke joint was Robert Chesterfield's greatest creation, in Bailey's humble opinion.

But that thought didn't last very long because she soon saw someone leaning against the wall, drinking a beer. It was Curtis the milkman.

She scowled.

Pat caught the look. "What's wrong? You need to sit for a while?"

Bailey nodded, and once they were seated on one of the couches, she gestured with her head. "I finally met Curtis."

"Oh, that's good. Curtis is great, and he is super fine! Don't you think?"

"I mean…he's not bad on the eyes, but that don't mean nothing to me. He treated me like he didn't approve of my marriage choice."

Pat squinted at her. "Are you sure? That doesn't sound like the Curtis I know."

"A man in town bumped into me and knocked one of my bags out of my hands—a white man. Curtis helped me and we got to talking. Everything was fine until he figured out who I was married to."

"Oh my God, Bailey. I'm so sorry. I can't believe he was rude to you. Was that why you called me?"

She nodded. "It was just a bad day, all the way around."

Pat looked over to where Curtis was standing with his beer. "Well, I can't fix everything about the craziness in the world, but you two are good friends of mine and I can fix that."

Pat stood, and to Bailey's horror, she sauntered over to where Curtis was standing. Curtis's expression brightened when he saw her and the two briefly hugged. He was all smiles—but then Pat pointed to where she was sitting and his expression immediately changed.

Bailey looked away as if searching for an escape route. But there was no escaping. She was in the middle of nowhere, and was going to have to deal with this.

She looked at them again and Pat was reading him the riot act. Bailey's stomach dropped. Having Curtis not like her felt like the school jock was friends with everyone she knew but thought she was Quasimodo! Besides, what happened to Curtis not wanting to act? All of a sudden, he had speaking roles.

She saw Curtis reluctantly nod his head and then he and Pat headed to where she was sitting. She quickly stood up, wishing she had kept her damn mouth shut.

A lot of things about yesterday had truly bothered her, but his abrupt change in attitude toward her had cut deep. She was fully prepared to go up against the white people in town, but she had never expected to be alienated from the Blacks.

"Bailey," Pat said with a broad smile. "I want to properly introduce you to my friend Curtis Jackson. And Curtis, meet my very good friend Bailey Banks."

Curtis sighed and forced a smile. "Bailey. Nice to meet you again."

"Hi, Curtis," she replied.

"Let's all sit and get to know each other."

Curtis reluctantly nodded and gestured for them to sit on the couch and he followed suit.

"So, I hear you're a newlywed and congratulations are in order."

Bailey nodded. "We've been married for about a month and a half, and just moved into our own house a week ago."

"It must be very exciting."

She smiled slightly. "It is."

Pat stood. "I'm going to get another beer. You two keep talking." She disappeared.

"So, how do you know Pat?" Bailey asked.

"We basically grew up together, went to the same school. My sisters were friends with her. How do you know her?"

"We worked together at the bank. When I got out of college, I got the job at the bank and Pat showed me around and helped me a lot."

He nodded. "Pat is good people. Sometimes she can be a busybody, but…"

"She has good intentions."

He straightened. "Look, Mrs. Banks—"

"Please call me Bailey."

"Bailey," he nodded. "I should apologize. I didn't mean to be rude the day I first met you."

"That guy that bumped into me was the one that was rude. I appreciate you stopping to help. You didn't have to—"

"I did. I was raised by Mrs. Jackson, and she taught me to be a gentleman—to everyone."

She gave him a wry smile. "Even to someone like me?"

He took a swig of his beer. "I have nothing against you."

"I guess I get the feeling you don't approve of my choices."

"Look, Mrs. Banks—Bailey—I don't need any trouble, and I need my job—"

Her brow shot up. "I'd never do anything to jeopardize your job. Look, Curtis, I don't know you, and I don't know why you'd judge me, but know this much about me: I'd never jeopardize a Colored man's job. You don't have to like me and I don't have to like you. Let's just leave it like that." She stood, but before she could walk away, Curtis was standing also.

"Wait. Bailey. I'm sorry. I truly have nothing against you. Look, you seem like a nice lady. I know Wingate and the people in it. Especially the white people." He shook his head and his expression became grim.

"This is the North, and people say things are different up here. And God knows I wouldn't want to be in the South right now. But it's not so much different. Whites just hide their intent a little better. Lord forbid they allow their Klan to march down Main Street. They just hide in the Governor's Mansion or the Sherriff's Department.

"So again, I apologize. But for the life of me, I don't understand how an obviously educated Colored woman would choose to marry a white man."

Bailey stared at Curtis — the man that said he didn't want to be an actor. The man looked like a super model, and could have been the true star of this production, and she wanted to applaud him. This man had thrown his whole entire self into that speech!

She had to do it justice. This was truth. This was education time.

Bailey drew in an angry breath. "You don't need to apologize to me, Mr. Jackson. You obviously know more about Bobby and me then we do. But here is the thing you don't know. We chose each other knowing how hard it was going to be, and that includes losing friends, family, and even acceptance from people we don't even know. And guess what? While it bothers me, even hurts me, I know my husband faces discrimination too, and he still looks at me as if I'm the best thing that ever walked into his life.

"It's hard knowing the whites in the world look down their noses at me because of my color. And I know some Negroes do the same because they think I want to be something I'm not. And those people don't even realize how much more work goes into the simple act of choosing to live your life with the one you love—openly, in front of God, your loved ones, as well as your enemies!"

Bailey gripped her purse, her heart thumping in her chest as she walked away. Most of the people had stopped dancing to look at her and Curtis. Pat was watching from across the room with a fresh beer in her hands.

Bailey was almost at the door when she felt Curtis's hand on her arm.

"Bailey. Wait." She turned, not wanting to go out the door because the community hadn't been finished, and she hadn't thought that far ahead.

She looked at the hand lightly gripping her arm and Curtis quickly released it and held up his hands.

"Bailey, I don't know why I said what I did. I know more good whites living here in Wingate than bad ones. But it's hard. The white women here are relentless. They throw themselves at me every time I turn around. I couldn't even speak in polite company the things I've seen them do in order to get my attention.

"There's never a day that passes when I don't wonder if I'm going to end up lynched by some redneck that thinks I have intentions on his woman." He drew in a shaky voice. "I have to smile extra and move quick so I don't give these women the impression I'm rejecting them. Because all it would take is one to whisper I'm uppity to get me killed. I think about that every single day of my life."

Bailey swallowed. Nobody could tell her this man wasn't a primo actor.

Pat was suddenly there between them. "Hey, guys...I'm so sorry. I thought if I left you two to talk it out—"

"It's fine, Pat. I think I understand Curtis a lot better. I...understand why he feels the way he does about me."

Curtis shook his head quickly. "No, Bailey, it's me that understands better. I judged you unfairly for something so stupid as who you chose to live your life with. Folks in Wingate have done that to me for years because they assume I..." He looked down in embarrassment.

"That you mess around with those white women," Pat filled in.

"Right. And whether I do or don't isn't anyone's business but my own. But rumors like that will get me killed. I guess I was just taking out my anger on someone else. Someone who doesn't deserve it. Please forgive me, Bailey. I don't think badly of you. I really don't. And I still think you're a highly intelligent woman."

They looked at her expectantly.

She nodded. "Of course, but there's nothing to forgive. Let's just put this all behind us."

"Let me buy you a beer," he said. And for the first time that night, she saw a light come on in his eyes.

"I'd better not. It's getting late—"

"Late?" He chuckled. "It's not even seven o'clock!" He looked at Pat. "She looks young, but she acts like an old married woman."

Pat laughed, and Bailey had to cover her mouth to prevent herself from doing the same.

"One beer, and then I should be getting home."

"Okay, just one."

Curtis hurried to purchase the beer and Pat nudged her.

"You see? He's not so bad."

She nodded and smiled.

Chapter Thirty-Five

They spent the next hour talking, mostly about music. Curtis seemed to know everything about bebop and all the musicians that made it popular.

Bailey had a hard time believing he had learned all of these facts just for this role. In fact, listening to him talking about music was really interesting, and she wished she knew about the music of this time period.

By eight o'clock, they each agreed it was time to leave and Pat had her back home by eight thirty. That left her only half an hour of filming before her cameras stopped for the evening. Bobby's car was parked in the driveway and she wondered if he had already turned in for the night. He had been working double-time over the last few days, thanks to her.

"You promise to do this again, won't you, Bailey?" Pat called while pulling out of the driveway.

"Yes, it was fun!"

"Okay, bye, sis!" She watched as Pat drove off and then heard the door open as Bobby stepped out onto the porch to greet her.

He looked after the car as it drove away. "Was that your friend, Pat? I didn't get a chance to meet her."

She walked to the house and he held out his arms for her. She slipped into a comfortable hug, to which he added a quick kiss to her forehead."

"Sorry, honey," she replied. "Maybe we can have her out for dinner one evening."

"Yes, we should do that." He led her into the house. "Did you have fun tonight?" His brow rose. "Did you have beer?"

She quickly placed her hand against her lips. "Just one." She peeked at him. "You don't mind, do you?"

"No. Where did you go?"

She opened the closet and hung up her hat and jacket. "Pat has a friend; Billy throws these house parties."

"A party in the middle of the week?" Bobby asked.

Bailey kicked off her shoes and padded into the living room with them in hand.

"He runs it like a lounge. It's in his grandmother's house—and I think he's doing a good bit of business." She sank onto the couch and sighed peacefully. "He charges a dollar for entrance."

Bobby sat down beside her and lifted her feet so they were on his lap.

"A dollar!" he paused to exclaim. "That's a lot to charge just for a party."

"Well, it's closer to being a lounge than a party. They had music from Delta blues to jazz, swing, and bebop. Everybody danced and drank beer, which they sold for a nickel. And you could get a plate of food also for just a nickel, and then a free drink with it.

"Ooo boy, I haven't eaten so good in so long. Billy's grandma cooked barbecued ribs, greens, potato salad, and cornbread." She got comfortable as he gently rubbed her feet. "One day, Bobby Bailey, I'm going to cook you some collard greens."

"Mmm, sounds good. Do you know how to cook collards?"

Bailey's eyes came fully alert with that question. She stared at him without commenting. Asking a Black woman if she knew how to cook collard greens?! Was he trying to get her Black card revoked?

He had the decency to blush. "What am I saying? Of course you know how to cook collard greens."

She relaxed and nodded in satisfaction at his response.

"How was work? Did you get your project completed?" she asked.

"No, but we're over the hump. They want to do an entire series on McCarthy and the witch hunts involving all his innocent victims. People like my parents automatically believed in a government conspiracy by the communists. But I feel most people our age see McCarthy as the true danger to American democracy."

"Will you get the byline?"

"No. Since it's a series, Mr. Adams wants us all to share in the credits."

She sat up and leaned in to snuggle next to him. His arm moved around her shoulders and he cradled her against his body.

"That's not fair! This is all your idea."

"It started as my idea—and I will get credit for. But it's really evolved since that suggestion. I guess I don't mind sharing the work. Besides, it will be very controversial, and Mr. Adams doesn't want the brunt of it to fall on any one person's shoulders. Also, at least I'll be home for breakfast and dinner again."

Well, she guessed that meant a return to spending the evenings making out. She wasn't really feeling that anymore.

"You look tired. Why don't you go to bed? I'll close the curtains and windows and then I'll be right there."

Bailey nodded and lifted her head and gave him a peck on the lips.

"Okay, honey. See you in a bit." She left the room. Wow, there was not even the tiniest spark—at least not for her.

Bailey took her bath, wishing for the hundredth time for a shower. She was certain people in the '50s had showers. And while the bath was a nice way to relax, it just wasn't always practical.

As she bathed, Bailey reviewed her scenes with Curtis. He was an amazing actor. She hoped she'd get to work with him more.

When she got out of the tub, she was surprised to see Bobby in his trundle bed, wide awake.

She gave him a curious look as she sat at her vanity to quickly wrap her hair.

"What are you still doing up? I thought you would have been long asleep by now."

"I am tired," he admitted. "Um...I thought we should talk." She gave him a quick look. What did she do wrong this time? "About what happened...in the bedroom."

Oh, jeez. Why did he have to bring that up?

"I am incredibly sorry!" His words erupted from him in a quick rush. "I swear nothing like that will ever happen again. Please don't think I'm a pervert—"

"Stop." He did. His face was filled with terror and had gone white. The poor guy probably thought she was going to file sexual harassment charges against him.

"I didn't even think any more about it," she lied. "It's a biological function—"

He sighed in discomfort. "We don't have to kiss anymore. We can go back to just hugging."

She shrugged. "Whatever you want."

He didn't say anything for a moment, and Bailey rubbed lotion into her hands and headed for her bed.

"Well." He stopped. "I mean, I think the kissing brought so much authenticity to Bobby and Bailey's relationship..."

"Then we can continue kissing. And I promise not to sneak up on you again while you're sleeping."

She pulled back her blankets and climbed into bed.

She was about to tell him good night when he finally continued speaking.

"I probably shouldn't say this, but...I feel as if I have to. So, I apologize if I'm speaking out of turn, but I've become attracted to you. I'm not talking physically!" he added quickly. "Although that is part of it. I felt a pull to you from the beginning, during the audition. You made me see things I hadn't really thought about before with anyone else; your story line, your enthusiasm, your wide-eyed eagerness and your humor. It's just...everything about you.

"I've tried to remain professional and...but I'm sure every time I look at you, you can see exactly how I feel. Sometimes I even think you can hear my heart beating in my chest.

"I know this is not the way a boss should feel about one of his employees! I know it's not right—especially with everything happening with my father. I'm not that man! And I would never want you or any other person to think I'd take advantage of my position.

"So, I felt as if I should say something because...I keep putting my foot in my mouth and making the stupidest mistakes in trying to put distance between us when the last thing I want is distance between us. I think about you, Bailey, while I'm in my office going over film and writing scripts. I'm thinking about you when I'm in this house, sleeping in this bed. I'm thinking about you when I sit opposite you and share a meal you prepared with me in mind.

"I know it's just a role, but this role is something I've always wanted. And I guess I just need to realize I need to separate myself—my true self—from Bobby and Bailey Banks and remember I'm Robert Chesterfield Jr. and you're Bailey Westbrook and this isn't 1954."

Bailey held her breath through Bobby's entire speech. When she remembered to breathe, she slowly sat up and stared over the side of the bed where she saw him lying there with his lower lip captured lightly between his teeth. His eyes met hers and just as she had always been able to see every inflection of his irises and the dilation of his pupils, looking at him now, she saw in his eyes the raw, naked fear of a man that had just jumped out of an airplane without his parachute.

Chapter Thirty-Six

Bobby and Bailey looked at each other, the silence stretching, and then he sat up. "Um...I should go." He began to climb out of his bed.

"Wait," Bailey said. "No, don't leave."

He gave her a hesitant look and then sat back down. "I don't expect you to...you know. I just had to say—"

"I wouldn't have had the courage to...I mean." She spoke hesitantly. "I *didn't* have the courage to say it." Bailey took a deep breath and did a free fall from the same damn plane.

"I think we both feel a connection."

He smiled. "I knew it! I knew I wasn't crazy. You're a good actress, but I knew."

Bailey smiled. "So, you think about me a lot?"

He closed his eyes and shook his head. "Too much. I don't even like anyone else touching your footage. I put it together myself—but not in a creepy way!" he added quickly.

Bailey giggled. "It's okay. I think about you all the time too."

They both sat there smiling.

"What made you say something?" she asked. "You have so much more courage than I do."

"No." He shook his head quickly. "I've been a nervous wreck all day. You would have thought I was an insane man if I didn't say something. It was just a leap of faith. I only took that leap because I just knew when we're together, it's..." he chuckled. "Beautiful."

If she smiled any more, her cheeks were going to go numb. "Where do we go from here?"

"Well, we're already married." His eyes got wide. "I didn't mean it like that! I just mean, we already skipped courting and moved straight to shacking up." He palmed his face, and Bailey hid her grin.

"It's weird," she admitted. "We're playing a married couple—newlyweds, at that. Do you think we feel this way because we're playing two people who love each other?"

He shook his head. "I can't speak for you, but..." His smile softened. "I knew you were special during your audition. You slipped right into the role, which was a given. It's what we wanted. But the way you made me feel, Bailey, as if I was really Bobby Banks and we were really married and starting our lives together...

"And the reason that's so special for me is because when I was a kid, I used to dream about a normal, traditional life, and that feeling stayed with me when I became an adult, which is why I had to create The '50s Experience.

"When you auditioned, you gave me that feeling again. I knew in that very moment I not only wanted you in the production, but I wanted to selfishly play opposite you."

She looked at him in confusion.

"You were meant to be Drew's wife."

"Drew? Are you for real?"

He smiled ruefully. "But I wanted to play opposite you. So...I guess from the beginning, I wasn't ever acting." Bobby looked away. "I know how that sounds..."

Bailey reached out and took his hand. He looked at their hands together and then gripped hers lightly.

"I know exactly what you mean! It doesn't feel like I'm acting. Whenever we're together, it's almost like being transported back to the '50s."

It made so much more sense. Bobby was never acting. In playing the role of her husband, he was just fulfilling a childhood fantasy. That's why it was so easy for her to fall for him. Through this production, he was living the life he had always wanted.

He was nodding enthusiastically. "This production is my life, Bailey. So, I knew by making you my—I mean, Bobby's—wife, I'd have to make some major changes to the story line. Like adding racism. In my perfect 1950s experience, I didn't think about civil rights or feminism, or even LGBTQ. But this year, we're delving into all of."

That pleasantly surprised her. "I didn't know."

"Yeah, we have someone who wants to come out on the show. They—I'm not sure of their pronouns— want to have a cross-dressing story line, and I'm obsessed with it." He looked at her sheepishly. He was still holding her hand and gave it a slight squeeze. "Not as much as I'm obsessed with our story line, though.

"It's not easy, because in doing the right thing for the show, I'm hurting Bailey." His smile was now completely gone. "You've probably been able to tell I get heavily effected by Bailey's sadness. After that barbeque..." He shook his head. "The scene that was the most pivotal for the entire season was the one that...crushed me."

This time, she squeezed his hand. "I think intuitively, I knew all of this already. I suppose it's the connection we're both feeling. But I'm not going to lie to you. It hasn't always been easy. The hardest thing is not knowing." He watched her intently, and she could tell he was taking in her every word. "I'm feeling anxiety and being weird about things I know are only an act."

He bit his lip slightly. "Bailey. I tried something new this year. In 1953, I controlled every aspect of each scene. But this year, I wanted to give control to the characters. I tell them what I expect, and I give them a rough idea of when I want it to happen, and then I let it go. So, honey, I honestly don't know what's going to happen when you step out of this house. But I can promise to tell you more about what I've instructed other actors to do.

"Like Curtis. I didn't expect him to come to me and ask for a speaking role. He told me he wanted to play a Black man that's fed up with his treatment in the white community. I didn't know he was going to give you the cold shoulder when he saw you in Wingate, and I didn't know you two were going to have such a dynamic confrontation at Billy's place. But it was amazing! I could have never written that scene. I don't even know if I would have wanted to write it."

"I was going to ask you about him. He surprised me, but he kind of reminds me of you in that it doesn't completely feel like he's acting."

Bobby nodded. "I know. We're developing a story line and it's going to be good. I'm reluctant to share it because I'm giving him free rein."

She sighed. "Look, I understand about not knowing and leaving a lot up to the characters. And in truth, the surprises have added to the authenticity. So, I get it. I need to be the one who stops trying to look at this as an acting job and just...get into the moment."

He kissed her knuckles and smiled. "You are an actress, and I appreciate what you bring to the table. And you're right that I'm asking you to go beyond acting. But it's up to you, Bailey. From now on, I'm going to leave my master copy of the script in the bathroom under the sink. You can read it anytime you want.

"I have a scene coming up tomorrow evening where I take you on a walk around the block and we finally meet Mr. Edelman. He says something to me and we have a confrontation."

"Oh, so it's your turn to be racially targeted."

He smiled. "Yep. But I'm sure Bobby doesn't go completely unscathed. I have a feeling his archnemesis, George McGee, has more against him than just simple rivalry. Luckily, his boss is forward-thinking. And Bobby's mom probably has plenty to say about his choice in a wife."

"Yeah! What's going to happen with that?"

His brow went up. "Do you really want to know?"

She twisted her lip. "Not really. I know Bailey has to behave as a proper 1950s housewife, regardless." She glanced down at their clasped hands. She liked holding Bobby's hand.

"So...what happens next?" she asked again.

"Well...I'd like to date you, Bailey Westbrook."

Bailey's eyes grew bright and her cheeks hurt from so much smiling.

"That's going to be hard to do when we work six days a week."

He shook his head. "Not at all. Bobby's taking you to a movie after dinner with Mom. And it's a real movie so...I guess that could be our first date."

She didn't know what to say because she was grinning so hard. "I like that." They would date through Bobby and Bailey. How surreal. But it was what she wanted, if she was going to be completely honest.

"It's like what I said before. Being my wife trumps being my girlfriend."

"Your girlfriend?" She tried to hide her grin.

His mouth opened and then closed. "Uh..."

"I'm just kidding. Neither Baileys will be dating anyone but you."

He grinned in relief. "Good, because Bobby doesn't play around. He's as serious as a heart attack about the woman he loves, and Robert Chesterfield is just Bobby living his dream life."

A thrill shot through Bailey at those words. He had said girlfriend, but in a roundabout way, he also said love. It was obviously too early to even think about love, but she got what he was saying. If she was Bailey Banks, then her world would be her husband — and with everything she was feeling, she was only a hop, a skip, and a jump from being that woman.

Bobby gave her hand a final kiss before releasing it. "We should get some shut-eye." He got up and turned off the light and then climbed back into his trundle bed. She sank beneath her covers. "I do have one request."

"Sure. Whatever you want."

"I'd like to be able to talk to you like this when the cameras stop rolling at night. I know you said you don't like coming out of character—"

"I can do that. I only said that about not coming out of character because I didn't want you to become...a different Bailey. But you're not. You are Bailey Banks." She heard him yawn. "Sleep tight, honey."

"Good night, Bobby."

"Good night, Bae."

Chapter Thirty-Seven

When Bailey awoke the next morning, the world seemed completely different. She smiled for a few moments while listening to Bobby's regular breathing. She had slept very well, and her night had been filled with wonderful dreams. She couldn't quite recall them, only the impression of her and Bobby, which had left her waking up feeling good.

She quietly climbed out of bed and went to the bathroom, where she quickly got ready for the day. When she crept out of the room, she heard Bobby stir.

"'Morning," he said with a yawn.

"Good morning."

"See you in a little bit," he mumbled.

She grinned. "Yeah, you will."

He chuckled sleepily.

"I'm going to cook you a big breakfast, so don't you oversleep."

"Oh? Okay. I'll be sure to be timely."

Bailey went to the kitchen wearing a grin. She wondered fleetingly how many couples in Wingate woke up wearing a smile like this. How many couples, in general?

Okay, she was going to have to get rid of the smile. She was, after all, a new housewife that had dragged herself out of bed in order to make breakfast and pack a lunch for her husband. Most people wouldn't find that a reason to smile—well, unless they had gotten some good loving the night before.

She had to stop herself from chuckling.

Okay. Big breakfast coming up!

She got the bacon in the oven the way Bobby did it and then set some sausage patties frying in the skillet. She got the grits going and then made French toast. She would have done pancakes, especially since they had the instant stuff, but this took the place of eggs. The coffee had just finished brewing when Bobby came into the room.

Her heart raced when she saw him entering the kitchen while straightening his tie. He never just walked into the kitchen. He was always pulling on his jacket or fiddling with his collar or tie. Why was he so cute?

His eyes locked on her and she saw him grin. "Good morning. It smells like Thanksgiving in here."

She went over to give him a casual morning kiss but she had been waiting to do this all night and all morning long—and she suspected he had as well. He put his hands on her hips and pulled her forward.

Bailey couldn't stop looking into his vibrant, blue eyes. He closed them and then kissed her. It was brief, but electricity still shot through her body. And when he pulled back, he placed his cheek on hers.

"'Morning," he said again. And this time it was like he was saying it to her, and not to Mrs. Banks.

"Good morning," she said, and then she couldn't help herself when she kissed him once more. He smiled and then she saw what she had been waiting for. His eyes dilated until the blue was a narrow ring. She drew in a relieved breath.

"Pour the coffee," she said while pulling back, "while I grab the milk."

He did, and then took his seat, staring at the spread of food. "What's the occasion? We just got married, so I didn't miss our anniversary."

She poured him a glass of milk and then took her seat. "You've been working hard for the last few days and I want my man to know that I appreciate it."

Bobby had already dived into the food. "Thank you, Bae." He grabbed another sausage patty. "I know what I'm having for lunch."

"What do you want for lunch?" she asked.

"A sausage and bacon sandwich made with French toast."

"We'll definitely have enough leftovers."

They ate and talked about nothing and everything. When he finally stood to head off to work, she handed him his packed lunch and they both knew what came next.

Bailey slid her hands up his chest and gave him a goodbye kiss. Again, he lingered long enough to press his cheek against hers.

"See you this evening. I'll be home on time," he spoke murmured while still cuddling.

"Okay," she replied breathlessly. "Have a good day." Neither made a move.

Bobby had to pull himself away. She watched him leave before remembering that a lot of people were watching them right now.

She turned to look at the mess in the kitchen and then with a sigh, Bailey headed off to the bedroom to get ready for her day.

Today was laundry day and this time, she was going to be smart about it. She wore slacks, a cute sweater, and her sneakers. She was all for heels and skirts while cleaning, but not walking out into the backyard and hanging clothes. She didn't need her heels sinking into the grass.

Bailey turned on the radio in the garage and felt more confidant working with the old-fashioned washing machine and wringer.

While her clothes were in the agitator, she pulled out one of the lawn chairs and read the paper while music played in the background.

"Hi, neighbor."

Bailey's head jerked up. She saw her neighbor waving at her from across the fence. It was Haley, the blonde bombshell.

Bailey put down her paper and waved. "Hi."

"I see you're enjoying this beautiful weather."

"It is beautiful." Bailey stood and walked over to the fence. "I'm actually doing laundry, but the clothes are still washing, so I'm just relaxing out here."

"I hate hanging laundry. I always imagine Jeff or Hank looking at my delicates."

Eww. Bailey realized she didn't want the world looking at hers either. She decided to hang her undies in the bathroom. And she'd hang Bobby's boxers there too, just in case there were perverts watching on stream.

"I've wanted to come by to apologize about what happened Saturday," Haley said. "It's one of the worst things about living in a small town. The people are small-minded. I personally don't have an issue with mixed relationships. Lucille Ball married a Cuban—or whatever Ricky Riccardo is; some type of Latin.

"I dated an Italian for a while. Anyway, I'm sorry they acted so ugly, and I'm sorry it took me so long to tell you. I'm Haley, by the way, in case you forgot."

"Would you like to come over for a cup of coffee, or maybe tea?" Bailey asked. It would be nice to have more allies in the neighborhood.

"Sure. You got anything harder than tea or coffee?"

"No. I should get wine—"

"No worries. Why don't you come over to my place and I'll make us cocktails."

"Okay." She was intrigued by how others lived. Helen's house was just way out there. And she still had to finish decorating her own house. The Sears and Roebuck catalogue had a lot to choose from, and not much of it was to her liking. But she still needed to stay with the times.

There was no back gate leading to her house, so Bailey told her she'd meet her at her front door.

Haley let her in with a broad smile. "Come in." Bailey stepped into the house and looked around.

The living room was eclectic. She had framed posters of cabaret performers and musicians. There was a suede fainting couch piled with pillows of every type. There was a frilly sofa and loveseat that looked too delicate for a hefty man to sit on comfortably.

The music playing from an old-fashioned record player sounded like Dizzy Gillespie. Exotic rugs covered her living room floor. She had a fireplace, but it had a sculpture inside instead of logs. Photos of all kinds rested on her mantel. But Bailey loved the Tiffany-style lamps on her mismatched side tables the most.

She loved the way the house had been decorated. It was an older style than fifties, but the vintage quality was evident.

"Your home is very nice."

"Thank you. Have a seat." Haley walked to a fancy wooden bar. "What's your drink of choice?"

It was barely noon, and she didn't really have a drink of choice. She drank a beer once or twice a year, and occasionally enjoyed a glass of Moscato or something equally as sweet. She had never developed a taste for hard liquor—although cocktails were supposed to be more palatable.

"I'll have whatever you're having."

"Good." Haley began preparing the drinks as she chatted. "I would ask how you like the neighborhood, but I'll just ask how you like your house."

Bailey smiled. "The house is great. We're still just starting out, so we still have a ways to go before we get it completely decorated."

"That's right. You're a newlywed."

"Yes. It's just been a few months."

"Your husband works for the newspaper, right?"

"Yes. He just got on there."

Haley walked over with two drinks. "Do you like old-fashions?"

"I've never had one." She accepted her drink. "But it's pretty."

"Then you'll like it. It's bourbon, but has oranges and a maraschino cherry.

"Thank you." Haley took a sip and Bailey did as well. Yep. This had real liquor. No fake drinks here. But it was also sweet and tasty. Thank goodness she'd had a big breakfast to soak up this liquor.

"How long have you lived in Wingate?" Bailey asked.

"I moved here with one of my husbands about five years ago. He was raised here. After the divorce, I got the house...and stuck in this hick town."

Bailey took another sip of the drink, warming up to it. "Where would you live if you weren't here?"

"Vegas," she replied without missing a beat. She sat opposite Bailey on the love seat and then lit a cigarette. She offered one to Bailey, who declined with a short shake of her head.

"That's where I dated the Italian. He was in the Mob."

"The Mob! Weren't you scared?"

"Not in the least. They're nothing but a bunch of teddy bears. And they know how to treat a lady — parties every night with movie stars and singers. And the gifts! I had diamonds and furs. But then I married that jackass, and look where it got me."

"You could sell and go back."

340

Haley sipped her drink. "I've thought about it. But even with all the fun, Vegas didn't have much security. The men are great, but there was always another pretty face just around the corner..." She took another draw from her cigarette. "I'd go, but only as a visitor.

"What I really need is a nice catch, like you have. Now a stable, good-looking fella is a real jackpot."

Bailey nodded and grinned. "I'd have to agree with that."

"So...does that gorgeous man of yours have a brother?" Haley watched her closely.

"No brother."

"Hmm," Haley said resolutely. "So, Bailey, what do you enjoy doing?"

She found Haley's questions a bit strange. "I've actually been too busy to enjoy much these days. But I used to enjoy reading and—"

"Have you ever read *Lady Chatterley's Lover*?"

"No..." What in the hell?

Haley leaped up and headed for a bookshelf. "You can read my copy." Bailey accepted the book. "I've highlighted the best parts."

"Okay."

"Go ahead and keep it. I've read it a million times."

"Thank you." Oh my God...what kind of 1950s swinger crap was this!

"You'll have to come over for dinner someday soon...with your husband, of course. I make a mean standing rib roast."

Bailey set down her glass. "I should probably get going. A housewife's work is never done."

"Oh. Ok." Haley led her to the door. "Well, I enjoyed the visit. We'll have to do it again soon."

"Yes. Of course. Thanks for the invite." Bailey left with her book in hand. When she reached her front door, she turned and saw Haley still watching her. She waved and went into the house.

As soon as she was inside, she gave the book a disgusted look before opening one of her side tables and stuffing it into the very back.

Had she just been given some woman's book of porn?

She went directly to the bathroom to wash her hands.

Did Robert write that scene?

She didn't want to know.

Chapter Thirty-Eight

Bailey had a pleasant buzz, but did finish up her chores. She did a few dance steps while hanging the clothes on the line and decided she was going to learn how to make cocktails.

Back in the kitchen, she got out the Betty Crocker Cookbook, flipping through it for the chicken casserole recipe. And then she simply closed the book.

She was just going to fry the chicken, make a pot of rice, and doctor up some vegetables. She had plenty of bacon grease saved in the refrigerator, and even she knew how to open up a can of green beans and toss in some diced onion, salt, and bacon grease.

Bailey got out the iron skillet and prepared to cook real food for real people. Forget the 1950s meals for now. Today, she just wanted something that would make her feel warm and comforted.

Bailey was singing along with Little Richard when the door opened. She hurried into the living room and leaped happily into Bobby's arms.

"Hey there," he said in surprise at the show of affection. They kissed a series of three times, each one leaving them both with a broader smile.

"Guess what happened?" she asked excitedly.

"What?" He was still holding her in his arms, and she was in no hurry to move away.

"I was invited to our next-door neighbor's house; the divorced woman, Haley. And she was really nice. And she made me a drink, and she gave me a book."

He gave her a knowing look. "A drink, you say?"

"Something with bourbon and oranges and a maraschino cherry."

He hugged her. "I see...how many did you have?"

"Just one. Why?"

"No reason. I'm happy there's another nice person in the neighborhood. Haley, you say?"

She nodded and gestured toward the kitchen. "She's the one that lives behind our house...in the house *behind* ours." Bailey giggled.

"Ok. I've seen her a time or two."

She helped him take off his hat and jacket. "Get changed, honey. Dinner's waiting. I fried chicken."

"That sounds good. I'll be quick." He gave her another quick peck before hurrying out of the room. She hummed and went into the kitchen to serve up their meal.

Dinner was the best. Not necessarily the best she'd ever prepared, but having dinner with him was like being back in her dream, where they were transported through time—free to be themselves, with no pretending; the real Bailey and Robert.

He loved the chicken, even though there were a few burnt spots on them. The cast iron skillet got a lot hotter than she had expected.

They talked about work and about Haley's house while enjoying the meal. Bobby had seconds, and then thirds, until there was no more chicken left and just a lone string bean lying on the serving dish.

He leaned back in his chair and rubbed his belly. "I enjoyed that."

"Was it as good as Miss Maybelle's?" she asked with a grin.

"Better. Miss Maybelle don't have nothing on my Bae."

She laughed and then stood and wrapped her arm around his neck and kissed him from behind. She gathered up the dishes and placed them in the sink.

"Let's go for a walk," he said. Bailey hesitated, and then slowly continued placing the dishes into the sink. "I need to work off this good cooking."

She had to plaster on a smile. "Okay. It's a beautiful day, and we should take advantage of this nice weather as much as possible before it turns cold. Let me just get cleaned up."

She hurried out of the room and went to the bathroom. Bailey turned on the water and then gripped the counter and closed her eyes.

She was shaking like a leaf.

Racial harassment, whether real or fake, still hurt.

She did not want to do this. She wanted to go for a walk with Bobby and enjoy the fall leaves. She wanted to watch the sunset and hold his hand. She wanted to look into his eyes and watch them go from light to dark.

She didn't want to go out there and have some no-name man believing she was less than any other person simply because of the color of her skin. And that went for everything else; religious belief, sexual orientation, gender, ethnicity...

Racism was the stupidest thing in the world, as were all the other *isms*. People sure could be stupid.

If not for...

Bailey stood up straight.

If not for people who risked their comfort, who took a stand, there would never be change. It wasn't easy. It was just necessary.

She left the bathroom and went to meet Bobby. They had something important to take care of.

The sun was bright and the weather warm and comfortable. Bailey and Bobby stepped out of the house and instead of strolling to the car, they headed for the sidewalk together.

She smiled at him, and he reached for her hand and gave it a firm grip. Despite the thrill that shot through her at the contact, the firm squeeze seemed to send a message;: *Here we go…*

The camera preceded them by a few feet this time, and Bailey wondered fleetingly how they were going to keep the cameraman's shadow from being in the shot. But she was sure they would figure it out.

"It's so nice out," Bobby said while looking around as they followed the cameraman. This obviously was not going to be a random walk. "I can't believe I allowed myself to be cooped up like a hermit for the last week."

"Well, it has been hectic with us just moving in and you starting a new job."

He shrugged. "True, but we have to make time to smell the roses, Bae. I don't want to turn into some boring old married couple."

"It will come together. Maybe we can have our date night Friday instead of Saturday, since I'll be throwing my first dinner party."

He kissed the back of her hand as they walked. "Sorry for having Mom out so soon, but she's anxious to see the house with the furniture in it."

Bailey raised a brow. "You sure she's not just anxious to make sure I'm taking proper care of her baby boy?"

He gave her a slight shrug. "There might be a bit of snooping involved. But I think our house is wonderful—especially considering we're just starting out."

"And," she added, "I think it was a good idea not to accept that dusty, hand-me-down furniture from the attic." Bailey went a bit out on a limb, but they did have all new furniture. When she first moved out on her own, the only new item she had for her house was a coffee pot.

"True," Bobby agreed. "And we won't tell her how much we're paying on that furniture."

She gave him a serious look. "But we're okay, right? Financially? Because I don't mind picking up some work—"

"No," he said firmly. "I promised you when I asked for your hand in marriage that I'd take care of you. And we are fine. We have to pinch a little, but we're doing good. And Friday date night will be good."

"Okay," she said with a satisfied sigh.

Bailey looked at some of the yards as they walked and wondered if she should be adding gardening to her long list of weekly chores.

She saw a few young men doing yard work, and as they were either Black or Hispanic, she knew they were the gardeners and not the homeowners. Bobby mowed on Saturdays, but was she supposed to plant flowers and such? She didn't have much of a green thumb. There were some bushes and a few patches of neat flowers already in place, but it might be nice to have a small herb garden. She'd consider it for the spring.

That thought made her blink. She was really planning her future here in Wingate. She peeked at Bobby, who was content to also gaze at the houses as they walked. She was making those future plans with a sexy man that was suddenly her husband—a man she knew very little about, but whom she strangely felt a connection with she had never felt with any other man.

He gestured to a house. "Maybe we should get some pink flamingoes." She looked at the pink plastic figurines.

"Good God, no."

"Why?" he chuckled. "It looks very tropical."

"We live in the Midwest." He conceded with a shake of his head.

She gestured with her head at a house across the street. "What about that giant crystal ball?"

He arched one brow. "How about a simple bird feeder?"

"I agree."

"Have you found anything in the Sears and—"

"What in the hell do you think you're doing?"

Both Bailey and Bobby turned. She hadn't even seen the older, white-haired man standing in his doorway as if he had been spying out of his window waiting to catch some kids getting their ball from his yard.

They stopped walking, Bobby's expression still casual. They had to turn as they had already passed the house, causing the cameraman to do a wide swivel.

"Hello," Bobby said.

The man came down his walkway with a perplexed yet angry look on his face. He was taller than Bobby, and despite appearing as if in his sixties, that looming height seemed intimidating. He stopped a few feet from them, staring at their interlocked hands.

"People been saying it, but I didn't think it was true..." the man said as if to himself.

"Is there a problem, sir?" Bobby asked curtly. Bailey simply stared.

"You walking down the street in broad daylight with a Negress and you ask me what the problem is? Ain't you go no self-respect, boy?"

Bobby gave her hand a reassuring squeeze.

"Hey! Watch your mouth, old man. I got plenty of self-respect."

"I can't believe my eyes," the man continued. "In this day and age, you do this in my neighborhood — with all the decent white girls out there —"

"Listen here, Mister, I have never raised my voice to one of my elders, but I won't stand by and let you badmouth my wife —"

"You did marry her! You damn fool! You don't marry a Negro, you take them behind a bush and have your fun and then settle down with a decent white woman!"

An angry, red glow began to creep up Bobby's face beginning at his neck.

"You're disgusting!" Bobby said. Bailey saw several neighbors looking out from their front windows, but a few actually came out onto their porches.

Was she supposed to say something? The real Bailey would have—but a year from now, in 1955 a 14-year-old Black boy would be tortured and murdered for supposedly looking at a white woman...

No. Bailey Banks wouldn't be saying a thing right now.

"Let me explain this so even a backwards redneck can understand," Bobby said in a voice that had gone loud—one she would have never recognized in a million years. "My wife is the smartest, kindest, and the most beautiful woman I've ever known. I am proud she accepted me as her husband—"

"What did you call me?" the old man asked. His look of awe and confusion had quickly become one of anger.

"You don't like it when someone calls you out your name; when they look down their nose at you!" Bobby continued. "It doesn't feel so good, does it?"

"Boy, I fought in a war, and I've served my country and I won't have some—" he stopped short of the N-word, but everyone heard it in their mind, in their hearts.

Bailey's heart began to beat rapidly in her chest. She had to remind herself this was all a part of a big, elaborate scene Bobby had planned.

"You're the trash!" the man continued with a sputter. "Sullying our decent neighborhood!"

Bailey tugged Bobby's hand. "Let's go—"

"Understand this, Mister—and this goes for any one of you that think like this one. My wife and I are not going to hide from you. We are not going to stop living and loving our lives just because it puckers your ass! If you don't like me or my wife, then you are beneath us, and we wouldn't care what you think in the first place!"

A woman across the street clutched her neck and looked appalled before hurrying back into her house. A couple next door to the old man whispered to themselves but only watched, their expression merely curious.

Bobby turned abruptly and led Bailey back in the direction of their home.

"I bet your parents are proud of you, boy!" the old man yelled after them.

"Edelman! That's enough! Leave them folks be," a woman said. Bailey didn't know who had stuck up for them. She looked at Bobby, whose jaw was clenched as he marched down the street with her in tow.

Chapter Thirty-Nine

Neither Bobby nor Bailey spoke until they were in their house and then Bobby slammed the door shut—right in the cameraman's face.

Oooo.

"That backwards asshole!" Bobby paced.

Hey…they were allowed to cuss like that?

He turned suddenly and looked at her. "Are you okay?"

She nodded silently and he hurried over to gather her in his arms. While he held her, rocking them both, Bailey heard the rapid beating of his heart.

"I'm so proud of you," she said. "I thought you were going to bop him in the nose for a minute."

He paused and then let out a stressed chuckle. "I wanted to. God…I wanted to."

"Somehow, I don't think that would have solved anything."

"But it would have made me feel good."

They rocked and held each other for a while.

"We were having so much fun and then that man—Edelman, I think they called him—he ruined it," Bobby whispered.

"Mhm." Bailey's eyes were closed as she pressed her cheek against his chest. "You told him we are not going to stop loving and living our lives."

"Mhm," he echoed. "Because it's the truth." He seemed to be enjoying the holding onto each other just as much as she was.

"I want to grow old with you, Bobby."

He stopped rocking and pulled back to look into her face, his arms still around her. He reached to tilt her chin up and then he kissed her.

To Bailey, it wasn't a kiss, because a kiss was normally two lips meeting, a sharing of affection. But he kissed her so thoroughly and so completely, it was as close to love-making as one could get with just the use of lips...and tongues.

She felt his tongue, bold as it flicked at her, and then Bailey did what came naturally. She sucked it.

Bobby paused; his lips parted as she had her way with his tongue. It was too sensual! Her body came awake, tingling in places that hadn't been touched by a man for longer than she cared to remember.

His hand came up where he held the back of her neck, fingers in her hair, and then he took over again. This time taking possession of her lower lip, gently drawing it into his own mouth as if it was a succulent piece of fruit.

He gave a soft, low moan and the sound sent a tremor throughout Bailey's body. Her breath came out in a rush as each of her nerve endings lit up.

Bobby lifted her until her feet were inches from the floor. He walked them quickly to the bedroom, her mind slowly awakening, pulling back from a wonderful dream.

They were on set—being watched by countless people all over the world. And two of those people were her aunt and uncle.

Bailey clung to him as Bobby quickly entered the bedroom and then sent the door shut behind them with his foot. He quickly deposited her onto the bed and then headed back to the door and slammed his hand onto the button that would stop filming.

Bobby then slid slowly down the wall until he was sitting on the floor, his face flush and still panting.

Bailey was propped on her elbows, watching in confusion. She sat up quickly.

"That..." Bobby said breathlessly, "was more than I can endure." He rubbed his hand through his hair and gave her a rueful smile. "God...you are going to be the death of me..."

She probably looked as confused as she felt. "Um...how much of that was acting?"

His cheeks grew red. "None of it...until I knew there was going to be no more filming for me."

She just gave him a confused look. Bobby cupped both hands in front of his crotch.

Oh!

"Oh."

"They could probably film from the waist up," he joked, still sounding embarrassed. "But I would not be very comfortable. I figured we could just wait it out here..."

She nodded.

"Besides, this is where they would have gone after that amazing kiss."

Bailey finally smiled. "That's true. Although it was pretty sexy, so they might have only managed to make it to the couch."

Bobby's eyes twinkled a bit, as if he was sure he hadn't offended her with yet another appearance of his erection. "Sorry about my stupid biological reactions!"

She just gave him a broad smile and a shrug. "Hey, yours is just visible, where mine isn't. But to be fair...I'm going to have to change these pants."

"What?" he exclaimed with a smile. And then he laughed. "Thank God!"

"Why are you thanking God about the condition of my undies?" she chuckled.

"Because," he looked at her again, "it means I'm not the only person that's horny as hell."

Neither of them were laughing now. Both watched the other, waiting. But Bobby was not going to do anything more.

"I don't..." Bailey began with a whisper, "...think it's natural to be this horny."

Bobby came to his feet and when he was standing before her—the bulge in his pants now showing all he'd been hiding, he knelt and kissed her. This time, it was gentle and slow.

"Do you have condoms?" she whispered.

"No." He shook his head. "I didn't—"

He hadn't planned or expected or thought she would...Bailey filled in all the blanks.

"But I can get them," he said, and then kissed her again. "But for now, I'm just interested in feeling how much wetter I can make you."

That statement would give him a lot more wetness to explore.

They had lain under the covers with most of their clothes gone—at least the items that covered up the most important areas. Bobby was just wearing an undershirt and socks while Bailey's sweater was gone, bra still on (despite it being pushed up to her neck for close to an hour), and pants and panties kicked to the foot of the bed.

No condom meant no penetration—but neither could say they missed it. They lay together in quiet contentment until Bailey said it was getting late and she needed to take her bath. Bobby asked if he could wash her back. And now they were in the big, cast iron tub together with her back against his chest while he went from snuggling the side of her face to burying his nose in her hair.

"I can't get my hair wet," she warned when she saw him reach up to touch it.

He leaned around to look at her face. "Really? Why?"

"Because my curls have to last until Saturday and if it gets wet, it's going to turn into an Afro."

"How did you wear your hair before the show?"

"Natural, which is why I'm not used to all this pressing and curling. And it was murder that week I had to do it on my own before meeting Juanita."

"Okay," he said. "I always like it. It's one of the things I look forward to." She turned her head to look up at him.

"Yeah?"

"I like when the cameras show you getting ready each day and how you pamper yourself. The last thing you do is put on the red lipstick. It's so sexy."

She chuckled. "Oh my God..."

He hugged her from behind. "I'm sorry if that sounds cringey, but it's not, it's just sexy. I read enough of the comments to see that a lot of the fans appreciate the same thing. Maybe not enough people take the time each day to pamper themselves. But for both men and women, the fan base likes watching you get ready each morning."

Bailey blinked. "Okay."

"I know you don't film your nighttime routine. But a lot of people have asked about the cold cream."

"Cold cream?"

"Yes. There's some on your vanity, and you can use it to remove your makeup or just as a moisturizer. They want to see you use it. I was thinking maybe a couple times a week you could change into some loungewear and show yourself taking off the makeup."

"Is that really a thing?" she asked.

"You would be surprised. I wouldn't suggest it with some because I doubt if they'd appear on camera without makeup, but you don't need it, you're so beautiful."

She grinned self-consciously. "Thank you. I didn't really wear makeup until this show."

"Really?"

"Yeah, just some lipstick and maybe eyeliner for a casting call. But I never got into the habit."

"Well, it's very natural on you. I like it both ways, though."

"I'll do the thing with the cold cream. In truth, it would be nice to kick out of my heels at the end of the day."

"You're getting better with them."

"You can tell?" she smirked.

"The world can tell. It's in the comments."

"Jeez. It's weird having people around the world commenting about me."

"I know," he sighed. "We are living our lives inside a glass bubble. And with a new relationship, it's especially weird. I think I'm saying the stupidest things because I get distracted looking at you."

Bailey hugged his arms that were folded across her body. "I do that too. Sometimes I just freeze, but then the actress slips in and takes over."

"You do? You always seem so perfect. I would have never thought you struggled."

"I do. All the time." She looked at her fingertips. "Ugh, I'm getting all wrinkly. We'd better get out."

It was weird putting on their nightclothes after being naked in the bath together.

When he reached down to pull out his trundle bed, Bailey stopped him.

"After what happened in this bed, I think it's okay for you and me to sleep together."

He rubbed his hand through his hair. "Are you sure? Because I don't want you to think I expected that."

"Unless you'd rather not—"

"No! I'd love to sleep with you."

"Okay," she nodded. "I'm going to wrap my hair now." He nodded and pulled down the blankets. "Did you want to touch it before I pin it?"

He stopped and looked at her quickly. "I...yes. You don't mind? I always heard that Black women don't let white people touch their hair." He sounded as if he was only half joking.

"Well don't ever do it without an invitation. It's best not to even ask." She sat down at her vanity and he came up behind her. "But you can touch mine anytime you want—as long as your hands aren't wet."

"Got it." He reached out and stroked some of her curls. "Soft," he whispered.

"Did you think it was going to feel like steel wool?"

"No." He rubbed her hair between his fingers.

"It's oiled, so unless I want the pillows stained, I need to keep it wrapped or wear a bonnet."

Bobby smiled and took a step back. He crossed his arms. "Okay. Now I get to watch you pin your curls without seeming like a perv peeking at you while pretending to be asleep."

"You are so silly." She quickly pinned her hair and Bobby asked to do the last one.

"Do you know those TikTok videos where they ask, show that you're dating a Black woman without saying you're dating a Black woman?" Bobby pointed to his handiwork. "This right here!"

She stood and gave him a kiss. "Oh, my goodness, you're dating a Black woman," she said playfully. "What will the world think!"

His smile disappeared as he put his arms around her. "The world doesn't think too highly of the name Chesterfield. If you Google my name, you'll see a lot of shit, and all of it is centered around my father. I just have the bad luck to share his name."

"I know what has been said about your father. But you're not him."

"I don't ever want you to feel as if I'm rushing you. I care about you, Bailey. And we can go as slow or as fast as you like because I'm putting the controls in your hands. It's the only way I can do things.

"I'll stop if you ever say the word. And I'll bring condoms, but it doesn't mean—"

She pressed forward to kiss him. "I know why you feel you have to say all of this, but I'm not judging you. And you don't have to tiptoe around me because I'm a big girl."

"But it's going so fast, and I don't want you to think—"

"That I have to sleep with the boss? I have never gotten that vibe from you. And if I had, I wouldn't be here now."

He let out a relieved breath and then kissed her again. "Let's go to bed, Bae."

"I like when you call me Bae."

"And I like when you call me Bobby and not Rob or Robert."

She nodded. "Noted."

They went to bed and climbed under the covers. Bailey moved to place her arm across his body and her head against his chest while his hand gently rubbed her arm. He kissed her forehead.

"Good night, beautiful. Today was the best day ever—even with that scene."

"It was a good scene and a good day. The best," she concurred. "Good night."

Chapter Forty

Bailey slept well in Bobby's arms, although she did find herself periodically waking up in disbelief it had really happened.

And when she awakened the next morning, it was to the sight of him gazing at her.

She covered her mouth to shield him from her breath. "How long have you been watching me?"

"Not long. I already turned off the alarm and…if you want to lay here and smooch for a while, I'm game."

"Not until I brush my teeth—"

He held her close and chuckled. "Two morning breaths cancel each other out. Or that's what I'm told." He leaned forward and tentatively placed his lips on hers.

She conceded because his lips were magical. They kissed for a while, and she was reminded how fulfilling a kiss with the right person could be.

After a while, she reluctantly drew back. "Ugh…I have to go to work."

"Really?" he joked. "Can you call in sick?"

"Nah. My boss is kind of a perfectionist."

"Shucks. How about we meet here tonight after work?"

"You have a date."

Bailey hurried to the bathroom and got prepared for her opening scene. When she returned to the bedroom, Bobby was lying in bed watching her.

"One more smooch for the road?" he asked.

"I don't know...since I just brushed my teeth, I'm worried my breath will give me an unfair advantage."

"I can't lie...I got up early and brushed my teeth."

Her mouth dropped. "What! You let me kiss you with morning breath?"

"But I promise I didn't mind. I didn't even notice—"

"Oh my God..."

He sat up. "Don't be mad, honey. I just wanted to kiss you so bad. I promise to wait to brush my teeth tomorrow."

She sighed, wondering how bad her breath had been. But he looked so cute with his tousled hair and crooked smile.

She went over to the bed but decided she'd better stay standing. She bent over and kissed his lips. When he reached up to place his hands on the back of her neck to pull her down, she giggled and sidestepped him.

"I'll see you for breakfast," she said while heading for the bedroom door.

"Fine," he replied.

Bailey had to straighten her face once she hit the kitchen. And whenever she forgot, she found herself smiling as she went about preparing breakfast.

She boiled half a dozen eggs, fried sausage patties, and got the toast ready to drop. Then she whipped up egg salad to make Bobby sandwiches for his lunch.

"That sausage smells good," she heard Bobby say as he entered the kitchen. For the first time, he caught her by surprise. He was behind her and snuggling her neck before she had time to fully turn.

"Morning," he murmured against her neck before placing a kiss on her lips.

Bailey was reminded of an old Erykah Badu song about wanting somebody to walk up behind her and kiss her on the neck.

"Good morning," she replied while nuzzling his freshly shaved cheek with her own. "Will you pour the coffee while I finish packing your lunch?"

"Yep." Bailey wondered if the world could see there was a difference in the way they acted this morning. They were no longer dancing around each other—they had already *done the dance*. She wanted to chuckle giddily at her joke.

After she had taken her seat, Bobby gave her a sly smile. "You know what today is?" He sprinkled salt and pepper onto his boiled egg.

"Friday?" she replied.

"Yes! And that means it's date night. I don't want you to cook dinner tonight. I'm taking you to a movie and dinner."

"Oh, that sounds like fun."

"That movie with Dorothy Dandridge and Harry Belafonte is playing at the Regal. It's supposed to be some type of remake of the opera Carmen. It's called *Carmen Jones*."

"*Carmen Jones*? It's a Negro opera?"

"I think so."

"Well, if it's got Dorothy Dandridge and Harry Belafonte in it, then it has to be good."

"It'll be like when we used to date," he said while reaching to hold her hand on top of the table.

"You're such a romantic, Bobby Bailey."

He kissed the back of her hand and they finished breakfast one-handed because they didn't want to stop holding hands.

This wasn't acting. This was them really enjoying each other's company. Actually being in the moment was completely different than acting as if they were. How did she ever think she could get away with faking this feeling?

When he got up to leave, he bent down to kiss her neck and then her lips from behind and again it gave her the biggest thrill.

"Have a good day," he said.

"You too."

"I'll be home on time. Love you."

Her heart went crashing in her chest. "Bye. Love you too."

It was time to think about work. Today was Friday and tomorrow, her mother-in-law would pay a visit and she didn't know what to expect. All she knew for certain was that the house had to be in perfect order.

She changed into her shorts and blouse so she could do her morning stretching. But this time, she opened up the Ponds cold cream and smeared a small amount on her face.

Oh no! She looked in the mirror and was reminded of a reverse minstrel act from the twenties! She grabbed tissues and wiped it off, but couldn't deny that afterwards, her face felt like satin.

She did her workout, opened the curtains, but only opened the windows in the bedroom, and then she got dressed for the day. She had liked wearing pants the day before, but it was time to get back to what made her a moneymaker; the dresses or skirts, the heels, and the makeup.

When that was done, she primped in front of the mirror for a bit and wondered what Bobby was thinking as he watched her.

Tonight would be date night—and the first date for her and her new boyfriend. Bobby said they would date each other through the show and that had been a genius idea. Bailey wondered again about what kinds of dates Wingate held and because Bobby was the producer, he could create some innovative ideas. What was that saying about necessity being the mother of invention?

He was in the process of creating an all-Black community because the story needed it. He could certainly create a hayride or a fair with a big old Ferris wheel to smooch on.

Stop thinking about him. You have work to do.

With a happy sigh, she turned on the radio and then washed the dishes, spending extra time wiping down the counters and going over the floor with a wet mop. Next, she waxed all the furniture instead of simply dusting, vacuumed the floors, and then cleaned both bathrooms—even though no one ever used the guest one.

Bailey quickly had the house to her satisfaction. She sat down at the kitchen table with the cookbook in order to plan out tomorrow's menu.

She would serve green beans. There was no question about it. Unfortunately, they would be canned. But she knew how to doctor them up. She had plenty of bacon grease.

They always had potato salad at home, but she wanted something nicer. Scalloped potatoes might be good, and she had plenty of potatoes, then there was cheese and cream. She checked the cookbook for the ingredients and found she had everything she needed.

Should she make another dish? No, that was enough. Plus, she had brown-and-serve dinner rolls.

Next was dessert. She needed to keep it simple—and 1950s. She had boxed chocolate pudding and she could make whipped cream easily.

Bailey smiled. She had just planned her first dinner party. And she should get a jump on it. She could make the pudding and the whipped cream now.

She found some cute dessert glasses and then pulled down the fancy serving dishes and gave them a good washing. As she made the pudding, Bailey's thoughts drifted to Bobby and all the things they had done the night before.

...and what she hoped would happen again tonight.

Bobby got home on time. She had changed into one of her nicer dresses; a forest-green wrap dress that fastened with four buttons in front. She even changed into real heels, noting that walking in kitten heels for the last week and a half had definitely honed her heel-walking skills.

Bobby's eyes grew large the moment he saw her and she beamed under his scrutiny.

"I think I'm going to have to take you to a fancier restaurant than just a burger joint." He pulled her into his arms but, conscious of her bright lipstick, only gave her a soft peck on the lips.

"I can change..."

"No, no, no. You look too beautiful." He released her and headed to the bedroom. "Give me a minute to change and we can head out."

Bailey turned off the radio and sat on the couch with the Sears and Roebuck catalogue. She had been looking at it earlier and swore that, once and for all, she was going to select something to decorate the house.

The doorbell rang and she looked up in surprise, wondering who would be visiting them. Maybe it was Helen. She had certainly rung her doorbell a time or two.

"Is that someone at the door?" Bobby called from the bedroom.

"Yes. I'll see who it is."

She went to the door and opened it.

On her front stoop were the couple she'd met at last weekend's barbecue. She did not remember their names, but they were her next-door neighbors on the other side from Haley. Geneva! That was the woman's name; but she couldn't recall the man's name for the life of her.

"Hello?" she greeted in confusion.

"Hi," Geneva said. "I hope we're not intruding. We're the Clines." The woman pointed to herself and then to her husband. "I'm Geneva and this is Jefferson."

"We met at the barbecue," Jefferson said with a broad smile.

"I remember," Bailey replied. Of course she remembered the welcome-to-the-neighborhood barbecue that hadn't been very welcoming.

"We were wondering if we could speak to you and your husband," Jefferson continued.

Bailey hesitated, and then remembered her manners. "Please come in."

Bobby came into the room just as they entered the house. He looked nice in navy slacks, shiny shoes, and a pullover sweater. He looked from the neighbors to Bailey with a questioning look. She gave a subtle shrug.

"Bobby, these are our neighbors Geneva and Jefferson Cline. We met at the barbecue." Bobby didn't reply, so she turned back to the Clines and politely gestured to the living room. "Come in."

Geneva looked around in surprise as they walked into the home.

"Your house is beautiful!"

Bobby stood next to Bailey and placed his arm around her waist.

"Thank you. Is there something we can do for you?" It wasn't rude, but it also wasn't very inviting. Bailey thought it sounded as if he was actually telling them to cut to the chase.

"We heard about the...exchange you had with Mr. Edelman yesterday," Geneva said apologetically.

Bobby's eyes hooded. "Yes. We had words."

Jefferson shook his head. "It was very unfortunate. Very unfortunate, indeed. But we wanted you to know we don't condone that type of behavior. We're not...confrontational people."

"We believe in live and let live," Geneva added as she rapidly nodded.

"Well, we appreciate the sentiment," Bobby said, relaxing a bit. "That's all we want as well."

"Jake Edelman is an old coot," Jefferson said. "He just feels very strongly about...certain things, and he doesn't know the right way to express himself."

"He's a war hero, you know," Geneva added.

"He's a bigot," Bobby said flatly.

Jefferson gave a half nod. "He has strong beliefs. But we don't all believe like he does."

Bobby sighed and nodded. "Won't you have a seat?" he finally relented.

She and Bobby sat close to each other on the couch while the Clines sat on the love seat. Bobby unconsciously reached for her hand and they sat comfortably with fingers interlocked.

Of all the people to come over in order to apologize on behalf of the neighborhood, she would not have expected the Clines. She remembered Geneva stating they'd gotten a security system, insinuating it had happened when they had moved into the neighborhood.

She just hoped they wouldn't expect them to play bridge with them every weekend. For one, she didn't know anything about bridge, and more importantly, she had no desire to dodge racial slurs while she was supposed to be having leisure time.

"What happened yesterday was unpleasant," Geneva said with a downturned expression. She leaned forward and gave Bobby and Bailey an earnest look. "Things like that should never happen—not here in our neighborhood."

Jeff nodded enthusiastically. "This is a good neighborhood," he insisted.

"It is," Bobby agreed while exchanging looks with Bailey. "It's why we chose it."

Jeff rubbed his chin. "But couples like you won't have an easy time of it here. In white communities," he said slowly.

"You might have an easier go in a Negro neighborhood. I hear there are some very nice ones," Geneva said with a forced smile.

"Places where you would never have to deal with the Edelmans of the neighborhood," Jeff added. "Some of us neighbors have been talking, and we can help you sell for a top price…"

Oh my God…Bailey realized what this really was.

Chapter Forty-One

"It's not that we don't think you're very nice people," Geneva said quickly. "Your property is very tidy—"

"We don't worry about you, per se. But if we allowed...well, it could affect the property. And we don't want our neighborhood to turn into a ghetto. This is a good neighborhood."

Bobby hadn't stirred once, and neither had Bailey.

"We want twice as much as we purchased the house for," Bobby finally said. "I'm sure you looked at the county records and know what we paid— neighbors like you generally do—"

"That's outrageous!" Jeff exclaimed.

Bobby stood and Bailey followed suit. "I think you and your friends have a lot to consider. I'll see you out."

"But we can make this worth your while," Jeff said while standing. "It could line your pockets with a few thousand we're all willing to scrape together." He gave Bailey a look. "You could start your life with a little extra. It can't be easy being newlyweds with a mortgage."

Bailey frowned. "You heard about the *exchange*, but do you understand we were doing nothing more than taking a walk and one of you so-called *good* people accosted *us*? Do you understand that the only threat that exists in this neighborhood is by people like you?"

"No." Geneva shook her head adamantly. "We would never act like Mr. Edelman. We are good people!"

"So you've said," Bobby said tightly. "I think you should leave, but before you do, I want you to know you won't be successful in running us out of this neighborhood. And if we ever do sell, it will be to someone just like us—*actual* good people whose race or religion won't factor into it."

"We aren't bad people!" Geneva said. But her husband just took her hand and led her to the door.

Bobby followed them. "Go back and tell your good people we won't be selling," he said tiredly. "We want to be good neighbors—but's a two-way street."

They left the house without another word and Bobby stood in the doorway and watched them disappear into their home.

"I can't believe that just happened," Bailey said as she came up to stand beside him.

He closed the door and looked at her with concern. "Honey, I want you to lock the doors from now on. And I don't want you taking a walk around the neighborhood without me—at least until things settle. If they ever settle."

She nodded and then hugged him. "I hate this."

He swayed slightly with her in his arms. "I do too. Do you want to move, Bae? Because we can move into a nice neighborhood with more diversity, or even into an all-Negro neighborhood—"

"No!" She looked up at him while still holding onto him. "These people are not going to run us out of our house. This is our home!"

He nodded. "It might be a battle."

She thought about that before answering.

"I knew what I was getting into. And I'd do it again because...our life together is worth it, Bobby."

He touched his forehead to hers. "I just don't want you to ever regret marrying me."

"And I feel the same."

He tightened his hold on her and pulled her closer until they were hugging. "You're everything I ever dreamed of, Bailey. People like that won't ever drive me away from you—it's only going to make me fight harder." He lifted her chin. "I'm not going anywhere, honey—until the day you convince me you don't want me anymore."

They drove into town for their date, but the mood had definitely changed. Bailey didn't try to talk to Bobby out of character as they drove. But she wanted to ask, why now? She had spent the day looking forward to having a real date and this had to happen right before.

She fiddled with the radio station while reminding herself the production came first, and as long as she was on this show, it always would.

They parked close to the theater, but still had to walk past a water fountain that had a Whites Only sign. At the theater, there were a lot of people in line because it was Friday and the end of the work week. Wingate likely didn't have much to do for entertainment. But she was surprised to see that at least half of the people present were Black. *Carmen Jones* had to be the big draw. Was this the 1950s version of *Black Panther*?

Bobby purchased the popcorn and drinks while the Blacks waited patiently for all the whites to be served. As she waited, she wondered how he felt knowing he was benefiting from his white privilege right now.

They entered their theater and then headed straight for the balcony because the lower level was whites only — even for a movie with an all-Black cast.

The balcony was filling up fast, but they found two seats together.

Several people looked at Bobby, since he was the only white man present. But he seemed at ease. She wanted to whisper in his ear that no, he shouldn't feel at ease right now. It was only Robert Chesterfield's white privilege that gave him a sense of security.

He should understand that he wasn't automatically accepted by the Blacks just because he had a Black wife — because not even she was automatically accepted.

But she snuggled with him and shared the popcorn and tried to enjoy these iconic Black actors on the big screen. But it was hard. It was really hard.

After the movie, as they drove to dinner, Bailey was able to get back into character. They talked about how good the movie was. Bobby mentioned Otto Preminger; the white director had been involved in a long-term relationship with Dorothy Dandridge during the filming. He began naming off other Black actresses of that era that were involved with white men.

But how many of these important white men of the '50s actually married these Black women?

She made a face. She was definitely not thinking about marriage.

Dinner was to be at an evidently new place on the outskirts of Wingate. This part of town was developing fast and looked as if it was going to be a town center. If this was Garden Hill, then it might even be nicer than Wingate.

They parked in a lot filled with other nice cars. And as they headed to the restaurant, Bailey saw there were no Whites Only signs. When they got closer to a brick building with a sign out front that read Madonna's, she began to hear dance music. Wait, was that live music?

"What is this place?"

He just grinned. A doorman greeted them with a broad smile.

"Welcome to Madonna's," he said while opening the door for them.

As they entered, she saw tables where people were eating but there was also a band on a bandstand. The Black musicians had a white singer but they were playing bebop. Below them was a dance floor where several people, Black *and* white, were dancing.

She gave him a quick look.

"This is a supper club. And it's integrated," he finally revealed.

A hostess led them to a table with a fancy, white tablecloth. A candle and the dim lighting made it very intimate.

"Wow," she said honestly. "This place is beautiful." It was decorated richly in powder blue and white, making it look like a little piece of heaven.

"It's new. I heard about it a few days ago," he said.

She looked over at the band and couldn't help tapping her feet to the music. The waiter came to take their drink orders. She ordered an old-fashioned, to which Bobby raised an amused eyebrow. He just had a beer.

For dinner, they both ordered the Steak Diane once learning the chef would prepare it tableside. It was such an extraordinary show, the other patrons turned to watch and once the chef set the dish on fire, everyone in the room applauded.

Bailey laughed and clapped as well. The meal was as delicious as it was beautiful.

"There's that beautiful smile," Bobby said while gazing at her.

She paused in eating to reach out to grip his hand.

"Thank you. I'm having fun."

"Good. Shall we dance?"

"Really?"

"I'm not a great dancer, but yeah."

She put her napkin on the table and the two headed for the dance floor.

A snappy dance number was playing and they couldn't help but move to the beat while trying to match the steps of the other dancers. They knew they weren't great at it; she was too afraid of twisting an ankle, while Bobby just danced like a crazy man.

Bailey laughed and clapped and danced and somehow, she forgot she had been annoyed. A while later, she felt as if she and Bobby were really on their first date—and it was a fantastic first date.

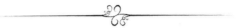

Back home, they finished their scenes in the living room, talking about how much fun they'd had before heading hand in hand to the bedroom.

Because it wasn't yet nine o'clock, as soon as they had the bedroom door shut, Bobby had to press the control to cut the cameras in the room.

He gathered her into his arms and looked down into her face. "Did you really have a good time?"

"I did. Madonna's is a game changer."

"I agree! We actually finished it earlier today."

"Wow. And that meal was amazing."

"It's a real working restaurant because this production is getting bigger."

"I saw the number of Black people in the restaurant. New hires, I gather."

"Yes. Many of them had their first shoot today."

"Well, it's great."

"I have to give credit to Bruce. He's been instrumental in following up on all my crazy ideas."

"They aren't so crazy. You're a visionary."

"I'm sorry our date almost got screwed." He frowned.

"Are you talking about us being invited to move elsewhere?"

"Yeah. That was supposed to have happened yesterday—after the Edelman encounter. But…well, we got sidetracked."

She grimaced. "For all the world to see."

He gave her an embarrassed grin. "I'm so sorry. I may have gotten carried away with the smooching."

"I think we both did."

"You don't have any regrets, do you?"

"Gosh no. But I confess, I didn't expect to be able to have fun after that encounter with the Clines."

Bobby glanced up momentarily before meeting her eyes.

"The way I see it, Bobby and Bailey are trying hard to make a normal life in a world that is far from perfect." He blew out a stressed breath. "Even you and I don't live in the decent world we might dream about.

"So they don't really have a choice but to make the best of a bad situation and to keep on living their lives. Even though you—or Bailey—felt down after what happened, it's the way she should feel. Don't you think? I mean, Bobby is going to do everything he can to show his wife that even though the ignorance is directed at her, he's going to be right there with her, defending her fearlessly and with no apologies. But yeah. She will feel like shit and so will he—they just might try not to show it.

"I felt like shit knowing some of the Black cast might miss part of the movie because all of the whites got served at the concession stand first. And in 1954, the Black people might resent seeing me with you. But I wouldn't show my wife if I felt intimidated by it."

She stared at him, feeling herself falling in love, seeing things in a way she hadn't before. But most importantly, trusting him.

"Are Bobby and Bailey going to make it?"

He touched his forehead to hers. "I hope so. But ultimately that's going to be up to us to decide. It's my hope they will, and they'll grow old together."

She smiled. If they did, then one day they would survive Jim Crow and see the first Black president of the United States. They would grow old with their children and grandchildren surrounding them. And hopefully, they would make strong friendships along the way.

"I..." she began, and then flushed. Bobby raised his brow and held his breath, waiting. "...love you."

He let out his breath and swiftly hugged her. "Bailey, if you believe in love at first sight, then I've loved you for months." He sighed happily while swaying with her in his arms.

Chapter Forty-Two

When Bailey woke up it was Saturday morning, and she did not want to face the day. Today her mother-in-law was coming to visit. Instead of getting up, she snuggled closer to Bobby, who reflexively tightened his hold on her before resuming his soft snoring.

She wouldn't allow herself to get too comfortable—but it would have been easy to do while wrapped in his strong arms.

"It's time to get up, beautiful.," Bobby murmured a few moments later.

She gave a soft groan. "But it's Saturday. People sleep in on Saturdays."

He placed a sleepy kiss on her forehead. "You have an eight a.m. hair appointment, remember?"

She pulled herself up into a sitting position and feigned an accusatory look. "I wouldn't be so tired if *someone* hadn't kept me awake all night smooching."

He smiled without opening his eyes. "But you're just too irresistible."

She got up and headed for the bathroom. He called her irresistible—but he had definitely resisted her last night.

They hadn't used the condoms he'd hidden in his underwear drawer. He looked apologetic when he showed them to her, but he didn't want her to accidentally expose them while putting away his clothes.

They spent the night kissing, talking, and when it was bath time, Bobby closed his eyes and grimaced.

"You bathe first and then I'll go."

She arched her brow. They had gotten hot and heavy with the kissing and he wanted to stop?

"You don't want to wash my...back?"

He gave her a wide-eyed look. "Yes. Very much so. Maybe too much." He drew in a deep breath as if he might want to kick himself. "But everything feels so perfect right now. I still get a thrill from watching you rub lotion into your hands!" He laughed and gave her an embarrassed look. "I don't feel like I'm missing anything by leaving those condoms in the drawer and fantasizing about the way you look while you're in the bathroom washing. So, you go first, and I'll go after you."

She found it ridiculously cute, even though they had already seen each other butt-naked and had explored all of the interesting parts of each other's bodies.

After all, it would be so easy to jump into having sex...but Bobby was right. There was something very sweet in just making out. So, she agreed with him that just kissing was pretty damn sexy, and once they'd had their baths and were in their nightclothes and her hair was pinned and wrapped, they'd resumed making out until they drifted off to sleep.

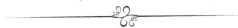

Bailey decided there was no way she was going to make a big, fancy breakfast, not when she had to prepare a ham dinner.

She poured Wheaties into two bowls and topped each with sliced bananas. By the time she got the coffee brewing, Bobby dragged himself into the kitchen with a yawn.

His tousled hair and stubbly cheeks were a far cry from the Bobby she was accustomed to seeing in the morning. His shirt and tie had been replaced by pajamas, a robe, and slippers, but she decided she liked seeing him like this more.

"Morning, honey." He leaned over to kiss her before taking his seat at the table.

"Morning. Did you sleep well?"

"I did." He poured milk onto his cereal, and she placed his coffee in front of him. "How about you?" he asked.

She shrugged. "I think I'm a little nervous about today. Maybe I should have cancelled my hair appointment."

"Bae, don't stress yourself. While you're at the beauty shop, I'm going to mow our lawn and head over to Mom's to do some chores for her. It's going to take all day. You know how Mom is."

No. She didn't. And that was the problem. But everything was ready to be tossed in the oven. She had even put the pineapple and cloves on the ham.

She inhaled deeply. "It's going to go well..."

"It will."

She sat and poured milk on her cereal and ate quickly so she had time to look presentable at Juanita's. The last time she was there, the ladies had been very fashionable, and she refused to look as if she didn't know what she was doing.

She put on a slimming dress with a matching jacket and while she worked on her makeup, Bobby came into the room and stripped out of his pajama bottoms right in front of the camera.

He was wearing boxers, but it seemed a bit risky. He then pulled on navy slacks and a sweater.

"Let me shave real quick and we can go."

"Okay, honey."

He paused on his way to the bathroom.

"You look beautiful."

She smiled. "Thanks."

"Don't be nervous. There's no reason to. We're family."

"I know, but this is my first time preparing a dinner for someone, and I just want everything to be perfect."

He kissed her forehead and went into the bathroom.

An hour later, he dropped her off in front of Juanita's.

"Don't worry about picking me up. I'll see if Pat can take me home or I'll catch the bus."

"Are you sure? I don't mind coming to get you."

"No, because you'll just have to go back to your mom's. I'll be okay. If I had thought about it, I would have asked Pat to pick me up on her way here this morning."

"Okay. Love you."

"Love you too."

As soon as she entered the salon, she was met with the fast-paced music of Little Richard—or someone that sounded just like him.

All the regulars were present and they greeted her as if they were old friends.

Juanita, tall and exotic, was dressed in a bright-orange pencil skirt, a pretty floral blouse...with sneakers on her feet. The low heels from last week were gone. Her hair was neatly pinned into a French bun with Betty Boop style pin curls framing her pretty face.

She was just styling another client's hair, and Bailey struggled to remember that the woman's name was Tracy.

Pat, who was sitting in another styling chair having rollers placed in her hair, wore a belted shirtdress that seemed tailored for her petite frame.

She called out to Bailey as she was hanging up her jacket. "I finally got this girl out of the house. We went to Billy's place and barely stayed long enough to get a buzz."

"You should have known I was going to be a killjoy," Bailey said as she took a seat in the waiting area until it was her turn. "I'm an old married woman now."

"In my day, married women didn't go to juke joints without they husbands," Miss Baker said with an eye roll. She was under the hair dryer, and Bailey didn't know how she'd managed to hear the conversation in the first place.

Pat crossed her legs and gave Miss Baker a pointed look. "Who said Bailey's husband didn't go with us?"

"Y'all didn't take that white man to a juke joint!" Miss Baker replied.

Betty sputtered and laughed. She finished placing the last roller in Pat's hair and led her to the dryer.

"I can see Bobby being comfortable at a juke joint," Bailey said while picking up a *Jet* magazine. "We went to that new supper club last night. Madonna's. And you know it's integrated."

"Ooo! I hear that place is ritzy," Tracy said. Juanita was spraying Final Net hair spray on her freshly curled hair.

"Charles and I are going tonight," Juanita said.

"You and Charles are getting pretty cozy," Jackie said as she got up to sit in the chair Pat had vacated. Betty draped a cape over her shoulders.

"It don't mean anything," Juanita said with a grin. "I'm taking things slow."

Tracy reached into her pocketbook and handed Juanita a dollar bill and two quarters.

"He's a cutie patootie." Tracy stood and put on her jacket. "You better not let the sun shine on that one."

"Oh, I'm keeping tabs on him," Juanita said. "But I'm also keeping my options open. Come on, Bailey. Let's see what we're working with today."

Bailey put the magazine down and sat in Juanita's chair. Juanita secured the cape around her and nodded in approval as she studied Bailey's hair. Meanwhile, the other ladies were talking about Negro men with good jobs and who were looking for wives.

Curtis's name came up and Bailey's ears perked.

"Curtis can have any woman in this town— including my married behind!" Tracy joked as she was leaving. "See y'all next week. I gotta hit the butcher shop before all the white women get there."

Everybody laughed at that.

"All right, honey. Let's get you washed," Juanita said while guiding Bailey into the back room.

The back room was still unfinished, but now had two washing stations; both modern. So that meant they still didn't film back here.

Bailey settled into the chair. She noticed Juanita had her hands on her hips, staring at her with a broad smile.

"What?"

Juanita quickly placed a finger against her lips, indicating for Bailey to whisper. "They're still filming out front now that we all got story lines."

"That's so good. I'm so happy for you guys," Bailey said in an excited whisper.

Juanita just looked at her with that broad grin. "You and Bobby did it, didn't you?"

Oh my God...

She gave Juanita a wide-eyed look.

"Look, I know it's none of my business. And you don't even have to say anything. But you two are on fire!" She quickly covered her mouth. "Girl, you're making interracial dating look sexy as hell!" Her voice had gone back to a whisper.

"We're that obvious?"

Juanita sat down in the other chair and leaned close, her face still split by a broad grin.

"I'm just saying...one day you two were watching each other like you didn't know what might happen next. And the next morning you two had this insane chemistry! When he puts his hands around you, it's like they're supposed to be there. When he kisses you now, it's like he knows you're all his. And, girl...you got that look whenever he comes into the room."

"Oh my God."

Juanita gripped her hand. "No! It's so cute! I have literally watched your last two days twenty times! We've been having watch parties every night at the factory. Nobody wants to wait until the weekend to watch the show!"

Betty came into the room and Bailey and Juanita jumped in guilt. Betty closed the curtain securely and rushed to them.

"So?" she asked in excitement. "Are you and Robert Chesterfield a real couple?"

Bailey's face was burning hot. Her aunt Mae was going to kill her.

"Guys…this is really new," Bailey replied, unsure how to answer. They hadn't talked about whether or not anyone should know.

Both ladies squealed, and Betty hurried back to the curtain. "I knew it!" she exclaimed before leaving.

Juanita stood and turned on the water. "Let's get you all beautiful for dinner with your mother-in-law. Is she going to give you a hard time? No! Don't tell me. We're going to watch tonight."

As Bailey got her hair washed and conditioned, her brain was in turmoil. What was going on? They were treating her like a movie star.

Chapter Forty-Three

Pat stuck around to give Bailey a ride home. As soon as they were in the car, Pat lit a cigarette and turned on the radio.

The cameraman was already in the back seat. That meant something important was supposed to happen. She prepared herself, hoping they just wanted to capture their friendship and that they weren't about to get profiled or something.

"Do you have any plans for tonight, you old married lady?" Pat asked.

"My mother-in-law is coming for dinner."

"Eww. That doesn't sound like fun. I was going to ask if you and Bobby might like to go on a double date. That new *Carmen Jones* movie is playing at the Regal."

"We saw it yesterday. Bobby and I had a date night. After the movie, we went to Madonna's."

"That's sweet. If I ever get married, my husband better take me out on the occasional date."

"Who are you going out with?"

Pat grinned. "Some guy I met at the factory. I got called in and this guy could barely keep his eyes off me."

"Oh?" Bailey grinned. "What's he look like?"

"He's a redbone. He's got curly hair and I don't think it's conked either. He has this moustache like Charlie Chaplin—but in a cute way." They laughed. "When we left work at the end of the night, he was dressed in a zoot suit!"

"Really? He sounds cute."

"He is. But it's a first date, and I thought it might be easier to break the ice with another couple."

"Aww. I'm sorry. I'll be enjoying the pleasure of my mother-in-law instead of having fun with you two."

"Didn't you two live with her?"

"Yeah, for a few weeks right after we got married."

"Well, how was she then?"

"Ugh."

"O...kay. I'm sure it'll be fine. And at least at the end of the day you can send her home."

"She didn't ever treat me bad. It's just that she treats him as if he's still a little boy. Plus, I'm evidently not good enough for him."

"That's every mother-in-law. And moms in general."

"Probably. I'll talk to Bobby. Maybe next week we can all go out together. He wants to make date night a weekly event."

Pat smiled. "That would be fun. I don't know Bobby well, and he's married to my friend."

"Oh well, there's not much to say. He's just a knight in shining armor."

When they got to the house, Bobby's car was still gone.

"Call me tomorrow and I'll tell you about my date, and you tell me how it went with dinner tonight," Pat called as she pulled out of the driveway.

"I will. Thanks, Pat."

Once inside the house, Bailey blew out a long breath. The ham needed to go into the oven and the dishes needed to get washed. She went into the kitchen and pulled on her apron and washed her hands.

After checking the Betty Crocker Cookbook, Bailey preheated the oven and pulled the ham out of the refrigerator.

While she waited for the oven to come up to temperature, she went into the dining room. They never ate in there, but she set the table with the nice china and glasses. She didn't want to put on airs, so she decided not to use the tablecloth.

Back in the kitchen, she put the ham in the oven, washed and dried the dishes, and retrieved the au gratin potatoes. She wanted them to be warm at dinner but she didn't want to risk putting a cold dish into a hot oven, so she set it on the counter. At the last minute, she decided to slice some tomatoes and cucumbers. It seemed her aunt always served them whenever they had a fancy dinner.

When everything was prepped, Bailey went around the house and gave it a once-over. She made up the bed, emptied the trash cans in the bathroom, made sure the curtains hung straight and that there weren't any fingerprints on any of the glass or metal surfaces.

Wow. She looked around in pride. This house was beautiful. It was a far cry from the empty house she had moved into two weeks earlier.

She was in the bedroom touching up her makeup when the phone rang. She quickly fastened the string of pearls around her neck as she hurried to answer.

"Hello?"

"Hi, Bae. I was just checking to see if you're ready for me and mom."

"Everything is ready." She'd taken the ham out of the oven an hour ago and it was still warm. The potatoes were bubbling in the oven and just needed to brown on top. She only needed to turn a low flame beneath the pot of green beans to get them hot again, and the dinner rolls had been buttered and were resting in a basket beneath a tea cloth.

Everything had turned out perfectly, without one snafu.

"Okay, honey. I'll see you in about twenty minutes."

"Okay. Bye."

Twenty minutes later, she heard the car pull up in the driveway and she hurried to the door.

This was making her almost as nervous as if she was meeting Bobby's real mother. But it wasn't just that—it was the expectation of another racial battle. And this one would be more important, because it was family.

She stood in the doorway as Bobby got out of the car and hurried to the passenger side to open the door for his mom.

The woman that stepped out of the car looked older than a mother would be. She was closer in age to a grandmother. Her silver hair was pulled back into a bun and she wore a modest dress, low heels, and very thick nylons.

Her pale, lined face had just a touch of pink lipstick and she seemed...severe.

When she spotted Bailey, her eyes immediately flitted away as if she hadn't seen her.

"Son, grab that pot."

"I'm getting it, Mom," Bobby said while opening the rear door and retrieving a large Dutch oven.

He then led his mother up the walkway to the house.

"Hi, honey," he greeted her with a broad smile.

Only then did Bobby's mother plaster on a broad smile of greeting. "Oh, there you are! Hello, Bailey."

"Hello, Mother Banks. How are you?"

"I'm fair to middlin'. My sciatic is bothering me. I had to have Bobby put some boxes up in the attic and pull down my winter decorations."

Bailey stepped aside to let them in. She gave a curious look to the Dutch oven Bobby was carrying.

"What's that?"

"Oh, that's a pot of Bobby's favorite minestrone. Give that to me, son. I'm going to put it on the stove because it's still hot."

"No, I'll do it. Take off your coat, Mom." Bobby headed to the kitchen with the pot while Mother Banks shook herself out of her coat and handed it to Bailey.

"I cooked dinner for us," Bailey said while her brow wrinkled. "I'm sorry, I thought you knew."

The older woman took off her hat and thrust it to Bailey. "We can have the soup today and you can have whatever you cooked tomorrow or another day. Bobby really likes my minestrone. I'm sure he's dying for it."

Bailey's expression literally froze. Bobby came into the room then.

"Mom, I already told you, we're not having the soup today. Bailey cooked a nice dinner for us."

He leaned over to kiss her.

Bailey smiled at her mother-in-law. "I made a ham with all the trimmings."

"In October? That's too close to the holidays." Mother Banks looked around with a sigh. "Well, show me this over-priced purchase you just had to make."

I do not like this woman, Bailey thought.

"It was a good purchase and a good investment," Bobby said, and gestured into the house.

"I'm just saying, you could have lived at the house for a while longer and saved money. Your father and I didn't run off and buy a house the moment we got married. You were three years old before we decided to move into a house."

"The difference is that we could afford a house."

She pursed her lips together as if mentally stating she wouldn't create a scene. Then she poked her head into the bathroom and gave the small room a thorough look before following them for the tour.

She didn't comment when Bobby pointed out particular pieces of furniture. She just nodded as if she had more to say but thought it best to keep quiet.

Bailey did catch her running her finger over items as if searching for dirt. She was confident there was none to be found.

Finally, they ended in the kitchen and Mother Banks looked at the new appliances and sparkling counters with a nod.

"You have a lot of house on your hands, but you really did a good job, son. It's very nice."

"Well, I can't take the credit for that. Bailey put in all the legwork in making this house a home."

"You picked the couch?" she asked Bailey.

"We both chose it," Bailey replied.

"It doesn't look like Bobby's style, but you can't expect someone to stay the same forever."

"Well, I am a grown-up now..." Bobby said.

Bailey hid a frown. "Dinner is ready. We can go into the dining room."

While Bobby and his mother took their seats, she retrieved the platters and bowls of food and placed them on the table.

"It smells so good," Bobby said while eyeing the spread. "Let's dig in."

Mrs. Banks placed a small portion of ham on her plate and when she picked up the serving spoon of green beans, she visibly grimaced.

"What is this?" she asked while studying the potato dish.

"That's au gratin potatoes."

"Did you say rotten potatoes?"

"No. Au. Gratin," Bailey replied. "It's French, I think. It's baked with cream, butter, and cheese."

"I'll taste of it," she said while spooning up the equivalent of one slice of potato with a bit of sauce.

Her plate looked like it wouldn't fill up a toddler, while Bobby's was practically overflowing.

"Mom, you're going to have more than that, aren't you?" Mrs. Banks glared at him. "Okay. Suit yourself."

Bobby had his mouth filled with food before his mother took her first tentative taste of green beans. She immediately lowered her fork and grimaced.

"Oh, I can't eat this. It's much too salty!"

"Mom, this is perfectly seasoned—"

"Well, honey, I can't help it—my blood pressure."

394

Bailey placed her hand over Bobby's and turned to her mother-in-law with a polite smile. "It's fine, Mother Banks. I don't want you risking your health with my overly flavored food." She turned to her husband. "Bobby, why don't you get your mother a bowl of minestrone soup."

Mother Banks smiled broadly.

"But you worked so hard—" Bobby began.

"It's fine."

After giving her a curious look, he got up and went into the kitchen for the soup.

The thing is, the food she'd prepared smelled delicious, and she knew it tasted just as good.

Her mother-in-law was being ugly, but it didn't hurt her. She was the one missing out on a delicious meal so she could eat a bowl of soup.

Bailey sliced into a thick piece of ham and placed it into her mouth. She savored it as she looked at Bobby's mother.

"This is my first time making a ham and I'm so proud of how it turned out. You know how sometimes ham is too dry?" She took another bite and closed her eyes to savor it. "Not this ham. It turned out so tender. Perfectly seasoned." Mother Banks watched her chew. "But I think the secret was the brown sugar and pineapple. Mmmm. Yep. That pineapple is perfect with the ham."

Bailey stabbed some green beans and savored a big mouthful. "I bet the bacon grease I seasoned these green beans with might have been the thing that didn't agree with you. Or maybe the grated onion. Or it could have been the black pepper and season salt.

Mmm. Mmm. Mmm," Bailey said as she practically smacked her lips.

Bobby returned to the dining room with a bowl of soup. He placed it in front of his mother. "Here you go, Mom."

Bailey took a big bite of potatoes. "Oh, my goodness, Bobby! Did you try the potatoes?! They are amazing!" She took another big bite and grabbed a warm, buttery role. "Mmmm…best meal ever."

Bobby took his seat and resumed eating. He grabbed another thick slice of ham and placed a piece into his mouth before he was even finished chewing his last bite.

Bailey thought he always made whatever he was eating look good, and this was no exception. Only this time, she could tell he genuinely enjoyed it.

"Mmm. Everything is delicious, honey. Simply perfect."

"Mother Banks, would you like a dinner roll with your soup?"

Bobby's mother was quietly sipping her soup. It looked like canned soup. She certainly hadn't made it from scratch.

"No, dear. I'm fine."

"How's your soup, Mom?" Bobby asked with a sly smile. He obviously had figured out what Bailey was up to.

"It's delicious," the older woman replied. "Are you sure you won't have some?"

"We'll have it for dinner tomorrow," Bailey replied for him. *Tomorrow when I'm off work and off set having a real meal with my aunt and uncle.*

After that, conversation was much easier; they basically talked about how good the food was and Mrs. Banks had nothing to complain about.

After dinner, they went into the living room and Bobby turned on the television while Bailey brought out the chocolate pudding on a tray.

Mother Banks gave her an apologetic smile. "I'm stuffed, dear. None for me."

Bobby grinned and picked up his dish of pudding. "Late-night snack for me, then."

Even though it was boxed pudding, it was delicious. She had to call her first dinner party a success—even if the one and only guest chose to eat canned soup instead.

Chapter Forty-Four

After Bobby drove his mother home, Bailey had to admit this was an amazing week and she wanted to cap it off right.

She unfastened her pearls and put them away then went to the bathroom, where she changed into her gown and robe, and she sat at her vanity to remove her makeup.

She reached for the Ponds cold cream and as she unscrewed the cap, she had to admit the fragrance was pleasant, as well as nostalgic. It was time to give the people what they wanted.

She hummed as she spread the cream over her face, concentrating on her lips and eyes. Then she wiped it off with tissues. After repeating, Bailey returned to the bathroom, where she thoroughly washed her face.

When she was once again sitting at her vanity, she pinned her freshly curled hair and carefully wrapped it. The audience never got to see this much of her nighttime routine.

She heard Bobby come in the front door and she hurried to greet him. It was not yet 9:00 p.m., so they had more filming to do.

"Hi, honey." She gave him a brief kiss.

"You're all ready for bed. Do you want to watch a little television? Jackie Gleason is still on."

"Yes! Let's do that."

He hurried out of the room. "You turn on the television while I get into my *loungewear*."

Jackie Gleason was funny, and they laughed and enjoyed the remainder of their evening together without mentioning her mother-in-law and her antics. They did, however, cuddle and share the occasional kiss.

At 9:00 p.m., Bailey sighed and turned off the television. She looked at Robert with an amused smile. "I need a drink."

He chuckled. "You did good today." He stood and gathered her into his arms for a hug.

"Thanks. Did you notice how I turned lemons into lemonade?"

"I did. Gloria was fuming when I drove her home." Bailey's smile slipped away. "She said the food smelled so good she nearly broke character and filled her plate with your dinner!"

Bailey threw her head back and laughed.

"We're not going to have any leftovers for next week. She made me promise to bring them to tomorrow's meeting."

"I think I changed my mind about your mom."

"I think Gloria does a good job for always claiming she isn't a real actress."

"But can you save the ham bone for bean soup? I'd like to make some pinto beans and cornbread next week."

"Hell yeah!" he exclaimed. She chuckled at his enthusiasm.

He held her hands. "Did you mean it about wanting a drink? Because it's Saturday night and you don't have work in the morning..."

"Do you want to go off the set?"

"We wouldn't need to. The cast has been gathering after filming for viewing parties. I hear it gets pretty exciting—and we can BYOB."

Bailey didn't tell him she'd already heard about it while at the beauty shop.

"Let's do it! I'd love to see some of the show with a crowd."

"Then let's change."

When they were in the bedroom changing and Bobby was trying to determine what she wanted to drink for the watch party, Bailey suddenly remembered something pretty important.

She turned to him quickly. He was just lacing up his sneakers and confirming they'd get a six-pack of beer.

"Oh..."

He looked at her. "Oh?"

She lightly gnawed her nails. "Everyone thinks we've...had sex—in real life."

Bobby's brow went up but he didn't speak.

"They also think we're a couple. I haven't confirmed anything! But I'm not sure how you want us to handle—"

"I know what everyone is saying. I've been hearing it whenever I go to the production company. Everybody's whispering and winking at me and making comments..." He sighed and stood and walked over to her. He rubbed her arms lightly.

"What we do is nobody's business. And I know to them it looks like we're moving fast. But they don't know I haven't been able to get you out of my mind since the day of rehearsals, when you sat opposite me and breathed life into Bailey Banks.

"I don't want to hide our relationship. But people are going to jump to conclusions either way —"

She put her arms around him and kissed him. He relaxed and they spent a few moments kissing. When their lips finally parted, he stared into her eyes, his sky-blue eyes growing darker and darker with each passing second.

"Bailey. Will you be my girlfriend?"

"Of course I will. Nothing would make me happier."

He gave her a grim smile. "There is a lot of baggage that goes along with dating me. My family isn't the most liberal, if you know what I mean."

"Your family is the last thing I'm thinking about." She gave him a quick peck on the lips, wishing to wash the concerned look from his face.

He smiled some, but it didn't fill his face completely. "I'm a very private person. I don't do interviews or talk to the press, and I certainly don't speak to people about my father. I also don't do non-disclosure agreements. I just trust that whatever you and I talk about will stay just between us."

"Bobby, we don't *ever* have to talk about your father, or anything you don't want to talk about."

He pressed his forehead against hers. "Okay." His smile had finally reached the rest of his face.

They picked up beer from the grocery store. It was closed and no one was around, but Bobby had a master key, so he went in and basically robbed them of beer and a big bag of potato chips.

It was nearly ten thirty by the time they reached the factory, and the lot was filled with cars.

"Is everybody in town here?" he asked while opening her door and grasping her hand.

"It looks like it."

She had never been to the factory. It was nice on the outside, with pretty landscaping. She wondered if they ever filmed inside. It was almost too nice.

Bobby led her through the front doors. She didn't see anyone—not one lone straggler.

As they headed down the corridor, she thought it looked like a school. There was a receptionist desk and casual seating. But things changed after they went through a second set of doors.

She could now hear loud talking and laughing, as well as the sound of obviously recorded voices.

She looked at Bobby and he gently gripped her hand. "Ready?"

"Yep."

They entered a dimly lit room. This looked as if it was a cafeteria. Vending machines sat off to one side, and there was a food service station at the rear.

Tables had been moved to the walls and chairs, including folding ones, had been set up neatly in the center of the room facing a large, portable screen.

There had to be close to sixty people present, and they all seemed to be very vocal about what they were watching.

"That's canned soup!"

"Gloria's eyes are watering! I bet she grabs a piece of ham—"

"It sho do look good!"

Bailey's face felt hot, and she knew her cheeks were red because on the screen was playing the scene that had just been filmed a few hours before with her, Bobby, and her mother-in-law at the dinner table.

Her feet seemed as if they had become lead.

Bobby gave her a concerned look. "Do you want to leave?" he whispered.

But it was too late for that, because several people had spotted them.

"Bobby! Bailey!"

And in that moment, a chant went up. People actually stood and applauded.

This was too surreal...

Bailey's heart was thudding in her chest at the unexpected attention.

"They're holding hands! I told you!"

The movie paused, and several people came up to greet them. Someone pulled over two seats for them and had them sit.

"Everyone voted to watch you two first, but we're going to fast-forward some because I think you're nearly done."

"That's fine by us," Bobby said. "We already know what we did. We want to see some other people."

People cackled at that.

Bailey saw some of the ladies from the beauty shop who waved at her and she waved back, even though she still felt a bit shell-shocked.

"All right, everyone!" someone called. "Let's settle down and finish up with Team Bailey so we can figure out who to play next."

Team Bailey...her brow was dotted with beads of sweat.

"Team Nadine!"

"Team Drew!"

People were shouting playfully over each other to watch their favorites next. Finally, the movie resumed. Bobby popped the tab of a beer and passed it to Bailey. She took a quick drink, and then another.

"You okay?" he leaned in to whisper. She nodded and gave him a half smile.

The stream did move forward, but slowed when they got to her doing her night routine.

"Yes! Use that cold cream!" People actually applauded when they saw her using it.

"See? I told you," Bobby whispered to her. She had to concede he was right.

By the time they got to the scene of them in their pajamas watching Jackie Gleason while cuddling, everyone in the room was oohing and aww-ing.

And by that time, the beer had settled Bailey's nerves and she could smile at how genuinely cute they looked. Yes. It was unmistakable. Anyone could see they were a couple.

Team Nadine was the winner for the next showing. She actually got up and bowed and curtsied playfully. She was a natural at all of this.

They hit the spotlights of Nadine's week, which included a visit to Mayor George's office.

Everyone began to hiss when he appeared on screen but evidently George was present, and he yelled for everyone to watch it, which sent more laughter through the crowd.

Bailey was having a great time—especially after two beers and a handful of chips.

Nadine and the mayor locked lips and everyone in the room whooped and hollered the way they had done when watching her and Bobby on screen. She stopped feeling self-conscious. It was all in good fun, and everyone was enjoying themselves.

When it was close to 1:00 a.m., Bailey yawned one too many times and Bobby told her it was time to go. He'd had one beer when they first arrived but then had switched to bottled water from the vending machine. Bailey thought he looked a little tired himself.

Back at the house, she got her bath first and by the time Bobby finished with his and climbed into bed, she was almost asleep. He pulled her close and she snuggled against his warm body.

"You're right," he yawned. "We're having a shower installed."

"Oh, thank God. I love my baths, but not when I'm tired like this."

"Go to sleep, Bae," he said while kissing her forehead.

"Good night."

"'Night."

Chapter Forty-Five

When Bailey woke up, she was alone in bed. She sat up with a yawn and looked around. The bathroom door was open and she could tell it was empty.

It felt very strange to wake up alone. She stretched and got out of bed, not bothering with the robe. That robe was a little too frilly for her liking. She hoped to be able to go shopping, and the first thing on her list was another pair of low heels and a different robe.

She went into the kitchen and heard the small radio that had been in the garage. A rockabilly song was playing and Bobby was busy at the stove.

"Good morning," she said.

He jumped and nearly dropped the egg he was holding. "I didn't hear you."

"That's because you're in here jamming to...who is this?"

"That's Buddy Holly." He came over and gave her a morning kiss. "You don't know about him?"

"I have to admit, I know very little about the musicians from the fifties."

"The music is one of the fun parts. There are a lot of things about the fifties that's not so fun."

"Don't I know it." She peeked over his shoulder. "What's for breakfast?"

"I thought we'd have eggs Benedict. We had the ham, and everything for a hollandaise sauce."

Was he for real? He just whipped up his own hollandaise?

"Where'd you get the English muffins?" Were they even invented in the fifties?

"I admit to getting up early to run to the grocery store."

Everything smelled and looked too good, so she didn't really care. "Mmm, I love eggs Benedict."

"I'm happy! I do too. Sit down and I'll pour you some coffee—or do you want something else to drink?"

"Just orange juice. I've never been much of a coffee drinker, and I'm beginning to develop a caffeine addiction." If she went for more than two cups she got antsy and jittery, not to mention having to run to the bathroom every hour.

Bobby went to the refrigerator for the orange juice. He moved so confidently around her kitchen. Yeah, this felt more like her kitchen than the one back in her apartment did.

She stared at him as he poured the orange juice to the backdrop of the rock and roll music. Why did seeing a man who was confidant in the kitchen look so damn sexy? She decided she was willing to think of this as their kitchen.

The eggs Benedict was suspiciously good. She decided these were the best eggs Benedict she'd ever eaten. Bailey was beginning to think he was secretly a chef.

"Bailey is going to have to up her cooking game," she said while chewing on the delicate ensemble of eggs, ham, and muffin. "I don't ever want another Egg McMuffin again."

"I don't mind Bailey's cooking." He slid a piece of muffin along his plate to collect some of the residual hollandaise sauce. "The truth is, I've had gourmet chefs prepare my meals since I was a kid. I know how to cook like this because I watched and learned. But even five-star meals can get old when you eat them every day of your life."

"So, you're saying bad cooking is a pleasant change?"

He shrugged and gave her a half grin. "Yes."

"You know that makes you basically perfect?"

"I try." He looked at the clock. "We should probably get a move on if we don't want to be late for the team meeting."

When she tried to help him with the dishes, he shooed her away and told her to get dressed and he was taking care of it.

She knew she was going to have to change out of her fifties attire once she got to the production office, so she just pulled on slacks, loafers, and a sweater.

She kept her makeup light and styled her hair so it didn't look too old-fashioned. Bobby was already dressed in jeans and a sweatshirt. He carried a bag with him to the car. When she gave the bag a questioning look, his response was simple.

"Leftovers from dinner. And yes, I saved the ham bone."

"What are your plans for the day?" he asked as they drove.

"I'll visit my aunt and uncle. It's an adjustment not talking to her on the phone at least every other day." He gave her an understanding look. "What about you? I know you don't always leave the set, but how do you decompress?"

He gave her a mysterious smile. "If we have time, I'll show you."

Now she was even more curious. For this, she was going to make time.

They reached the production office with plenty of time to spare.

"Okay, so tell me how you spend your spare time."

"Okay, let me drop these leftovers off in the conference room, then we can go to my office."

After that was accomplished, he clasped her hand and led her down several corridors. Whenever they saw others, they were always greeted with smiles and hellos. She didn't know anyone, but was cheerful— unlike the night before, when she'd been overwhelmed. She definitely wanted to go to more watch parties, and she swore to herself the next time, she wouldn't be so weird.

When they finally got to the office, Bobby quickly moved a stack of paperwork to a bookshelf.

"Sorry about the mess. I promise, I'm usually tidier than this."

Bailey looked around curiously. There was a lot to look at. The office was large, and it seemed every available space was filled. The bookshelves held more boxes and bins for papers than it did books. But there were a few knickknacks; a small model airplane, a laughing Buddha sculpture, several records, and photographs of people and places. She saw him in a few of them; out with friends (including some cute girls), boating, at the beach, and other places that seemed International.

His infamous father appeared in only one photograph, and that was apparently a family shot with his mom, siblings, and a much younger Bobby.

The desk sat in front of a large picture window and held a computer with two large monitors. It was stacked with more files that he quickly moved to place in a file cabinet.

"These are new cast members. I've been looking at their bios and developing their scripts," he explained.

She saw a whiteboard on the wall with notes scrawled on nearly every available space. There was a map pinned to another wall and she walked over to look at it. He came over to stand beside her.

"This is the new community of Garden Hills. I really think we can have it fully operational by Christmas, and we should be able to use many of the locations by Thanksgiving."

She gave him a look of awe. "How do you keep all of this straight?"

He shrugged and looked tired. "I take plenty of notes; but it also helps that I love what I do."

"But this doesn't look like chill time…"

"Oh no. Not here." There was an adjoining room and he opened the door and proudly turned on the lights.

There was a drum set. A real drum set with the cymbals and all.

"You play drums?"

"And work out." He gestured to workout equipment off to one side.

This room was much neater than the others. There were posters on the wall of music groups she wasn't familiar with. There was also a comfy couch with a pillow and folded blanket he obviously used for naps.

Bobby took a seat behind his drums and picked up a pair of drumsticks he had sitting in an old coffee can. He began to play a simple beat that grew in intensity until it was full-on music.

Bailey knew nothing about drumming. She had always appreciated guitar and piano, but never thought very much about the drums. But she could clearly see Bobby was a good musician.

When he finished his solo, he hit the cymbals and immediately quieted them with two fingers while pointing the drumsticks at her as she applauded.

"You're really good at that! I had no idea you were a musician!"

He got up and set his drumsticks back in the coffee can. "I played in a band for a few years when I was a teenager. I've done some session work." He gestured to a poster of an album cover.

"A few of my friends are in The Buddha Kings. Have you ever heard of them?"

"No." She shook her head.

"Yeah. That's the problem. No one's heard of them, and they're pretty good." He looked around in pride. "I keep this room soundproof, just in case I want to bust a move at eight in the morning."

"Bust a move?"

"This right here…" He turned on a stereo, and a song from an eighties boy band began playing. He shook his hips and did a few dance moves before cutting off the music with another shrug.

"Once upon a time, I thought I'd like to be Justin Timberlake — but I can't dance or sing."

She hugged him. "You are still very accomplished."

"Thank you."

They smooched for a while before he said they were going to be late and should probably get to the meeting.

The conference room had even more people in it than before and they were all eating the ham.

Some looked at them guiltily as they walked into the room.

"I grabbed some plates and forks from the canteen..." Helen admitted.

"Eat up. That's why I brought it," Bobby said.

Bailey noted that the cold green beans and potatoes au gratin were already gone. They ate it cold?

Bailey saw her mother-in-law approach. Wow...did she ever look different! This morning she wore soft makeup, and her gray hair was layered over her shoulders. Dressed in khaki slacks and a button-up blouse, she looked like a woman in her fifties instead of seventies.

She was holding a plate of ham, green beans, potatoes, and two dinner rolls — and she had the biggest smile on her face.

"Bailey! You are...evil!"

Bailey's brow went up. "Oh..."

Her face was still split in a broad smile. "I'm Georgia, by the way. And I've been thinking about this ham and potatoes and green beans *all* night long!" Bailey grinned while Georgia ate a forkful of the food. "This is fantastic. Now, I'm going to be perfectly honest." She glanced at Bobby, who was just smiling and shaking his head at her. Everyone else had gathered around to listen to Georgia.

"I saw how you made pot pie last week. And when Bob showed me the script and it said I was supposed to criticize everything about the meal, I said to myself, I can't eat that cooking! I'm old, and I got diabetes!" People began to chuckle. "So, it was my idea for me to bring an alternative dish, and it turned out to be just the right touch of rude and self-preservation."

She was really hamming it up, and Bailey was laughing along with everyone else.

"But when I saw that meal on the table" — she shook her head — "That's when I knew I'd messed up. Honey, that soup I ate was terrible, and you were killing me describing how good your meal was. I almost lost it when you apologized for your overly flavored food."

Everyone was in stitches, but Bobby had to finally get them seated so they could begin the meeting.

Bailey was definitely more at ease. The entire cast was so nice.

Bobby introduced the new hires and one of them was Curtis the milkman. They exchanged smiles as Bobby explained he was going to have a role as an activist along with several other Black cast members.

Finally, he introduced the man that played Mr. Edelman, the racist neighbor. He stood and bowed slightly to the others.

"Hello. My name is Guy. I'm happy to be part of the show."

Everyone welcomed them all. Guy met her eyes and quickly looked away before she could give him a smile of greeting.

"So, just in case you didn't know," Bobby said while prepping the laptop to show some film clips, "There's a nightly watch party at the factory starting at about nine thirty p.m. I think I saw some of you there last night..."

"I was out way too late," Pat admitted with a chuckle. "I may have drank a little bit more than I should have." Most people laughed and agreed. But Guy gave Pat a cold, hard glance before looking away. Bailey didn't think she had misunderstood his expression. He didn't like Pat, or something about her.

"I just want you all to know the watch parties are perfectly fine, but it's up to you to make sure you're on time and prepared for filming the next day."

"Yes, sir."

"We will!"

He began playing a stream. "For the second week in a row, Team Bailey wins top clip of the week." Everyone whooped and applauded, and those sitting closest to her clapped her back and nudged her good-naturedly.

"The clip with the most comments was Bailey and Bobby's kiss after their run-in with Mr. Edelman."

"It wasn't that kiss, it's what happened after that kiss!" Helen said. Bobby just blushed.

"Here's the clip of their exchange with Mr. Edelman...and the infamous kiss afterwards."

Everyone sat enthralled as the clip played, including Guy. He may not have had an opportunity to ever see himself on film before and she wondered what he thought. He just held his head up proudly with a slight smile on his face.

Next, they were in the house and she and Bobby were sharing their electrifying kiss. Of course, there were oohs and ahhs and strong applause when they went off to the bedroom together.

Guy was the only one staring at the table with gritted teeth.

Bobby raised his hands and had them quiet. His cheeks were almost red enough to glow. She found his shyness so endearing. "You all may have already figured this out, but Bailey and I are a couple—"

"Of course, you are!"

"You've been a couple! Y'all just didn't know it!"

"Well..." he said with a big smile. "You all know it now."

There was congratulations from everyone— except from Guy, who sat stiffly, trying not to look at anyone.

"Okay, moving on," Bobby said quickly. "The second-most popular scene goes to Team Nadine." Jackie and Tracy both applauded, as they represented both teams.

Bobby showed a clip of Nadine speaking to the adoption agency, who told her they had the identity of her daughter but she had declined to meet her. Nadine broke down and cried, and it was so heartbreaking. Jackie and Tracy were there to comfort her.

Applause erupted after that heartfelt scene.

Bobby passed out scripts. "I always say this, but for the new cast members that don't know me, you'll see that your scripts won't tell you what to say. The production team is just here to tell you what to do. You make the decision on how you're going to achieve that goal. You own your role. You make your character, not me, nor the other writers.

"If you don't have any questions, we can conclude until next week. Any script changes will appear in your mailbox, so be sure to check for them daily. Have a good week."

Everyone rushed out to make their phone calls or link to the Internet before returning to the set. Once the room was empty, he pulled Bailey into an embrace.

"I guess it's time for you to leave."

"Yeah. I need to call my aunt and uncle and I'll head out."

"When you get back call me, and I'll pick you up and drive you back to the house. I'll send you a text so you'll have my cell number."

"It might be late," she said.

"I'll probably be here working late. I have a lot of things to coordinate for next week."

She hadn't even bothered to look at her script. She was going to make it into what she needed it to be, regardless.

He kissed her. "Good job on another successful week."

"Good job to you, as well."

"I'm going to miss you," he said with a sigh.

"You'll be busy, and I'll be back before you know it."

He just pressed his forehead against hers. "I know."

1954 Pepper Pace

Chapter Forty-Six

Bailey called her aunt and uncle's house as she headed for her car. She had a few messages—sales calls, but none from Aunt Mae.

As the phone rang, she made a mental note to bring back her winter coat and gloves, and she also needed another change of clothes.

"Bailey, is that you?"

"Yes. Hi, Aunt Mae. I'm on my way to the house."

"Hmph. I'll see you when you get here."

Hmph? Bailey paused. "Is everything okay?"

"We'll talk about it when you get here." Her aunt's voice seemed to suggest she really wanted to talk about "it" now.

Crap. That kiss was about to catch up with her. Bailey hurried to her car. "Aunt Mae, you might as well tell me now. I have a two-hour drive and it's going to make it seem double if I have this on my mind."

"Chile, why you embarrass me like that? I had some of my friends from the neighborhood come over to watch the show. I'm bragging about you! And you go open that can of green beans and serve it to your mother-in-law. Bailey..." It was almost as if she could see her aunt's head shaking forlornly.

Bailey stopped in her tracks in complete disbelief that of everything that happened this past week, the canned green beans was the thing that had triggered her aunt.

"You did so good with that ham, and you had to go and open up a can of green beans? It ain't even hard to make 'em fresh."

"Oh..." was all Bailey could say.

"When you get here, I'm going to give you a lesson on how to cook. The way you make your grits...why you get those short-cooking ones? This is all my fault. I'm so embarrassed..."

Bailey was a little tickled and very much relieved.

"Okay. I can use as much help as I can get."

"I know. I should have never sent you out into the world without at least knowing how to make an egg salad sandwich the right way. You ain't put a lick of sweet pickle relish in it! How you going to put mayonnaise and mustard but no pickle relish?"

"I forgot to pick some up."

"Well, that boy is a saint for eating that mess. You get on over here so we can go grocery shopping."

"Yes, ma'am."

"Okay. I'll see you in a little bit. Drive safe. Love you."

"I will. Love you too."

Bailey shook her head and got into her car. She put in her favorite CDs, sang at the top of her lungs, and just enjoyed the freedom of being herself for a while.

Her phone trilled, indicating a text message and she hazarded a quick glance and saw an unknown number, but a kissy smiley face.

Yeah, she was going to save that ASAP.

When Bailey finally pulled up into the driveway, her aunt came out to stand on the front porch with a broad smile on her face. Despite her recent tongue-lashing, Bailey couldn't help her own smile.

She enjoyed being on the show, getting to act and being recognized for her efforts. In hindsight, even the bad parts had to be considered a learning experience. But not talking to her aunt on a regular basis was harder than anything the show had thrown at her thus far.

Aunt Mae pulled her into a long hug. When she finally pulled back, she patted Bailey's hair. "You look so pretty. Come on in here while I get my purse and coat. It got chilly out here."

Bailey chuckled. "We're really going grocery shopping? I thought you were kidding."

Her aunt looked back at her with a raised brow. "No. I'm not kidding. Isn't there a farmer's market in town?"

"No. I don't think so." She followed her aunt into the house and the smells of past meals, carpet deodorizer, and her aunt and uncle wrapped her in a warmth of nostalgia. Bailey realized that while she liked her new house, it probably wouldn't really feel like home until it smelled like her and Bobby, with a hint of all the meals they shared.

"Every town in the '50s had a farmer's market, or at the very least, some places to buy corn and melons off the side of the road." Her aunt pulled on a light coat and picked up her pocketbook. "The Black people always went to the farmer's market. That's why we know how to make vegetables taste so good. Come on, I'll drive."

"Where's Uncle Dewbug?" Bailey asked as she looked around. "I didn't get a chance to say hi."

"He went to lay down. You know he's out for the count once he gets some food in his belly. He'll be awake by the time we get back. Did you eat?"

"Yes, ma'am. Bobby made breakfast."

She huffed. "That boy know if he wants to eat good, he better learn to cook."

"Aunt Mae, I'm not bad!"

She was just met by her aunt's playful chuckle.

Bailey had to admit, she didn't mind the drive to the market. It was like old times. They got caught up on all the gossip she'd missed out on. They were so absorbed in chitchatting that their time at the market went fast.

Aunt Mae didn't like the way the tomatoes looked and explained she had to pay attention to what was good based on the season. For that reason, they picked up a lot of collards, two cabbages, sweet potatoes, apples and oranges, and squash.

"Squash." Bailey wrinkled her nose. "Not that. I don't want to learn to cook that."

"Chile, squash is easy, and you are a grown-up now. You might just like it now." Bailey made a face just like she had when she was a kid. "Well, I'm going to make a squash casserole and you can just take some back to that husband of yours."

Bailey gave her a swift look. Did she buy all of this thinking she was going to take it back to the set? "Oh, Aunt Mae, I can't take back a bunch of prepared food. It won't fit into the story line."

Her aunt gave her a confused look. "What you just said doesn't fit."

"What do you mean?"

"That mother-in-law got to come to the house, but I didn't. I heard you speak of me; your aunt Mae. So, I figured your character visits your aunt and uncle every Sunday just like the real Bailey does, right?"

Bailey considered that. It seemed feasible Bailey would do that. "Yes. That sounds right."

"Then your character's aunt Mae wouldn't send you home without a bunch of good fixin's—especially knowing you can't cook and you're a newlywed. You have to represent Black culture, baby girl, just like you have to represent the '50s. We just wouldn't act like that."

Bailey wasn't so sure if Bobby or the rest of the crew would agree. She tried to remember if there was anything in the contract that discussed bringing back items from off set. But she wasn't going to argue with her aunt. She'd figure something out.

They got back to the house and Bailey had to admit, she was excited about learning how to prepare these dishes; especially the greens.

By that time, Uncle Dewbug was awake and in his favorite chair watching sports on television.

"Hi, baby girl." He greeted her with a big bear hug.

"Hi, Uncle Dewbug. How you been?"

His brow raised as he regarded her. "I've been very concerned about you, little girl."

"Me?"

"More specifically, you and that man you're living with. I have eyes. I see what's going on."

A hard blush pushed up Bailey's neck to warm her cheeks. But surprisingly, it was Aunt Mae that came to her defense.

"Oh, Bug, Bailey has common sense. And it was pretty obvious the boy liked her for a long time before she even realized it. Now they're on the same page."

Bailey gave her aunt a shocked look.

"Oh, don't look so surprised. I used to be young once." She placed a bag of groceries on the breakfast bar. "Bernie, run out and get the last bag, will you?"

"Yes. But I want you to be careful. That boy is still a Chesterfield, and more girls have come out about the daddy paying them off to keep quiet. If there was truly justice in this world, they'd put that man *under* the jail!"

Bailey stopped them before her uncle could leave the house for the remaining grocery bag. "Guys, I wanted to tell you something I feel is good news, and I hope you'll feel the same. Bobby — Robert — and I have decided we want to date. He's...my boyfriend now."

Uncle Dewbug's worried expression intensified. "You just be careful," he said, and he went out to the car. But Aunt Mae was the one that surprised her the most today.

"Bailey, there ain't nothing wrong with opening up to someone you care about. And it's so easy to see he cares for you and you feel the same. I like that boy if he's anything like the man he plays on the show. And since you are just like the girl on the show, I have to think he's a good person."

Bailey relaxed. "He is. And I really do like him."

Her aunt gave her hand a pat. "Anybody watching the show can see that. Now come on. These vegetables ain't going to wash themselves and we ain't got all night."

They washed and removed the stems from the collards and talked about something different; a topic she and her aunt had never discussed before.

One moment Bailey was talking about how well she was being received by the fans and the rest of the crew, and the next thing she knew they were talking about something even deeper.

"When I was a teenager, I seen a man get spit on by a bunch of white teens and I wanted to do something. I was so outraged for that man, and I could see he had to hold himself back from doing something about it.

"In the end, I just walked away and he did the same, because one man could not have done anything but get beat down, put in jail, or worse.

"When I was young, I didn't do much to fight the system. I saw bad things, but I knew I didn't have the power to change them. I just followed the same course everybody before me followed.

"And sometime later I heard about the civil rights movement. I thought about that day a lot. I even joined some protests before my mama found out and beat my tail."

"You never told me."

"I know, but I'm not proud. I didn't do nearly as much as I could have. Because I was scared. And that day, so long ago, I had not been strong enough to stand up on my own, or to back up another person that needed my help. Because I was scared.

"I have always wondered what would have happened if I had stepped forward, and someone else had done the same. And if all the people that had witnessed what I'd seen had joined forces, and maybe we would have started our own civil rights movement."

"There had to be a lot of moments where people fought back, and sometimes they won and sometimes they lost," Bailey said.

Aunt Mae paused and leaned her elbows against the sink front. "You know what keeps people complacent? It's fear of the unknown. Some people a long time ago were heinous enough to figure out fear is the best way to control another human being, and they made fear into an art form.

"By cutting others down with insults, treating them as inferior, and scaring them with violence, humans can control other humans very easily. One overseer controlled a plantation of slaves. A group of soldiers led twenty times their numbers to gas chambers, and tens of thousands of Indians were led down the Trail of Tears by what would amount to a handful of soldiers. All because of fear."

"That's true," Bailey agreed quietly.

Aunt Mae resumed slicing through layers of freshly washed collards. "But people aren't so easily tricked once you figure out fear has crippled you more than anything else. Me and that man that got spit on could have easily taken on those teenagers. I guess that's why I like your show. They're telling the truth. They're *showing* the truth."

Chapter Forty-Seven

That conversation stayed on Bailey's mind as she drove back to the set later that night. It was just another reason she knew joining the production of 1954 had been a good decision.

She did not consider herself anywhere near in the league of those that pioneered the movement. But she was aware that what was happening with this production went beyond entertainment. And everyone that contributed to the story line was bringing awareness to the truth.

And just maybe, everyone was a little afraid.

Part of the truth was, her aunt was right when she'd sent a care package home with her. Family would play a pivotal part of their lives, especially a family that supported her decisions. And she wouldn't dare write her aunt and uncle's story as being less than what they truly were to her.

It was after ten when she got back to the set. She stayed in her car and texted Bobby.

"I'm back. Can you come to the lot? I brought something."

"Intrigued." He texted back. "On my way."

He was there in moments. He had probably even run. She got out of the car and he pulled her into a hug and swift kiss before looking over her shoulders at the car.

"What? Did you bring a puppy or a kitten?"

"No!" she laughed. "Do you want a puppy or kitten?"

"I thought about it. But I think it's too much for now. How was your visit?"

"It was great. It's always good." She moved to open the trunk. "My aunt and uncle always seem to bring something important about the fifties to mind." She stepped in front of the open trunk before showing him the contents.

"So, let me explain—"

"Uh-oh," he said.

"No. It's nothing bad. I figure that each Sunday while I've been away, Bailey is off visiting her aunt and uncle. And maybe even sometimes you come along."

He nodded. "Yeah, that sounds right."

"Bailey would be very close to her family, since we know Aunt Mae and Uncle Dewbug raised her. So, it would only make sense that Aunt Mae would send her a care package home…"

His brow went up. Bailey finally stepped aside and showed him the two bunches of greens, a bag of green beans, the two large squash, and two fairly decent tomatoes.

He looked at the items. "We'd have to get rid of the plastic before we take it to the house—"

She looked at him in pleasant surprise. "You're okay with this?"

"Yeah, it makes perfect sense. We just need to talk about your aunt and uncle more during the show. But what smells so good?" He moved aside the bags and saw a glass casserole dish that was half-filled with squash casserole.

Bailey lightly bit her lower lip. "Aunt Mae was convinced I'd like her variation of squash casserole now that I'm an adult. And she was right. So, she sent the rest home with me…"

Bobby threw his head back and laughed. "I think I love your aunt already."

She clapped her hands together happily. "We can keep it?"

He pulled her into a kiss. "What we can do is eat it before we go home. I don't think the cookware is 1950s, so just to be safe, we'll keep it here."

She smirked. "Of course. Let's eat it now, even though we could keep the dish in the cabinet where no one would see it..."

"But I'm so hungry now," he said playfully. "Why does it smell like Thanksgiving dressing?"

"Because the recipe calls for a box of stuffing mix."

She grabbed the bag of vegetables while he kept hold of the warm casserole and they headed back to the office.

When they got back to the house, she put the vegetables in the refrigerator with the exception of the tomatoes, which Aunt Mae warned her to place on the windowsill and to never store in the refrigerator unless they were cut.

Bobby's belly was full because he'd eaten all of the remaining casserole once Bailey had explained she couldn't eat another bite.

Aunt Mae had shown her how to cook half of the collard greens, fresh green beans, smothered cabbage, the proper way to make grits, the proper way to make egg salad, and just in case she needed to know, the proper way to make cornbread.

And of course, the fruits of her lessons had to be consumed by someone. They had talked and ate, and it had been just like old times.

When everything was put in place, Bailey looked around at her neat kitchen and nodded in satisfaction. She saw Bobby leaned against the kitchen entrance with a sly smile on his face.

"I have a little surprise too."

"What is it?"

He held out his hand for hers and she took it tentatively. He led her to the bedroom and she grew suspicious—but in a good way.

Had he changed his mind about having sex? That didn't really sound like an appropriate surprise, although she thoroughly missed smooching.

But once in the bedroom, he walked her straight through to the connecting bathroom and she remembered and got excited.

"Did you—?"

He beamed as she took in a new, white shower curtain. Which meant there would be a brand-new shower.

"Ta dah!" he exclaimed.

"Oh my gosh, we just moved into the twenty-first century!"

"They did have showers well before the '50s, and even though I like the way this house looked without it—I have to admit, this is much more convenient."

"Well, I love it!"

"Then it was well worth pulling one of the plumbers off the Garden Hills project to get it done today."

"Oh! Speaking of Garden Hills, my aunt says the show should have a farmer's market. I'm not talking about right away, because I know you're busy. But it was a way to save money—plus you said there are farmers and they can make extra money selling to all the new people."

His eyes brightened.

"You are brilliant—you *and* your aunt!" He hugged her and swung her around. "That is a great idea..." He seemed suddenly in deep thought. He gave her a quick look. "I need to make some notes...do you mind? I know we haven't seen each other all day..."

She grinned. "Of course I don't mind. I want to take a long, hot shower." She didn't tell him she was also pretty tired, and after the shower, wrapping her hair and getting ready for bed, she'd probably be out for the count.

He kissed her and as a second thought, lingered for a second kiss that lasted several minutes before she pulled back.

"Okay, if you're going to take those notes you'd better do it or neither of us are going to get around to our plans."

"Right." With one last peck, Bobby hurried to his office.

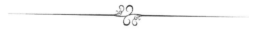

When Bailey woke up the next morning, she was snuggled against Bobby. She had fallen asleep before he had come back to bed, and while she knew she might do that, she had honestly thought she'd wake up the moment he climbed in beside her.

She must have been more tired than she thought, or she just slept better with him beside her. It was probably a little bit of both.

If she had been tired, then she knew he definitely was. Lord only knew when he'd finally gone to bed.

Bailey got up as quietly as possible and crept to the bathroom, where she prepared for her opening scene. She looked forward to a brand-new week and had scanned her script before leaving her aunt and uncle's house. Predictably, it revealed nothing about what she'd have to prepare for ahead of time. There wasn't even anything like, Bailey does her chores. Bailey goes to the grocery store. Monday through Friday it simply said, "Bailey's daily routine." But on Saturday it said, "Date night."

That meant Bobby didn't have anything planned—which she honestly doubted, or he was truly allowing her to write her own script.

Once she was finished in the bathroom, she went to the bed and leaned over to place a kiss on Bobby's forehead. He truly was sound asleep because he jerked in his sleep a second before his eyes opened.

"Hey, sorry to wake you, honey," she whispered. "But I'm about to start my scene and I didn't want you to oversleep."

"Thank you, Bae. I won't fall back asleep."

"What time did you come to bed?"

"It was a little after midnight. I had plenty of sleep." He reached up and pulled her down for a kiss. "I'm sorry I missed our bedtime date."

"Me too. But it just means we'll have more to look forward to tonight."

"Yep."

She gave him one last kiss and left the room.

For breakfast, Bailey prepared sausage patties, French toast, and scrambled eggs.

She packed Bobby two ham and cheese sandwiches with the leftover ham from Saturday. She packed the last serving of chocolate pudding from dinner with her mother-in-law, and finally, because she knew Aunt Mae would be watching, she bypassed potato chips and packed him the last of the carrot sticks with a side of ranch dressing.

There. Aunt Mae would not be able to find fault with today's meal.

Bobby came into the room just as she poured the coffee.

"Morning, Bae." He pulled her in for a kiss, being careful not to get burned by the percolator.

"Morning. Did you sleep well?" Bailey took her seat.

"I did. But I think I ate too much at your Aunt Mae's house."

"Why do people tend to want to feed you?"

He chuckled. "It must be my boyish looks."

"Speaking of boyish, I have to remember to call your mom and thank her for that soup. I didn't need to make lunch or dinner yesterday."

He nodded while chewing enthusiastically. "This French toast is good, Bae."

"Is it really?"

"Yes, it is."

"Thank you," she said with a beaming smile.

As soon as he left for work, Bailey quickly set out the two empty milk containers in their metal crate on the porch along with this month's payment.

She wasn't sure what time Curtis made his delivery to their neighborhood, but she wanted to catch him and say hi. Even though he now had a recurring role, she wanted to tie him to her story line whenever possible.

That was the same with Helen. She had been her first friend on the set, but the neighborhood was also racially divided. She just wasn't sure whose court the ball was in now.

She supposed she'd be taking the bus to the grocery store today. There wouldn't be a Black-owned store for several more weeks. Today there would be two things she wasn't looking forward to facing; sitting in the back of the bus, and having the white customers get served before her.

Well, one thing for sure was that nothing was going to get done until she got dressed for the day — no stretching today. Today was going to be another busy one.

She was sitting at the vanity styling her hair when she saw the milk truck pull up across the street. Bailey quickly applied her lipstick and slipped on her shoes and hurried to the front door.

She hoped she wouldn't come off like a desperate housewife, but she wasn't dressed in anything fancy despite the fact that she would be going into town. She'd chosen the dark-blue skirt and one of the short-sleeved sweaters that felt like cashmere.

She looked out the living room window, waiting for Curtis to appear on her porch. Soon enough, she saw him with his carrier filled with dairy products.

As soon as he stooped to pick up her empty containers, Bailey opened the front door.

He looked up at her with a surprised smile. "Good morning, Mrs. Banks."

"Call me Bailey."

He nodded. "Okay, Bailey. Good morning."

"Good morning to you, as well."

"Did you have a good time at the juke joint the other night?" he asked as he glanced at her order form. He then began to place her items into her carton.

"It was fun. I had a great time."

"It's a nice place to hang out at the end of a long day." He pocketed her payment and picked up her basket and handed it to her. "Maybe I'll see you there again."

"Do you go there a lot?" she asked while accepting her basket.

"A few times a week."

"I'll go back if for no other reason than another plate of food."

He chuckled. "You're right about that food!" He glanced to the side before looking back at her. "I better go. I don't want your neighbors jumping to conclusions. Two Negroes talking will send tongues wagging."

"You're right. We're obviously conspiring about something. Thanks, Curtis. I'll see you around."

"I'm sure we will. Have a good day."

She was happy they'd had their run-in and made up before meeting here. She saw in him another potential friend. She closed the door and put away her items and sat down to make out her grocery list.

"Pinto beans," she said aloud. "Toilet paper. Oh! And sweet relish. Fresh fruit; whatever looks good. A loaf of bread. Ground beef." She tapped the pen to her lip as she thought. "Some chili would be good with the leftover beans." She jotted that down on her list.

"Meat loaf tonight, and I can soak the beans for tomorrow. Yep. That's done!"

The doorbell rang. She looked up in surprise. This wasn't in the script.

She went to the door curiously, hoping it wasn't the Clines back to whittle down her resolve to move out of the neighborhood. She was going to be very curt if it was.

It was Helen, standing on her stoop fidgeting uncomfortably.

"Hi, Helen. Come on in."

Helen smiled, visibly relaxing. "Sure. Thanks."

"Wait," Bailey said before she could step across the threshold. "You're not here to convince me to move out of the neighborhood, are you?"

"No!"

Bailey grinned. "Then come on in."

She came in and gave Bailey an apologetic look. "I heard about what happened and I'm so sorry. People can be terrible, and I'm not just talking about Mr. Edelman."

"I have some coffee brewed. Do you want to sit down for a bit?"

"Yes. That sounds nice." Helen followed her into the kitchen and sat at the table while Bailey got their coffee and a box of cookies. "The Clines had some nerve! I can't imagine what I'd do if my neighbors asked me to move. I told Hank about it. I called him while he was on the road. He agreed it was a lousy thing to do. Thanks, dear." She accepted her coffee.

"I can't say I'm completely surprised."

"I am! That takes some gall to do something like that!"

Bailey sat down and gave the woman across from her a meaningful look. "I really appreciate your kindness, Helen."

Helen quickly shook her head. "It's not kindness. It's friendship."

Bailey smiled. "Yes. Friendship. Have some cookies?"

Helen grimaced. "I'm trying to lose fifteen stubborn pounds..." She picked up a cookie. "I'll exercise extra tomorrow."

Helen was funny. Bailey was happy she had an ally in the neighborhood. And a friend.

"I came over to ask if you want to go shopping together. I know you go on Mondays."

"I did have plans to go shopping today. I was going to take the bus, but I'd much rather go with you." Besides, she might even get served at the same time Helen did if they were together.

"Perfect! I have to do my shopping too. I heard about a diet that's guaranteed to cause you to lose weight, even in the first week. You have to ingest a tapeworm, but somehow, they take it out when you get too skinny."

"Oh. I don't know about that one," Bailey grimaced.

"You're right. It sounds extreme."

They talked like that, as if they were old friends, all the way to the grocery store and back.

Chapter Forty-Eight

Bailey awoke when she felt the bed dip. She rolled over and Bobby slipped his arm beneath her head and gave her a kiss.

"What time is it?" she asked.

"Just after midnight," he whispered, and settled with her snuggled in his arms. "Go back to sleep, sweetie."

"It was a good day," she said sleepily.

"It was a good shoot," he agreed.

She was about to drift back to sleep when the difference between those words caught her attention. "Do you only call it a good day when there's drama?"

"Hmm?" he asked.

She lifted her head to look at him. "I don't know what I'm talking about..." she finally said, and lay back down to snuggle tiredly against him again. "I remember hearing somewhere that every scene has to have conflict in order to be a good scene, and we had absolutely no conflict today."

"Oh." Bobby sat up and looked down at her. "I guess there are rules to storytelling like there are rules to acting. But...the way I see it, the people who are watching our show and making it popular don't care about rules. It's a balance, right? No one wants to see too much of either; especially not the bad." He sighed. "I'm just listening to the audience. They're engaged when they see all the terrible things Bailey's going through but they're happy when they see her happy. It's a balance."

The next day, Bailey thought about balance when it was another good day but couldn't decide if that made for good scenes. When she and Helen went for a walk with the cameraman following behind them and there was no Mr. Edelman or the Clines to harass her, it felt good. It felt successful.

And on Wednesday, when she and Pat talked on the phone about her date with the guy at work and she invited them to date night with her and Bobby on Friday, Bailey called it another good day.

On Thursday she cleaned and cooked wearing heels and bright-red lipstick. Her bean soup with ham had been spot-on and the cornbread made from scratch was light and fluffy. She called it another good day because the only conflict she had was Bobby's late-night gas from eating three bowls of beans.

But by the time the weekend rolled around, Bailey realized what truly made the difference between a good scene and a good *day*. Her day had decidedly stopped being good, but it most likely made for the best scene 1954 had ever had, and would most likely have for a very long time.

"Good morning, Bae." Bobby greeted her by snuggling her from behind and placing a kiss on her neck.

"Good morning, honey," she said happily. "I figured we'd have a light breakfast."

He smiled crookedly before rubbing his belly. "Thanks, honey…it was a bit of a rough night."

"Yep. I told you not to have that extra bowl of beans." He sat down and bit into his buttered toast while looking at the big bowl of grits in front of him.

"That's a big bowl of grits."

"Eat it with sugar and butter. You'll like it."

He gave her a dubious look before reaching for the sugar bowl and sprinkling a liberal amount of sugar onto it.

She opened the refrigerator. "What do you want for lunch?"

"Do we have any more of that egg salad? That recipe you got from your aunt was good."

"Yes, we do." She grabbed the last of the egg salad, the lettuce, and sliced one of the tomatoes she'd gotten over the weekend. She quickly whipped up a salad and topped it with the egg salad.

"Mm, this is good." She looked behind her and saw he'd already eaten most of the bowl of sugared grits. She was happy he'd tipped her off that he liked it that way but his character would never know it if she didn't introduce it to him.

"Do you want more?"

"Just a little more."

After she sat down with her cup of coffee, she asked if he'd remembered to make the reservation for Madonna's.

"Yep. Eight o'clock on the dot."

"I can't wait to meet this zoot suit-wearing man of Pat's."

"Maybe I should wear a zoot suit."

"Maybe not."

He chuckled and stood. "I'd better go."

"Have a good day," she said after receiving a kiss on the cheek.

"Love you," he said as he headed out of the room with his lunch.

"Love you too." Those words were coming natural now, even though they had yet to say them after the cameras stopped filming.

The after-filming make-out sessions were still hot and heavy, and she still looked forward to them. Those make-out sessions still had not led to anything more than touching and kissing—which Bailey still found very exciting. Very.

After Bobby left, Bailey got changed, did her stretching exercises, but then had to quickly start the laundry if she wanted it all washed and dried before Bobby got home.

It was a cold October morning, and soon she was going to have to switch from workout shorts to something more season-appropriate. In the meantime, she threw on a sweater and hoped Haley Brinkman wouldn't be watching her from over the fence. She had no desire to chitchat while her teeth chattered.

After getting the items hung out to dry, Bailey made quick work of her remaining chores. It went quickly because she had a good excuse not to get gussied up. She'd later have to get completely made up for double-date night and she refused to do it twice. She simply slipped on ankle-length pants and a pair of loafers.

Dressing casually as a 1950s housewife meant you still had to be presentable in case of an unannounced guest—and of course, for the cameras.

She decided to call Helen to see if she wanted to take another walk. But Helen happily explained Hank was home and they planned to spend the weekend catching up on…private time.

Okay then.

She went out to the clothesline to see if her washing was dry enough to bring it in. Nope. She was not looking forward to hanging clothes out to dry in the winter. Aunt Mae said laundry went outside regardless of the weather — with the exception of rain. And if it had to come in before it was completely dry, then it was hung over radiators and doors. Bailey decided she'd hang clothes in the garage before she'd stomp around in the snow dealing with frozen clothes.

When her stomach began to rumble, she made a peanut butter and jelly sandwich with a glass of delicious whole milk Curtis delivered. She ate while leafing through the Sears catalogue, dog-earing the corners whenever something interested her.

She still had yet to actually order something but when she got to the shoes, it was going to be game on!

She went out and checked the clothes. They were finally dry, and Haley still hadn't shown up. It was turning out to be another stress-free day and that made her happy.

Bobby would be home in about an hour, so she decided to finally get ready. The supper club was considered fancy, but she was limited on her fancy clothing. She decided on one of her wrap dresses, the pearls with the matching earrings, and her nice coat and gloves.

She styled her hair by pinning it up into a French twist. Her curls were fading fast, even with pinning them each night, and she looked forward to visiting Juanita tomorrow for a refresh.

Bailey reapplied her makeup and checked her appearance in the mirror. She patted her belly. The pooch had disappeared, and things definitely felt looser. Soon she'd *have* to get a new wardrobe.

When Bobby got home, she hurried to greet him at the door.

"Va-va-va-voom!" he said with a raised brow. She appreciated his enthusiasm, even though he'd already seen her wearing the same dress.

She still did a quick pose and twirl before he pulled her into a hug. Men in the '50s liked to make sure you knew it was time for loving. Instead of being cringey, it was sexy seeing his confidence and self-assuredness as he took control.

"How was work?"

"It was good. Mr. Adams put a date on when we can go forward with the McCarthy poll."

"That *is* good." She took his coat and hat and hung them in the closet.

"We're thinking first week in November. You'll still do the poll in the Negro neighborhoods?"

"Yes. I'll even ask Pat if she might want to help."

"That would be nice. We can bring it up tonight at dinner. Speaking of dinner, I'm starving. Any chance I can have a snack before we meet up for dinner?"

"Of course."

He loosened his tie. "Okay, let me get changed."

She turned off the radio and put on the evening news so they could snack while watching television.

She placed cookies on a tray along with a glass of milk for him and a cup of hot tea for herself. She knew he liked dunking his cookies, and she'd already had her limit on milk for the day.

They watched television, ate their snack, and made conversation about the most random things before it was time to meet Pat and her date at the club.

She stared in awe at how far the development had come in less than a week.

Garden Hills was beginning to look like an actual community. There were so many construction crews working on separate projects that Bailey knew the cost had to be out of this world. She glanced at Bobby, who was smiling proudly.

He was using his money to fund this. This project had to work.

"It's shaping up," he said, as if reading her mind.

"Do you really think we'll be able to go door-to-door here by the first of November?"

"I'm thinking about trying something different. Instead of everything being in real time, I'd like to splice shots together of you just knocking on doors and speaking to people."

"That's a great idea. That way, the cameras won't pick up the construction crews."

"Right."

She gazed out at all the sights. "This is amazing. Whenever you decide to stop filming the show, you can open this up for visitors like they do at Renaissance festivals."

He didn't respond.

Chapter Forty-Nine

Pat and her date, Marvin, were waiting for them at the entrance. She and Pat kissed cheeks while Marvin and Bobby shook hands. He was dressed in a zoot suit, but Bailey had to admit it was pretty cool-looking.

His hair was slicked back and he had a pretty-boy moustache. It's what she always thought of those men that probably spent more time in the mirror than she did—which was probably most men.

He was handsome with his hat tilted to the side and his shiny shoes. Pat looked equally good in a form-fitting dress that had ruffles at the hem, which was sure to flare out when they danced.

She was definitely going clothes shopping. Besides, she was young and newly married. Wouldn't she have cute clothes from when she used to hang out and date?

"This club is rocking," Marvin commented while tapping his feet to the beat of the live music. Once again there was a singer, this time a Black man that shouted and got the dancers riled up.

The hostess led them to their table, but Marvin was anxious to get up and dance.

"Let's cut a rug, baby!" he said while taking Pat's hand.

"Don't you want to order drinks first?" she asked while chuckling. But she got up with him.

Marvin turned to Bobby off-handedly. "Order us a couple of beers. This music is hitting me in all the right places."

Bobby grinned. "You got it." Once they were out on the dance floor, Marvin led Pat into some very intricate dance steps. They swung and spun and hopped and skipped. Marvin had to be a professional.

"Do you want to dance?" Bobby asked nervously.

"Um..." She was going to have to practice if this was going to turn out to be a regular hangout. "How about we wait for something slower?"

He nodded in relief.

The waitress came, and Bobby ordered beers for them all. Pat and Marvin danced through another song while she and Bobby studied the menu for something new to try.

Finally, Pat pulled away from Marvin and headed back to the table patting her chest as if she was winded. Marvin followed reluctantly, as if he could live out on that dance floor.

He picked up his beer and took a long drink. "Thanks, brother. You get this round and I'll get the next."

"Yep." He turned his attention to Pat. "Bailey told me you just started at the factory. That's rotten how they let you go from the bank."

"Yeah, but I hear my replacement isn't nearly as efficient as I was."

"They don't care about that girl's efficiency," Marvin said dismissively. "They only care about that 'image.' " He made air quotes.

Bobby nodded thoughtfully.

Pat took Bailey's hand and squeezed it. "This place is great; the music, the vibe, everything!"

"It's a little pricey," Marvin complained.

Pat gave him a sharp look. "Well, I don't mind going half on the bill—"

"No, no. I'm not saying that," he quickly replied, and gave Bobby an embarrassed laugh as if to say, ladies these days don't know how to take a joke. "I'm paying for everything." He put his arm on the back of her chair possessively.

Bailey's smile faltered. That was creepy, as if he assumed this date gave him rights to her.

"You two check out the menu while I take my wife out for a spin on the dance floor." The music wasn't exactly a slow song, but it wasn't fast-moving bebop either.

"Oh, we already know what we're going to have," Marvin replied.

Pat lowered her menu. "We do?"

"Yes, I scoped the menu on my way home yesterday and the Caesar salad sounds perfect."

"Salad?" was the last Bailey heard before Bobby had her out on the dance floor.

"It doesn't look too good for Marvin," Bailey commented.

"He seems a bit pushy," Bobby said before he began doing his version of the boogie-woogie. He wasn't bad at it, but her woogie to his boogie left a lot to be desired. Still, she laughed and had fun clapping her hands at her man when he went into a frenzied solo.

They returned to the table after only one dance. Pat applauded them while Marvin slouched and drank a second beer. He'd only bought one for him and Pat.

"You sure know how to cut a rug, Bobby," Pat said.

"You've obviously been around plenty of Coloreds," Marvin said while glancing at Bailey.

"No," Bobby shook his head. "Not really. I guess I'm just not too embarrassed to look ridiculous trying my best."

Good answer! Good answer! Bailey wanted to yell as if she was on the *Family Feud* show.

The waiter came and took their orders. They allowed Pat and Marvin to order first. Sure enough, they ordered the Caesar salad and when asked if they wanted to add chicken, Pat blurted out yes.

Bailey ordered the same, even though she actually wanted to try the beef stroganoff. Bobby ordered the Caesar salad as well, also *splurging* on the added chicken.

"May we get a bottle of wine, please?" Bobby requested.

"Put that on our bill!" Marvin said.

"No. I have it," Bobby said while passing the waiter his and Bailey's menus.

"Thanks, my man," Marvin said. He took Pat's hand again. "Let's dance."

Pat followed him good-naturedly, but Bailey could tell she wasn't really up for more dancing.

Eventually, the food came and the salad was outstanding. They did have to fill up on dinner rolls, though.

Bailey finally had an opportunity to ask them about helping with the poll.

"You know, Bobby works for the paper, and he has a great idea to take a poll on the opinions on Joseph McCarthy after all that red scare nonsense."

"So many people from my mom's generation really bought into it. But I wonder how many people only followed those ideas because they worried about what others might think. And now that he's the one that's being censored, I think it would make a great article."

"I don't think Negroes cared as much about being invaded by communists as the whites," Pat said.

"A communist never enslaved my pappy," Marvin added.

"It would be a great way to hear those opinions," Bobby said with excitement. "People who had liberal ideas were mainly targeted. If I was more of an important person, and if his crazy ideas weren't determined to be baseless, I might have been blackballed or even thrown into jail just for falling in love with my wife."

Marvin looked at him. "Yeah, man. That's right."

"I'm going to be conducting the polls in the Negro areas of town and I could sure use some help," Bailey said.

"It sounds like fun. Count me in!" Pat said.

"You mean going door-to-door? For free?" Marvin snickered. "That sounds too much like work for me."

Pat leaned forward. "I'll do it with you. Just let me know when."

Bailey grinned. "Thank you, sis!"

Marvin poured himself another glass of wine.

Bailey could have stayed for the rest of the night, but Bobby began to yawn right around the time Marvin suggested he and Pat split a dessert.

"I'm so sorry," he apologized. "Work has been mad lately."

Pat brightened as if she was being rescued. "It's fine." She looked at Marvin. "It has been a long day..."

"You want to leave? We haven't done hardly any dancing."

"Maybe next time?" He eventually nodded.

As they went out to the parking lot, they hugged and shook hands and said they'd see each other again.

Three of the people present probably knew that when they did, it wouldn't include one of them...

Bobby and Bailey sat in the car. It was well after nine so if they returned home, there would be no filming.

"Watch party?" he asked hopefully. She enthusiastically agreed.

They drove to the factory laughing about their evening. "I told Marvin to make it a terrible date—but I didn't tell Pat..."

"Oh my God! You and your authenticity."

"But it worked," he grinned. "Did you see her face when he ordered salad for her?" Bobby laughed.

"That was an asshole thing to do."

"He's not really an asshole. He's pretty cool. And he's going to be a regular. I just don't want anyone to think that all the African-American characters are one-dimensional."

"One-dimensional?"

"If there has to be good and bad whites, then there should also be good and bad Blacks. Don't you think?"

"Do you think there is such a thing as a bad Black person?" She stared at him. His brow creased as he looked at her. She suddenly burst out laughing. "I'm just messing with you."

He laughed in relief.

Once again, the watch party was fun. They were playing clips of Nadine when they arrived and only showed the events of the double date once Pat and Marvin arrived about an hour later.

He had changed out of the zoot suit and he laughed at himself good-naturedly as he watched himself on the big screen. Pat turned to Bobby and playfully glared at him.

"I'll have you know that we had to get hamburgers after leaving the restaurant!" Everyone laughed. Bailey loved the energy of the cast and crew, especially at the watch parties. She liked having date night but hoped they'd make the watch parties a regular occurrence.

Saturday morning, Bailey hummed while she prepared breakfast. It was going to be a big one, since Bobby had been such a good sport to eat light when he could have had a steak last night.

She made instant pancakes — Aunt Mae was going to have something to say about that! She fried sausage and scrambled eggs and diced up canned peaches and thawed frozen strawberries and finally she warmed the maple syrup.

When Bobby came into the room wearing his robe and slippers, with tousled hair and stubbled cheeks, she could not have been more attracted to him.

"Good morning." He pulled her into his arms and they kissed for what seemed like a full minute.

"Last night was fun—" she began.

"...despite..."

"Yeah. I wonder how long that's going to last. But I guess I'll find out at my hair appointment."

"Okay. Let's have lunch at Maybelle's after I pick you up."

"Really? After all that money we spent at Madonna's last night?"

"We actually didn't spend that much. It does pay to be thrifty."

"What a sweet way to put it."

Later, they drove into town. Once again, no one harassed her—not with Bobby watching her walk into the beauty salon. And while she was there, Pat cracked jokes at Marvin's expense and Miss Baker made snarky jokes while Juanita raved about the movie *Carmen Jones*.

If life was good when things ran smoothly, then why couldn't a reality show be the same way?

She left feeling very comfortable with her beauty shop family. Bobby was waiting in the car reading the paper and listening to rockabilly when he saw her and joined her at the sidewalk so they could walk to Miss Maybelle's. She was definitely going to have a big, juicy burger and a chocolate milkshake.

"Bobby?" a female voice said. "Bobby Banks?"

They turned. A young white woman had just stepped out of a different beauty salon.

She had coiffed, black hair that contrasted drastically with her pale-ivory skin. She had vibrant, green eyes that couldn't be real and her makeup was perfect.

It only took her a moment to take all of that in. It took her longer to realize Bobby was staring at her in shock. He didn't even speak.

"It is you." The woman glanced at their clasped hands and turned to Bailey. "Who is this?"

Who is this?

"What...what are you doing here?" he stuttered.

"I moved back to town a few days ago."

Bailey waited for Bobby to make introductions, but he didn't. She saw his eyes weren't looking at the woman's face, he was staring lower, and his face had lost its color.

Bailey followed the line of his vision and she realized this pretty woman was heavily pregnant.

"Who is this?" Bailey asked. "Bobby?" she prompted when he failed to reply.

"Bobby and I were a couple not too long ago," the woman replied. She placed a hand on her belly. Bailey's eyes moved from her prominent pregnancy to her face.

"I had intended to speak to you about this alone," she said to Bobby. Her eyes shifted briefly to Baily before her gaze returned to him. "But I suppose there is no better opportunity than now. Yes, Bobby. This is your baby."

ACT III

Chapter Fifty

This is your baby.

Bailey repeated those words mentally.

She looked at the woman, waiting for Bobby to tell her she was crazy or to ask her who she was or to say it was impossible.

But Bobby said nothing.

That's when it sank in. Bailey looked at Bobby. He just stared wordlessly at this ex-girlfriend…soon-to-be baby mama?

"Bobby?" she whispered. He finally looked at her as if remembering she was a part of the grand scheme of things and his expression took on a shocked look.

"Bailey…I didn't know."

"Oh my God…"

Is this real? Did Robert Chesterfield knock up one of his actresses—no, his *costar* from 1953?! Was she repeating history in 1954?

Bailey turned and walked away from him, from them.

"Wait, Bailey!" Bobby caught up with her and stopped her by taking hold of her arm. "I didn't know. I swear I didn't know about any of this!"

As she looked at him, Bailey was unsure if he was acting or if he was talking out of character. She yanked her arm from his grasp.

"But it's possible, right? You had…sex with her?"

His eyes flinched and he looked away, no longer meeting her gaze.

"Bobby!" the girl called. "Are you going to just leave me standing here?"

He barely looked over his shoulder at her. "Paula, I am talking to my *wife!*" He put his hand on Bailey's arm again. "I'll explain everything when we get home."

Bailey saw the girl, Paula, give him an exasperated look before turning and walking away.

She blew out a breath and held out her hand. "Give me the keys to the car."

He blinked in surprise. "Why?"

"Because I'm going home, and you have some things to discuss with...with the mother of your child."

"Bae, please. It's not what you're thinking—"

She pulled from his grasp again and turned to walk away. "Then I'll just take the bus—"

"No, wait. Here. Take the car."

He passed her the keys and tried to hold her hand but she snatched it away. She didn't want him to touch her. At this moment, she didn't know what his touch meant.

He had set her up again, and this time it was in the cruelest way possible. Even if he had not knocked up his ex-costar, he had sprung this on her for her reaction, all to further the show. And to not explain to her what was about to happen and how this affected them on a personal level was just beyond anything she could accept.

"We have to talk—"

"Not to me," she replied angrily. "Go talk to the mother of your child!"

He ran his hands through his hair and looked back at Paula, who was retreating. Bailey turned and went to the car. She thought she was happy Bobby hadn't followed her until she got into the car and saw him running after Paula.

She started the car and drove off.

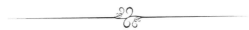

By the time Bailey got home, she wondered why she had run off. She'd had time to digest things, and also to realize she didn't like the idea of this other woman being with her husband...no, boyfriend.

Robert Chesterfield wasn't an actor, he just pretended to be Bobby Bailey. With that said, she knew when he saw that girl, he was just as surprised as she had been.

Bailey got out of the car and went into the house. She was more aware of the camera than she'd ever been before. She sat on the sofa and just rested her head on the back as she sat there and just tried to figure things out.

Think, Bailey. Think.

If the real Robert didn't know this woman was going to appear, was it because he'd hired her but wasn't sure when she'd show up, or was it because he hadn't known about her at all?

So that was one scenario. The other was that this Paula had also been his girlfriend — in both real life as well as on the set. He had known all along she was pregnant, but hadn't expected her to show up on set.

She shook her head. That was disgusting, if that was the case. They had spent literally hours talking about everything under the sun after the cameras stopped rolling. He would have had an opportunity to say, oh, by the way...I dated one of the actresses and we're going to have a baby.

Bailey jumped up and went to the telephone. She picked it up meaning to call Pat but then slowly put it down. First, Pat probably wouldn't be home yet. Second, what was she going to say? My husband is having a baby with his ex-girlfriend but I have no details because I ran off?

She went into the kitchen. Why didn't they have anything to make a drink with because right now, she just needed something to take away her anxiety. She had to be natural, to be Bailey Banks and not Bailey Westbrook wondering if she had been a fool. Wondering if she could continue to play this role with a man she didn't know...

She found herself staring out the back window at Haley's house.

Before she knew it, she was heading out the back door, through her gate, and standing on Haley's front porch ringing her bell.

Haley answered with a bit of surprise. She was holding a cocktail, and the sound of jazz music wafting from her house sounded very inviting.

"Hello, neighbor. Come on inside," Haley said with a broad, inviting smile.

Bailey couldn't even force a smile, but she went inside. "Sorry to just drop in. I know we're not really..."

"Friends?"

Bailey gave her a guilty look. "It's hard to always know where you stand..."

"Are you okay, hon? You look a little stressed. Let me make you a drink."

"Okay." She followed her into her eclectic but neat home. Haley went to the bar. "I remember you liked the old-fashioned, but how about a whiskey sour?"

"Or just the whiskey," Bailey muttered.

"Oh. That bad. Let's take it slow. Have a seat, hon."

She sat on the love seat and again took in her surroundings.

Haley had rollers in her hair but it was also wrapped in a colorful cloth. She was wearing makeup and dressed in slacks, heels, and a shirt that was knotted in a way that showcased her flat tummy.

"You caught me at the perfect time. I have a date later tonight—"

Bailey quickly came to her feet. "Oh! I'm so sorry—"

"No! Sit." She came around the bar with two cocktails and passed the fresh one to Bailey. "It's not until later this evening. A good party doesn't jump off until after nine."

They both sat on the love seat, knees practically touching. Bailey took a sip of her drink. Whew, it was strong, but also slightly sweet, and good.

Haley lit a cigarette and offered it to Bailey, who declined with a quick shake of her head. "No thank you. This is very good."

"You don't do much drinking, do you?" Haley said while appraising her.

"Not much. Maybe a beer or a glass of wine." In the real world, she just hadn't done things like going out to bars or clubs. Living with her aunt and uncle had made it impossible to be one of the "fast" girls, and once out on her own, she'd been preoccupied with her career.

"You know, if you want to be a good hostess, you have to know how to make drinks. I can show you sometime if you like."

"Really?"

"Yes. Of course." Haley picked up a nearby ashtray and set the cigarette in it.

Bailey didn't know why she noticed the ashtray was clean. There were no butts or ash in it. Did Haley even smoke? The idea of them acting in a role-play streaming series hit home. She was still an actress, even when her head was not in the part.

"I'm sorry I haven't come around more. And thanks for the book. Honestly, things have been hectic."

"Because you're a newlywed. I remember those days—trying to be so perfect. Oh. I heard about what they're trying to do to you and your husband."

"What?" Bailey blinked.

"Trying to get you to move out."

Bailey sighed. "Oh. Yes. Because we're just such horrible people."

"They're just ignorant."

"Ignorant people are dangerous people."

Haley bit her lip and quickly picked up her cigarette. "I don't know if you know this. But Guy Edelman is in the Klan."

Bailey's heart leaped. "I...didn't know."

"It's a topic no one wants to broach. But those very same people that want to buy your house and get you out of the neighborhood aren't necessarily doing it because they dislike you, but because they want to avoid race issues; Edelman's type of race issues."

Really? The Ku Klux Klan was part of the story line now?

"Do you think we're in danger?"

"What I think is that while there are a lot of people who are against you being here, there are many who don't want to see violence or hate in this neighborhood, whether it's from Negroes or the Klan.

"And there are those that believe people should mind their own business. I'm one of those people. And as someone who has been given a number of…unsavory titles, I am not going to condemn anyone else.

"So. You ask if you are in danger. No. I think everyone, including you and your husband, want the same thing. And that is a good, safe neighborhood." Bailey nodded. "You're a nice person. Some people don't give me the time of day." She took one last draw from her cigarette and crushed it out. "They think just because their men ogle me, I'm interested in them.

"To some, a pretty, single women is a threat that's as bad as a Negro man. If you don't believe that, then just ask Marina. She thinks everyone in town wants her idiot husband Al when, in fact, it's Al trying to get into everyone's pants."

Haley got up to refresh her drink. "I'm sorry. I don't mean to be a gossip. I despise the town gossips — basically because I've always been the topic of discussion. Do you want another one, hon?"

"No. This one is going to my head."

"Yeah…I may have gone a bit heavy with the whiskey. So. What brought you to my house? I know it wasn't to get into my pants. Or was it?"

"No, not!" Bailey replied quickly. Haley chuckled.

"I'm kidding! I have a dirty sense of humor. I hope you don't mind. But really? Was it because of the issues with the neighborhood? Or no…did you and that tasty hubby of yours have a fight?"

Tasty?

"Bobby and I don't really fight." Bailey finished her cocktail. "I just wanted a drink and someone to talk to." Bailey took her glass and got up to return to the bar.

"Then let's do."

"Oh. I don't know —"

"Look, Bailey. Being a housewife is boring. I know. I've been there. Have you had to make dinner for the boss yet?"

"No. Not yet —"

"And there's going to work functions and hosting events and being home for hours at a time with nothing to do.

"If you're lucky you meet a few interesting people, get together, have a little fun…"

Haley returned with the drink and passed it to her. "I wasn't so heavy-handed with the whiskey this time." Bailey accepted the second drink. "Is it good?" Bailey took a drink. It tasted the same, but she nodded and smiled.

"Like I said. If you're lucky, you will meet some people who also like having fun. And they'll be allies to you and your husband — like being a part of a private club."

"Club?" Bailey said. She thought about the supper club. "Have you been to new club, yet?

Madonna's?" she asked, trying not to slur her words. She was getting a teeny bit...high.

"No. I haven't been to Madonna's. Do you recommend it?"

"I do. And it's integrated."

"That's even nicer. We should do a double date sometime."

Bailey nodded. "Yes. I'm sure we...Bobby and I, would like that."

"What kind of things do you and Bobby like to do?"

She shrugged. "Whew. It's getting warm in here."

"You don't hold your whisky well," Haley chuckled again. Bailey laughed.

"You're right." She put her cocktail on the table and nearly spilled it. "I should probably get going." She stood and headed for the door.

"Are you sure? You just got here."

"Yeah, but I may need to lie down for a minute."

Haley laughed again. "Okay. But you promise to come back sometime?"

"Yes. I promise."

"And bring your husband."

"I will."

"And I'll bring my friend."

"That sounds nice. Like a double date. We just had a double date yesterday."

"Oh?" Haley grew more interested.

"Yeah. It was with my friend Pat and her new guy. He was a bit of a jerk. But it was still fun. Something to do." She reached for the door. Haley kissed her cheek, her lips lingering a bit.

"Come back soon."

Bailey nodded. "Okay."

She left and hurried across the yard to her front door. She turned to see Haley watching. She waved, and Haley did the same.

When she turned back around, her brow shot up.

A baby. The Klan. Swingers...or gay neighbor — not sure which. That was a lot!

When Bailey opened the front door, Bobby quickly turned to her. He was on the telephone.

"She just walked through the door. Okay. I'll have her call you later. Bye." He hurried to her. She shut the door slowly. "Where were you? I saw the car and your coat and purse were here but you weren't."

"Who were you talking to?" she asked.

"Pat. I thought maybe you two had gone off..." He gestured to the address book. "I was about to call your aunt and uncle next."

She shook her head. "I was just next door."

"Honey, you have no idea how bad I feel about what happened."

"What did happen, Bobby? Is she carrying your child?"

He licked his lips and sighed. "I think so. Yeah. The dates line up."

Bailey crossed her arms in front of her. For the moment, she didn't feel any of this. She was numb to this pregnancy arc. Because this wasn't real. This was acting. She was not a part of this scenario and wouldn't be — not in her real life. That was just too much to ask of any new relationship.

She thought about Bailey Banks. She had to be true to her right now. Right now, she was Bailey. What would Bailey feel right now?

"How many months is she? We've been married two months."

"And we dated six months before and" — he swallowed uneasily — "she's going into her ninth month."

"Really? You were having sex with her right up until you met me?" she asked incredulously. "Or...did you cheat?"

Chapter Fifty-One

"God no. I never cheated! I would never do that. Can we sit down? Please?"

She purposely moved to the chair so he wouldn't sit next to her and Bobby seemed to get that as he sat on the edge of the couch across from her.

"I met Paula at the *Gazette*. We dated for a little more than a year. When I realized we were dating but she wasn't someone I wanted a long-term relationship with, I ended it."

Bailey shook her head. "What does that mean? Exactly?"

He seemed to think about it for a moment. "When someone dates for a year, I guess you have to decide if it will lead to marriage.

"I knew Paula wasn't the woman I wanted to be married to. I liked her—but she liked me more. That wasn't fair to her. I just had to end it. And it hurt her. She thought we were heading to something permanent, while I knew she wasn't the one."

He rubbed his eyes tiredly.

"Bobby."

He looked at her quickly.

"Why didn't you use protection? You had to know what could happen—"

"We did, Bae. Believe me, it was something I was very insistent on. But I will admit that on more than one occasion…things got out of hand." He wouldn't meet her eyes. "I'm sorry, Bae. Maybe two or three times that happened." He sighed and leaned back with his head against the back of the couch.

To Bailey, he looked defeated. She rubbed her tired eyes. She wanted to lay down. The whiskey sour had numbed her some, but had also caused her to want to retreat.

She did not want to act. She did not want to pretend. She just didn't want to do *this*.

But she had to.

"What did you and Paula talk about after I left?"

"She wants to raise the baby...here in town." He sat up slowly with a sigh and looked at her again. "She came back to town despite her mother's wishes. Her parents kicked her out and she's living with her older sister and her husband." He sighed again. "Her mother wanted her to pretend she was a widow of a war veteran but she said no to that. I think that was a good idea."

He sighed again and leaned forward with his fingertips touching. He looked at her hard. "If this is my child, then I want to support...him."

"Him?" Her voice quivered.

He nodded. "She's having a boy."

She blew out a long breath.

"Bae—"

She held up her hand to stop him. "What else did you two talk about?"

"Nothing much. I just told her, of course, I'd be there for my kid."

"If it's yours."

He nodded. "If it's mine. We can have a blood test after he's born."

"In the meantime, everyone is going to know you're married to one woman while you're having a baby with another. What are people going to say?"

"That's something I have never been concerned with," he said off-handedly. "Not for me. But it's a lot for you and for...her."

She stood up. He stood up too.

"I'm going to make dinner."

"We can...I'll pick up something, burgers or a fried chicken dinner."

She hesitated. "Okay." She needed something to do, like concentrate on cooking a meal, but she also needed him to leave for a while.

The conversation they were having wasn't the conversation she needed to have with him. And after those drinks, she could barely keep from asking the real question that was beating in her skull.

Is this your baby in real life?

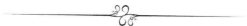

Bobby went out to get dinner. Bailey changed out of her clothes and removed her jewels and put them away. She rubbed Ponds cold cream onto her face and wiped off her makeup, taking her time while doing each task.

After her hair was pinned and wrapped, Bailey went to the bathroom but made sure to be quick. It took her five minutes to use the toilet and change into a gown. She wasn't going to hide. Her heart was breaking for Bailey Brooks. But so were the hearts of Bailey's fans.

Her dream life was crumbling, and it felt like a real loss. Some of it was because her boyfriend had possibly fathered a child just like her persona's husband.

Tears welled in her eyes and she wasn't completely acting. Not completely…and maybe not at all.

She wiped them away with a tissue and continued removing her makeup.

When Bobby returned home with a bag of burgers and fries and two melting milkshakes, she remembered that before all hell broke loose, she had been looking forward to a juicy burger.

They sat down to eat, and it was indeed juicy and messy, but it sat like a rock in her belly.

Bobby watched her as he too seemed to force himself to eat. He never had a hard time eating — even when it was basically garbage.

"Have you told your mom yet?"

"I'll go over and talk to her tomorrow. I think this deserves a face-to-face meeting. You'll be telling your aunt and uncle during your weekly visit with them…I guess they'll hate me now."

She opened her mouth, but then closed it.

"Don't hate me, Bailey. Please don't hate me." His voice broke. "You have to know this isn't the life I wanted for us. I love you so very much, honey, and I blame myself; not her, and not the child. I knew right from wrong!"

"*I'm* supposed to be the mother of your children!" she shouted. "I'm not supposed to see some other woman saying she's about to have a baby with *my* husband! That's not the life I wanted for myself either, Bobby!"

"I know, Bailey. I know. You deserve better. But please don't leave me. Please."

He sniffed back his tears, but they still spilled down his cheeks. And then Bobby just gave in and sobbed.

"You don't know how long I dreamed for you, Bailey. I dreamed for the person I would want to go through life with.

"Every girl I knew has always been the same—pretending to be what they think an adult should be, acting like their mothers or my mother. Acting. Not being themselves. You laugh with your eyes, and I see your heart when you smile. And when you touch me, I feel your love and not just"—he wiped his eyes and swallowed so he could look at her without sobbing—"not just someone that thinks, he's a good catch.

"You do not play games. You are authentic, and I love you. You are what I am trying so hard to be."

Bailey stood and he looked at her with fear, as if she would walk away.

Bailey went around the table and held Bobby against her. He buried his head against her breast and she thought she could feel his fear and his relief as his arms went around her waist while tightly holding onto her.

"I'm not leaving. I am not going anywhere. I love you, Bobby, and we are going to work through this."

He gripped her gown as if he was hanging onto her. She felt him nod and she stroked his head and kissed the top of it repeatedly. She whispered to him they would get through it, she would be by his side.

They stayed that way for a long time and then moved to the bedroom, even though it wasn't yet nine o'clock. There was no more to film. For now, this scene was finished.

Chapter Fifty-Two

After the door to the bedroom was closed, they simultaneously reached for the stop filming button. They met each other's eyes in surprise and Bobby withdrew to allow her to press the button.

She had never thought she would do that. Having control, power, was nerve-wracking, but exhilarating. She had just stopped the filming on what had to be the most important scene in the history of The '50s Experience LLC.

"First," Bobby said before she could even turn fully to face him. "Paula's baby is not mine. I have never had sex with her!"

Bailey didn't even say anything, she just hurried to him and hugged him in relief.

He held onto her. "Babe, I am so sorry. I wanted to stop filming half a dozen times. I knew what you were thinking, and I'm so sorry it caused you any amount of stress."

Whatever stress and anxiety she'd been feeling fell away instantly. She loved her character of Bailey Banks and had fallen in love with Bobby Banks, but Robert Chesterfield was who she was with, and that relationship was still solid and still budding.

"I'm so happy to hear you say that," she said while holding him. "I saw the look on your face and I didn't know what to think."

"I know." He kissed the top of her head and her forehead. She pulled back enough to look up into his face.

"You didn't know she was going to show up?"

"No. Not at all. I didn't expect to ever see her again. She wasn't invited back this season."

"I see—"

He was already shaking his head. "No. No. There is so much you don't know. We are going to need to sit down for this."

"Shit."

"We might as well go back out into the living room." Tension started to fill her again as she followed him. They sat together on the sofa and he took her hand.

"Let me start out by saying that I never had sex with Paula."

Bailey's heart sank further.

"The way you and I haven't had sex? Because we're doing everything but..."

He shook his head. "No. It's nothing like us. We only played the role of lovers. Paula is an actual actress and she was one of the first we hired to enhance the production. We hoped she'd help me feel natural behind the cameras.

"While I never felt anything for her, not even the smallest inkling of attraction, we did become friendly and several times she, me, and Bruce would go off set together for drinks or for food. We had fun and we hung out a lot.

"I didn't initially realize she was developing real feelings for either me or Bobby—I can't say which. So, we would shoot a scene and if there was kissing involved, it began to seem as if she had convinced herself it was more real than it actually was."

Bailey lightly bit her lip. She definitely understood, and could feel for Paula. Bobby Brooks was hard not to fall for—especially if 1953 Bobby was anything like 1954 Bobby.

"I noticed during filming, her character seemed to push towards marriage. I hadn't thought about marriage for Bobby. And she kept bringing it up whenever we hung out, even after I told her I wasn't sure I wanted a regular role on the show.

"Finally, it all came to a head when we had a kissing scene and she turned it into a make-out session. I kind of went with the flow but after filming ended, she went for it again."

He shook his head and sighed. "I had to tell her I liked her as a friend, but not as anything more. I thought she understood…but honestly, I wasn't really comfortable with onscreen intimacy after that.

"And I got a surprise when she began dating Bruce."

Her brow went up. "Your ex-costar is dating your production manager?"

"No…I mean, I didn't think they were still going. I had to have a frank discussion with Bruce about her coming on to me and they stopped hanging around each other. I had long since stopped hanging with them together. I assumed they had ended it.

"And when it was time to discuss 1954, we were both in agreement she wouldn't be returning. Maybe I should have discussed whether or not they were still seeing each other but he never brought it up, and I figured it wasn't any of my business."

"So, Bruce is the father of Paula's unborn baby?"

"I would assume so."

"Wow." Bailey massaged her forehead. "This isn't a reality show—it's a soap opera."

Bobby stood. "I need to call him. This was out of line."

He picked up the old-fashioned phone and began to dial.

"Bruce. Yes, I'm pissed! Of course I am. And Bailey isn't happy either. You are? Okay." Bobby hung up.

"What happened?" That was the quickest conversation she'd ever heard, even if it was just one-sided.

He came back to sit down beside her. "He figured we'd have words, so he's on his way over to talk to us both."

"I'm going to get dressed." She went back to the bedroom and pulled on slacks and a sweater. By the time she was dressed, she heard Bruce Adams come into the house.

"What were you thinking?!" Bobby asked. He was more angry than she'd ever seen him—angrier than she'd ever expected to see him.

Bruce held up his hands but he had the nerve to be smiling. He was holding an iPad in one hand.

"I know, Bobby. You have every right to be mad. But you need to see something." He thrust the iPad at his boss after tapping on it briefly. "Hi, Bailey. Sorry to barge in."

Bobby accepted the iPad but glared at it.

"Check out those numbers."

Bobby frowned. "Is this right?"

"Yes, brother! These numbers are real."

Bailey came over to see what they were looking at. It looked like comments, but they were rolling in so fast they were impossible to catch.

"But look at the numbers!" Bruce insisted.

Bobby's brow shot up. "Holy shit…"

"That's half a million in less than one day!"

Bobby looked at Bruce. "Holy shit!" he repeated.

"I know, right?"

Bailey stared from one to the other. "What does this mean?"

"It means we're getting new subscribers, repeat watches, and the comments aren't stopping! It means, Bailey my dear, we have surpassed our *year's* goal!

Bobby threw his head back and began to laugh. He picked up Bailey and swung her around.

"Bae! We have made it!"

She gave him a crooked smile. "Congratulations."

He gave her a big kiss. "I need to go to the office! Is that okay?" he asked.

"Yeah. Go. But do we know what's going to happen next with the pregnancy story line?"

"There are just so many possibilities…" Bobby's smile remained but his eyes grew cloudy as he seemed to think of hundreds of story lines. But he did finally turn back to Bruce. "But there are to be no more secrets between us—"

Bruce raised his hands innocently. "I'm sorry! I'm really sorry, but it worked the way I knew it would. And you have to admit, Bobby; when it comes to the show, you're a control freak. You gotta give me some room for my ideas too."

"But *you* have to admit that everything I brought to the table turned out right."

"It has."

"Still." Bobby glanced at Bailey and reached for her hand. "This caused a lot of unnecessary strife."

Bruce's expression grew serious. "Look...I know you two are a couple now. I have to be honest with you both. A week ago, Paula contacted me. At first, I blew her off. We haven't talked in months and things were a little...well, I'm sure Bobby can tell you all about it." He directed the last to Bailey.

"Anyway, she told me she was pregnant and I was the father." He sighed. "I wasn't expecting that." But then he smiled. "The idea of being a father is strange, but she's so very mellow about everything. Well, we inevitably started talking about the show and it was like, hey, if she was still on the show, then Bobby would be grappling with fatherhood right now..." He shook his head. "I had to do it. And, Bobby, I knew you would nix it—for various reasons. But if it didn't work, then I knew we could write her off again very easily by saying she's lying about the paternity of her baby."

"There are so many possibilities..." Bobby said again to himself.

"Right!" Bruce said.

Of course, Bobby was right; there were so many possibilities. But Bailey couldn't help but wonder if this was a mistake.

Chapter Fifty-Three

Bobby and Bruce left to talk about strategy. It was just after nine on a Saturday night and she was too anxious to sleep. She suddenly had an idea.

Hurrying to the phone she called Pat, hoping she was home and not out on a date with Marvin or even at the factory. Helen was closer, but she was probably doing things with her hubby, and Haley was just next door—but she'd had her fill of that one for one evening. Luckily, Pat answered the phone.

"Hey, Pat—"

"Oh my God, girl! I was on my way to the factory to watch the day's shoot. I saw that heffa Paula came back! You don't know how much I wanted to run out of the beauty shop so I could hear what was going on, but this is better! Are you able to talk about what's going on? Please say yes, please say yes…"

Bailey giggled. "Yes. But I warn you, there isn't much to tell. Bobby's out at the production lot with Bruce. I'll probably know more tomorrow—"

"I'll come over. Give me fifteen. I'll bring beer."

"Sounds good. I want to know all about Paula."

"Yeah, that's a story right there. I'll see you in a bit."

When Pat arrived, they hugged like sister-friends. She passed the beer to Bailey and hung her jacket in the closet.

"Okay, what happened after you left the shop?" Pat sat on the couch with wide eyes, her elbows on her knees and her chin resting on her palms.

Bailey thought she looked like a little kid sitting at a campfire waiting for a ghost story. She explained what happened as if she was the village storyteller. Pat exclaimed in all the right places, even biting her nails a few times. Bailey didn't bother talking about her scene with Haley, even though it was pretty interesting. She figured for now, the main story had to do with Paula.

When she was finished, Pat sat back in contentment. "Wow. So, is it Bobby's baby?"

She shrugged. "I don't know how they're going to play it out, but Bobby thinks it is."

"Who...?" Pat quickly closed her mouth.

"What?" Bailey prompted.

"Uh...nothing."

"Do you want to know if Robert Chesterfield is the father of Paula's baby?"

"You don't have to answer. It's not my business —"

"No. It's fine. I suppose everyone is going to figure it out anyway. But Bruce is the baby's daddy."

"Oh...shit." Pat said slowly.

"Why shit?"

"Girl, Paula really wanted to get with Robert. But he wasn't feeling her so she called herself trying to make him jealous by flirting with Bruce. I guess they did the deed..."

Both girls opened another beer and speculated on the nature of Paula's return.

"Bobby said they declined to ask her to return for 1954 because it had become uncomfortable."

"Yeah. That's called being fired. She was always all over him. And she got jealous too. If there was a pretty white girl in the vicinity, then she was nasty."

"Nasty?"

"Oh yeah. Now I wasn't there, but I heard that during the team meetings she'd always criticize anyone she thought of as a threat. She'd put down their acting, poke holes in their scenes, and was basically a bully. She wouldn't give a hand up to anyone for fear they'd do better. That was one selfish bi-otch."

"But why would Bobby tolerate someone like that on his set?" Bailey asked.

"In 1953, he was always behind the scenes. Not like he is now. He didn't always see what the rest of us did. But eventually, he did. I think he knew she was nothing but a gold-digger. I just hope I don't have any scenes with her because I am not the one."

Bailey couldn't help but chuckle. She definitely had a pleasant buzz from her beers and the whiskey sours before.

"Well at the moment, she's just a girl carrying another man's baby. She's no threat to me."

"True. Just remember you got what she wants, and as long as you do, no matter how friendly she might act, you will always be her biggest nemesis."

"Honey. Wake up." Bailey was awakened by soft kisses on her face. She tried to open her eyes but they felt as if they had weights on them. When she moved, her head began to pound.

"Oh, my head…"

Bobby climbed into bed beside her even though he was fully dressed. "Oh. My poor baby," he crooned. "I saw the beer cans and I watched the clip with you and Haley and her infamous whisky sours. I'm not surprised your head isn't on right."

Bailey rubbed her eyes as she remembered last night. "Pat came over..." She sat up quickly and looked at the clock. It was twenty to eight. "Oh my God! Why did you let me oversleep?!"

He propped himself up on the pillow and watched her with a smirk.

"You needed the sleep...and I kind of overslept myself. I fell asleep at the production office and you didn't even notice," he pouted.

She slammed the bathroom door behind her so she could pee. "Did you and Bruce plan out the rest of the year?" she yelled.

"Not exactly," he called back. When she returned to the room after brushing her teeth and washing her face, she saw he had made up the bed.

"Oh gosh. I don't have time for makeup." She pulled on the same clothes she wore the night before.

"Nobody's going to care if we're a little late."

"But we're always late!"

"I'm the boss...so..."

She checked her hair in the vanity mirror after removing her scarf. She fluffed it with her hands. It was going to have to do.

"Okay. I'm ready to go."

"Sorry we don't have time for breakfast, but maybe we can stop somewhere after the meeting."

They got into the car. "That would be nice," she replied while getting buckled in, "but it would cut into my time with my aunt and uncle."

"True. We'll have to figure something out."

She wondered what that meant, but was more interested in what he and Bruce had talked about.

"So how is this pregnancy story line going to play out?"

"Definitely, Bobby will be the father." Bailey couldn't help that her heart sank a little. "But with just a bit of guidance from Bruce and me, I expect us all to tell our own stories."

Of course he was going to say that.

"What if Bailey decides she doesn't want to stay with Bobby?"

He flashed her a quick look. "Is that what you think might happen?"

She stared at him. "Would it be allowed? You once told me that if Bailey wanted to leave Bobby, then it would be okay because you'd just hook up with Pat."

He snorted. "I was just being an ass. That was never going to happen. But I really did mean that if Bailey wanted to leave Bobby, then she can. Just…be prepared to have him chase her to the ends of the earth."

She smiled. "He really does love her, huh?"

"With every inch of his heart." They smiled at each other and he took her hand and squeezed it.

When they got to the production office, they hurried down the corridors hand in hand. They didn't have much time to say hello or to comment on yesterday's shoot to all the passersby watching them curiously.

When they got to the meeting, the projection screen had been pulled down. Hank was sitting behind the laptop and everyone turned to stare at them when they arrived. Hank paused the film and Bailey saw herself frozen in time, wiping off her makeup as tears filled her eyes.

Today no one was laughing or cutting up. Everyone was serious.

Bailey's eyes fell on Paula, who was sitting quietly. She gave Bailey and Robert a half smile.

"We decided to get caught up while we waited for you two," Hank said. "Team Bailey had the highest rank, by far." She remembered Hank was part of the production team, so obviously he would know.

Someone applauded and then everyone did. Paula applauded the loudest. As Bailey stood there looking and feeling awkward, everyone began to express how good her scenes were, how deeply they felt her anger and pain.

Several people had kind words they directed at Bobby—but she found it funny there was a bit of animosity directed at him as well.

And there were the half-hearted congratulations directed at Paula for her return. But it was plain those weren't authentic. Either people remembered her being a bully last year or they just didn't like that she had thrown a monkey wrench in a relationship people saw as something that made them feel good.

It wasn't fair, because there were good people here that weren't the sum of the role they had been assigned to play. And yet it was necessary—even Guy Edelman being a part of the Klan.

But good or bad, Paula was necessary too. Because even though Bailey'd had the best week, without any conflict, no one was going to break viewing records just to watch her being happy.

Chapter Fifty-Four

The day's meeting finally warmed up once Bobby took over the reins from Hank—especially after he introduced Paula's return and everyone realized what was actually going on.

"Let's welcome Paula to 1954." There was polite, if not subdued, applause. "Some of you will remember Paula from last season as Bobby's love interest.

"Paula will have a feature role on the show so soon she will have her own team, which will be headed by Bruce Adams. And speaking of Bruce, let me be the first to congratulate Paula and Bruce on the soon-to-be birth of their child."

At clarification, everyone's congratulations became more authentic, as the fans in the room realized Paula was no threat to Robert and Bailey's real-life relationship.

The congratulations rang out. They still might not like that her appearance had caused a rift between Bobby and Bailey, but it evidently had not caused one between Bailey and *Robert,* so she had obviously been given a slight reprieve.

The remainder of the meeting went well, with Team Nadine coming second in the rankings and Team Drew a close third. They watched a few minutes of their highlights, and Bobby pulled up some slang phrases he wanted them to incorporate on air.

"I know some of these might sound corny, but it also brings realism to the production, especially for the younger crowd. We don't have any beatniks on our team at the moment, which is good because it is literally a different language. Cash is called bread, you're wigged-out if you're mad, crazy means good, and boss is okay.

"I won't ask you to go far, but stop calling people assholes and call them party-poopers or a wet rag.

"And again, segregation is real. It's a rare thing for Blacks and whites to interact comfortably. No one should be doing it unless it's scripted. You guys are amazing. I absolutely have no complaints. Just remember to do your research on your days off, and if in doubt, leave it out. That's all for the week—your scripts are short, but read them, please. We don't want you messing up someone else's plans because you didn't show up at a location you were scripted to be."

Everyone got up, excited to hit the phones or get on the Internet.

While Bailey waited to walk out with Bobby, Paula came up with her hand held out to shake Bailey's hand.

"It's nice to formally meet you," Paula said. She looked a lot prettier without the heavy 1950s makeup. She might have been in her late twenties or early thirties. Her dark hair was pulled up into a messy top knot and although her skin was pale, without the white face powder she looked fresh and youthful, with a splattering of freckles across her nose. Up close, Bailey decided her eyes were green.

She was pretty.

Bailey shook her offered hand. "Nice to meet you too. Welcome back to the set."

"Thanks."

"How are you getting settled in?" Bobby asked.

"It's a big house. I'm sure it will feel a lot smaller once you hire the sister and brother-in-law."

Bailey suddenly thought about her having an actual baby on set.

"Will it be hard having a baby while you're filming?"

"I think it's the best scenario. I'll be able to work with my baby and when either of us needs to go off the set, Bruce will have a nanny to look after him here in the production office." Paula placed her hand on her belly. Bailey decided she was probably right, although being a '50s housewife was hard enough without a baby in the equation.

"You'll definitely get as much help as you need," Bobby assured her.

"Well, I'm sure I'll be fine — but things might be a bit tough for my character. Thank goodness Bobby is going to pay child support before the baby's born or she won't have any cash."

Bailey raised a brow because this was something they hadn't discussed. Not that she minded. She would mind more if Bobby *didn't* want to help.

But what Paula said was definitely true. The cast had to make do with the money they would actually make if it really was 1954 — and an unwed mother probably made less than the Blacks.

"It's going to be tough," Bailey said. "Luckily, you'll be living with your sister and her husband."

"Not as lucky as if she was living with her child's father."

Well that sure as hell wasn't going to happen. Bailey looked at Bobby.

He shrugged. "That's the beauty of this open scripting. None of us have any idea what might happen."

Bailey refrained from saying he knew he would be paying her child support before the baby was actually born, so he did know some things that were going to happen…

Instead, she checked the clock. "I'd better get going. It's a long drive home."

"Sundays are you days off?" Paula asked.

"Yes, although I don't know why I chose that day. It doesn't give me much time off."

"I might choose Mondays." She turned to Bobby. "So, Rob, you and I might be able to do a scene together since Bailey won't be available."

Why did Paula feel as if she had to talk to Bobby when Bailey wasn't around?

Bailey pushed that thought out of her mind because she didn't want to hate on the girl just because of her discussion with Pat.

"Sure. Bobby's going to do a scene with his mother this afternoon where he tells her about the pregnancy. Our characters should probably meet up to discuss things after." He looked at Bailey. "Since Bailey visits with her aunt and uncle on Sundays, then when we film on Monday, we can talk on camera about the child support and whatever Paula and Bobby discuss."

"Monday? I don't think so," she replied.

"Really? Why not?" Bobby asked.

"Because Bailey isn't spending the night at her aunt and uncle's place. I think as soon as she gets home from her visit, she'd expect Bobby to tell her about the conversation with his mother and his ex."

He nodded. "Yeah. You are right. We'll have to play the scene of you and me talking about it off camera, but I think it's fine, since we'll be filming the actual conversations. Good call, Bae."

Bailey gave Paula another smile. "If you two want to talk, I can go ahead and leave—"

"No. I'm going to walk you out." Bobby turned to Paula. "Will you be around for a while?"

"I was going to talk to Bruce and get a ride back into Wingate. But if you're going into town, I'll stick around and get a ride with you."

"Perfect," Bobby said while placing his arm around Bailey and leading her out of the room. "I'll meet you in Bruce's office."

"Okay. Maybe we can all grab lunch," Paula called after him. "I'm eating for two, as much as I hate to admit it."

"Yeah, sounds like a plan," Bobby said.

Bailey looked over her shoulder as Paula's eyes shifted to her.

"Nice to meet you, Paula."

"You as well, Bailey," she replied with a quick smile.

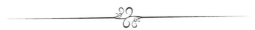

"Are you sure you can't stay long enough to have lunch with us?" Bobby asked as she closed her locker and pulled on her coat.

"Sorry, honey. I don't want to keep them waiting too long." She glanced at her cell phone. "Aunt Mae has already called me once—probably to see when I'll get there."

Bobby pulled her into a kiss. "I miss you on Sundays." Bailey put her arms around his neck and felt a tingle building throughout her body.

"I miss you too. It's been hectic the last few days."

They kissed, allowing it to build in intensity until they had to stop or end up locked in Bobby's office for a prolonged make-out session.

He rested his forehead against hers after the kiss ended.

"I love you, Bailey." He looked into her eyes. "Is it too soon to say that? Because I say it every day to Bailey Banks, but I also mean it for you too."

The sensations in Bailey's body went from tingle to earthquake.

"It's not too soon. I've been in love with you since before I even became your girlfriend. It just feels so natural."

He caressed her as he stared into her eyes. "It does. You are everything I've ever wanted. Everything."

She smiled. "How do you know? We've only known each other a few weeks."

"But you feel it too. It's almost as if I'm reincarnated in this century but we've shared a love that goes back decades."

She nodded rapidly. That is exactly how she felt. It was as if she and Bobby Banks were really a couple that shared an actual history filled with love and loyalty. And through Bobby, she had fallen in love with the real man behind the character.

"I love you, Robert Chesterfield." She kissed his lips and felt his heart pounding against her breast. "But I'd better go."

He released her with a smile. "Let me walk you to the car." He took her hand and she knew he wanted her to stay, but he was too kind to ask it of her.

Bailey had driven off the set before pulling up Aunt Mae's voice message.

It was left yesterday, and she was expressing her *supreme* dislike of the "trollop" that was claiming to be carrying Bobby's baby. Aunt Mae was telling her to get a DNA test as soon as possible and not to believe anything until she saw it in black-and-white.

Bailey smiled and shook her head. She decided to wait until she got to the house before explaining everything. It would give them some good conversation.

Chapter Fifty-Five

Bailey was starving when she got to her aunt and uncle's house. She just hoped her aunt wasn't going to make her go shopping and teach her how to cook something that might take hours to finish. If so, she was going in for leftovers she was sure to find in the freezer.

She didn't have to worry. The house smelled of gumbo, a dish Bailey absolutely loved.

Uncle Dewbug gently took hold of her arms even before she could take off her coat and he stared at her closely.

"Are you still with that Chesterfield boy?"

"Yes. Why?"

"After that stunt he pulled with that baby?"

She gave him another hug for caring about her so much. "Uncle Dewbug, it's just a show. Robert isn't that child's father. If you must know, the production manager is the father of the child."

He just gave her an uncertain look. Aunt Mae crossed her arms in front of her. "Stop trying to stress the girl out! Bobby is a good man and he loves Bailey, and if *he* loves Bailey, then Robert Chesterfield loves Bailey."

Her husband just huffed and walked away.

"Don't mind him," Aunt Mae whispered, and led her into the kitchen. "But tell me the child isn't Bobby's. Please tell me it's not."

She gave her aunt a serious look while removing her coat and draping it over a kitchen chair. "Are you sure you want me to tell you what's to come? Because I don't want to spoil it for you—"

"Chile, I want to know! Is he, or isn't he?"

"He is."

"Shit!" she said, and made a face. Bailey covered her smile. Aunt Mae hardly ever cursed. "Why y'all go and write that into the show? You two got it bad enough!"

Bailey went to the sink to wash her hands. "The truth is, I don't really like it myself. But I know it's necessary. It's just like when you watch your stories and someone gets kidnapped by the Mob even though they live in the suburbs."

"You ain't going to leave that boy, are you?"

Bailey turned and gave her a mischievous look. "Should I?"

"If you do, I'll disown you!" But then she grinned and leaned close to whisper, "That boy looks like Paul Newman when he was in *Cool Hand Luke*. It's those eyes of his. Don't tell your uncle I thought a white man was good-looking though. He'll never let me live it down."

"He's probably had a crush on a white woman."

Her aunt moved to the pot of simmering gumbo. "The closest thing to a white woman he's ever had a crush on was Lena Horne."

"I'm going to have to look these people up."

"You don't know who Paul Newman is? *Cat on a Hot Tin Roof? Butch Cassidy and the Sundance Kid?*"

"I know the names. I just can't picture the faces."

"Oh?" She spooned gumbo into large bowls. "Well after lunch, we'll pull up some pictures of Paul Newman."

"And Lena Horne."

"Yeah, her, too."

Lunch was delicious, and Bailey had two helpings of gumbo and two big slices of garlic bread.

When she told them about how much Bobby had enjoyed her cooking from last week, Aunt Mae said she was going to send him a plate of food. Uncle Dewbug scowled.

When lunch was over, she had Bailey pull up pictures of Paul Newman. Her aunt forgot about Lena Horne.

Bailey's visit with her aunt and uncle was great, as usual. But she didn't stay late. She wanted some off-camera time with her sweetie.

"You don't mind, do you?" Bailey asked, worried they thought she was trying to tell them she didn't like their company. She did love her time with them, but she also missed Bobby and after the harrowing day they had, she really wanted to reconnect with him.

"I'm just happy you come to see us at all. It's going to be winter before you know it and I don't want you on the roads for so many hours. If you want to Zoom chat, it's perfectly fine."

Bailey's heart leaped in excitement. "Really? You wouldn't mind?"

"Of course not," Aunt Mae said.

Uncle Dewbug was watching the game on television. "You can bring that young man here to meet us."

Bailey's brow went up. "Bring Bobby here?"

He turned and gave her an innocent look. "Yeah. We should meet him, don't you think?"

Bailey looked at Aunt Mae, who gave her an excited nod. "I'll cook a big meal. If he's not too busy, that is. He's an important man."

"I'll talk to him about it and I'll let you know next Sunday."

Bailey decided to call Bobby as soon as she got on the road.

He answered immediately.

"Hey," he said happily.

"Hey, back at you. I'm on my way home early."

"Great!"

"You haven't eaten yet, have you?"

"We had lunch, but it was much earlier. I'll be ready for dinner though."

"Good, because Aunt Mae packed you damn near half a pot of gumbo."

"Oh my God. I love your aunt."

"Truthfully, I think she has a crush on you."

"Oh? Is she as cute as you?"

"Of course. Oh, and my uncle invited you to come to the house. But we all realize you're busy, so it doesn't have to be any time—"

"Yes."

"Yes?"

"Yes. I'd love to meet your aunt and uncle." Bailey grinned so hard her cheeks began to ache. "You still there? Hello?"

"Yeah. I'm here. I'm just happy. My favorite people in the world in the same room would be mighty nice."

"You're so sweet. But I want you to get off the phone. You don't need to be talking and driving. But call me when you get here and I'll drive us home."

She was talking hands-free and wasn't ready to get off the phone. She wanted to know what he and Paula had talked about. But they had plenty of time to talk so she didn't object.

"Okay, babe. I'll call you as soon as I get there."

"I love you."

Bailey smiled again. "I love you too."

"The next time you talk to your aunt, tell I love her too."

Bailey laughed. "Okay. I will."

"And don't leave out your uncle."

"Oh…I think we'll leave him out."

"Whatever you think is best. Be safe. I'll see you soon, Bae."

Bailey hung up feeling very happy.

Bailey sent Bobby a text as soon as she hit the lot. By the time she was parked and had opened the trunk, he was coming out of the building. He jogged over to her and pulled her into an embrace.

"Hi," he said after a brief kiss.

"Hi," she grinned. He gave her a longer kiss and they didn't part for a full minute.

"Let's get you home. It's cold out here."

"Is it?" she whispered, almost delirious from that powerful kiss.

He grinned. He grabbed the food and they transferred it to their car, then they headed for home.

"Did you and Paula shoot a scene today?" she asked.

He turned down the radio. "Yep. So did me and Gloria. Instead of me telling you about the scenes, I'll play them for you."

"Oh yeah. That'll be better."

"So how was your visit with your aunt and uncle?"

Bailey recapped the evening while Bobby listened closely. She got a sense he was very interested in her family's dynamic. It made her curious about his. She never initiated conversations about his family, leaving it to him to bring it up—which he seldom did. But she was curious.

"You don't visit with your family?" She might be curious, but she vowed never to ask him about his father.

"No. I FaceTime with my mother occasionally. But my family dynamic isn't the norm. Mom and Dad—especially my dad—were always off somewhere doing things. They're jet-setters. So, it was common for me to go weeks without seeing them. And even when they were home, we had nannies or teachers that dealt with us.

"Having kids was not going to put an end to my parents' fun." He gave a forced grin before glancing at her. "I spent the best part of my childhood at my grandma and grandpa's house. My mother did not come from wealth, but her parents were comfortable, and yet chose to live modestly.

"That's where I got my love for the fifties lifestyle."

"You're a millionaire, but you prefer your grandparents' lifestyle. That says a lot about why I like you so much."

He covered her hand with his own. "This is going to sound completely tone deaf, but if you're a kid that's always been wealthy, you don't notice it. And I certainly didn't feel privileged. All I knew was I'd rather have my mom and dad than horse riding lessons."

When they got to the house, Bobby took possession of the gumbo as if it was a treasure chest. She offered to trade him while she heated up the food if he set up the laptop.

Before she knew it, they were in the kitchen with bowls of gumbo, garlic bread, and Bobby's laptop spread out before them.

"I spoke to Gloria first, so I'll play that clip first." She had to force herself not to quiz him about the revelation.

She was happy she didn't, because she truly got a feel for their audience as she sat in anticipation for her mother-in-law's reaction.

Gloria greeted him by wringing her hands and asking what was so important he couldn't just talk to her over the phone. Bobby had her sit down and explained that Paula had come back to town and she was pregnant.

Bobby's mother asked how far along she was and when he told her, she just closed her eyes and said a little prayer. She then chastised him, and he didn't say a thing to defend himself.

Bailey gave Bobby a sympathetic look. "She went in hard on you."

"Yeah," he said with a lopsided grin. "If it had been my father, I might have been taken out to the woodshed."

They quieted as Bobby finally got a word in edgewise. He apologized, but explained there was no one was more disappointed than he was in himself.

When he told her this could destroy his marriage, Gloria went off again and asked him what his child would think of him for marrying a Negro.

Bobby then used his stern man voice when asking what that had to do with anything.

Gloria just clamped her mouth shut and shook her head.

When Bailey looked over at Bobby, his expression was serious as he either critiqued the clip or relived it.

Bobby turned off the video. "Thoughts?"

She nodded as she considered her words. "It seems like a discussion a mother might have with their son other than to say you should have wrapped it up."

He grimaced. "Yeah, but I'm not sure how much a '50s mom would say."

"I don't know either, but it was a good scene. Now I'm ready for the main event."

He chuckled and navigated to the new clip.

"How are the views?"

"Still phenomenal," he replied in excitement. "We'll easily triple our subscribers this year." He reached over to hug her. "And that has to do with you."

"Us," she corrected.

But he shook his head. "No. This is you. You're a really good actress. If this show was more mainstream, you'd be famous right now." She felt her face warm at the compliment.

"Thank you."

"You will be famous." He gave her another crooked smile. "Let's play this. I'm beginning to get sleepy."

"You have been doing a lot."

"It never ends." He pressed play.

Chapter Fifty-Six

Bobby had apparently gone to Paula's home where she was living with her sister and the sister's husband.

She was back to her heavy makeup while her black hair was a heavily teased up-flip. Despite her eyes being green instead of violet, she reminded Bailey of Elizabeth Taylor.

She was dressed in a green maternity blouse and a black skirt with sensible kitten heels.

He entered the large house with his hat in his hand and greeted her as if they were strangers and not like a man that had knocked her up at least eight months ago.

She was polite when she offered to take his hat and coat. They went into another room and she again was polite when she offered him tea and cookies, which she poured before he even accepted the offered refreshments.

"My sister and her husband went out to give us time to talk. They aren't very happy with you, or me."

"I didn't know," he explained. "Why didn't you tell me?" He glanced down at her belly.

"Well, I didn't think you'd get married months after we broke up," she snapped.

He blew out a long breath. "I didn't either. But why did you wait so long to tell me? I've been married for over two months. You've been pregnant eight."

"You broke up with me, Bobby."

"But you're having my kid!"

"Don't raise your voice," she said.

His mouth snapped shut. "I'm sorry."

She sipped her tea. "You broke up with me and I thought you'd try to get me to end my pregnancy. I was...not in a good place, and I didn't want you to influence my decision. But I didn't intend to keep it a secret. It's just, when I was going to tell you, I heard you were engaged."

Bobby looked away.

"So, you're happily married?" she asked with a voice that had grown softer.

He looked uneasy. "Yes. I'm happily married."

She placed her teacup back on the table and inhaled as if that was a hard thing to hear.

Bailey was impressed. She actually felt sorry for her.

"I'm sorry things between us didn't work out, Paula. I didn't want to prolong a relationship I knew wasn't going to..."

"Go anywhere?" She smiled. "Well, with the exception of having your way with me."

"That's not fair," he replied calmly. "It wasn't always me that initiated that."

She frowned. "I know. I was a big girl."

"Let's not blame each other. A baby is going to be born. The question is...are you keeping him?"

"Of course."

Bobby nodded quickly. "Okay. And for the record, I would not have tried to talk you out of having the baby."

"If I had..." She looked away and seemed to gather her courage before looking at him again. "If I had told you before you married *her*, would you have...married me?"

He took a long time to answer. "I would have done the responsible thing. But I don't know if that would have been the right thing."

Her eyes teared up. "I didn't realize you disliked me as much as you did."

"I didn't! It was never like that. I cared about you then and I care about you now. I just want to do the right thing. I'll take care of my child. Of course, I'd want a paternity test—"

"Oh my God!" she cried. "Do you think I was doing *that* with other boys?"

"I don't think that," he said quickly. "But I want to do everything right, and legally, and I think that's going to be part of it."

Her chin tilted upward. "Of course. I have no issue with proving you're the father. It's just one more step in this terrible nightmare."

"Hey," he said softly. "I'm sorry. This isn't easy for anyone. But I promise to be decent and do the right thing. Always."

She sighed and nodded. "Then can you help with expenses before the birth? The only reason I ask is because I obviously can't work, and there are things he'll need. I saved some money, but—"

"Paula, I'll help. Just call me at the office." He stood and retrieved his wallet and gave her a business card. "Do you need any cash now?"

"Not now. My sister has a friend can get me a second-hand crib and some used baby clothes. But the hospital bill worries me."

"I don't want you to worry about that," he sighed. "I'll talk to Mr. Adams and we'll start from there."

She nodded. "Thank you." She stood. "You should probably go before my sister and brother-in-law come home. He's not...very even-tempered where you're concerned."

Bobby stood and nodded once. "I would feel the same, I guess." She showed him to the door and the last thing he did before leaving was to apologize.

"I'm sorry for what's happened. I should have been more responsible."

"If I had known you had no intentions of marrying me..."

He closed his eyes and nodded, then left.

Bobby turned off the clip and Bailey sighed. "Wow. That was powerful."

"Yes," he agreed. "It feels a bit too close for comfort."

"I guess that's every man's nightmare."

He nodded. "Being in a brand-new relationship and having something like that crop up. Hell yeah, that's a nightmare."

"Is that why we haven't...?"

"No, honey!" He gripped her hand. "I love you. Anytime you think we should move forward in our relationship, I'll be more than ready and willing.

"But in truth, I enjoy the intimate moments we already share. We're very new and still learning each other. And I admit to liking that. I have been in relationships where it was all based on sex and if that's what is agreed upon, then it's fine—but it's never great, at least for me." He rubbed his hair in embarrassment. "Sorry about bringing that up, but it's true." He looked deeply into her eyes, his sky-blue irises fluctuating in size as his pupil grew larger, darkening his eyes.

"Honestly," she replied while taking both of his hands in hers. "With us living *and* working together, I think we should leave more for later…exploration."

He grinned broadly. "You found the words I couldn't."

She stood. "I'm going to shower and get ready for bed, and maybe we can finish this discussion beneath the covers?"

"Woot! Yes!" He stood. "You shower while I finish up here. I want to wash that gumbo dish and put it in the trunk so we can take it back to your aunt and uncle's house next week.

She kissed him. "Thanks for agreeing to go."

"Agreeing?" He grinned. "I look forward to it."

Later that night, after they enjoyed intimate time together, Bailey had to admit that lack of intercourse didn't mean lack of intimacy. She was happy Bobby had such a rare way of looking at sex. If he'd been a different type of man, then this week's narrative might have truly been like life imitating art.

Chapter Fifty-Seven

It was a strange feeling to head for the kitchen on Monday morning and to feel one way but have to act a totally different way.

In real life, Bailey felt upbeat and positive because she and Bobby had hit a critical milestone in their relationship. They had both said those three magical words; I. Love. You. He was interested in her, and not just what lay between her thighs, and was also enthusiastic about meeting her family.

How could she not want to smile and dance when her heart and soul were soaring?

She had done so well in this show because it was manifesting what she actually felt. She showed pain she actually felt, along with joy and passion.

Bobby thought that one day, she would be widely known for her acting skills. But was it truly acting if she was just role-playing? Which required more ability, scripted acting or improvisation?

Well, she was about to find out.

Bailey turned on the kitchen light. She stood there for a moment looking around listlessly, getting into character, becoming Mrs. Baily Banks.

As if waking up, Bailey moved to the refrigerator and opened it. She got out milk and put on a pot to begin the oatmeal.

She quietly made breakfast and put together a quick lunch of sandwiches and chips, then Bobby walked into the room. She could tell he hesitated before approaching her and he placed his hands lightly on her hips. Bailey turned quickly with a forced smile so he could place a kiss on her lips and not on her neck.

The neck-kiss was that special place, and it meant too much when they were going through so much turmoil. But she loved him. This was her husband, and she didn't want to change that.

She placed her hand on his neck and accepted the kiss. He gave her a half smile and took his seat.

"Were you...able to sleep?" he asked.

She sat and poured her coffee. "Not much. I tossed and turned a lot." She added cream and sugar and stirred listlessly.

"I did too."

"What are we going to do?" she asked. "What happens next?"

He sighed tiredly. "I'll speak to Mr. Adams, and I'll see whether my insurance covers the medical bills."

"Can't you just go to HR?"

"It's still going to get back to him. Everyone will know. I'd like to head off any fallout."

"Fallout?" Bailey's brow stitched. "What do you mean?"

"There's been some talk around the office. Nothing to worry about." He reached out and covered her hand.

"Talk? About what?"

"Just stupid, snide remarks. Mostly from people who wanted my position."

"Are you getting bullied at work, Bobby?" she asked with concern. "Why didn't you tell me?"

He lifted her hand and kissed her knuckles. "I wouldn't call it bullying. People say things that get back to me, whether intentionally or not." He shrugged. "I don't let people like that bother me, Bailey—if you didn't figure that out already. People beneath me can't hurt me with their words—not unless they hurt the ones I love."

She smiled and squeezed his hand. "But if you ever need to talk about things that happen at the office—"

"I'm not going to bring that poison home to our house." He continued to eat. She nibbled her oatmeal, mostly picking the berries and chewing them slowly.

"Did...she say anything about me? Paula?"

He glanced up at her and paused in chewing. "I promise, I told you everything we discussed."

"You would have married her if she had told you about the pregnancy earlier."

He put down his spoon. "Bae, once I met you, there was no way I could have ever been happy with someone else. But if she had told me before I ever knew you—then yes. It would have been the right thing to do."

She nodded and ate.

When Bobby finished breakfast, he kissed her cheek and allowed his hands to linger on her shoulders as she sat, struggling with her oatmeal. He picked up his lunch and turned to leave.

"I'll see you this evening," he said over his shoulder.

"Bye, honey. I love you."

She felt him pause from behind her. "I love you, Bae." And then he was gone.

Bailey sat there until she had finished her coffee and then she went to the bedroom to begin her day.

Bailey was fluffing her hair in her vanity mirror when she glanced out the window and saw Curtis's truck parked across the street.

Damnit! She forgot to put the used bottles out and to leave payment.

She slipped on her kitten heels—because she still needed to look good despite how she felt—and she hurried to the kitchen for the checkbook. After she hastily wrote the check, she poured the last of the milk from one bottle into a cup. She'd have it for lunch, and she grabbed the milk crate with the other bottle and carried it to the front door.

Damnit! He had already left her order. She looked down the street and saw him wheeling his cart to a house two doors from hers. She had never met those people, and she had no intention of running up on him while he was dealing with his customers.

Bailey waited patiently until his cart was empty and he returned to the truck to refill it.

When she hurried toward him, he smiled and waved. It was nice seeing a friendly face. She smiled and shrugged.

"I always seem to be late."

He accepted her carton and check. "Not a problem. I'm not always on time myself. Although there are certain people on my route that will complain if I'm not there at exactly the same time with their milk. They swear it's going to go sour, even when I explain the truck is refrigerated." He rolled his eyes and grinned. "So, Mrs. Bailey Banks, when are you going back to Billy's?"

She shrugged, but liked the idea of getting away for a while. "I don't know. I went with Pat, but she just started a new job. I'll call her tonight and ask her about it."

"Okay, well, I'll meet you guys there. I'll call her later."

"Okay. I better let you get back to work before your regulars get mad at you."

He turned briefly to look up the street. "Yeah..." he said slowly. "Bailey, don't go walking alone down Birch Avenue. Some of the people can be bad news."

She looked into that direction. Her expression suddenly became serious. "You mean Mr. Edelman."

He gave her a quick look. "You've already been warned about that one—or did you learn about him by experience?"

"Experience—my husband, anyway. I'll just say he had a few words against race mixing when he caught us walking together."

Curtis's brow furrowed. "I'm sorry to hear that. But he's bad news, and he's the real deal. You and your husband will do best to steer clear."

"I believe it. I was told he was in the Klan." Curtis nodded. "You better get going," she said honestly. "I'll see you at Billy's or—next week when I run after your truck."

He chuckled as he went to the back of his truck. "You're funny. I'll talk to you later."

"Bye."

She turned to head back to her house and saw the curtains from the Clines' front window quickly flutter closed.

She made a face. Well, here comes more gossip.

Chapter Fifty-Eight

The first thing Bailey did was to return the checkbook to the drawer. She pulled out the ledger and sat down to write in it—but discreetly, she was quickly scanning her script.

Was there anything in it about Billy's or Curtis? She had merely scanned it. But with the exception of two pieces of information, everything else was pretty bare. Tuesday, Quinton would visit for an encyclopedia sale (which they couldn't purchase, as it wasn't in the budget). At the bottom of the page was a key that advised that the Piedmont Grocery Story was open in Garden Hill. Also, the Wingate Farmer's Market was open for business and was located on the outskirts of Wingate and Garden Hill—it was integrated.

She retrieved a notebook so she could come up with a shopping list. After quickly scanning the pantry and refrigerator, she had a modest list.

She called Helen.

"Hey, I was going to come by," her neighbor said. "Do you want to go shopping?"

"Yes. I just got behind. Meet you at your house?"

"Yep. I'm grabbing my jacket as we speak. See ya!"

She met Helen and the cameraman at Helen's car. The latter was already in the back seat, shooting from the lowered window. Bailey waited until Helen was at the car before loudly speaking.

"Hey. Hank is gone?"

"Yep." They got into the car. "He left at about five this morning."

"I know you said you don't mind, but it has to be strange having your husband gone all week."

Helen lit a cigarette. "I'm used to it now. We've been married for twelve years." She gave Bailey a quick look. "Before you ask, I was just ten years old when I got married."

Bailey grinned. "I figured it was something like that."

"Hank is great—and don't get me wrong, but how can you women stand seeing your men all day long?"

"I love it. But...I am happy he leaves for work." Both women chuckled. "Hey, I need to get some veggies. Do you want to hit the farmer's market?"

"That sounds like a good idea. If we time it right, we can have lunch." Bailey sighed. She supposed it was a good time to segue—besides, why else was the cameraman in the car?

Helen looked at her quickly. "Everything okay?"

"Money might be tight for a while," Bailey huffed. "For about eighteen years."

"Bailey!" Helen's eyes flashed happily. "Are you...?"

Bailey shook her head quickly. "No. Not me." Helen gave her a questioning look.

"Before I met Bobby, he dated another woman. They were together for about a year before Bobby ended it. They just weren't a good match, he says. They were apart for about two months when we met." Bailey licked her lips and dove in.

"The other day, we saw her downtown. She's pregnant."

"What! Oh my God…"

"She's eight months. And no, neither of us cheated. And yes, he thinks it's his child."

"Oh my gosh, Bailey." She gave the younger woman a sympathetic look before quickly squashing out her cigarette. "What are you going to do?"

Bailey shook her head. "We're going to help financially—"

"No, not him; you?"

"What can I do? I can't leave him over a stupid mistake he made in another lifetime. If this is his kid, he wants to be a part of the baby's life."

"What a mess…" Helen said. "You know I'm here for you. Even though we haven't known each other very long, I count you as a friend."

"Thanks, Helen. I feel the same. Some might find it strange a Negro and a white woman can be friends, but it doesn't feel odd to me."

"Quite honestly," Helen said, "I've always been this way. I had a Negro nanny, and my best friends were Nanny Joy's children. If anyone ever mistreated them, my parents were there to protect them—and everybody knew it. She was our family.

"During the Depression, a lot of poor people changed. My parents did. They didn't look down their noses at others and they taught us kids to be the same way."

"I'm happy there are people in this world that feel that way, Helen. I just learned Mr. Edelman is in the Klan. Did you know about that?"

"Yes. They march through town on the Fourth of July, and he's darned proud of it; backwoods, redneck hick!"

"This is insane," Bailey sighed. "Everything seems to be going against us—from the Clines asking us to move, to Mr. Edelman calling out Bobby, and now this with Paula." She reached into her purse for a handkerchief and used it to dab at her moist eyes.

"Oh, Bailey, honey. I can't imagine walking in your shoes. But I can tell that you are a mountain among simple boulders. I think that's what drew me to you. But even a mountain has to break some. I just want you to know, I get it. If you ever need to lose it, I'm here as a shoulder...or an ear."

Bailey chuckled back her tears. "Thank you. I feel isolated sometimes. I was raised in Dayton and I'm still navigating this place. But I have met a few people I can count as a friend—and that includes you."

Helen smiled wryly and gave her hand a quick pat.

The farmer's market was huge. There were some outdoor stalls where people sold everything from flowers to seasonal produce. There was also an inside area where you could find almost everything food-related. There were fresh-baked cookies, handmade pasta, pies and cookies, meats and seafood of all kinds, and even cooked food.

"I don't know where to begin..." Bailey said in awe.

"I hope you made a list."

She dug into her pocketbook for the list and gave it a dubious look. How could she be forced to adhere to these few meager items when there was a cornucopia of food here? But she was on a budget. So, with a sigh and a brief smile, she tried not to look at the other enticing items.

Bailey had never considered grocery shopping exactly fun, but the farmer's market had a festive air. People walked around eating corn on the cob or candied apples while toting bags of groceries.

Once Bailey had her few items, she was happy to follow Helen around as they chatted and joked with each other.

"Oh, my goodness. I need to get off my feet!" Helen said while gesturing to a nearby café. "Let's get some lunch and take a break."

Bailey grimaced. "I...need to stay on budget—"

Helen waved off her words. "Don't worry about it. It's my treat."

"Oh, Helen. I don't know…"

"You'd be doing me a favor. I haven't been out in a while. I could use some girl-time. I love my big, sweet hubby, but...he's not the biggest conversationalist." Helen gave her puppy dog eyes. "What do you say?"

"Okay," Bailey conceded. "And thank you."

The café was small and quaint. They had chicken salad sandwiches with a side of fruit. It was delicious.

"I think I'd happily never step into the grocery store or butcher shop in Wingate ever again," Bailey said.

"Really? I love the butcher shop," Helen said. "The grocery store isn't much to speak about, but the butchers are so nice. When they give you a sample, you could make a meal out of it!"

Bailey just stared at her. "I suppose it's a different experience depending on who you are."

Helen's expression took on a look of surprise. She leaned forward. "But they aren't segregated..."

"No," Bailey agreed. "But if you're a Negro, you wait until everyone else is served, and sometimes that can be a long time."

Helen nodded apologetically. "You're right. It's not fair."

"And unnecessary. Here, they serve everyone equally; first come, first served."

Helen looked around. "True. But in all fairness, there are just as many Negroes here as there are whites. That's because the market is so close to Garden Hill. Some whites won't come here, you know."

Bailey sipped her iced tea. "Their loss."

Helen grinned at her. "You're right. The ones that won't come are probably those hoity-toity ones that expect to be served before everyone else."

Bailey gave her a surprised grin.

Chapter Fifty-Nine

By the time Bailey got home, she had to rush to make dinner. Since breakfast had been oatmeal, she wanted something more substantial for dinner.

It looked like it was going to be meat loaf.

Bailey had intentionally skipped the cliched '50s meal. It wasn't that it was difficult. Even she probably couldn't mess up meat loaf. But it was so unimaginative. It was the quintessential 1950s meal—overly recognized.

But it was also quick, and with a can of green beans, some mashed potatoes and buttered slices of bread, dinner was ready in about an hour.

"Hi, honey," she greeted Bobby as he stepped tiredly from the car.

He gave her a smile. "Hi, Bae." He kissed her and stepped into the house.

She helped him off with his coat, a frown on her face. Where was the passionate kiss he usually greeted her with? Or the wolf whistles?

"Bad day?" she asked.

"Not the greatest..."

"Oh no. What happened?"

"Well, I talked to Mr. Adams." His expression became grim as he placed his briefcase on the floor by the door. "I got a big lecture about fraternizing with a coworker—even though everyone knew we were an item—and we weren't the only two from the office dating." He sighed and headed for the bedroom. "Let me get changed. Dinner smells great."

Bailey watched him walk into the bedroom with concern. She didn't like seeing him so lifeless—as if the weight of the world was on his shoulders.

She'd fallen in love with the Bobby Bailey whose eyes flashed with dark desire when he looked at her. He was a man that could barely keep from touching her, and whose optimism carried them forward even when she had doubts.

She put her hands on her hips and pursed her lips. If he couldn't be the rock, then she would have to be.

Bobby took his seat at the table. He smiled when he saw the meal.

"I love meat loaf with red sauce."

"That's how we always had it."

"My mom always made it with gravy." He cut into the meat loaf with his fork and placed a large slice into his mouth. "Mmm," he hummed. "Delicious. This has so much flavor."

"It does?"

"Yeah. This is really good. Everything you cook has so much flavor. My mom believes too much spice is bad for the stomach."

"No wonder you like my cooking so much—even the stuff that's not so great."

He flashed her a playful look. "Hush, now. I'll gladly eat whatever you put on the table as long as you put a little season on it."

She took a bite of food and although it might be a bit dry, he was right, it had great flavor. Besides, she put a little extra sauce on it and it became easier to swallow.

To her credit, Bailey didn't bring up the meeting with Mr. Adams while they ate. A man that came home as stressed as Bobby had deserved to eat his meal in peace.

But he brought it up on his own.

"It looks like my insurance covers the birth, but it won't cover any prenatal visits, since I'm not married to her. Also, my insurance will cover the paternity test—but only because they'll make me pay back the hospital costs if it turns out the baby is not mine."

"I see. I'd gladly go into debt if that could be the outcome."

"I know." His expression turned grim and she reached out and lightly gripped his hand. He gave her an appreciative smile.

He cleared his throat. "Things might be a bit tight for a while…"

"I understand," she said.

"Mr. Adams thinks I should get an attorney. It's free through the paper. He doesn't want me to get cheated on child support, but I want to be fair, not just affordable." Bailey nodded when he looked at her as if he hoped she understood.

"I don't know that I want to antagonize her by getting an attorney. Mr. Adams might be a bit judgmental about the situation, but he also wants to make sure she's not just out for my money."

"You know her. Is that possible?"

He shook his head. "I don't think's the case. I'm not a rich man, and she doesn't stand to come out of this smelling rosy." He ran his hand through his hair, messing it up. "I just feel so bad. What was I thinking?"

"Honey, it was a mistake, okay? This isn't going to be easy on anyone. That's why we have to stay strong. I can get a job—"

"No. Hell no!" he said adamantly. She gave him a surprised look. He reached out and took her hand, an apologetic look returning to his face. "I'm sorry. I didn't mean...it's just that I don't want you to have to work. When I married you, it was my dream to give you a life better than the one I took you from."

"My life was pretty good, Bobby. I didn't mind working—"

"But I mind it." She closed her mouth at the intensity in his eyes. "It will be a struggle, but we will get through it. We just have to cut some corners..." Bailey nodded. He lifted her hand to his lips and kissed her knuckles. "I love you so much, Bailey. And I'm so sorry."

She squeezed his hand. "We'll make it work. We might have to eat some extra leftovers."

"I like leftovers, especially meat loaf sandwiches."

"And we can put a hold on date night—"

"No." Bobby shook his head. "We're going to need as many date nights as we can get. We'll just have to do free things and put a hold on places like Madonna's."

"Definitely."

"There is a free hayride Saturday."

"And the park is always fun. Also, we both enjoy snuggling in front of the television."

He smiled at her. "You're a gem, Bae. I don't deserve you."

"Don't say that. We've faced a lot. But if I have to go through this, I want it to be with you. I love you,

Bobby, with every fiber of my being. We are going to weather this storm. And I don't care about the material things. I just want you."

He closed his eyes and lowered his head as if a weight had fallen from his shoulders.

That night as Bobby and Bailey lay in bed, she was relieved to be able to shed Bailey Banks and slip into her own reality. Bobby's expression lost its tension as soon as they closed the bedroom door.

They had made-out until their lips were sore and she had gotten a beard burn on her cheeks. After slathering a layer of Ponds on her cheek, they were snuggled in each other's arms in contentment.

"How were the comments for the day?" she asked.

"Well, Bobby has definitely earned some critics. Some viewers are really pissed at him for ruining the fantasy, while others relate, and they feel for them both.

"I can't say I enjoy being on the negative side of the fans, but the views are still rising, so no complaints from me."

"That's good."

"You know, you are the most unaffected woman I've ever met," he said while pulling back to look at her in awe.

"What do you mean?"

"Babe, you are a star. You never ask about what the fans say about you, or even how many comments you get."

Her cheeks grew warm as she tried not to grin. "I am affected. I just don't know how to...process it. So, I tend not to think about it."

He leaned forward and kissed the tip of her nose. "You are so sweet."

"If you say so," she grinned, embarrassed. One of the reasons Bailey liked acting was so she could pretend to be someone else. She didn't ever hate her life, but it wasn't easy being that kid who didn't have a mother and father. She had been that child was ultra-aware of all the pitfalls of life. She had prepared herself for an accident or misfortune at nearly every turn of the corner. It didn't stunt her, but the blinders had been removed from Bailey's eyes much too soon in her young life.

"Soooo. Full disclosure." Bobby inhaled long.

"Uh-oh." Bailey met his eyes.

"Nothing bad. I mean...not really bad."

"Okay, am I getting lynched?"

"No." He rolled his eyes, unamused. "I think we need to cross over story lines, which is why I've brought Quinton to Team Bailey. But I'd like to do it with everyone."

She gave him a look of interest. That idea excited her. She had been interested in the three other people she had met on the day she'd arrived on set.

"I love that idea. Nadine's story line is very popular, and people seem to really like Drew. Poor Quinton doesn't seem to be doing all that well..."

"Yeah, and he's a very good actor. But the story lines he's forming with the others in the boardinghouse just haven't picked up. It's just that everyone else's stories are so much better." Bailey nodded in understanding. His brow knit. "So, my idea is to have someone from Team Bailey have an affair with him."

Bailey propped herself up on her elbow. "Whoa. That's big."

"I know. But if we can get some of Team Bailey's viewers invested in Quinton's story, it might help his ratings."

"Well, who's the lucky woman?"

"Uh...I don't know."

"Come on, Bobby—"

"No, I'm serious. I don't know. I'm allowing Quinton to decide."

Bailey wasn't sure if she completely believed that. He had to have an idea who he wanted to play the love interest, but she'd see how it played out without being pushy.

"Who are the contenders?" Bailey asked.

"Any female on the team is a prospective love interest."

"Wow. Oh! How far are we going to take the swinger story line?"

"How far do you want to take it?" He winked at her.

"Well, how badly do you want ratings?"

He just chuckled. "Not that bad. Honestly, I don't know how far I want to delve into that, but it was a thing. I have had some ideas about who Haley could swing with, but not all parties are on board."

Now she sat up fully. "Okay, now you have to tell me. No playing!"

He sat up in bed as well. "Shirley and Carl."

Her eyes grew big as she pictured Shirley in her wannabe blonde bombshell getup. And what about poor Carl, who was more interested in eating than acting.

"I guess the holdout is Carl?" she said.

"How did you guess? Shirley is on board, but Carl is adamant he is not making out with anyone."

She grinned. "I'm surprised Carl is even considering being in front of the camera." He'd nearly flipped out when he thought Bailey had actually broken down in real life after the scene at the barbecue.

"Carl wants to stay on the show to be an ally to Bobby and Bailey."

"I haven't seen any of the story lines for the other neighbors." Working six days a week made difficult. "But if Shirley wants to act and Carl doesn't, then it seems obvious Quinton and Shirley should have an affair."

He gave her an inquisitive look. "Not Haley?"

"Well, you can get actual actors to swing with Haley — or maybe someone from another team."

Bobby lay down, his expression thoughtful. Uh-oh...she knew what was coming.

He quickly sat up and gave her an apologetic look. "I have to go to the office — "

She just grinned. "I know that look. It's fine."

He smiled sheepishly. "You're the best." He kissed her and hopped out of bed to hurry off to his office to make notes.

Chapter Sixty

The next day seemed to move much smoother for the Banks family. They had cereal for breakfast and Bailey packed meat loaf sandwiches to send Bobby off to work with.

Bailey did her exercises and dressed for the day. She was just finishing up with her vacuuming when she heard the doorbell ring. She hurried to check the front window and saw a man standing on her doorstep. A large briefcase was at his feet.

Bailey patted her hair to make sure it was still in place and answered the door.

The man standing on her stoop gave her a broad smile. "Hello. May I speak to the lady of the house?"

"I am the lady of the house," she replied.

He only paused for a beat. "Hello, ma'am. My name is Quinton Young." He held out his hand to shake and she politely offered her hand.

Quinton didn't look much different from the last time she'd seen him, although he was dressed in a nice suit and a nice coat and hat. He didn't look to be older than his mid-thirties. With thin, brown hair that was becoming sparse on top, Quinton was almost nondescript. He was a bit stout, but neat, and probably stood just under six feet. He reminded her of Bruce Willis back in his *Die Hard* days.

"I'm with the American Encyclopedia Company—"

Bailey shook her head. "I'm so sorry. I'm not interested—"

"I'm actually here to offer you a free gift." He bent down and opened his briefcase and removed a small box, which he offered to her.

She gave him a curious look before accepting the box.

"It's yours. Regardless of whether you purchase a set of encyclopedias today, we're giving you a free gift for just giving me ten brief minutes of your time. At the end of the ten minutes, if you aren't interested in the books, I'll leave, and you keep the gift."

She gave him a doubtful look. "I don't want to waste your time."

He just smiled. "No waste. In fact, it's a win-win. You accept the gift and give me ten minutes of your time and regardless of whether I make a sale, I get to sit down for a few minutes." His pleasant chuckle put a grin on her face.

Quinton was doing good. She nodded. "Okay. Come in."

"Thank you, Mrs.?"

"Banks. Bailey Banks."

"It's a pleasure to meet you, Mrs. Banks." He stepped into the house and looked around. "You have a beautiful home. That free gift of yours will make a perfect addition to this home. Go ahead and open it."

Bailey grinned and opened the box. Inside was a delicate music box. She opened the lid and a soft, tinkling melody could be heard. He was right, it would look good on her fairly empty sideboard. It was much better than a rosy-cheeked cherub playing a harp, or a sad-eyed puppy dog.

"It's beautiful."

"And it's all yours. Where should I give my presentation?"

"Oh." She gestured to the living room. "Please have a seat. Would you like a cup of coffee?"

He sat on the sofa. "Yes. Thank you very much."

Bailey went into the kitchen, happy to be able to entertain someone that didn't have an attitude problem.

She quickly put together a tray with coffee and cookies and carried them out to the living room where Quinton had set up a display of encyclopedias.

"Please serve yourself while I turn off the radio."

"Oh. No need to do that. I like bebop."

"You do?" She turned the music down some but didn't turn it off.

"Yes, and jazz. Have you ever been to the new supper club?"

"Madonna's? Yes! I love that place."

"I've been there for the food, but ended up loving the music."

She sat down with a smile and added cream and sugar to her coffee.

"Thank you for the coffee," he said. "It doesn't look cold out there but if you walk around for hours on end, you begin to feel it. But don't get me wrong. I love selling encyclopedias.

"Many people think owning encyclopedias is just about furthering your education—but these books represent more than that for me. Yes, you can gain knowledge of history—both American and foreign—as well as politics and current events. There's an area that goes over economics, psychology, even a medical dictionary.

"But, Mrs. Banks, what I particularly like about our encyclopedias is the world they open up for people." Quinton picked up a beautifully sheathed leather-bound book.

"This section talks about the Orient. Look at the beautiful images. You truly feel as if you're traveling into another world." He leafed through until he reached another section. "And here is the dark continent of Africa. You can practically hear the tigers roar." He handed her the book and she leafed through it with interest.

"I don't know about you, Mrs. Banks. But I've often experienced the solitude of my own mind where oftentimes my imagination is my best friend. Many of my clients are women just like you. Many of them have access to all the current magazines but it doesn't carry them away into a new world with new experiences. I sell knowledge, but I also sell the fantasy."

She watched him, intrigued. Quinton did have a quality about him that drew you in. She understood why he was hired, and knew all he needed was a better opportunity.

"Well, it certainly is intriguing. The pictures are gorgeous."

Quinton took a few moments to explain about the covering and how it was bound. Bailey listened politely.

"As much as I would love to own this beautiful set, I have to be honest and tell you I'm a newlywed. And well...things have been tight..."

He gave her an understanding smile. "That's the beauty of purchasing through my company. We can offer you the ability to pay this beautiful set off over the course of a year—or even two. It basically amounts to pennies a week."

Bailey reluctantly put the book down. It would look good on their empty bookshelf. And as much as she wanted to help Quinton out, she had to practice restraint.

"I'm sorry. We just moved in, and we're still finding ways to cut corners."

He gave her a polite smile. "No worries. I completely understand. May I leave my card? You might change your mind at some time in the future, or even know someone who might be interested." She accepted his card and he stood. "I appreciate your time, Mrs. Banks. And thank you for the coffee and the hospitality."

Bailey led him to the door. "Are you sure you don't want the gift back—"

"No," he said adamantly. "I have tens of those in boxes at home."

After Quinton left, she retrieved the music box, listening to it play for a while before she found the perfect place to put it.

When Bobby got home that night, he didn't look nearly as defeated.

"Hi, honey." He kissed her, this time pulling her close for a deep kiss.

She grinned. "Good day at work?"

"Well, it wasn't bad. But what makes it a great day is coming home to my beautiful wife."

He took off his coat. "Saturday, we'll conduct the poll. I brought home the questionnaires."

"I'll call Pat and Helen after dinner," she said while hanging up his coat.

Dinner was meat loaf casserole and salad. It looked like trash; leftover meat loaf, green beans, and canned corn covered with a jar of brown gravy — but it tasted good.

"We had a visitor today," she said.

He paused in chewing. "Oh?"

"Yes, an encyclopedia salesman, of all things."

"Oh." He stabbed his food. "Were you interested?"

"No. But we got a free gift out of it." She got up and hurried to the front room for the music box. She returned and handed it to him.

He gave it a critical look.

"It's so pretty, don't you think?"

"It's nice." He handed it back to her with little interest.

After dinner, while he worked in his office, she called Helen.

"Hey, sorry to bother you, but I have a favor to ask."

"No bother. I just finished talking to Hank. He likes to call me when he's having dinner so it's like we're eating together."

She told her about the poll and Helen was very enthusiastic about it.

"Count me in!"

"We'll meet up Saturday afternoon. Bobby has a few of his coworkers working around town. If you can hit our neighborhood, I'll be visiting Garden Hills and the Negro areas."

"Sure thing," Helen replied. "I can ask a few of the ladies in the neighborhood to help out."

"Yes, if you think they'd help."

"They'll be volunteering for the newspaper, and that's all that really matters — at least in their eyes."

"Let's talk tomorrow. Why don't you come over for lunch? I owe you."

"You owe me nothing, Bailey. But I'll be over for lunch. See you, hon."

"See you."

She hung up feeling optimistic. And yet there was something nagging at her mind.

Maybe she had been too hasty when she told Bobby she'd only do the poll in the Black neighborhood. She was missing a big opportunity for the show in not opening the door to possible conflict.

She couldn't play it safe if she wanted to make 1954 meaningful.

Damn.

Chapter Sixty-One

Both Bobby and Bailey felt wide awake after filming, so they decided to go to the factory for the watch party.

This evening, Bobby didn't turn on the radio to listen to his rockabilly. "I've been thinking…"

Bailey gave him a quick look. "Why did my palms begin to sweat?"

He grinned. "Not all my ideas are scary."

"No. I'm only kidding. What's your idea?"

He squinted at the road as if in deep thought. "I'm going to allow the cast to use a personal streaming device while on set."

"Wow. Really?" She was very surprised. One thing she knew about Bobby was that he liked having complete control, and he wouldn't be able to completely regulate something like that.

"Since we've had these watch parties, I realize how much people really need to connect with each other. We have teams, but I noticed we're all invested in the bigger picture. We need to keep that growing."

"How is allowing people to have their computers going to help that? I mean, I completely agree that I've seen nothing but camaraderie where the cast and crew is concerned. But personally, if I had my cell phone, I already know I'm going to be tucked in a corner watching TikTok videos."

He nodded. "When we made the rule that people can only use those devices while at the production office or after the weekly team meeting and days off, I didn't anticipate how everyone runs out of the meeting to hit the phone or Internet."

"Yeah, the after-meeting stampede."

"In hindsight, it's understandable. My idea is to have an Internet café at the factory. I wouldn't exactly allow people to take those devices onto the filming set. It would only take one cell phone ring captured on film to cause me to lose my shit. I still don't actually trust that people won't sneak them onto the set. But I want everyone to have more access to the outside world and more access to watch the show."

He looked over at her. "You spend your free time with your aunt and uncle, and it gives you no time to watch your scenes or to even read your comments. You have a crazy amount of fans, Bae."

She grinned sheepishly. "I have to admit, it would be nice to watch the parts of the show that interest me." And that didn't exactly include watching herself. She was really intrigued with who Quinton was going to connect with when he started his affair. And there was more to watch than Nadine and Drew. What was happening with Pat and her new beau? What did Miss Baker from the beauty shop do when she wasn't having her hair done? And her interest also included the Clines, as well as others from the neighborhood.

Did it make her a voyeur that she wanted to peek into their lives? She supposed that was the appeal of reality television.

"I like your idea, and I think everyone is going to love it," Bailey said. She was already making plans to watch all of her neighbors — and stream some music — and catch up on current events.

The next morning at breakfast, Bobby didn't eat his French toast with the enthusiasm she was accustomed to. She knew she had cooked it right. It might be just a touch soggy in the center but he liked soft eggs, so this shouldn't be much of a stretch...

He finally met her eyes. "I have to visit Paula today."

She paused in bringing her coffee cup to her lips. "Okay."

"I need to tell her about the insurance. Also, I want to give her a little bit of money."

She took a small sip of coffee. "Yes. You should." She refused to ask him how much. He should just tell her without her having to ask. Right?

But he just chewed his eggs without looking at her.

"Helen's coming over today. We're going to talk about the poll Saturday." She tried to turn the conversation to something that should interest him. But it didn't work.

Bobby put his fork down. "Your beauty appointment Saturday will have to be cancelled. I'm sorry, Bae, but I needed to use that money to have enough to give to Paula."

Her mouth dropped. Her hair appointment? No. Not that. She couldn't go back to having scary hair.

"I have a little bit of money left from doing the shopping. It's enough for the beauty shop."

He nodded, and seemed too ashamed to meet her eyes. She reached out and touched his hand. "Are you going to see her after work?"

"Yes. Don't wait for me for dinner. I don't know how late I'll be."

"I'll keep a plate for you on the stove."

"Thank you. I'd better get going." He hadn't even eaten half his food.

Bailey looked at his plate. "But you didn't finish breakfast."

He bent down to kiss her cheek. "I don't have much of an appetite this morning." She got up and handed him his lunch.

"I made grilled cheese and a thermos of tomato soup."

He offered her a smile. "That sounds good."

"Have a good day," she called as he headed out of the room. "Love you!"

"Love you!" he called back before leaving.

She frowned in concern. She didn't like seeing Bobby so down, even though she knew that's the way it needed to be played. She hoped this story line wouldn't put too much stress on her favorite couple.

For her and Helen's lunch, Bailey decided to continue with the tomato soup and grilled cheese theme. She felt a little bad that it wasn't anything fancy but she added some ham to it, which made it a bit nicer.

Helen came to the house filled with enthusiasm, and even before saying hello she was announcing good news. "I already got three people on board, and I'm sure I can get more."

"That was quick," Bailey said while taking her jacket and hanging it in the closet.

"Remember, we're a bunch of bored housewives. Ladies are dying for things to do."

"Shhh. Don't let our husbands hear you say that," Bailey joked. She led Helen to the kitchen. "I have the poll questions. We can go over them while we have lunch."

"You know," Helen said while touching her chin, "I can call the other girls and we can all get together. Plus, it will give them an opportunity to finally meet you, Bailey. Then they can see just how nice you are."

It was a good idea...but Bailey was thinking about how to stretch the grilled cheese sandwiches. If she cut them into sticks, she could make two more sandwiches and easily stretch them—but if she cut them into squares, she could call them canapes! And she could serve the soup in dainty teacups with a dab of cream on top.

"Forget I even suggested it," Helen said quickly.

Bailey smiled. "I think it's an excellent idea. Call them and invite them over."

The other ladies were at her house within fifteen minutes. That was one good thing about the '50s. Housewives were typically ready at the drop of a dime.

The first woman to arrive was Mary, who shook her hand politely while looking her directly in her eyes. She had short, dark hair and freckles. She was probably only a little older than Bailey.

Her intensity was evidently not a sign that she didn't like Bailey because Mary was very enthusiastic about her dislike for Senator McCarthy, so it probably wouldn't be easy to hide.

Next was Sue, who walked into the house and looked around with interest — only acknowledging Bailey with a faint hello. She was closer to Helen's age, in about her mid-thirties. She was blonde, and Bailey was happy to see that not all blonde women felt the need to look like Jayne Mansfield or Marilyn Monroe.

Sue was possibly a bit overdressed, with no less than ten pieces of costume jewelry.

And finally there was Anita, who hugged Helen and then turned to Bailey and hugged her too. Anita was the oldest of the group and appeared to be in her late forties to early fifties. Despite that, she seemed the most youthful. She even wore two short pigtails with her black bangs cut starkly short. She also wore cat's-eye glasses, saddle shoes with ankle socks, and a calf-length pleated skirt and cashmere sweater. Wow.

"So nice to finally meet you, Bailey!" Bailey couldn't help the smile that tugged at her lips. Anita had a child-like quality, amplified by the Band-Aid on her knee and fading bruise beneath her eye as if she'd run into a door. Her short nails even had peeling yellow polish.

"It's nice to meet you. I'm happy for your help with the poll."

"My pleasure. Helen says it will be fun — and I'll be able to get out of the house." She winked at Bailey.

"Please make yourself comfortable. I have some snacks. Would you like tea or coffee? I also have sweet tea."

"Sweet tea sounds good."

Once everyone was together, they talked easily, and all seemed enthusiastic about the poll. Also, no one seemed to think the grilled cheese and tomato soup was a stupid idea. In fact, there were only two squares of grilled cheese left and none of the soup.

Who didn't like grilled cheese and tomato soup?

Anita liked it so much, she had seconds.

They each took the poll themselves and then went over the answers, which led to a lively discussion on political repression, which of course led to talk of racial repression—because it was technically impossible for whites to be in the company of a Black person without the topic of race coming up.

Helen opened her notebook, and they were determining how to divvy up the streets each would poll when Bailey cleared her throat.

"I know I said I'd be working in the Negro areas, but I think I want to visit some houses in our neighborhood too."

Everyone grew quiet. Helen quickly smiled. "You and I can go together."

Bailey nodded, "Okay. As long as we don't go down Birch Avenue. I want nothing to do with anyone on Edelman's street."

Helen's mouth formed a large O. "Bailey, I didn't mention—and I probably should have—that Anita's last name is Edelman."

Bailey turned to look at sweet Anita. The older woman gave her a sheepish smile.

"Guy's my brother."

Chapter Sixty-Two

No one said anything. Bailey just stared at her while blinking.

How did such a sweet lady end up related to a man that would stop strangers walking down the street in order to chastise them about being of different races?

Anita shrugged sheepishly. "I do know my brother is a cranky old so-and-so. But he's not so bad if you get to know him—well, not you, particularly..." Anita gestured to Bailey.

Helen quickly rushed in. "Guy and Anita couldn't be more different."

"Your brother is in the Klan..." Bailey whispered.

"True, but he can't rule my life, despite how much he thinks he can." She looked over at the others in the room. "You know how men can be. They have no more life experience than you, but they think they know your life better than you do!"

Mary agreed. "You are so right about that. Phillip once complained I let the water run too long when I rinsed the dishes.

Bailey blinked, still in shock that they were sitting here talking casually as if having a Klansman in the family wasn't a big deal. How did you handle that when you were the Colored host of such a shindig?

After the ladies left, Helen lingered behind. She gave Bailey another apologetic look.

538

"I didn't realize you knew about Guy being in that horrible club."

Bailey was almost speechless. "That horrible club? You mean the one that lynches people like me?" she said incredulously.

"No. No," she said quickly. "It's not like that! They're just a bunch of good ol' boys that get together talking nonsense. They like to put on that stupid outfit and march, but that's about it."

Bailey just stared at her. "I think that's pretty bad..."

Helen sighed. "It is. But Anita isn't like that. She's a very nice person."

"...Who thinks her brother is a good person to anyone but people like me."

"Bailey, trust me when I say, Anita's just a sweet lady that got the short end of the stick when it came to family. She's a spinster who lives with her brother in their childhood home. He's nothing but a self-important dipstick. But he's not a dangerous person. And Anita's a sweetheart."

"Okay," she finally conceded. "If you say it's okay, I'll trust you."

Helen touched her hand. "Thank you. And I'm sorry I didn't tell you about Guy. I know a lot of people think of me as nothing but an empty-headed gossip, and maybe I do have a tendency to put myself in the middle of things. But this time, I thought I was doing the right thing."

"It's fine. I appreciate everything you've done, and for your friendship. See you Saturday?"

"Yep. I'll send the ladies out earlier, but I'll see you when you get home."

After Helen left, Bailey closed her eyes and leaned tiredly against the closed door.

As Bailey got everything cleaned after the meeting with the ladies, she thought about what to make for dinner. It had to be something that would keep easily covered in the oven or on the stovetop.

It was time to refer to the Betty Crocker Cookbook. After leafing through it for a while, tuna casserole was the winner. She had all the ingredients, and even though she had never made it, she'd eaten it enough times. Also, it was foolproof.

As it baked in the oven, she checked the time and decided to call Pat.

"Hi, Pat. This is Bailey. You're not busy, are you?"

"Hey, sis," Pat said. "No. Is everything okay?"

"Uh...not really. There's just so much going on right now. I could really use a friend."

"Okay...now I'm worried. Do you need me to come over?"

"Would you mind? I mean, we can talk over the telephone. Bobby's not here, he'll be out late—"

"Then I'll come over. You sit tight. I'll be there in a flash."

Pat hung up and Bailey sighed.

Pat truly was over in a flash. They hugged and Bailey grinned.

"You didn't have to dash over."

"I wasn't doing anything. I live in that big house by myself, and even though Marvin keeps hinting about coming over...I'm just not sure about him yet."

"He's really handsome."

Pat followed her into the living room. "And he knows it."

They got comfortable on the sofa. "Do you want something to drink? I don't have any beer, but I do have iced tea."

"Actually, you said Bobby's going to be home late?"

Bailey smiled ruefully. "Yes."

"Why don't we hit Billy's place? He's got beer, and it's cheap."

"You know, I was just talking to Curtis about when I was going back to Billy's. And cheap sounds perfect right now."

"What's going on, sis? Are your neighbors getting you down?"

Bailey rolled her eyes and told her all about being politely invited to leave the neighborhood.

"The icing on the cake is finding out the neighbor Bobby argued with is a part of the Klan."

"Oh my...I don't want to blaspheme, but Christ-on-a-handrail!"

Bailey stood and began to pace.

"That's not even the worst of it." She stopped in front of her friend and wrung her hands. "Bobby's ex-girlfriend came back to town."

"Oh, don't tell me that heffa wants to get back with him!"

"It's not that. She's pregnant, and she says Bobby is the father."

Pat covered her mouth as if it was the first time she had heard this story. Bailey had to hand it to her and her acting skills. It was a touch over the top, but so authentic to the situation.

"He wasn't cheating!" Bailey added quickly. "She's almost in her final month and we didn't get together until he ended it with her." Pat was staring at her. "Don't look at me like that, Pat. She was out of the picture by the time we got together."

"Okay, okay. I'm not doubting you. It's just really close…"

"I know. And I also know everyone in town is going to think I'm the other woman and I broke them up!"

Pat stood. "The last thing worth worrying about is what other people think."

Bailey rubbed her temples. "You're right. Most people are already thinking the worse of me for marrying a white man."

Pat rubbed her shoulder. "It takes guts to lead your life on your own terms. Don't start worrying about other folks now. Your enemies will be happy to see you fail—so you can't."

She looked at her. "You're right. I don't live for what others think. If I did, then Bobby and I would have never gone out on our first date."

"Let's get out of here," Pat said. "I think you need a break."

"I may as well. After this week, I'll be holding onto every dime just to be able to afford my beauty shop visit."

Pat's eyes widened. "It's that bad?"

"Yes. Bobby's giving her money to afford things for…you know…the baby."

Pat just rubbed her arm.

Bailey left a quick note for Bobby explaining she went to hang out with Pat and dinner was in the oven along with a quick salad in the fridge.

The ride to Billy's juke joint was nice because there was no cameraman present to ride in the back seat.

It gave Bailey an opportunity to comment that she would like to see Curtis there. She didn't want their scenes together to only take place on her front stoop.

"I can call him once I get there by saying we need him to buy us free beer."

"Yeah! Good idea! But don't tell Bailey about it until after you do it, because she'll be all shy about it."

"Should I call Marvin?" Pat asked.

"He might hog all of Pat's attention, and Bailey wouldn't want you to leave her completely alone with Curtis. They aren't going to have an affair or anything."

"Why not?" Pat asked seriously.

"Do you think they should? I really don't want to go that route. An affair would destroy the integrity of what I hoped having an interracial relationship would show the world about how hard those relationships were."

"If you did have an affair, those fans of yours would leave you lickety-split." Pat grimaced. "Oh man...I'm beginning to talk like I live in the '50s even in my free time."

Bailey chuckled, but then gave her a serious look. "Before this story line, I was truly having a hard time separating Bailey Banks from myself. Are you having problems like that?"

"No. For me, it's strange living in character when I don't have a story line. My script will say, Monday, Pat goes to work, comes home and does her normal routine. Tuesday, Pat goes to work, comes home and does her normal routine."

Bailey nodded. "Same here. Bobby said he does that so we can write our own story line. But man, it's not easy."

"Right? I know the endgame, but I can't really do much about ushering in civil rights to Wingate when there's not a completed Black community to rally. So basically, I spend a lot of time rattling around that big house because I can't even drive around Garden Hill until it's complete. And I don't want people thinking I'm a drunk, so I can't even hang out at Billy's place every night."

"What about Marvin?"

"He's cool, but I don't want to depend on him to float my story line. I mean, don't get me wrong. I like that Rob is giving us so much power to write our stories, but I feel like I'm pretty boring. Some of us have even thought about a crime story line, or even a murder mystery." She shrugged. "But I don't know."

Bailey agreed it was hard, but could Bobby actually be expected to write full scripts for every actor on the show? No. If the cast wanted a compelling story line, they would have to create it themselves. And that was more than fair.

Chapter Sixty-Three

When they got to Billy's, Pat handed the man two singles before Bailey could stop her.

"Pat! You paid last time," Bailey said as they entered the small house. "Here, take this dollar—"

"No. You're going to use that money to pay for your hair visit Saturday. We are getting together Saturday for the poll, right?"

"Uh...stop changing the subject..." Bailey began as she followed her friend into the room. The music wasn't quite as loud, and was more bluesy than bebop. Several people were slow dancing in the middle of the floor while others were standing around chatting and drinking from bottles of beer.

"I'm not changing the subject. Things for you are tight right now, but I'm sure they won't be that way forever. And when things change, then you can get me, okay? Now put that money away before Billy comes along and snatches it out of your hand!"

Bailey gave Pat a half smile and put the money back in her pocketbook.

"If you got a dime, you can get us both a plate of food. Smells like fish fry. Mmm, mmm, mmm. Grab us food and I'll be right back." Pat headed in the opposite direction from the food. "And get me a beer!" she called over her shoulder.

"Okay," Bailey said.

She got the food, which was indeed a piece of catfish, fried potatoes, and coleslaw. By the time she was trying to figure out how to hold the food while getting their drinks, Pat was beside her taking a plate of food out of her hands.

"Where'd you run off to?" Bailey asked.

"I called Curtis."

"Why'd you do that?" Bailey's brow rose.

"Who else is going to pay for the rest of our beers? Let's grab those chairs over there."

Bailey followed Pat and they were able to snag the chairs.

"Oh!" Bailey said. "I meant to tell you, I decided to do part of the poll in my neighborhood. I'm going to tag along with Helen for a few houses."

Pat watched her as she munched on her fish. "I thought you were going to have the whites poll the whites and us Negroes poll other Negroes."

"That was the plan. But I met some of the ladies today that will be conducting the poll, and I really feel I should show my face more."

"Well, you are there to stay. You might as well."

They talked about when they'd meet up Saturday, and Bailey was happy Curtis showed up after their meal was finished.

He looked good in navy slacks and a sweater with a shirt beneath it—no tie. Pat waved him over and he leaned over and gave her a brief hug and shook Bailey's hand.

"You ladies are a bad influence."

"What?" Bailey asked in surprise.

"It's a work night." He looked around and spotted a chair, which he brought over.

"Would you like another beer?" he politely asked.

"Yes. Thanks, Curtis. And you should grab yourself some fish. It's delicious!"

"I just had dinner. But save my seat."

He went off to get the beers.

"He's such a nice guy," Bailey commented. "Have you two ever been...you know?"

"Curtis and me? No way! I grew up with him. He's like a brother. Plus, he always has too many girls interested in him. See? Look at those girls over there about to make their move on him."

Several women were eyeing Curtis, and they probably weren't acting.

He returned a moment later with beers. Pat mentioned the poll, and Curtis seemed interested and invited them to come to his house when they were polling if they wanted to practice on him. It led to a conversation about the senator and once again, Curtis proved to be very knowledgeable. It helped because beyond knowing McCarthy was behind the blacklisting of several famous people, she knew little else.

They ended up dancing together when the music got fast again. The three of them jumped up and down and laughed and did the popular dance steps.

Her two beers had made everything easy and fun. But it was getting late, and she should get home.

"Aww," Curtis said. "It's still early. And I know for a fact you're the only one of us that don't have work tomorrow."

"I'm also the only one that's married and whose spouse isn't present."

Pat looked at her watch. "Goodness, you're right! It's getting late."

"Next time, bring the hubby," Curtis said.

Bailey looked around at all the brown faces. "I don't think the people here would approve of that."

Pat touched Curtis's arm to draw his attention. "This place is ours. When we get off work where the boss is paying whites more than us for doing the same work, this is where we come."

"Or when you're still called boy every day you're at work," Curtis added.

"Or," Bailey added, "when your neighbor is in the Klan and his sister tells you he's a good person to everyone else."

Curtis and Pat looked at her in shock.

"Oh...well, damn." Everyone laughed, and she and Pat made their way out of the little juke joint.

If she had to be honest, she wished she could stay for another hour.

Bailey tried not to scowl when she saw the cameraman waiting for them in the back seat of Pat's car. It meant they probably wanted them to discuss serious matters, but she didn't want to do that. She'd had a surprisingly good time, and she wasn't going back to being morose.

"That was fun," Bailey said. "Thanks for inviting me out."

"I wish we could hang out more." Pat started the car and lit a cigarette.

She wanted to say it might be a while before she could go out like this again, but that would just open up the conversation to money and saving and eventually, Bobby and his baby's mama.

"We'll definitely do that. How are things going with Marvin?"

"Ah, Marvin. You know, he kinda grows on you. He sent me flowers. I woke up and there was a bouquet on my front stoop…"

They got back to the house a little after eight, and Bailey leaned forward and gave Pat a quick kiss on the cheek.

"See you Saturday! And thanks again for doing this."

"Any time, sis."

Bailey hurried past their car, and just as she reached the front door, it opened. Bobby looked at her, his eyes quickly scanning her before he stepped aside.

"Hi, honey," she said, and gave him a brief kiss. Bobby took her coat and hung it in the closet. Bailey paused at his silent greeting.

"You got my note I was with Pat, right?"

"Were you drinking?" he asked.

She gave him a surprised look. After a moment, Bailey shook her head and headed for the kitchen without answering. She saw that the tuna casserole was now on the stovetop and a big hunk of it had been eaten. There was also a used plate, glass, and silverware in the sink.

Bobby followed her into the kitchen. "Bae, I'm working really hard, and you're going out and spending money we don't really have on drinks with your friends."

"I spent a dime, Bobby; one dime!"

His eyes swept her form. "How many beers did you have?"

"I had two, if that's okay with you." He stared at her. "Pat paid." She intentionally didn't mention Curtis. First, what in the hell was going on with him? Second…what the hell?!

Bobby sighed in annoyance. He went to the refrigerator and pulled out the container of milk.

"Why are you so angry?" Bailey asked. "There's nothing wrong with a drink or two every few days."

Bobby shook his head. "Just drop it, Bailey."

Her head tilted. Did he just use her first name? She rotated her neck until she heard it crack.

"Wait a minute. What *are* you so mad about? All of a sudden you have a problem with me having a drinking or going out with a friend when you were the one who encouraged me to get out of the house."

He went to the cabinet for a glass. "I'm not going to argue with you about it." But then he put the glass on the table and glared at her. "But I would think you should understand without me explaining it to you, I wouldn't want my wife getting free drinks from our friends. We don't need handouts!"

Bailey's mouth parted. "I'm not taking handouts…"

"Did you really need to go out drinking that badly? Is your life that bad?"

She just blinked. Bailey slipped off her heels and turned and began running water in the sink to begin washing the dishes.

She heard him walk up behind her.

"Bae…" His tone was different, not as combative. "I'm sorry."

Bailey washed the first dish without responding.

Bobby walked slowly to stand beside her. She continued to ignore him.

"Don't be mad at me," he said in a pleading tone.

She suddenly turned to look at him. "Are you done being mad at me?"

He swallowed. "Yes."

"Good. Because I am not your punching bag. When things go wrong, you do not get to come home and take it out on me."

This time, he was the one who blinked at her. He nodded. "You're right. I didn't mean to do that." He reached for the plate she had just washed. She released it and he rinsed it and picked up the towel and dried it.

"I love you, Bae," he said. "I'm sorry for how I acted."

She picked up the glass and washed it and handed it to him. He rinsed it and dried it.

"I love you too."

Chapter Sixty-Four

After that scene, they headed for the bedroom. It was a little after nine p.m. Bobby hit the stop filming button the way he normally did. He then quietly gathered Bailey in his arms and hugged her.

"They had their first fight," he whispered.

She hugged him back. "Yeah." She felt him gently rub her back. "How are we going to play this?"

He leaned back and cupped her face. "I don't know. I'm just playing it by ear." He kissed her. "You do smell like smoke and beers, though."

Bailey wrangled out of his arms. "I'm going to take a shower!"

Once they were both showered and in bed, Bobby pulled her close. "I think I'm going to get a bunch of hate mail. But I loved the way you handled him. 'When things go bad, you do not get to come home and take it out on me,'" he mimicked.

She chuckled. "I do not sound like that."

He kissed her cheek and pulled her close.

"But on a serious note…"

Bailey looked at him curiously. "What?"

"I've been thinking about removing liquor from the set."

Bailey sat up slowly while Bobby tracked her with bright-blue eyes.

"Because of me?"

He sat up too. "I don't think Bailey's drinking is problematic." He chuckled. "This is 1954, after all. I'm supposed to be greeted every day with a cocktail." Bobby sighed and looked at her seriously. "But I think in the wrong hands, liquor could compromise filming.

"You know I like authenticity. But last year, there weren't as many crewmembers. And a lot of them spend a great deal of time drinking socially."

"Has anyone gotten drunk on set?" she asked in concern.

"No. But at the rate we're going…"

"Are you sure you want to do that?" He raised a questioning brow, allowing her the opportunity to continue. "Many of the cast members have never acted before this. But I think they get bored."

"Bored? How is that possible! Everyone should be concentrating on coming up with a good story line."

She nodded in agreement. "And some of them have been. Others need…direction."

He thought about it. "You are right. But we have so many people—and we need many people. But not all of them can have starring roles."

"True," she agreed.

"So, those that can't come up with an interesting story line won't get featured. That's only fair. There's only a finite number of spots."

"I know. But those people that don't have a designated story line—the dancers and the factory workers and the people that fill up the market. They're all on set day in and day out with nothing to do but live a fake life on a set."

"They're just doing what they'd do if they were at home, right?"

"No. At home they have a community, a network, friends and family. I just think the clubs and bars are necessary—and the liquor."

Bobby didn't answer for a few moments. "You're right. There are too many people with not enough to do."

"Are you going to go into your office to write down notes?" she asked.

Bobby's thoughtful expression cleared. "No." He grabbed her and pulled her back down to the bed, where they snuggled. "I won't kill the alcohol on set, but I will make sure each of the team leaders give a talk against excessive drinking."

He changed the subject. "The crew knows about my ideas for the Internet café at the factory and we should have it done by the weekend."

"Everyone's going to like that," she smiled.

He grunted and closed his eyes.

"Tomorrow, we have to talk about Bobby's meeting with Paula."

"How did that go?"

"Well, I think it's fantastic. But Bobby probably wouldn't agree."

"Aww," she groaned. "I'm too tired to sit up again. Can we just make out some more?"

He snickered tiredly. "Yes. I could always use some Bailey-love." He squeezed her butt and nipped her chin.

Bailey gave in for a while before growling. "Nooo, tell me how the meeting went."

Bobby rolled onto his back. "Well, Paula wants Bobby to have his marriage with Bailey annulled so he can do the 'right thing' and marry her."

Bailey shot up in bed.

"What?!"

Did she hear that right? Paula wants Bobby to divorce her so they can get married?

"Maybe we should discuss it on camera?" he suggested.

"Too late for that!" Bailey crossed her arms in front of her. "I can't believe she actually suggested that. Who does that?"

He sat up again. "Someone who doesn't believe that a marriage between a white man and a Black woman is legal."

Her mouth parted. "I remember seeing a movie about the Lovings, where a white man and Black woman were married in the '60s. He went to jail because of it." She shook her head and gave him a horrified look. "Bobby, we are not going to make that a story line." She would put her foot down on that.

He quickly shook his head. "No. First of all, I have no desire to play the role of a prisoner. Second— and more importantly, Ohio repealed their anti-miscegenation law back in the 1880s." He pointed to his temple. "That's one of the first things I researched. No. Bobby and Bailey's marriage is completely legal."

Bailey relaxed. "All right. Still, that was low-down." Bobby grinned and nodded.

"It took me by surprise."

She looked at him. "So how are we going to play it? Bailey might have a few choice words for her."

"Well...I don't know that Bobby will tell Bailey."

"What?"

He wore a thoughtful expression. "Think about it. Bobby's not leaving his Bailey, and he'll want peace between them."

Bailey made a face. "You really don't think she should be told?"

"Hey, if this was me, I'd tell you. But the way things were back then, Bobby would have thought he had to run things a certain way—meaning he has to act like the head of the household.

"I won't call Bobby a chauvinist. But he does believe he has to take care of the household and be the breadwinner. It was a sense of pride for him to be able to buy the house, have a car, a television, *and* afford to allow Bailey to be a housewife."

"He'd rather see their family sacrifice than allow Bailey to get a part-time job?"

"Yes. Unless it becomes absolutely necessary."

"Wow," Bailey grimaced. "Times have changed. Most men would agree that having a wife help with the finances wouldn't be the end of the world."

Bobby gripped her hand. "How do you want to handle the situation?"

Bailey thought about it instead of answering off the top of her head.

"I think your idea is a good one. But if Bailey finds out he's keeping secrets, it might affect the trust she has in him."

"I understand." He sighed. "It's kind of sad, don't you think?"

She leaned in and put her head on his shoulder. "Yes. But you were right that it's a good story line. And the ratings are still growing?" She looked up at him.

"That's another thing. Paula is getting a lot of views, as well as positive comments."

Bailey pulled back to look at him again. "Really? She's interfering with Bobby and Bailey's happiness. A few days ago, everybody hated her."

"Right, and a lot of people still despise her. But she's changing the tide. She's actually in love with Bobby. The scene we filmed Sunday showed her staring at a picture of them together. She held it to her chest and placed it in her treasure box.

"And then today when they argued about Bobby's marriage, after he left, she broke down and cried and began talking to her unborn baby.

"It was brilliant. People began responding positively to her. She's a sympathetic character. They're tuning in to her story line to see what she's plotting."

Bailey didn't know what to say. She was missing out on a lot by not having the ability to watch the show. But she couldn't believe Paula had people's sympathy.

"Then there are Bailey's scenes," Bobby sighed. "Of course, they are still the top ranked. But..."

"But?"

"We got a few comments where people want Bailey to fall for Curtis the milkman, but just as many demanding we don't let her have an affair."

"Jeez." Bailey looked at Bobby warily.

"What do they want me to do? I'm sure they have opinions."

His brow gathered. "They want you to beat up Paula."

Bailey threw her head back and laughed. "Oh my God. They do realize she's pregnant, right? If I put my hands on her they'd lock me up and throw away the key."

He nodded. "Some comments want Bobby and Bailey to take Paula's baby and raise it as their own."

She froze. "Please tell me you're not considering that."

"I'm not considering it."

"Okay, because I can barely get my chores done as it is." The last thing she could ever imagine is trying to follow her story lines while also looking after someone's baby.

"A reality show isn't the best way to raise another person's baby. Of course, if we had our own baby that would be different."

Bailey's heart leaped. Did he just say what she thought he'd said?

"Do you want to have kids someday?" She made sure to add *someday*.

"Yes. I think I'd like a kid or two. What about you?" His gaze on her was steady.

It was always strange when discussions with a new boyfriend turned to serious life questions. It always felt as if they were speaking in code about what they wanted from the relationship they were in. But of course, you couldn't say things like, yes, I want to have kids with you someday. So you just had to talk in general.

It was so awkward.

"I'd like to have kids—but after I pursue my career as an actor."

He nodded and kissed the knuckles of her hands the way Bobby Banks always did. She smiled shyly.

"Tomorrow at breakfast, we can discuss Paula — but it might be better if we can hold off until after work."

"I agree." She stifled a yawn. "Sorry. I guess I'm more tired than I thought. Being a 1950s housewife is harder work than I ever anticipated."

"Especially when she goes out drinking and dancing with her friends."

She scowled as they lay back down in each other's arms. "She's still young—"

"And married," he added. "A lot of men would have a problem with their wives going out drinking with a handsome, single man."

She grinned. "Don't tell me you're jealous," she joked.

"You can play that how you like," he replied dryly. "But there may be consequences and repercussions."

She smirked and looked at him. "Such as?"

"Don't worry about it." He kissed the tip of her nose. "Get some sleep. You're tired."

She closed her eyes as if his words willed them to do just that.

"I love you, honey," he whispered a few minutes later.

Bailey smiled. "You sneak and say that when I'm too sleepy to reply."

"No I don't," he murmured with his lips pressed to her forehead. "I don't sneak. I just say it while you're sleeping."

"Why do you do that?"

He took a while to answer and she almost fell asleep. "Because I don't need you to say it back."

She chuckled. "I hate that; the obligatory I. Love. You. But I do love you."

He lightly squeezed her shoulder. "I know."

Chapter Sixty-Five

The next day, Bailey went about making breakfast while she thought about last night's revelations.

Paula had come back to the production with guns blazing. Unlike some of the other actors, she knew exactly what she had to do to be a success on this show.

Was it possible Paula's story line could really take over the top spot?

Yes. It was.

Bailey didn't think she would mind if she wasn't number one week after week—if that honor went to Nadine, Drew, or Quinton. But not to someone that had tried to seduce her boyfriend last season.

If Bobby had been one to have sex with just anyone, then this could have been a totally different issue. She wondered how long Bruce Adams had known about this love child of his.

She sighed and began oven-frying strips of bacon. She would make BLTs for Bobby's lunch and they could have bacon, eggs, and grits for breakfast.

She had just put the pot of grits on the table on a trivet when Bobby came into the room. She fiddled with his tie nervously as he looked at her before his eyes shifted to the table.

"Good morning. Breakfast looks mighty fine." He gave her a quick peck on the lips.

"Thanks. BLTs for lunch. Do you want an apple or a banana?"

"A banana," he said while taking his seat and tucking his napkin in at his collar. "It looks like they might go bad soon."

She noted he was back to being uneasy while in her presence. She'd have to test that theory and try to spot if he stared at her when she thought he wasn't looking.

"I can make banana pudding when that happens. I'll have to call Aunt Mae for her recipe. I'm sure Betty Crocker can't make it as good as my aunt's."

"That's something I haven't had in a while."

She got up from the table. "I need to put whipping cream on the milk list before I forget!"

Bailey went to the kitchen drawer for her list and studied it while leaning against the counter. Wait. Did they really need two containers of milk each week? They almost had to rush to drink up the last few sips…it would save money.

She discreetly peeked over at Bobby.

He was staring at her!

He quickly picked up a slice of bacon and concentrated on eating it.

Her heart warmed. They might have argued the night before, but Bobby Banks was still enthralled by his Bailey.

She took her seat and smiled at him. "Done. I'll say there will be a batch of banana pudding on Saturday—or I can take them to my aunt's when we visit Sunday and have her make it."

He paused while chewing. "Do your aunt and uncle…know?"

She put down the cup of coffee she had raised to her lips.

"No. I thought maybe we should tell them face-to-face when we see them Sunday."

Bobby licked his lips and nodded. "I guess they'll go back to hating me again."

"They never hated you."

"Your uncle sure wasn't in love with the idea of you marrying out of your race. I know he still calls me 'that white boy.'"

"What? No, he doesn't."

"I'm sure they're going to rub it in your face that you should have married that nice young man from their church."

Bailey rolled her eyes. "Don't worry about my aunt and uncle thinking bad about you. I will slip to my aunt that you remained a complete gentleman with me and I was a virgin until our wedding night."

He inhaled. "Thank you. Are you sure you want me there? Maybe I should—"

"It will look better if you're there."

He nodded. "You're right." Bobby quickly drank the last of his coffee.

"I'd better get going," he said while standing. He kissed her cheek from behind.

"Have a good day," she said. "I love you, Bobby."

He paused and then kissed the top of her head.

"I love you, Bae."

When Bobby came home that evening, Bailey decided to allow him to at least change clothes and sit down for dinner before she brought up Paula.

But he beat her to it.

"I gave Paula money yesterday; ten dollars. I was thinking I should do it every two weeks."

She nodded. "Twenty dollars a month...it's going to be tight, but I think we can afford it. Have you given any more consideration to getting a lawyer?"

"Well, I think I'm giving more than most men would. Some wouldn't help her out at all. She said she wants to move out of her sister's house. It wasn't supposed to be long-term and...well, that costs money."

Bailey frowned. "Bobby, you can't support her entire household *and* ours."

He sighed. "I know."

"She is not your responsibility. After the baby is born, I'm sure she'll get a job." She gave him a piercing look. "Unless you don't want her working either."

He gave her a guilty look. "If she works, who is going to take care of the kid?"

Her eyes got big. "You can't tell me you're thinking about supporting her completely?"

He shrugged and shook his head. "I don't know. If I had the money, then yes. Yes, I would support the mother of my child."

All Bailey could do was look at him incredulously.

...I would support the mother of my child...

Bailey's eye twitched. Was the emotion she was feeling coming from modern-times Bailey, or 1950s Bailey? Because right now, she wanted to throw this dry, day-old tuna casserole into the garbage and hop in the car and drive to...*where?*

"You asked me," he said while chewing a bite of food.

"I don't want you to think I'm one of those women that wouldn't want her husband to take care of his *outside* child."

Bobby froze.

"Every child needs the love and support of his mama and his daddy—and that's emotional *and* financial. I do want your son to be well taken care of because he is yours. But *she* doesn't get to have *my* husband support her when he can barely support me!"

Bobby glared at her before he dropped his fork and stood. "You know...I think I need to go for a walk."

Her teeth clenched tightly so she didn't break character and tell him not to walk out that door while she was in the middle of expressing herself.

Bailey threw up her hands. "Fine. Walk away if you don't want my opinion." She stood and took his plate of food to the garbage, where she scraped the contents off the plate and into the trash. He watched her and she turned and glared at him.

"Do you want me to keep my mouth shut? Do you want a wife that just nods her head and says yes dear?'

"Yes. That would be nice. You trusting my decisions and allowing me to do the right thing would be pretty good right now, Bailey. Some support right now wouldn't hurt."

She crossed her arms. "Support? I haven't been supportive?" She gestured to the table, which still had her plate of food. "I'm eating day-old tuna casserole and you yelled at me for letting my friends buy me a bottle of beer!"

Bobby rubbed his hands through his short-cropped hair before meeting her eyes. "You're right. And I'm sorry. I don't know how many women would have been as understanding as you have been. Right now, I feel like a failure. I'm making my wife go without in order for my child's mother not to have to struggle.

"It's not fair to you." He held out a tentative hand to her. Bailey accepted it slowly. "You're my priority."

"The baby—"

"No," he interrupted. "*You* are. A baby's needs are limited; a comfortable place to sleep, food, diapers..." He gently pulled Bailey into his arms. "But you are right. I know you're in my corner. This is just...my guilt speaking."

Bailey sighed and hugged him. "Let's not argue. It's not going to get us anywhere."

"I hate arguing with you." They swayed together.

"I do understand how you feel, honey," she said. "It's because you're a good man that you want to do as much as you can." She pulled back slightly to look at him. "You're not a failure, Bobby. There aren't many men who would be able to handle this situation with as much grace and dignity. And I'm very proud of you."

He smiled. "You are? Because that's the last thing I thought I'd hear you say."

Bailey placed her head on his chest. "I want to be a part of this process."

"Okay." He kissed the top of her head. "I need your support, Bae. Because I can't get through this without you. I need you."

"I need you too."

He made a pleased hum. "This Sunday, before we go to your Aunt Mae and Uncle Dewbug's, we'll work on the weekly budget together and we will find a way to pull together enough for your weekly hairdresser visit."

"I can also clip coupons."

"We'll make it work. This is my main purpose in life." They rocked together for a while longer in silent contentment.

Chapter Sixty-Six

When Saturday morning finally arrived, Bailey was anxious. There was a lot that was supposed to go on.

She made oatmeal for breakfast and then quickly got ready for the day. She would be doing plenty of walking, so she had to find something to wear that would complement her loafers.

She decided on a pleated navy skirt, sweater, and blouse. She looked young, like a schoolgirl, but that wasn't necessarily bad. People weren't rude to schoolgirls.

Bobby blinked when he saw her. "If I don't get questioned for marrying outside my race, I'm definitely going to be questioned for being seen with an underaged girl."

She chuckled. "So, I guess pigtails would be out of the question?"

"Oh, jeez..."

Once they arrived at the hairdresser, he opened Bailey's door and gave her a quick kiss.

"What are you going to do while I'm here?" she asked.

"I think I'll poll around Mom's neighborhood after I cut her lawn."

"Good idea."

She went into Juanita's and greeted the ladies. Of course, it was a good visit. Juanita let her and Pat poll the customers and it was good practice. Bailey laughed a lot. They gossiped about people she didn't know, she tapped her feet to the cool music of the time, and she tried not to laugh when Miss Baker criticized Pat's "fast" ways.

"When y'all go out polling, you should come to Miss Nadine's house. She'll probably participate. She Negro-friendly," Jackie said.

Everyone laughed at that. It led to a discussion about who would be the secret abolitionist in town. Mayor George was definitely not on that list.

When her hair was finished, Bailey felt rejuvenated. She was happy about Jackie's suggestion to visit Nadine. She wondered if Bobby had thought about featuring the other regulars during the various polls.

As usual, he was waiting for her when she left the salon. Bobby hopped out of the car when he saw her.

"I don't know if I should give you a wolf-whistle while you're wearing that schoolgirl outfit, but you definitely deserve one."

She got in and saw a cameraman in the back seat. That was always awkward. Plus, she could have used a few minutes to kick back.

"How did your polling go?"

"I'm not surprised that most everyone I talked to is still sympathetic with him. Folks from my mother's generation still believe in the communist boogeyman hiding around every corner."

"I am curious about the different demographics. Jackie suggested we poll in the richer neighborhood where she works."

"That's a great idea. I'd love to get the mayor's take on things. Maybe you and I can come back to town this evening and poll some of the common folk?"

"I think we have a plan."

When they got home, Bailey walked across the street to Helen's house. She had her satchel with her polling items and felt important. Hank answered the door.

"Hi, Bailey. Come inside. Helen's changing her shoes."

Hank reminded her of John Goodman back in the days when he starred in the show *Roseanne*. He was big, but appeared as sweet and snuggly as a teddy bear.

"Is that Bailey?" Helen called from somewhere in the house.

"Yeah," Hank replied. "I told her you'd be right down."

"I'll be right down, hon!" Helen called.

"I just said that..." Hank gestured her into the living room. "Would you like something to drink?"

"No. I'm fine. Thanks." She spotted a new set of encyclopedias on the bookshelf. "Oh, you two bought the encyclopedias."

"Yep. Helen wanted them so she could beat me at Scrabble."

Helen came into the room. "Aren't they lovely?"

"They are. The salesman stopped at my house too. I had to decline."

"That's probably because you discuss major purchases with your husband first," Hank said dryly.

"I didn't break the mint, dear," Helen replied.

Bailey glanced from Hank to Helen. Oh...

"Let's go," Helen said as she retrieved a cardboard file folder. "You look adorable. I polled a few people already. You had the right idea wearing flats."

They went out the door, and of course the cameraman was waiting for them. Bailey quickly turned to say goodbye to Hank. Helen ignored him. Yikes, they were fighting.

As soon as the door closed, Helen made a face. "Ugh, he irks me sometimes. He's on the road all the week. He gets to see the world, and just because I want to read about far-off places, he calls me a spendthrift!"

Bailey was unsure how to respond. "That nice salesman said they had a payment plan."

"Exactly!" They walked down the street together. "So...he was awfully nice, didn't you think?"

"He was. I got a free music box—even though I didn't buy the encyclopedias."

"I got that and a glass-blown rose."

"I didn't get a rose."

"Well, I think it was a purchase gift. It's so pretty. I think Hank is just jealous because some other man gave me a flower."

Bailey chuckled, but inside she groaned. No. Not Quinton and Helen. She really liked Hank. Well, Helen was the textbook lonely housewife.

"How many houses have you visited so far?" Bailey changed the subject.

"I got to six before I changed my shoes. Plus, I wanted to be back home before you got there. Everyone's agreed to it so far." She gave Bailey a quick look. "Maybe you should let me begin and then once they agree, you can ask the questions."

"Yes, that sounds good. I polled eight people at the hair salon. Of course, no one turned me down since they were stuck in the styling chair."

They reached the first house on the street they decided to work. It was several blocks from their own. Helen rang the bell and a middle-aged woman answered curiously.

"No thank you. We don't want any," she said before Helen had an opportunity to say anything, and then made to close the door.

"No, we're not selling anything. We're conducting a poll for the *Gazette* and wanted to know if you would like to answer a few short questions."

The woman looked from Helen to Bailey. "The *Gazette*, you say?"

"Yes, ma'am. We wouldn't take much of your time."

She looked at Bailey distrustfully. "Well, okay. I guess it'll be all right."

Bailey discreetly made a face. She was dressed like a schoolgirl! How did she come off as dangerous?

The poll went fast. The woman didn't even offer them a seat once Bailey began reading the questions. The woman was, not surprisingly, in favor of Joseph McCarthy, despite the hearings, which she thought were slanted against him.

They thanked her for her time, which she barely acknowledged before shutting the door.

"Well, she was a peach," Helen commented sarcastically.

At the next house, a man answered. He looked a bit suspicious, but let them in after explaining that his wife was out shopping. He too was in favor of McCarthy, but didn't think there were communists around every corner. He was simply in favor of him because he served in War World II.

They polled for an hour and a half and only one person declined. It was a woman that took one look at Bailey, said no, and then slammed the door in their faces.

Bailey checked her watch. "We did good. I'm going to head back home so I can poll in the Negro neighborhood with Pat."

"Okay. I'm going to keep at it for a few more hours. Good luck."

"You too."

Bailey walked home. A car with several teens drove past and honked their horn at her. She looked around and walked faster in case they went around the corner and came back to harass her.

Bobby wasn't home. He had probably gone out polling too. She left the polls on the cocktail table for him to go over and then she called Pat.

The drive to Garden Hill did not include the cameraman, as there was too much construction still going on.

"Oh my gosh, Pat," Bailey groaned. "This feels like real work, going door-to-door. It reminds me of when I used to work at a fast-food joint and keeping that polite face and voice."

"Did you get hit with any racism?"

"Not really. But no one seemed to enjoy seeing me at their front door. Where are we going first?"

"Well, that depends. Do you have money for lunch?"

Bailey dug into her change purse. "I have sixty-two cents."

"Perfect. Then we'll go visit my friends at the farmer's market and get some empanadas and tacos. They're a penny each. And after watching you and Bobby fight over accepting gifts, I am definitely not going to offer to buy you lunch."

Bailey laughed. "For a penny each, I can afford to buy *you* lunch. Uh...but I won't. Bobby might ask me about the missing pennies," she joked.

Pat didn't laugh. "Yeah, he's turning into a *basic* man."

"What do you mean?"

"Well, he used to be awesome; always looking at you with those googly eyes, touching you and wishing you'd touch him. I've never dated outside of my race, but I would not have minded having a Bobby Banks of my own." Pat rolled her eyes. "But now he's tangled up with too much crap. And not telling you about what Paula said when he gave her that money...that kinda pissed me off."

"You mean about her wanting him to leave me and marry her?"

"Hell yeah!"

"I was hoping he'd tell me after our fight. And I still haven't watched that scene."

"Oh! I heard about him allowing us streaming devices at the factory after nine. I think the demise of the watch parties are imminent. Everyone wants to watch something different."

"I hate to hear that. I didn't go often, but it really felt like a party."

"I know. Drew even showed up a few times. I wish he was in my story line. He is *fine!* Do you think Rob is up for another swirl couple?"

Bailey chuckled. "You should bring it up in tomorrow's meeting."

"I'm kidding! I don't think that's the direction we're taking for my story line. Even though I'm pretty sure Drew wouldn't mind." She winked at Bailey.

"What do you mean?"

"He's got this PTSD story line, and he told a buddy he left someone important behind in Korea. We know the girl is Korean because he mentioned he couldn't bring her back because his granny wasn't down with the swirl. But whenever he has an episode, he mumbles something about a baby."

"Wow!" Bailey said. "That is really interesting." Her friends were really enhancing their stories. "Oh! I think Helen and Quinton are going to have an affair!" Bailey said.

"They already kissed!" Bailey covered her mouth. Pat gave her the side-eye. "C'mon, Bailey. I know Rob has an iPad or smartphone you can sneak and watch."

"Yeah...but I generally let him tell me what's happening."

"Girl, you are missing out! So, after mass flirting, Helen bought the encyclopedias, right? And before Quinton left, he turned back and asked her if she'd like to get a cup of coffee with him because it was a little lonesome for him too. Because you know, she mentioned that her husband, Hank, was on the road all the time and she wanted to explore the world through the books. Girl, it was really kind of sexy!"

"Okay…so when did they kiss?"

"After they had coffee. He walked her to her car and then swooped in for that kiss. Girl, you could see Helen's pulse in her neck!" Pat began laughing. "I'm telling you, that story line is about to explode."

Bailey sighed. "Wow. I'm going to watch it for sure." She narrowed her eyes. "You know what's weird? I saw Hank today and he seemed a little upset. Do you think there are some real feelings between them?"

Pat shook her head. "All I know is that an on-set relationship isn't rare. Look at you and Rob. And last year, Paula sure wanted it to be her and Rob."

Bailey mulled that over.

Chapter Sixty-Seven

They had penny tacos and then polled Pat's friends at the farmer's market. Each were anti-Joseph McCarthy.

They decided to go to Curtis's house next. Bailey found herself looking forward to seeing his setup, since he'd been on set the year before.

Curtis lived in a small, neat house out in the farmlands near the factory. His car, which was parked in his driveway, was big and old-fashioned, and not flashy like Pat's.

They rang the bell and Curtis answered with a broad smile. "Come in."

Bailey looked around in shock. His impeccable house was very mid-century-decorated. As the town milkman, Curtis would be financially stable and could afford all the bells and whistles, from a powder-blue suede sofa to a gorgeous wooden console that was opened to expose a record player— currently spinning some instrumental jazz. It was filled with record albums, and more were displayed on a matching bookcase.

The home was modern without looking like *The Jetsons*. This was exactly the way she wanted her and Bobby's house to be decorated. Not that it was likely to happen under the current circumstances.

"Your house is lovely," Bailey complimented.

"Thank you. It's still a work in progress." He gestured to the wall. "I just got these jazz prints in something called the modernist style."

"It's really cool," Pat said while studying them.

"Do you ladies want a beer?" he asked.

"Sure. Thanks," Pat replied.

"Water is fine for me."

Curtis's brow went up. "Water? I can make you a cocktail. My bar is fully stocked."

"Oh…I don't hold my liquor as well as I should, and I have plenty more houses to hit."

He chuckled in understanding. "I'll be right back."

She and Pat sat down and gathered their paperwork.

"I'm in love with this house," Bailey whispered to her friend.

"I told you he was a catch," Pat replied.

They stayed at Curtis's house for a full half an hour. He served them crackers and pate. It was so good. He was an amazing host. She had to up her game in that department.

They reluctantly left with Curtis pointing out some places they might want to go, but Bailey was anxious to poll Nadine, so they went there next.

Bailey remembered the impressive house. It looked like an old-fashioned manor. They hesitated before going up the walkway.

"Should we go around back?" Pat whispered. No microphone was going to catch that question.

"We'd better," she replied.

They went around to a side door and rang the bell. Jackie answered with a big smile.

"There you are!" She hugged them both and ushered them in. She was dressed in a gray maid's outfit with the obligatory white apron. At least she didn't have to wear a bonnet to hide her perfectly coiffed hair.

Tracy hurried into the room and exclaimed equally as happily—even though they had all just seen each other four hours ago.

"We already told Miss Nadine about your visit, and she said she'd be happy to help. Come on, she's in the study."

Pat and Bailey followed practically on tiptoes. They looked around, trying to capture every one of the rich decorations. Bailey had been here before, but then it had just been an empty space filled with boxes. And Pat had likely seen this when she watched Nadine's stream, but she acted as if it was the first time for her too.

"This is so pretty," Pat whispered. Tracy knocked on a door and then opened it.

"Miss Nadine, these are the girls I was telling you about."

Nadine's eyes lit up when she saw Bailey, although she downplayed it with a casual smile. She stood and ushered them into the room.

"Ah, ladies. Of course, please come in. Have a seat. Would you like some refreshment?"

"No," Pat said. "We don't want to take up too much of your time—"

"Nonsense. I'm not busy at all." She turned to Tracy. "Tracy, can you bring us tea, please?"

Tracy nodded with a smile. "Certainly, Miss Nadine."

"We really appreciate your time," Bailey said.

"I understand this is for the *Gazette*."

"Yes, it is."

"And my name won't be used?"

"Not at all!" Pat replied. "We won't use your address or anything else that can identify who you are."

Nadine nodded. "Good. I happen to know McCarthy, and he's a jerk."

Bailey's brow shot up. "You know him?"

"I met him at a few fundraising parties." Nadine reached for a cigarette. "He's a drunk."

Her and Pat's eyes had grown big. Nadine offered them cigarettes and Pat accepted one. Nadine lit it for her.

"You learn a lot about a person when you're at a party. Give them some booze and you'll learn a lot more."

She relaxed and crossed her legs. Bailey was in awe of Nadine. She was a standup comic by profession, but she was also a primo actress. Her words fell with ease. She told them a few stories about famous people she'd met. It was always at some type of party.

By the time Tracy returned with the tea, Nadine had already put them in stitches.

It was no surprise that when they finally got around to the poll, Nadine's answers were decidedly on the liberal side. She mentioned how "ridiculous" the witch hunt against homosexuals was, which earned her extra brownie points in Bailey's book.

After finishing their tea and crumpets, Bailey and Pat thanked Nadine again and excused themselves.

Bailey left wishing there was a way she and Nadine could film more with each other.

After leaving Nadine, they went to Garden Hill and polled for a few more hours before Bailey said it was too close to dinnertime to keep knocking on people's door. In the Negro neighborhoods, they might be invited to stay and eat.

When she got home, Bobby was already there, papers spread on the kitchen table while he busily scribbled on a legal pad. A half-eaten sandwich was on a nearby plate along with half a bottle of Coca-Cola.

"Hi, honey," he greeted her, rising to give her a kiss. "How did it go?"

"Good, but is that your lunch or dinner?"

He chuckled. "I think both. I started with cookies and milk...um, you might want to buy some more. But yeah, I ended with this."

"I'm sorry. I can make dinner—"

"No, I'm not hungry—unless you just want something for yourself."

"God, no." She rubbed her belly and sat down opposite him. "People give you food when you randomly knock on their door." She pulled the polls from her bag and placed them on the table.

"Wow," he said.

"It really did go well. I think this poll is going to be an eye-opener. Most of the Negroes we spoke to were totally against the senator. Several didn't have televisions and hadn't watched the hearings, but still sided against him purely by word of mouth.

"Surprisingly, I met a wealthy woman that actually met him and she said he was a jerk. That is a direct quote."

Bobby laughed and gathered up the papers. "I have my work cut out for me. Are you game to hit one more neighborhood?" He looked at the clock. "It's just before four, and we might be able to hit a few houses before the dinner hour."

"I'm game."

"Great. We might be able to even out the poll if we talk to a few working-class whites." They drove back into town. The cameraman didn't join them in the car, but instead of spending the time breaking character, they were content to drive in quiet silence while listening to that ghastly rockabilly music.

Once in town, Bobby parked and led her toward the boardinghouse.

"I figured we could use the *one stone method*; working class white men all in one location."

Bailey instantly recognized the building. It was where Quinton lived!

They walked to the front stairs, where several men were sitting and smoking cigarettes. A few of them tipped their hats at her, which put her at ease. Unfortunately, none of the men present was Quinton.

"Hi, fellas. I was wondering if I can have a bit of your time. I work at the *Gazette* and we're taking a poll on the opinions on Joseph McCarthy."

There was some grumbling, but apparently not about participating in the poll, just about McCarthy himself.

They were taking a tally on the various opinions when the door opened and none other than Helen Swanson stepped out of the boardinghouse. She was moving so fast, she didn't see Bailey and Bobby until she had reached the stairs.

The look of horror in her eyes could not have been manufactured. She obviously had not seen this in her script.

Quinton opened the door. "Please, Helen. Let me walk you to the door."

Ohhh…

Chapter Sixty-Eight

Helen and Bailey locked eyes, both with mirroring expressions of shock at seeing the other.

"Uh," Helen stuttered. "I took a poll—" she said while turning to look back at Quinton.

Someone chuckled lewdly. "I bet she did." And then several men began to laugh.

"Shut your damn mouths!" Quinton snapped. "There're ladies present!"

The schoolboy laughter immediately stopped.

"We can get together later to collect all of the polls from the others," Bailey said.

Helen nodded and then hurried down the rest of the stairs. Bobby nodded to her and she simply nodded back before hurrying down the street.

Bailey glanced at Quinton, who followed her with his eyes for a few moments before he turned and walked back into the building.

If Bailey was a director, she would have called: *"And SCENE!"* because that was a slam dunk! Bobby made that happen. She wanted to break character so bad! She wanted to turn to him with a Cheshire cat grin and ask how he had managed to maneuver that situation without letting her or Helen in on it.

Instead, she kept her excited surprise to herself and finished jotting down the answers to the poll questions. A few minutes later, she and Bobby were thanking the men for their time.

As they headed back to the car, Bailey looked at Bobby with wide eyes, but there was no cameraman following them to record their reaction.

Shit!

She had to keep her mouth shut.

But when they reached the car, she was grateful when she saw the cameraman in the back seat, just waiting to capture all the juicy reactions.

Bobby didn't say a thing as he started the car. The radio started, and Bailey reached over and swiftly cut it off.

"Did you see?" she asked incredulously.

"I did." He pulled out of the parking space.

"Well, aren't you going to say something?"

He inhaled deeply. "I can say that I don't intend to ever be friends with Hank now."

"What?" She looked at him curiously. What in the heck was he talking about?

Bobby glanced at her. "I can't be friends with a man knowing his wife is messing around with another man behind his back! I'd want to tell him."

"Oh. Poor Hank. Maybe...maybe there's a reasonable explanation for what we saw..."

Bobby snorted. "I don't think so, Bae. It wasn't the fact that she came out of the boardinghouse. It was the look on her face when she did."

Bailey shook her head. "I know that guy."

Bobby's head swiveled to look at her. Now he wore a frown. "How?"

"He's the encyclopedia salesman."

"Jeez..." Bobby was frowning even harder. "And he was in our house?"

"Yeah."

"Well, what did he do?" he asked excitedly.

She gave him a look of surprise. "Nothing! What are you asking?"

"Did he come on to you?"

"No! What? Do you think he's a roving sex salesman? Going door-to-door asking women if they want a little something on the side?"

Bobby's mouth twitched. He was trying not to laugh. Bailey had to chuckle.

"Why would I need him when I can barely keep up with you?" she said with a smile while looking out her window.

She saw from the corner of her eyes that Bobby perked up and grinned.

When they got home, Helen's file folder was waiting for them on the front stoop.

Bobby reached down to scoop up the files. "My God! There's probably a hundred polls in here!"

They went inside, and Bobby immediately went to the kitchen, where he gathered all of the paperwork that was scattered on the table.

"We did better than I expected."

"You don't think we need to go out anymore?" Bailey asked while tying on her apron.

"No. Although I might have wanted to poll a few more prominent areas...but I think this shows what the average man thinks." He reached out and pulled her in for a hug and a kiss the way he used to do before things got tense between them. "Thanks for your help and for organizing the ladies. I could not have done this without you." He kissed her again, and this time, they lingered in it.

Bobby gave her a look filled with desire. "I'll be in my office."

"Okay. Dinner won't be long." She watched his strong, broad back and tight tush as he walked out of the room. He was one sexy man. Of course, she had no choice but to fall for him.

They had dinner, which were all the leftovers placed in a casserole dish over a bed of noodles and covered with a can of gravy. It wasn't pretty to look at, but it tasted surprisingly...acceptable.

After dinner, they watched television while cuddled on the couch and went to bed as soon as the clock hit nine.

And for Bailey, that's when the best part of her day began.

Chapter Sixty-Nine

Bailey was the one to hit the stop filming switch the moment Bobby shut the bedroom door behind them.

"How did you get us at the boardinghouse at the same time Helen and Quinton were there!" she asked in excitement. She felt like Pat whenever she had to explain all of the scenes Bailey had missed. She was as excited as a fan.

Bobby grinned sheepishly. "I didn't know it would work." He sat down in the chair to remove his shoes while she sat in her vanity chair and watched him.

"Well, as you now know, Quinton selected Helen to have an affair with. The look of surprise on your face was priceless!" He chuckled. Bailey grinned. She wasn't going to tell him Pat had already told her about it. She didn't want him to know they talked out of character at times. Even though she was the producer's girlfriend, it was still a rule.

"Quinton and I planned the big reveal at the boardinghouse. I went to his team meeting and together, we figured out the way to do it.

"I would be in charge of getting you and me there at about dinnertime. If you would have said you wanted to eat, I would have taken us to Maybelle's for dinner with the last of our money as a way of celebrating, but then I would have said, let's hit the boardinghouse first—blah blah blah."

"Right. But how did you get Quinton and Helen there?"

"I put it in her script that she was to go to the boardinghouse to see Quinton on the pretense of asking him to participate in the poll. But it was up to Quinton to keep her there until we got there.

"I have no idea how he kept her there, what they did, but by her lack of lipstick, I have a good idea."

Bailey chuckled and clapped her hands together. "This is just the boost Quinton's story line needed!"

"Do you think we should go to the watch party?" he asked.

She nodded. "I want to see people's reaction! I want to see my reaction."

He laughed. "I told you, the look on your face was priceless."

The watch party was in full force when they got to the factory, and even though the next room had the streaming devices, none were being used.

She and Pat were evidently wrong. The demise of the watch parties wasn't even close. The cast and crew still found it more important to have fun together than to just hit the Internet.

When they walked into the room, people hooted and hollered.

"Replay it!" people were yelling.

"How many times am I going to have to watch my wife cheating on me?" someone shouted. Was that Hank? The entire room fell out in laughter.

"Sorry, Hank!" That was Quinton! This time even Bailey couldn't stop laughing.

"I ain't sorry!" came Helen's loud response. "I'm finally getting some."

They were dying in laughter, so it took a few moments before the scene rolled back to Helen nervously approaching the boardinghouse. Quinton had been sitting on the stoop, smoking with the other men, and he greeted Helen happily. She stuttered and tried to laugh away her nervousness as she explained about the poll and thought he might participate.

From there, it moved fast. He invited her inside, got them refreshments and they got comfortable, talked, joked about her exercise routine going nowhere. And Quinton said the magic words. Not I love you, but: you look perfect the way you are.

The make-out scene was *hot,* and Quinton had become a lot cuter.

There was a slight interruption as someone came into the room. It was Paula and Bruce. Several people greeted them, and Bobby stood and waved them over.

Bobby grabbed an empty chair for Paula and Bruce did the same for himself. Bailey was sitting on one end, with Bobby obviously sitting next to her, then Paula and Bruce on the other end. They whispered greetings to each other as the scene resumed.

They watched Helen and Quinton kiss a while until Hank spoke up.

"Can we skip ahead? Please!" Everyone laughed again, including Hank.

They skipped ahead until Bobby and Bailey arrived.

Oh my God, why had she worn that skirt with those loafers? All she needed was a bow on her head to look like the caricature schoolgirl. Bobby looked great, though. He was dressed in khaki pants, a madras shirt and a beige, zip-up jacket. None of his clothes hid what she knew he possessed; big arms and muscular legs.

His normally perfectly coiffed blond hair had fallen onto his forehead, which gave him a very casual look. They did look good together.

Bailey watched herself as she warily took stock of the men on the stoop. Bailey nodded at herself in approval. It was the way she would have intentionally acted the scene if she wasn't already unconsciously doing so.

A few minutes later when Helen came out the door, everyone cheered when Bailey's mouth dropped and her eyes practically bulged.

Whatever camera they used was good because it zoomed right on her face. A second later, the camera zoomed in on the shocked and surprised expression on Helen's face.

Of course, it brought more laughter. When the shot widened to show Bobby's face, the laughter intensified as his eyes swiveled from one to the other.

It was so fun! Bailey couldn't remember laughing so much. She looked over and saw that Bobby and Bruce were doing the same. Paula, on the other hand, just sat there with a prim smile. Periodically, she would lean toward Bruce and whisper something and he'd pat her hand or put his arm across the back of her chair.

Once when she did, he got up and asked if anyone wanted a refreshment. Everyone declined, and once he was gone, Paula turned to them with a smile.

"I get awfully thirsty. I think this baby's a vampire."

"I'm happy you came out," Bobby said. "You see, no one booed you."

"Well, not today," she replied with a smile.

"It's all in good fun," Bobby replied.

"Maybe someone should mention that what one person thinks of as good fun, another person might find insulting."

Bobby just gave her a wry smile.

Bailey looked back at the screen. Did Paula really expect Bobby to chastise people at their own watch party? He certainly didn't regulate it.

She mentally shrugged it off.

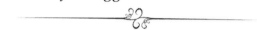

They stayed long enough to watch several more scenes that didn't include her. They said goodbye to Paula and Bruce, and then took a quick tour of the Internet café. She wasn't sure what Bobby planned to call it, but that's basically what it was. There were comfortable seats, as well as tables set up for several people to sit together.

There were now a few others present, either getting their Internet fix on, or on Internet calls. One lady even stopped her and Bobby to ask if they wouldn't mind saying hello to her mother.

Bailey was surprised but happy to take the time to ask how the mom was enjoying the show and to hear her feedback. When it turned to "treacherous" Paula, the daughter gave them apologetic looks while trying to hush her mom.

"Oh, she's nice in real life," Bailey said with a polite smile while exchanging looks with Bobby.

"That's not what my daughter says."

The daughter was very embarrassed. Bailey and Bobby quickly said their goodbyes and headed outside.

When they were in the car, Bailey asked the question that had been on her mind.

"Paula's having a hard time on the show?"

"She's gotten a lot of negative comments. I told you, it's getting better, but when she comes to a watch party and people boo her, she says it makes her feel like an outsider."

"You're not really going to tell people to stop doing it, are you?"

"You don't think I should mention it?"

"I don't. Not unless it turns into bullying."

He nodded, but didn't indicate whether he intended to follow her suggestion.

Chapter Seventy

The next morning, Bailey woke up to soft kisses on her cheeks, nose, and eyelids.

"Wake up, babe," Bobby whispered.

Bailey groaned but refused to open her eyes. "Oh no...already? Didn't we just go to sleep?" she muttered.

Bobby chuckled. "I made breakfast."

Bailey's eyes popped open and she dragged herself up in bed. They hadn't gotten to sleep until nearly 3:00 a.m.

"Is there coffee?"

"Plenty."

Bailey dragged herself out of bed and Bobby stood. She took a double -take. He was already dressed and shaved.

"Damn, you're dressed."

"Yep, I tried to let you sleep as long as possible, but we need to be out the door in about forty-five minutes."

Her eyes widened as she dashed for the bathroom. Thank goodness she'd forced herself to shower the night before. It was a habit she needed to maintain for the show. "Sorry, honey, but I'll have breakfast after I'm dressed!"

"Go, go, go!" he cheered.

Bailey quickly got ready for the day. It was autumn and growing cold, so she dressed in jeans and a cashmere sweater. Not wanting to destroy her pretty curls, she simply fluffed them with her fingers until her hair was voluminous.

Makeup was simple, just liner and lip gloss. She dashed into the kitchen and Bobby thrust a mug of coffee at her.

"Oh, thanks! Breakfast smells so good. What is it?" She sipped the hot coffee. He had put the right amount of sugar and cream into it, and she sighed in appreciation.

"Bacon and eggs, but I toasted some bread and turned it into a sandwich so you can eat it in the car if you want."

She was hungry, and had no intentions of leaving a portion of her meal on her sweater. "Give me five minutes and I'll be finished." She was finished eating in four.

They got into the car and a short time after, arrived at the production office.

"I need to grab some things from my office," Bobby said. "If you want to go on to the meeting, you can let everyone know we'll start soon."

"Okay," she nodded. After all, she was the one that made them late—at least it was only by about ten minutes.

She hurried to the meeting and was surprised to see Bruce working the overhead. She saw a scene with Paula and Bobby.

"Hey, Bailey," he said when he saw her. Everyone greeted her.

"Hi. Sorry we're late. Bobby had to grab something. He'll be here shortly."

She took a seat at the large conference table between Helen and a neighbor whose name she didn't remember. Helen nudged her in greeting and she smiled at her before giving her attention to Bruce.

"So, as I was saying," Bruce continued. "The direction we're going is sure to be dynamic." He looked over at Paula, who was beaming. "I just want to remind you that we're all a team. And although we have fun and it's a good time—especially when we're at the factory watch party—please keep in mind that words can hurt."

Bruce stared out at the group. Bailey tried to keep the surprise from her expression. The quiet that ensued was laced with disbelief. When Bailey looked at Paula, she wore a smug smile.

Bailey recognized the smile. She'd seen it before on the face of the high school cheerleader that called her Porky Pig during gym class. It mirrored what she'd seen on the face of an ex-boyfriend when he started seeing someone else and no longer cared for her. She'd seen it plenty of times over the years, worn by bullies, coworkers, and managers that had self-esteem issues.

Bruce continued. "If you think you're saying something that's funny, but the other person isn't laughing…then it's probably better to keep it unsaid. Okay? Let's not have a toxic work environment."

People were looking around at each other in question—everyone except for Paula, who seemed oblivious to the confusion as she continued to smile.

The door opened and Bobby hurried in. He caught sight of Bruce.

"Hey, Bruce." He seemed surprised. "Oh, cool. Thanks for taking up the meeting. What are we looking at?" He stared at the projection screen.

"I was showing the scene between Bobby and Paula where she reveals she wants him to break up with Bailey. It's among the most popular scenes of the week."

Bobby was studying notes. "Cool," he said absently. He took over the meeting, apparently oblivious to the quiet confusion still on the faces of the team members.

Bruce hung around, sitting next to Paula while Bobby handled the projector.

"Guys, Team Bailey is number one yet again."

There was some soft clapping, but none of the hoopla that generally accompanied that announcement.

"How do you guys like the café at the factory?"

The enthusiasm slowly returned as people voiced their happiness at being able to get on the Internet during the week.

"I have some pretty big news." Bobby's brow had gone up as he turned his attention to Helen. "Helen's apparently leaving our team and joining Team Quinton."

Bailey looked at her friend in surprise and noticed that Helen seemed equally as surprised. She still smiled at the applause and congratulations.

Bobby paused as he studied his notes.

"Hendrix and I thought it might be good to keep Quinton and Helen's story line tight by having her on his team," Bruce said while reclining casually in his seat with his arm on the back of Paula's chair.

Bobby looked at Bruce and raised a hand as if to say, WTF?

597

"Okay...nice to be in the loop." Bobby did not sound happy.

"It's a good idea," Bruce reiterated.

Bobby ignored him and turned his attention to Helen. "You can probably float between teams. I'll leave that up to you. You're still Bailey's neighbor and friend."

Helen nodded in what seemed to be relief.

"It is a good opportunity," Bruce directed to Helen. "You'll be able to get much more exposure on Quinton's team."

The remainder of the meeting progressed normally. Bobby did contradict Bruce without knowing when he announced that Quinton and Helen's affair was the top scene of the week, Helen getting busted by Bobby and Bailey was second, and third was Paula asking for Bobby to annul his marriage with Bailey.

Bailey saw Paula's expression had gone sour.

Did Paula put Bruce up to moving Helen to Quinton's team? Quinton was a good actor, but his team had never hit a top ranking. Paula's scene would have been number one if not for Helen and Quinton's affair...

Bailey dismissed that idea. Why was she giving that woman more power than she had?

After the meeting, the normal stampede to the lounge didn't occur, probably because everyone had visited the Internet at the factory.

Bailey leaned toward Helen. "I'm going to hate not seeing you at our meetings."

"I will too, hon. But do you still want to go shopping on Mondays? I still want a friendship with Bailey—"

"Me too!" Bailey said. "And yes, Bailey's going to be poor. She's going to need you more than ever," Bailey chuckled.

Helen smiled in relief. "Okay. I wasn't sure..."

Bailey understood. "Helen, having you leave the team wasn't my idea," she whispered.

Helen studied her eyes and both ladies looked over at Paula. Helen leaned in before rising out of her chair.

"You watch your back."

And then Helen was heading out the door.

Bruce, Bobby, and Paula were at the front of the room talking softly. Bailey joined them and Bobby put his arm around her waist.

"Hi, Bailey." Paula smiled at her.

"Hi."

"We have to go," Bobby said.

"Oh, I thought we'd have lunch and discuss some of my ideas for this coming week," Paula said. She looked at Bruce. "All of us...and Bailey too."

"We can't," Bobby said. "We're having lunch with Bailey's family."

"Oh..." Paula looked from Bobby to Bailey. "This is beginning to sound serious," she chuckled.

Bobby's brow moved up. He shrugged. "Yeah."

"Oops." She raised her hand defensively, her smile even more broad. "I didn't mean to get too personal."

"We'd better go. We have a long drive. Take a look at your script and if you want to discuss it, we can do it while Bobby's at work."

While Bobby's at work...Did Paula come to the office to talk to Bobby while he was here during the week?

Bailey decided she and Bobby were going to have a nice, long conversation when they got in the car.

Chapter Seventy-One

"To be honest with you," Bobby said after a moment of listening to Bailey's concerns, "I don't care about Paula's little power plays. What bothers me is the way Bruce has been going behind my back.

"First it was hiring his baby's mama without telling me. Now he moves one of my regulars to a different team. I will have words with him about that. I think Bruce forgets that the company—and the show—is *my* baby."

"It was very weird when he chastised the team for bullying people under the guise of trying to be funny."

Bobby shook his head. "I don't know what's up with him lately." He gently rubbed her knee as she drove. "You know what? Let's put talk about work behind us. It's all I think about all day, every day."

Bailey smiled. "You're right. No more talk about work." She shrugged. "Well, until we get to my aunt and uncle's house. They will want to pick your brain."

He leaned his head back against the headrest and grinned. "I look forward to that, Bae. I just want something normal. Just for a few hours."

She covered his hand, still on her knee, with hers.

The ride to Bailey's aunt and uncle's house seemed to go too fast as Bailey pointed out places she used to hang out as a teen.

"Did you have a lot of boyfriends?"

She scoffed. "No! I lived with my aunt and uncle, remember? They were not going to allow me to run around acting 'fast.'"

"Fast? People really still use that word?"

"My aunt and uncle did."

"So, you weren't fast?"

"I was slow. I didn't have my first boyfriend until I was sixteen years old. Actually, I kissed a boy when I was in kindergarten and he said he was my boyfriend. But then I saw him kissing another girl an hour later!"

"Oh my God, I'm so sorry, Bae," he said with a straight face. "Do you want me to go find that fool? I'll bust him up."

She giggled. "Bust him up?"

Bobby flexed an arm, exposing his impressive bicep even beneath his sweater.

When they pulled up into the driveway of her childhood home, Bailey tried to see it from Bobby's perspective. He was, after all, a millionaire. It was hard to see him in those terms as a man that lived on a budget of $4,500 a year.

They got out of the car and Bobby looked around. He was the type that took in everything around him while visibly weaving information about it. She wondered what his brilliant mind's eye saw.

Her aunt and uncle opened the door and came down the porch to greet them.

"Hello!" Aunt Mae hugged her, even though she was grinning at Bobby. After releasing Bailey, she went up and hugged him.

He hugged her tight without the obligatory pat on the back, as if he really appreciated the affection.

"Nice to meet you, ma'am."

"I'm Aunt Mae," she said while pulling back.

"Aunt Mae," he grinned.

Uncle Dewbug hugged her and kissed her temple before thrusting his hand out to Bobby. Bailey noticed her uncle was holding himself up really tall, almost as if he was puffing out his chest.

"Nice to meet you, sir. Thank you for inviting me," Bobby said while shaking his hand.

Uncle Dewbug didn't offer to allow him to call him uncle.

"Come inside. You two must be tired. That's a long drive."

"It's not long if you have good company." He took Bailey's hand and followed them inside the house.

"You have a beautiful home," Bobby said while taking in everything.

Aunt May had taken their jackets.

"It's nothing like what you're probably accustomed to."

"I don't know about that," Bobby replied. "I've lived in plenty of museums, but only a few places that felt like home."

Uncle Dewbug grunted. "I know that's right."

"Well, come in and sit down," Aunt Mae said.

"Do you mind if I go to the bathroom?" Bobby asked. Aunt Mae pointed out the direction. When he was gone, the older woman looked at Bailey and her eyes were practically glowing.

"He's much cuter than I thought! How can you stand it?!"

"He's short," her uncle commented before Bailey could respond.

"Uncle Dewbug," Bailey chided. "He is nice."

"Hmph," he grunted.

They got settled in the living room, where Aunt Mae brought out refreshments using her fancy glasses. It was iced tea, potato chips—the fancy kettle kind—and her fancy homemade French onion dip.

Bailey thought she should have told her aunt to be herself. Not that she would have listened. Aunt Mae stared at Bobby with stars in her eyes while her uncle watched him suspiciously.

The two talked about sports for a few minutes and when her uncle determined Bobby was a Bengals fan, he was somewhat redeemed.

"This dip is amazing," Bobby said while chewing.

"I'll be sure to give the recipe to Bailey."

Bailey looked at her aunt. "Isn't it on the back of the Hidden Valley Ranch pack?"

Her aunt looked at her as if she was appalled. "That's the white—I mean—the way *other* people make it! I add my own touches!" She turned her attention back to Bobby. "I hope you like pork chops and smothered cabbage."

Bobby's eyes brightened as he nodded. "Yes, ma'am—"

"Aunt Mae, not ma'am."

"Aunt Mae. I haven't had pork chops in years, and I like cabbage." He looked at Bailey. "I don't know what smothered cabbage is though."

"You're going to love it!" She got up and headed for the kitchen. "Don't talk about anything interesting while I'm cooking!"

"Okay." Bailey gave Bobby a crooked grin.

They didn't talk about anything of great interest, in Bailey's opinion. Uncle Dewbug had turned on the football game and was watching it while giving commentary to Bobby, who had relaxed and was watching intently, cheering whenever there was a good play.

Things had taken a turn for the positive when her uncle offered Bobby a beer and was chatting comfortably about the players on the field.

Bailey got up and placed a hand on Bobby's shoulder. "I'll be right back. I'm going to help Aunt Mae in the kitchen."

He looked up at her with a smile. "Okay, Bae."

She tried to see if there was a silent plea for her not to leave him alone, but he seemed to genuinely enjoy talking to her uncle about boring sports.

She went to the kitchen and saw her aunt with the phone propped up on her shoulder as she stirred a pot of "this" and flipped the contents of a pan of "that."

"Yes, girl. I told you, he is sitting in my living room as we speak! Oh, I gotta go. I'll call you later."

"Aunt Mae, who was that?" Bailey asked.

Aunt Mae waved her hand dismissively. "Nobody. Just Carol from up the street. She always bragging about something." She winked at Bailey. "Now I got something to brag about. But I brag about you too!" she quickly added. "But Carol can't afford the streaming thingamajig. Sometimes the ladies come over to watch the show, but only the parts with you. I ain't got time to entertain all day and all night."

Bailey shook her head and hid her smile. "Let me help."

"No, everything is basically done. I just gotta put on this last batch of pork chops. You go out and keep your man company. I am worried about y'all."

"What do you mean you're worried?"

Aunt Mae leaned in again and whispered, "That Paula-girl. She is bad news. Did you know she's trying to break you and Bobby up?"

Bailey just stared at her aunt. "Aunt Mae," she said slowly. "It's not real..."

Her aunt picked up a long fork to check the chops. "I know it's not real, Bailey. But you better keep an eye on that chick." She looked at Bailey again and lowered her voice once more. "Or you're going to find yourself with Curtis the milkman and she's going to end up with Bobby, *and* you're going to think it was your idea. That's how people like her do things."

Bailey thought about how Helen had been moved onto a different team.

Aunt Mae sighed and put down her fork. "Look. You and I need to have a heart-to-heart. I know you like Curtis. He's a sweet man, and I can tell he's a good man. But you are a married woman and it is not appropriate."

Bailey's heart began beating too fast as she stared at her aunt. Was she joking? She was talking to her as if Bailey Banks was real.

"Aunt Mae...it's just a show."

Aunt Mae rolled her eyes. "Bailey, I don't have dementia! I know you're on a show and none of it's real." Bailey's body relaxed. "I'm obviously not talking about *you*! I'm talking about Bailey Banks."

"You do keep saying *you*..." Bailey murmured.

"Yes, but both of you are my niece, right? So, I'm obviously talking about the other Bailey. Keep up, girl! I'm trying to save your marriage."

Bailey sighed and nodded, deciding she wouldn't argue.

"Now, this is what you need to do; you need to go and have a talk with that would-be husband-stealer."

Bailey looked at her, intrigued. "Really?"

"Yes! And don't ask Bobby's permission. He's going to say no—or he's going to want to be there with you."

Bailey rubbed her cheek. "Okay, go on."

"Well, I think you're doing okay with everything else, especially how you laid into him when he tried to put you in your place. But, stop being a whiny baby!"

"A whiny baby?" she said in surprise. "What am I whiny about?"

"Girl, you got it good. You got a big, pretty house and a husband that isn't asking you to go out and work. You waste too much food. You don't know how to shop. And why are you eating out so much? Stop eating at that juke joint! You are married. You shouldn't even be at a juke joint!"

Bailey listened intently. "I can't go out with my friends?"

Her aunt picked up her big fork and flipped the pork chops. "That's why you're giving googly eyes at Curtis."

Bailey's mouth dropped. "I'm not!"

Aunt Mae smirked. "Whatever you say. But's not how it looks on film. And I think Curtis is a little too interested."

Bailey bit her lip. Had her attempts to be friendly been misconstrued?

"I think it's just the way it looks on film. I'm—I mean, Bailey—is not interested in Curtis."

Bobby came into the room holding two empty beer bottles. "Sorry to interrupt…" He looked from Aunt Mae to Bailey. "Dewbug sent me for more beer."

Aunt Mae pursed her lips with widened eyes. "No interruption at all. Dinner is almost ready. I'm going to set the table…"

Bobby nodded and threw away the empty beer bottles and looked at Aunt Mae thoughtfully. "Aunt Mae, can I ask you a question?"

"Sure, baby," she replied.

"Would you like to visit the show?"

"What?" she blinked. Bailey even blinked.

"Well…" Bobby's brow had gathered as if he was in deep thought.

"This is just an idea I've been toying with, but I'd like you and Bailey—Bailey Banks—to be able to talk on the phone. And I want you to have candid conversations, just like the one you were having when I came in." He held up his hands defensively while quickly shaking his head.

"I'm sorry! I wasn't trying to eavesdrop, but I loved what you two had to say! If we could have that type of dialogue on the show—obviously not where you know things Bailey hasn't told you, but you giving her advice—and she could confide in you things she's feeling, it would give such an amazing dynamic to the show."

Aunt Mae's eyes had gone as wide as saucers.

"Aunt Mae, the pork chops are getting too brown..." Bailey said while craning her neck at the sizzling meat.

Aunt Mae stared at Bobby in excitement. "You want *me* on the show?"

"Well, your voice," he replied. He looked at Bailey, who had gone to the skillet and was removing the pork chops. "I've been thinking about it ever since you started telling me stories about your aunt and uncle. It's another touch of realism." Bailey turned off the flame with a smile.

"I love it. But how would that work with her not on set?"

"We could set up a separate line; an entirely different phone in this house. It would only connect to our house on set. It could be set up so her voice would be heard on film without requiring anyone to see her, the way we do when you're talking to Pat or Helen."

He looked at her aunt. "What do you think, Aunt Mae? Would you like to be a regular on our show?"

Chapter Seventy-Two

"Would I get paid?" Aunt Mae asked.

"Maybe not at first. This is just an experiment—"

"I'll do it," Aunt Mae interrupted.

"Well, if your role is successful, we can offer you a contract and you'd be on salary."

"I can't wait to tell the ladies!" Aunt Mae exclaimed while doing a little shimmy.

Bobby grinned. "We'll work out some guidelines. Just simple things, like not calling Bailey when you see something sad or interesting happening that might interrupt the flow—"

"No!" Mae shook her head adamantly. "I wouldn't do that!"

"And we wouldn't want you to stay on the telephone too long—maybe ten minutes max—"

"Ten minutes?!" She scowled before her face straightened. "I can make that work."

"We'll play with it and work it out."

Bailey was taking the food to the dining room when she called over her shoulder, "How soon can we start having my aunt call?"

Bobby followed her. "As soon as we set up the new phone." He looked over at Mae, who had followed them with the skillet cornbread. Her smile was so big it spread from ear to ear. "I'm on a real television show—or movie. I don't know what it is, but I'm an actress!"

"You are," Bailey agreed with a chuckle.

Uncle Dewbug came into the room looking at them curiously. "What's going on? Is it time to eat?"

Bailey was surprised her uncle didn't ask to be on the show. That might not have been a great idea, since most of the time he just grunted or scowled when he wasn't napping or watching television.

After dinner, Aunt Mae wanted to watch the show. She talked more than she watched, asking Bobby questions about everything under the sun.

Bobby was happy to answer, and never got tired of talking about a subject he loved; 1954.

Uncle Dewbug sipped his beer and peered at the screen. "How much something like this cost you?"

"Uncle Dewbug!" Bailey exclaimed.

Aunt Mae lightly slapped his arm. "Bernie, what did I tell you? Don't start no mess!"

"All right, all right," he scowled.

Bobby fought to hide his amusement. He reached over and took Bailey's hand.

By nightfall, they had packed up the leftovers at Aunt Mae's insistence and Uncle Dewbug's chagrin.

"Can you leave me one of those pork chops?"

"No!" Mae admonished. "Your blood pressure." They walked them to the car. "Now don't forget to make those biscuits I told you about. I made them every morning. Y'all eat too much white bread."

"Okay, Auntie."

"You won't mess it up; just one cup of self-rising flour and one cup whipping cream. And don't forget what I told you about opening the curtains so early."

"Right. Only open them when I'm ready for people to visit. I'll call you when the phone is installed and you can tell me the biscuit recipe again."

"Oh! That's good," she clapped.

"Mae," Uncle Dewbug said while putting his arm around her ample waist. "Let them folks get home. It's already getting dark."

She reached up and cupped Bailey's face and gave her a kiss and hug. She then did the same to Bobby. Uncle Dewbug hugged and kissed Bailey but then thrust his hand quickly out to Bobby, as if he didn't want him getting any ideas about becoming too personal. But then as an afterthought, he slapped the younger man's shoulder.

"It was a pleasure to finally meet you, sir," Bobby said respectfully.

"I said to call me Dewbug or...Uncle Dewbug is fine."

Bobby nodded, and Bailey could tell it wasn't something her uncle had expected to do, but he had grudgingly begun to like the younger man.

A few minutes later, Bobby shook his head slowly as they drove out of the neighborhood. "They are amazing." He looked at Bailey. "Just like you described."

She grinned. "Thanks. For better or for worse—but I'm crazy about them."

"I'm used to something...different," he said. She glanced at him as she drove. His smile had faded. "My father barely spoke to us unless it was the obligatory topics, like grades. My mother, at least, showed more interest, but I believe my siblings and I were just considered an investment for her to keep my dad."

"Don't you speak to any of them?" she asked, hoping he would open up more about his life outside of set.

He shrugged. "There's nothing to talk about. I keep up with Mom, but haven't talked to my siblings in probably a year. I'll drop them a Christmas card and my mom will probably try to set up a holiday get-together. We'll all pretend to be too busy, and that will be that."

"That's sad."

He gave her a brief smile. "It's okay. Thank goodness I had my grandparents for a while so I knew what to strive for."

Bailey nodded, but wondered if the '50s had become an obsession for the young, rich man that lived a humble existence in a fantasy world.

As Monday morning arrived on set, Bailey Banks went to the kitchen and made oatmeal and toast. Bobby's lunch was peanut butter and jelly sandwiches and a thermos of milk.

The night before, they had discussed how they were going to handle the Banks's visit with her aunt and uncle—which had not gone nearly as good as it had for Bailey Westbrook and Robert Chesterfield.

Bobby came into the kitchen rubbing his eyes, causing them to become red and tired-looking.

"How'd you sleep?" she asked as she gave him a kiss on the lips. He held her, his arms around her hips as he replied, "Not so good. Your aunt and uncle hate me."

"They didn't say—"

"They didn't have to." He moved to take his seat. "Your uncle thinks I'm even more of a liability to you than when I was just 'that white boy.'" Nice touch, Bailey thought. "Now I'm a *white boy* with a bastard kid on the way."

She sat down and stirred her oatmeal. "People can think what they want. Some were just waiting for a reason to be able to say I told you so. Some truly want us to succeed, even though they might not agree with what we are doing. And some are just going to hate us regardless." Bobby watched her without blinking.

"I've been thinking that right now, we are at our most equal." Bailey lowered her spoon as she looked at her husband lovingly. "Part of me felt as if you wouldn't understand how I felt being looked down on. I always wanted to be stronger than I felt, and I hid part of myself from you.

"Now that I see you doing the same thing, it makes me realize how silly it was to worry about people who had no hold on our happiness. Those people didn't stop us from getting married, and they are *not* going to influence our happiness."

Bobby dropped his spoon and rounded the table and got down on his knees beside her. He wrapped his hands around her body and placed his head against her breast.

"I love you, Bae. I love you so much..."

Those words Bailey spoke were to become her new mantra.

After Bobby left for work, she left her payment on the front porch for Curtis along with her empty milk containers without trying to visit with him.

She did her exercise, got dressed, cleaned the kitchen, and checked the time. As she opened her curtains, she looked across the street to see if Helen had opened hers.

She had.

Bailey had scanned her script and for Monday it simply read she would go shopping with Helen.

She was strangely excited at the prospect of learning what Helen had to say about getting caught coming out of Quinton's apartment.

Chapter Seventy-Three

Bailey quietly rapped on Helen's door. She had considered calling first, but didn't want to waste any dialogue on telephone conversation.

Bailey wasn't the producer, but she was beginning to think like one.

Helen opened the door with a tentative smile. "Hey there, Bailey. Come on in while I grab my jacket." She looked up at the sky nervously. "It sure is getting cold. I think we might get some snow for Halloween."

"You might be right," Bailey said while stepping inside. "But I'm hoping for another Indian summer. By the way, thanks again for all your help this weekend. Getting the ladies together and taking me out around the neighborhood was more than I ever expected."

"Uh...sure." She pulled on a jacket with a guilty expression on her face.

As they went to the car, Bailey was not even the tiniest bit surprised the cameraman was already in the back seat waiting for them.

"Did Bobby get the polls he needed?" Helen asked as she started the car.

"Yes. He got more than enough, actually. He'll know the results by mid-week."

"Great." Helen chuckled nervously. "You know, I happened upon that encyclopedia salesman while I was out."

"Oh?" Bailey replied casually.

"Yes, when I saw you and Bobby at the boardinghouse. That guy lives there and we ended up talking."

Bailey's brow rose slightly. "Yeah...he was really interesting to talk to."

"He is!" Helen nodded. "Quinton is his name..."

"Oh, that's right. So...what was his stance on McCarthy?"

"He thinks he's an ass," Helen said while relaxing. "We actually think a lot alike. We both voted for Stevenson over Robert Taft, even though he was an Ohioan. We're both die-hard Democrats. Hank was more concerned with getting an Ohioan into office than getting a Democrat elected." She stopped. "Well...that's neither here nor there."

"It sounds like you made a new friend."

Helen glanced at her before turning her attention back to the road.

They did their shopping at the farmer's market and even though Bailey wasn't able to use the coupons she had clipped from the newspaper, she saved a great deal.

When she bought a paper bag of potatoes, the owner threw in a few extra because he said she had a pretty smile. When she purchased fish she intended to try her hand at frying, the fishmonger went through several pieces, locating the best ones for her.

The fresh vegetables sometimes cost less than the canned ones, and when she selected two grapefruit that had gone soft, the salesman offered them to her for pennies.

Helen politely asked if she wanted to stop for lunch but when Bailey declined, she seemed relieved. Bailey noticed her friend's groceries contained more salad and cottage cheese than usual. She was not going to ask her if she was starting a new diet—not even to further the show. That was just too impolite. But Helen brought it up all on her own.

"Say, do you mind if we make a run into town? I want to stop at the record store and pick up a new exercise record I've been hearing about."

"Sure," Bailey said. "I'm game."

"I'm going to change the way I've been eating. No more cookies and cake. And I want to tone up—not necessarily lose weight," she added matter-of-factly. "You know, there are men in the world that appreciate women with...uh...ample curves." Helen turned and looked at her shapely behind.

They giggled.

Once they were at the record store, Bailey checked out some record albums as Helen shopped. The bebop and jazz section was small, and she saw barely any of the musicians she had learned about while at the juke joint or at Juanita's.

She checked out the magazines. There wasn't a *Jet* magazine in sight. After they left the record store with Helen's exercise records and a *Vogue* magazine, she said she needed to stop at the grocery store for salad dressing they didn't have at the farmer's market.

Bailey did want to pick up another package of toilet paper and she needed feminine products— although she felt the latter shouldn't have to come out of their limited budget, so she dismissed it for the time being.

Bobby had only left her ten dollars for the weekly budget, which was supposed to cover groceries, the milkman, and her salon visit—along with any other necessities that might arise. She intended to stretch that allotment as thin as necessary because she was not giving up her beauty shop visit.

While at the grocery store, she saw the self-rising flour and almost grabbed it before she remembered she already had regular flour, baking powder, and baking soda at home.

She put it back on the shelf and just purchased the toilet paper. Somebody was going to supply her with free sanitary napkins or this would turn out to be a completely different type of show than intended!

As they drove back home with the cameraman still in the back seat, Bailey decided it was time to have a certain discussion with her neighbor and new friend.

In reality, Bailey wouldn't even consider sharing such personal information with someone she'd just befriended mere weeks ago...but this was a reality show, after all.

"Helen."

"Yes, hon?"

"I should probably mention, I'll be counting my pennies for the unforeseeable future—if you haven't already noticed."

Helen's brow dipped. "Is it because of *the baby?*" she whispered the last.

"That and being newlyweds...but mostly that."

"Hmph," Helen said. "She must be hideous. Bobby doesn't strike me as the type to love them and leave them."

Bailey almost laughed out loud before she caught herself, biting the inside of her cheeks to stop the laughter. Helen was obviously not happy with Paula.

"I had an opportunity to see her. She's far from hideous. She's actually really pretty."

Helen looked at her. "What are you two going to do?"

"The child's mother wants to raise him here in town, and Bobby is going to give her money monthly to help support him. Financially, we can make it work. But emotionally..."

Helen gave her hand a pat. "Your world is breaking."

Bailey nodded, and felt her eyes well with tears without even trying.

"He's amazing, Helen. Please don't get me wrong. It's just...*I* was supposed to have his children. This was supposed to be *us*, not *them*."

"Bailey, I'm sure Bobby doesn't want it to be this way."

Bailey forced a smile and dug into her pocketbook for a tissue. She dabbed her eyes. "This has just been so much to handle. I thought the hardest thing about my marriage would be how to make a chicken pot pie." They both chuckled.

"I guess I just don't know what my life will look like once he has a baby with someone else. He wants to be a part of this child's life. Where will I fit in? Do I even...want to fit in to that part of his life?"

Helen covered her mouth and after a long sigh, she spoke. "Bailey, there's no shame in backing away from this—especially if you don't think you can have feelings for the child. If Bobby wants him, and it sounds as if he does, then you will have to want him too. Because if you don't think you can love this child, it will not work."

Bailey sat there for a long time before she replied. "You're right. But I just don't know."

Chapter Seventy-Four

Since they had leftover pork chops from dinner at her aunt and uncle's the day before, Bailey decided not to risk reheating them and turning them into dry hockey pucks. Instead, she cut up some onion and threw them into a skillet with a can of prepared gravy and a little cream.

She made fresh mashed potatoes and the last of the smothered cabbage. It smelled delicious, and while credit for the majority of it fell on her aunt, she was happy to take some of the credit for figuring out how to repurpose it.

There was also leftover cornbread she reheated, along with throwing together a sliced tomato, cucumber, and onion salad dressed with salt, pepper, vinegar, and a pinch of sugar. Her aunt always had little side dishes that didn't quite go along with the meal; like a bowl of cottage cheese and some sliced cucumbers she served with meat loaf and green beans, or pickled beets with a side of onions and tomatoes she served with pinto beans.

Uncle Dewbug always ate the side dishes with the same gusto he ate the main course—regardless of how odd they were.

Bobby got home in a happy mood. He grinned and pulled her into a big hug.

He stepped away from her. "Mr. Adams loved the poll results! He's going to make it a feature for three full days, with the results appearing in the Friday issue!"

"Friday? Isn't that the big one?" she asked in excitement.

"The biggest!"

"And you get the byline?" Her eyes were huge.

"I do indeed!"

Bailey squealed and jumped into his arms while Bobby swung her around before setting her back onto her feet.

"I think we should celebrate," he said. "Friday date night?"

"Okay..." she agreed, without bringing up the issue of money.

"There's a Halloween hayride this weekend, and it's free."

"That sounds like my kind of date," she grinned. "I can pack some hot chocolate."

"Do we have marshmallows?"

"No, but I can buy some."

"No," he said quickly. "As long as we have cookies, I'm good."

"We have cookies."

He gave her one last peck on the nose before going off to change for dinner.

Judging by the way Bobby inhaled dinner, the meal was a success. He even ate the cucumber, tomato, and onion salad without looking at it strangely.

She brought up her conversation with Helen and they briefly speculated about the nature of Helen's friendship with the encyclopedia salesman.

She decided she wouldn't make it a habit, gossiping about Helen. It just didn't seem right to talk about her friend. Bobby then brought up a funny incident that occurred in the office. They laughed and chatted easily. And after dinner, instead of watching television, Bobby turned on the radio and they listened to the Platters, Perry Como, and Rosemary Clooney.

They slow danced, holding onto each other as if they were courting for the first time without a chaperone. Bailey rested her head on Bobby's shoulder and as they swayed to "Mambo Italiano," she wondered why people didn't do this more often.

Later that night, once filming had ended and they were in the bedroom, Bailey took off her sensible heels and slipped on sneakers.

"Do you mind if we go to the factory tonight? I want to take a look at some scenes from the show."

"We can," Bobby replied. "But you can just use the iPad in the office if you prefer." He pulled her in for a kiss. "You having your own Internet at home is one of the perks of having the producer as your boyfriend."

"Are you sure you don't mind?" She didn't want him to think she wanted special favors. Well...save for one or two, like not having to pay for feminine products.

"Can I get free feminine products?"

He nodded. "I can arrange that. I'll bring them home tomorrow from the production office—unless you just want to go to the factory now—"

"Tomorrow is fine. I'm really tired. It seems like Helen and I travelled all over the city in one day."

"I saw."

They determined that he would bring home her "lady products" stowed in his briefcase, since the 1950s man probably didn't openly make such purchases for their wives.

"But for the record," he joked, "I would be the exception."

She kissed him in appreciation. "It's a good thing you're actually a twenty-first-century man."

"By the way, Bruce and I had that well-needed talk."

"Okay. Well hold on a sec." She sat down on the bed with her elbows on her knees, watching him intently. "This is much more interesting than watching scenes."

Bobby sat in the chair to remove his own shoes. He gave her a hesitant look. "Well...I didn't tell you this before, but about a week ago, Bruce and I had a talk. I told him I wanted a bit more free time, and I was going to give him more responsibility on the show. He's been asking for it for years. And while I know I can be a bit controlling where this company and show is concerned, I recognize that Bruce is more than qualified to run it without me.

"I thought he would have jumped at the opportunity. Instead, he accused me of being...preoccupied by you."

Bailey gave him a look of surprise. "Me? Really?"

Bobby leaned back in his seat and shrugged. "I handle all of your scenes, and I won't allow him to let anyone else do your editing until after I leave the production office to come home. And even then, I have pretty strict rules on how I want you filmed. So, I suppose he's not completely wrong."

Bobby leaned forward as his eyes locked onto hers. "But I have a vision of how I want us to be, and I've been able to make that come true—not just for me, but for the viewers. If I'm preoccupied, then it's only for the good, because Bobby and Bailey gave us our first profits ever for the show. And our segments have consistently been number one."

Bailey watched him, feeling a variety of emotions about what he was saying.

Bailey thought he worked too hard, never taking time for himself with the exception of brief respites in his office playing drums or working out. Who could exist like that? Never dating, barely communicating with family, and no friends outside of the set. He definitely needed to find time for himself; time when he didn't have to think about the show.

Bailey also knew he did all of the editing on her scenes. He had told her that once before. But she didn't realize his production manager—the second-in-command behind him—found it problematic. Bruce seemed to be saying he had taken on the brunt of Bobby's other duties. And Bobby was asking him to take on even more.

Bruce was about to be a father. Maybe it was something he literally was unable to handle.

"After that failed conversation, I pretty much let it go. I shouldn't have to explain that I need time to enjoy my life too. He knows better than most that my obsession isn't with a person, but with an object; this show.

"Today I told him I appreciated him stepping up to handle more of the story line and scripts, and overseeing the Garden Hill build. But I wasn't on board with him moving my core group without discussing it with me first."

"How did he feel about that?" Bailey asked while trying not to think about his use of the word *obsession*, when before he had just used the word *preoccupation*.

"It went over about as well as expected. We were about to start arguing, and my life is going in a good direction. I'm happy for the first time since...I can't even tell you."

Bailey reached over and took his hand, squeezing it with quiet encouragement. Robert Chesterfield was a sweet man, even if in some ways he was also a strange one. But she loved him with all of his quirks and idiosyncrasies.

He pulled her up, urging her off the bed and onto his lap. She put her arms around his shoulders. He pressed his forehead against her arm before offering her a soft smile.

"Maybe things are changing. A month ago, I would have chewed his ass. Today...I couldn't exactly blame him, when I gave him the added responsibility and he does something in a way I wouldn't."

"What are you going to do?"

"I basically told him not to mess with my team. And I gave him control of the others."

"You did? Are you sure about that?"

"You don't think I should? Because I want to spend more time with you, Bae—outside of Wingate and cameras. After going to your aunt and uncle's home, I realized the way I've been living has been insane. I need more than this show."

"Then, I don't think what you said was wrong. I guess I just mean, is it something you think you can handle — giving up so much control?"

"As long as he doesn't mess with us. There won't be any more Paulas or illegitimate babies in our future. I'm not saying it was a bad idea, but there won't be any more of that.

"Besides, I already have a complete story line planned out for this team."

"With the civil rights movement?" she asked.

"Yes. But trust me not to go into details. Even Pat doesn't know the full scope, and she's the focus of it."

"Okay." She hugged him. "As long as there are no more kids or exes."

"Noooo," he chuckled. "No more kids, and definitely no more exes."

Chapter Seventy-Five

Bailey got onto the Internet in the home office, sitting at the desk in what she thought of as Bobby's big leather chair. He left her alone, even closing the door after he'd gotten her signed on. He'd taken his laptop, stating there was always work to get caught up on. And he retreated to the kitchen with a glass of milk and some cookies.

The very first thing she did was navigate to her account where she read some of her comments. She tentatively replied to some, thanking them and giving her appreciation. Others, she had to bite her tongue and ignore; especially when people said she should "learn her place."

Another critique was on her looks. There were a group of people that thought she wasn't good enough or pretty enough for Bobby.

"You don't appreciate him!"

"A man like him wouldn't go for someone so unattractive."

"Let him go to the white girl!"

Still, there were others that felt the opposite; she deserved what she got for marrying a redneck. Or she needed to get with the milkman because he was cuter than her husband.

She remembered what Bobby had said in one of the team meetings about ignoring the bad comments. It did take restraint, but she'd much rather her positive commenters call out the ignorance of others. Besides, the bad ones were few and far between. Also, like Bobby said, no one could completely hide when they paid so much for the stream.

When she grew tired of that, Bailey located Paula's stream. The pregnant woman's day was far more interesting than she wanted to admit.

She lived with her sister and brother-in-law, who constantly criticized her for ruining her reputation, her prospects at ever finding a decent man, and for being a laughingstock.

It was actually pretty sad...until she moved back to the scene where Paula had propositioned her husband.

She scowled as she watched a pregnant woman trying to seduce her man.

She grabbed his hand and pressed it to her stomach when the baby kicked—her hand lingering on top of his until he had to slip out of her grip.

"I dream of being a family," she said. "Don't you miss me at all? We would be better together..."

Bailey had to pause the stream and stand up and pace.

Bobby had just been so polite. He should have told her off, smacked her hand away.

After a moment, Bailey was calmed down enough to continue watching what had taken place. No wonder so many people who knew her were angry.

Paula hadn't been subtle, at all.

Finally, Bailey heard what she'd been waiting to hear from Bobby. Paula mentioned annulment, and Bobby told her he didn't want to hurt her feelings, but the truth was, he never loved her, and never once considered marrying her—not then and not now.

"I love my wife, and I'll never leave her. I'm sorry things have been rough on you. But you had choices…more than I did."

Bailey found herself smiling. After Bobby left her house, Paula did indeed break down in frustrated tears. But the act of cradling her stomach didn't seem at all endearing.

To Bailey, she just looked like a woman trying to manipulate an audience into sympathizing with her.

Bailey scowled again and switched off her stream.

She turned to Helen's channel, feeling like a voyeur. But she had to admit, she had more fun watching her friend. Helen knew many of the neighbors, and there was barely a day that went by when she didn't have company or didn't go out visiting. She could hop in her car and do just about anything, from going to a movie, to grabbing an ice cream cone.

When Hank came home, they spent one day a week playing cards with neighbors. Hank was fun too, and they seemed to have a good relationship.

It was a shame she was going to have an affair when he was so loving—at least when he was at home.

Helen and Quinton didn't talk today but when she tuned in to watch his stream, she saw he picked up his phone several times before hanging it up. He must know Hank's schedule.

Bailey tuned in to watch Pat, who seemed to be getting closer to Marvin. After work he'd come to her house, and she told him not to expect much for dinner and had cooked them bacon and eggs with toast.

He ate it the same way Bobby did; as if it was his last meal.

She was curious about the ladies from the beauty shop, but found that while Juanita and Miss Baker were regulars, it didn't mean they had all-day streams. The same went for the neighbors, Curtis, and the extras.

She got what Pat had said about the boredom. It must be tedious to be on call all day long, but not to know exactly what parts would be placed on film.

It was getting late, and she could only peek in on Drew and Nadine.

This was addictive. If she wasn't careful, she'd spend all evening watching the show.

For the next few days, Bailey followed the routine of filming during the day and watching the daily takes in the evening. Bobby didn't complain, maybe because he got more work done when he didn't spend hours making out with her.

Not to say they completely stopped with that part of their relationship.

Holding and kissing each other through the night became less frantic the more they grew comfortable with each other.

On Wednesday, Bobby announced that the phone system to her aunt and uncle's house was finally operational, and she could phone her beginning Thursday. Bailey was so excited, she was giddy.

She cooked breakfast of oatmeal and toast. Aunt Mae was probably right; they ate too much store-bought bread. Between toast for breakfast, Bobby's sandwiches for lunch, and her occasional PB&J a few times a week, they easily went through a pack of bread weekly.

Maybe she should bake her own bread. No. She was not going to spend hours kneading and proofing bread each day. She needed her aunt to once again "teach" her this biscuit recipe.

Finally, the time came, and Bailey tried to act as casual as possible when she picked up the phone in the kitchen and dialed the special number.

"Hello?" came a tentative, almost shaky voice.

"Hi, Aunt Mae. It's me."

"Oh, Bailey. How are you today?" she asked stiffly, enunciating each word.

Bailey's brow began to bead with sweat. Everything in her told her she should probably hang up the phone and "abort mission!" but she pushed through.

"I'm good. You're not busy, are you?"

"I'm not busy. No."

Okay…usually Aunt Mae went on and on about what she'd been doing for the last hour, if not the last day.

"That's good, because I need that biscuit recipe you were telling me about the other day."

"Biscuit recipe…" she said blankly.

Oh God. Aunt Mae was freezing up.

"Do you mean the one with the two ingredients?" she asked.

"Yes, the easy one."

"You just need one cup of heavy whipping cream and one cup of self-rising flour."

"That is easy."

Crickets.

"Yes," her aunt finally said.

"What if I don't have self-rising flour?"

"Uh...you should go to the store and get some."

Bailey hid a smile. That was a very Aunt Mae response.

"Well, we have all of this regular flour. Can't I just use that?"

"No. The purpose of using the two-ingredient method is to make it easy. If you're going to use regular flour, you might as well cut in shortening, then measure your salt and your baking powder."

"Every time I do, they get so hard."

"All right, Bailey." She sounded exasperated, but she chuckled. "You can turn regular flour into self-rising. But please tell me you have White Lily flour?"

"It's not White Lily..."

"Bailey! How did you come from my house and not know you always keep two types of flour? Go next door and borrow a cup of flour and call me back."

"What?" Her eyes grew large.

"I am sure your neighbors have White Lily."

"But, Aunt Mae —"

"No buts! Call me back. Bye."

Bailey stared at the dead phone. Did her aunt really just hang up on her?

With a sigh she grabbed a bowl and headed for the living room, where she looked out the front window to see if Helen's car was there.

It wasn't. Helen was out early today. It wasn't even noon. Bailey sighed and went outside and marched to Haley's house.

Haley gave her a surprised look. She was dressed in a robe with a fur collar and fur slippers. Her hair was wrapped, and the front showed silver clips holding her bangs in place.

"Bailey. Come in."

"Hi, Haley. I'm so sorry to barge in on you like this—"

Haley closed the door and waved her hand dismissively. "Don't worry about it. I have a date tonight and I want to look extra gorgeous. Would you like a drink?"

Yes. "No. I just came over to see if you have any White Lily self-rising flour. I need it for a recipe."

"White Lily? I sure do." She headed for the kitchen and Bailey followed in surprise that the swinger next door had a specific type of flour she'd never even heard of.

"I don't do much baking, so no telling how long it's been here."

She opened her pantry, and there was a brand-new package of the flour.

"Wow." Bailey looked at Haley's well-stocked pantry. Including every cooking ingredient known to man, she also had numerous bottles of whiskey, bourbon, and several six-packs of beer.

Haley chuckled. "I do a lot of entertaining. Although I don't bake, I make a mean beef Wellington. If you and your husband will ever accept my invitation for dinner, I'll make one."

Bailey's mouth dropped. "Definitely. Let me talk to Bobby about it."

"Well, I'll relinquish my prized Saturday if you're free this weekend."

Bailey smiled and nodded. "I think we are. But I'll check with my husband."

"Fantastic!" She got a pen and paper and wrote her phone number on it. Bailey accepted it. "I think I gave this to you before, but here it is again. Ring me, and let me know so I can get the beef."

"I can call you tonight. Oh, your date —"

Haley made a shooing motion. "That's not until eight." She opened the package of flour. "How much do you need?"

"Just a cup. And thank you so much!"

"A cup? Sweetheart, take half the bag." She poured the flour into Bailey's bowl.

"Oh...are you sure?"

"Yes. It sounds like you'll get more use out of it than I will."

"Thank you, Haley," she said in actual appreciation. "I should get back to my recipe." She gestured to the door. "But I'll call you a bit later."

Haley walked her to the door. "Talk to you later, Bailey."

That was the first time she'd gotten out of house without being half drunk.

Chapter Seventy-Six

Once back home, Bailey called her aunt again.

"Hello."

"Hi, Aunt Mae. I got the flour!"

"I told you everybody would have it."

"Yes. You were right."

"You'll need to turn the oven to four fifty, and they bake for twenty minutes. I brush the top of my biscuits with cream before I put them in the oven."

"That sounds good."

"What are you going to make with them?"

"I'm not sure. But I want enough for breakfast tomorrow."

"You can have breakfast for dinner. You can make sausage and gravy and have it again for breakfast."

"That's a good idea!"

"I got a recipe for that too. But you're going to need to write this down."

Her aunt was warming up. She wasn't quite smooth, but was getting better. She detailed the recipe, making sure she understood it, just like her aunt would normally do.

Although they had been talking for a while, Bailey decided she'd give her aunt an opportunity to talk about something deeper.

"Is Uncle Dewbug still upset?"

Aunt Mae took a long time to answer. Bailey was just about to tell her it was okay not to answer when she did.

"Your uncle loves you, baby. And Bobby was just beginning to grow on him.

"We would have preferred you married a Negro, but anyone can look at Bobby and see he's committed to you and your marriage. But in our time, race-mixing only happened when a white man took advantage of a Black woman.

"I think your uncle can't stop thinking the situation could have easily been swapped, and you could have been in other woman's shoes."

Bailey gnawed her lips, but deep down, she was screaming internally. Her aunt was back!

"Times are different. Bobby loves me and I love him, and we want the same thing anyone would want. And what happened with that girl was an accident. One he's ashamed of."

"I know, Bailey. I know. Just give your uncle time. He has to relearn Bobby's character."

"Okay. I know. I just hope you and Uncle Dewbug will be in our corner because soon, we're going to be the talk of the town and there won't be many."

"Honey, I am always in your corner. Even if I'm annoyed or angry, I will always be supportive of you — even if I don't always agree with you."

Bailey sighed. "I understand. I better get off the phone if I want to have dinner ready. I'll call you tomorrow to let you know how the meal turned out."

"Okay. I love you, baby."

"I love you too." Bailey hung up, suppressing her grin. Even though it began shaky, it ended very well.

Bobby should consider Aunt Mae's inclusion in the show a definite success—if for no other reason than the biscuits and gravy turned out fantastic!

As they ate breakfast-for-dinner, she thought about how nice it was Haley had given her enough flour that she'd have enough to make a double batch of biscuits the next day.

"Do you like beef Wellington?" she asked, thinking about Haley's invitation.

"I don't know what it is, but I'm sure I will since it has the word *beef* in it. As long as it's not like Welsh rabbit."

"Welsh rabbit? Aunt Mae makes a delicious rabbit stew, is that what it is?" She watched him cut through half a biscuit and drag it through the sausage gravy before it disappeared into his mouth.

"No," Bobby replied while chewing enthusiastically. "It's cheese sauce over toast. When I saw it, it was like a smack in the face!" He chuckled.

"When'd you have that?" she asked while laughing too.

He pursed his lips momentarily, his smile disappearing. "Paula made it."

"Oh. Well," she said dismissively. "Our next-door neighbor Haley invited us to dinner Saturday. I think we should go. She's been nothing but nice to me."

"Sure. As long as beef Wellington isn't just cheese sauce or something."

She smiled. "I'm pretty sure it's roast beef."

"I like roast beef," he replied.

I hope that's not a hint because on our budget, you'll be getting meat loaf twice a week...

"What brought on an invitation to dinner?"

Uh-oh. She definitely didn't want to tell him she'd had to borrow some flour. He was pretty sensitive about that kind of thing, and today had been a good one.

"I just think we should get to know the neighbors better," she hedged. "Especially the nice ones, and Haley's always been friendly."

He shrugged. "Okay."

They finished dinner. Bobby had eaten five biscuits to her three, leaving one biscuit and an iron skillet that had practically been scraped clean of every inch of sausage gravy.

Bailey decided she'd get up early the next morning to make the double recipe of the biscuits.

Later, as they snuggled on the sofa watching first the news and then *Arthur Godfrey And His Friends*, Bobby dozed off. He was so adorable, she snuck kisses on his face until he jolted awake, only to smile when he saw her face.

"Let's go to bed early," she said suggestively.

He nodded and lowered the shades and locked the doors as she cut off the television and carried their empty glasses of milk and plate of cookies into the kitchen.

Bailey covered her mouth as she yawned, waiting for him to join her. When he did, he placed a loving arm around her waist and they retreated to the bedroom, closing the door behind them.

And that is where the scene ended for Bobby and Bailey Banks—but not for Robert Chesterfield and Bailey Westbrook, who had an entirely different nighttime routine.

She changed out of her dress and into shorts and one of Bobby's T-shirts while he bathed. Using the alone-time, she hurried into the home office to catch up on her daily fix of scenes.

Yay! Quinton had finally gotten up the nerve to call Helen! He asked if they could meet for coffee and Bailey shook her head internally screaming, *NO! Girl, don't you know some nosey neighbor is going to see you!* Luckily, Helen was smart enough not to get caught out in public having coffee with the single, attractive encyclopedia salesman. Instead, she said she'd meet him at the farmer's market.

That was good. Not that Bailey knew the ins and outs of having a clandestine affair, but she would think an "innocent" meeting while at the market was pretty good.

After peeking in on Helen, she got to spend time catching up on Drew, who was still single despite being super cute and having deep dimples. But he also had PTSD and was emotionally unstable. Still, in the world of fiction, a man like that was a catch.

Nadine was killing it with her affair with the mayor. They nearly got caught kissing by the mayor's wife, who had made a surprise visit to the office.

She checked in on Pat, who had gone to the juke joint with Marvin and had eaten mouth-watering fried catfish and fries, drank tons of beer, and laughed and danced the night away.

It was late by the time she got her shower. Bobby was already in bed going over script changes. He placed his laptop in the bedside drawer when she climbed in beside him. They cuddled, kissed, talked a bit, and kissed some more before eventually falling asleep with her face tucked comfortably beneath his chin.

Chapter Seventy-Seven

When Friday rolled around, Bailey hurried through the laundry. A) It was cold out. B) Doing laundry out in the cold garage was insane...which was basically the same as A. And C) Today was date night and they were going on a hayride.

Bailey remembered when Bobby told her that although they didn't have a traditional relationship, he planned to date her while on the show. Bobby and Bailey's date nights would then be *their* date nights. It made it feel so special because although she saw her boyfriend every single day, she looked forward to the idea of them doing special things together.

Bobby had not told her anything about what to expect on the date, only promising he didn't have any sinister plans up his sleeve, like a Klan march or something along those lines. The only drawback was since Friday was payday, he'd have to visit Paula first in order to give her money.

Bailey wasn't worried about the money now that she knew how to make her $10 weekly budget work...although it was true that Paula did get $20 a week. Of course, Paula didn't have a husband to take care of her other expenses. But on the other hand, those *other* expenses were probably being covered by her sister and brother-in-law...

Okay, no! She was not here to count some other woman's money!

Bailey went through her list of daily chores, figuring out she could wear one of her wrap dresses, which looked pretty fancy although it was lightweight and comfortable enough to do housework in.

Bailey had also broken in the kitten heels, so she barely even noticed them on her feet until about 2:00 p.m. when she kicked them off long enough to sit in the reclining chair for a short 20 to 50 winks.

After she ironed the clothes that were dry, she folded and put them away and went back out for the ones that had needed a bit more time, ironing and putting them away as well.

Dinner tonight was just leftover ham and beans with cornbread. She'd also figured out that on her busy days, she would plan for leftovers. And besides, a hayride was a perfect time to have a second day of beans, since no one would know when Bobby got a case of gas.

By 4:00 p.m. she had the kitchen table set for dinner but decided to leave the bean soup warming on the stovetop, since she knew Bobby would be late due to his visit with Paula.

She hurried into the bedroom and got dressed for a hayride. Bailey didn't exactly know what hayride clothing was, but knew what was right for fall weather; the wool circle skirt with both of her petticoats. To resolve the itchiness, she also wore the petti-pants that had been tucked in the back of her lingerie drawer.

She also chose a cashmere sweater set—the outer sweater, she draped over the couch until it was time to leave.

With wool socks and boots, Bailey was ready for an impromptu blizzard!

She reapplied her makeup, pinned up her hair so it would look nice even with her wool bucket hat, and she primped in front of the mirror.

Every day was dress-up day on the set of 1954, but today was especially so. She felt excited to go out seeing the sights while on the back of a wagon, or hopefully it would be a carriage. She and Bobby would snuggle beneath blankets and sip cocoa.

Bailey went into the kitchen to make the cocoa—although she would need Bobby to get home so she could use his thermos. She checked the time and saw it was half past five.

She packed some cookies, stirred the beans, noting they were beginning to become dry so she added some water. She put the cornbread back into the oven with the heat turned off, hoping it would stay warm without turning hard.

She checked the time again. It was almost six. She looked out the back window, hoping they wouldn't lose too much daylight. She was beginning to get warm, so she went into the bedroom and removed the petticoats, placing them on the bed so she could quickly slip them back on.

At six thirty, Bailey turned on the television and sat on the couch, not really paying attention to any of the shows.

It was quarter to seven when the phone finally rang. She ran to answer it before it even had time to ring a second time.

"Bailey!"

Her heart leaped at the frantic sound of Bobby's voice. "Bobby?"

"I'm so sorry I'm late. I'm at the hospital. Paula's having the baby."

Bailey blinked, her brows rising in surprise. "Now? But isn't it too early?"

"It is. She's just in her eighth month. Honey, I won't be home until much later. I'm so sorry —"

"No. It's okay. But is everything going to be okay?"

"She's in with the doctors now, and no one has let us know much."

"Us?"

"Her sister and sister's husband. Plus, her mother and father are here."

"Okay." Bailey rubbed her forehead. "Call me when you find out more."

"I will. Bae...I might be a father tonight."

She inhaled sharply and smiled softly. "You will be the most amazing father."

"Thanks, honey. I love you, Bae."

"I love you. Call me."

"I will! Bye!" And then he hung up.

Bailey slowly returned the phone to its cradle. She then sank onto the sofa with her elbows planted on her knees and her hands folded in front of her.

Bobby called about an hour later.

"Did the baby come?" she asked anxiously. This wasn't real, she had to remind herself. When Paula did actually have her baby, she was going to have to leave the set for a while. She couldn't imagine having a newborn on set — but she also couldn't imagine working every day without having her newborn with her.

"Well, honey, I'm not a father yet. It was a false alarm."

Bailey didn't reply immediately. "That's a good thing. It will give the baby a bit more time."

"Yes, but it really scared me. Look, I'm coming home. I just need to call my mother first."

"Oh. Right," she said. Of course he would keep his mother in the loop. She was definitely going to peep that scene when it came time for her to pull out the iPad. "I'll see you when you get home."

They disconnected, and Bailey changed back into her everyday dress. She put away her petticoats and hung up the rest of her clothes and sat at her vanity, where she spread cold cream on her face.

She couldn't afford to waste the tissues, so Bailey used a washcloth to wipe off her makeup before scrubbing her face clean in the bathroom sink.

When Bobby got home, she greeted him at the door and took his coat and hat. He pulled her into a long hug, swaying with her long after he would have normally released her.

"I'm so sorry we missed our date night," he said against her neck.

"It's okay, honey."

He pulled back. "I'll make it up to you. I promise."

She gave him a smile. "Are you hungry?"

"No," he said quickly. "I grabbed a burger in the cafeteria." He went into the living room and slumped into the armchair and held out his hand for her. When she was within arm's reach, he pulled her onto his lap and hugged her. It was as if he needed her there as reassurance she wouldn't leave him. She kissed his forehead, hoping he felt her complete support.

"So, what happened?" she asked.

"When I went to drop off the money, she wanted to talk about…baby names," he forced out.

"Did you decide on one?" she asked easily.

He looked at her, meeting her eyes in a way he hadn't done in a while.

"Robert the third." Bailey nodded slowly. He continued to watch her. "Robert Alan *Banks* the third." Bailey said nothing. "Is that okay, honey? Because even though we haven't talked much about having our own baby…maybe you might want to have our own son named after me."

"Who's to say we'll even have a son?" she said in a voice that sounded thin even to her own ears. "Who's to say we'll have kids at all?"

"We will," he said resolutely. He rested his head against her breast and closed his eyes. "I want our babies, ones that look like *us*—more like us than we look like us."

Bailey lay her head on the top of his head. *Why do you have to be so perfect, Bobby Banks?*

Chapter Seventy-Eight

That night, Bailey didn't feel like watching Paula fake her labor on replay. She decided to take a night off from watching the show.

"What do you want to do?" Bobby asked before taking off his shoes. "Do you want to go to the factory?" They were in the bedroom, door shut, stop-filming button pressed.

She shook her head. "No. Can we just do something different?"

"What would you like to do?"

She shrugged. "I don't know. I just want time with you in a place that doesn't look like the fifties."

Bobby smiled. "I have an idea. Change into pants and sneakers and meet me in the living room."

"What do you have up your sleeve?" she asked while a slow smile covered her face.

"You'll see."

Once in the car, Bailey checked the time. It was nearly half past nine. Where could they go at this time of night?

She looked at Bobby, who wore a slight smile, but it was one of genuine enjoyment. Bobby reached over to grip her hand.

"I really am sorry we missed date night," he said, his brow gathered. Was he annoyed with Paula, or just unhappy about not being able to follow through with his plans?

"I am too." She sighed in acceptance. "But I keep remembering the way you explained that this story will unfold due to the way the characters interact with each other. I like that. I like that the story line is more alive for me because I get to make my own decisions." She shrugged. "I won't lie and say it hasn't been challenging, but the more I get used to it, the more I prefer this role-play to scripted scenes."

He seemed to think deeply about her words. "It was born out of necessity once the actors began to grow. There was no way we could write complete scripts for everyone."

"Yeah, I figured that out when my scripts started saying, 'Bailey will go about her day-to-day routine.'" She chuckled.

"Yeah, but once I knew you could handle writing your own story line, I left you to it. And I'm happy I did." He shook his head and grinned. "I suppose you're reminding me that as one of the players, I too fall under that rule."

"No. You don't need me to remind you of that. Only that the story becomes richer with the occasional unexpected occurrence."

"*Occasional* being the pivotal word."

They reached the production office and Bobby entered the garage and parked. She waited for him to hurry over to open her door, still impressed by that show of courtesy.

Once she was out of the car, instead of heading for the entrance to the building, he turned to unlock the car parked next to them with a gentle twirp-twirp of the key fob.

Bailey glanced over at the entrance to the building and then back at the shiny, black car Bobby had unlocked. She slipped into the cool leather seats of the BMW. She didn't know much about cars, and couldn't say what type or year the BMW was, but it was understated luxury as opposed to her car, which was a 1988 Cadillac Brougham that was about the size of a boat but had been lovingly cared for by her uncle before being handed down to her.

He shut her door after making sure all of her bits and pieces were inside and then he slid into the driver's seat and started it up with just the press of a button. The engine was so smooth, it barely made any sound.

Noting her look of surprise, Bobby winked at her and then reached for a leatherbound CD case. He pulled out of the parking garage while slipping in a CD he'd selected.

When the music filled the car, Bailey didn't know what she had expected—maybe more rockabilly; but certainly not the cool, soulful song "Fair Chance" by Thundercat.

"You're a Thundercat fan?" She could not hide the sheer surprise from her voice.

"Yeah." He looked at her. "Do you like him?"

"Yes." She suddenly wondered why she thought it was so weird. Music was boundless, enjoyed by people of all races and ages. Even she liked some vintage rock as much as she liked soul music.

"I listen to this playlist whenever I get off set." He pressed the next song and she didn't recognize it, but it was jazzy, with nice mellow drums, horns, and strings, and yet still managed to be infused with plenty of soul.

"Do you know this?" he asked.

She shook her head, but grooved to the mellow swells and dips of the drums and piano.

" 'City of Mirrors' by BADBADNOTGOOD."

"I've never heard of them. This is cool." She nodded her head to the beat. "You have an eclectic taste in music." His forehead wrinkled.

"I feel like everyone does, don't they? Who listens to only one type of music?"

"My aunt Mae and uncle Dewbug. They only listen to oldies."

He chuckled. "Okay. You're right. I like basically everything—everything that sounds good. I don't care about genres or things like that."

Something occurred to her as she remembered Bobby was a musician. "Have you ever recorded any of your music?"

"Well, I was a session player. Do you know the group The Sunburned Penguins?

"Yes," she grinned and her smile froze. Wait, was he actually saying he played with them?

TSP had been a popular alternative group that had its heyday right around the time Pearl Jam was at its height of popularity. At that time, everyone was trying to release songs sounding like them. TSP was one of the few that had been successful.

"You played with TSP?"

He smirked at her surprise. "A few times. But not under my real name."

She stared at him in awe. "You have a pseudonym?"

He started to laugh. "Something like that. I mean, let's be honest, how many musicians want a rich, right-wing politician's son hampering their street cred?"

Bailey just blinked at him. "What is your pseudonym?"

"It's silly..." A red tint had begun to creep up his neck.

"Tell me," she begged.

"Mike Smith."

Bailey was quiet. "Mike Smith? Just Mike Smith. Why?"

He stared ahead as he drove, the smile on his face frozen in place. "Because it's simple and normal. A guy named Mike Smith would just become part of the background. He would never stand out."

If she was the son of a notorious politician, she was sure she would want the same. She reached out for his hand and squeezed it reassuringly.

Chapter Seventy-Nine

They drove for a while, speaking of music and nothing more until Bobby pulled into the crowded parking lot of a little hole-in-the-wall pub. A worn sign stated the name of the establishment was Scotty's Place.

As Bobby opened her car door, she gave him a curious look and he shrugged. "This is where I come when I want to get off the set." His words were casual, and even his lips tilted into a happy smile. But his eyes were apprehensive as he watched her.

"Okay," she said simply, and he took her hand and led her up the worn wooden planks of the walkway where an outdoor seating area was empty due to the season.

As soon as he opened the door, Bailey could tell the live band was pretty decent. They were playing a funky instrumental tune that sounded somewhat familiar. And with alarm, she realized it was "WAP" by Cardi and Megan.

She grinned in amusement. People were on the dance floor jamming to the tune; older, young, Black, white, just a mixture of people having a good time.

He led her to the bar and a pretty bartender smiled, her eyes lighting up the moment she saw him.

"Yo, Mike! Where you been, mate? It's been a minute." She had an English accent, or perhaps Australian. Bailey wasn't good with such things. She had never actually met anyone with that type of accent.

The woman was tall, even a few inches taller than "Mike," with long, brunette hair she wore in a top tail. She was slender, gorgeous, and they were obviously friends.

"It's been busy," Bobby replied with an easy smile.

"Yep, you're the man that's always so busy."

The woman's attention turned to Bailey. She scanned her quickly, noted their locked hands, and made a split-second assessment of her looks before offering her a welcoming smile.

"And who do we have here?"

"Mel, this is my girlfriend, Bailey. And Bailey, this is Melvina; the cook, bartender, and bouncer of this fine establishment."

Mel wiped her hand with a rag that hung from the waist of a half apron before thrusting it to Bailey to shake.

"Melvina?" Mel smirked at Bobby. "Dude, I told you I'm never going to tell you what Mel stands for, but it's definitely not Melvina." Her handshake was firm. "What do you two want to drink?" she asked.

"Beers?" Bobby asked while looking at Bailey with a raised brow.

"Yeah, that's fine," Bailey nodded.

He turned back to Mel. "Whatever you have on draft."

Mel slung the rag across her shoulder as she moved to retrieve two tall pilsner glasses.

"Only the finest; PBR."

"I love that stuff." He grinned mischievously.

Bailey looked at him, "PBR?"

"Pabst Blue Ribbon. It's kind of…" Bobby began.

Mel looked at him with a slight smirk before turning to Bailey as she poured up the brews.

"PBR started out as a working man's drink; cheap and cold. Then the hipsters got hold of it and it became fashionable. But just like hipsters to jump ship as soon as something goes mainstream. So, it's basically back to the working class."

She slid the beers to them and accepted Bobby's credit card. That meant she had to know his real name. The name thing was just a bit of fun between them.

"Are you playing tonight?" Mel asked.

He picked up both beers. "Nah. I just want to spend time with my girl. Talk to you later."

He led them to an empty two-seater table. Bailey looked behind her to say goodbye and saw the gaze Mel had on her face as she stared at Bobby's back. The woman turned quickly away when caught wearing such a look of longing.

He set the beers down and pulled out her chair before she could do it for herself.

She smiled at him in gratitude. She knew she had a good man in Bobby. Others evidently knew it too.

Bobby took his seat and took a sip of the beer before taking her hand and kissing the back of it. He gazed over at the stage where a man was crooning in the style of Prince.

Bailey sipped her beer and found herself swaying slightly to the gentle beat and the singer's low falsetto.

"That's pretty," she said as the singer crooned over and over that he just wanted to feel numb.

"It is. What do you think of this place?"

Bailey watched the people slow dancing, chitchatting, or just enjoying their beers.

"I like it," she said honestly. "The vibe here is so chill."

He nodded and seemed satisfied. "I'm happy." He looked down at the table, where he traced the wood pattern with a free fingertip. "I think so many people think rich people only go to the country club. And I'm a member of several...but I like this place better than any of them."

"Why is that?" she asked while peering at him closely.

He met her eyes. "Because, for the most part, people here leave their pretenses at the door."

"And you can be Mike Smith and melt into the woodwork?"

He chuckled. "Well, the regulars know who I am. They're just too polite to mention it."

They were there for about half an hour before he led her to the dance floor, not accepting her shy refusal to get up. With a chuckle, she finally went along with it, happy he'd had her change into jeans so she didn't look too out of place. And of course, despite his fifties clothing, he just looked like a hipster.

Bobby pulled her into his arms and they began to slow dance to a fast song. He didn't care and as they swayed in each other's arms, she forgot about all the people around them.

As song after song played, Bobby and Bailey were content to stay in each other's arms while listening quietly to the pub's diverse playlist of music.

Much later, as they drove back on set to their home, Bailey sighed in contentment.

"Can we go back there sometime?"

He looked at her. "Yes. I'll take you there as often as you want."

"That can be our real-life date night place," she offered. "But I still want on set date nights."

Bobby chuckled. "Definitely, honey." He gazed out at the road in easy contentment. "Thanks, Bailey."

"Thanks for what?" She hid her yawn.

"For understanding me. I've gone out with girls that thought I was weird because of my interests, the music I listen to and the way I choose to live."

Bailey's head was leaned against the headrest. "Those girls were so boring. This life is the most fun I've ever had. Honestly."

His head jerked to her. "Me too." He seemed amazed as he just stared at her, and even in the darkness, Bailey could see the blue of his eyes recede as the blackness of his pupils took over.

When they got to the house, Bobby reached out for Bailey even before he locked the door. He pulled her to him and kissed her with more than his normal enthusiasm.

Bailey wrapped her arms around his neck and accepted his kisses, his tongue, and the way his body molded to her every curve.

One of his hands lightly gripped the base of her neck while the other moved slowly over her back, past her hips, only to rest on the swell of her butt.

Bobby's lips trailed from her lips to her jaw and neck, where he laced her collar bone with soft, tender kisses.

Bailey moaned with a quiet sigh. She had always resisted being too vocal when they made out. It seemed as if to vocalize it would be to push their self-imposed boundaries. The quiet enjoyment of kissing, along with the light touches, pushed the boundaries of their control. Giving in to the moans of pleasure she had to force herself to swallow would have been more than she could bear—and she knew it would push Bobby over the edge.

But today had been one filled with so many new discoveries. His hands on her body, his kisses against her skin felt like home. Bobby was her home in a strange place.

When he heard her moan, his hand moved up to grip her breast, squeezing with an urgency he seldom gave in to. His mouth parted and his tongue located hers, sparring with it before he closed his lips and sucked it into her mouth with a harsh groan.

"Bailey..." he sighed. His hand moved beneath her shirt, where it slipped urgently beneath her bra.

Bailey did something similar when her hand crept beneath his shirt to lightly graze the muscles of his abdomen. The soft hair there moved beneath her nails and his muscles jerked as he drew in a sharp breath.

Bobby pulled back long enough to stare into her eyes. Hers were just as dark as his. He quickly lifted her, both of her legs going around his body. He kissed her lips as he walked her to the bedroom.

"...love you, Bailey. I love you..." he murmured against her lips.

Once in the bedroom, he stopped long enough to fumble open the top chest of drawers, where he retrieved one of the condoms.

Chapter Eighty

Bailey felt the soft soreness of recent lovemaking—the type after a long period of abstinence.

She came fully awake and listened for Bobby's light snores. His arm was draped over her, and his hand cupped her naked belly. He was the big spoon and she was the little one. She could feel his nude body pressed along the back of her and although they spooned often, they had never done it in the nude.

Bailey smiled to herself. She relived the last few hours, including their date at the pub. It had been a beautiful evening. She could reminisce about it for hours, but they didn't have hours. She hadn't showered as she usually did the night before and shooting would begin in a few hours.

Bailey slipped carefully from his grasp and out of the bed. She padded on tiptoes to the bathroom feeling the chill in the air and wishing for Bobby's warmth.

As she showered, the bathroom door opened. And a moment later, the shower curtain was pulled back to reveal Bobby's stubble-covered face.

"Do you want your back washed?"

She spied a condom packet in his hand and smiled. Two birds with one stone…

Later, as they lay in bed dressed in their nightclothes in order to prepare for the morning scene, Bobby kissed Bailey's fingertips while she gazed at him lovingly.

"Every little thing about you, mesmerizes me," he whispered. "How did I hold back for so long?" He smiled with a blush and pulled her into his arms.

She paused long enough to kiss him.

"I love you," he whispered.

"I love you too." She settled against him, and he yawned.

"We have a few more hours before shooting begins. Let's get some sleep."

"Mmm," she muttered while tucking her head into its place beneath his jaw. "It's going to be a long one. We have dinner with Haley."

He rubbed her back. "Yep."

She hesitated. His short response didn't give her any idea about what to expect. Haley certainly added dimension to the story, and Bailey didn't want them to end up at odds with each other. But by the same token, no woman would sit idly by if another woman was hitting on her husband.

She felt herself begin to doze as she eventually decided that whatever happened would just happen.

She was awakened later with soft kisses to her forehead and face. When she opened her eyes, she saw the soft glow of the sun streaming past the shades.

"Do you want to sleep in?" Bobby peered down at her with sky-blue eyes that still struck her with their brightness. "It's Saturday, and we can begin filming from the bedroom." He seemed wide awake. How long had he been watching her sleep?

She rubbed the sleep from her eyes. "It's tempting." She yawned into her fist. "But I don't want to be late for the beauty shop."

He kissed her hair. "What did your hair look like before?"

She propped her chin on the back of her hands, which were planted on his chest. She looked at him pleased he wanted to know.

"I had microbraids. I was never the type that had the patience to visit a beauty salon on a regular basis." There were times when she'd gone three months before a touchup. "But going to Juanita's is more than just a place to get my hair done. It's like a little community."

In so many ways, Bailey could forget she was being filmed as the ladies cut up.

"Your salon visits are popular—all of them are, not just yours." He reached up to touch the hair that fell past her scarf. "It's about time for me to get a haircut, myself."

She reached up and stroked a blond curl that had fallen onto his forehead.

"Not too short, okay? No military cut or anything. I love your hair."

He grinned. "Okay."

She pulled herself out of his warm embrace and he held onto her hand until she chuckled and headed for the bathroom to begin her day.

Bailey had run out of Haley's self-rising flour so there would be no biscuits and sausage gravy this morning—which is what her appetite craved. One of the pitfalls of living in the '50s was that she couldn't make a quick stop at her favorite fast-food joint. And even if she didn't want fast-food, she couldn't snack on Doritos at 1:00 a.m. or crack open a bottle of sparkling water.

And maybe that's why when they'd split some loaded fries with their beers last night, it had felt like a feast.

She quickly put last night out of her mind; otherwise, it might show on her face when filming this morning.

She was still in awe she and Bobby had made love, but also it had far exceeded anything she'd ever experienced with other lovers.

She caught herself smiling as she remembered she'd never been in love before. And that was the difference.

Once again, she forced herself to change her thoughts as she began making the oatmeal.

Not long after, Bobby came into the room carrying the Saturday morning paper. He kissed her neck from behind, tickling her slightly with his stubble.

"Good morning."

"Morning," she replied while turning. She then gave him a proper kiss as he settled his hands on her hips. They both smiled, allowing their lips to brush after the kiss.

He reluctantly pulled away to pour himself coffee before taking his seat at the table.

"Did you sleep well?" Bailey asked, settling into her role as the wife that had been forced to miss her date night because the "baby mama" had put on some unnecessary drama.

"Eh..." he shrugged. "Okay, I guess."

She had spooned oatmeal into bowls and brought them to the table.

"I was thinking," she began. He peered at her and lowered the paper. "Maybe you should take Paula's money to her on Saturdays. That way, it won't interfere with our date nights."

He nodded. "And I can handle that and visit my mom while you're at the hair salon. Brilliant."

"Brilliance is born out of necessity," she replied with a smirk. "I need for our date nights to be uninterrupted by drama."

His brow rose but he grinned. "Yes, ma'am." He spooned oatmeal into his mouth and gave an appreciative nod.

"We still have dinner with our neighbor—Haley, is it?"

"Yes. Haley Brinkman. I think we should make room in our budget to bring a bottle of wine."

He nodded. "We can get that when I pick you up after your appointment." He opened the paper again, but this time, he grinned. "Look at this, Bae."

He passed the paper to her and she laughed and clapped her hand over her mouth in actual pride.

"Honey! Your poll!" The full page was taken up with the poll results. The headline stated:

How McCarthy and His Policies Are Viewed By The Citizens of Wingate. Written by Robert Banks, Editor and contributing author.

Bailey got up and threw her arms around him. "We have to frame this and hang it in the office!"

He pulled her down onto his lap. "This is just the beginning, Bae. Mr. Adams told me he likes the fresh ideas I'm bringing to the paper. He says I'm sweeping out the stale ideas." He smirked mischievously. "That put a couple of the fellows on their toes." He kissed her. "I couldn't have done it without your help, and that includes the help of the other ladies."

"I'll be sure to thank them."

They looked over the results and it wasn't surprising that McCarthy's popularity had taken a nosedive.

She couldn't linger long; she quickly finished up the kitchen dishes, having learned that washing as she went made the cleanup quicker.

Afterwards, Bailey dressed casually in a skirt and a powder-blue blouse. Her curls were still in good condition but she pulled her hair back into a French twist, allowing enough of her bangs to swoop down across her forehead.

She applied her makeup a bit heavier than she would normally wear it. Most people at the salon looked like fashion models, and she certainly didn't want to look like chopped liver next to them.

After leaving the bedroom, Bailey found Bobby in the living room watching the morning news with the newspaper spread out before him.

Instead of simply reading it, he had his ink pen and was taking notes in the margins and circling other items.

"What are you doing?" she asked as she came to stand next to him.

"Forever searching for the next big story." He glanced up at her and did a double-take. "Look at you...are you sure you don't have a new man hidden away in that beauty shop?" He stood and pulled her close for a kiss.

She only gave him a quick peck before pulling back so as not to smudge her lipstick.

"There's no chance of that ever happening. I simply don't have the time for an affair."

His brow furrowed. "Okay…I guess that's good news."

Bailey laughed and headed for the closet for her coat.

Chapter Eighty-One

"What are you going to do while I'm getting my hair done?" Bailey asked after Bobby opened the car door for her. She could tell he wanted to touch her—hold her hand.

But PDA in 1954, even if it wasn't between two race-mixers, would not have been completely accepted. Instead, he leaned against the car and shoved his hands into the pockets of his slacks.

"The grass is slowing, so I don't think I'll need to mow. But I'll go to my mom's house and visit with her a while."

"Then when you get back can go pick up the wine—"

"It is you." The voice was coming from behind her where she stood on the sidewalk.

She turned to see none other than Mr. Edelman. The old man wore black pants held up by suspenders and a wrinkled, white shirt. He also wore a jacket, with a black felt hat pulled down on top of his head, which concealed most of his silver-white hair. He really looked like Archie Bunker from the old TV show *All in The Family*.

Edelman's face was etched with anger, and red blotches had sprouted on his cheeks and had completely covered his neck. In his hand was a folded newspaper. Ah...this morning's paper.

"You wrote these lies."

"Edelman." Bobby straightened, removing his hands from his pockets as if he might need to do more than verbally defend himself. "If you're referring to the article about Senator McCarthy, I assure you, these are strictly the opinions of *your* friends and neighbors."

"I knew you were a communist the first time I saw you!" Mr. Edelman spat. "I've been at that paper where you work, and believe me, buckaroo, I'll have you fired!"

Bobby crossed his arms and Bailey saw his jaw clench. "The paper is completely behind the article." He spoke in a mild voice, despite the color that had crept onto his own face. "But feel free to offer a review on this or any other article the *Gazette* prints. We completely believe in freedom of speech."

Edelman snorted and turned away. He caught sight of Bailey and walked past her, barely avoiding knocking into her.

Bobby quickly moved forward to make a grab for Edelman, but Bailey stopped him with a hand on his forearm. She shook her head and squeezed it gently.

He met her eyes and in that second, Bailey saw that Bobby had become lost in the scene. With a few blinks, he brought himself back.

Jeez, she frowned. Bobby hadn't been acting. If she hadn't caught his arm, what would he have done to Guy?

While Bailey got her hair done, she tried her best to have the same amount of fun she normally did during her Saturday visits to the salon.

Juanita hinted at a deeper relationship between her and her beau. Pat regaled them with stories about the factory and dates with her cheapskate boyfriend.

Of course, Miss Baker had to complain about something.

People came and they went. The gossip was plentiful, the music danceable, and the jokes always a bit raunchy.

But Bailey couldn't prevent her brain from unwanted speculations. She hoped her acting was as good as others seemed to think, because all she could think about was how far Bobby's quirkiness extended. She sometimes got the lines blurred, and evidently, so did he.

Bobby and Bailey were dressed in their "good" clothes for dinner with Haley.

Bobby wore a navy suit with slim pants that was completely unlike the khaki-colored slacks with their big cuffs he normally wore to work, along with a dark suit jacket and tie. With his shiny, black dress shoes and freshly cut hair laid back with pomade, he looked very '50s, and Bailey could now see how his aunt could compare him to Paul Newman.

She bit her lower lip when she looked at him with hands in his pockets the way men these days never could because they were all wearing skinny jeans.

But he was looking at her the same way. Bailey wore a burnt-orange cocktail dress with a matching waist-length jacket. She was also wearing high heels, not just those training kitten heels she'd thought were so hard to get used to. Thank God she'd trained with them because she walked smoothly in the pointy, black high heels.

She had pulled on stockings with actual seams along the back and clipped them on with an actual garter. This she did in the bathroom because although it was something done often in the '50s, nowadays, it would definitely make for a fetish scene.

For makeup, Bailey went with a harsh cat's-eye look. She'd wanted a light one but her hand had slipped and she'd had to overcompensate. It still looked good. She'd told Juanita about her dinner at the neighbor's—to which Miss Betty asked if it was dinner with *whites*. Once everyone knew Haley was white, Juanita had given her a special hairdo. It was an updo with side bangs and a teased mound on top.

As Juanita had teased her hair with a rattail comb and copious amounts of hairspray, Bailey had tried not to squirm.

"Won't this make my hair nappy on top?"

"Yep."

Juanita instructed her she'd just have to wear a beehive for the next week until she came back to have all the hairspray washed out.

For the finishing touch to her outfit, Bailey put on the pearls along with the matching pearl earrings.

The results were obviously good because with her "uniform" in place, Bobby seemed to forget how to speak.

"You look..." he said softly.

When he didn't finish, she grinned. "So do you."

He went to the closet for her coat and she shook her head and indicated she wanted the fur wrap. It wasn't made of real fox fur, despite the faux fox tails that hung from one end.

Once securely wrapped, he squeezed her shoulders and dipped his head to move his lips lightly along her jaw line, his body firm against her side.

Yeah, there was going to be some loving tonight, especially when she let him remove the stockings and garter.

Chapter Eighty-Two

Bobby and Bailey were sitting on the love seat at Haley's house. Each was holding a martini and smiling at Haley and her friend Jack.

Jack had been an unexpected addition to dinner — at least on the part of Bobby and Bailey.

"I read your article about McCarthy," Haley said while sitting next to Jack with a fresh drink in hand. "It's amazing how so many people support him."

Bobby nodded briefly. "It shows how the difference in generations have such a vast difference in opinions," Bobby replied.

Jack looked from her to Bobby. "That was you that wrote that article?" Jack was good-looking, with dark hair, dark eyes, and a rugged chin. He had that Don Draper from *Mad Men* look. He had been basically quiet over the last fifteen minutes, mostly discreetly watching Bailey.

"Yes," Bobby confirmed. "I wrote the article, but I can't take credit for those results. I would have liked to see them more on the liberal side — "

"But Wingate is a neighborhood with old people who have old ideas," Haley interrupted. She gave Bobby a winning smile. "It's nice to live next door to a couple of modern-thinking people." She turned to Jack. "I told you these two weren't the average couple with outdated ideas."

Jack's eyes swiftly took in Bailey's crossed legs. "Obviously."

"So, what do you do, Jack?" Bobby asked.

"I work with my hands."

Haley chuckled and leaned against him. "That you do."

Jack laughed. "I manage a construction crew."

"Jack's going to own his own construction company."

Jack shrugged. "Well, that's a work in progress."

Haley hooked her arm around his. "You'll do it, baby."

Jack responded to Bobby and not Haley. "Who wouldn't want to be an entrepreneur? But the economy doesn't favor that. Sometimes it's better to be safe than sorry. Being a foreman is nothing to sneeze at, you know?"

"True," Bobby agreed. "Especially if you like what you do."

"He's meant to work with his hands," Haley replied suggestively.

Jack untangled his arm from hers but then put it around her shoulders. He kissed her lightly. "You said you were going to behave."

Haley pouted. "That's no fun..."

Bobby and Bailey exchanged quick looks.

Haley jumped up. "Oops, gotta check the roast. I hope you like it rare. It's the only way to have a beef Wellington." She dashed to the kitchen.

Jack looked at Bailey. "Haley says you two are newlyweds."

"We've been married almost three months," Bailey replied.

"Do you like this suburban life?" he asked her.

"I..." she tried not to outright lie. "...probably need more time to decide."

Bobby gave her hand a light squeeze but directed his attention to Jack. "We've faced the ugly side of having neighbors—especially older ones in an older neighborhood."

Jack sipped his martini. "That's why it's so surprising a lady like Haley doesn't want to live in one of those fancy high-rises. She likes this small-town life, despite always complaining about it."

"There is something to be said for it when you come upon good people like Haley," Bailey said. "She's been so kind to me."

He smiled at her but didn't reply.

"Are you from Wingate?" Bobby asked. He sipped his drink but had been nursing it since they'd arrived. Bailey had done the same. It was a bit strong.

"Hell no. I moved here from New York—Manhattan." He leaned forward. "The money is in these little midwestern towns. The new trend is in cookie-cutter homes. I don't even have to think about how to build a ranch-style house. I could probably do it in my sleep!" Jack laughed. "No. If not for the work I'd be back in New York, lickety-split."

Haley returned then. "Oh, New York! I love the Big Apple! Have you two ever been?"

Bobby and Bailey both shook their heads.

"You have to go!" Haley exclaimed. "Especially Harlem! It's the Negro mecca!"

Bailey's brow went up and she smiled. "I heard the music is fantastic."

"If you like music, then Harlem is the place to be. I never danced so much as when I was at the Cotton club."

Jack smirked. "The Cotton Club isn't a Negro establishment. None of those clubs on Lennox Avenue are. If you want to see where the real parties are then you'll go to Spanish Harlem and hit the cabarets and lounges there."

"You're right. I was around too many mobsters. We were always at those ritzy clubs with the ritzy rich." Haley clapped her hands together and beamed. "The roast is ready. We can meet in the dining room. Bring your drinks, we'll have martinis and that wine you two brought."

They filed into the dining room and Bailey noted it was more traditionally decorated, although still had bits of whimsy.

There was a nice-sized dining room table with matching chairs and a china cabinet. Only instead of china, the cabinet held painted dolls and clowns.

The paintings on the wall consisted of barely covered nudes. Some even looked like Haley. The walls were painted a dark green, which might have made the room dark if not for about twenty candles that created a warm glow.

"I love how you decorated this room," Bailey said. "Your entire house is so pretty."

"Thank you. I had those pictures commissioned from an amazing artist when I lived in Hollywood. He painted Jane Russell—but it wasn't quite as sexy as mine."

Everyone gazed at her semi nudes before Bailey moved to take her seat and Bobby quickly pulled her chair out for her. Jack did the same for Haley. Haley looked at her beau.

"Jack, why don't you carve the roast? And mind you don't tear the puff pastry."

He sliced through the beef, revealing rare medallions surrounded by pate and lightly browned pastry. Bailey didn't often like the sight of red juice seeping out of her meat, but she had to admit it looked and smelled delicious.

In addition to the beef Wellington was roasted asparagus, pureed carrots, and thyme roasted red potatoes. Haley took a great deal of pride in announcing each dish.

Bailey gave Haley an appreciative look after biting into the flavorful roast. "This is delicious."

"It is," Bobby replied enthusiastically. Neither of them were exaggerating. Bailey wondered if it had been catered.

Haley gave them knowing looks. "My mama taught me the best way to a man's heart is through his stomach, so I made sure to learn to cook."

"She was a wise woman," Jack replied while chewing.

It seemed to Bailey the conversation became easier as they ate and talked, and the pinot noir didn't hurt.

"Have you joined a bridge group yet with the rest of the old fogies...or do you prefer more youthful entertainment?" Haley asked while sipping her wine.

"I don't know if playing bridge is our thing," Bobby replied. He slipped the last bit of roast into his mouth. Haley rose and quickly slid another slice of roast onto his plate and added potatoes and asparagus.

"There you go," Haley said. "There's plenty for seconds, and even thirds." Bobby smiled appreciatively.

"We've been kind of busy," Bailey said. "You know, with the new house. But we've gone out a few times." She exchanged looks with Bobby. "But we might be more of the stay-at-home type." He nodded his agreement.

"What?" Jack smiled. "You can't tell me a pretty girl like you didn't get swamped with dates."

Bailey shrugged. "I was a college girl, and I took my studies seriously. It cost my aunt and uncle a lot to help me get through college. After that I got a job at the bank and...well, here I am." She smiled and shrugged.

"Pretty and educated," Jack observed.

Bailey blushed. "Thank you."

"Bailey's accomplishments don't stop there," Bobby added. His eyes twinkled in a way that said he'd definitely enjoyed the food and drink. "She's a fine decorator, a good cook..." Bailey rolled her eyes at that and Bobby placed his hand over hers. "You're getting there, Bae." He turned his attention back to Jack. "The best thing might sound like a cliché, but my wife is also my best friend."

"That is so sweet," Haley said. "Without trust, no relationship can prosper. Isn't that right, Jack?"

Jack was looking at Bobby steadily. "That's true. Everything in life is about respect and trust. If your relationship has that, then...you can explore so many possibilities..."

Bobby cocked his head inquisitively but then raised his wine glass. "I toast to that."

Haley raised her glass and the rest followed suit. "Trust and respect."

"So, how long have you two been a couple?" Bailey asked.

Haley smirked. "We're not actually…a couple."

"We're friends," Jack concurred. "Good friends."

"Oh, I'm sorry —" Bailey began.

"It's fine," Haley said with a wave of her hand. "Neither of us believe in the constraints of…" Haley looked into the air as if in deep thought. "…traditional relationships."

Jack shrugged. "She just means we're free to date whomever we like." His eyes lingered on her. "What kind of man would I be to clip her wings…"

"It's not that I have anything against marriage." Haley poured more wine into her glass and topped off Bobby's glass, leaving the bottle empty. "I love the idea of marriage, just not the boredom that goes along with it."

"We haven't had time to get bored," Bobby said while exchanging looks with Bailey as if to confirm his words.

"I agree…I'm still trying to get a handle on being a housewife."

"Well, you must promise me you two won't ever turn into a bunch of stuffy suburbanites!"

"That's not likely to happen," Bobby smirked. "Half the neighborhood wants us out."

Haley waved her hand and lit a cigarette. "Don't worry about them. I have friends that are open-minded and loyal. I'll introduce you. I have a feeling you two will fit right in."

She suddenly leaned forward. "Say, you two should come to our next mixer. It's couples only, and best of all, they are very open-minded — the way we are."

Bobby's brow went up and he gave Bailey a glance before nodding his head. "We don't know very many couples. But if they are as friendly as you and Jack, then we'd be happy to meet them."

Okay then, Bailey thought. Here we go with the swingers story line...

"That sounds like fun. But maybe everyone should be made aware we're an interracial couple—"

"Oh," Haley smiled. "You aren't the only ones." She patted Bailey's hand and allowed it to linger. "Relax, Bailey. I told you our friends are open-minded, just like me and Jack."

Chapter Eighty-Three

"They were so nice," Bobby said as they entered their house.

"I know. I'm so happy you finally got a chance to meet her."

Bobby helped her take off her fur, where he hung it in the closet.

"Yeah, I am too. If only all of the neighbors were as friendly," he replied.

"Right. I was wondering if we would ever fit in," Bailey said, and Bobby pulled her into his arms.

"Haley is right; we need to meet more young couples like us."

"And one of them is a mixed-race couple! Maybe they can give us pointers on adjusting."

"It'd be nice to compare notes, but I don't agree that we need any help adjusting." He kissed her nose.

"True," she conceded. "I think it's everyone else that needs to adjust to us."

It was Sunday, Bailey's day off. She stretched in bed. It felt good to linger.

She turned and snuggled against Bobby's nude body, appreciating the hard lines and the soft down of the hair on his chest. He stretched, and eyes still closed, he wrapped his arms around her and pulled her close.

"Morning," he mumbled.

"Good morning. We should sleep in."

He turned while facing her, his hands moving up and down her arm. "That sounds wonderful. But that might have to wait until next week. When we have today's meeting, I plan to tell everyone we'll be transitioning to using Zoom calls for the meetings." He sat up. "I know you spend Sundays with your aunt and uncle, but I was hoping next Sunday, you'd join me for lunch with my mom. I want to introduce you two."

Bailey nodded. "Okay." Her voice might have been calm, but she was nervous. While meeting a boyfriend's parents was a big step, she wasn't sure what this meeting meant. Was he doing it because her aunt and uncle had invited him to dinner, and he felt as if he had to reciprocate? Was this the visit that said, Mom, this is the one?

"So, what are your plans for the day?" Bobby asked as he got up to dress.

"Well, I'd like to visit my aunt and uncle, and maybe talk to them about doing video conference meetings in the future. What about you?" she asked.

He quickly pulled on his boxers. "I have some ideas for certain characters and I want to get them written out."

"Did you write Jack's character?"

He grinned. "I just put in his script that he was to follow Haley's lead." He turned to her as he zipped up his pants. "Aren't you going to ask about the swinging story line?"

She smirked. "I'd be pretty surprised if Bobby wanted to be into something like. I think I'll let it play out on its own."

He nodded while smiling.

They had bacon and eggs for breakfast, along with toast and large cups of coffee to get them through the busy day.

They arrived at the meeting in a timely manner — for probably the first time ever — and Bailey was surprised to see that not only was Helen missing, but so was Paula. The latter didn't bother her at all.

Bailey just enjoyed seeing the faces of her teammates, both old and new.

"Many of you will see that your scripts will give you new objectives; some short-term, while others will be long-term." He passed out scripts as he spoke, handing one to Bailey. "Not everyone will get a script, and it doesn't mean you will be cut from production. We need every warm body possible. It just means you will go through your day-to-day activities as normal."

Bobby perched himself on the edge of his desk and looked out at them as if they were students and he was the fun, nerdy teacher.

"It wouldn't hurt to also touch up on phrases and history. I appreciate those that contributed to the discussions on McCarthyism. But I also need you to speak about music and books and other local news. So, I pulled some information together and you'll find it on the cast's docking page."

"Who's got time to study history?" Juanita frowned. "When I get out of the hair salon, get dinner and spend on-screen time dating, I don't even have time to hit the factory to relax."

A few people quietly agreed.

"That brings up another topic," Bobby said. He nodded at Juanita. "And thank you for bringing that up. What do you all think about holding our weekly meetings remotely instead of dragging ourselves all the way to the production office?"

"Hell yeah!" Hank exclaimed.

There wasn't a person present that didn't like the idea.

"Well," Bobby continued while holding up his hands to quiet everyone. "I know your time at the factory is part of your free time. And I don't want to impede on that by turning it into more work." He stood and reached into a cabinet, where he pulled out several iPads. "So, from this moment on, everyone will be able to take this home—"

The cheer of gratitude was so loud it drowned Bobby out. He continued with a laugh. "Look, guys, I'm taking a big leap of faith. This is only to be used after filming. *And*, if I catch sight of anyone's iPad in a shot, I'm going to take them from everyone. And I'm going to announce who the offender was. So..." Everyone chuckled. "Just be careful."

The meeting ended with everyone in high spirits and clutching their electronic devices as if they were gold bars. Bailey had scanned her script and the only direction it pointed to was she was to be open for a phone call from Pat, and Monday she'd get an unexpected visitor.

Once the room was empty, she went up to Bobby and held the script up. "An unexpected visitor?"

"Anita," he confessed.

"Mr. Edelman's sister?"

"Yep."

"Okay..." Edelman had remained the morose old man that barely acknowledged anyone, and unsurprisingly, she still didn't like him.

He pulled her in for a kiss. "Don't worry. She has the direction on how the visit will go. And it was her idea. I like it."

Bailey kissed him. "Okay. I won't ask for any more hints."

"Good. Now how much time do you have before you leave for your aunt and uncle's house?"

"Well, it depends..."

His hands rested on her waist. "Tell your aunt and uncle hello and thank them for dinner last week. Drive safe. And if your aunt has any leftovers..."

Bailey laughed and kissed him. "Duly noted."

Dinner with her aunt and uncle did result in plenty of leftovers. And surprisingly, some of Aunt Mae's friends were also there for dinner. All, including Aunt Mae, were disappointed Bobby hadn't come along.

"Aunt Mae, this is our time."

"Yes, but I still see you and that young man is in need of some good home cooking!"

Bailey suppressed the urge to roll her eyes. "So, remember when you said it would be okay to do Zoom meetings instead of driving out here once a week?"

"Of course! Baby girl, I know you're young and you don't have much free time. And I'm sure you want to spend some of your off day with your beau."

"She lives with him, Mae." Uncle Dewbug scowled. "How much more time do you think they need?"

Bailey's face warmed, and she quickly changed the subject. She'd successfully avoided an embarrassing conversation about shacking up with a man she had only just met. And she didn't want to explain that being with Bobby didn't feel like she'd only just met him.

She didn't even understand it herself. She was a sensible girl, but Bobby had quickly taken root in her heart in a way no other man ever had—not even one that had been a much longer-term relationship.

She wanted to tell them she was meeting his mother next week, but she still had too many questions and decided to wait until after it was done.

They confirmed Thanksgiving together, and her aunt made sure she invited Bobby.

"I'll invite him, but he's a Chesterfield. Maybe he has rich-people plans." She was only half joking.

Aunt Mae huffed. "Well, I hope you don't have any plans to fly off to Acapulco with that family. Don't get me wrong, I like Bobby. But that daddy of his is a snake in the grass!"

Uncle Dewbug's brow dipped low. "If he tries any shenanigans with you, you tell me. I'll do to him what them other daddies should have done when he got caught with them girls."

"Believe me," Bailey said. "I will never be caught alone with Robert's father. I doubt if he'll ever even introduce us. We haven't talked much about the man, but I get the feeling he doesn't completely approve of his father."

She didn't want to probe too deeply into Bobby's personal life, but she was curious about his exact stance where his father was concerned.

After she left her aunt and uncle's house—along with leftover pot roast and fixings—Bailey's curiosity caused her to stop at a local McDonald's. It wasn't to grab some fast food, but to power up her iPad and Google Robert Chesterfield Jr.

Chapter Eighty-Four

Robert Allen Chesterfield Junior is the second child and first son of ex-congressman Robert Allen Chesterfield Senior and his first wife, Gloria Margaret Chesterfield (nee Straub).

The fact page went on to give age and approximate wealth. It talked about two prior girlfriends. One was the daughter of a B-lister movie star. The other was the daughter of a senator.

Bailey studied the photos of Bobby with the other girls. Both were pretty, but it was strange seeing him with someone that didn't look like her. But just because a man dated outside of his race once didn't mean he always had. She was apparently the first Black girl.

In one picture, the two appeared to be on the red carpet. He looked good in a tuxedo, and the brunette was dressed in a fashionable gown—probably something she wouldn't be able to afford if she saved for a year.

The next photo was a lot older, and he looked barely twenty years old. He was with a group of friends seated around a table with the backdrop of the ocean. He was laughing and having fun, and the girl that clung to his arm was pretty, and probably as rich as he was.

She moved on to the rest of the information, which stated he lived in Los Angeles. Well, that wasn't true. Bailey closed out that information and moved to the next piece.

Robert Chesterfield Jr. purchases LLC with help from Daddy. Disgraced congressman Robert Chesterfield is rumored to be the silent partner is his namesake's venture into reality television.

The younger Chesterfield is producing a show that explores life in the 1950s Midwest. The streaming reality series will have no Hollywood actors, while certainly having a Hollywood budget.

The show is being marketed to the rich friends and family of Chesterfield's parents at a staggering price of five thousand dollars a month for full access into the small-town life—

Bailey closed the article. It was mean-spirited. Also, she didn't like feeling as if she was spying on her boyfriend. Just because he was a public figure and had an Internet presence didn't mean what was written was truthful. People didn't like his father, and that meant they probably wouldn't like him either. Besides, what did she expect to find by searching for him on the Internet?

She resumed her drive and arrived at the production office just as the sun was setting.

"Hey, honey. I'm here," she said into her cell phone once she was parked.

"I'm on my way out. Did your aunt send me food?"

"Of course. You gave her a role in the production. She'll probably send you food for the next year."

"Good."

When Bailey met Helen for their weekly excursion to the grocery store, the two friends hugged and talked as if they hadn't seen each other in a year instead of just a week.

"Oh, Bailey!" she exclaimed after a few moments of shopping. "I gotta tell you something!"

"What?" Bailey asked.

Helen nipped her bottom lip lightly. "I...I met someone."

Bailey's brow went up. "Are you saying you...?"

"I'm not having an affair!" Helen added quickly. "Well...not yet."

"Helen!" Bailey grabbed her hand. "We need to sit and have a cup of coffee. I'll gladly go off budget a little for this!"

"I don't dare." Helen lowered her voice. "I don't want anyone to overhear." They continued shopping, their steps slower as they kept their heads close.

"Is it the encyclopedia salesman?"

Helen nodded. Her cheeks were flushed. "His name is Quinton. Oh, Bailey, he's so sweet. Don't get me wrong. I love Hank, but he takes everything for granted. He thinks his laundry washes itself and the food just magically appears on his plate. To be honest, I like it when he's gone during the week. And I wasn't looking to fall for someone else. I've never done anything like this before. You believe me, don't you?"

"Of course I do."

"I know it's bad, but Quinton makes me feel young and beautiful again. He makes me feel wanted. No. Desired."

Bailey smiled. "Every woman should feel that way. But, Helen, where do you see this going?"

Helen lightly drew her lip in again. "I don't know. I honestly don't know. Do you think it's crazy a woman can love two men at once?"

"Do you think you love Quinton?"

Red crept up her neck and engulfed her face. "Maybe. It's so silly. I just met him! But all I do is think of him. I go to sleep with our phone conversations on my mind, and I wake up not able to wait to tell him good morning."

Bailey listened to Helen sing Quinton's praises and she felt bad she hadn't been watching the story after hours. The truth was, she really was beginning to buy into Bobby's narrative. The story line was much more satisfying when she allowed it to unfold naturally.

Also, there was the fact that she was involved with more interesting nighttime endeavors now that her and Bobby's relationship had moved to the next level.

But as she listened to Helen, something told her there was more than acting going on with her and Quinton. Well, one thing was for certain, 1954 was much more interesting when there was someone there to hold your attention.

When Bailey got home, she very nearly forgot about the scheduled visit with Anita until the doorbell rang. She jumped and made a weird squeaking noise.

Bailey took off her apron and hurried to the door, happy she hadn't changed into something more relaxing after her trip to the grocery store.

A pot of chili was already simmering away on the stove, so she didn't have to worry about that, and she hadn't whipped up the cornbread yet.

She dutifully looked out the front window and saw the small woman standing on her front stoop.

She plastered on a look of confusion, although it wasn't completely false, and she opened the door.

Anita smiled and waved. It was such a youthful thing to do despite her being a woman in her fifties, that Bailey smiled. She stepped out onto her porch instead of inviting the semi-stranger into her house.

"Hello," she greeted.

"Hi. I'm Anita Edelman. I helped with your husband's poll."

Anita was just as quirky as ever. Today, instead of pigtails, her ultra-black hair hung to her shoulders, where it was cut as blunt as her bangs.

She still wore the cat's-eye glasses and had on a big, wool coat, as well as loose, black pants that looked like they might have been made of felt. On her feet were black boots that were far from feminine. She had a different bruise on her cheek, as if she was a clumsy adolescent with a penchant for walking into doors.

"I remember you, Anita," Bailey said. "And by the way, thank you. I asked Helen to send you my thanks—"

"Oh, she did. And it was my pleasure."

Anita didn't speak, and Bailey stepped aside and opened her door. "Would you like to come in?"

"Sure. Thank you."

Anita came in and walked right to the living room, where she unbuttoned her coat and sat on the sofa.

"Would you like something to drink? I have Coca-Cola, and there is coffee. Or I could make some tea—"

"Coca-Cola," Anita said. Bailey hurried into the kitchen for two Cokes and two glasses of ice. She sat opposite Anita on the edge of the armchair.

"The article my husband wrote was a big success. A lot of people in town participated."

"I read the article. I managed to get to it before my brother did. You're probably wondering what I'm doing here," Anita said after pouring cola into her glass until it nearly fizzed over.

Bailey eyed the near disaster, imagining cleaning sticky beverage off the rug. But Anita managed to save that from happening by taking a big slurp of the foam.

Afterwards, she settled back to look at Bailey. "I was there when Guy threatened your husband." Bailey nodded, but waited for her to continue. "That was a bad thing for him to do. My daddy always said there are two things you don't do; take what ain't yours, and mess with a man's money."

Obviously, Anita was playing the role of a woman her aunt would have called a little *off*. She talked like a child of about ten.

"You're a Negress, but that ain't even the worst thing in the world." Anita leaned forward. "Worse than that is being in the KKK and doing bad things to people."

"I agree," Bailey said slowly. "Anita, does your brother do bad things to people?"

Anita drank some Coke and looked into the distance. "Only to Negroes and Jews. But they don't do those things in town. Guy says everybody will point fingers at him if he gets involved in business here." She met Bailey's eyes. "But he might. He been talking about it a lot lately—especially after that newspaper article your husband wrote."

Bailey's breath caught. "Your brother's planning to do something to my husband?"

"Not Klan business. But he's going to try to get your husband fired. He's got a whole lot of people willing to say he lied on that poll. But I know no one did. But he's going to get people to say it just the same."

Jesus... "I appreciate you telling me this. I'm sure it's probably hard to go against your brother."

Anita touched her bruised cheek. "Yes. But Daddy said right is right and wrong is wrong. And Guy is wrong for this."

Bailey's brow was gathered. "Does your brother hit you, Anita?"

Anita shrugged. "Sometimes he belts me if I get too mouthy."

"But you're his sister!"

Anita shrugged again. "I'm a burden, is what I am. I ain't never gonna get married on account I can't tolerate men. I rather love a woman; but Guy says that's a sin. So, he has to take care of me. Sometimes, it makes him mad." She gave Bailey a fearful look. "I ain't supposed to tell nobody about me liking girls. But it's okay to tell you since you're a Negro, right?"

"It's okay to tell me because I'm a friend."

Anita nodded enthusiastically. "You are Helen's friend. She's a nice lady—I don't like her, though! Not like that!"

"It's fine." Bailey tried to smile, but it didn't feel authentic. What kind of monster was Guy Edelman?

Anita hopped to her feet. "I gotta go before Guy gets home. He always wants to know where I've been." She thrust her glass to Bailey. It only had ice. She'd drained it. "I don't know why he thinks it's so bad I'm a spinster. He ain't never been married either!"

She went to the door, with Bailey following. "I appreciate the information, Anita. Your brother won't find out from us what you told me."

"That's good. If he finds out I've been running my mouth, he'll get BIG mad."

"Anita…" The woman turned and looked at Bailey before walking out the door. "Is there any place else you can go—you know, to live?"

"Why would I do that? We have a great house. The best in the neighborhood. Guy thinks the Negroes are going to eventually turn our street into a slum." She gave Bailey a half smile. "But I look at your yard, and it's prettier than some of the white people's yards. It sure made Guy mad when I pointed that out. Don't tell anybody, but I like Mr. Curtis, the milkman. He always smiles and says nice things to me."

Bailey nodded. "He is kind."

Anita hurried out the door. "Bye, Bailey. Sorry I can't come back to visit. You're a nice lady."

"It's okay, Anita. I understand. Take care of yourself."

Anita hurried down the street.

Chapter Eighty-Five

Bobby's chili and cornbread sat untouched as he listened to his wife.

As soon as he'd sat down for dinner, Bailey told him about Anita's visit.

"I'm not even worried about him trying to get me fired," Bobby said tightly. "I'm more worried about him using his sister as a punching bag."

"I hate it too. But, babe, he's in the Klan, and my focus is on that. I know you don't have the same...experience. But I know what they do to people like us. US, Bobby! Race-mixers!"

He stood and pulled her into his arms. "I'm not a Negro, Bae. But I work for a newspaper. I'm not wearing blinders. But I'm also not going to run." He sighed. "My dad had a gun—"

"Oh, Bobby!"

"I know, honey. I know." He kissed her forehead. "I don't want to have to shoot anybody. But let someone set foot on this property that intends to do harm to me or mine and I will blow a hole straight through their heads!"

She closed her eyes and rested her head against his chest.

I hate 1954.

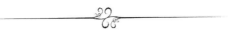

When Pat called Bailey on Tuesday, there was lots to talk about. She didn't dare tell Aunt Mae about her conversation with Anita out of fear her aunt might clam up out of rage—or even worse, go out of character.

And talking to Helen about her concerns about Edelman seemed pointless. So, Pat ended up being the one who got an earful.

"Look, sis," Bailey heard Pat say with unmistakable worry. "Under normal circumstances, I would never say this. But maybe you and Bobby should really consider leaving that neighborhood and moving to Garden Hills. I mean, they are building a very nice community here. I'm not saying it won't be a little hard, because there are Coloreds that dislike race-mixing just as much as whites. But at least no one here will be burning a cross in your front yard."

Bailey sighed, actually considering Pat's suggestion. If she truly lived in 1954 without the same understanding of equality she had been raised with, would she truly choose to live in this all-white neighborhood?

"Maybe this is something Bobby and I will have to really consider," Bailey finally conceded. "I love this house, Pat. This is our first home together and we've already made so many memories. But I'm beginning to not feel safe here."

"I'm so sorry, sis. You know...I've been attending meetings. Me and Marvin. It's at the old church on Kennedy Avenue. Negroes are getting together, talking about a revolution."

"Are you talking about a race war?" Bailey asked incredulously.

"Why did you all of a sudden sound like a white girl?" Pat chuckled. Bailey smiled too. "No. We're not talking about creating a war. But we are talking about ending our acceptance of racism. Bailey. This has got to end. We can't continue ignoring the mistreatment, accepting Jim Crow, being bullied and mistreated. I can't continue ignoring it."

"I hate it too," Bailey said. "People think being someplace other than the South means being a Negro is easy."

"Right. Did you know Mayor George has denied the raises for all non-white city workers? That includes the Hispanics, and even the Jews. And I know you've seen more of those Whites Only signs."

"Yes," she sighed.

"Bailey, there's a rally this Friday. You and Bobby should consider attending. He'd be the only white face, but he's married to you—so we'll give him a pass."

Bailey smiled. "I don't know if Bobby will want to come. But I know I do."

"Good, sis. The more people we can get, the better our chances for success."

That night when Bobby got home, they didn't snuggle on the couch or watch *The Honeymooners*. They talked. They sat at the kitchen table and they discussed moving, Edelman, and attending Pat's meeting.

Bobby's eyes were lit with a fire she'd never seen. "Yes, I'll go. But as much as I want to be a different type of man, Bae...I don't know how far I'm willing to go with this. I have you, a home, and a baby to take care of. This could affect my job."

She squeezed his hands. "But I want to be involved."

"I'm afraid," Bobby said after a few minutes. "I'm scared of something happening to you. I hear about these sit-ins that have been going on. People are getting beat by the police, even when they're being peaceful. If someone hurts you, Bae..."

She swallowed. "They *are* hurting me, Bobby. And you too. And if we have children and don't do anything, they're going to hurt them as well. I have to believe people are ready for a change. Look at Helen and me. Look at Haley Brinkman, and even Anita. Those white people didn't have to reach out to me— to us—and yet they have. I have to believe there are more good people than ignorant ones."

He kissed her hand. "I love you so much. I'm in it with you, all the way."

"Baby girl, what is on your mind?"

"What?" Bailey's brow shot up. "Aunt Mae, what do you mean?"

"I have been telling you about that jezebel Janice Sturgis from down the street, and the scandalous way she has been flirting with the mailman and you only said uh-huh. I think if I would have said a parade of African wildebeest was roaming downtown Dayton you would have just said, 'Oh really...'"

Bailey cracked a smile. "I'm sorry." Bailey stretched the phone cord until she could plop down into one of the kitchen chairs. She had not talked to her *real* Aunt Mae about the sudden direction change in the show, but the way she watched, Bailey was sure she was aware.

Mae was giving her a subtle hint that she wanted to be included—at least in the sage manner Aunt Mae had acted throughout her entire life.

Well, Bobby had included her in the show for a good reason, and she trusted her aunt's acting. Over the last few days, she had cut up enough that Bobby would end the day laughing at her way of wording things.

"Aunt Mae has so many fans. People want to see what she looks like. Bailey, if she wasn't married to your uncle, I'd hire her to join the crew in a second."

Bailey had to ask him not to tell her aunt or she just might leave Uncle Dewbug for a year.

Okay. She would stop holding back her aunt's involvement. With a sigh, Bailey pretended to tentatively broach the subject. "Aunt Mae, I've been seriously thinking about us moving out of this neighborhood and into an all-Negro one."

"You have?" Aunt Mae replied, sounding authentically surprised.

"Yes. There's a new community here that's all-Negro—and I'm not talking about a slum, either. I've heard good things about it from my friend Pat. They are forming a community committee, they have a Negro-owned bank and a Negro-grocery store that is scheduled to open in time for Thanksgiving. There are parks, theaters—"

"That sounds nice. But you and Bobby sank all of your savings into that house you're living in. And I swear you love it almost as much as you love that husband of yours." Bailey looked down with a sigh.

"Have you had more problems with them neighbors of yours?"

"There's just one neighbor, really. I told you about that poll Bobby created."

"Yes. About that McCarthy character. He been treating some white people the way they've been treating Coloreds. I know all about him."

Bailey told her about Mr. Edelman's threats to Bobby and how he was even going to go as far as to make it seem as if Bobby had manufactured the votes in order to invalidate the results.

"That is vile," her aunt shot back.

"Bobby already talked to his boss about it, and they have all of the polls with addresses and signatures, so he's not worried about his job. But that man already hated us for all the reasons people like him hate people like us. And when his plan fails, I think he's just going to try something else. Aunt Mae, Bobby brought a gun into the house!"

"Oh, Bailey!" Aunt Mae cried. "I warned you against this! I knew this kind of mess was going to happen!"

Bailey rubbed her temple. "Aunt Mae, please. I didn't tell you so you could say I told you so!"

"I'm not trying to tell you I told you so! I'm trying to tell you your marriage is more than the average marriage. It's more work, more roadblocks, and more heartache. There are so many people like you and Bobby that didn't make it, baby girl. They were hung from trees, drowned in rivers, beaten and imprisoned—including people that did a whole lot worse in the eyes of the ignorant people of the world.

"But you and Bobby are smart, and I know you went into this with your eyes open. It's like those white people you've made friends with. You just got invited to one of their parties! You are a good person, Bailey, and you opened yourself to them with the same grace you've always allowed people into your life — and that includes a white man that couldn't help but fall in love with you."

Tears unexpectedly began to wet Bailey's eyes. Oh my God...Aunt Mae was killing it. But her speech had touched her on another level — beyond her being able to act in a reality show that was airing to a bunch of privileged rich people. It touched her that she was speaking truth to a bunch of privileged rich people that called you disrespectful, unpatriotic, or accused you of stirring a pot that needed to be doused if you spoke about racial disparity in any other forum besides entertainment.

"Aunt Mae, I don't know what to do...I want to stand up and fight, but I'm so scared. I don't want Bobby to lose his job or get hurt or...but there's a meeting Friday. People are getting together to talk about the mayor's racist agenda, and about making Wingate a community for *all* people. I talked Bobby into going, but what if I made a mistake? What if we lose everything we've been trying so hard to hold onto?"

She heard her aunt sigh. "That's not a decision anyone but you and Bobby can make for yourselves. I certainly won't think badly of you regardless of the decision you make. When I was a little girl..." Aunt Mae sniffed. "Well...let's just say there have always been people that spoke up and *showed* up! Little Linda

Brown tried to go to an all-white school. I read about what she went through. A *little girl*. But because of her, we finally won the right to send our kids to the good schools where the white kids go!

"If you ask me what you should do, all I can say is you are already doing it."

Tears had spilled from Bailey's eyes and she quickly sniffed and wiped them away. "Thank you, Aunt Mae. I love you."

She could hear the tears in her own aunt's voice as she replied, "Well, you are welcome. You'll call me after you go to the meeting, right?"

"How—?" Bailey chuckled. "Yes, Auntie. I will call you after we go." Her aunt knew she didn't have any other decision but to attend.

What a week. A meeting for civil rights on Friday, and a swingers mixer on Saturday. Hello, 1954.

Chapter Eighty-Six

Bobby and Bailey walked hand in hand into the Garden Hills Church of God and Christ. Signs pointed them to a large room where folding chairs had been set up in front of a stage.

People were milling around, and she was suddenly reminded of when she'd asked Bruce Adams about the number of people of color on set and the number had been so low he could basically name them.

Now, it was a different story. There weren't just Blacks present, but Hispanics one Asian man...and another white man; Carl from the picnic—Carl who had announced that the only reason he'd agreed to stay in front of the camera was to be an ally for Bobby and Bailey.

He was standing at a table of refreshments holding a cup of coffee. When he saw her look in his direction, he gave her a partial smile and a head nod of agreement. He then popped the remains of a cookie into his mouth.

His wife Shirley was nowhere in sight. Bailey returned the short greeting.

Pat hurried to them and she hugged Bailey and did the same to Bobby.

"I'm so happy you two came." She looked around in pride. "Look at the turn out and still more people are coming.

Bailey saw a number of faces she recognized, including the women from the beauty shop and Curtis Jackson—Milkman Curtis.

"Thank you for inviting us," Bobby said. Marvin was by Pat's side and they shook hands.

"I'm happy to see you were interested in attending." Marvin said.

Bobby nodded. "Bailey and I have basically been here for a while now."

Marvin's shoulders relaxed and he smiled and clapped Bobby on the back. "Yes, sir. You two have been on the front lines. Come on in and let me get you a cup of coffee."

Bobby allowed Marvin to lead him away as she and Pat talked. Pat held her hand enthusiastically.

"Oh, sis. I'm so happy to see you! We actually managed to get in touch with a representative of the NAACP who agreed to attend the meeting."

"Oh my God," she craned her neck to look around. "That's big, Pat! It's not Thurgood Marshall, is it?"

"No," Pat said. "Mr. Marshall is pretty busy after his big win with the Brown versus Board of Education case. A lot of communities are being fueled by that win and are forming committees just like this one. Sis," Pat said proudly. "What's happening now is a movement; a real movement. This is big."

Friday night, as the cameras stopped rolling and Bobby and Bailey had retreated to their bedroom, Bailey jumped into his arms.

"Babe, that went so well!"

He held her close, his forehead touching hers. He didn't respond but they held onto each other for a while, just swaying together. After a minute or two, he met her eyes.

"I need to do some homework tonight."

She smirked. "It's been a minute since you've had to do that. Sure, honey. Are you going to the production office?"

"No, I can use the office here."

Bailey noted that his expression was serious.

"Is everything okay? Didn't you think it went well?"

He finally smiled as his blue eyes locked onto hers. "Better than I ever imagined."

"You know, I'm happy you chose Pat to usher in the civil rights movement to Wingate. Her enthusiasm is so real! I'm loving it."

His brow gathered as he looked at her. "She is good. We have a great team and" — he blew out a long breath — "it's going to be tough. But we're working to make it awesome."

"Don't tell me!" she said. "I want it to be authentic when I find out what you two have up your sleeves."

He nodded and kissed her. "All parties are sworn to secrecy. And besides, it's not my story line." He gave her a pointed look before kissing her nose before leaving the room.

Bailey cocked her head. She had no doubt it would be hard, but over the weeks, she had grown as an actor and she would make sure that when the time was right, she would react as Bailey Banks and not with the confusion of Bailey Westbrook.

The next day when she went to the beauty salon, Bailey expected they would discuss yesterday's meeting, as everyone present had been there. But no one brought it up.

Was this the way it was in the '50s? You protected your friends and neighbors by not openly discussing or speculating about the meetings?

Instead, they talked about how good the cookie lady's butter cookies were today and how some days they were a tiny bit burnt around the edges. They talked about the Big Joe Turner concert in Cincinnati where there was going to be a rhythm and blues revue. Apparently, people had taken Bobby's suggestion to do more research on the current events of the time.

Juanita paused in doing the head she was pressing and hurried over to turn off the radio. She put on the "Shake, Rattle and Roll" record by Big Joe Turner, and Pat and a few of the other ladies began to dance. Bailey clapped and tapped her feet from her position under the hair dryer.

No. She didn't hate 1954. It was actually pretty cool.

At the house, she got dressed in a black cocktail dress with her high heels.

Juanita had done an amazing job with her hair, trimming it so it really did make her feel as if she was Dorothy Dandridge—well, maybe not quite as pretty.

Bailey studied her trimmed-down body in the full-length mirror and straightened the seam down the back of her nylons.

No. She took that back. She would embody the spirt of Dorothy Dandridge. She was beautiful.

When she returned to the living room, Bobby was holding a bottle of wine. He gave her a confused look.

"Do you take wine to a party?"

"I think so. I've never been to a mixed-race party, but Colored people wouldn't be caught dead going to a party without bringing their own booze."

Bobby gnawed his lip and nodded. "Okay. Wine, because that's our booze of choice."

"I don't know, honey. I'm beginning to develop a taste for cocktails."

He gave her a light kiss on the lips. "We can't afford to cultivate that mentality."

"Fine," she smirked.

"And by the way, how is it possible you get more beautiful each day?"

"I'm not," she replied shyly. "A little makeup and a visit to the hair salon goes a long way."

He shook his head and when she tried to pull away, he held her close. "No. You are breathtaking. In every way, Bae."

"You're not so bad yourself, Mr. Banks."

The drive to the party was uneventful—mainly because there wasn't a cameraman in the car with them. Bobby did, however, turn on his rockabilly music, and she had to admit she didn't altogether dislike it. In fact, she found herself once or twice singing along to a catchy tune.

They drove towards Garden Hills, in the newly developed area Bobby had worked so hard on.

Even though it was dusk, she saw the people driving or walking down the streets. They were people that actually lived here in this new community, and not just waiting to act out a role.

People went in and out of shops and buildings and houses just as if this was the world outside of a massive set.

She looked at Bobby in awe, who acknowledged her with a smile as he continued driving down the street of a world he had created.

That article that hinted that Robert Chesterfield Jr. had sunk his daddy's money into a project doomed for failure should really be looking at this now, because they had completely missed the point.

Chapter Eighty-Seven

They drove down a nice residential street. The houses were all new, but someone had taken the time to weather some of the wood for some houses. Mature trees had been planted, and someone had taken enough attention to detail to make things look old—even going as far as leaving a broken-down car in someone's driveway. Bailey was completely in awe.

They walked hand in hand to the house. She clutched her fur wrap close and prided herself on not twisting her ankle in the high heels.

Once Bobby rang the doorbell, the butterflies in Bailey's gut turned into bats. What in the hell was about to happen?

A man opened the door. He wore a pleasant smile, appeared to be in his mid-thirties, and instead of a suit and tie he wore a turtleneck sweater.

"Hi. You must be Bobby and Bailey," he greeted. He was nice-looking while also fairly nondescript. He had thinning, brown hair and a thin frame and fleetingly reminded her of that actor from the show *YOU* about an unlikely serial killer.

"Hello," Bobby replied while handing him the bottle of wine—which had put a dent in their weekly budget.

The man accepted the wine with a gracious thanks and with an exaggerated swing of his arm, gestured them inside.

"I'm Garrett. Come in."

Once inside, Bailey took in the stylish house. It was every 1950s enthusiast's dream. Bailey had looked at some classic 1950s furniture before showing up on set and this house had items that meant whoever lived here most certainly had money and status.

"Bailey! Bobby!" Haley hurried to them. She took Bailey's hands and kissed her cheek. She then placed her hands on Bobby's shoulders and kissed his. "I'm so happy you made it." Garrett slipped Bailey's fur from around her shoulders and offered to take Bobby's coat and hat.

"Thank you for the invitation." There were at least eight other people present, and indeed one was an African-American man that looked over at them in interest.

Bailey's eyes got wide when she saw someone she recognized sitting on the couch, trying to pretend she hadn't noticed them.

"Isn't that one of the ladies from the picnic?" Bailey asked.

Haley smirked. "Shirley? Yes. Come on. Let's say hi, and I'll introduce you to the folks."

It was funny seeing Shirley here at the party while her husband Carl was nowhere in sight. They had just seen Carl at the civil rights meeting the day before, and Shirley hadn't been anywhere in sight. Hmmm, so Shirley was a swinger, but apparently Carl wasn't...

"Shirley. You remember Bobby and Bailey."

Shirley turned to look at them in an exaggerated manner. "Oh! Of course. Hello, neighbors."

Shirley still looked like an overly made-up Marilyn Monroe. Her platinum-blonde hair was over-teased and kind of ratty looking on top while neat bangs framed her face. Her lipstick was too orange and her cheeks too red. She wore a tight, orange dress—not form-fitting, but tight.

Whereas Haley looked the picture of perfection. She wore a sweater dress that hugged every trim line of her body. Her pointy-toed heels perfectly matched the red color of her dress. Her makeup was artful, with dark-lined eyes and brightly painted lips. She could be a model, Bailey thought.

Bobby and Bailey greeted Shirley politely, although their last encounter with her hadn't been altogether positive.

Garrett appeared with a pretty, dark-haired woman at his side. She, too, had an easy smile.

"Bobby, Bailey, this is my wife, Connie."

Connie shook their hands. "You two are good-looking, just like Haley said."

"Oh. Well, thank you," Bobby replied with a smile.

"What can I get you two to drink?"

"Wine is fine," Bobby replied while looking at Bailey, who concurred with a nod.

"Red or white?" Garrett asked while heading to the bar.

"White," Bobby said.

"Let's introduce you to our friends," Connie said while eyeing Bobby closely. She took his hand as if she was his kindergarten teacher.

Bobby just chuckled and agreed. He reached out and took Bailey's hand with his free one.

Nearly everyone in the room besides Shirley seemed to be a couple. But Jack wasn't present. It soon became obvious that Haley was here with another *friend*. She hung onto this man's arm as if he was a life preserver at the sinking of the *Titanic*.

The only other Black person present was introduced as Jess. He was probably in his late thirties, and was almost as handsome as Curtis except instead of being dark brown, Jess had a café au lait complexion and curly hair that might indicate he was biracial.

"I hear you two are newlyweds," Jess said after shaking Bobby's hand and giving Bailey's fingertips a gentle squeeze. "Congratulations."

"Thank you," Bailey replied.

His wife, Leslie, was a white woman, also pretty, but she seemed older. Her eyes scanned Bailey's face and body.

"Jess and I have been together five years, but only married for one."

"Technically," he chuckled, "we're probably newlyweds also, but we had our honeymoon period years ago." He put his arm around Leslie's shoulders and she peered at Bailey while barely looking at Bobby.

Most everyone they'd been introduced to, both male and female, seemed preoccupied with Bobby — either because behind the scenes he was their boss, or because he just looked damn good.

Bailey was always the shy one, but she found the little mixer to be pleasant and she was comfortable with everyone — even Shirley, who eventually loosened up and talked to her and Bobby.

"I'm sorry about how things went at that barbecue," Shirley said. She was sipping a cocktail, and seemed to be feeling nice. Having drinks with real liquor certainly made acting a bit easier, Bailey decided.

"Don't worry about that," Bailey said. "I'd rather know who I'm dealing with than wonder who's really on our side…"

Shirley glanced away. "Well, I almost didn't show up. We don't use our last names for a reason, and Carl isn't into this…"

Bobby looked at her with a curious lift of his brow.

"What do you mean?"

"I just mean that regardless, you will be mindful of our discretion."

Bobby shrugged and nodded. "Yeah. Bailey and I don't really have anyone to gossip to."

Shirley seemed relieved, and Haley just watched each of them without comment.

The doorbell rang half an hour after they arrived and after Garret answered the door, he had Jack with him.

Everyone greeted Jack with enthusiasm. Bobby and Bailey exchanged glances, as if waiting for the drama.

Instead, Haley got up and greeted Jack with a passionate kiss. The PDA was surprisingly bold. Bailey glanced at the guy Haley had been hanging onto and he just smiled indulgently.

They drank, ate hors d'oeuvres, and listened to Sinatra and Bennet. And then Connie got up and put on a slow record. She pulled Garret up to dance with her and the two began to sway together. He kissed her lips, and the two seemed to be in their own little world.

Jess got up but instead of taking his wife, Leslie's, hand, he took Shirley's. She got up without reservation and began to dance slowly with him, their bodies close and their movements slow and very intimate.

Bailey glanced at Leslie, who wasn't paying any attention to her husband and Shirley, but was watching her. Bailey tried to hide the look of surprise from her face.

Haley rose and took Bobby's hand. Bobby gave Bailey a silent look as if asking her permission and Bailey gave an almost imperceptible shrug.

Bobby put down the glass of wine he had been nursing and rose to slow dance with Haley.

Bailey barely had time to watch before Jack rose and offered his hand to her.

Oh my God...Jack? Why couldn't Carl be here? At least she somewhat knew Carl—well, she knew he was a gentleman and an advocate.

She accepted Jack's hand and followed him to the impromptu dance floor.

His body was close as they began to move together. He guided her into the slow dance, his hands at a respectable distance on her body. After a few seconds, she began to relax. He wasn't going to jump her bones. They were just dancing.

She hadn't done this with anyone but Bobby. Jack was much taller and more thickly built. He smelled good, and she appreciated that he was being gentle, even though she knew something was probably going to have to happen soon. Right? These were swingers, after all.

But when Bailey managed to peek at Bobby and Haley, she was just swaying with him, chatting quietly, and while he seemed a bit stiff, he smiled a little and responded quietly to whatever they were discussing.

Bailey relaxed even more. Some couples snuggled and exchanged kisses, but no one was making out on the dance floor. She'd seen worse at Billy's juke joint.

After two songs, Connie changed the record to dance music and the mood changed and became lively. Bobby even continued dancing with Haley, but Leslie interrupted her and Jack.

"Do you want to cut a rug, Bailey?" she asked.

Bailey looked at Jack for his okay and he nodded and thanked her for the dance.

Bailey began moving to the music the way she had learned over the last few weeks, swinging her arms and hips in opposite directions while barely moving her feet. It was the only way for her not to risk breaking her ankles on what felt like stilettos on her feet.

"I'm happy you came," Leslie said. "We need to meet more mixed-raced couples."

"Have you met many here in Wingate?"

"With Mayor George in office?" Leslie snorted. "Most don't come out in the open."

"What made you and Jess be open about your relationship?"

"We wanted to live our lives the way that felt right for us. So, we found people like us, and for the last two years we've been doing so many things I never thought I'd have the courage to do."

Bailey nodded. "I know what you mean."

Leslie smiled. "Yeah. I know you do."

Garrett turned the music down and raised his cocktail.

"Hey, everyone. Listen up. I want to thank Bobby and Bailey for joining us tonight.

"Thank you for inviting us," Bobby replied. He was still on the dance floor, but had also switched dance partners.

"Well, everyone has gotten a chance to meet you. And we all agree that you're our type of people." Connie came to stand beside Garrett.

"We want to invite you to join our group." She looked around the room, and everyone present nodded in agreement.

"We keep our numbers small. At any given time, we never have more than twenty couples. You will learn that those in our group represent a fairly vast placement in our city. We are doctors, lawyers, a politician—"

"As well as housewives and entrepreneurs," Connie interrupted. "We enjoy life, and indulging in what we enjoy about life." Connie and Garrett exchanged knowing looks.

He turned back to look at Bobby and Bailey. "If you accept our invitation, then know that we respect discretion and won't tolerate drama of any kind—but we will be your support system for more than just lovemaking. We'll be your allies—"

Bailey saw Bobby bite his lip. Her brow went up. This was the moment where she had to pretend to be shocked. Except, Bailey didn't want to be that pearl-clutching individual she was supposed to be.

No. She didn't want to have an open marriage—not as Bailey Banks, or even Bailey Westbrook. But she also didn't want to reject these people. She actually liked them—well, not Shirley—but everyone else.

"We appreciate the invitation—" Bobby said.

"And we'll think about it," Bailey replied. Bobby looked at her. "We...uh, you know, we...have things to talk about."

"Of course," Garrett replied. "You'll let Haley know your decision. You're newlyweds, but...that doesn't mean you can't explore passion." Garrett looked out at the crowd. "We've been behaving ourselves but the witching hour grows near, and it's time to let our hair down."

Haley hurried to Bailey and grabbed her hand. "I'm so happy you're open-minded about this!" While she was speaking, Shirley began boldly making out with some guy that wasn't her husband, and Jess started touching Connie.

Bobby came to stand next to Bailey. He took her by the elbow.

"If you'll excuse us a moment, Haley." He gently guided Bailey away a few feet. "What in the hell?"

"Don't make a scene," she whispered while plastering on a smile. He plastered on a fake smile too. "Are you out of your ever-loving mind? I'm not allowing another man to put his hands on my wife!"

Bailey nodded politely at someone who raised a glass to her and Bobby. "And I'm not letting you sleep with another girl."

Bobby sighed in relief. "Okay. So can we just get out of here before someone gets naked?"

"Yeah."

They went up to Haley, who was just about to become sandwiched between Jack and her other *friend*.

"Uh...we are going to leave—" Bobby said.

"No...things are just about to get fun!" she cried.

Jack pulled Haley closer to him. "Let them go home and think about things." He looked at Bailey. "There should be no regrets."

Bailey swallowed, and Bobby grabbed her hand and pulled her to the closet where their coats were hanging.

Garrett came over. "Are you sure you're ready to leave?" he asked with a friendly smile. "You don't have to participate. We have a hands-off policy for those going through initiation—I mean, unless you want—"

"No," Bobby said resolutely. "We have so much to talk about." Bailey gave him a nervous look.

"Of course." Garrett's eyes lingered on Bobby.

Oh...

"We hope to see you soon," Garrett said, but Bobby was pulling her out the door while waving goodbye.

They were halfway to their car before she saw the cameraman waiting in the back seat for them.

Oh, yay! The trip home had to play out for the audience.

Bobby started the car with quick, angry movements and pulled down the street as if he was preparing for a drag race.

"Don't be mad," Bailey began, wishing the cameraman wasn't present so she and Bobby could have a big laugh.

"I just want to know how long you knew what kind of party that was?" he asked tightly.

"Uh...when Garrett talked about lovemaking. I had no idea Haley was inviting us to a swingers party!"

Bobby's lips pursed and he glanced at her and slowed his driving. "Okay."

"Well, when did you figure it out?"

"When Haley's other boyfriend showed up, I started getting suspicious. Especially when no one but us thought it was strange."

"And you didn't tell me?"

He raised his hands and gave her a look. "How? We were surrounded."

She sighed. "But didn't you like them?"

His brow dipped. "I mean...they were friendly. But that's because they wanted to have sex with us!"

"When you put it that way..."

"Bailey, you aren't genuinely considering—"

"No! I'm not. But just because they have peculiar sex habits doesn't mean they can't be good friends to have." Bobby scowled. "Think about it. Garrett said they are doctors and lawyers, and even a politician—"

"Who are not going to allow their reputations to be destroyed by a hint of scandal. Bae, these are the scenarios that appear in those magazines they keep hidden behind the counter at the grocery stores! People that get involved in this kind of thing go missing."

"You think?" she asked.

"I know." He took her hand. "I want friends in high places too. But not if Garrett has to have his way with me."

She smirked. "You noticed that too?"

He nodded. "And I saw how Jess's wife was watching you. I'm just not into all of that. You're enough for me."

"But if you ever get bored…"

"You worry me."

"I'm kidding!" He gave her a suspicious look. "Bobby! I don't want anyone but you!"

He kissed the back of her hand.

Chapter Eighty-Eight

That night, after the cameras stopped rolling, Bailey and Bobby practically fell on the floor laughing. They even went to the factory to get everyone's take on the party.

While there weren't nearly as many people present as when the parties first began—now that everyone had their own means to watch the show—there were still enough to roar in laughter at Bobby and Bailey's reaction to learning they were at a swingers party. Team Bailey still seemed to be the most popular clips, and being a part of such a popular production felt good.

The next day, as Bailey entered the hairdressers, she vowed she was not going to gossip about last night's party with anyone—not even Pat.

She did wonder if it was scripted that Helen knew about Haley and Shirley. But if there was to be drama about their secret lives being uncovered, it was not going to come from her.

Saturday night, Bailey felt a touch of nerves as she anticipated meeting Bobby's mom IRL. When she asked what she was like, Bobby just shrugged and said she was the perfect socialite. That didn't help Bailey determine what to expect.

As Sunday morning rolled around, the two slept in, enjoying the fact that they didn't have to rush to the production office for their weekly team meeting. In fact, Bobby put on a shirt and kept on his sleep shorts as he powered up his computer to begin the meeting.

Bailey felt awkward sharing his space, so she moved to the kitchen with her iPad.

"You are so silly," Bobby laughed at her as she waited for him to begin the meeting. "Everyone knows we're together—that we live together." He measured coffee into the percolator while she side-eyed him.

"I know, but..." She didn't know how to explain that she felt it best to separate their personal from business life when it came to the show. How was that possible when the show was essentially their personal life was hard to decipher, but she was going to try.

Once everyone was invited into the virtual meeting, Bailey saw that not everyone kept their personal and private lives separate. Paula was in bed. And that wasn't a big deal. She was in her eighth month of pregnancy, after all. But Bruce was obviously there, and walking in and out of the shot as he brought her breakfast in bed.

Since everyone could see Bailey's face, she fought to control her expression and to remain passive. But the breakfast in bed thing during a team meeting seemed a little forced to her.

As Bobby conducted the meeting from the other room, Bailey took a moment to look at the other members of her team. She was being a little nosey as she checked out what she could see of their living space.

Guy Edelman peered into the camera quietly. His face took up much of the screen so she couldn't see anything behind him. He was just as passive as he was during the physical team meetings, not speaking to anyone, but observing.

Anita was there in her own screen looking nothing like the woman that had shown up at her door days earlier. She wore a ponytail and a fresh face—free of makeup...and bruises. She was mostly quiet, but smiled in a friendly way and contributed to any open discussions.

When the meeting ended, Bailey knew this modernized way of doing things had been a success. Bobby might not have ever decided to do things this way if not for the fact that he wanted as much free time with her as he could get.

And after the meeting, they hopped back into bed and enjoyed a few hours of *free time*.

"Mom is staying at the Hilton. She loves their brunch," Bobby said as they drove his BMW into downtown Cincinnati. "Have you ever been?"

"No. Is it nice?"

"Very."

"What brings her into town?"

"Me. She knows I'm not flying all the way to LA. So, unless she wants to FaceTime me, she has to come here."

"You and your mom aren't very close, are you?"

He gave a half smile. "We...respect each other's differences."

Bailey mulled that over, trying to understand it.

He reached out for her hand. "Don't worry. My mom isn't someone you have to worry about."

Again, something that didn't completely put her at ease.

The Palm Court was ritzy without making her feel as if she was out of place in her nice 1950s skirt and cashmere sweater. The style felt familiar, with its art deco influences.

Bobby called his mother from his cell phone to let her know they were waiting by the entrance.

"Mom. We're here. We'll be by the elevators. Okay, see you in a bit."

Bailey stroked a curl behind her ear. She had told Juanita to give her a style that wasn't too flamboyant — meaning, no teased bouffant. She liked the soft curls that framed her face.

"You look pretty." Bobby took her hand reassuringly. "Don't be nervous."

"What if she hates me?" she finally asked.

He chuckled. "Even if she did, she would never cause a scene. It wouldn't be proper."

"Babe," she scowled. "That is not reassuring."

"I love you. And that's all that matters."

Bailey smiled too. He was right.

When the elevators opened, several people exited but it was easy to see which person was Bobby's mom.

She was petite, probably no taller than five feet four. She was pretty and blonde — which meant nothing when beauty was the result of manufacturers, and hair color could be obtained from a bottle. But she also looked like Bobby. She had passed her facial expression and mannerism down to her son.

She hurried to him the moment she spotted him and gave him a hug and a kiss on the cheek. She patted his bicep.

"Have you been working out?"

"Hi, Mom. I have to find some way of staying active." He turned to Bailey. "Mom, meet my girlfriend, Bailey. Bailey, this is my mom, Joanna."

Bailey stuck out her hand, wishing Bobby hadn't introduced his mother as simply Joanna. She had been raised to address her elders as Missus or Mister.

"It's nice to meet you, Mrs. Chesterfield."

Joanna scowled. "Well, you are the polite one. I'm Joanna, dear." She pulled Bailey into a hug a moment before softening her expression with a smile. "I no longer go by that name. Not since my divorce."

Bailey could have kicked herself.

"My mom uses her maiden name; Dorsette."

"Oh. I'm sorry —"

"Nonsense," Joanna said with an annoyed wave of her hand. "I just don't like being reminded of that man."

Bobby offered her mother his arm and she hooked her hand around it naturally. He then took Bailey's hand.

"Let's grab a seat while there is still a good selection." Bobby guided the two women into the restaurant.

Bailey's nerves didn't settle, so she went into actress mode. She plastered on a calm face and subtle smile while listening to Joanna chatting to her son as they located their seats.

"So, Bailey, how did you meet Robert?"

"We actually met on set."

"Yes. I told you, Bailey is in the production," Bobby said.

"But you didn't say that's how you two met," Joanna replied. "How do you like the show? I know it's hard to be candid with your boss here," Joanna joked.

Bobby made a face. "You just made it weird by calling me her boss. I manage the production."

Joanna made a face. "You *own* the production."

"I try not to be anyone's boss." A waiter came and got everyone's drink order.

"I guess what Robert means," Bailey said while adopting Bobby's given name, "is the show allows so much input from the cast that we basically write our own scripts—I mean, with direction from the production crew, of course." Bobby didn't reply, and Joanna watched her with interest. "But," Bailey added, "to answer your question, I enjoy working on the show, and I love the direction it's going."

"What's it about, again?" Joanna asked while digging into her purse for her compact so she could check her face.

Bailey looked at Bobby. His mother didn't watch the show? She didn't even know what it was about? Her aunt knew every nuance of a show her loved one was involved in.

"It's about the wonderful 1950s," Bobby replied with thinly veiled sarcasm. He stood. "We should get our food, it's kind of late."

When they returned to their seats from the buffet, they ate and talked casually. Joanna asked Bailey about herself but didn't dig too deeply. She filled Bobby in on the other members of his family and spoke briefly about a friend or two.

Bobby listened, laughed when he was supposed to, but didn't seem overly enthused about anything they discussed. It was weird, considering her conversations with Bobby had always been filled with passion. But they were artists, and what they were passionate about was a common denominator for them both. His mother, on the other hand, liked talking about her trips and rich people she'd rubbed elbows with.

"Robert. Can you get us a selection of desserts?" Joanna asked. "Bring some chocolate truffles if they have them. I do adore the truffles here."

"Sure." He gave Bailey a quick look. "I'll be right back."

Joanna picked up her glass of prosecco and took a sip.

"Have you met Robert's father?"

"No, I haven't."

Joanna stared at her, blue eyes meeting brown ones in a stare that was so much like her son's.

"Good," she finally said. "One day, you will." Joanna put her glass down and placed her folded napkin on top of her plate, indicating she was finished eating. She met Bailey's eyes again.

"When you do, you come and see me."

Bailey frowned in confusion. "I don't understand."

"Call me, visit me, write me. I don't care how you do it. But you talk to me." Joanna gazed out at where her son was filling a plate with a selection of goodies.

"But do yourself a favor, and try to avoid that meeting for as long as you possibly can."

Bailey felt a shiver go up her spine. "Okay."

Joanna looked at her. "Every girlfriend Bobby has ever had, has been hit on by Robert's father." Joanna's lips formed a thin line in a face that suddenly seemed to look older. "And that includes ones that were just teenagers."

Bailey's lips parted. "Does he know?"

"I think he does. But not through me. And most of them were too embarrassed to tell him. So, they told me."

Bailey didn't know how to form the next question, but it burned in her. She had to ask it and consequences be damned.

"And what did you do?"

Joanna's eyes flashed something that could have been guilt, or regret. "Not enough."

A teenaged girl had come to her revealing her husband had acted inappropriately and she hadn't done enough. What in the fuck did that mean?

Bailey looked away.

"My son doesn't let too many people in. He's very careful when it comes to relationships. You're the first I've met in years."

Bailey still didn't look at her. "That doesn't mean there hasn't been others. It just means you didn't get to meet them."

"Honey," Joanna said. "I might not know everything about my son, but I do know this; he wants my approval for everything. And sadly, he wants his father's too. So, one day, you will meet him."

Bailey met Joanna's eyes. "If I come to you, what are you going to do? Give me money to keep me quiet?" She instantly regretted the bitter words that came from her mouth. This was Bobby's mother. But she was also an enabler for a monster.

But Joanna didn't look angry. She held the hint of a smile. "If you need it, then yes. But you come to me so I can collect the evidence to put that bastard behind bars for the rest of his life. He'll discredit you. But he won't pull that on me."

Bailey's eyes widened as she saw the fire behind blue eyes that could move between calm to vengeful rage in just a flash.

Bobby returned with the plate of dessert and Joanna looked at him with a broad smile. "Now we need coffee. I'll be up all night, but you can't have good chocolate without good coffee."

Bailey looked from Joanna to Bobby. Is that where he learned how to act so well?

Chapter Eighty-Nine

"What did you think of my mom?" Bobby asked as they drove back to the set.

"I like her." It was true. Despite the fact that she'd lived the life of a jet-setter and her children were left in the care of others, and even though she had probably stayed with her husband even after learning he was a sexual predator, Bailey could sense she had regrets. And really, no one went through life the exact same as they had begun it.

Bailey decided she would only judge Joanna based on how she treated her, and so far, she was facing tough situations head-on.

"Do you think she liked me?"

Bobby looked out at the road and seemed to think before answering. "Yes." Bailey watched him, trying to read between the lines.

He answered her unspoken question without looking at her. "She wanted to talk to you privately or she wouldn't have sent me off for a tray of desserts she only took one bite of. And no...I don't want to know what you two talked about. All that matters is you like her and she likes you."

Bailey nodded and watched the scenery in quiet contentment.

Bailey and Bobby eased into the week with barely any fanfare. There was drama—but nothing dealing with their story line. Like when Helen and Quinton had dinner at an out-of-town restaurant, but then she got into a fender-bender on the way back home. When Hank found out about it, he questioned why she was so far out of town and his suspicions were rising.

A big one was with Mayor George trying to introduce an ordinance instilling a curfew for the residents of Garden Hills—a town that housed and entertained mainly people of color.

The civil rights group was going door-to-door asking people to sign a petition. Bobby even wrote an article about it, pointing out that the NAACP's attention had been drawn to the issue.

By the following week, Mayor George had pulled back on the law change.

Aunt Mae's daily phone calls had become a high point. The fans wanted more of her and her old stories, humorous observations, and perfectly timed advice.

"I was thinking," Bobby said as he climbed into bed one night. "Do you think Aunt Mae would consider paying a visit to the set?"

Bailey shot up in bed. "Do I? Heck yes! That would make her life, Bobby."

"I was thinking we could host Thanksgiving here at our house. It will be a perfect segue to the holiday hiatus."

"Oh. That's not going to fly with fake-mother-in-law."

"I know, right? So, imagine having your aunt and my fake mom here with a new wife, all trying to cook a Thanksgiving meal together."

"You know what? That's freaking brilliant!" Bailey paused and narrowed her eyes in thought. "On this one, I want to be included in directing the script—but we won't tell my aunt or your mother how to react."

Bobby nodded. "Agreed. I'm giving you complete control of the story line."

Bailey gave him a surprised look. "Are you serious? You barely do that for Bruce." Her face changed into a knowing expression. "You're just too busy with that big, secret project of yours, am I right?"

He grinned sheepishly. "It's huge, and there's a lot of elements to it."

Bobby had been working hard at the production office and after hours in the at-home office. She hadn't seen him working this hard since he'd created Garden Hills.

She had hoped that once they got to the tail end of that project, Bobby would relax for a bit. But like the typical workaholic, he had found something even bigger to work on.

The thing was, this one didn't seem to fill him with the same pride creating the all-Black community had. He seemed stressed-out but whenever she pointed it out, he would smile and plaster on a look of contentment.

She had to let it go. He wanted the story line to be right. And she had no doubt it would be. He just had to believe he had the Midas touch and their viewership was growing because of it.

"Speaking of Thanksgiving, Aunt Mae invited you to dinner with us."

"Oh." His expression fell. "I'd love to, but my family is having one of their rare get-togethers and I said I'd attend. I tried to get out of it by saying I'd be busy on set, but they're all flying out. There's no way I'm getting out of it." He made a face. "I was going to invite you, but we still haven't worked everything out…"

"I have you all the time," she said with a sigh. "I guess I can give you to your family for a day."

He looked at a spot in the distance. "Dad will be there, *and* Mom. It's not going to be fun, but neither was willing to forgo an opportunity to have all the kids and grandkids in one place."

"Oh…" She reached out and clutched his hand, happy she wasn't going to be there.

"Do you know what I really want to do?"

She scowled. "Bobby, we just did it—"

"No," he chuckled. "Not that. Well, I always want to do that. But I think we should hold a family day here on the set. Not on Thanksgiving Day, but maybe the week before, and everyone can invite their friends and family to see what things look like behind the scenes."

"Dang. You are just overflowing with great ideas."

"Well, people make a huge sacrifice being on a show like this. And their families have to be curious."

"We can make it a Friendsgiving."

"Yes! We can even make a potluck at the factory."

"Oh my God, I love it!"

He pulled her back down and snuggled against her. "Now for that other thing I like doing…"

Bailey sat in one of the metal fold-up chairs at the civil rights meeting. Bobby wasn't there, but he'd come to the last two. He felt it was just as important as she did, but he was working on an article that was a big departure from the current events articles he normally wrote.

He was working with a news reporter who was doing an expose on Mayor George. Rumors about an illegitimate child had come to light, and all Bobby would say about it is there was a lot more the mayor was hiding.

Curtis passed out cups of coffee to her, Pat, Marvin, and Carl.

They had become "meeting" friends. Carl was surprisingly great in the role of a white civil rights activist. He was the gung-ho revolutionary that talked about sit-ins and boycotts, while Marvin and Curtis warned him they had to ease into it. They first needed the support of the Negro community. Bailey knew the three men were working on the scripts together. They just played off each other too easily.

"There can't be a revolution without an army." Marvin spoke while they all waited for the meeting to begin.

"Army?" Pat said. "Let's just focus on bringing awareness to the cause."

"Yeah," Bailey agreed. "The city is just waiting for a reason to push through another ordinance keeping us from gathering. We have to remain peaceful."

"That joke of a mayor will just make up whatever scenario he needs," Carl said.

"That's why we need friends in the local television channels," Bailey said. "Bobby is working on that."

"We got allies." Pat nodded in approval.

Carl grinned. "I have friends that choose to remain behind the scenes. But they support what we're doing, and they're helping to fund the movement."

Marvin gave Carl a soul slap. "That's great, man. Money is just as important as having warm bodies."

The meeting was called to order, and everyone turned their attention to the speaker.

Bailey was so excited to tell Aunt Mae the good news about being in a spot on the show she could barely sit still in her seat in the car.

She had invited Bobby to Sunday dinner at her aunt and uncle's house because he absolutely had to be the person to tell her. He'd happily agreed to come along, but insisted on driving. Great tunes, a cool car, and wonderful company—Bailey was not going to object.

Uncle Dewbug met them at the door and shook Bobby's hand while clapping him on the shoulder.

"Nice to see you again, son. Come on in, you two. Mae's in the bathroom." He leaned in to whisper loudly, "She's always sneaking fiber in those health shakes she makes us drink every morning but it's starting to backfire on her!" He laughed.

"Uncle Dewbug!" Bailey chastised while holding back her grin. "Auntie's going to be mad with you telling her business."

He made a dismissive sound. "Bobby's family now that he's given my wife something to occupy her time besides how to keep me healthy."

"Thanks, Dewbug. I appreciate that," Bobby said. "But your wife is absolutely an asset to the show. Has she told you about her fan mail?"

"Me and all the neighbors and everybody at church. You want a beer? I'm watching the game."

"Yeah, I'll join you," Bobby said while taking a seat as Uncle Dewbug retrieved the beer.

Bailey looked on in pride at how comfortable the two were with each other.

When Aunt Mae came into the room she gave Bailey a quick hug, but then fawned over Bobby, asking if he was hungry and commenting on the number of biscuits he could eat in one sitting.

"I'd eat more if Bailey made more," he said.

"I gave her that recipe because as accomplished as my niece is, she's no wiz in the kitchen."

Bailey scowled at her aunt's good-natured jibe. "Now I'm not even sure if I want Bobby to tell you the good news."

Aunt Mae's eyes grew big and she looked at Bailey, then to Bobby, and finally down at Bailey's empty ring finger and her shoulders sank a little.

"What news?"

Uncle Dewbug even turned down the game to listen, although his face was filled with warning. Maybe she shouldn't have started off the announcement like that.

"Well," Bobby said. "You've done so well on the show, your fans have been begging for more Aunt Mae airtime." Aunt Mae smiled proudly. "I was hoping we could convince you to make a guest appearance on the show. We were thinking—"

Aunt Mae began screaming as if she had caught the Holy Ghost. Poor Bobby's face went white and he jumped, ready to catch her before she fell to the floor in a fit.

Aunt Mae threw her hands into the air and danced around in a big circle, whooping and hollering all the while.

Bailey laughed and clapped. "I think my aunt has accepted your invitation."

Chapter Ninety

The week leading up to the Friendsgiving celebration was a busy one. Everyone decided Saturday would be the best day to hold it. And that would mark the first day of the week-long winter break.

When they returned from hiatus, they would be ready to film the actual Thanksgiving scenes. It seemed everyone had something big planned. When she had chatted with Helen on the way to the grocery store, she had hinted she and Quinton were going to "seal the deal." There was also a rumor that Nadine was going to end her affair with Mayor George due to his conservative/racist views. And Bobby revealed Drew was going to discover his girlfriend's secret— that she worked in a strip joint.

There were so many things that were coming up on the horizon, Bailey was just happy her time was going to be preoccupied with the civil rights story line and upcoming baby.

Paula had moved in with Bruce and was only going to come to set on Saturdays, when she could film collecting money from Bobby. It was time to prepare for her real-life birth. But on the set, things were progressing much quicker. Paula's forwardness was even more pronounced; inviting Bobby to touch her belly when the baby kicked, reminiscing about the "good times," speculating about what life would have been like if he could raise his child full-time like a true family...

Ugh.

They were definitely going to have to get together to discuss their eventual first meeting. But Bailey no longer felt Paula could do anything to infiltrate her and Bobby's real-life relationship. And she sensed Paula had figured that out as well. She and Bruce were settling in together—for better or for worse.

She had one last scene to film where she would go into labor right before the hiatus. Once they returned, Bailey had no idea what to expect.

Hectic was an understatement. It wasn't just the culmination of the high points of the various story lines. But also, Bailey needed to consider her potluck contribution. She had considered chicken and dumplings as a joke—but found she actually wanted people to enjoy her food. Also, she was the girlfriend of the producer. Bobby was going to cater the main course, but that didn't absolve her of contributing something.

She was still thinking about it.

But the biggest thing was that Bobby's secret story line was going to be revealed sometime this week. She was scared, but excited.

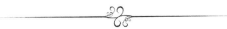

There was a knock on her door early Monday morning and Bailey jumped and let out another embarrassing little squeak. There hadn't been anything written in her script about a visitor. She was still in her exercise clothes; shorts and a shirt, and her hair was still wrapped.

She hurried to the door and peeped out the front window. It was Curtis, wearing his white milkman uniform and neat cap.

She opened the door and poked her head out.

"Hey, Bailey." They had long ago lost the formality and were solid friends. "Sorry to ring so early."

"Oh! I didn't mess up on the payment, did I?" she asked.

"No. No, that's not it. Your order said you needed whipping cream but we're out of it. I'm sorry, but with Thanksgiving, we just didn't order enough."

"Oh," she smiled. "That's fine. I'll stop at the store today and pick some up."

He made a face but smiled. "Sorry for the inconvenience. Now I have to go around to everyone on my route and announce the same thing." He handed her the milk crate and turned away with a wave. "See you at Friday's meeting!"

"See you." Bailey closed her door and put the items in the refrigerator.

She adjusted her shopping list and got ready to go shopping with Helen. When she walked out the door forty minutes later, she was surprised to see the cameraman standing on her front stoop waiting for her.

She tried to keep her face even, but she wondered what was about to go down. She knocked on Helen's door and when her friend opened it, even she seemed surprised by the presence of the cameraman.

Helen didn't invite her inside, since the cameraman's presence meant they were supposed to do something significant outside.

"We should stop at the butcher's shop. They have fresh turkeys at a good price," Helen said as they headed for the car.

"Well, I'm happy I'm leaving the preparation of the turkey to either my aunt or my mother-in-law. I'm going to let them battle that out." Bailey saw Helen pause and look down the street.

"The milk truck is still here. I've never seen the milkman this late."

"Oh, yeah." Bailey peered down the street to where the familiar truck was parked. "He had to tell everyone that ordered whipping cream they were out."

Helen got into the car. "Luckily for everyone concerned, I don't have to make dessert."

Helen fiddled around while the cameraman got settled in the back seat and they drove off.

As they drove past the Edelmans' house, they finally saw Curtis heading back to his truck. His posture said he was pissed, annoyed, or frustrated. She soon saw why when she saw Guy and his sister, Anita, standing on the porch.

Anita was holding the milk crate and Guy was glaring after Curtis. He saw Bailey in the car and his eyes locked onto her, sending a chill down her spine at the obvious dislike she saw reflected at her—even at a distance.

Damn. He played the role of disliking her a little too easily.

"Poor Curtis," Helen said as she drove past. "Having to deal with people like Guy."

Bailey turned to Helen, getting a sense of why the cameraman was there. "What's the deal with his sister?"

"Anita?" Helen glanced at her. "Anita's nothing like her brother. I wouldn't have brought her around you if she was."

"No, I know she's nice. She came by the house to apologize for her brother threatening Bobby's job after that poll. But did you see all those bruises?"

Helen made a face. "You know she's a little...different."

"Yeah."

"Everyone keeps an eye out for her. She's always getting hurt. She's a little accident-prone."

Bailey's brow gathered. "Do you think that's all there is to it?"

Helen glanced at her. "You don't think..."

"I don't know. She just kept talking about how hard her brother was on her." Bailey decided not to "out" Anita. Her sexual preferences were her own business.

"Oh, Bailey, I don't know. I can't imagine someone hitting that poor, sweet woman. She's like a child, and she's so sweet."

"I don't know," Bailey sighed. "I'm probably too suspicious. I just don't like that man."

"No one does, except for maybe other people like him."

When they got to the butcher's shop in town, Bailey decided she would pick up a small pot roast that would be perfect for one dinner and leftover sandwiches.

But the shop was extra crowded, and the butchers made her wait so long, even though Helen had already gotten her order, she had to intervene and order Bailey's roast for her. The butcher knew what

Helen was doing and wasn't as nice to her as he had been the first time.

"You know, there is a perfectly good butcher at the farmer's market that realizes money is green regardless of whether it comes from a Colored or a white hand."

The butcher turned red and replied with forced politeness, "Have a good day, ma'am."

Helen stormed out of the shop. "That's it. I'm never going back to that place! I can't believe how long they made you wait! We would have been there an hour!"

"Well, I appreciate you helping me, but…" She looked back at the shop, where three other Blacks patiently waited to be helped.

Helen followed her gaze, the cameraman capturing everything.

"Maybe I should have…" Helen closed her mouth as if realizing that whatever she suggested, wouldn't be enough.

As they headed for the car, Helen looked at the Whites Only sign in the window of a restaurant as if she had never seen it before.

That night after the pot roast dinner, Bailey called Pat.

"You know what?"

"What?"

"We should boycott the butcher shop in town."

"Hell yeah! I hate that place. Ever since Bill retired, it's taken a turn. Maybe we can hold a boycott before Thanksgiving and hit them in the pocketbook! Good idea, sis."

"Yes. That's perfect. And after Friday night's rally, hopefully we'll get more people interested."

"I'll call Nathan. We should push Friday's meeting up and maybe get some flyers printed before the rally."

"I can ask Bobby to print the flyers."

"Perfect! I love this idea."

Bobby was watching her curiously. "Flyers?" he asked.

"I don't want to go back to that butcher. And I'm sure I'm not the only one."

"Right," Bobby agreed.

"I think we should pass out some flyers at Friday's rally about boycotting."

He nodded. "Good idea. If someone draws them up, I just need a few hours to get them printed."

Bailey snuggled against him and gave him a peck on the lips. "I love you."

He hooked his arm around her waist. "This is my fight too."

On Tuesday, Bailey was putting her best foot forward in trying to defuse any potential problems with the Thanksgiving menu.

"Mother-in-law Banks offered to make the turkey—"

"What?" her aunt exclaimed. "Who comes to someone else's house for dinner and brings the main course?! No. The turkey is made at *your* house."

Bailey slouched in the kitchen chair. "Well...Bobby kinda told her I've never made a turkey before and—"

"And she took it upon herself to just offer to cook it? Without consulting you first?"

Bailey opened and closed her mouth. "Uh...yeah."

"Hmph," Aunt Mae snorted. "Who is the woman of your household, little girl?"

"Me," Bailey answered quietly.

"Then you call that woman and tell her you will be making the turkey. You do that or you will forever be a pushover."

"But...what if she refuses to come to dinner?"

"That would be rude. People like her always want to give off a good appearance. You've told me about her nasty-nice attitude when you were living there for those few weeks. I'm going to tell you now, when people like that pull back from your life, you have to remember the choice was on them and them alone."

"You're right. But I just want everything to go right. Plus, I don't know how to make a turkey."

"Well, of course you don't. *I'm* going to make the turkey. But I'm going to make it at your house!"

Bailey chuckled behind her hand. Aunt Mae was funny as hell.

"I guess I can call her and tell her to bring the dressing—"

"Uh...no. Dressing and turkey are an extension of each other. I'll have the broth and drippings, and therefore *I* should make the dressing."

"Oh my goodness," Bailey sighed. "You make one version of dressing—but promise you won't make a party size. Then I'll let Mrs. Bailey make her version."

Aunt Mae sighed. "I guess. But I'm bringing collard greens."

Bailey rubbed her forehead. "I'm making the collard greens. And I'm making the mashed potatoes and the gravy—"

"Not the gravy!" her aunt exclaimed. "You don't have the drippings! How are you going to make the gravy? You going to pick up packaged stuff?"

"Okay. You make the gravy and a dessert."

"Okay." Aunt Mae sounded satisfied.

"I'd better go. I'll talk to you tomorrow. Now I have to call my mother-in-law."

"Girl, you got this."

"That's easy for you to say. Bye, Auntie. Love you."

"Love you too."

When they disconnected, Bailey called Bobby's mother's house. This wasn't scripted, so she hoped she answered. But this is the kind of thing Bobby encouraged them to do; enhance their own story lines without constant direction from the production crew.

"Hello?" Mrs. Banks answered as if she'd had to rush to the phone. What did she do all day? She was retired, and didn't have a regular story line.

"Hi, Mrs. Banks. This is Bailey." There was no response, so Bailey quickly continued. "I wanted to talk to you about the Thanksgiving menu."

"Oh. Right. Bobby said this will be your first time preparing a Thanksgiving meal. Of course I'll help. I bought a turkey that's thawing out in the refrigerator as we speak. I know your family will be attending, and I suppose they will have a healthy appetite, so I was sure to get a big one—"

"I didn't realize you were going to do that. I wanted to make the turkey."

"You?"

"Yes. My aunt would help me, of course."

"Well, what am I supposed to do with a ten-pound turkey, Bailey? You should have said something before I started thawing it out," she complained. "What a waste."

It was on the tip of Bailey's tongue to remind her that no one had told her to go out and purchase the main course for someone else's celebration. But she bit back her words.

"I can send Bobby over to pick it up. And I'm sorry, but I'd like to make the turkey. It's my first Thanksgiving with my husband in our home. I'm sure you understand," Bailey said, trying another tactic: guilt.

Mrs. Banks sighed. "I guess that will be okay. I can bring the dressing. Bobby is pretty picky when it comes to dressing." Bailey smirked, not believing Bobby had ever been particular about food. "I'll bring the green beans and sweet potato casserole. Is that okay with you?"

"Sure. That sounds perfect."

"Well okay, Bailey. I hope you know what you're doing. Turkey isn't easy to make, especially a big one."

"My aunt makes a delicious turkey and she's going to teach me what to do. I have to learn if I want to take care of my family."

"Well...I suppose I can come over sometimes and help you learn how to cook for my son."

Bailey made a face. "That would be nice, Mrs. Banks. Thank you. I'll have Bobby call you when he comes home about picking up the turkey."

"Okay, Bailey. Bye."

Bailey hung up and sighed. Navigating opinionated in-laws wasn't easy. Luckily, she liked both parties in real life.

The next day, Pat called with good news.

"The meeting was moved up to tonight. Can you and Bobby make it?"

"I'll ask him when he gets home, but I'll definitely be there."

"Great. I'll talk to you then. I have a few other people to call."

"See you tonight."

Bailey hung up, feeling guilty that dinner tonight would have to be tomato soup and grilled cheese sandwiches. She'd fancy it up with ham. But it was budget-friendly, and with tonight's meeting, it was also quick.

Bailey was dancing happily to the tunes playing on the radio while she vacuumed when the front door opened and Bobby came in.

What in the world? It was way too early for him to be home. It was just after lunch.

"Hey, honey," she said after turning off the vacuum. "What are you doing home so early? You didn't forget your lunch, did you?"

Bobby's brow was gathered. "Bailey, I wanted to come home before you heard the news on the television or radio."

She walked over to him. Was this it? Was this the moment he had been working toward for the last few weeks? Anxiety caused her belly to feel strangely empty.

"What is it, Bobby?" she asked, and he took her hands.

"Honey. Curtis...Curtis was just found lynched. They found his body in a field by the new construction..."

Bobby was talking, but Bailey had to look at his lips to understand him, reading them to put together the meaning of his words.

"Wait a minute," she interrupted. "Did you say Curtis was...?"

He closed his eyes briefly and met her eyes. "He was found hanging. Lynched."

Chapter Ninety-One

They were sitting on the couch, and Bobby was still holding her hand.

"Curtis showed up to work this morning and had gone out on his route, but never showed up at any homes. His boss called the police and...they found his truck first, and them him.

"Oh my God," Bailey had already said half a dozen times. She was trying to play the role while at the same time trying to reconcile why the story had to take such a tragic turn. She looked at Bobby, knowing she couldn't ask him the real questions she had in her head.

Curtis had been killed off the show. This wasn't some sci-fi movie where they could kill off a character and bring them back. Curtis would no longer be on this show.

Had Bobby done this intentionally? Had Curtis been written off the show because of his popularity? Because there were still viewers that thought that ever since the reappearance of Paula, Bailey and Curtis should hook up.

No. Bobby wasn't insecure. But this was much too big to just hit everyone with it!

She was still shaken when she remembered there was much more that had to play out.

"Do you think Pat knows?"

He shook his head. "I don't know."

Bailey jumped up, more to have something to do than as a need to keep the story moving forward. "I have to call her..." She dialed Pat's number, not expecting her to answer, since this was the middle of the workday, and she didn't.

Bailey cursed and hung up. "She's still at work..."

There was a sudden frantic ringing of the doorbell. Bobby jumped up.

"Don't answer!" He hurried out of the room and she stood there, confused and a little scared.

When Bobby returned to the room, he was holding the gun. Bailey moved back. Wait? Was this going to turn even more violent?

"Bobby..." she said, nearly breaking character in her fright.

"Stay behind me," Bobby said as the doorbell continued to shrill. He hurried to the door and Bailey stayed back, her stomach twisting as she waited for the next thing to unfold.

Bobby swung the door open with the gun pointed down at his side. He relaxed a bit when he saw it was Anita Edelman. The woman rushed into the house without invitation. Tears were in her eyes.

"I think my brother did something bad."

Bobby shut the door. "You're Edelman's sister?"

Anita's head bobbed up and down as she bit her nails. "Guy's my brother, and he did something really bad."

Bobby turned to look at Bailey, who finally came forward and placed a hand on Anita's shoulder. "Come inside. Tell us what happened."

Anita sat on the couch, sniffling and chewing her nails. "My brother was awfully mad when the milkman rang the bell the other morning. He wasn't asleep or anything, but he don't like it when people call too early. I answered the door and the milkman said there wouldn't be any whipping cream in today's order.

"He was real nice," Anita said while looking at Bailey. "Just like you are. He said if I needed it in time for Thanksgiving, I should probably go to the grocery store early before they ran out too. We stood there and talked for a while. Well, I talked mostly, but he was nice, and didn't ask me to shut up."

Anita frowned and drew in her lower lip. "But Guy came out to see what was taking me so long and when he saw me talking to a Negro man, he accused him of flirting with me." Anita shook her head adamantly. "But he wasn't doing that! He's just a nice person. Plus, my brother knows I don't even like men..."

Bailey's hands were folded tightly in her lap as she listened. They had orchestrated this so perfectly...it had been playing out ever since that poll when she'd first been introduced to Anita.

"Guy got real mad with the milkman and called him bad names and said he was dangerous. But he's not. He's been our milkman for a long time and nothing dangerous ever happened because of him!"

"Go on," Bobby said gently.

"Guy got on the phone and started talking to somebody about how uppity the Coloreds were getting; moving into his neighborhood, holding meetings, and working white men's jobs."

Bailey couldn't even look at Anita when she said those words and had to close her eyes.

Bobby stood up and began to pace. "Jesus," he whispered.

"Guy went to one of his meetings last night. And he was gone early this morning. When he came home a little while ago, he said he took care of...well, he said the bad name. He said he wouldn't be messing around with any more white women."

Bailey looked at Anita again. "Will you tell the police this, Anita?"

Anita swallowed, but nodded her head. "I will, because I don't want him to hurt the milkman. He's always been nice to me. And I think...well, I think him and his friends already have."

Bobby picked up the phone, and Bailey could hear him speaking to the police.

An hour later, two sets of police showed up on Bobby and Bailey's quiet street. One set was at their house gently asking Anita questions while another set was at the Edelmans' house taking Guy in for questioning.

As the police led Anita out to the cruiser to finish questioning her at the station, Bailey and Bobby followed them outside and stood on their front stoop. All of the neighbors were outside, talking, watching, waiting.

Haley was the first to approach. Her eyes were red, so she must have already heard the news.

"Is it true?" she asked Bailey and Bobby. "Did that maniac Edelman have something to do with what happened to Curtis?"

Haley had formed the tears Bailey hadn't been able to manufacture. This was just too much, too fast. She and Haley hadn't talked much since she'd explained that as newlyweds, the swinging scene just wasn't for them. Haley had taken it in stride, but hadn't gone out of her way to invite her over for any more of her famous cocktails.

Helen rushed over, and Bailey saw Quinton standing in her doorway with a look of concern.

Now there seemed to be a new kind of friendship forming between them, a bond of mutual disbelief at the loss of a beloved character.

"They're taking him in for questioning now," Bobby replied. "I want to go to the station with Anita. I don't want her there without someone with her." He squeezed Bailey's hand. "Will you be all right alone? I don't know how long I'll be —"

"Go. You need to be there." He was the neighbor. He had heard the confession, and he worked with the local newspaper. Yeah, he had to be there.

He kissed her and hurried to jump into his car and drive off.

"I can't believe Curtis is gone," Haley said in a shaky voice. Tears streamed down her face. When Bailey looked at Helen, she saw her eyes were also filled with tears.

Her own eyes were dry, but her heart was in turmoil. This wasn't right. She couldn't play this out with two white women. Not when her Black friend had been murdered because of his race! No!

Bailey shook her head. "I have to..." She turned back to her house. "I have to make some calls. I'm sorry."

"It's okay," Helen said gently. "Call me if you need me."

All Bailey could do was nod before closing the door behind her. She walked to the phone as if she was a robot. "Aunt Mae. Something bad happened..."

Aunt Mae wailed on the phone, reminding Bailey she had watched Curtis's character far more than Bailey ever had. He was someone she had liked, even though she had never met him.

Bailey explained about what had probably happened with Guy Edelman and her aunt listened intently, interjecting the occasional sob and prayer.

"I'm sorry, Auntie. I have to call my friend Pat. I haven't been able to get in touch with her, and she and Curtis…" The words froze in her mouth and she had to force them out. "She and Curtis grew up together."

"Go ahead, baby girl. Call your friend."

Bailey hung up and dialed Pat's number again.

This time, the phone was picked up quickly. "Pat."

"Bailey!" Pat sobbed into the phone. "He's dead. Curtis is dead!"

"I know, honey. I know."

"They killed him. They hung him…"

Tears finally welled in Bailey's eyes as she listened to Pat's heartbreaking words.

When Bobby came home, it was just after 9:00 p.m. but they didn't stop filming. He pulled her into his arms and held her and Bailey sagged against him, emotionally exhausted with all the speculations swirling through her head.

"Guy Edelman confessed." Bailey pulled back and blinked.

"What? He confessed?"

Bobby's lip formed a grim line that was far from happy. "He said Curtis has been...doing things to his sister."

"Oh my God..."

"Of course, he's lying. But...he was released."

She flashed him a look of surprise. "He's been released? He confessed to lynching a man!"

Bobby rubbed the back of his neck. "He confessed to lynching a Negro man that he says has been doing things to his sister...his sister who has mental disabilities."

Bailey's nose flared as she glared at Bobby. "That's some utter *bullshit*—"

He touched her arms. "I know."

"That's just...BULLSHIT!" she yelled while moving out of his touch as if untangling herself from something that had trapped her. "I don't want Curtis to have to go out like *that!*" Bailey was shaking her head and glaring at him.

Bobby looked away. After a moment he walked away, which gave her a moment to gather her thoughts and to remember this was a show. Curtis wasn't really dead. He was probably at the factory right now, watching this play out.

Bobby returned with the gun and she gave him a wary look. He checked it and looked at her with a stony expression that seemed far from anything she had ever seen on his face before.

"Guy is out there. He said he acted alone, but there's no way that old bastard overpowered Curtis. If he or any of his friends show up here, I will kill him."

Bobby sat down on the couch and stared in the direction of the front door.

The scene ended there, and Bobby placed the prop gun into its safety case as if it was real. He did that before even speaking to Bailey. But once the gun was out of sight he looked at her sadly, no touching, no words. He just looked at her as if he was a complete asshole.

She stood in the living room facing him, just as quiet, but disappointment was all that showed on her face.

"This was too big to not let me in on..."

"I know. But it wasn't my choice." Her expression became questioning. "This was Curtis's idea. Long ago, when he first agreed to be on the show, he said he'd only do it if he could die in a blaze of glory."

"What the−?" Her mouth hung open.

"I thought him dying was kind of cool back then too. But then Pat and I started working out this angle, and when we factored in Curtis's request...well, it all just made sense."

Her shoulders sagged. Curtis had asked to go out like this? "He asked to be lynched?"

Bobby nodded. "It was his idea. Hell, Bailey. This all makes me uncomfortable as hell. So, I left it to them to work it out. This is Pat and Curtis's story line. I swear, I had no input."

She lowered her eyes from his, feeling guilty for even thinking he'd done things for the wrong reason. She quickly moved to close the space between them and they hugged. She could feel Bobby's heart thudding in his chest, and she knew he could either read or sense every doubt she had felt.

"I'm sorry," she said. "I'm sorry I tried to blame you."

"It's okay," he whispered against her cheek. "I wanted to tell you, but Curtis and Pat were adamant that no one know, especially not you because you are so amazing when it all comes out in front of the camera.

"I knew it could backfire, and it almost did. You were more pissed than sad."

She looked at him. "I'm still pissed. This story line…" She was shaking her head.

"…will all turn out good. Trust and believe. Okay? Curtis is where he wants to be; working with The '50s Experience LLC as the head of research and development—behind the scenes, where he prefers to be."

She sighed in relief. "You hired him to the production crew?"

"I wanted him in front of the cameras, but I'll take him behind them any day."

He drew her into a hug and this time, she settled against him and stayed there. "Okay."

Chapter Ninety-Two

Bobby asked if she wanted to go to the factory to watch the show and Bailey declined. She still didn't know how she felt—well, she knew how she was feeling and she didn't want to share with anyone, not even Bobby.

So, she went into the office and sat alone and went through all of the scenes that had to do with Curtis's murder. Watching it was sometimes disgusting, sometimes devastating, and one hundred percent heart-wrenching.

Bailey cried more watching it than she did acting it. That made sense, though. Instead of coming off cold and unfeeling, she just seemed shell-shocked. As she watched and wiped away her tears, Bailey had to remind herself this was just a show. This was acting. This wasn't real.

But when she saw Guy Edelman's smug expression as he sat in the police station lying about the interaction between Curtis and his sister as the production crew artfully merged the reality with his lies, Bailey couldn't stop the anger.

Edelman had never looked so lively as he did when cursing out a Black man, when joking with the good ol' boys down at the police station. The police cracked jokes with him and treated him as a guest instead of what he really was.

She closed out, having hit her limit. Bobby was already sleeping when she retreated to the bedroom and she took a shower and wrapped her hair and when she finally climbed into bed, Bobby moved to her as if they were magnets.

Bailey snuggled against him, thankful she had a man that saw the ugliness in racism, and her man had devoted his show into showing that ugliness back to society. Would it mean anything?

Only time would tell.

On Thursday, Mayor George announced there would be a curfew in Garden Hill to prevent retaliation due to the unfortunate death of a Negro man.

Retaliation. A no-name Negro man.

Bobby and Bailey had an argument. Not a real-life one, but one for the cameras.

"I don't want you to go," he said resolutely.

She gave him a surprised look. "How can you think I won't go to a rally after what happened to Curtis?"

"Bailey, I understand how you feel, but it's dangerous—"

"Everything is dangerous. Being a good person is dangerous! Speaking up for yourself is dangerous—"

He shook his head. "And we will fight. But I'm going to fight with words. I'm writing an article about Curtis and about how his lynching has affected the Negro community. After I do, you know how everyone will label me. But I'm willing to take that because right is right and wrong is wrong."

Bailey looked away. "I'm happy you're doing that. But what about me? I knew Curtis as more than the milkman. He was my friend!"

Bobby rubbed her arms. "I'm sorry. I know you're hurting. I am too. I only knew him from the meetings, but everyone that speaks of him talks about how good he was. But, Bae, you are my priority.

"That rally is going to get violent. The mayor has the police ready to disperse any Negro gathering with force! I won't let something happen to you! My biggest nightmare is something like what happened to Curtis happening to you, and I'm not going to just sit back and let it!"

She gave him a sad look. "Then you shouldn't have married a Negro woman." She walked away.

In the end, Bobby put a hold on his article and went to the rally with her.

It was held right in the city center of Wingate. As Bailey saw the police bordering the park, she had another jolt of reality while they were acting; this really did happen in her country's recent history. Except they would have already begun clubbing and spraying everyone with hoses.

Bobby and Bailey walked hand in hand to where the others had begun to gather, and Bailey saw it was impossible to call this a Negro gathering.

Almost half of the people present were white, and they were standing side by side with the Negroes in outrage, in horror, and in solidarity.

In the end, the police didn't break up the gathering. The mayor was in his limo watching from behind the police barricade and he undoubtedly recognized some of his supporters in the crowd. Bailey even saw Nadine holding hands with Jackie and Tracy.

When Bailey saw Pat, they ran up to each other and hugged and began to sob as if they truly had lost a dear friend. Marvin stood watch over them and after a few minutes, Bobby felt reassured enough in Bailey's safety to retreat with his pen and pad of paper in hand to interview the crowd.

Bailey saw Helen and Quinton, openly holding hands. She saw Haley, as well as a number of people from the swingers club. Carl was there, but she didn't see Shirley. She did, however, see every single Black person that had been hired by The '50s Experience LLC.

As Bobby and Bailey filmed their Friday-morning scene over breakfast, the couple locked hands and ate quietly—no apologies or explanations exchanged or needed. The love between them was so obvious, they didn't have to speak it into the cameras.

Bobby called around lunchtime to say that Paula had gone into labor and he didn't know when he'd be home.

She smiled. "Your son is about to be born."

"Oh God. What a time for my son to come into this world…"

"He's got a good man to guide him."

"Thanks, honey. I love you so much."

"I love you too. Call me as soon as you can."

"I will! I gotta go!"

Bailey sighed and sat quietly on the couch. After a moment, she lay down and drew her knees up and held onto them in a fetal position.

As far as she was concerned that was the last scene of the season for Bailey Banks. She had given all she intended to give.

The morning of the Friendsgiving was a welcome relief. Bailey had a big ham in the oven so she couldn't drive with Bobby to the production office to pick up Aunt Mae and Uncle Dewbug.

She wanted to be there to see their faces when they first set foot on set, but she wasn't taking any chances with the ham.

She had just taken it out of the oven when the front door opened.

"This is it," she heard Bobby say.

Bailey ran into the room to see her aunt and uncle looking around curiously. She flung herself at them as if she hadn't just seen them less than a week ago.

"This is so pretty!" Aunt Mae said after Bobby had taken her coat and hung it up. "It looks just like it does on the television set."

"Let me show you around," Bailey said proudly.

"Show me to the bathroom," Uncle Dewbug said.

They didn't stay too long. Her aunt and uncle wanted a tour of the town before they went to the factory.

"Ugh. That's where that evil Mr. Edelman lives," her aunt said while pointing at his house.

Bailey scowled. "Yeah. That's his house."

"I don't know how y'all can live that close to a killer. Maybe y'all should move to Garden Hills."

Bobby shrugged. "That's always a possibility." He exchanged looks with Bailey, who didn't reveal anything with her expression. She wasn't sure. She guessed it would depend on how things played out with her murderous neighbor.

They drove downtown, and Bailey saw her aunt visibly shudder when she saw the Whites Only sign in front of a water fountain. When they drove past the park where they'd held the civil rights rally, her aunt peered out the window with a smile of pride, as if she had been with them in spirit.

They eventually got to the factory, and Bobby went ahead with the ham and to check that the caterers were getting things set up.

Aunt Mae discreetly pointed out characters she recognized. When she pointed out Drew, he turned and came over to them, shaking hands with her aunt and uncle and giving Bailey a brief hug.

"You did one hell of a job with that story line," he said.

"Thanks, but when you walked in on your girl giving a lap dance, I almost fell on the floor." He grinned sheepishly.

"Well, I hope you give her a chance," Aunt Mae interjected. "In that economy, a good job was hard to find. I bet she's one of those ride-or-die gals."

Drew cracked up laughing and gave Aunt Mae a hug.

Uncle Dewbug quickly became bored with meeting people and went off to help Bobby set up the food.

Bailey and Aunt Mae spotted Pat, and her aunt hugged her as if she was just as much her niece as Bailey was. They talked very easily, and Pat stayed around as the two introduced her aunt and uncle to other cast members. Several of them greeted her as if they were fans of hers, which tickled her beyond measure.

There was a bit of a crowd around the refreshment stand and it soon became obvious why. Curtis was standing there surrounded by a number of admirers. They were laughing and clapping him on the shoulders as if trying to convince themselves he wasn't dead.

He was so good-natured about it, and went around hugging and laughing with everyone as he explained he was not done with the show but would be working behind the scenes.

Curtis spotted her and broke away from his fans. They hugged, and he grinned like a Cheshire cat.

"Are you okay?"

She gave him a crooked smile, happy he'd asked her.

"I am now."

He hugged Pat and returned Aunt Mae's hug, doubling up on it when he realized she was *the* Aunt Mae.

"You are just so much more handsome than on television." He chuckled at her statement.

"Thank you. I think you'll enjoy being on the show — at least more than I did."

"But you were so good at it!"

"I just wanted to be a part of something new. I never wanted to be a milkman. But it was that or lawn boy."

Bailey made a face. "Yeah. I gotcha."

"I really do like the job Rob gave me. I get to do what I love best, research the era and help develop the story line."

She gave him another brief smile. "Then I'm happy."

Some of the cast from another team came up to them and began talking to Bailey about how much her story line had touched them.

"You make me push myself as an actress just so I can appear as authentic as you. Do you have any pointers?"

Bailey gave the woman a surprised look. "Thank you. Sometimes, I just don't feel as if I'm acting."

Aunt Mae wanted to use the bathroom, and Pat took her while Bailey talked to the two admirers.

"Oh! Look who showed up!" Curtis exclaimed. He moved to give someone a big bear hug and Bailey's smile faltered when she saw who it was. Guy.

Curtis smiled so hard, Bailey wished she could elbow him and tell him to chill. Guy looked at her and his big smile dropped by fifty percent.

"Hi, Bailey," he said politely.

"Hi, Guy."

"Who is this lovely lady?" Curtis asked as he looked fondly at a woman about her aunt's age. She was pretty, with a chocolate-brown complexion and long, gray dreadlocks.

Guy turned and put his arm around the waist of the woman. "This is my wife, Brook. Brook, this is my good friend Curtis."

Brook broke away from her husband and pulled Curtis into a huge hug. "Of course I know who this fine young man is!"

Bailey's eyes were probably hanging out of her head.

Guy was married to a Black woman?

He gestured to Bailey. "And this is Bailey."

Brook turned to her and before hugging her, she placed her hands on Bailey's cheek. "Hi, honey. Oh, you are just so adorable." She turned to look at her husband. "You're right. She looks like Eden." Brook turned back to Bailey. "That's our daughter." She kissed Bailey's cheek and hugged her for a long time.

Bailey blinked in confusion while returning the hug. She looked at Guy, who smiled fondly at his wife before turning that fond smile on her.

Wait. What?

Brook finally pulled back when Bobby joined them with her uncle in tow.

"And this is Bobby," Guy said. "Bobby, this is my wife, Brook."

It seemed tears appeared in Brook's eyes as she gazed at Bobby. She cupped his cheeks too before hugging him just as closely as she had hugged Bailey.

She suddenly chuckled and swiped at her eyes. "I'm sorry. You two remind me so much of me and Guy; your story, the fears, the love, and the commitment."

Guy reached out and clasped her hand and Bobby gave Bailey a quick look, letting her know he hadn't known Guy was in an interracial marriage either.

"We lived the life you two are portraying on the show," Guy said shyly. "Except I didn't dare bring my illegitimate child home."

Brook gave him a poke in the side with her elbow.

"He's kidding! Besides, it's too late in the game for you to be springing any new babies on me."

Others had gathered around in curiosity. They all seemed just as shocked as she was that the bigot of the show actually was not a bigot.

Aunt Mae returned with Pat and her expression hardened when she set eyes on Guy. But as she watched, she realized *this* Guy wasn't the same one that had killed the much-favored character of the show.

"I love this show so much," Brook gushed to Bobby. "But I'm ready to have my husband back home."

Guy looked at Bailey, even though she hadn't said a word. "But we did come to a mutual agreement that if I did get this role as the show's antagonist, I'd put my entire self into it.

"As much as I despise cowardly men like Edelman, I know how important it is to show just how despicable they are. No one needs to find anything redeeming about monsters like him." His eyes moved from Bailey's to Bobby's.

"Thanks for giving me the opportunity." They shook hands, and people began gushing and applauding them.

Curtis placed a friendly arm around Guy's shoulder. "After you go to prison for my murder, you should help with research and development. There's not enough research that can top actually living in the '50s."

Brook snuggled against her husband. "Oh, Guy can tell you a story or two. We marched with King, we did sit-ins, and he drove people to work free of charge when we boycotted the buses…"

"Oh my gosh," Bobby said as he watched them heading to the dining area. "Can you believe that?"

Bailey just shook her head. "He was such a freaking good actor…" Bailey didn't finish her thought, which is that in his heart, he was just a shy guy portraying the horrible people he'd encountered.

"Okay, can we grab a plate? Or does the cast get to eat first?" Uncle Dewbug asked anxiously.

"No." Bobby clapped his hand together. "Let's go eat!"

"Let's grab a seat by Brook and Guy," Bailey said. "I want to hear some of these stories about the past."

"Don't ask for too many stories," Bobby said as he placed his arm around her. "Some of them might appear in next season's show."

The End

About The Author

Pepper Pace creates a unique brand of Interracial/multicultural romance. While her stories span the gamut from humorous to heartfelt, the common theme is crossing racial boundaries.

Pepper Pace Books

STRANDED!
Juicy
Love Intertwined Vol. 1
Love Intertwined Vol. 2
Urban Vampire; The Turning
Urban Vampire; Creature of the Night
Urban Vampire; The Return of Alexis
Urban Vampire; The Final Battle
Wheels of Steel Book 1
Wheels of Steel Book 2
Wheels of Steel Book 3
Wheels of Steel Book 4
Angel Over My Shoulder
CRASH
Miscegenist Sabishii
They Say Love Is Blind
The Throwaway Year
Beast
A Seal Upon Your Heart
Everything is Everything Book 1
Everything is Everything Book 2
Adaptation book 1
Adaptation book 2
About Coco's Room
The Witch's Demon book 1
A Bubble of Time
SHORT STORIES/NOVELLAS

~~***~~

The Way Home
MILF
Blair and the Emoboy
Emoboy the Submissive Dom

1-900-BrownSugar
Someone To Love
My Special Friend
Baby Girl and the Mean Boss
A Wrong Turn Towards Love (An Estill County
Mountain Man Romance)
True's Love (An Estill County Mountain Man
Romance)
The Miseducation of Riley Pranger (An Estill County
Mountain Man Romance)
Christmas Redemption (An Estill County Mountain
Man Romance)
The Delicate Sadness
The Shadow People
The Love Unexpected
The Vinyl Man
Punishment Island
Super G
Awakening
1954
COLLABORATIONS
~~***~~

Sexy Southern Hometown Heroes
Seduction: An Interracial Romance Anthology Vol. 1
Scandalous Heroes Box set
Secrets of the Elite
WRITTEN UNDER BETH JO ANDERSEN
~~***~~

Snatched by Bigfoot!
Bigfoot's Sidepiece
Mated to the Bigfoot!
WRITTEN UNDER KIM CHAMBERS
~~***~~
The Purple World book 1

Sign-up to the Pepper Pace Newsletter!

1954 Pepper Pace

http://eepurl.com/bGV4tb

Made in the USA
Middletown, DE
25 June 2022

67785086R00435